"Paul   r t w o
best

...on, a great hero, war
excit... what ...ore can you people wa...
– *Black Tears*

"More intricately crafted and exciting story.
More scenes of martial heroics. More moments
of rug-pulled-out-from-under-your-feet treachery.
More triumphs. More setbacks.
More tragic moments, senseless deaths, fear,
brutality, relief, love, joy of life."
– *SF Site*

"The book is brisk and vivid, and as ever full
of surprises and painful reversals. People don't
just die in Kearney's novels, they die badly,
with a credible but not overwhelming edge
of realistic pain and squalor."
– *Infinity Plus*

"This was a page-turner in every sense, and I
read it in two sittings. It might have been one
but for having to work for a living."
– *Rambles Magazine*

Other Books by Paul Kearney

The Way to Babylon
A Different Kingdom
Riding the Unicorn

THE MONARCHIES OF GOD SERIES
Hawkwood's Voyage
The Heretic Kings
The Iron Wars
The Second Empire
Ships From The West

THE SEA BEGGARS SERIES
The Mark of Ran
This Forsaken Earth

The
CENTURY
of the
SOLDIER

PAUL KEARNEY

SOLARIS

This omnibus first published 2010 by Solaris
an imprint of Rebellion Publishing Ltd,
Riverside House, Osney Mead,
Oxford, OX1 0ES, UK

www.solarisbooks.com

ISBN: 978 1 907519 08 6

The Iron Wars © Paul Kearney 1999
The Second Empire © Paul Kearney 2000
Ships From the West © Paul Kearney 2002

10 9 8 7 6 5 4 3 2 1

A CIP catalogue record for this book is available from the
British Library.

Designed & typeset by Rebellion Publishing

Printed in the UK by CPI Bookmarque, Croydon, CR0 4TD

The Story so Far

FIVE CENTURIES AGO two great religious faiths arose that were to dominate the entire known world. They were founded on the teachings of two men: in the west, St. Ramusio, and in the east, the Prophet Ahrimuz.

The Ramusian faith rose at the same time that the great continent-wide empire of the Fimbrians was coming apart. The greatest soldiers the world had ever seen, the Fimbrians had become embroiled in a vicious civil war which enabled their conquered provinces to break away one by one and become the Seven Kingdoms. Fimbria dwindled to a shadow of her former self, her troops still formidable, but her concerns confined to the problems within the borders of the homeland. And the Seven Kingdoms went from strength to strength – until, that is, the first hosts of the Merduks began pouring over the Jafrar mountains, quickly reducing their numbers to five.

Thus began the great struggle between the Ramusians of the west and the Merduks of the east, a sporadic and brutal war carried on for generations, which, by the sixth century of Ramusian reckoning, was finally reaching its climax.

Aekir, greatest city of the west and seat of the Ramusian Pontiff, finally fell to the eastern invaders in the year 551. Out of its sack escaped two men whose survival was to have the greatest consequences for future history. One of them was the Pontiff himself, Macrobius, thought dead by the rest of the Ramusian kingdoms and by the Church hierarchy. The other was Corfe Cear-Inaf, a lowly ensign of cavalry, who deserted his post in despair after the loss of his wife in the tumult of the city's fall.

By the time Macrobius's escape was announced, the Ramusian Church had already elected another Pontiff, Himerius, who was set upon purging the Five Kingdoms of any remnant of the Dweomer-folk: the practitioners of magic. The purge caused Hebrion's young king, Abeleyn, to commission a desperate expedition into the uttermost west to seek the rumoured Western Continent, led by his ruthlessly ambitious cousin, Lord Murad of Galiapeno. Murad blackmailed a master mariner, one Richard Hawkwood, into navigating the voyage, and as passengers and would-be colonists they took along some of the refugee Dweomer-folk of Hebrion, including one Bardolin of Carreirida. But when they finally reached the fabled west, they found that a colony of lycanthropes and mages had already existed there for centuries under the aegis of an immortal Archmage, Aruan. Their exploratory party was wiped out, only Murad, Hawkwood and Bardolin surviving.

Back in Normannia, the Ramusian Church was split down the middle as three of the Five Kingdoms recognized Macrobius as the true Pontiff, while the rest preferred the newly elected Himerius. Religious war erupted as the three so-called Heretic Kings – Abeleyn of Hebrion, Mark of Astarac and Lofantyr of Torunna – fought to retain their thrones. All succeeded, but Abeleyn had the hardest battle to fight. He was forced to storm his own capital, Abrusio, by land and sea, half-destroying it in the process.

Farther east, the Torunnan fortress of Ormann Dyke became the focus of Merduk assault, and there Corfe distinguished himself in its defence. He was promoted and, catching the eye of Torunna's Queen Dowager, Odelia, was given the mission of bringing to heel the rebellious nobles in the south of the kingdom. This he undertook with a motley, ill-equipped band of ex-galley slaves, which was all the king would allow him. Plagued by the memory of his lost wife, he was, mercifully, unaware that she had survived Aekir's fall, and was now the favourite concubine of the Sultan Aurungzeb himself.

The momentous year 551 drew to a close. In Almark, the dying king Haukir bequeathed his kingdom to the

Himerian Church, transforming the Church into a great temporal power. And in Charibon two humble monks, Albrec and Avila, stumbled upon an ancient document, a biography of St. Ramusio that stated that he was one and the same man as the Merduk Prophet Ahrimuz. The monks fled Charibon, but not before a macabre encounter with the chief librarian of the monastery city, who revealed himself to be a werewolf. They ran into the teeth of a midwinter blizzard, collapsing into the snow.

And now all over the continent of Normannia, the armies are once more on the march.

The
IRON WARS

In thy faint slumbers I by thee have watched,
And heard thee murmur tales of iron wars...

– Henry IV, Part I

This book is respectfully dedicated
to the memory of
Richard Evans

PROLOGUE

IN THE SWEATING nightmare-fever of the dark he felt the beast enter his room and stand over him. But that was impossible. Not from so far, surely –

Oh, sweet God in Heaven, overlord of Earth, be with me now...

Prayers, prayers, prayers. The mockery of it, he praying to God, whose soul was black as pitch and already sold. Already lost and consigned to the fires of eons.

Sweet Ramusio, sit with me. Be near me now in this lost hour.

He wept. It was here, of course it was. It was watching, patient as a stone. He belonged to it. He was damned.

Soaked in perspiration, he opened his gummy eyelids to the all-embracing dark of his midnight room. Tears had fled down the sides of his neck as he slept and the heavy furs of his bed were awry. He gave a start at their lumpen, hairy shape. But it was nothing. He was alone after all, thank God. Nothing but the quiet winter night wheeling in its chill immensity beyond the room.

He scratched flint and steel together from the bedside table, and when the tinder caught, transferred the seed of sparks to his candle. A light, a point of reference in the looming murk.

Utterly alone. He was without even the God he had once reverenced and to whom he had devoted the best years of his life. Clerics and theologians said that the Creator was everywhere, in every niche and pocket of the world. But He was not here, in this room. Not tonight.

Something else was coming, though. Even now he could sense it hurtling through the dark towards him as unstoppable as the turning sun, its feet hardly setting down upon the dormant world. It could cover continents and oceans in the blink of an eye.

The furs on his bed gave a twitch, and he yelped. He clawed his way to the headboard, eyes starting out of his head, heart hammering behind his ribs.

They gathered themselves into a mound, a hulking mass of hair. And then they began to grow, bulking out in the dimness and the candle-flame, the room a sudden playground of moving shadows as the light flickered and swam.

The furs rose and rose in the bed, towering now. And when they loomed over him, tall as some misshapen megalith, two yellow eyes blinked on in their midst, bright-hungry as an arsonist's flame.

It was here. It had come.

He fell on his face amid the damp linen sheets, worshipping. Truly *here* – he could smell the musk of its presence, feel the heat of the enormous form. A drop of spit fell from its maw and sizzled as it struck his neck, burning him.

Greetings, Himerius, the beast said.

"Master," the prostrate cleric whispered, grovelling in his soiled bed.

Be not afraid, its voice said without a sound. Himerius's reply was inarticulate, a gargle of terror.

The time is here, my friend, it said. *Look up at me. Sit up and see.*

A huge paw, fingered and taloned like some mockery of man and beast, raised him to his knees. Its pads scorched his skin through the wool of his winter shift.

The face of the winter's wolf, its ears like horns above a massive black-furred skull in which the eyes glared like saffron lamps, black-slitted. A foot-long fanged muzzle from which the saliva dripped in silver strings, the black lips drawn back taut and quivering. And caught in the teeth, some glistening vermilion gobbet.

Eat.

Himerius was weeping, terror flooding his mind. "Please master," he blubbered. "I am not ready. I am not worthy –"

Eat.

The paws clamped on to his biceps and he was lifted off his feet. The bed creaked under them. His face was drawn close to the hot jaws, its breath sickening him, like the wet heat of a jungle heavy with putrefaction. A gateway to a different and unholy world.

He took the gobbet of meat in his mouth, his lips bruised in a ghastly kiss against the fangs of the wolf. Chewed, swallowed. Fought the instinct to retch as it slid down his gullet as though seeking the blood-dark path to his heart.

Good. Very good. And now for the other.

"No, I beg you!" Himerius wept.

He was thrown to his stomach on the bed and his shift was ripped from his back with a negligent wave of the thing's paw. Then the wolf was atop him, the awesome weight of it pinioning him, driving the air out of his lungs. He felt he was being suffocated, could not even cry out.

I am a man of God. Oh Lord, help me in my torment!

And then the sudden, screaming pain as it mounted him, pushing brutally into his body with a single, rending thrust.

His mind went white and blank with the agony. The beast was panting in his ear, its mouth dripping to scald his neck. The claws scored his shoulders as it violated him and its fur was like the jab of a million needles against his spine.

The beast shuddered into him, some deep snarl of release rising from its throat. The powerful haunches lifted from his buttocks. It withdrew.

You are truly one of us now. I have given you a precious gift, Himerius. We are brethren under the light of the moon.

He felt that he had been torn apart. He could not even lift his head. There were no prayers now, nothing to plead to. Something precious had been wrenched out of his soul, and a foulness bedded there in its place.

The wolf was fading, its stink leaving the room. Himerius was weeping bitterly into the mattress, blood trickling down his legs.

"Master," he said. "Thank you, master."

And when he raised his head at last he was alone on the great bed, his chamber empty, and the wind picking up to a howl around the deserted cloisters outside.

PART ONE

MIDWINTER

The spirit which knows not how to submit,
which retires from no danger because it is formidable,
is the soul of a soldier.

– Robert Jackson,
A Systematic View on the Formation,
Discipline and Economy of Armies, 1804

ONE

NOTHING ISOLLA HAD been told could have prepared her for it. There had been wild rumours, of course, macabre tales of destruction and slaughter. But the scale of the thing still took her by surprise.

She stood on the leeward side of the carrack's quarterdeck, her ladies-in-waiting silent as owls by her side. They had a steady north-wester on the larboard quarter and the ship was plunging along before it like a stag fleeing the hounds, sending a ten-foot bow-wave off to leeward which the weak winter sunlight filled full of rainbows.

She had felt not a smidgen of sickness, which pleased her; it was a long time since she had last been at sea, a long time since she had been anywhere. The breakneck passage of the Fimbrian Gulf had been exhilarating after the sombre gloom of a winter court, a court which had only recently emerged from an attempted coup. Her brother, the King of Astarac, had fought and won half a dozen small battles to keep his throne. But that was nothing compared to what had gone on in the kingdom that was her destination. Nothing at all.

They were sailing steadily up a huge bay, at the end of which the capital of Hebrion, gaudy old Abrusio, squatted like a harlot on a chamberpot. It had been the rowdiest, most raucous, godless port of the western world. And the richest. But now it was a blackened shell.

Civil war had scorched the guts out of Abrusio. For fully three miles, the waterfront was a smoking ruin. The hulks of once-great ships jutted out of the water along the remnants of the wharves and docks, and extending from the shore was a wasteland hundreds of acres in extent. The still-smoking wreck of the lower city, its buildings flattened by the inferno which had raged through it. Only Admiral's Tower stood mostly intact, a gaunt sentinel, a gravestone.

There was a powerful fleet anchored in the Outer Roads. Hebrion's navy, depleted by the fierce fighting to retake the city from the Knights Militant and the traitors who had been in league with them, was a force to be reckoned with, even now: tall ships whose yards were a cat's cradle of rigging lines and furiously busy mariners, repairing the damage of war. Abrusio still had teeth in plenty.

Up on the hill above the harbour the Royal palace and the monastery of the Inceptines still stood, though pitted by the naval bombardment which had ended the final assaults. Up there, somewhere, a king awaited them, looking down on the ruins of his capital.

ISOLLA WAS SISTER to a different king. A tall, thin, plain woman with a long nose that seemed to overhang her mouth except when she smiled. A cleft chin, and a large, pale forehead dusted with freckles. She had long ago given up trying for the porcelain purity that was expected of a courtly lady, and had even put aside her powders and creams. And the ideas which had prompted her to don them in the first place.

She was sailing to Hebrion to be married.

Hard to remember the boy who had been Abeleyn, the boy now become a man and a king. In the times they had seen each other as children he had been cruel to her, mocking her ugliness, pulling at the flaming russet hair that was her only glory. But there had been a light about him, even then, something that made it hard to hate him, easy to like. "Issy Long-nose," he had called her as a boy, and she had hated him for it. And yet when the young Prince Lofantyr had tripped her up in the mud one winter's evening in Vol Ephrir, he had ducked the future King of Torunna in a puddle and smeared the Royal nose in the filth Isolla stood covered in. Because she was Mark's sister, and Mark was his best friend, he had said. And he had wiped the tears from her eyes with gruff, boyish tenderness. She had worshipped him for it, only to hate him again a day later when she became the butt of his pranks once more.

He would be her husband very soon, the first man she would ever let into her bed. At twenty-seven she hardly worried about that side of things, though it would of course be her duty to produce a male heir, the quicker the better. A political marriage with no romance about it, only convenient practicalities. Her body was the treaty between two kingdoms, a symbol of their alliance. Outside that, it had no real worth at all.

"By the mark eleven!" the leadsman in the bows called. And then: "Sweet blood of God! Starboard, helmsman! There's a wreck in the fairway!"

The helmsmen swung the ship's wheel and the carrack turned smoothly. Sliding past the port bow the ship's company saw the grounded wreck of a warship, the tips of her yards jutting above the surface of the seas no more than a foot, the shadowed bulk of her hull clearly visible in the lucid water.

The entire ship's company had been staring at the war-wrecked remnants of the city. Many of the sailors were clambering up the shrouds like apes to get a better view. On the sterncastle the quartet of heavily armed Astaran knights had lost their impassive air and were gazing as fixedly as the rest.

"Abrusio, God help us!" the master said, moved beyond his accustomed taciturnity.

"The city is destroyed!" one of the men at the wheel burst out.

"Shut your mouth and keep your course. Leadsman! Sing out, there. Pack of witless idiots. You'd run her aground so you could gape at a dancing bear. Braces there! By God, are we to spill our wind with the very harbour in sight, and let Hebrians brand us for mooncalf fools?"

"There ain't no harbour left," one of the more laconic of the master's mates said, spitting over the leeward rail with a quick, hunted look of apology to Isolla a second later. "She's burned to the waterline, skipper. There's hardly a wharf left we could tie up to. We'll have to anchor in the Inner Roads and send in a longboat."

"Aye, well," the master muttered, his brow still dark. "Get tackles to the yardarms. It may be you're right."

"One moment, Captain," one of the knights who were Isolla's escort called out. "We don't yet know who is in charge in Abrusio. Perhaps the King could not retake the city. It may be in the hands of the Knights Militant."

"There's the Royal flammifer flying from the palace," the master's mate told him.

"Aye, but it's at half mast," someone added.

There was a pause after that. The crew looked to the master for orders. He opened his mouth, but just as he was about to speak the lookout hailed him.

"Deck there! I see a vessel putting off from the base of Admiral's Tower, and it's flying the Royal pennant."

At the same second the ship's company could see puffs of smoke exploding from the battered seawalls of the city, and a heartbeat later came the sound of the reports, distant staccato thunder.

"A Royal Salute," the leading knight said. His face had brightened considerably. "The Knights Militant and usurpers would never give us a salute – more likely a broadside. The city belongs to the Royalists. Captain, you'd best make ready to receive the Hebrian King's emissaries."

Tension had relaxed along the deck, and the sailors were chattering to each other. Isolla stood on in silence, and it was the observant master's mate who voiced her thought for her.

"Why's the banner at half mast is what I'd like to know. They only do that when a king is –"

His voice was drowned out by the pummelling of bare feet on the decks as the crew made ready to receive the Hebrian vessel that approached. As it came closer, a twenty-oared Royal barge with a scarlet canopy, Isolla saw that its crew were all dressed in black.

"THE LADY HAS arrived, it would seem," General Mercado said.

He was standing with his hands behind his back, staring out and down upon the world from the King's balcony. The whole circuit of the ruined lower city was his to contemplate, as well as the great bays that made up Abrusio's harbours and the naval fortifications that peppered them.

"What the hell are we going to do, Golophin?"

There was a rustling in the gloom of the dimly lit room, where the light from the open balcony could not reach. A long shape detached itself soundlessly from the shadows and joined the general. It was leaner than a living man had a right to be, something crafted out of parchment and sticks and gnawed scraps of leather, hairless and bone-white. The long mantle it wore swamped it, but its eyes glittered brightly out of the ravaged face and when it spoke the voice was low and musical, one meant for laughter and song.

"We play for time, what else? A suitable welcome, a suitable place to stay, and absolute silence on anything regarding the King's health."

"The whole damned city is in mourning. I'll wager she thinks him dead already," Mercado snapped. One side of his face was gnarled into a grimace, the other was a serene silver mask which had never changed, not in all the years since Golophin had put it there to save his life. The eyeball on the silver side glared bloodshot and lidless, a fearsome thing which cowed his subordinates. But it could not cow the man who had created it.

"I know Isolla, or did," Golophin riposted, snapping in his turn. "She's a sensible child – a woman now, I suppose. As importantly, she has a mind, and will not fly into hysterics at the drop of a glove. And she will do as she is told, by God."

Mercado seemed mollified. He did not look at the cadaverous old wizard, but said: "And you, Golophin, how goes it with you?"

Golophin's face broke into a surprisingly sweet smile. "I am like the old whore who has opened her legs too many times. I am sore and tired, General. Not much use to man nor beast."

Mercado snorted. "That will be the day."

As one, they moved away from the balcony and back into the depths of the room. The Royal bedchamber, hung heavily with half-glimpsed tapestries, carpeted with rugs from Ridawan and Calmar, sweetened with the incense of the Levangore. And on a vast four-poster bed, a wasted shape amid the silken sheets. They stood over him in silence.

Abeleyn, King of Hebrion, or what was left of him. A shell had struck him down in the very instant of his victory, when Abrusio was back in his hands and the kingdom saved from a savage theocracy. Some whim of the elder gods had caused it to happen thus, Golophin thought. Nothing of the Ramusian deity's so-called mercy and compassion. Nothing but bitter-tasting irony to leave him like this: not dead, hardly alive.

The King had lost both his legs, and the trunk above the stumps was lacerated and broken, a mass of wounds and shattered bones. The once boyish face was waxen, the lips blue and the feeble breath whistling in and out over them with laboured regularity. At least his sight had been spared. At least he was alive.

"Sweet Blessed Saint, to think that I should ever have lived to see him come to this," Mercado whispered hoarsely, and Golophin heard something not far from a sob in the grim old soldier's voice. "Is there nothing you can do, Golophin? Nothing?"

The wizard uttered a sigh that seemed to start in the toes of his boots. Some of his very vitality seemed to flicker out of him with it.

"I am keeping him breathing. More, I cannot do. I have not the strength. I must let the Dweomer in me grow again. The death of my familiar, the battles. They leached it out of me. I am sorry, General. So sorry. He is my friend too."

Mercado straightened. "Of course. My apologies. I am behaving like a maiden aunt. There's no time for handwringing, not in days like these... Where have you put his bitch of a mistress?"

"She's accommodated in the guest apartments, forever screaming to see him. I have her under guard – for her own protection, naturally."

"She bears his child," Mercado said with an odd savagery.

"So it would seem. We must watch her closely."

"Fucking women," Mercado went on. "Another one here now for us to coddle and to step around."

"As I said, Isolla is different. And she is Mark's sister. The alliance between Hebrion and Astarac must be sealed by their marriage. For the good of the kingdom."

Mercado snorted. "Marriage! And when will that be, I wonder? Will she marry a –" He stopped and bent his head, and Golophin could hear him swearing under his breath, cursing himself. "I have things I must attend to," he said abruptly. "Enough of them, God knows. Let me know if there is any change, Golophin." And he marched out as if he were about to face a court martial.

Golophin sat on the bed and took the hand of his King. His face became that of a malevolent skull, anger and hatred pursuing each other across it until he blinked, and then a huge weariness settled in their place.

"Better you had died, Abeleyn," he said softly. "A warrior's end for the last of the warrior kings. When you are gone, all the little men will come out from under the stones."

And he bowed his head and wept.

Two

By God, Corfe thought, *the man knew how to breed horses.*

The destrier was dark bay, almost black, and a good seventeen hands and a half high. A deep-chested, thick-necked beast with a lively eye and clean limbs. A true warhorse, such as a nobleman alone might ride. And he'd had hundreds of them, all three years old or more, all geldings. A fortune in horn and bone and muscle – but, more importantly, the makings of a cavalry army.

His men were encamped in the pastures of one of the late Duke Ordinac's stud farms. Three acres of leather tents – also the property of the late duke – had been pitched in scattered clumps by the four hundred tribesmen who remained under Corfe's command. The makeshift camp was as busy as a broken ants' nest, with men and horses, the smoke of cookfires, the clinking of hammers on little field-anvils, the vastly intricate and familiar and, to Corfe, wholly invigorating stink and clamour of a cavalry bivouac.

The gelding danced under him as it seemed to catch the lift of his spirits and he calmed it with voice and knees. He had mounted pickets half a mile out in every direction, and Andruw was two days gone with twenty men on a reconnaissance towards Staed, where Duke Narfintyr was arming against the King with over three thousand men under his banner already.

Stiff odds. But they would be farmers' sons and lesser nobles, peasants turned into soldiers for the day. They would not be the born warriors that Corfe's savage tribesmen were. And there were very few infantry troops on earth who could stand up to a heavy cavalry charge, if it were well handled. Professional pikemen perhaps, and that was all.

No, Corfe's worst enemy was time. It was trickling through his fingers like sand and he had none to spare if he were to find and defeat Narfintyr before being superseded by the second army that King Lofantyr had sent south.

Today was the third of the five Saint's Days that scholars had tacked on to the last month of the year to keep the calendar in step with the seasons. In two days' time it would be *Sidhaon*, the night of Yearsend, and then the cycle would begin anew, and the season start its slow turn towards the warmth and reawakening of spring.

It seemed long overdue. This had been the longest winter of Corfe's life. He could hardly remember what it was like to feel warm sun on his face, to walk on grass instead of trudging through snow or quagmire. A hellish and unnatural time of the year to be making war, especially with horse-soldiers. But then the world had become a hellish and unnatural place of late, with all of the old certainties overturned.

He considered this second army on its way south to deal with the rebels it was his own mission to destroy. A certain Colonel Aras, one of the King's favourites, had been given a tidy little combined force with which to subdue the southern nobles, as the King had clearly expected Corfe to make a hash of it with his barbaric, ill-equipped command. He had enemies behind as well as in front, more to worry about than tactics and logistics; he had to be something of a politician as well. These things were inevitable as one rose higher in rank, but Corfe had never expected the intricacies and balances to be so murderous. Not in a time of war. Half the officers in Torunn, it had seemed to him, were more intent on winning the King's favour than on throwing the Merduks back from Ormann Dyke. When he thought about it, a black, beating rage seemed to hover over him, an anger which had had its birth in the fall of Aekir, and which had been growing silently and steadily in him ever since, without hope of release. Only wanton murder could hope to ease it. The killing of Merduk after Merduk down to the last squalling dark-skinned baby until there were no more of them left to stink out the world. Then perhaps his dreams would cease, and Heria's ghost would sleep at last.

A courier cantered up to him and, without flourish or salute, said: "*Ondrow* come back."

He nodded at the man – his tribesmen were picking up quite a bit of Normannic, but still had little notion of the proper forms of address – and followed him as he cantered easily up the hill that dominated the bivouac. Marsch was there, and Ensign Ebro, with three pickets. Ebro slapped out a salute, which Corfe returned absently.

"Where away?"

"Less than a league, on the northern road," Marsch told him. He was rubbing his forehead where the heavy *Ferinai* helm had begun to chafe it. "He's in a hurry, I think. He pushes his horses." Marsch sounded faintly disapproving, as if no emergency were important enough to warrant the maltreatment of horses.

"He's swung round then," Corfe said approvingly. "I'll bet he's been taking a look at our rivals in the game."

They sat there watching the score of horsemen galloping up the muddy northern road with the clods dotting the air behind them like startled birds. In ten minutes the party had reined in, the horses' nostrils flared and red, their necks white with foam. Mud everywhere, the riders' faces splattered with it.

"What's the news, Andruw?" Corfe asked calmly, though his heart had begun to thump faster.

His adjutant tore off his helm, his face a mask of filth.

"Narfintyr sits in Staed like an old woman at the hearth. Farmers' boys, his men are, with a few nobles in fifty-year-old armour. None of the other nobles have risen – they're waiting to see if he can get away with it. They've heard of Ordinac's fate, but no one thinks we are regular Torunnan troops. The gossip has it that Ordinac ran into a war-party of Merduk deserters and scavengers."

Corfe laughed. "Fair enough. Now, what news from the north?"

"Ah, there's the interesting part. Aras and his column are close – less than a day's march behind us. Nigh on three thousand men, five hundred of them mounted – cuirassiers and pistoleers. And six light guns. They have a screen of cavalry out to their front."

"Did they see you?" Corfe demanded.

"Not a chance. We crawled on our bellies and watched them from a ridgeline. They're bound by the speed of the guns and the baggage waggons, and the road is a morass. I'll bet they've cursed those culverins all the way south from Torunn."

Corfe grinned. "You're beginning to talk like a cavalryman, Andruw."

"Aye, well, it's one thing firing them, quite another coaxing them through a swamp. What's to do, Corfe?"

They were all looking at him. Suddenly there was a different feeling in the air, a tenseness which Corfe knew and had come to love.

"We pack and move out at once," he said crisply. "Marsch, see to it. I want one squadron out in front as a screen. You will command it. Another to herd the remounts, and a third as rearguard under Andruw here. The lead squadron moves out as soon as they can saddle up. The rest will follow when they can. Gentlemen, I believe we have work to do."

The knot of riders split up, Andruw's party heading for the horse herd to procure fresh mounts. Only Ebro remained beside Corfe.

"And what am I to do, sir?" he asked, half resentful and half plaintive.

"Get the baggage mules sorted. I want them ready to move out within two hours. Pack everything you can, but don't overload them. We have to move quickly."

"Sir, Narfintyr has three thousand men; we are less than four hundred. Hadn't we better wait for Aras to come, and combine with him?"

Corfe stared coldly at his subordinate. "Have you no hankering for glory, Ensign? You have your orders."

"Yes, sir."

Ebro galloped off, looking thoroughly discontented.

THE PERFECT INDUSTRY of the bivouac was shattered as the officers rode around shouting orders and the tribesmen hurried to don their armour and saddle their horses. Marsch had found a store of lances in the late Duke Ordinac's castle and the troopers ran to collect theirs from the forest of racks that sprouted between the tents. The tents themselves were left behind, as they were too heavy to be carried by the pack mules that comprised Corfe's baggage train. The stubborn, braying beasts had enough to bear: grain for a thousand horses for a week, the field-forges with their small anvils and clanking tools. Pig-iron for spare horseshoes, and extra lances, weapons and armour, to say nothing of the plain but bulky rations that the men themselves would consume on the march. Twice-baked bread, hard as wood, and salt pork for the most part, as well as cauldrons for each squadron in which the pork would be steeped and boiled. A million and one things for an army which was hardly big enough to be an army at all. Ordinarily, a field force would have one heavy double-axled ox-drawn waggon for every fifty men, twice that for cavalry and artillery. Corfe's two-hundred-strong mule train, though it looked impressive en masse, could barely carry anything by regular military standards.

The vanguard moved out within the hour, and the main body an hour after that. By midday, the bivouac they had left behind them was populated only by ghosts and a few mangy dogs who hunted through the abandoned tents for left-behind scraps of food or leather to gnaw on. The race had begun.

WINTER WAS HARSHER in the foothills of the northern Cimbrics than it was in the lowlands of Torunna. Here the world was a brutal place of killing grandeur. Twelve thousand feet high and more, the Cimbrics were nevertheless shrinking, their ridges and escarpments less severe than further south. Trees grew on their flanks: hardy pine and spruce, mountain juniper. In this land the River Torrin had its birthplace. It was already a splashing, foaming torrent two hundred feet wide, an angry spate flushed with the offpourings of the mountains, too violent in its bed to freeze over. It had a hundred and fifty leagues to run before it became the majestic and placid giant which flowed through the city of Torunn and carved out its estuary in the warmer waters of the Kardian Sea beyond.

But here in its aeons of flood it had broken down the very mountains which surrounded it. Here it had carved out a valley amid the peaks. To the north were the last heights of the western Thurians, the rocky barrier which held in the hordes of Ostrabar, so that they had been forced in their decades of invasions to take the coastal route in order to break out to the south, and had come up against the walls of Aekir, the guns of Ormann Dyke. To the south-west of the river were the Cimbrics, Torunna's backbone, home of the Felimbric tribes and their secret valleys. But this gap, carved by the course of the Torrin, had for centuries been the link between Torunna and Charibon, west and east. It had been a highway of Imperial messengers in Fimbria's days of empire, when Charibon itself had been nothing more than a garrison fortress built to protect the route to the east from the savages of Almark. It was a conduit of trade and commerce, and in later days had been fortified by the Torunnans when the Fimbrian Hegemony came crashing down and men first began to kill in the name of God. And now there was an army marching along it, an infantry army whose soldiers were dressed in black, who carried twenty-foot pikes or leather-cased arquebuses. A grand tercio of Fimbrian soldiers, five thousand of the most feared warriors in the world, tramping through the blizzards and the snowdrifts towards Ormann Dyke.

THAT WAS THE noise he heard and could not account for. It was a sound he had never before heard in his life, and it carried over the creak of wood and leather, the clink of metal on metal, even the crunch of the snow.

Feet. Ten thousand feet marching together in the snow to produce a low thunder, something felt rather than heard, a hum in the bones.

Albrec opened his eyes, and found that he was alive.

He was utterly confused for a long minute. Nothing about him was familiar. He was in something that swayed and lurched and bumped along. A leather canopy over his head, chinks of unbearably bright light spearing through gaps here and there. Rich furs encasing him so that he could hardly move. He was bewildered, and could not think of any events which might have added up to the present.

He sat up, and his head exploded into lights and ache, clenching his eyes tight shut for him. He struggled an arm free from his coverings to rub at his face – there was something about it, something strange and whistling in the way he breathed – and the hand appeared bound in clean linen. But it was wrong, it had no shape. It was –

He blinked tears out of his eyes, tried to flex his fingers. But he could not, because they were no longer there. He had a thumb, but beyond his knuckles there was nothing. Nothing.

"Merciful God," he whispered.

He levered free his other hand. It, too, was bound in cloth, but there were fingers there, thank the Blessed Saints. Something to move, to touch with. They tingled as he wiggled them, as though coming to life after a sleep.

He felt his face, absurdly shutting his eyes as if he did not wish to see what his touch might tell him. His lips, his chin, his teeth in place, and his eyes the same. But –

The breath whistled in and out of the hole which had been his nose. He could touch bone. The fleshy part of the feature was gone, the nostrils no longer there. It must look like the hole in the face of a skull.

He lay back again, too shocked to weep, too lost to wonder what had happened. He remembered only shards of horror from a faraway land of dreams. The fanged grin of a werewolf. The dark of subterranean catacombs. The awful blankness of a blizzard, and then nothing at all. Except –

Avila.

And it came back to him with the speed and force of a revelation. They had been fleeing Charibon. The document! He fumbled frantically with his clothes. But his habit was gone. He was dressed in a woollen shift and long stockings, also of wool. He threw aside his furs and crawled over them, lurching as whatever he was inside swayed and bumped along. He scrabbled at the knots which held shut the leather canopy at his feet, the tears finally coming along with the realization of what had happened. He and Avila had been caught by the Inceptines. They must be on their way back to the monastery city. They would be burnt as heretics. And the document was gone. Gone!

The canopy fell open as he yanked at the drawstrings with his fingered hand, and he fell out and thumped face first into the rutted snow.

He clenched shut his eyes. There was warm breath on his cheek, and something soft as velvet nuzzled his ruined face.

"Get away there, brute!" a voice said, and the snow crunched beside him. Albrec opened his eyes to find a black shape leaning over him, and behind it the agonizing brightness of sunshine on snow, blinding.

Another shadow. The two resolved themselves into men who seized his arms and hauled him to his feet. He stood as confused as an owl in daylight.

"Come, priest. You are holding up the column," one said gruffly. The pair of them tried to stuff him back into the covered cart he had been riding in. Behind them, another such, drawn by an inquisitive mule, and behind that a hundred more, and a thousand men making a dark snake of figures in the snow, all in ranks, pikes at their shoulders. A huge crowd of men standing in the snow waiting for the obstruction ahead to be cleared, the cart to begin moving again.

"Who are you?" Albrec demanded feebly. "What is this?" They perched him on the back of the two-wheeled cart and one disappeared to take the halter of its mule. They started off again. The column moved once more. There had been no talk, no shouting at the delay, nothing but patience and abrupt efficiency. Albrec saw that the second man who had helped him, like the first, was dressed in knee-high leather boots rimmed with fur and a black cloak which looked almost clerical with its hood and slit sleeves. A plain short sword was hanging from a shoulder baldric. Attached to the harness of the mule he led was an arquebus, its iron barrel winking bright as lightning in the sun, and beside it was a small steel helmet and a pair of black-lacquered metal gauntlets. The man himself was crop-headed, broad and powerfully built under the cloak. He had several days of golden stubble glistening on his chin, and his face was ruddy and reddened, bronzed by days and weeks in the open.

"Who are you?" Albrec asked again.

"My name is Joshelin of Gaderia, twenty-sixth tercio. That's Beltran's."

He did not elaborate, and seemed to think that this should answer Albrec's questions.

"But *what* are you?" Albrec asked plaintively.

The man called Joshelin glared at him. "What is that, a riddle?"

"Forgive me, but are you a soldier of Almark? A – a mercenary?"

The man's eyes lit with anger. "I'm a Fimbrian soldier, priest, and this is a Fimbrian army you're in the midst of, so I'd be watchful of words like 'mercenary' if I were you."

Albrec's astonishment must have showed in his face, because the soldier went on less brusquely: "It's four days since we picked you up – you and the other cleric – and saved you from wolves and frostbite. He's in the cart behind me. He was less beaten up than you. He still has a face, at all events, just lost a few toes and the tips of his ears."

"Avila!" Albrec exclaimed in joy. He began to scramble down from the cart again, but Joshelin's hard palm on his chest halted him.

"He's asleep, like you were. Let him come to himself in his own time."

"Where are we going, if not to Charibon? Why are Fimbrians on the march again?" Albrec had heard rumours in Charibon of such things, but he had dismissed them as novices' fancies.

"We're to relieve Ormann Dyke, it seems," Joshelin said curtly, and spat into the snow. "The fortress we built ourselves. We're to take up the buckler where we set it down all those years ago. And scant gratitude we'll get for it, I shouldn't wonder. We're about as well trusted as Inceptines in this world. Still, it's a chance to fight the heathen again." He clamped his mouth shut, as if he thought he had begun to babble.

"Ormann Dyke," Albrec said aloud. The name was one out of history and legend. The great eastern fortress which had never fallen to assault. It was in Northern Torunna. They were marching to Torunna.

"I have to speak to someone," he said. "I have to know what was done with our belongings. It's important."

"Lost something, have you, priest?"

"Yes. It's important, I tell you. You can't guess how important."

Joshelin shrugged. "I know nothing about that. Siward and I were told to look after the pair of you, that's all. I think they burned your habits – they weren't worth keeping."

"Oh God," Albrec groaned.

"What is it, a reliquary or something? Were there gems sewn into your robes?"

"It was a story," Albrec said, his eyes stinging and dry. "It was just a story."

He crawled back into the darkness of the shrouded cart.

THE FIMBRIANS MARCHED far into the night, and when they halted, they deployed in a hollow square with the baggage waggons and mules in the middle. Sharpened stakes were hammered into the ground to make a bristling fence about the camp, and details were ordered out of the perimeter to collect firewood. Albrec was given a soldier's cloak and boots – both much too large for him – and was sat in front of a fire. Joshelin threw him cracker-bread, hard cheese and a wineskin, and then went off to do his stint as sentry.

The wind was getting up, flattening the flames of the fire. Around in the darkness other fires stitched a fiery quilt upon the snow-girt earth, and the loom of the mountains could be felt on every horizon, an awesome presence through whose peaks the clouds scudded and ripped like rolling rags. The Fimbrian camp was eerily quiet, save for the occasional bray of a mule. The men at the fires talked in low voices as they passed their rations out, but most of them simply ate, rolled themselves in their heavy cloaks and fell asleep. Albrec wondered how they endured it: the heavy marching, the short commons, the snatches of sleep on the frozen earth with no covering for their heads. Their hardiness half frightened him. He had seen soldiers before, of course: the Almarkan garrison of Charibon, and the Knights Militant. But these Fimbrians were something more. There was almost something monastic in their asceticism. He could not begin to imagine what they would be like in battle.

"Hogging the wineskin as usual, I see," a voice said, and Albrec turned from the fire.

"Avila!"

His friend had once been the most handsome Inceptine in Charibon. There was still a fineness to his features, but his face was gaunt and drawn now, even with a smile upon it. Something had been stripped from him, some flamboyance or facet of youth. He limped forward like an old man and half collapsed beside his friend, wrapped in a soldier's greatcloak like Albrec, his feet swathed in bandages.

"Well met, Albrec." And then as the firelight fell on the little monk's face: "Sweet God in heaven! What happened?"

Albrec shrugged. "Frostbite. You were luckier than I, it seems. Only a few toes."

"My God!"

"It's not important. It's not like we have a wife or a sweetheart. Avila, do you know where we are and whom we are with?"

Avila was still staring at him. Albrec could not meet his eyes. He felt an overpowering urge to put his hand over his face, but mastered it and instead gave his friend the wineskin. "Here. You look as though you need it."

"I'm sorry, Albrec." Avila took a long swig from the skin, crushing in its sides so that the wine squirted deep down his throat. He drank until the dark liquid brimmed out of his mouth, and then he squirted down more. Finally he wiped his lips.

"Fimbrians. It would seem our saviours are Fimbrians. And they march to Ormann Dyke."

"Yes. But I've lost it, Avila. They took it, the document. Nothing else matters now."

Avila studied his hands where they were gripped about the wine-skin. The flesh on them had peeled in places, and there were sores on the backs of them.

"Cold," he muttered. "I had no idea. It's like what we were told of leprosy."

"Avila!" Albrec hissed at him.

"The document, I know. Well, it's gone. But we are alive, Albrec, and we may yet remain unburned. Give thanks to God for that at least."

"And the truth will remain buried."

"I'd rather it were buried than me, to be frank."

Avila would not meet his friend's glare. Something in him seemed cowed by what they had been through. Albrec felt like shaking him.

"It's all right," the Inceptine said with a crooked smile. "I'm sure I'll get over it, this desire to live."

There were soldiers around them at the fire, ignoring them as if they did not exist. Most were asleep, but in the next moment those that were awake scrambled to their feet and stood stiff as statues. Albrec and Avila looked up to see a man with a scarlet sash about his middle standing there in a simple soldier's tunic. He had a moustache which arced around his mouth and glinted red-gold in the firelight.

"At ease," he said to his men, and they collapsed to the ground again. The newcomer then sat himself cross-legged at the fire beside the two monks.

"Might I trouble you for a drink of the wine?" he asked.

They gazed at him at a loss for words. Finally Avila bestirred himself and in his best frosty aristocratic tone said: "By all means, soldier. Perhaps then you will leave us alone. My friend and I have important matters to discuss."

The man drank deeply from the proffered wineskin and pinched the drops from his moustache. "How are you both feeling?"

"We've been better," Avila said, still haughty, every inch the Inceptine addressing a lowly man-at-arms. "Might I ask who you are?"

"You might," the man said, unruffled. "But then again I might not choose to tell you. As it happens, my name is Barbius, Barbius of Neyr."

"Then perchance, Barbius of Neyr, you will leave us, now that you've had your drink of wine." Avila's haughtiness was becoming brittle. He was beginning to sound shrill. The man only looked at him with one eyebrow raised.

"Are you an officer?" Albrec asked, staring at the man's scarlet sash.

"You could say that." Off in the darkness an invisible soldier uttered a half-smothered guffaw.

"Perhaps you would tell us what happened to our belongings then," Avila said. "They seem to have been misplaced."

The man smiled, but his eyes had the glitter of sea ice, no gleam of humour to warm them. "I might have thought some gratitude was in order. My men, after all, saved your lives."

"For which we are duly grateful. Now our things, where are they?"

"Safe in the tent of the army commander, never fear. My turn for questions. Why were you fleeing Charibon?"

"What makes you think we were fleeing the place?" Avila countered.

"You were perhaps taking a constitutional in the blizzard, then?"

"It is none of your business," the young Inceptine snapped.

"Oh, but it is. I saved your lives. You'd be frozen wolf-bait had my men not found you. I believe I am due an answer to whatever questions I have the urge to pose, plus some common courtesy in their answering."

The two monks were silent for a few seconds. It was Albrec who finally spoke.

"We apologize for our lack of manners. We are indeed grateful for our lives, but we have been under some strain of late. Yes, we were fleeing the monastery-city. It was an internal matter, a – a power struggle in which we became embroiled through no fault of our own. Plus, there was a heretical side to it..."

"I am intrigued," the Fimbrian said. "Go on."

"I saved certain forbidden texts from destruction," Albrec said, his mind racing as it concocted the tissue of half-truth and outright lie. "They were discovered, and we had to flee or be burned as heretics. That is all there is to it."

Barbius nodded. "I thought as much. The text you were carrying with you – is it one of these heretical documents?"

Albrec's heart leapt. "Yes, yes it is. It still exists, then?"

"The marshal has it in his tent, as I told you." He seemed to lose interest in them. His gaze flicked out to the surrounding campfires where his men lay close to the flames in weary sleep. "I must go. Call by the marshal's tent in the morning and you shall have your belongings back. You may stay with the column as long as you wish, but be warned: we travel to Ormann Dyke, and the longer you remain with the army the worse the roads will become, the less easy for you to make your own way in the wilderness."

"If you could spare us a couple of mules we could be on our way by tomorrow," Albrec said eagerly.

Barbius's cold eyes sized up the little monk squarely.

"Whither will you go?"

"To Torunn."

"Why?"

Albrec was momentarily confused, sure he had said too much, given something away. He faltered, and it was Avila who spoke, his voice dripping with scorn.

"Why, to throw in our lot with Macrobius and his fellow heretics, of course. My enemy's enemy is my friend, as they say. It's a hard world, soldier. Even clerics have to rub along the best they can."

Barbius smiled again. "Indeed they do. I will see you in the morning, then." He rose easily, and it was Avila who called him back as he turned to go.

"Wait! Where is this commander's tent? How shall we find it? This camp is as big as a town."

The Fimbrian shrugged, walking away. "Ask for Barbius of Neyr's headquarters. He commands the army, or so I am told."

THREE

"I DON'T LIKE it, my lady," Brienne was saying as she fussed with the pins in Isolla's hair. "No one will tell me anything, not even the pageboys."

"If they won't spill their confidences to you, there is truly something wrong with the world," Isolla said wryly. "That's enough, Brienne. I can't bear it when you fuss."

"You've an impression to make," Brienne said stubbornly. "Would you have these Hebrians think you were come from some backwater court where the ladies still wore their hair down on their shoulders?"

Isolla smiled. There was no arguing with her maidservant sometimes. Brienne was a minx of a woman, tiny and slim with raven hair and flashing hazel eyes. Her skin possessed the flawless paleness which Isolla had once yearned for, and with a crook of her little finger she could set men staring and stammering. But she was no light-headed giggler. She had sense, and was the closest thing to a friend Isolla had ever had, if she did not count her brother Mark. Mark the King, who loved his sister and who had sent her here to wed a man of whom she knew virtually nothing. A man who was mysteriously absent.

"You don't think he's dead, do you?" she asked Brienne.

"No, my lady. Not dead. I ventured to suggest that to one of the cooks and was almost brained by a ladle for my pains. They're very touchy, the palace staff. No, it's my belief something happened to him in the battle to retake the city. He was wounded, that's plain, but no one knows or will say how badly. It's unsettling. I was in Abrusio as a girl – you know my family hailed from Imerdon – and it was a godless place then, teeming with foreigners and heathens, everything to be had for a price. It's different now. All that is gone."

"War is apt to put a dampener on things," Isolla said, studying herself in the dressing mirror. "That will do, Brienne."

"No powder, my lady?"

"For the fiftieth time, no. I'll not have myself painted like a mannikin, even for a king."

Brienne pursed her lips in disapproval, but said nothing. She was utterly devoted to her mistress, the woman who had befriended the kitchen-wench and raised her to the level of body-servant. And she knew how conscious Isolla was of her plainness, and suffered for her when the other ladies at court whispered behind the backs of their hands. The Princess of Astarac could sit a horse as well as a man, and she had both a man's bold way of striding on her long coltish legs and a man's bluntness in speaking. And she read books, books by the hundred it was rumoured. A strange way for a noblewoman to carry on. But Mark the King would have nothing said against his sister and her eccentric ways, and it was even rumoured that he discussed high policy with her in the quiet of her apartments. Discussing politics with a woman! It was unnatural.

Brienne felt the feminine barbs more keenly than her mistress, for they had long ago lost their sting for Isolla. She wanted to see her lady happy, married, with child. All the things that a woman ought to be. But she knew that for Isolla life held more, not merely because she had been born a princess, but simply because of the woman she was.

There was a knock on the door. Isolla rose smoothly from the dressing table and said: "Enter."

A footman stepped in, in Hebrian scarlet. He bowed. "My lady, the wizard Golophin asks if he might be admitted."

"Golophin?" Isolla's brow creased, then smoothed. "Yes, of course. Show him in." And when the door had closed again: "Quickly, Brienne. He likes wine. And bring some olives."

Her maidservant rushed out to the anteroom whilst Isolla composed herself. Golophin, Abeleyn's mentor and teacher – and, she had heard, his closest friend. Perhaps now she would learn what was ailing the invisible King of Hebrion.

Golophin entered with little ceremony beyond a courtly bow. She was shocked at his appearance, the desiccated look of his flesh. The man was no more than an animated skeleton. The eyes, however, missed nothing.

"My thanks for receiving me so informally, lady," the old wizard said. He had the deep voice of a singer or orator, music all through it.

They sat and looked at one another for a moment whilst Brienne bustled in with the wine and olives. Golophin's gaze was frank and open. *He's sizing me up*, Isolla thought. *He's wondering how much he can tell me.*

The old wizard poured for them both, saluted her with a tilt of his glass, drank his entire gobletful at a draught and poured himself another. Isolla sipped at hers, suppressing her surprise.

Golophin smiled. "I am trying to regain my lost strength, lady, and perhaps I am trying to forget how I lost it. Pay me no mind."

She liked his frankness, and sat without saying a word. She somehow realized that it would be better if she were not to make small talk.

"Are your apartments to your liking?" Golophin asked absently.

She had been given a vast, lonely suite that belonged to some long-dead Hebrian queen – Abeleyn's mother, perhaps. The rooms were hideous, with sombre tapestries and hangings and devotional pictures of Saints. The furniture was huge and heavy and dark-wooded. The place felt like a mausoleum. But she nodded and said: "They are very fine."

"Never liked this place myself," the wizard admitted. "Abeleyn's mother Bellona was a fine woman, but a bit austere. I see you've pulled the hangings away from the balconies. That's good. Lets in what sun there is in this black month of the year." He threw back another glass of the wine. Isolla thought privately that it was not the third or even the fourth glass he'd had that morning.

"I remember you as a child," he said. "A patient little creature. Abeleyn liked you, but had the cruelty of all small boys. I hope you do not hold it against him."

"Of course not," she said, rather coldly.

He smiled. "You have a head on your shoulders, lady, or so I am told. That is why I am here. Were you another tinsel-brained princess, you'd be kept in the dark and told whatever we thought you'd believe. But I have a feeling that will not suffice. That is why I am willing to do what I am about to do."

Ah, she thought, and straightened. "Brienne, leave us."

Her maidservant exited the room with a piteous look. Golophin rose from his chair and paced about the floor like some huge cadaverous bat, his mantle billowing out behind him. No – he was more of a raptor, a starved falcon, perhaps. Even his movements were as quick and economical as a bird's, despite the wine he'd quaffed.

He went to the far wall, pulled back the hideous tapestry that hung there and pressed hard on the stone. There was a click, and a gap appeared, rapidly broadening into a low doorway.

Isolla sucked in her breath. "Magic."

He laughed. "No. Engineering. The palace is riddled with hidden doors and secret passageways. Now you must come with me."

She hesitated. She did not like the look of the hole he was gesturing at. It might lead anywhere. Was there some kind of plot afoot?

"Trust me," Golophin said gently. And then she saw the suffering in his eyes. There was a grief there that he held bottled up as tightly as a genie of eastern myth. Despite herself, she rose and joined him at the secret door.

"I am going to take you to meet your betrothed," the wizard said, and led her into the darkness.

ISOLLA HAD SEEN bale-fire before, as a child. A ball of it hovered above Golophin's head in the dark and lit the way for them. But it was a guttering thing, like a candle almost burnt down to the wick. She suddenly realized that the old mage was damaged in some way – something had stolen away his strength and made him into a caricature of what he had once been. It was the war, she guessed. It had drained him somehow.

The passage they trod was smoothly made out of jointed stone, and it rose and wound like the coils of a snake. There were other doors off its sides, leading to other rooms in the palace, Isolla supposed. She knew she, a foreigner, was being trusted with some of the secrets of the palace. But then she'd be Hebrion's queen soon enough anyway.

They halted. The bale-fire went out and there was a grating of stone. She followed the wizard's lean back through a low door like the one in her own chambers, and found herself in a high-ceilinged room that was almost totally dark. A rack of tall candles fluttered by the side of a massively ornate four-poster bed, and she could make out weapons on the walls gleaming in the gloom. Maps and books and more of the dull hangings. A bedstand with jug and ewer of silver. And everywhere engraved or embossed, the Hebrian Royal arms. She was in the King's chambers.

"Speak normally. No whispers," Golophin told her. "He is far away, but not gone, not entirely. It may be that a new voice will reach him as a familiar one might not."

"What – ?" But Golophin took her arm and led her to the side of the huge bed.

The King. Her horrified eyes took in what was left of him at a glance, and her hand flew to her mouth. This thing was to be her husband.

Golophin was watching her. She sensed a protective anger in him that was not very far from the surface. She brought her hand down and touched Abeleyn's where it lay on the coverlet.

His features she recognized: the dark hair as thick as ever despite the threads of grey. The face she had known as sun-brown was as pallid as the sheets behind it. She was surprised to feel grief, not for herself who was to be joined to this wreck of a man, but for Abeleyn, the high-spirited boy she had known who had pulled her hair and said cruel things about her nose. He had not deserved to end up like this.

"What was it?" she asked, uncomfortably aware of Golophin's hawk-like scrutiny.

"A shell. One of our own, God help us, in the moment when the battle was won. I was able to seal the stumps, but I had already exhausted myself in the fighting and could do nothing more. It would take a great work of theurgy to heal him completely, something I'm not sure I would be capable of even if I were at my full strength. And so he lies here, his mind in some fathomless limbo I cannot reach. We have made discreet enquiries for Mindrhymers, but those who were not murdered under Sastro di Carrera's regime fled to the ends of the earth. The Dweomer cannot help Abeleyn. His own will must pull him through, and whatever human warmth we can give." Here he glared at Isolla as if he dared her to contradict him.

But she was not so easily cowed. She released the unconscious King's hand and faced the old mage squarely. "I take it there will be no wedding until the King is brought to himself again."

"Yes. But there *will* be a wedding. The country needs it. We may have slaughtered Carrera's retainers and expelled the surviving Knights Militant, but there are still ambitious men in Hebrion who would stoop to seize a crown if they saw it fall."

"You cannot fool the world for ever, Golophin. The truth will out, in the end."

"I know. But we have to try. This man has greatness in him. I will not abandon him to rot!"

He loves him, she thought. *He truly does.* And she warmed to the fierce old man. She had always responded to lost causes, had always sided with the underdog. Perhaps because it was how she had always seen herself.

"So you brought me here to join your little conspiracy. Who else knows the true condition of the King?"

"Admiral Rovero, General Mercado, and perhaps three or four of the palace servants whom I trust."

"The whole city is in mourning."

"I had to put out a bulletin on the King's health. He is dangerously ill, but not dying. That is the official line."

"How long do you think you can keep the hounds leashed?"

"A few weeks, maybe a couple of months. Rovero and Mercado have the army and the fleet firmly under control, and in any case Hebrion's soldiers and sailors fairly worship Abeleyn. No, as always, it is the court we must worry about. And that, my dear, is where you come in."

"I see. So I am to make reassuring noises about the palace."

"Yes. Are you willing?"

She looked down at the wrecked King again, and felt an absurd urge to ruffle the dark hair on the pillow. "I am willing. My brother would wish it so anyway."

"Good. I did not read your character wrong."

"If you had, Golophin, what would have become of me?"

The old man grinned wolfishly. "This palace would have become your prison."

FOR THE LADY Jemilla, the palace had indeed come to seem like a prison. Ever since the retaking of the city she had been shepherded and watched and guarded like some prisoner of war. And she had not seen Abeleyn once in all that time. That old devil Golophin was always there to put her off. The King was too ill to see anyone but his senior ministers, he said. But the rumours were running like wildfire about the palace: that Abeleyn was dead and already buried, that he was too horribly scarred to see the light of day, that his injuries had turned him into an imbecile. In any case, the triumvirate of Rovero, Mercado and Golophin – always Golophin – were running Abrusio as though they wore crowns themselves. It galled her beyond measure that she, who bore the King's heir, should be put off and shuffled about as though she were some troublesome trull whose swelling belly could be ignored. And then, worst of all, the Princess of Astarac had arrived with due state to be married to the father of Jemilla's child. Or to the man everyone thought was the father, it made no odds – not now.

Things were slipping through her grasp with every passing day. This wedding must not happen. Her child must be recognized as the rightful heir. And if Abeleyn were as near death as everyone supposed, then surely it made sense to secure the succession. Couldn't they see that? Or must they be made to see it?

She lay naked on the wide bed in her suite. The short day was almost over and the room was dark but for the blaze of a fire in the huge hearth that dominated one wall. At least they had quartered her in the palace. That was something. She regarded her body in the firelight, running her hands up and down it as a man might with a horse he meant to buy. The swelling was visible now, a bulge that marred the otherwise perfect symmetry of her shape. She frowned at it. Childbirth. Such a messy, painful affair. Even messier if one sought to avoid it. She remembered the blood and her own shrieking the night she rid herself of Richard Hawkwood's first child. Nothing could be worse than that.

Her breasts were filling out. She cupped them, ran her slender fingers down her abdomen to where the hair sprang in ebony curls at her crotch. She stroked herself there absently, thinking. She thought of her body as an instrument, a tool to be utilized with the utmost efficiency. It was her key to a better life, this flesh and all that it contained.

She sprang up, pulled round her shoulders a robe of Nalbenic silk and padded barefoot to the door. A moment to gather herself, to rehearse her words, and then she yanked open the heavy portal in a rush.

"Quickly, quickly – you there!"

There were two guards, not one. She must have caught them as they were changing shifts. It made her hesitate, but only for the fraction of a second.

"There's something in my room – a rat. You must come and look!"

The two soldiers were members of the Abrusio garrison, veterans of the battle to retake the city. They were rough, untutored swordsmen who had not been told why they were to guard the lady Jemilla's door, only that her every move was to be reported direct to General Mercado. They hung back, and one said: "I'll get your lady's maidservant."

"No, no, you fools. She can't abide rats any more than I can. Get in there and kill it for me, for God's sake. Are you men at all?"

Jemilla was beautifully unkempt, one shoulder gleaming pale as ivory above the robe she clutched together at her breasts. The two soldiers looked at one another, and one shrugged. They marched into her chambers.

Jemilla followed them, shutting the door behind her. The soldiers poked under the bed, along the wall hangings.

"I believe it's gone, lady," one of them said, and then said no more but simply stared. Jemilla had dropped her robe and was standing incandescently nude before them, touching herself, her body undulating like a willow in a breeze.

"It's been so long," she said. "Won't you please help me?"

"Lady —" one of the men said hoarsely. He held out a hand as if to ward her off.

"Oh, please. Do this thing for me, just this once." She approached them as they stood, thunderstruck. "Please, soldiers. Just this once. It's been so long, and no one will ever know."

The men's eyes met for the briefest moment, and then they moved in on her like wolves on a lamb.

FOUR

THE MEN WERE drooping in the saddle when the lead riders of the screen came in sight of Staed. Corfe called a halt – it was by then the middle of the night – and after seeing to their mounts the tribesmen sank to the ground and slept without fires to warm them, pickets out every hundred yards around the bivouac.

Corfe, Marsch and Andruw stole up to the rising ground that hid them from their objective and took a look at the port itself in the starlit night. It was bitterly cold, and flakes of snow were running before the wind like feathers. The ground was frozen stiff as stone, which was all to the good. It would be better for the horses. Nothing worse than a cavalry charge bogged hock-deep in mud.

Staed was a largish port of some ten thousand people, one of the prosperous coastal settlements that the Fimbrians had founded centuries before in their drive to populate what was then a wilderness dominated by the Felimbric tribes. It had done well for itself. Corfe could see the massive breakwaters that protected the harbour and held in their arms over a score of vessels: galleys of the Kardian, probably hailing from one of the Sultanates, and some caravels, the seaworthy little ships that were the lifeblood of trade in the Levangore. Down by the harbour was the old fortress – in which Duke Narfintyr had his headquarters, no doubt, his ancestral seat. It was tall under the stars, a castle built before artillery. Nowadays walls were squat and thick to resist bombardment. But three hundred men would not fit in that keep, much less three thousand. Where had he them quartered?

They lay on the hard earth with the cold slowly sinking into them, the warmth of their bodies chilled by the metal armour they wore. The world was vast and starlit and bitter with winter. A few lights burned in Staed and in the keep which dominated it, but the rest of the sleeping earth seemed dark as a cave.

This country had been Corfe's home once. He had been born in a farmer's hut not two leagues from where he now lay. He had been a farmer's son for fourteen years, before he followed the tercios north to Torunn to go for a soldier. It was the only profession allowed to the lowest class of commoners in Torunn, those tied to the land by the obligations to their feudal lords. For the poor, it was soldiering, or serfdom. An age ago it seemed, that last morning on the farm, a time back in the youth of the world. There was no familiarity in the dark hills, nothing for him here that he could recall. He remembered only his mother, small and patient, and his father, a broad, taciturn man who had worked harder than any human being he had ever known before or since, who had not stopped his only son from going for a soldier, though it would mean there would be no one around to look after him in his old age.

Old age. They were ten years dead, worn out by a lifetime of backbreaking labour. Dead in their fourth decade so that nobles like Narfintyr might hunt and drink fine wine and foment rebellion. That was the way the world worked. Ironic that the peasant's son would come back with an army intent on destroying the noble. There was a sweetness in that which Corfe savoured.

It was Marsch who discovered the enemy camp, with his eagle sight. A scattering of fires to the south of the town, on a hillside. There was no shape or regularity to them. They might have been sparks fallen from the forge of some sky-borne god. Corfe studied them, somewhat puzzled.

"No camp discipline. They're spread over damn near half a mile. What are their officers thinking of?"

"There's folk in the castle," Andruw said quietly. "Lights and such. Do you think Narfintyr is in there, or out in the field with his men?"

"It's a cold night," Corfe said with a smile. "If you were one of the old nobility, where would you be? And if his senior officers are out of the cold with him, then that would explain the slackness of their men's bivouac. But doesn't he know that there's an army approaching him? It's criminally remiss of him to sleep separately from his command, even if he is a bone-headed nobleman."

"We made sixty miles in the last eighteen hours," Andruw reminded Corfe. "It could be we've stolen a march on them. Maybe they're expecting Aras's column and no more, and it's still twenty-five leagues behind us, a week at their pace."

Corfe considered it. The more he thought, the more he was sure that he had to move at once. Now. If he delayed the attack a day there was every chance his men would be discovered, and there went the advantage of surprise, which was vital when he faced the odds he did.

"We attack tonight," he said.

Andruw groaned. "You can't be serious. The men have had no sleep in two days. They've just completed a hellish forced march. For God's sake, Corfe, they're flesh and blood!"

"It's to spare their flesh and blood that I want to hit the enemy tonight. They can sleep all they want once we've broken Narfintyr's men."

"The colonel is right," Marsch said. "We have them where we want them. Such a thing may not happen again. It has to be tonight."

"God's blood, but you're a couple of fire-eaters," Andruw said, resigned. "What's the plan then, Corfe?"

Their colonel was silent for a few seconds, watching the haphazard collection of campfires that was the enemy camp. It was on a slight hill – at least they had had the sense to choose the higher ground – but if he squinted, he could make out a deeper darkness in the night on the far side of the camp. A small forest. Probably they had camped near it for the convenience of the firewood. Something clicked into place in Corfe's head. Finally he said: "Have you ever hunted boar in a wood, Andruw?"

THE STARS WHEELED in their courses, the cold deepened. It took two hours to get the squadrons in position, the men staggering with tiredness, half of them afoot in accordance with Corfe's plan. It was one of the most wearing and difficult exercises in the field, Corfe thought as he sat his horse waiting for his men to get into position. A night march, when body and brain are drunk with exhaustion. Men can sleep as they march, blinking awake as their knees start to buckle. They begin to see bright lights and hallucinations in the night. Shadows become living things, trees move and walk. He had experienced it all himself. He hoped he had not pushed his willing tribesmen too far.

He had four squadrons about him, two hundred men mounted and sitting still as graven statues while their horses breathed pale plumes of smoke into the frigid night air. Thank God for the surplus horses. Every one of them was on a relatively fresh mount. Only ten men remained back at their camp with the rest of the remounts and the baggage. As always, he was staking everything on one throw of the dice. He had not the numbers to do otherwise.

His cavalry were deployed in a two-deep line on a slope to the north of the enemy camp, between it and the outskirts of Staed itself. From where he was he could see the sea glittering under the clear night sky off to his left. Ahead, perhaps half a mile away, the campfires burned by the hundred, guttering low as dawn approached.

The rest of his men, on foot, should by now be on the southern side of the enemy campsite, getting into position under Marsch and Andruw. Their approach and deployment would be concealed by the wood there, and the northern edge of the treeline would be their start point. They were the beaters, their job to wreck havoc and flush the enemy in a confused mass from the camp into the open. Like flushing a boar out of a hazel brake on to the spears of the hunters. Corfe had no reserves. Everything depended on speed, darkness, surprise, and the sheer unbridled savagery of his men.

And there it began. A surf of shouting in the night, the shrieking war-cry of the Felimbri, a sound to chill the blood. Corfe's mount twitched and fidgeted under him at the distant sounds, while around him the other mounted men seemed to straighten in the saddle, their exhaustion forgotten.

Marsch and Andruw were in the enemy camp. Men would be stumbling from their tents half awake. They would be fumbling for weapons in the firelit dark, running from unknown attackers. They would have no time to don their armour or to form up. Their officers would not have a chance. If any rallied and got a hold of themselves, Marsch and Andruw were under orders to butcher them, to annihilate any sign of organized resistance. Otherwise, their task was to simply panic the enemy, make him run north. Into the waiting arms of Corfe's Cathedraller cavalry.

A few scattered arquebus shots, flashes followed by bangs. The shouting grew louder. Men screaming and yelling in fear, pain, anger. Blooming flames startling bright in the fleeing darkness. Someone was setting the tents on fire. Shadows and shapes running past the flames, the campfires blinking on and off as men went by them. This was the hardest part, judging when the enemy was in the open, far enough out of the camp so that Corfe's charge would not carry them back into it. He could see them now. There was a mass of men in streaming retreat, a mob rather than an army, hundreds of them fleeing north towards the town with the tribesmen slashing at their heels, not giving a moment in which they might reform and dress their ranks. In the confusion they would not even realize that they outnumbered their attackers.

Now. Corfe hoped his men would recognize the signals he and Andruw had tried to teach them. He turned to Cerne, the burly tribesman on his right hand.

"Sound me the *Advance*."

Cerne wet his lips and put a hunting horn to them. It was an unorthodox kind of cavalry bugle, but it did the trick and it was somehow fitting that these men should be summoned to battle with the clear, high call of the chase, the hunting call of their own mountains.

The first line of heavily armoured horsemen began to move forward. A walk at first, then a trot. Metal clanking in the night air, the muffled snorting of horses. A sound that was almost a deep hum: the thumping of a myriad of hooves on the hard earth.

Corfe moved ahead of his men, lance upraised. He had to keep them in line, keep the cohesion of the unit until the last moment, like clenching the fingers into a fist for the blow. This was new to them, this keeping of a formation while mounted, and though he had drummed it into them as far as he could on their journey south he still could not be sure if they would remember the drills in the heat of approaching battle. So he stayed ahead of the line, something for them to focus on.

A canter. The line was becoming ragged as some men drew ahead, the horses jostling each other. The enemy was a black crowd of faceless shapes two hundred yards ahead. They were still fighting Marsch and Andruw's men to their rear and the fire of the burning camp silhouetted them. They would be blinded by the light of the flames and would not be able to see what was approaching them out of the night. But they would hear the hoof-thunder, and would pause, afraid and uncertain.

"Charge!" Corfe screamed, and levelled his lance. Cerne blew the ringing five-note hunting call of the Cimbric foothills. The horsemen spurred their mounts into a raging flat-out gallop, and the lances came down like a wood and iron hedge.

Corfe felt his mount go up and down small dips, rising and falling with the shape of the earth. Someone stumbled – he glimpsed it out of the corner of his eye, and there was the scream as a horse went pinwheeling. A rabbit hole, perhaps. They were blind to whatever was below the hooves of their mounts, an unnerving experience for a horseman, especially when he is encumbered by armour and lance, his vision, such as it is, circumscribed by the weighty bulk of an iron helmet. But the men held together, shrieking their shrill, unearthly battlecry. A hundred armoured troops on a hundred heavy horses, lances out chest-high. They crashed into the enemy at full career, like some iron-shod apocalypse come raging out of the dark, and trod them into the ground, impaled them, crushed them, knocked them flying.

Corfe was able to see more clearly. The burning campsite made the night into a chaotic, yellow-lit circus of toiling shadow, the flash of steel, faces half seen and then ridden down, stabbed at with the tall lances or hacked down with swords.

There was no coherent resistance. The enemy could not form ranks, and the cavalry hunted them like animals, spearing them and knocking them off their feet. It was murder, pure and simple. Those who could were running through the gaps in Corfe's first line, now a series of struggling knots of horsemen brought to a standstill by the press of bodies and beasts around them. They ran to what they thought was salvation – northwards towards Staed and the castle of their overlord.

And these staggering survivors who kept running were hit by Corfe's second line, which Ensign Ebro now brought screaming out of the night at full gallop. Another thunderous wave of giant shadows which resolved itself into raging eyes and hooves and wicked piercing iron, not horsemen at all but some terrible fusion of beast and man out of nightmare myth. They smashed their way through mobs of men, dropping broken lances and drawing swords to slash and stab, whilst under them the trained destriers reared up to bring down shattering hooves and bit and kicked in tune with their riders.

Corfe was not surprised to hear some of his men laughing as they whirled and swung and stabbed relentlessly in that maelstrom of slaughter, their exhaustion forgotten, their blood rising in that strange, reckless exaltation that sometimes comes upon men in combat. They were born horse-soldiers, well-mounted and in the midst of battle. They were doing what nature had created them to do. Corfe realized in that moment that in these few he had the kernel of what could be a great army, a force to rival Fimbrian tercios. With ten thousand of these men he could wipe anyone who opposed him off the face of the earth.

THE SUN ROSE at last in a bloody welter of cloud out of the glittering sea. Shadow lingered in the folds of the hills and there was a ground mist which hid the battlefield like a shroud pulled over for decency's sake. Morning, in all its chill greyness, and the aftermath of the night.

It was *Andaon*, the first day of the Year of the Saint 552. Over seven hundred corpses littered the field, and of those only thirty were from Corfe's command. Duke Narfintyr's army was a dismembered wreck. More than a thousand prisoners taken, scores more ridden down and killed in the pursuit all the way to the outskirts of Staed. A few hundred had mustered some shreds of discipline and had fought their way clear of the trap; they were in the hills now, their way to the town barred by the heavy cavalry. They could stay there. Corfe's men were hollow-eyed and quaking with tiredness, the adrenalin of the battle dying. And they had lost heavily in horses: the carcasses of more than eighty of the big destriers littered the field.

Corfe stood beside his steaming, quivering horse, grimacing at the flap of flesh some blade had taken out of its shoulder. This was the worst part, the part he hated, when the glory of the fight gave way to maimed men and animals and the trembling aftershock of battle. When one had to look at the contorted and broken faces of the dead, and see that they were one's fellow countrymen, killed because they had been ordered to leave their small farms and do the bidding of their noble masters.

Andruw joined him, bareheaded, his blond hair dark with sweat. His usual jauntiness was subdued.

"Poor bastards," he said, and he nudged the body of a dead boy – not more than thirteen – with his foot.

"I'll hang Narfintyr, when I catch him," Corfe said quietly.

Andruw shook his head. "That bird has flown the coop. He got on a ship when word of the battle reached the town. He's out on the Kardian, probably making for one of the Sultanates, and half his household with him. The piece of shit. But we did our job, at any rate."

"We did our job," Corfe repeated.

"A night cavalry charge," Andruw said. "That's one for the history books."

Corfe wiped his eyes, knuckling his sockets until the lights came. The tiredness was like a sodden blanket hanging from his shoulders. He and his men were shambling ghosts, mere wraiths of the butchering demons they had been during the fight. He had two hundred of them overseeing the slow, limping progress of the prisoners back to town, whilst the rest looked after their wounded comrades and scoured the battlefield for anyone who might have been overlooked and who was lying still alive under the sky. Others under Ebro were commandeering Narfintyr's castle and all it contained, setting up a crude field hospital and collecting anything in the way of provisions that Staed had to offer. So many things to do. Clearing up after a battle was always much worse than the preparation for one. So many things to do... but they had won. They had defeated a force many times their own, and at such slight cost to themselves that it seemed almost obscene. Not a battle, but a massacre.

"Have you ever seen men such as these?" Andruw asked him wonderingly. He was staring at the Cathedrallers, who shambled about the field leading their worn-out horses, their armour cast in the strange and barbaric style of the east. They looked like beings from another world in the morning light.

"On horseback? Never. They make Torunnan cuirassiers look like boys. There is some... energy to them. Something I have never seen before."

"You have made a discovery here, Corfe," Andruw said. "No – you are creating something. You have added discipline to savagery, and the sum of the two is something awesome. Something new."

They were both drunk. Drunk with fatigue and with killing. And perhaps with more than that.

"A few of the surviving local notables are waiting for us in the town," Andruw said more briskly. "They want to treat for peace and hand in the arms of their retainers. They have no stomach for fighting, not after this."

"Do they know how few we are, the shape we're in?" Corfe asked.

Andruw grinned evilly. "They think we've two thousand men out here, everyone a howling fiend. They don't even know which country we hail from."

"Let's keep them in ignorance. By God, Andruw, I'm as feeble as a kitten, and I feel like lord of the world."

"Victory will do that," Andruw said, smiling. "Me, I just want a bath and a corner to pitch myself in."

"It'll be a while before you have either. We have a busy day ahead of us."

ALBREC HAD NEVER known any soldiers before, not even the Almarkan troops of the Charibon garrison. He had assumed that men of war were necessarily crude, rough, loud and overbearing. But these men, these Fimbrians, were different.

A blinding white snowscape that reared up in savage, dazzling mountains on both sides. Snow blew in flags and banners off the topmost peaks of the Cimbrics to his right and the Thurians to his left. This was the Torrin Gap, the place where west met east. An ancient conduit, the highway of armies for centuries.

Fimbrians had marched here before, back in the early days of the empire when they had been a restless, eternally curious folk. They had sent expeditions north-east into the vast emptiness of the Torian plains where now Almark's horse-herds grazed. They had been the first civilized men to cross the Searil River into what was now Northern Torunna, and their parties of surveyors and botanists had crossed the southern Thurians into what was now Ostrabar. They had been a nation full of questions once, and sure of their own place in the world. Albrec knew his history; he had pored over untold volumes relating to the Fimbrian Hegemony when he had been assistant librarian in Charibon. He knew that the western world as it presently existed had largely been created by the Fimbrians. The Ramusian kingdoms had each been provinces of their empire. The capitals of the western kings had been built by Fimbrian engineers, and the great highways of Normannia had been constructed to speed the passage of their tercios.

So he felt strangely as though he were back in time, lost in some earlier century when the black-clad pikemen of the electorates had reigned supreme across the west. He was in the company of a Fimbrian army marching east, something which had not been seen in four hundred years. He felt oddly privileged, as if he had been given a glimpse of a larger world, one in which the rituals of Charibon were archaic irrelevancies.

But he was not sure what to make of these hard-faced men who were, for the moment, his travelling companions. They were sombre as monks, laconic to the point of taciturnity, and yet generous to a fault. He and Avila had been completely outfitted with cold-weather clothing and all forms of travelling gear. They had been given mules from the baggage train to ride when every man in the army marched on foot, even its commander, Barbius. Their hurts had been doctored by army physicians with terse gentleness, and as they were completely inept their rations were cooked for them at night by Joshelin and Siward, the two soldiers who seemed to have been assigned to look after them: two older men who had been relegated from the front rank of fighting infantry to look after the baggage train, and who accepted their extra duties without a murmur.

"An incredible society, it must be, in Fimbria," Avila said to his friend as they rode along near the back of the mile-long column.

"How is that?" Albrec asked him.

"Well, so far as I can make out, there is no nobility. That's why their leaders are called electors. They have a series of assemblies at which names are put forward, and the male population vote for their leaders, with each man's vote counting for the same as the next, whether he be a blacksmith or a landowner. It's the merest anarchy."

"Strange," Albrec said. "Equality among all men. Have you noticed how free and easy the men are with our friend the marshal, Barbius? He has no household worth speaking of, no bodyguards or retainers. And he keeps no state, except for a tent where the senior officers meet. But for the fact that they do as he says, there's no difference between him and the lowliest foot-soldier."

"It is incredible," Avila agreed. "How they ever conquered the world I'll never know. Were they always like this, Albrec?"

"They had emperors once, and it was the choosing of the last one that sent the electorates into civil war and provided the opportunity for the provinces to break away and become the Seven Kingdoms."

"What happened?"

"Arbius Menin, the emperor, was dying, and wanted his son to succeed him even though he was a boy of eight. Sons had succeeded fathers before, but they had been men of maturity and ability, not children. The other electors wouldn't stand for it, and there was war. The empire crumbled around their ears while Fimbrian battled Fimbrian. Narbosk broke away from Fimbria entirely and became the separate state it is today. The other electorates finally patched up their differences and tried to win the provinces back, but they had bled the country white and no longer had the strength. The Seven Kingdoms arose in place of the empire. The world had changed, and there was no going back. Fimbria retreated in on itself and no longer took an interest in anything outside its own borders."

"Until now. This time," Avila said grimly.

"Yes. Until this day."

"What changed their minds, I wonder?"

"Who can say? Lucky for us something did."

Joshelin came alongside them, leading his train of mules, his weathered face aflame with the cold and the pace of the march.

"You sound like a student of history," he said to Albrec. "I thought you were a monk."

"I used to read a lot."

"Aye? What about that book you were so keen to get back from the marshal's tent? Is it worth reading?"

"Whatever it is, it doesn't concern you," Avila said tartly. Joshelin merely looked at him.

"Only the ignorant are too poor to afford courtesy," he said. "Inceptine." He slowed his paced so that the two monks drew ahead of him again.

Albrec touched the ancient document that was once more hidden in the folds of his cloak. Barbius had given it over with not even a question as to its content. The little monk had received the impression that the Fimbrian marshal had a lot on his mind. There were couriers – the only Fimbrians who ever went mounted – coming and going every day, and camp rumour had it that they were in contact with General Martellus of Ormann Dyke, and that the news they bore was not good.

Soon the time would come when the two monks would have to break away from the army and strike out on their own towards Torunn, whilst the column continued to follow the eastern road to the Searil River and the frontier. Already, Albrec was rehearsing in his head what he would tell Macrobius the High Pontiff. The document he bore seemed like a millstone of responsibility. He was only a humble Antillian monk. He wanted to turn it over to someone else, one of the great people of the world, and let them bear the burden. It was too heavy for him alone.

The two clerics rode south-east in this manner with an army as escort. Three more days of sitting foul-tempered mules, sharing the nightly campfires with the soldiers, having their slow-to-heal injuries dressed by army physicians. The Fimbrians were all but quit of the Torrin Gap by that time, and were setting foot in Torunna itself, the wide, hilly land bisected by the Torrin River that rolled for a hundred leagues down to the Kardian Sea. It was largely unsettled, this region, too close to the blizzards that came ravening out of the mountains and the Felimbric raiders that sometimes came galloping down in their wake, even in this day and age. The most populous towns and settlements of Torunna were on the coast. Staed, Gebrar, Rone, even Torunn itself, were ports, their eastern sides flanked by the surf of the Kardian. The interior of the kingdom still had great swathes of wilderness leading up to the mountains where none went but hunters and Royal prospectors and engineers, seeking out deposits of ore for the military foundries to plunder and turn into weapons, armour, cannon.

The Fimbrians left the snow behind at last, and found themselves marching through a country of pine-clad bluffs teeming with game. Antelope, wild oxen and wild horses abounded, and Barbius allowed hunting parties to leave the column and pot some meat to eke out the plain army rations. But of the natives of the kingdom, the Torunnans themselves, they saw no sign. The land was as deserted as an untouched wilderness. Only the ancient highway their feet followed gave any sign that men had ever been here at all.

But the highway forked, one branch heading off east, the other almost due south. The eastern road forded the Torrin River and disappeared over the horizon. Some sixty leagues farther, and it would end at the fortress of Ormann Dyke, the marching army's destination. The southern way had three hundred winding and weary miles to go before it too ended, at the gates of Torunna's capital.

The army camped that night at the fork and Albrec and Avila were invited to the marshal's tent. They ducked under the leather flap and found Barbius awaiting them, but he was not alone. Also there were Joshelin and Siward, and a young officer they did not recognize.

"Take a seat, Fathers," Barbius said with what passed for affability with him. "We soldiers will stand. Joshelin and Siward you know. They have been your... guardian angels for some time now. This is Formio, my adjutant." Formio was a tall, slim man of about thirty. He seemed almost boyish compared to his comrades, though perhaps this was because he lacked the traditional bull-like build of most Fimbrians.

"We have come to the parting of the ways," Barbius went on. "In the morning the column will continue toward Ormann Dyke, and you will go south to Torunn. Joshelin and Siward will go with you. There are all manner of brigands in these hills, more now since Aekir's fall and the war in the east. They will be your guards and will remain with you as long as you need them."

Albrec chanced a look at Joshelin, that grizzled campaigner, and was rewarded with a glare. Clearly, the old soldier was not enamoured of the idea. He remained silent, however.

"Thank you," the little monk said to Barbius.

The marshal poured some wine into the tin cups that were all there were to be had in camp. He and the two monks sipped at it, while Formio, Joshelin and Siward sat staring into space with the peculiar vacancy of soldiers awaiting orders. There was a long, awkward silence. Clearly, Marshal Barbius was not a believer in small-talk. He seemed preoccupied, as if half his mind were elsewhere. His adjutant, too, seemed subdued, even for a Fimbrian. It was as if the two of them were burdened with some secret knowledge they dare not share.

"It only remains for me then to wish you Godspeed and good travelling," Barbius said finally. "I rejoice to see you both in such good health, after your travails. I hope you find journey's end what you wish it to be. I hope we all do..." He stared into his cup. In the dim tent the wine seemed black as old blood.

"I will not keep you from your sleep then, Fathers. That is all." And he turned from them to the table, dismissing them from his mind. Joshelin and Siward filed out silently. Avila looked furious at the curt dismissal, but he drained his wine, muttered something about *manners* and followed the two soldiers outside. Albrec lingered a moment, though he was not sure why he did.

"Is the news from the dyke bad, Marshal?" he asked.

Barbius turned as though surprised to find him still there. "That is a matter for the military authorities of the world," he said wryly.

"What should I say to the Torunnan authorities if they ask me about it?" Albrec persisted.

"The Torunnan authorities are no doubt well enough informed without seeking the opinion of a refugee monk, Father," the younger adjutant, Formio, said, but he smiled to take the sting out of his words, un-Fimbrian in that also.

"The dispatches I send out daily will have kept them up to date," Barbius said gruffly. He hesitated. There was some enormous pressure on him; Albrec could sense it.

"What has happened, Marshal?" the little monk asked in a low voice.

"The dyke is already lost," Barbius said at last. "The Torunnan commander Martellus has ordered its evacuation."

Albrec was thunderstruck. "But why? Has it been attacked?"

"Not as such. But a large Merduk army has arrived on the Torunnan coast south of the mouth of the Searil River. The dyke has been outflanked. Martellus is trying to extricate his men – some twelve thousand of them, all told – and lead them back to Torunn, but he is being caught between the two sides of a vice. He is conducting a fighting withdrawal from the Searil, pressed by the army that was before the dyke, whilst the new enemy force comes marching up from the coast to cut him off." Barbius paused. "My mission as I see it has changed. I am no longer to reinforce the dyke, because the dyke no longer exists. I must attack this second Merduk army and try to hold it off long enough for Martellus's men to escape to the capital."

"What is the strength of this second army?" Albrec asked.

"Perhaps a hundred thousand men," Barbius said tonelessly.

"But that's preposterous!" Albrec protested. "You have only a twentieth of that here. It's suicide."

"We are Fimbrian soldiers," Formio said, as if that explained everything.

"You'll be massacred!"

"Perhaps. Perhaps not," Barbius said. "In any case, my orders are clear. My superiors approve. The army will move south-east to block the Merduk advance from the coast. Mayhap we will remind the west how Fimbrians conduct themselves on the battlefield."

He turned away. Albrec realized he knew he was ordering his men to their deaths.

"I will pray for you," the little monk said haltingly.

"Thank you. Now, Father, I wish to be alone with my adjutant. We have a lot to do before morning."

Albrec left the tent without another word.

FIVE

POWER IS A strange thing, the lady Jemilla thought. *It is intangible, invisible. It can sometimes be bought and sold like grain, and at other times no amount of money on earth can purchase it.*

She had some power now, some small store of it to wield as she saw fit. For a woman in the world she had been born into, it was impossible to possess the trappings of power as men possessed them. Armies, fleets, cannon. The impedimenta of war. It was said that the most powerful woman in the world was the Queen Dowager of Torunna, Odelia, but even she had to hide behind her son the King, Lofantyr. No Ramusian nation would ever tolerate a queen who ruled alone, without apology for her sex. Or they had not thus far at least. Women who possessed ambition had to use other means to gain their ends. Jemilla had realized that while she was still a child.

She held the lives of two men in the palm of her hand, and that power had gained her her freedom. Allowing herself to be taken by the two guards had been unpleasant but necessary. She blocked out of her mind the acts she had performed for them in the dark firelight of her chambers, and reminded herself instead that with one word she could have them hanged. It was not permitted for palace guards to couple with noble ladies in their care. They knew it – they had done so as soon as their lust was spent and she had risen from the bed still shining with their effluent, laughing at them. Which was why she was free to wander the palace whenever one of them was on duty outside her door.

Such a simple thing. It worked with common soldiers as easily as it worked with kings.

It was well after midnight, and she was prowling the palace corridors like a wraith wrapped in hooded silk. She was looking for Abeleyn.

The Royal chambers were guarded, of course, but there were untold numbers of secret passageways and tunnels and alcoves in the palace, some of which predated Abrusio itself, and it was in search of these that she was out here creeping in the echoing dark. Abeleyn had told her of them months ago, one airless night in the lower city when they were both spent and sweat-soaked with the late summer stars glittering beyond the window and two of the King's bodyguards discreet as shadows in the courtyard of the inn below. He used the secret ways of the palace to come and go as he pleased, without fanfare or remark, and take his pleasure in the riotous night life of Old Abrusio below, as free and easy as any young man with a pocketful of gold and a nose for mischief. It was – had been – a glorious game to him to roam the backstreets and alleys of the teeming city, to wear a disguise and drink beer and wine in filthy but lively taverns, to feel the buttocks of some lower city slut wriggling in his lap. And to be their king, and they not know it. Perhaps to forget it himself for a while, to be a young man with nothing tripping at his heels, a high-living gentleman and no more.

There had been a light to him, Jemilla thought, not without regret. Something that had nothing to do with being a king but was part of the man himself. He had been easy to like, pleasant to bed, the boy in him counting for more than the monarch. But then the summer had ended, and this winter had come hurtling down upon the world full of blood and fire and powdersmoke. And Abeleyn had changed, had grown. There were times after that when he frightened her, not with any threat or violence, but simply with the steady stare of his dark eyes. He had become a king indeed, much good it had done him.

Her feet were bare, slapping slightly on the floors. She carried her slippers under her mantle; they slipped and slid in the slumbering palace, and only a few oil-fed lamps burned in cressets up on the walls, throwing a serried garden of light and dark about her and making of her hooded shape a cowled giant down the passageways. One hand for her slippers, the other curved protectively about her swelling belly. One good thing about the nausea that overwhelmed her most mornings – it kept her thin. Her face was unchanged. Only her breasts had grown, the nipples often stiff and sore. Apart from her belly and breasts, the rest of her was as lithe as it had always been.

Except... Oh, no. Not now.

Except for this thing. She appropriated a vase and ducked behind a curtain with it, then pulled her silks aside and squatted over it and sighed in relief as liquid gushed out of her. Oh, such a God that visited such indignities upon women.

She left the vase behind and pattered along as fast as she might. Abeleyn had told her how to come and go from his chamber to other rooms in the palace when he had been drunk, and she had been pretending to be. But it had been a long time ago, or seemed so. She was not sure if she could remember the exact places, the things to do. And thus here she was in the moonless chilly night, running along palace corridors in her bare feet, dodging sentries and yawning servants running midnight errands, and, absurdly, pushing at walls and feeling behind hangings and pressing loose stone flags. But it was somewhere here, in the guest wing of the palace. Some secret entrance which would admit her to the hidden labyrinth of passages and, finally, to the King's presence. If the King still breathed and they had not had his corpse spirited away and secretly buried days ago. She would not put anything past the wizard, Golophin. But she had to know if Abeleyn were truly alive, if he were too maimed ever to recover – there were terrible rumours flying about the palace. Only then would she be able to decide what her own course of action might be.

Movement in the passageway ahead. She shrank into the shadows, heart beating wildly, bladder suddenly ready to burst again. Thank God for the darkness of her mantle.

"– no change, none at all. But I have seen this kind of thing before. We need not despair, not just yet."

It was the wizard's voice, that skeletal fiend Golophin. But who was with him? Jemilla edged farther down into the dark. There was a cold, bobbing light approaching which she knew was unnatural: the wizard's unholy lantern. She found a heavy tapestry at her back, an alcove where the palace servants had stowed brushes and brooms away from the genteel eye, and she slipped in there gratefully, peering out through a chink she left for herself, watching the cold light approach.

Yes – Golophin. The werelight gleamed off his glabrous pate. But there was a woman with him in rich robes, a hooded mantle much like Jemilla's own. Two pale hands threw back the hood and Jemilla saw a white face, the coppery glint of hair. An ugly woman, a face with little harmony to recommend it, but there was strength in it. And she carried herself like a queen.

"I'll keep visiting him, then," the woman said in a voice as low and rich as a bass lute. "Mercado's men are still looking, I suppose?"

"Yes." The wizard's voice was musical also. A pair of beautiful voices, oddly matched. And at strange odds with the features of their owners. Who might this aristocratic but plain woman be? Her accent was strange, not of Hebrion, but it was cultured. It was of some court of other.

They were three yards away. Jemilla put her hand over her mouth. Her heart was thumping so loudly she could hear the rush and ebb of her blood in her throat.

"No luck, I am afraid," the wizard went on. "The kingdom has been scoured clean of the Dweomer-folk. I doubt Hebrion will ever be host to them in any numbers again. We are a dwindling people, we practitioners of the Seven Disciplines. One day we will be only a rumour, a lost tale of ancient marvels. No, there will be no mighty mage uncovered in time to heal Abeleyn. They are all fled or dead, or lost in the uttermost west... And I am a broken reed at best. No, we must continue to do what we can with what we have."

"Which is precious little," the woman said.

They were moving past her. Jemilla caught a hint of the woman's expensive scent, saw the hair piled up on her head in great coils of copper fire, the only thing of beauty about her other than her voice. Then they had turned the corner and were gone.

She waited a while, and then left her hiding place, her breath coming fast. As silently as a cat she retraced their steps, and came up against a dead end. The corridor ended with an ornate leaded window through which she could see the lights of the city below, the mast lanterns of ships in the ruined harbour, the glimmer of the cold stars.

She began investigating every inch of stone in the walls, tapping, pressing, poking. Perhaps half an hour she was there, her heart beating wildly, bladder painfully full again. And then she felt a click under her fingers and a section of the wall, perhaps a yard square, moved in with a suddenness that almost made her fall. She staggered as the grave-cold air came whispering out of a lightless hole in the wall. A glimpse of steps leading down, and then nothing but the blackness.

She shivered, her toes growing numb with the wintry blast. It looked an awful place to go in the dark hour of the night.

She padded quickly back up the corridor and took a lamp down from its cresset. Then she put her slippers over her frigid feet and, shielding the flame from the cold draught, she entered the passageway.

A metal lever here, on the inside. She pulled it down and the door shut behind her, almost panicking her for a second. But she cursed herself for a fool and went on, angry with herself, hating the composure of the plain woman who had been with Golophin, hating them both for being privy to the secrets of the palace, for being so close to the hub of power. Hating everyone and everything indiscriminately because she, Jemilla, must lurk and creep in cold passages like a thief though she bore the King's heir. By the blood of the martyred saints, they would pay for making her do this. One day she would serve them all out. Before she died, she would call this palace her own.

Doors and levers like the one she had entered by on both sides. She itched to try every one, but knew somehow that they would not take her where she wanted to go. The door to the King's chambers would be marked, she felt. It would be different.

And it was. The passage wound for hundreds of yards in the bowels of the palace, but at its end there was a door taller than the rest, and set in the door was an eye.

She almost dropped the lamp. It blinked at her, meeting her own horrified gaze. A human eye set in a wooden door, watching her.

"Sweet Lord of Heaven!" she gasped. It was an abomination, set here by that bastard wizard. She was discovered. She almost turned tail and ran, but the harder Jemilla, the one who had aborted Hawkwood's first child, who had coldly set out to seduce the youthful King, made her stand still, and think. She had come this far. She would not turn back.

It made her insides squirm even to approach the thing. How it stared! She shut her own eyes, and jabbed it as hard as she could with her thumb.

Again, harder. It gave like a ripe plum, and burst. Her thumb went in to the first joint, and she was spattered with warm liquid. When she opened her eyes there was a smeared, bloody hole in the door and her mantle was streaked with clear and crimson gore. She turned away, bent and vomited on the stone floor, dappling her slippers.

"Lord God." She wiped her mouth, straightened and pushed at the door.

It gave easily, and she was in the King's bedroom, a place she knew well.

She paused, wondering if the alarm would be raised quickly, if Golophin the demon was even now raging towards her with terrible spells on his lips to blast her out of existence. Well, she was where she had wanted to be.

She approached the great ornate bed in which she and Abeleyn had cavorted in the humid nights of late summer, the balcony screens flung wide to let in a breath of air off the sea. Candles burning now, as there had been then, and Abeleyn's head on the pillows.

She stood over the prostrate King like a dark, bloody angel come to fetch his soul away. And realized why they hid him here, why there was nothing but rumour about his condition.

She touched the dark curls, for a moment feeling something akin to pity; and then wrenched away the covers with one violent tug.

A tattered fragment of a man below them, naked to her gaze, his stumps muzzled in linen wraps. His chest moved as he breathed, but the pallor of death was about him, his lips blue in the candlelight, the eyes sunken in their sockets. He could not be long for this world, the King of Hebrion.

"Abeleyn," she whispered. And then louder, more confidently: "*Abeleyn!*"

"He cannot hear you," a voice said.

She spun around, the lamp-flame guttering wildly. Golophin was standing behind her as silently as an apparition. She could not speak: the terror closed her throat on a scream.

The old mage looked like something unholy made incarnate by night shadow and candle-flame. His eyes glittered with an inhuman light, and one of them was weeping tears of black blood down his cheek.

"My lady Jemilla," he said, and glided forward across the stone with never the sound of a footfall. "It is late for you to be up. In your condition."

She was more afraid than she had ever been in her life, but she fought a swift, soundless battle with her terror, mastered herself, composed her face.

"I wanted to see him," she said hoarsely.

"Now you have seen him. Are you happy?"

"He's dead, Golophin. He is not a man any more." Her voice grew calmer by the second, though she was calculating furiously, wondering if a scream would be heard if uttered here. Wondering if anyone would come to investigate it. The old mage looked like some night-dark prowling fiend with his bright eyes and skull-like countenance.

"I bear the King's heir," she said as he approached her.

"I know." He was only pulling the covers back up over the King's exposed body. She could almost smell the fury in him, but his actions were gentle, his voice controlled.

"You cannot touch me, Golophin."

"I know."

"You had no right to keep me from him."

"Do not talk to me of *rights*, lady," the wizard said, and his voice made her hair stand on end. "I serve the King, and I will do so to the last breath in my body or his. If you do anything to injure him, I will kill you."

Said so quietly, so calmly. It was not a threat, it was a statement of fact.

"You cannot touch me. I bear the King's heir," she said, her voice a squeak.

"Get out." Venom dripped from the words. Hatred hung heavy in the air of the room between them. She felt that violence was not far off. She retreated from the bed, one shaking hand still holding the lamp, the other cradling her abdomen.

"I will be treated according to my station," she insisted. "I will not be shut away, or be forgotten. You will not muzzle me, Golophin. I will tell the world what I bear. You cannot stop me."

The old mage merely stared at her.

"*I will have my due*," she hissed at him suddenly, venom for venom.

She could not bear his eyes any longer. She turned and left the room without looking back, aware that he watched her all the way, never blinking.

SIX

"HERE HE COMES," Andruw said. "Full of piss and vinegar."

They watched as the knot of horsemen drew near, pennons billowing in a breeze off the grey sea. And behind them nearly three thousand men in full battle array waited in formation, the field guns out to their front, cavalry in reserve at the rear. Classic Torunnan battle formation. Classic, and unimaginative.

"Do you know this Colonel Aras?" Corfe asked his adjutant.

"Only by reputation. He's young for the job, a favourite of the King's. Thinks he's John Mogen come again, and is too easy on his men. He's had a few skirmishes with the tribes, but hasn't seen any real fighting."

Real fighting. Corfe was still amazed at how much of the Torunnan army had not seen any *real* fighting. Torunnan military reputation had been built up by the men of the Aekir garrison, once considered the best troops in the world outside Fimbria. But the Aekir garrison were all dead, or slaves in Ostrabar. What was left were second-line troops, except for Martellus's tercios at the dyke. And now it was these second-line troops that would have to take on the Merduk invasion, and beat the armies which had taken Aekir. It was a chilling prospect.

The rest of his own men, the Cathedrallers, were drawn up behind him in two ranks. Scarcely three hundred of them able to mount a horse out of the five hundred he had started south with. His command was being inexorably worn down, despite the victories he had won. The men needed a rest, a refit, fresh horses. And reinforcements.

Aras's party reined to a halt in front of Corfe and Andruw. Their armour was shining, their horses well-fed. They wore the standard Torunnan cavalry armour, much lighter than the

Merduk gear Corfe's men had. Corfe was keenly aware that he and his men looked like a horde of barbaric scarecrows, clad in scarlet-daubed Merduk war harness, eyes hollow with weariness, their mounts scarred and exhausted.

"Greetings, Colonel Cear-Inaf," the lead rider opposite said.

A young man, red-haired and pale, his freckles so dense as to make him look suntanned. He had the big hands of a horseman and he sat his mount well, but compared to Corfe's troopers he seemed a mere boy.

"Colonel Aras." Corfe nodded. "You have a fine command."

Aras sat visibly straighter in the saddle. "Yes. Good men. Now that we have arrived, we can get on with the business at hand. I take it Narfintyr and his army have decamped from the vicinity, else you would not be here." And he smiled. Corfe heard some of the tribesmen muttering angrily behind him. They understood enough Normannic to grasp what was being said.

"Indeed," Corfe answered civilly. "I fear Narfintyr is far away by now. But you're welcome to try and catch him if you like."

Aras's smile grew brittle. "That is why I am here. I am sure your men have striven nobly under you, but you must now leave it to me and my command to get the job done."

Corfe was very tired. He had almost forgotten what it was like not to be tired. He was too tired even to be angry. Or to boast.

"Narfintyr has fled across the Kardian," he said. "My men and I have destroyed his army. There are over a thousand prisoners locked in the halls of his castle as I speak. I leave the last of the mopping up to you, Colonel. I am taking my command north again."

There was a pause. "I don't understand," Aras said, still struggling to smile.

"We've done your job for you, it seems, sir," Andruw said, grinning. "If you doubt us, there's a pyre to the south of the town with seven hundred corpses on it, still smouldering. Narfintyr's finest."

Aras blinked rapidly. "But you... I mean, where are the rest of your men? I thought you had only a few tercios."

"We're all here, Colonel," Corfe told him wearily. "There were enough of us to do what was needed. You can stand down your own men. As I said, we leave for the north at once. I must get back to the capital."

"You can't!" Aras blustered. "You must stay here and help me. You must attach your men to my command."

"God's eyes – have you been listening?" Corfe barked. "Narfintyr is gone, his army destroyed. You cannot give me orders – you are not my superior. Now get out of my way!"

The two groups of riders remained opposite each other, the horses beginning to dance as they picked up the tension from their masters. Corfe had intended to have a civilized meeting, a military conclave of sorts where he would fill Aras in on the current situation. They were, after all, on the same side. But instead he found he could not bear the thought of trying to brief this arrogant puppy. His unravelling patience had finally frayed entirely. He wanted only to be on the move again, to get his men some well-earned rest. And to go north, where the real battlefields were. There was no time for bitching and moaning.

One thing, though, that he could not forget.

"Before we depart, Colonel, I must inform you that I must leave behind some score or so of my wounded who are too badly injured to travel. They're billeted in the upper levels of the keep. Those men are to be looked after as though they were of your own command. I will hold you accountable for the well-being of each and every one of them. Is that clear?"

Aras opened and shut his mouth, his pale face flushed. Behind him, one of his aides muttered audibly: "Playing nursemaid to savages now, are we?"

It was Andruw who nudged his mount forward until it was shoulder to shoulder with the speaker's.

"I know you, Harmion Cear-Adhur. We went to gunnery school together. Remember?"

The man Harmion shrugged. Andruw grinned that infectious grin of his.

"One of these savages behind me is worth any ten of your parade-ground heroes. And you – you only got those haptman bars by kissing the arse of every officer you were ever placed under. What have you to say to that?" Andruw's grin had become wild, giving his grimed face a slightly demented aspect. He had his right hand on his sabre.

"Enough," Corfe said. "Andruw, get back in ranks. You are out of order. Colonel Aras, I apologize for my subordinate's behaviour."

Aras got hold of himself. He cleared his throat, nodded to Corfe and finally asked in a civil tone: "Is it actually true? These men of yours have defeated Narfintyr?"

"I do not make a habit of lying, Colonel."

"You are the same Colonel Cear-Inaf who was at Aekir and Ormann Dyke, are you not?"

"I am."

Aras's face changed. He cleared his throat again. "Then might I shake your hand, Colonel, and congratulate you and your men on a great victory? And perhaps I can prevail upon you to stay here for one more night and partake of my headquarters' hospitality. I can also have some equipment and spare mounts sent over to your men. If you do not mind my saying so, they look as though they need it."

Corfe rode forward and took the younger man's hand. "Courteously put. All right, Aras, we'll remain another night. My senior ensign, Ebro, will acquaint your quartermaster's department of our needs."

AND SO THEY remained, the two little armies encamped upon the muddy plain north of Staed. Aras had wanted to billet his men with the townspeople, but Corfe talked him out of the idea. The local people had suffered enough lately, and they were Torunnans, after all, not some conquered nation. It was enough that they went hungry to provision the soldiers who had lately swamped their countryside, and that their sons had died by the hundred whilst fighting those soldiers.

The camps of the Cathedrallers and Torunnan regulars were kept separate, and between them were Aras's headquarters tents. The Torunnans seemed at first dubious, then curious, and small parties of men from both camps met at the stream where the horses were watered, and there took wary stock of each other, like two dogs sniffing and circling, unable to decide whether to go for each other's throats.

Aras's column was remarkably well stocked with all manner of military supplies. He sent over to the Cathedraller lines waggons full of new lances, pig-iron, charcoal for the field forges, fresh rations, forage and sixty fresh horses.

Corfe, Andruw and Marsch watched them come in. Big-boned bay geldings with matted manes and wild eyes.

"They're only half broken," Andruw pointed out.

"What did you expect – the best of his destriers?" Corfe asked him. "If they had three legs apiece I'd still take them. What think you, Marsch? Do they amount to much?"

The big tribesman was looking over the snorting, prancing new arrivals with a practised eye.

"Three-year-olds," he said. "Only just lost their stones, and still feeling the loss. They'll quiet down in time. My men will soon break them in."

"Why is this Aras suddenly kissing your backside, Corfe?" Andruw asked thoughtfully.

"It's obvious. We head for Torunn tomorrow, back to the court. He wants us to give a good account of him, maybe even let him share in some of the glory."

Andruw snorted. "Fat chance."

"Oh, I'm not going to disparage him before the King. I won't make any friends that way either. But he won't steal the glory my men bled for."

THERE WAS A feast that night in Aras's conference tent, a huge flapping structure thirty feet long and high enough to stand upright in. All his officers were there, dressed, to Corfe's astonishment, in court uniforms, complete with lace cuffs and buckled shoes. There was a Torunnan soldier acting as waiter behind every one of the folding canvas chairs which seated the diners, and the long board table blazed with silver cutlery and tableware. As Corfe, Andruw and Ebro walked in, Andruw laughed aloud.

"We must be lost, Corfe," he muttered. "I thought we were supposed to be on campaign."

Corfe was seated at Aras's right hand at the head of the table, Andruw farther down and Ebro near the bottom. Marsch had declined to come. He had to see to the settling in of the new horses, he said, though Corfe privately thought that the prospect of using a knife and fork terrified him as no battle ever could.

"Some of my staff brought down several deer last week in the march south," Aras told Corfe. "They're tolerably well hung by now. I hope you like venison, Colonel."

"By all means," Corfe said absently. He sipped wine – good Candelarian, the wine of ships – from a silver goblet, and wondered how large Aras's baggage train had to be to sustain a headquarters of this magnificence. For an army of under three thousand it was ridiculous.

As the wine flowed and the courses came and went, the table set up a respectable din of talk. Ensign Ebro, Corfe saw, was in his element, regaling the other junior officers with war stories. Andruw was eating and drinking steadily, like a man making up for lost time. He was seated beside an officer in the blue livery of the artillery, and the two were engaged in a lively discussion between wolfed-down bites of food and gulps of wine. Corfe shook his head slightly. The field army of Aekir, John Mogen's command, had never done things thus. Where had the pomp and ceremony which permeated the entire Torunnan army come from? Perhaps it had to do with soldiering to the rear of an impregnable frontier. Apart from himself and Andruw, no man here had ever fought in a large-scale pitched battle. And with the fall of Aekir, the frontier was no longer impregnable. An entire army, over thirty thousand men, had been destroyed in the city's fall. The only truly experienced soldiers left in the kingdom were those at the dyke with Martellus. Once again, Corfe felt a thrill of uneasiness at the thought. Had he been Lofantyr, he would be conscripting and drilling men by the thousand, and marching them off to Ormann Dyke. There was a leisurely nature to the High Command's strategy that was downright alarming.

Aras was talking to him. Corfe collected his thoughts quickly, mustering his civility. He had precious little of it to spare these days.

"I suppose you have heard the rumours, Colonel, you having been at the court for the arrival of the Pontiff."

"No. Tell me," Corfe said.

"It seems hard to credit it, but it would seem that our

liege lord has hired Fimbrian mercenaries to reinforce Ormann Dyke."

Corfe had heard as much in the war councils of the King, but his face betrayed nothing. "How very singular," he said, and sipped at his wine.

"Yes – though there's other words I'd rather use. Imagine! Hiring our ancient overlords to fight our wars for us. It's an insult to every officer in the army. The King has never been greatly loved by the rank and file, but this has enraged them as nothing else ever could. It makes it look as though he does not trust his own countrymen to fight his battles for him."

Corfe privately thought that in this at least the King was showing some shred of wisdom, but he said nothing.

"So now we have a grand tercio of them marching across Torunna as if they owned it. Fimbrians! I wonder they can still fight at all after having locked themselves behind their borders for four hundred years."

"I am sure that Martellus will know what to do with them," Corfe said mildly.

"Martellus – yes – a good man. You know him, I suppose, having served at the dyke."

"I know him."

"He's not a gentleman, they say – a rough-and-ready kind of character, but a good general."

"John Mogen was no gentleman either, but he could fight battles well enough," Corfe said.

"Of course, of course," Aras said hastily. "It is just that I think it is time the new generation of officers was given a chance to prove their mettle. The older men are too set in their ways, and the world is changing around them. Now give me a couple of grand tercios, and I'll tell you how I'd relieve the dyke..." and he launched into a detailed description of how Colonel Aras would outdo Martellus and even Mogen, and send the Merduks reeling back across the Ostian River.

He was drunk, Corfe realized. Many of the officers there were by now, having thrown back decanter after decanter of the ruby Candelarian, their glasses blood-glows brimming in the candlelight. Outside, Marsch and the Cathedrallers would be making their cold beds in Torunnan mud, and up along the Ostian River, a hundred and thirty leagues away, the bones of the men who had once been Corfe's comrades in arms would be lying still unburied.

I'm drunk myself, he thought, though the wine had curdled in his mouth. He hated the black mood that settled upon him with ever increasing frequency these days. He wanted to be like Andruw or Ebro, able to enjoy himself and laugh with his fellow officers. But he could not. Aekir had set him apart. Aekir, and Heria. He wondered if he would ever know a moment's true peace again, except for those wild, murderous times in battle when all that existed was the present. No past, no thought of the future, only the vivid, terrifying and exhilarating experience of killing. Only that.

He thought of the night he had bedded the Queen Dowager of Torunna, his patron. That had been like battle, a losing of oneself in the sensations of the moment. But there was always the aftermath, the emptiness of awakening. No, there was nothing to fill the void in him except the roar of war, and perhaps the comradeship of a few men he trusted and esteemed. No room for softness there, no place for it any more. He had his wife's face and her memories stored away in that inaccessible corner of his mind, and nothing else would ever touch him there.

"– but of course we need men, more men," Aras was saying. "Too many troops are tied down in Torunna itself, and more will be sent south to guard against any fresh uprising. I suppose I can see the King's reasoning. Why not let foreigners bleed for us at the dyke, and harbour our own kind until they are truly needed? But it leaves a bad taste in one's mouth, I must say. In any case, the dyke will not fall – you should know that better than anyone, Colonel. No, we have fought the Merduks to a standstill, and should be thinking about taking the offensive. And I am not the only officer in the army who thinks this way. When I left the court, the talk centred around how we might strike back along the Western Road from the dyke and make a stab at regaining the Holy City."

"If all campaigns needed were bold words, then no war would ever be lost," Corfe said irritably. "There are two hundred thousand Merduks encamped before the dyke –"

"Not any more," Aras said, pleased to have caught him out. "Reports say that half the enemy have left the winter camps along the Searil. Less than ninety thousand remain before the dyke."

Corfe tried to blink away the wine fumes, suddenly aware that he had been told something of the greatest importance. "Where have they gone?" he asked.

"Who knows? Back to their dank motherland perhaps, or perhaps they are in Aekir, helping with the rebuilding. The fact remains –"

Corfe was no longer listening. His mind had begun to turn furiously. Why move a hundred thousand men out of their winter camps at the darkest time of the year, when the roads were virtual quagmires and forage for the baggage and transport animals would be nonexistent? For a good reason, obviously, not mere administration. There had to be a strategic motive behind the move. Could it be that the main Merduk effort was no longer to be made at Ormann Dyke, but somewhere else? Impossible, surely – but that was what this news suggested. The question, however: if not at Ormann Dyke, then where? There was nowhere else to go.

A sense of foreboding as powerful as any he had ever known suddenly came upon him. He sobered in a second. They had found some way to bypass the dyke. They were about to make their main thrust somewhere else – and soon, in winter, when Torunnan military intelligence said they would not.

"Excuse me," he said to a startled Aras, rising from his chair. "I thank you for a hospitable evening, but I and my officers must depart at once."

"But... What?" Aras said.

Corfe beckoned to Andruw and Ebro, who were staring at him, bowed to the assembled Torunnan officers and left the tent. His two subordinates hurried to keep up with him as he squelched through the mud outside. Andruw saved the bewildered and drunken Ebro from a slippery fall. A fine drizzle was drifting down, and the night was somewhat warmer.

"Corfe –" Andruw began.

"Have the men stand to," Corfe snapped. "I want

everything packed and ready to move within the hour. We move out at once."

"What's afoot? For God's sake, Corfe!" Andruw protested.

"That is an order, Haptman," Corfe said coldly.

His tone sobered Andruw in an instant. "Yes, sir. Might I ask where we are going?"

"North, Andruw. Back to Torunn." His voice softened. "We're going to be needed there," he said.

TORUNNA SEEMED THE hub of the world that winter, a place where the fate of the continent would be decided. Around the capital, Torunn, the hordes of unfortunates from Aekir were still squatting in sprawling refugee camps beyond the suburbs of the city. They were foreigners, bred to the cosmopolitan immensity of a great city which was now gone. And yet at day's end they were Torunnan also, and thus the responsibility of the crown. They were fed at public expense, and materials for a vast tented metropolis were carted out to them by the waggonload, so it seemed to an observer that there was a mighty army encamped about the capital, with the smoke and mist and reek and clamour of a teeming multitude rising from it. And also the stench, the disease, and the disorder of a people who had lost everything and did not know where to go.

The nobility of Normannia were fond of heights. Perhaps it was because they liked to see a stretch of the land they ruled, perhaps it was for defensive purposes, or perhaps it was merely so they were set apart from the mass of the population who were their subjects. There were no hills in Torunn to build palaces on, as there were in Abrusio and Cartigella, so the engineers who had reared up the Torunnan palace had made it a towering edifice of wide towers interconnected with bridges and aerial walkways. Not a thing of beauty, such as the Peridrainian King inhabited in Vol Ephrir, but a solid, impressive presence that frowned down over the city like a stooped titan. From the topmost of its apartments and suites one might on a clear day see the glint of white on the western horizon that was the Cimbric Mountains. And on a still spring morning it was possible to see fifty miles out to sea, and watch the ships sail in from the Kardian Gulf like dark-bellied swans.

But now the mist that arose from the camps walled in the city like a fog, and even from the highest towers it was impossible to look beyond the suburbs of Torunn.

ODELIA, THE QUEEN Dowager, sighed and rubbed her hands together. Slim fingers, impeccable nails – the hands of a young woman but for the liver spots which dotted them and reminded her of her age. The cold seemed to have settled in her very marrow this winter – this endless winter. She had fought against time for so very long now that it was with instant resentment she noted every fresh signal of her body's decay, every new ache and pain, every subtle lessening of her strength. She would repair the waning theurgy of her maintenance spells tonight – but oh how she so wanted that young man in her bed again, to feed on his vitality, to feel his strength. To feel like a woman, damn it. Not a queen slipping into the twilight of old age.

No one knew for sure how old she was. She had been married to Lofantyr's father King Vanatyr at the age of fifteen, but the first three children they had conceived together in their joyless fashion had died before they could talk. Lofantyr had survived, and her womb was barren now. And Vanatyr was dead these fifteen years, having choked on something he ate. She smiled at the memory.

There had been three lovers in her life in the decade and a half since her husband's death. The first had been Duke Errigal, the regent appointed to advise, guide and educate the thirteen-year-old King Lofantyr upon his coronation. Errigal had been her creature, body and soul. She had ruled through him and her son for five years, until Lofantyr attained his majority, and then she had ruled through Lofantyr. But her son the King was rising thirty now, and more and more often he brushed her advice aside and made decisions without consulting her. In short, he was learning to rule in his own right.

Odelia hated that.

Her second lover had been John Mogen, the general who had been Aekir's military commander, one of the greatest leaders the west had ever seen. And she had truly loved him.

Because he had been a *man*. A great man, devoid of manners, culture or breeding, but with a roaring humour and an art of remembering everything he was ever told, everyone he ever met. His men had loved him too: that was why they had died for him in their tens of thousands. She had helped along his career, and it was she who had procured for him the military governorship of the Holy City. She had never dreamed it could fall with him in command. And she had grieved for him, weeping her tears into her pillow at night, furious with her lack of self-control. It had been six years since she had last exchanged so much as a word with him.

And now there was this new lover, this embittered young man who had served under her beloved Mogen, who had seen him die. She knew full well that in advancing him she was indulging in a form of nostalgia, perhaps trying to recapture the magic of those years when she had ruled Torunna in all but name, and Mogen had been her knight, her champion. But she would allow sentiment to take her only so far, and the darkness of these times was something different, something new. She believed she could smell out greatness as surely as a hound scenting a hare. Mogen had possessed it, and so did this Corfe Cear-Inaf. In her own son, the King, there was no vestige of it at all.

As if summoned by her musings, her maid entered the chamber behind her and curtsied. "Lady, His Majesty –"

"Let him in," she snapped, and she closed the balcony screens on the rawness of the day, the reek of the refugee camps and the roaring bustle of the city below.

"A little short of late, aren't you, mother?" Lofantyr said as he came in. He had a heavy fur-lined cloak about him; he hated the cold as much as she did.

"The old are permitted impatience," she retorted. "They have less time to waste than the young."

The King seated himself comfortably on one of the divans that sat around the walls and warmed his hands at the saffron glow of a brazier. He looked around.

"Where's your playmate?"

"Asleep. He caught a kitten, and he is so decrepit now he needs to gather his strength before tackling it." She nodded towards the ceiling.

Lofantyr followed her eyes and saw up in the shadowed rafters a spiderweb fully twelve feet across. At its centre his mother's familiar crouched, and twitching in a corner was a small web-wrapped bundle that uttered a faint, pathetic mewing. Lofantyr shuddered.

"To what do I owe the honour of this visit?" the Queen Dowager asked, gliding across the floor to her embroidery stand and seating herself before it. She began selecting a needle and a bright silken spool of thread.

"I have some news – more of a rumour, actually – that I thought might interest you. It is from the south."

She threaded the needle, frowning with concentration. "Well?"

"The rumours have it that our rebellious subjects in the south have been subdued with unwonted speed and ease."

"Your Colonel Aras made good time then," she said, baiting him.

"The rumours say that the rebels were beaten by a motley group of strangely armoured savages under a Torunnan officer."

She kept her face impassive, though her heart leapt within her. The needle stabbed through the embroidery board and into her finger, drawing a globule of blood, but she gave no sign.

"How very intriguing."

"Isn't it? I will tell you something else intriguing. As well as the refugees from Aekir, we have encamped at our gates almost a thousand tribesmen from the mountains *with* their mounts and weapons. Cimbriani. Felimbri, Feldari. A veritable melting-pot of savages. They have sent a delegation to the garrison authorities saying that they wish to enlist under the command of one Colonel Corfe, as they call him, and that they will not leave the vicinity of the city until they have seen him."

"How very curious," she said. "And how have you dealt with them?"

"I do not want a horde of armed barbarians at my gates. I sent a few tercios to disarm them."

"You did what?" Odelia asked, very softly.

"There was an unfortunate incident, and blood was shed. Finally I surrounded their camp with artillery and forced them to give up their arms. They are now in chains awaiting transfer to the Royal galleys to serve as oarsmen." Lofantyr smiled.

Odelia looked at her son. "Why?" she asked.

"I don't know what you mean, mother."

"Don't seek to play games with me, Lofantyr."

"What has irked you? That I made a decision without first running to your chambers to consult? I am King. I do not have to answer to you, whether you be my mother or not," the King said, his pale face flushing pink.

"You are a damned fool," the Queen Dowager told her son, her voice still soft. "Like a child who destroys something precious in a fit of pique and cannot have it mended afterwards. Look beyond your own injured pride for a moment, Lofantyr, and consider the good of the kingdom."

"I never consider anything else," the King said, at once angry and sullen.

"This man I have sponsored, this young officer – he has ability beyond any of your court favourites and you know it. We need men like him, Lofantyr. Why do you seek to destroy him?"

"I will promote my own war leaders. I will not have them chosen for me!" the King exclaimed, and he stood up, his fur cloak billowing around him.

"Perhaps you will be allowed to choose your own when you have learned to choose wisely," Odelia told him. Her skin seemed almost to glow and her eyes were alight, like emeralds with the sun refracted through them.

"By God, I do not have to listen to this!"

"No, you do not. A fool never likes to listen to wisdom when it crosses his own desires. Think, Lofantyr! Think not of your own pride but of the kingdom! A king who is not master of himself is master of nothing."

"How can I be master of anything when you are always there in the shadow, spinning your webs, whispering into the ears of my advisors? You have had your day in the sun, mother, now it is my turn. I am the King, damn it all!"

"Then learn to behave like one," Odelia said. "Your antics are more those of a spoilt child. You surround yourself with creatures whose only goal in life is to tell you what you want to hear. You place your own absurd pride above the good of the country itself, and you refuse to listen to any news which conflicts with your own ideas of how the world should work. The men bleeding on the battlefields are the glue which keeps this kingdom together, Lofantyr, not the fawning office-seekers of the court. Never forget where the true power lies, what the true nature of power is."

"What is this, a lesson in kingship?"

"By the blood of the Saint, were I a man I'd thrash you until you shrieked. You're so blinded by protocol and finery you cannot hear the very footfalls of doom come striding across the world."

"Don't become apocalyptic on me, mother," her son told her, scorn in his own voice now. "We all know the witchery you practise – it is common knowledge at court – but it cannot help you predict the future. Your gifts do not lie that way."

"It does not take a soothsayer to predict the way the world is going."

"Nor does it take a genius to understand your sudden interest in this upstart colonel from Aekir. Does it help you to forget your age to take a man young enough to be your son to bed?"

They stared at each other.

Finally Odelia said, "Tread carefully, Lofantyr."

"Or what? It is all over the court – the Queen Dowager bedding the ragged deserter from John Mogen's vanished army. You talk to me of my behaviour. How do you think yours reflects upon the dignity of the Crown? My own mother, and a ragged-arsed junior officer!"

"I ruled this country when you were a snotty-faced child!" she cried shrilly.

"Aye, and we know how you managed that. Errigal you bedded too. You would prostitute yourself a thousand times over if it would seat you any nearer the throne. Well, I am a grown man, mother, my own man. You are not needed any more."

"You think so?" Odelia asked. "You really think so?"

They were both standing now, with the hellish radiance of the brazier between them, illuminating their faces from below so that they were transformed into masks of flame and shadow. Above them, the giant spider that was Arach had awoken and its legs were gently tapping the web it clung to, as though readying itself for a spring. Lofantyr peered up at the thing; it was uttering a low keening, something like an anguished cat's purr.

"Stop meddling in the affairs of state," Lofantyr said more calmly to the Queen Dowager. "You must give me a chance to rule, mother. You cannot hang on for ever."

Odelia inclined her head a trifle, as if in gracious agreement. Her eyes were two viridian flickers mingled with the yellow flame-light.

"Release the tribesmen," she said in a reasonable tone. "Let him have them. It can do no harm."

"Arm the Felimbri? Is that what you want? And you were the one who cautioned me about hiring the Fimbrians!"

"They will obey him. I know it."

"They are savages."

"Maybe if you had given him a command of regulars at the beginning this problem would never have arisen," she said, her voice cutting.

"Maybe if you had not –" he began, and stopped. "This bickering does neither of us any good."

"Agreed."

"All right, I will release them. Your protégé can have his savages. But they will receive no assistance from the military authorities. He is on his own, this Aekirian colonel."

Odelia bowed her head in acceptance.

"Let us not fight, mother," Lofantyr said. He moved around the brazier and held out his hands.

"Of course," his mother said. She took his hands and kissed his cheek.

The king smiled, then turned away. "There are couriers from Martellus on their way in from the gates. I must see them. Will you come with me?"

"No," she said to his retreating back. "No, see them alone. I have my work to do here."

He smiled at her, and left the room.

Odelia sat a moment in the quiet he had left behind, her eyes hooded, their fire veiled. Finally she picked up the embroidery board and hurled it across the room. It cracked against the far wall in a tangled mess of snapped wood and fabric and thread. The maid peeped in at the door, saw her mistress's face, and fled.

THE BLACK-BURNT STONE of Admiral's Tower seemed somehow in keeping with the tone of Abrusio in these times. Jaime Rovero, admiral of Hebrion's fleets, had his halls and offices near the summit of the fortress. In a tall chamber there he paced by his desk while the smell of sea water and ashes came sidling in from the docks below, and he could hear the gulls screaming madly. A winter fishing yawl must be putting in. All his life he had been a seaman, having risen from master's mate aboard a caravel to command of his own vessel, then of a squadron, then a fleet, and finally the very pinnacle of his career: First Lord of the Navy. He could go no higher. And yet he would look down on the trefoil of harbours that the city of Abrusio encircled and – seeing the ships there, the hiving life of the port, the hordes of dock hands and mariners – he would sometimes wish he were a mere master's mate again with hardly two coppers to rub together in his pocket, and the promise of a fresh horizon with the next sunrise.

The door was knocked and he barked, "Enter!" and straightened, blinking away the memories and the absurd regrets. One of his secretaries announced, "Galliardo Ponera, Third Port Captain of the Outer Roads, my lord."

"Yes, yes. Send him in."

In came a short, dark-skinned man with an air of the sea about him despite fine clothes and an over-feathered hat. Ponero made his bow, the feathers describing an arc as he swung his headgear in a gesture he imagined was elegance itself.

"Oh, stow that courtly rubbish," Rovero grated. "This isn't the palace. Take a seat, Ponero. I have some questions for you."

Galliardo was sweating. He sat in front of the massive dark wood of the admiral's desk and soothed down his ruffled feathers.

Rovero stared at his visitor silently for a second. He had a small sheaf of papers on his desk which bore the Royal seal. Galliardo glimpsed them and swallowed.

"Calm down," Rovero told him. "You're not here on corruption charges, if that's what you're thinking. Half the port captains in the city turn a blind eye now and again. It's the grease that turns the wheels. No, Ponero, I want you to have a look at these." He tossed the papers across the desk at his trembling guest.

"They're victualling warrants. Royal ones," Galliardo said after a moment's perusal.

"Bravo. Now explain."

"I don't understand, your excellency."

"Those two ships, outfitted and victualled at Royal expense and carrying Hebrian military personnel, were readied for sea in your section of the yards. I want to know where they were headed, and why the King sponsored their voyage."

"Why not ask him?" Galliardo said.

Rovero frowned, an awful sight.

"I beg your pardon, your excellency. The fact is the ships were owned by one Richard Hawkwood, and the leader of the expedition and commander of the soldiers was Lord Murad of Galiapeno."

Rovero's frown deepened. "*Expedition*? Explain."

Galliardo shrugged. "They were carrying stores for many months, horses for breeding – not geldings, you understand – and sheep, chickens. And there were the passengers, of course..."

"What about them?"

"Some hundred and forty of the Dweomer-folk of the city." Rovero whistled softly.

"I see. And what of their destination, Ponero?"

Galliardo thought back, back to the tail end of a summer that now seemed years ago. He remembered clinking a last glass of wine with Richard Hawkwood in the portside tavern by his offices which had seen so many partings, the backs of so many men who went into tall ships and sailed towards the horizon, never to return. Where was Richard Hawkwood now, and his ships, his companies? Rotting in the deep perhaps, or wrecked on some cragged rock out in the unmapped ocean. One thing Galliardo knew: Hawkwood had been meaning to sail west – not to the Brenn Isles or the Hebrionese, but west as far as his ships would take him, farther perhaps than anyone had ever sailed before. What had become of him? Had he found at last the limits of the turning world and set his foot on some untrodden strand? Galliardo would probably never know, and so he deemed it safe to tell the admiral what he knew of the Hawkwood expedition despite the fact that Richard had enjoined him to secrecy. Richard was probably dead, and beyond the consequence of anything Galliardo might do. The Hawkwood line had ended: his wife, Estrella, had died in the howling inferno that had been Abrusio scant weeks ago.

"West, you say?" Rovero rumbled thoughtfully when Galliardo had told him.

"Yes, excellency. It's my belief they were trying to discover the legendary Western Continent."

"That's a fable, surely."

"I think Hawkwood had some document or chart which suggested differently. In any case, he has been gone for months with no word sent back. I do not think he survived."

"I see." Rovero seemed strangely troubled.

"Is there anything else, Excellency?" Galliardo asked timidly.

The admiral stared at him. "No. Thank you, Ponero. You may go."

Galliardo rose and bowed. As he left the room and negotiated his way through the dark maze that was the interior of Admiral's Tower, sharply lit memories came to his mind, pictures from what seemed another age. A hot, vibrant Abrusio with a thousand ships at her wharves and the men of a hundred different countries mixed in her streets. The *Gabrian Osprey* and the *Grace of God* sailing out of the bay on the ebb tide, proud ships plunging into the unknown.

As he came out into the cold grey day of the winter city, Galliardo whispered a swift prayer to Ran the God of Storms, the old deity many seamen sought to placate when they were a thousand miles from land or priest or hope of harbour. He prayed briefly for the souls of Richard Hawkwood and his crews, surely gone to their long wave-tossed rest at last.

SEVEN

YEAR OF THE SAINT 552

DIM THOUGH THE winter afternoon was, it was darker yet in the King's chambers. It seemed to Isolla that lately she had been living her life by candlelight and firelight. She sat by Abeleyn's bedside reading aloud from an old historical commentary on the naval history of Hebrion, glancing every so often at the King's inert form in the great postered bed. In the first days she had been here she had constantly been prepared for some sudden show of life, some twitch or opening of an eyelid, but Abeleyn lay as still as a graven statue, if a statue could occasionally break into loud, stertorous breathing.

She stroked his hand as she read, the book propped on her knees. It was dry stuff, but it gave her a reason to be here, and Golophin believed that Abeleyn might yet be recalled to himself by the sound of a voice, a touch, some external stimulus which none of them had yet discovered.

It never for an instant occurred to her to wonder what she was doing here, by the bedside – or perhaps the deathbed – of a man she scarcely knew, sitting reading aloud to a man beyond hearing, in a country that was not her own, in a city half ruined by fire and the sword. Her sense of duty was too deeply ingrained for that. And there was an innate stubbornness too which her maid Brienne could have vouched for. A willingness to see something through to the end, once it was undertaken. She had never run away from anything in her life, had braved the snide asides of the Astaran court ladies for so long that it slipped like water from the feathers of a duck. She knew her brother the King loved her, also. That was one of the unshakable pillars of her life.

And he wanted her here with this man, or what was left of him. Isolla could no more have shirked this task than she could have grown wings and flown back to Astarac. Life was not to be enjoyed, it was a thing to work at, to be carved and polished and sanded down until at its end some form of beauty and symmetry might be left behind for others to see. Happiness was rarely a factor to be considered in that process, not when one was born to royalty.

The door opened softly behind her. One of the palace servants, an old man who was one of the few entrusted with the reality of the King's condition. He stood unsure and silent behind her, coughed quietly.

"What is it, Bion?" She knew all their names.

"My lady, the King has a... a visitor, who insists on being admitted. A noblewoman."

"No visitors," Isolla said.

"Lady, she says that my lord Golophin expressly gave her permission to see the King."

Isolla put away her book, intrigued but wary. Half the nobility of Hebrion had blustered or wheedled at the door at some point, eager for a look at Hebrion's invisible monarch. Golophin had turned them away, but he was indisposed. Something had happened to his eye – he was wearing a black patch over it – and even his febrile energy seemed to be fading.

"Her name?"

"The lady Jemilla." Bion seemed ill at ease, perturbed even. He could not meet her eyes.

"I'll see her in the anteroom," Isolla said briskly, unwilling to admit even to herself that she was glad of the interruption.

The lady was pale-skinned, raven dark-haired · and assured: a doppelganger of half a dozen who had made Isolla's childhood a misery. But things were different now.

The lady paused a moment as Isolla entered, black eyes watchful, gauging. Then she swept into an elegant curtsey. Isolla acknowledged this with a slight bow of her head. "Please, be seated."

They took up positions on small, uncomfortable chairs with their robes spread out around them like the plumage of two competing birds.

"I hope I see you well, lady," Jemilla said pleasantly.

A series of vapid exchanges essential to courtly conversation, all of which were meaningless, a convention. How had the lady Isolla found Hebrion? Cold, was it not, at this time of year, but more pleasant in the spring, surely. The summer far too hot – best to retreat to a lodge in the mountains until the turning of the leaves. And Astarac! A fine kingdom. Her brother the very model of a Ramusian monarch (his current heresy and excommunication blithely passed over). The lady Jemilla held a roll of parchment in one fine-fingered hand. It stirred Isolla's curiosity, and pricked her into a fine-tuned wariness even as the empty talk slid from her mouth.

"So Golophin agreed that you be admitted to see the King," Isolla said at last when the polite phrases had run their course.

"Yes, indeed. He and I are old acquaintances. The palace is like a village really. One cannot help but get to know everyone – even the King himself."

"Oh, indeed?" Isolla's face gave nothing away, but there was an apprehension growing in her.

"Such a man! Such a monarch! He is greatly loved, lady, as I am sure you are aware. The kingdom is riddled with worry for him. But the dearth of news as to his progress has been quite worrying." She put out a hand as Isolla stirred. "Not that I mean any reflection on Golophin or the worthy Admiral Rovero, you understand, or General Mercado either. But the people who bled for Abeleyn have a right to know, as do the great men of the kingdom. After all, if the King's convalescence is to be a long one, then it is only proper that some other personage of fitting rank be nominated to help steer the course of the kingdom. These... *professionals* are very well in their way, but the common folk like to see good blood at the head of the government. Do you not agree?"

There it was, the gleam of steel through the velvet. Jemilla smiled. Her teeth were small, fine, and very white. Like those of a cat, Isolla thought. Could Golophin actually have given this creature leave to see the King? No, of course not. But what was she to do, tell this lady she lied, to her face? And what was in that damned parchment?

Isolla's face, unknown to her, grew severe, forbidding almost. It was what her brother Mark called privately her "beat to quarters expression."

"I will not speculate on the policies of the man who is soon to be my husband, nor on those of his closest and most trusted advisors. It would not be fitting, you understand," Isolla shot back, watching the little barb slide home. "And unfortunately, the King is very fatigued today, and unable to receive anyone. But be assured, lady, I will convey to him your best wishes and hopes for his recovery. I am sure they will hearten him mightily. And now, alas, I too am not mistress of my own time. I am afraid I must bring this delightful interview to a close." She paused, expecting the lady Jemilla to get up, to curtsey and to leave. But Jemilla did not move.

"Forgive me," she said, purring, "but I am afraid I must beg your indulgence for a few moments more. I have here" – the parchment at last – "a document of sorts which I have been charged to deliver to you, as the King's betrothed. Little do I, a mere woman, understand of these things, but I believe it to be a petition signed by many of the heads of Hebrion's noble families. May I leave it in your hands? It would be a weight off my mind. Thank you, gracious lady. And now I must bid you farewell." A curtsey, only just as deep as custom demanded, and a swift exit, the triumph flashing in her eye.

The bitch, Isolla thought. *The scheming, insolent bitch*. She cracked open the seal – it was the house seal of some highborn princeling or other – and scanned the long scroll which fell open in her hands.

A petition all right, and the names on it made Isolla purse her lips in a silent, unladylike whistle. The Duke of Imerdon, no less. The Lords of Feramuno, Hebrero and Sequero. Two thirds of the highest aristocrats in Hebrion must have their signatures here – if the document were genuine. She would have to check that, although did not doubt that it would be genuine. Who was this Lady Jemilla anyway? She was not married to anyone of rank, or she would have taken his name instead of parading around under her own. A husband's name was the label of a woman's stature in this world.

And what did this petition request? That the King reveal himself to his anxious subjects and prove that he was the ruler of Hebrion, not the triumvirate of Golophin, Mercado and Rovero. Or, if he were too ill to do so, that a suitable nobleman, one whose bloodline was closest to the King, be named Regent of Hebrion until such time as the King himself was capable of ruling again. Second, that access to the King's person be granted for the signatories, his noble cousins, whose concern for him was overwhelming. Third, that the aforementioned triumvirate of Golophin, Rovero and Mercado be broken up, these gentlemen to resume their proper duties and station and allow the kingdom to be ruled by whomsoever the Council of Nobles decreed Regent. And, by the way, the Council of Nobles – an institution that Isolla, for all her reading on Hebrian history, had never heard of – would be convening in two sennights in the city of Abrusio to debate these matters, and to call on the King to marry his betrothed Astaran princess and give the kingdom the joyous spectacle of a Royal wedding, and perhaps, within due time, an heir.

There it was, the gauntlet tossed down before her. Marry him or go home. Produce him, upright and breathing, or let the nobles squabble over his successor. It was what it amounted to, for all the flowery language. Isolla wondered how deeply Jemilla was buried in this thing. She was more than a mere errand-runner, that was plain.

"Bion!" Her voice snapped like a whip.

"My lady?"

"Ask the Mage Golophin if he will receive me at once. Tell him it is a matter of the direst urgency. And be quick about it."

"Yes, my lady."

Hebrion had just gone through one war, and now it was to suffer another; but this one would be played out in the corridors of the palace itself. Strangely enough, Isolla was almost looking forward to the prospect.

EIGHT

IT DEPRESSED CORFE to see Torunn again in the numbing
drizzle of the new year, the smoke of the refugee camps
hanging about it like a shroud and the land for miles around
churned into a quagmire by the displaced thousands of
Aekir. They were still squatting in the hide tents provided
by the Torunnan authorities, and seemed no nearer than
before to dispersing and rebuilding their lives.

"Our glorious capital," Andruw murmured, his usual
good cheer dampened by the sight, and by the swift miles
they had put behind them in the last week. They had killed
twenty-three horses in the retracing of their steps north, and
even the tribesmen of the command were sullen and stupid
with exhaustion. They had had enough, for the present. Corfe
knew he could push them no further. Perhaps that depressed
him too. He was as tired as any of them, but still all he could
think of was getting out of here, up to the battlefields of the
north. Nothing else held any attraction for him.

This, he thought, is *what my life has become. There is
nothing else.*

The long column of filthy, yawning cavalry and silent
mules wound down from the higher land overlooking the
capital and came to a halt outside the city walls amid the
tented streets of the shanty town. The folk of Aekir stared at
the hollow-eyed barbarians on the tall warhorses as if they
were creatures from another world. Corfe stared back at
them, the white lightning-fury searing up in him at the sight
of the muddy children, their ragged parents. These had once
been the proud citizens of the greatest city in the world. Now
they were beggars, and the Torunnan government seemed
content to let them stay that way. He felt like dragging King
Lofantyr out here and grinding his face into the liquid filth

of the open sewers. When the warmer weather came, disease would sweep through these camps like wildfire.

He turned to Andruw and Marsch. "This is no damned good. Get the men bedded down beyond the camps, away from this."

"We've no bedding, no food – not even for the horses," Andruw reminded him. As if he needed reminding.

"I'm aware of that, Haptman. I'm going into the city to see what can be done. In the meantime, you have your orders." He paused, and then added reluctantly. "You might want to slaughter a couple of the pack mules. The men need meat in their bellies."

"God's blood, Corfe!" Andruw protested quietly.

"I know. But we can't expect too much. Best to prepare for the worst. I'll be back as soon as I can."

He turned his horse away, unable to meet Andruw's eyes.

He felt as though the anger in him could set the world alight and take grim satisfaction in its burning, but it left him feeling empty and cold. His men depended on him. If needs be he would lick the King's boots to see them provided for.

The sentries at the main gate forgot to salute, so outlandish did he appear in his crimson Merduk armour. He turned over the options in his mind and finally pointed his horse's nose towards the courtyards and towers of the Royal palace. His patron would, perhaps, be able to do something for him. He had passed the first test she had set him, at any rate.

"COLONEL CORFE CEAR-INAF," the chamberlain announced, a little wide-eyed.

The Queen Dowager turned from the window. Her hands fluttered up over her face and hair. "Show him in, Chares."

Her chamber was warm with braziers and blood-coloured tapestries. A pair of maids sat quiet as mice in a corner. At a look from her they rose and left by a concealed door. She awaited him with regal poise, though her heart thumped faster in her breast, and she felt a winged lightness there she had not known in many years. It both cheered and irritated her.

He clumped in. He seemed to love that outlandish armour of his, but at least he had doffed the barbaric helm that went with it. He was a mud-stained, bloody harbinger of war, out of place, uncomfortable-looking. His face had aged ten years in the few weeks since she had seen him last. The light in his eyes actually unnerved her for a moment, she who had faced down kings. There was a strength and violence there she had not noted before, a reined-in savagery.

"So," she said quietly. "You are back."

"So it would seem." Then he collected himself, and went down stiffly on one knee, clods of dirt falling from his boots. "Your Majesty."

"I told you before, I am 'lady' to you. Get up. You look tired."

"Indeed, lady." He rose as slowly as an old man. There was blood on him, she noted, and he stank of old sweat and horse and burning.

"For God's sake," she snapped, "couldn't you have bathed at least?"

"No," he said simply. "There was nowhere else to go. We have only just got in." He swayed as he stood, and she saw the deep bone-weariness in him. Her lips thinned, and she clapped her hands. Chares entered at the main door, bowing. "Your Highness?"

"Have a bath brought here at once, a fresh uniform for the Colonel and a couple of valets who know their job."

"At once, Highness." Chares withdrew hurriedly.

"I haven't the time," Corfe said. "My men –"

"What do you need?" she demanded.

He blinked stupidly, as if the question had caught him unawares.

"Quarters for three hundred men, and food. Stabling for nearly eight hundred horses and two hundred mules. Fodder for them, too."

It was her turn to be taken aback. "Horses?"

The shadow of a smile. "Spoils of war."

"I'll see to it. You have been busy, it seems, Colonel."

"I did what was expected of me, I believe." Again, that ghost smile. This time she returned it.

His armour was rusted to his back. The buckles had to be cut free by two owl-eyed palace valets while a flurry of others brought in a bronze hip-bath and filled it full of steaming water, kettle upon kettle of it until there was a mist hanging in the room. Others carried in fresh clothing and footwear. The Queen Dowager withdrew behind a screen, stifling a laugh when she heard Corfe curse away the flunkeys who fussed over him. She sat herself at her writing desk and in her swift, stabbing hand drew up the necessary orders, sealing them with her signet. It was the twin of her son the King's. That much authority she retained. She snapped her fingers for a servant.

"Give this to the Quartermaster-General," she told him, "and be quick, too." She raised her voice. "Colonel, where are your men?"

A grunt, the clump of a boot hitting the floor. "By the southern gate, outside the camps. Haptman Andruw Cear-Adurhal commands at the moment. You'll find them by the smell of roasting mule."

THE ATTENDANTS LEFT at last, and she heard him splashing in the bath beyond the screen. It would be over the palace in minutes, that the Queen Dowager had a muddy colonel of cavalry bathing in her private chambers. It was a signal she sent out quite deliberately. People would tread more warily around her protégé as a result. It was his reward for the passing of the first test.

And besides, she liked having him here.

The splashing had stopped. "Corfe?"

She peered round the screen. He was asleep in the bath, arms dangling over its sides, mouth open.

She rose and approached him, silent as a spider in her court shoes. The floor around him was a mess of mud and water. As she crouched by his side it soaked the bottom of her skirts.

Some of the lines faded when he slept. He seemed younger. His forearms were scarred with old wounds, and the bathwater was bloody where a more recent one in his thigh had reopened. She touched the wound, running her hand over him under the water. She closed her eyes and the gash healed under her fingers. The bleeding stopped.

He came awake with a violent start that sent the bathwater spraying. His hand gripped her wrist. "What are you doing?"

"Nothing," she said softly. "Nothing at all." She leaned over and kissed his bare shoulder and felt him tremble under her lips.

"You don't fear scandal much, do you?" he remarked.

"As much as you."

His hand, calloused from rein and sword-hilt, caressed her cheek gently. For a second he seemed almost a boy. But the second passed. The lines settled in his face again. He hauled himself out of the bath and reached for a towel to cover himself. He seemed almost bewildered.

"I must get back to my men."

"Not yet," she told him, her voice becoming harder as she rose with him. "Your men are being looked after. You, I need here for now."

"For what, payment?"

"Don't be a fool," she snapped. "Get dressed. We have much to discuss."

He held her eyes for a moment, and she was sure her need for him would betray her, spill out of her and plead with him. She turned away. The attendants had left decanters of Gaderian, a joint of venison, apples, cheese, fresh bread. She poured herself some of the blood-red wine whilst he towelled himself dry and pulled on the black Torunnan infantry uniform which had been left for him. As a cavalryman, he should have been in burgundy, and she thought it would suit him, but she knew also that he would prefer black.

"Eat something, for God's sake," she ordered. He was standing motionless as though on parade, obviously hating the court version of the uniform, the lace cuffs, tight collar and buckled shoes.

He seemed to experience some kind of inner struggle. It flitted across his face.

"Your men are being fed as we speak," she said. "Stop playing the noble leader and get something into your own stomach. You look half-starved."

At last, he unbent. She saw it was all he could do not to wolf down the food like an animal. He made himself chew it slowly, and sipped at the wine. Again, the tiredness in his face making him look so much older. How old was he? Thirty? Not much more, perhaps even less. He took a seat by one of the glowing braziers with a brimming wine glass in one fist and a chunk of bread in the other, taking alternate bites and sips. Finally he paused, conscious of her eyes on him, and said, "Thank you" in a low voice.

She sat down opposite him, wishing she'd had time to ready a few rejuvenating spells. She was very aware of the liver spots on the backs of her hands. She hated herself for feeling so absurdly self-conscious.

"You are your own courier, it seems," she said. "I take it the business in the south was concluded satisfactorily?"

He nodded. "Aras is still down there. I left him the last of the mopping up."

"Your tribesmen did well."

"Amazingly well." For the first time some real warmth came into his voice, and his face became more animated. He gave her a brief outline of the short campaign, neither boasting nor deprecating. When he was done she looked at him in some wonder.

"So the Felimbri make soldiers. If we'd known that twenty years ago it would have saved the country some grief. You are down to three hundred now, you say."

"Yes, plus some two dozen wounded I had to leave with Aras."

She smiled, glad to be able to give him the news. "It's lucky your savages acquitted themselves so well. There are a thousand more of them currently awaiting you at the north gate. News travels fast in the mountains, it appears." Better not to tell him that these men had almost been sent to the galleys by the King. He would find out soon enough.

His eyes were glittering, fingers whitening around the wine glass. "By the Saints –" He bowed his head and for an astonished instant she thought he might weep, but she heard him give a strangled laugh instead. When he looked up the relief was engraved in his features like the words on a tomb-top. She saw then how tautly strung he was, and had some inkling of the strain that bent him.

The wine glass shattered in a spray of scarlet.

"Forgive me." He shook the liquid from his fingers, grimacing. His palm was gashed and trickling blood.

"Corfe..." she said, and took his bloody hand, pulled him across to her. It was like tugging on the branch of an unyielding tree for a moment, before he gave in. He knelt on the floor and buried his face in her lap with a sigh. Summoning the Dweomer, she smoothed away the slash in his palm, restoring the skin as though she were shaping warm wax. As the spell worked the energy in her flickered. She felt her years dragging at her limbs, age baying for her life.

He would have risen, but she held him there, suddenly needing his youth close to her.

"You can rest a while. The Merduks have drawn half their army off from the dyke. Campaigning has finished for the winter. I will see to it that your men have all they need." *Stay with me.*

"No." He raised his head. His eyes were dry. "It's just begun. I believe they've outflanked the dyke somehow. Martellus is in trouble, I know it."

The soldier again. He had retreated from her. She let him go, and he rose to pace about the room, pausing to stare at his healed hand and then at her.

"You *are* a witch then."

"Indeed," she said wearily. "What nonsense are you talking about the dyke?"

"It's a feeling, nothing more. Has Martellus sent any dispatches lately?"

"Not for ten days. But the roads are bad."

"He's cut off already then."

"Oh, for God's sake! Are you an oracle, who knows this through intuition alone?"

He shrugged. "I know it. For what purpose would the Merduks mobilize a great army in the depths of winter? They are making another assault, that's clear – but not a head-on one this time. They're doing something else, something we have no idea of. And time is not on our side. I must go north."

She saw she could not move him. "You need rest, you and your men. I'll have couriers sent to the dyke. We'll find out the truth of it."

He hesitated. "All right."

Their eyes locked. Odelia knew there was greatness in him, something she had glimpsed before with John

Mogen. But there was something else, too. An injury that refused to heal, old agony which racked him yet. She thought it might be that pain which drove him on, which had changed him from the lowly ensign of Aekir to the man who stood here now, his star on the rise. But still, the pain was always there.

She rose in her turn and padded over to him, wrapped her arms about him and kissed him on the lips, crushing her mouth against his.

"You will come to bed now."

He was still tense, resisting her. "I have not yet reported to the King. And I must see these new recruits..." He faltered. "Why?" he asked. There was genuine puzzlement in his voice.

She grinned fiercely. "I want you there, and you need to be there too."

At last he smiled back.

FIFTY LEAGUES, A crow might fly, north-north-east from the room where Corfe and the Queen Dowager shared a bed. Across the empty hills that bordered the Western Road, itself a brown swampish gash across the earth with old corpses littering its length. Thousands had died along that road, lying down in the mud and rain in the retreat from Aekir and the trek from Ormann Dyke, relinquishing their grip on a life that had become a waking nightmare.

But now Ormann Dyke was burning.

The smoke could be seen for miles, a black, thunderous reek of destruction. Men were fighting in the midst of it. A thousand Torunnans, valiant with despair, struggled vainly to stem the onslaught of the Merduk army. The enemy had already crossed the Searil in force and was overrunning the three-mile length of the Long Walls, which for the first time in their proud history were about to fall to an assault.

The rest of the dyke's garrison was in full retreat, its artillery spiked and left behind to burn, its stores destroyed, the men marching with nothing more than the armour on their backs and the weapons in their hands. Their comrades left behind at the dyke were buying time with their lives, precious hours of marching which might yet save what was left of Martellus's army.

The army moved in a vacuum. Around it, the countryside was alive with harassing clouds of enemy light cavalry which severed communications with Torunn and the south. No one in the capital even suspected that Ormann Dyke had fallen. The Merduk light horse had already slain half a dozen couriers which Martellus, in desperation, had sent south.

THIRTY LEAGUES AWAY, another column of troops, this time black-clad Fimbrians, their pikes resting on their shoulders, their fast pace eating up the miles in a deadly race. They were coming in from the north-west, the last direction the Merduk High Command was looking. Their mule-mounted scouts ranged far ahead of the main body, seeking out the whereabouts of the third army in the region. striving to come to grips with it before it might descend upon Martellus's flank and complete the destruction of the dyke's garrison.

AND THE THIRD army, the largest of the three, had left behind the ships that had transported it across the Kardian Sea and was steadily making its way north-west to cut off Martellus's retreat. In its van rode the elite Merduk cavalry, the *Ferinai*, and behind them the shock troops of the *Hraibadar*, armed now with arquebuses instead of the spears and tulwars with which they had assaulted Aekir. War elephants by the score marched like mobile towers in their midst, and others in the rear hauled huge-bored siege guns through the mud whilst alongside strode the men of the *Minhraib*, the feudal levy of Ostrabar, and regiments of horse-archers from Ostrabar's new ally the Sultanate of Nalbeni. A hundred thousand men moving in four columns, each several miles long. And in the middle of this moving multitude trundled the chariot of Ostrabar's Sultan, Aurungzeb the Golden; to its rear were the eighty heavily laden waggons transporting the Sultan's household, his campaigning gear and his concubines. Aurungzeb liked to go to war in style.

"They've gone," Joshelin said with low harshness. "You can get up off your bellies, priests."

Albrec and Avila rose out of the tall grass they had been skulking in. Behind them Siward stood and slapped out the burning end of his slow-match, then replaced the end in the clamp on his arquebus.

"What were they?" he asked his fellow Fimbrian. "Foragers, or scouts?"

"Scouts. Merduk light horse, a half-troop. A long way from the main body, I'm thinking. Where are the Torunnans? Looks like they've given over the whole damn country to the enemy."

Albrec and Avila listened to the exchange in shivering silence. They were wet through, mud-stained and hungry and their legs wobbled under them, but the two old soldiers seemed to be built out of some other substance than mere human flesh. Twenty years older than either of the two monks, and they were as fit and hardy as youths.

"Must we go farther today?" Avila asked.

"Yes, priest," Joshelin told him curtly. "We've done scarcely eight leagues today by my pacings. Another two or three before dark, then we can lie up for the night. No fire, though. The hills are crawling with Merduks."

Avila slumped. He rubbed a hand over his face and said nothing.

"Do you think the capital is safe yet?" Albrec asked.

"Oh, yes. These are merely part of the enemy screen. He sends out light cavalry so that we can learn nothing of his movements, while he learns all about ours. Basic tactics."

"How ignorant we are, not to know such things," Avila said caustically. "Can we ride now?"

"Yes. The mules have had a good rest these last three leagues."

Avila muttered something venomous none of them could catch.

They had been four days travelling, the two monks and the two Fimbrians. During that time they had marched and ridden harder than Albrec had ever thought it possible for the human frame to bear. They had spent fireless nights shivering against the mules for warmth, and had eaten salt beef and army biscuit through which the weevils squirmed. Joshelin reckoned that another three days would see them in Torunn, if they continued to elude the Merduk patrols. Those three days loomed ahead of them like a long period of penance. Albrec found it easier to think only about putting one foot in front of the next, or getting to the next rise on the horizon. He had not even had the energy to pray. It was only the crinkling bulk of the ancient document he carried which kept him on his feet at all. When it was safe with Macrobius in Torunn, his mind as well as his body might know some peace at last.

At day's end Albrec and Avila were numb and swaying on the backs of the two mules. Nothing in their lives had prepared them for this unbelievably swift, unencumbered travel across a wilderness. Their feet were blistered, the stumps of Avila's lost toes weeping blood and fluid, and their rumps were rubbed almost raw by the crude pack-saddles. When the little party finally stopped for the night, the two monks were too far gone to care. They had not even the energy to dismount. Their companions looked at each other wordlessly for a long moment, and then Siward began to lift the monks down off their steeds whilst Joshelin unpacked an entrenching tool and began to dig a hole.

They had halted in the eaves of a small wood, mostly spruce and pine with beech and pale-trunked birch on the outskirts. Farther in, the coniferous trees grew closer together, and their needles carpeted the ground, making the travellers' footfalls soundless as a cat's. Night was fast setting in, and it was black in the wood already. Beyond it, the wind had picked up into a whine that roamed across the Torunnan hills like winter's courier. Albrec thought that never had he felt himself so lost, or in such a place of desolation. During the day they had passed abandoned farms and had helped themselves to food from their larders. They had even sighted a roadside inn, as deserted as a mountaintop. The entire population of Northern Torunna, it seemed, had fled at the coming of the Merduks. Would the Torunnans ever make a stand and fight?

When Joshelin had dug his hole to the depth of his knees, he threw aside his entrenching tool and began gathering wood from under the deciduous trees at the outskirts of the forest. Siward threw the two shuddering monks a couple of greasy, damp blankets, and then unsaddled and rubbed down the mules before fitting them with bulging nosebags. The animals were so tired he did not even hobble them, but merely tied their picket ropes to a nearby tree.

An owl hooted in the ghost-dark of the wood, and something – a fox, perhaps – yipped and barked far off, the sounds merely adding to the emptiness.

There was a flash, a jump of sparks that revealed Joshelin's face bent and puff-checked as he blew on the tinder. A tiny flame, smaller than that of a candle. He fed it as delicately as if he were tending a sick baby, and when it had grown a hand's breadth, he lifted the small pile of twigs and needles into the trench he had dug and began feeding it with larger limbs. He looked as though he were peering into some crack in the earth that led to Hell, Albrec thought, and then dismissed the image as unlucky.

The fire grew, and the two monks crawled over to its warmth.

"Keep it going," Joshelin told them. "I have things to do."

"I thought we were to have no fire," Avila said, holding his hands out greedily to the flames. His blanket stank as it began to warm.

"You looked as though you needed it," the Fimbrian said, and then strode off into the darkness with his sword drawn.

"Ignorant fellows," Avila muttered. His eyes were sunken, and the firelight writhed in them like worms of yellow light.

"Their bite may not be quite so bad as their bark, I'm thinking," said Albrec, blessing the warmth and the gruff thoughtfulness of their companions.

Chopping sounds, breaking wood, and then the two soldiers returned to the firelight holding a rough screen-like structure they had created out of interlaced branches stuffed with sods of turf. They planted it in the ground on the side of the fire trench that faced the border of the wood, and at last sat down themselves, pulling their black military cloaks about them.

"Thank you," Albrec said.

They did not look at him, but threw over a wineskin and the provisions bag. "You'll eat well tonight, at any rate," Joshelin said. "That's dainty fare we picked out of that farm."

They had a chicken, already plucked and gutted, bread that was several days old but which nonetheless seemed like ambrosia after Fimbrian hardtack, and some apples and onions. The chicken they spitted over the fire, the rest they wolfed down along with swallows of rough wine which in Charibon they would have turned their noses up at. Tonight it slid down their throats like the finest of Gaderian vintages.

Siward produced a short black pipe from the breast of his tunic and filled it from a pouch at his waist, and he and Joshelin smoked it in turns. The pipe smoke was heavy and strong and acrid. There was some tang in it that Albrec could not quite identify.

"Might I try it?" he asked the soldiers.

Siward shrugged, his face a crannied maze of light and dark in the fire-laced blackness. "If you have a strong head. It is *kobhang*, from the east."

"The herb the Merduks smoke? I thought it was a poison."

"Only if you take too much of it. It helps keep you awake and sharpens the senses, so long as you do not abuse it."

"How do you obtain it?" Albrec's curiosity awoke, taking his mind off his exhaustion.

"It is army issue. We get it along with the bread and salt horse. When there is no food to be had, a man can keep going for weeks by smoking it."

"And can he then stop smoking it if he has a mind to?" Avila drawled.

Joshelin stared at him. "If he has the will."

Albrec took the pipe Siward proffered rather gingerly and sucked a draught of the bitter smoke deep into his lungs. Nothing happened. He returned the pipe to its owner, rather relieved.

But then his aches and pains dimmed to a comfortable glow. He felt a new strength seeping through his muscles and his body became as light as a child's. He blinked in wonder. The firelight seemed a beautiful, entrancing thing of bright twisting loveliness. He put out his hand towards it, only to have his wrist grasped by the hard fist of Joshelin.

"One must be careful, priest."

He nodded, feeling foolish and exhilarated in the same moment.

"I haven't seen you smoke it before," Avila said to the Fimbrians.

Siward shrugged. "We are getting tired. We are men also, Inceptine."

"Well, bless my soul," Avila retorted, and wrapped himself in his evil-smelling blanket.

They took the chicken off the spit and ripped it into four pieces. Albrec was no longer hungry, but he ate the scorched meat anyway, no longer able to taste it. His mind felt clear as ice. His worries had vanished. He began to chuckle, and then stopped himself as he found his three companions were watching him.

"Marvellous stuff. Marvellous," he muttered, and fell back into the soft pine needles, snoring as soon as he was horizontal.

Avila threw a blanket over him. It had holes in it from other nights spent lying close to campfires.

"I will dress your feet in the morning," Joshelin told him.

The young Inceptine nodded distantly and took a huge swallow of the wine. "What will you do when you have escorted us safely to Torunn?" he asked.

The two Fimbrians glanced at each other and then into the fire. "We will await further orders from the marshal," Siward said at last.

"You don't believe you'll get any further orders, though. Albrec told me his intentions. Your marshal is leading his men to their deaths."

"Mind your own matters, priest," Joshelin hissed with sudden passion.

"It is no matter to me," Avila said. "I only wonder that you had not thought out what will become of you when you have run this errand for him."

"As you say," Joshelin grated. "It is no matter to you. Now get you to sleep. You need a lot of rest if you are to keep up today's volume of whining on the morrow."

Avila looked at him for a long minute, and finally his face broke out into a smile.

"Quite right. I would hate to let my standards slip."

NINE

HE THOUGHT SHE looked younger in the morning light than she had the night before. He lay propped up on one elbow watching her quiet sleep, and in him a storm of feelings and memories fought for the forefront of his mind. He wrestled them back brutally, slammed a door in their faces, and was able for some few precious seconds to lie there and watch her, and be almost content.

Her eyes opened. No morning bleariness or process of awakening. She was instantly alert, aware, knowing. Her eyes were green as the shallows of the Kardian Sea in high summer, a bewitching, arresting green. His wife's eyes had been grey, quick to humour, and holding less knowledge in their depths. But then his wife had died still a young woman.

"No grief," Odelia said quietly. "Not on this morning. I will not permit it." Her words were imperious but their tone was almost pleading. He smiled, kissed her unlined forehead, and sat up. His moment of peace had passed, but that was to be expected. He did not wish for more.

"I must away, lady," he said, feeling like some swain in a romantic ballad. To connect himself back to reality, he swung his feet off the bed and on to the stone floor. "I have a thousand men waiting for me."

"What is one woman, set against a thousand barbarians?" she asked archly, and rose herself, naked and superb. He watched her as she slipped a silk robe about her shoulders, her hair spilling gold down her back. He was glad she was not dark. That would have been too much.

He pulled on the court uniform he hated, stamping his feet into the absurd buckled shoes. They seemed as insubstantial as cotton after the weeks in long cavalry boots.

A discreet knock at the door.

"Yes," Odelia said, never taking her eyes off Corfe.

A maid. "Highness, the King is in the antechamber. He wishes to see you at once."

"Tell him I am dressing."

"Highness, he will not wait. He insists on entering immediately."

Odelia met Corfe's eyes, and smiled. "Find yourself a corner, Colonel." Then she turned to the maid. "Tell him I will see him now, in here."

The maid scurried out. Corfe cursed venomously. "Are you out of your Royal mind?"

"There's a tapestry behind the headboard which will serve admirably. Make sure your toes do not stick out below it."

"Saint's blood!" Swallowing other oaths, Corfe dashed across the room and concealed himself there. The tapestry was loose-woven. He could see through it as though through a heavy fog. His heart hammered as cruelly as if he were going into battle, but he found time to wonder if he were not the first man ever to hide in that spot.

The King of Torunna entered the Queen Dowager's bedchamber seconds later.

Odelia sat down at her dressing table with her back to her son and began brushing her golden hair.

"An urgent matter indeed, if you must burst in on me before I am even dressed," she said tartly.

Lofantyr's eyes swept the chamber. He was sweating, and looked like nothing so much as a frightened boy in the schoolmaster's study.

"Mother, Ormann Dyke has fallen."

The brush stopped halfway through the gleaming tresses.

Corfe thought that his heart had stopped with it. Almost he stepped out from behind the tapestry.

"Are you sure?"

"Merduk light cavalry have been sighted scarcely ten miles from the city walls. General Menin sent out a sortie which destroyed or captured an enemy patrol. One of the enemy was found to have this on him."

Lofantyr proffered his mother a small leather cylinder, much scuffed and stained.

"A dispatch case," Odelia said mechanically. She snatched it out of her son's hands and ripped it open, tapping out the scroll of parchment within. She unrolled and read it, the sheet quivering like a captured lark in her hand.

"Martellus's seal – it's genuine enough. Dated the day before yesterday. The courier must have made good time ere they caught him. Blood of the merciful Saint, he's on the march, trying for the capital. Ten thousand men, Lofantyr. We must send out a host to meet him."

"Are you mad, mother? The countryside is swarming with the enemy. General Menin's sortie barely made it back to the walls alive. We must ready ourselves for a siege here, and Martellus must fend for himself. I cannot spare the men."

Odelia raised her head. "Do you jest with me?"

"It is the considered advice of the General Staff," the King said defensively. "I concur. I have already given orders that the Aekirian refugee camps be broken up and their occupants shipped south. The fleet is at anchor in the estuary. We will bleed the Merduks white before the walls."

"As they were bled at Aekir and Ormann Dyke, no doubt," the Queen Dowager said. "My God, Lofantyr, think about what you are doing. You are abandoning a quarter of the country and its people to the enemy. You are throwing away Martellus and his army – the best troops we have. Son, you cannot do this."

"The necessary orders are being written out as we speak," the King snapped. "I'll thank you to remember who is monarch of this kingdom, mother." His voice had grown shrill. Perspiration glittered on his temples. He snatched Martellus's dispatch out of her hand. "From now on, the affairs of state are no business of yours." His eyes swept the chamber, passing over the two wine glasses, the rumpled clothing. "I see you have other things to keep you occupied, at any rate. I shall send a clerk round for the seal you still possess this afternoon. Good day." He bowed, wild-eyed, turned, and spun out of the room, wiping the sweat from his forehead as he left.

There was a moment of silence, and then Corfe came out of his hiding place. The Queen Dowager was sitting at her dressing table, chin sunk on breast. She looked up at him as he emerged from behind the tapestry and he saw to his shock that there were tears in her eyes, though her face was set as hard as that of a statue.

"God knows how I ever gave birth to that," she said, and something in her voice made the hairs on Corfe's nape stand up.

She rose. "The fool had not the courage to take the seal outright – he must send a lackey to do it for him. Well, I am forewarned, which is something. You must have a set of orders, Colonel, something suitably vague so that you may not be accused of overreaching yourself. I shall see to it at once."

Corfe was already at the door, his arms full of his old uniform, rusting Merduk armour, the sabre baldric over one shoulder. "What would you have me do?" he asked harshly, pausing.

"Save Martellus, if you can. Use the tribesmen awaiting you at the gates. You can have nothing else. If I read this dispatch correctly, Martellus is still at least a week's march away."

"An infantry march," Corfe told her. "My men will do it in half the time." He hesitated. "Do you really think my tribesmen can make a difference?"

"I would not be sending you else. How soon can you move?"

He turned it over in his mind. His men were exhausted, as were his horses. He had a thousand new recruits, who had to be integrated into his command.

"I need at least a day. Two, probably," he replied.

"Very well."

Corfe turned to go, but she called him back.

"One more thing, Colonel – two more, in fact. For the first, there is a Fimbrian grand tercio on the march out there, trying to intercept the southern Merduk army. It may well be closer to you than Martellus is. I shall not presume to teach you tactics, but it might be best to combine with it ere you launch into the enemy."

Corfe nodded. His mind was racing, juggling the information, trying to make a plan, a sense of it.

"And the other," the Queen Dowager went on. "I shall write out a commission for you which will await your return. If you can save Martellus and the Fimbrians, you shall be a general, Corfe."

He looked at her unsmilingly. *I am tasting the carrot,* he thought. *When shall I feel the stick?* But all he said was "Goodbye, lady," before striding out the door.

HIS MEN HAD been billeted in an empty warehouse down by the river. They were lying there with nothing to cover them, on a stone floor which was inadequately strewn with straw. Heaped around their sleeping bodies were opened barrels of salt pork and hardtack and kegs of the weak beer which the Torunnan military quaffed daily. They had torn down some of the timber sidings of the building's interior to make smoky fires. In the collective fug of the warehouse, the tribesmen stank and the smoke smarted Corfe's eyes. He roused Andruw, Marsch and Ebro, and the trio stared at him as though he were a ghost, their eyes red-rimmed pits, the filth of the march north still slobbering their clothing.

"What ho, the popinjay," Andruw said, rubbing his eyes, managing a tired grin.

Corfe began removing the court uniform and donning his old one. He felt furiously ashamed to be clean and well dressed while his men lay like forsaken vagabonds upon the straw-strewn stone. "I thought you would be billeted in regular barracks," he said, savagely angry.

"It's all they could find, apparently," Andruw told him. "I don't give a damn. I'd have slept in a ditch, the men too. The horses are being well looked after, though. I made sure of that. They too have straw to lie on."

"Let the men sleep. You three come with me. We have work to do."

His three officers obeyed him like laboured old men. The expression on Corfe's face quelled any questions they might have had.

Torunn in winter, like all the northern cities, was a choked quagmire, the streets running with liquid mud, commoners splashing through it ankle-deep, their betters on horseback or carried in sedan chairs or sitting in carriages. It was a weary trek through the crowds under a thin drizzle, but the rain woke them up. Corfe was glad of it. He could still catch the scent of Odelia on his skin, even over the stink of his scarlet armour.

Companies of Torunnan regulars elbowed aside the crowds of civilians at frequent intervals, all heading towards the city walls. The capital was crawling with activity, but there seemed to be no panic, or even unease as yet. The news of Ormann Dyke's fall was not yet common knowledge, though it was known that the refugee camps about the city walls were about to be broken up. As the foursome made their way to the northern gate, Corfe filled in his subordinates on the situation. Andruw became silent and glum. Like Corfe, he had served at the dyke, but for longer. He had friends with Martellus. The dyke had been his home. Marsch, by contrast, seemed uplifted, almost merry at the thought of meeting a thousand more of his fellow tribesmen.

The prospective recruits were encamped a mile from the walls, out of the swamp of the refugees. They had posted sentries, Corfe was gratified to see, and as he and his three comrades puffed up the slope to meet them a knot of riders thundered out of their lines, coming to a mud-splattering halt ten yards away. The lead rider, a young, raven-dark man as slender as a girl, called out in the language of the tribes, and Marsch called back. Corfe heard his own name mentioned, and the dark rider's eyes bored into him.

"I hope they don't put too much store by appearances," Andruw muttered. "We should have ridden."

The dark rider dismounted in one fluid movement, and came forward. He was shorter even than Corfe, and he wore old-fashioned chainmail of exquisite workmanship. A long, wickedly curved sabre hung at his side, and Corfe noted the light lance dangling from the pommel of his horse's saddle.

"This is Morin," Marsch said. "He is of the Cimbriani. He has six hundred of his people here. The rest are Feldari, and a few of my own people, the Felimbri. He has been elected warleader by the host."

Corfe nodded.

The dark tribesman, Morin, launched into a long and passionate speech in his own language.

"He wishes to know if it is true that his men are to fight the Merduks only," Marsch translated.

"Tell him it's true."

"But he also says that he will fight the Torunnans too if you wish. They tried to enslave his men when first they arrived, and had them disarmed. Three were killed. But then they were released again. He" – Marsch sounded apologetic – "he does not trust Torunnans, but he hears you were an officer under John Mogen, and so you must be an honourable man."

Corfe and Andruw looked at each other. "Torunnan military courtesy is as famed as ever, I see," Andruw murmured. "I'm surprised they didn't bugger off back to the mountains."

"They want to fight," Marsch said simply, whilst beside him Ensign Ebro, a prime example of Torunnan military courtesy, glowered at the ground.

"Tell Morin," Corfe said, holding the eyes of the dark tribesman, "that as long as his people serve under me, they shall be treated like men, and I shall speak for them in everything. If I break faith with them, then may the seas rise up and drown me, may the green hills open up and swallow me, may the stars of heaven fall on me and crush me out of life for ever."

It was the ancient oath of the mountain tribes which Marsch and the rest of the Cathedrallers had once sworn to him. When Marsch had finished translating it to Morin, the dark tribesman instantly fell on one knee and offered Corfe the hilt of his sabre – and Corfe heard the same words coming back at him in the rolling tongue of the Cimbriani.

His little army had just grown by a thousand men.

TEN

IT WOULD TAKE not two days but three to get the command ready for the road north. Thirteen hundred men and almost two thousand horses, plus a baggage train of some two hundred mules. The entire column had been fitted out in the discarded Merduk armour which lay mouldering in a quartermaster's warehouse, and the new men's gear was lathered in red paint, just as that of the original Cathedrallers had been. They had looked somewhat askance at the Merduk equipment at first. Unlike Marsch and his five hundred, they possessed their own weapons and wore finely wrought mail hauberks, but Corfe had insisted that they don the same armour his original command had fought in down south. Also, he wanted heavy cavalry, the shattering impact of an armoured charge. Half of the newcomers had powerful recurved compound bows of horn and mountain yew and bristling quivers hung from their cantles, but they were now outfitted with the lances of the Merduk heavy horse. They were to be shock troops, pure and simple.

Thirteen hundred men, a thousand of whom had never been part of a regimented military command before. Corfe organized them into twenty-six troops, fifty strong each, and sprinkled the three hundred survivors of his original command throughout the new units as NCOs. Two troops made up a squadron, and four squadrons a wing: thus three wings, plus a squadron in reserve to guard the baggage and spare horses. Corfe made Andruw, Ebro and Marsch wing commanders, Ebro almost speechless with gratitude at being given a real command at last.

All very well on paper, but the reality was infinitely more complex. It took a day and a half to equip the new men and reorganize the command. Morin, it turned out, spoke good Normannic and Corfe detailed him as his adjutant and interpreter. The tribesman was none too pleased at not having command of a wing, but he knew nothing of the tactics that Corfe meant to employ, and had to be content with the promise of a field command at a later date. As it was, his pride was satisfied with relaying Corfe's orders as though he had given them himself.

The command was heterogenous to an extreme, liable to sub-divide along the lines of tribe. The new men saw themselves as Cimbriani or Feldari rather than Cathedrallers, but once they had a few battles under their belt, Corfe knew that would change.

Their camp was a buzzing maelstrom of activity, night and day. Andruw and a couple of squadrons busied themselves with the collection of stores from a reluctant and somewhat outraged Torunnan quartermaster's department, and had it not been for the goodwill of Quartermaster Passifal his men would never have been issued a single piece of hardtack. Others were occupied having the horses shod and the armour reconditioned, while Corfe conducted formation drill on the blasted plain north of the capital and the battlements of the city were lined with fascinated, and in some cases derisive, spectators.

He worked his men hard, but no harder than he worked himself. By the third day the three wings were able, with a certain amount of cursing and jostling, to move from road column to line of battle at a single trumpet call from Cerne, Corfe's bugler. Their efforts would have made a Torunnan drill-master stare, but the end result was well enough, Corfe thought. There was no time to teach them any of the niceties. The image which chiefly disturbed him was that of his men breaking formation and reverting to some tribal warband, especially if they happened to push an enemy into flight. He impressed upon them, at campfire gatherings interpreted by Morin, that they were not to break from the line or advance without direct orders from their wing commanders. There was some muttering at this, and someone shouted out from the darkness at the back of the crowd that they were warriors not slaves, and they did not have to be taught how to fight.

"Fight my way," Corfe shouted back. "Just once, fight my way, and if I don't bring you to victory, then you may fight any way you please. But ask Marsch and his Felimbri if my way is not the best."

The muttering died down. The men now knew of the battles the original Cathedrallers had fought in the south, the odds they had overcome. Corfe realized he was on trial. If he led these men to defeat, initially at any rate, then he would never be able to lead them with confidence again. They respected ability, not rank, and deeds rather than flowery declarations.

On the night before they moved out, he was summoned to meet the Queen Dowager again. He turned up at her chambers in his old, ragged uniform, aware of the whispers that followed him through the palace. Rumour was running like fire through the city: Torunn was about to be besieged as Aekir had been, the King was about to abandon the city to the enemy and pull the garrison south, a treaty was to be signed, a deal to be struck. Martellus was dead, he was victorious, he was a hostage of the Merduks. No one could tell fact from fiction, and already thousands were fleeing Torunn, lines of carriages and waggons and handcarts and trudging people heading south. At Aekir there had been hope, even confidence, that as long as John Mogen led them and the walls stood they would prevail. Here, hope was fleeing with the mobs of refugees. It sickened Corfe to his stomach. He was beginning to wonder if anything of the world he knew would survive another winter.

ODELIA WAS ALONE when he was shown in, sitting by a brazier with the shadows high and dark on the walls about her. "Lady."

Something scuttled away from the flame-light too quickly for him to make out, but the Queen Dowager did not stir. "You have been lucky, Colonel."

"Why is that, lady?"

"You have been almost forgotten about. Thus far, you have been overlooked."

Corfe frowned. "I don't know what you mean."

"I mean that my son the King has forgotten you in the... excitement of the present time. But someone else – Colonel Menin, or I should say now General Menin – has just been made aware of your existence. The sooner you are away from the city the better."

"I see," Corfe said. "Does he mean to make a fight of it?"

Odelia smiled unpleasantly. "I do not know. I am no longer privy to the workings of the government. My instincts tell me that the King is timid and his general is a buffoon. Menin's lackeys have been watching your men drilling. Tomorrow morning you will receive a new set of orders. You will be ordered to turn over your command to another, more... amenable officer who only today arrived from the south."

"Aras," Corfe hissed.

"The very same. According to him, you left your work there half done, and he had the lion's share of the fighting to do while you hot-footed it back to the bed of the Queen Dowager." Odelia's smile was like a scar across her face in the firelight.

"I left wounded with him, the dastard."

"I have had Passifal quarter them in an out-of-the-way place, don't worry. But you have to get into the field, Corfe, before they ruin you."

"We leave at dawn. Or sooner, with this."

"Dawn should be safe enough. But no fanfare. A discreet exit is called for, I think."

"When have you found me anything but discreet, lady?"

She laughed suddenly, like a girl. "Don't worry, Corfe. Just make sure that when you come back you have laurel on your brow, and I will do the rest. I still have strings to pull, even in the High Command. But that is not why I asked you to come here. I have something for you." She threw aside a cloth to reveal a long, gleaming wooden box. Intrigued, but chafing at the waste of time, Corfe stepped closer.

"Well, open it!"

He did as he was bidden, and there, set in silk padding, was the shimmer of a long, bright-bladed sword.

"It's yours. Call it a lucky charm if you like. I've had it sitting here these six years."

Corfe lifted the sword. It was a heavy cavalry sabre, only slightly curved, double-edged for all that, with a plain basket hilt, the grip wire-bound ivory darkened with another man's sweat. An old, iron sword which had seen use – there were several tiny nicks in the blade. Looking closer, he saw the serpentine gleam of pattern welding.

"It must be ancient," he said, wondering.

"It was John Mogen's."

"My God!"

"He called it *Hanoran*, which in old Normannic means 'The Answerer.' It was an heirloom of his house. He left it here before he went to take up the governorship of Aekir. You may as well have it." Her voice was off-hand, but her eyes bored into him, twin peridot glitters.

"Thank you, lady. It means much to me, to have this."

"He would have wanted you to have it. He would have wanted it to taste blood again in an able man's hands rather than lie here gathering dust in an old woman's chambers."

Corfe looked at her, and he smiled, the joy of the sword's light, deadly balance upon him. The hilt fitted his hand as though it had been made for him. On an impulse, he knelt before her and offered it to her.

"Lady, for what it is worth, know that you have one champion at least in this kingdom." He raised his dancing eyes. "And you are not so old."

She laughed again. "Gallantry, no less! I will make a courtier of you yet, Corfe." She rose, and indeed in that moment she looked young, a woman barely into her third decade, though she must have been almost twice that. *She's beautiful*, Corfe thought, and he admired her. One slim-fingered hand stroked his cheek.

"That is all, Colonel. I won't keep you from your barbarians a moment longer. You must, *must* leave at sunrise. Fight your battle, come back with Martellus and his men, and I guarantee they will not be able to touch you."

He nodded. The Answerer slid into his scabbard with hardly a click, though it was an inch too long. He took the battered sabre which he had carried from Aekir and tossed it into a corner with a clang. Then he bowed to her and left the room without a backward glance.

But Odelia the Queen Dowager retrieved his discarded sabre and placed it in the silk-lined box which had once housed Mogen's blade, and then set the box aside as gently as if some great treasure were stored therein.

THE GREY HOUR before dawn, chill as a graveside. And in the broken hills that bordered the Western Road to the north of Torunn, a small party of weary travellers paused to look down on the sprawl of the Torunnan capital in the distance. Torches burned along the walls like a snake of gems trailed across the sleeping land, and the River Torrin was wide and deep and iron-pale as the sky began to lighten over the Jafrar Mountains in the east.

Two monks, two Fimbrian soldiers and two half-dead mules, all stained with the mud of their wanderings. They stood silent as standing stones in the sunrise until the shorter of the two monks, his face hideously disfigured, went down on his knees and clasped his hands in prayer. "Thank God, oh thank God."

The soldiers were looking about them like foxes for whom the hunt is on, but the hills were empty but for wheeling kites. "You shall have your fire, then," one of them said to the monks. "I doubt the Merduks will venture so close to the walls."

"Why not continue into the city?" Avila protested. "It's barely a league. We can manage that, I'm sure."

"We'll wait until it's fully light," Siward retorted. "If you approach the gates now you're liable to be shot. Torunn is all but under siege, and the gate guards will be jumpy. I've not come this far to finish with a Torunnan ball in me."

There was no more argument, and indeed the two monks were hardly able to advance another step. They had walked all night. Joshelin and Siward unloaded the bundle of faggots which one of the mules bore and began busying themselves with flint and tinder, after throwing the flaccid wineskin to their charges. Albrec and Avila squirted wine into their throats for want of a better breakfast, and sat gazing down on the last Ramusian capital east of the Cimbric Mountains.

"The Saint must have been watching over us," Albrec said. His voice trembled. "What a penance this has been, Avila. I have never known such weariness. But it refines the soul. The blessed Saint –"

"There are horsemen approaching," Avila cried.

Joshelin and Siward kicked out the nascent campfire, cursing, and threw themselves upon the ground, hauling the exhausted mules down with them.

"Where away?"

"My God, it's an army!" Avila said. "There – a column of them. They must have come out of the city."

Even the crannied features of the two Fimbrians fell with despair. "They are Merduks," Siward groaned. "Torunn has already fallen." Grimly, he began loading his arquebus while Joshelin worked furiously to light the slow-match.

"They are in scarlet," Albrec said dully. "Sweet Saints, to think we came this far, only to end like this."

It was indeed an army, a long, disciplined column of heavily armoured cavalry over a thousand strong. They bore a strange banner, black and scarlet, and some sang as they rode in an unknown tongue which sounded harsh and savage to the two cowering monks. The horsemen's line of march would take them within yards of the foursome, and beyond the hollow in which they hid the country was wide open for miles around. There was nowhere to run.

Albrec prayed fervently, his eyes tight shut, whilst Avila sat dully resigned and the two Fimbrians looked as though they meant to sell their lives dearly. The head of the column was barely a cable's length away, and the two soldiers were gently cocking their weapons when they heard a voice shout out in unmistakable Normannic:

"Tell Ebro to keep his God-damned wing on the road! I won't have straggling, Andruw, you hear me? Blood of the Saint, this is not a blasted picnic!"

Albrec opened his eyes.

The lead horsemen reined in and halted the long column with one upraised hand. The monks had been seen. A knot of troopers cantered forward, the thin birthing sun flashing vermilion off their armour. Their banner billowed in the cold breeze, and Albrec saw that it seemed to represent a cathedral's spires. He stood up, whilst his three companions tried to pull him down again.

"Good morning!" he cried, his heart thumping a fusillade in his breast.

The leading rider walked his horse forward, staring. Then he doffed his barbaric helm. "Good morning." He was dark-haired, with deep-hollowed grey eyes. He reminded Albrec of the two Fimbrians behind him. Hard, formidable, full of natural authority. A young man, but with a middle-aged stare. Beside him was another hewn out of the same wood, but with a certain gaiety about him that even the outlandish armour could not dim. In the early light the pair looked like two warriors of ancient legend come to life.

"Who are you?" Albrec asked, quavering.

"Corfe Cear-Inaf, colonel in the Torunnan army. This is my command." The man's eyes widened slightly as the rest of Albrec's companions finally stood up. "Would you folk happen to be Fimbrians, at all?"

"We two are," Joshelin said proudly. He held his arquebus as though he had not yet decided whether or not to fire it. "From the twenty-sixth tercio of Marshal Barbius's command, detached."

The cavalry colonel blinked, then turned to his comrade. "Get them going again, Andruw. I'll catch up." He dismounted and held out a hand to Joshelin, whilst behind him the long column of horsemen began moving once more. Hundreds of soldiers, all superbly mounted, weirdly armoured, many with tattooed faces. If they were Torunnan troops, they were certainly like no soldiers Albrec had ever seen or heard of before.

"Where is Barbius?" this Colonel Corfe Cear-Inaf demanded of Joshelin even as he gripped his hand.

"Why would you want to know?" the Fimbrian countered.

"I wish to help him."

ELEVEN

"AND THESE PAIR are from Charibon, you say?" Colonel Corfe Cear-Inaf asked Joshelin. "They are clerics, then. What are you two, emissaries from the Pontiff?"

"Not quite," Avila told him dryly. "Charibon's reputation for hospitality is vastly exaggerated. We decided to seek our earthly salvation elsewhere."

"They're heretics, like you Torunnans," Joshelin said impatiently. "Come bearing some papers for the other holy man you have stashed away here. Now I've told you, Torunnan, the marshal and the army were a week away from the dyke when we left them, headed south-east towards the coast. But listen – they go not just to link up with your Martellus. The marshal also means to assault the flank of the Merduk army coming up from the Kardian Gulf."

"They have a high sense of their own prowess, if they think they can assault an army that size and live," Corfe said shortly. His eyes bored into the Fimbrian before him. "And a high sense of duty, also. I salute them for it."

Joshelin shrugged fractionally, as if suicidal courage were part of the normal make-up of any Fimbrian soldier.

"You cannot catch up with them before they make contact with the enemy," he said. "I take it your mission is to preserve the dyke's garrison."

"Yes."

"With thirteen hundreds?"

"I also have a high sense of duty, it seems."

The two soldiers looked at one another, and the glimmer of a smile went between them. Joshelin unbent a little.

"You are cavalry, so mayhap you will move swift enough to be of use," he admitted grudgingly. "What are your men? Not Torunnans."

"They are tribesmen from the Cimbrics."

"And you trust them?"

"Insofar as I trust any man. We have shed blood together."

"You know your own business, I am sure. What of the Torunnan King? Is your command all he is sending out?"

"Yes. The King is very... preoccupied at present. He prefers to stand siege in Torunn and await the Merduk assault here."

"Then he is a fool."

Albrec and Avila caught their breath, awaiting some outburst in reply to this comment, but Corfe only said, "I know. But we will bleed for him nonetheless."

"That is as it should be. We are merely soldiers."

The long column of horsemen had passed them by, the rearguard a dark bristle in the distance. Corfe raised his eyes to it, and then straightened, mounting his restive destrier. "I must be on my way. Good luck to you on your errand, priests. If you meet Macrobius, tell him that Corfe sends greetings, and that he does not forget the retreat from Aekir."

"You know Macrobius?" Albrec asked wonderingly.

"I travelled with him, you might say. A long time ago."

"What manner of man is he?"

"A good man. A humble one – or at least he was when I knew him. The Merduks cut out his eyes. But men change, like everything else. I can't answer for him now."

He turned to ride away, but Joshelin halted him. "Colonel!"

"Yes?"

"It may be that Barbius will not be so easy to find, nor Martellus either. Let me ride with you, and I will set you upon the right road at least."

Corfe looked him up and down. "Can you ride?"

"I can stay on a horse, if that's what is needed."

"All right, then. Get up behind me. We'll find you a mount from the spares. Good day, Fathers."

The warhorse leapt off into a canter with Corfe upright in the saddle, Joshelin clinging on behind him, as elegant as a bouncing sack. Siward followed his comrade's departure with thin lips, and it was with real disgust in his voice that he turned back to the two monks who were his charges.

"Well, let's get you down into the city. I may as well see it out to the end."

THE ANTECHAMBERS OF the new Pontifical palace were large, bare halls of cold marble and stuccoed ceilings. Little gilt chairs stood in rows, seeming too frail to bear anyone, and the new Macrobian Knights Militant stood guard like graven mages, gleaming with iron and bronze. Someone had unearthed a few score sets of antique half-armour from a forgotten arsenal, and the Knights looked like paladins from another age.

The antechambers were busy, teeming with clerics and minor nobles and messengers. Macrobius, whom Himerius in Charibon had labelled a heresiarch, was spiritual leader of three of the great Ramusian kingdoms of the west, and even in time of war the business of the Church – this new version of it, at any rate – must go on. Bishops had to be reconsecrated in the new order, replacements had to be found for those who remained faithful to the Himerian Church, and the palace complex was full of office-seekers and supplicants whose contributions to the Church's coffers had to be rewarded. A new Inceptine order was being organized, and in fact all the trappings and facets of the old Church were here being duplicated at high speed, so that the Macrobians might be considered worthy rivals to the unenlightened of Charibon. Albrec, Avila and Siward stood amid the crowds and stared. The Merduks were baying at the gates, and still men haggled here, seeking novitiates for second sons, exemptions from tithes, tenancy of Church lands.

"Life goes on, it seems," said Avila, not without bitterness. He had been the most worldly of clerics, and an aristocrat to boot, but he surveyed the worldly strivings of the New Church with much the same weary amazement as Albrec.

"We must see the Pontiff," they told a harried Antillian who was trying to organize the throng.

"Yes, yes, no doubt," and he walked on self-importantly, dripping disdain.

The two monks stood like a couple of lost vagabonds, and indeed that is what they were – disfigured, ragged and filthy. Albrec hobbled after the Antillian. "No, you don't understand, Brother – it is of the utmost urgency that we see the Pontiff today, at once!" He tugged at the cleric's well-tailored habit like a child harassing its mother.

The Antillian snatched himself away from the diminutive tramp. "Guards! Eject this person!"

Two Knights Militant strode forward, towering over the pleading Albrec. One seized him roughly by the shoulder. "Come, you. Beggars wait at the door."

But then there was a blur of dark movement, a whistle of air, and the Knight was smashed off his feet by the swing of Siward's arquebus butt. The Fimbrian dropped the weapon, whipped out his short sword, and the second Knight found its glittering point in his nostril.

"These priests will see the Pontiff," Siward said evenly. "Today. Now."

The hubbub in the antechamber died away, and there was a silence, all eyes on the ugly tableau unfolding before them. More Knights came striding up the hall, swords unsheathed, and for a moment it looked as though Siward would be cut down where he stood, but then Avila spoke up in a clear, ringing aristocratic voice:

"We are monks from Charibon, bearing important documents for the eyes of Macrobius himself! Our protector is a renowned Fimbrian officer. Any mistreatment of him will be seen as an act of war by the electorates!"

The Knights had frozen as soon as the word "Fimbrian" came out of Avila's mouth. The Antillian's jaw dropped, and he stammered:

"Put up your swords! There will be no blood shed in this place. Is this true?"

"As true as the nose on his face," Avila drawled, nodding at the sweating Knight who had two feet of steel poised at the aforementioned feature.

"I will have to see my superior," the Antillian muttered. "Put up your swords, I tell you!"

Weapons were sheathed, and the hall began to glimmer with talk, speculation, surmise. Avila clapped the narrow-eyed Siward on the shoulder.

"My friend, that was as good as a play. I'm only sorry you did not have the opportunity to spill his entrails on the marble." Siward said nothing, but picked up his arquebus, kicking aside the other, still-senseless Knight as he did so. No one dared interfere.

An Inceptine appeared, heavy-jowled and glabrous. "I am Monsignor Alembord, head of His Holiness's household. Perhaps you will be so good as to explain yourselves."

"We did not travel here through blizzards and wolves and marauding armies to bandy words with a lackey!" Avila cried. He was obviously enjoying himself. "Admit us to His Holiness's presence at once. We bear tidings that must be heard by the Pontiff alone. Thwart us at your peril!"

"For God's sake, Avila," Albrec murmured, helping the Knight Siward had knocked down to his feet.

Monsignor Alembord seemed torn between alarm and fury. "Wait here," he snapped at last, and jogged off with the unfortunate Antillian in tow.

"You should have been a passion-player, Avila," Albrec told his friend wearily.

"I'm sick of being abused, especially by fat insects like that Inceptine. It's time to stop sneaking around. Things need to be stirred up a little. Ramusio's beard, do they think they tore down the Church only to build a doppelganger in its place? Wait until the Pontiff sees the tale you carry, Albrec. If he's a decent man, as that fellow Corfe seemed to think he is, then by the blood of God we'll make sure he shakes the world with it."

PART TWO

INTO *the* STORM

You must never drive your enemy into despair. For that such a strait doth multiply his force, and increase his courage, which was before broken and cast down. Neither is there any better help for men that are out of heart, toiled and spent, than to hope for no favour at all.

– Rabelais

TWELVE

IT WAS THE thunder of the distant guns that drew them. It muttered beyond the horizon like the anger of some subterranean god. Artillery, by battery, and the rolling crackle of arquebus fire. Morin dismounted and laid his ear to the ground, listening to the unseen engagement. When he straightened there was a look of something like wonder on his face.

"Many, many men, and many big guns," he said. "And horses, thousands of horses. War echoes though the earth."

"But who is it?" Andruw asked. "Martellus or Barbius? Or both?"

The other members of the party, Corfe included, looked at Joshelin. The grizzled Fimbrian sat upon a restive Torunnan destrier looking tired and irritable. He was not a natural-born horseman, to put it mildly.

"It will be the marshal," he said. "We have not gone far enough north to intercept Martellus. We must be forty leagues from the dyke still. I would wager that Martellus's host is two or three days' march away."

The little knot of horsemen were half a mile in advance of the main body, though both Ebro and Marsch were detached for now, leading squadrons out on the flanks and destroying any Merduk skirmishers they came across. Corfe intended the approach of his men to remain a secret. As at Staed, if he could not have numbers on his side, he'd best have surprise.

"How far, Morin?" Corfe asked his interpreter.

"A league, not more."

Thirty minutes, perhaps, if he were not to wind the horses for a charge. He would have to leave at least one squadron with the mules... Corfe's mind raced through the calculations, adding up the risks and probabilities. He needed to make a reconnaissance, of course, but that would eat up valuable time. A reconnaissance in force, then? Too cumbersome, and it would throw away surprise. With his numbers, he needed to pitch into the Merduk flank or rear for preference. A head-on charge into a large army's front would simply be throwing his men's lives away.

"I'm going forward," he said abruptly. "Morin, Cerne, come with me. Andruw, take over the command. If we're not back in two hours, consider us dead."

THE ROAR OF battle grew as they advanced. It ebbed and flowed, dying away sometimes and rising up again in a furious barrage of noise that seemed to make the very grass quiver. The three horsemen began to see stragglers running singly or in small groups about the slopes of the hills ahead, Merduks by their armour. Every army shed men as it advanced, like a dog shedding hair. Men grew footsore or exhausted or bloody-minded, and even the most diligent provost guard could not keep them all in the ranks.

Finally they rode up the side of one last bluff, and found themselves looking down like spectators in a theatre upon the awesome spectacle of a great battle.

The lines stretched for perhaps two miles, though their length was obscured by toiling clouds of powder smoke. A Fimbrian army was at bay there, fighting for its life. Corfe could see the fearsome bristle of a pike phalanx, eight men deep, and on its flanks thin formations of arquebusiers. But there were other western troops present also. Torunnan cuirassiers, perhaps three hundred of them, and several thousand sword-and-buckler men and arquebusiers intermingled, struggling against immense odds to extend their flanks. So Martellus was here. The dyke garrison must have marched more quickly than Joshelin had given it credit for. They had joined up with the Fimbrians, and for the first time in history were fighting shoulder to shoulder with their ancient foes. So few of them. Martellus had lost over half his command.

The Merduk host they were pitted against was vast. At least thirty or forty thousand men were hammering against the western lines, and Corfe could see more coming down from the south-east, fresh formations on flank marches which would encircle the western troops. The battle to their front was no more than a holding action. When the Merduks had their flanking units in place they would attack from all sides at once and nothing, not Fimbrian valour nor Torunnan stubbornness, would be able to resist them.

Look for a thin place, a weakness. Somewhere to strike which would lever open the enemy lines and sow the greatest confusion possible. Corfe thought he saw it. A long ridge ran to the left rear of the western battle-line, part of the outlying chain of hills which came trailing down from the south-western heights of the Thurian Mountains. The North More, men called them. Already, Merduk regiments were on the ridge's lower slopes, but the crest was empty. They had moved down from the summit to get within arquebus range, and there was nothing but emptiness behind them. Why should they look to their rear? They did not fear the arrival of Torunnan reinforcements. They were so intent on annihilating Martellus and Barbius that they had left themselves vulnerable. A strong blow would break open the trap there, might even roll up the enemy right flank. That was the place. That was what he must do.

"Back to the command," he told his two companions, and they set off at a full gallop for the column.

A HASTY COUNCIL of war during which Corfe outlined to Andruw, Ebro, Marsch, Joshelin and Morin his plan. Morin had become very quiet, but his eyes were shining. Clearly, he was in favour of attacking. Marsch was as imperturbable as always – Corfe might have been ordering him to go and buy a loaf of bread – and Joshelin obviously approved of anything which might help his countrymen. But Andruw and Ebro both looked troubled. It was Andruw who spoke up. "You're sure about this, Corfe? I mean, we've faced long odds before, but this…"

"I'm sure, Haptman," Corfe told him. Time was wasting, and men were dying. He was chafing to be off. "Gentlemen, to your commands. I will lead the column. No trumpets, no damn shouting or cheering until I have you all in position and you hear Cerne give the order to charge. You have five minutes, then we move on my order."

The Cathedrallers were on the move less than ten minutes later. They shook out into three parallel columns, each over four hundred men strong. Corfe, Cerne and Morin made a little arrow of riders at their head. The monumental, earth-trembling roar of the battle ahead was rising to a climax. Corfe hoped he would not find the western forces completely swept away when they reached the top of the ridge. There would be nothing for it then but a headlong retreat to Torunn, the inevitable brutality of another siege. Defeat utter and final. He found himself mouthing childish prayers he had not uttered in decades as his horse ascended the north-west slope of the ridge that hid the battlefield from view. He had never felt so alive, so *aware*, in his entire life.

They were still fighting, but they had their right flank hopelessly encircled. A dozen Fimbrian pike tercios there had gone into square and were completely surrounded, a sea of the enemy breaking against the grim pike points and falling back, the Fimbrian formation as perfect as though it were practising drill on a parade ground. In the centre, the Fimbrians and Torunnans were close to being overwhelmed. Their line had given ground, like a bow bending, and was now concave. Soon, it would break, and the western armies would be split in two. Only on the left, scarcely half a mile from where Corfe's men were forming up on the ridge, was there any hope.

The Merduks on the left still had not manned the crest of the hill, and the Cathedrallers spread out along it in battle-line, four horses deep. Corfe could see some of the enemy below pointing at the newly arrived cavalry on the hilltop, but they would also see the Merduk armour they wore. He had a few minutes on his side.

The Cathedrallers were in position. A line of horsemen six hundred yards long, four ranks deep, completely silent, spectators of the vast carnage in the valley below them. Their scarlet armour gleamed in the thin sunlight, their banner flapped in the raw wind. Some of the enemy were becoming worried now about the motionless cavalry on the hill. A few hundred men had spread out into skirmish-line to counter any move round the Merduk right flank.

Corfe cantered over to Andruw and put out his hand. "Good luck, Haptman. If we don't meet again, it's been an honour serving with you."

At that, Andruw grinned, gripping Corfe's iron gauntlet in his own. "We have seen some sights, Corfe, haven't we?"

Corfe took up the position he had assigned for himself in the middle of the front rank. He turned to his trumpeter. "Cerne, sound me the *Charge.*"

Cerne, a heavily tattooed savage who would gladly have died for his colonel, raised his horn to his lips and blew the five-note hunting call of his own hills. Corfe drew out John Mogen's sword, and it flashed like summer lightning above his head. Then he kicked his mount into motion, whilst around him the line began to move, the ground shook at the thunder of over five thousand hooves, and the battle-paean of the tribes issued from a thousand throats.

THE MERDUKS IN the valley looked up, and the Torunnans and Fimbrians who were fighting their desperate battle for survival saw a long line of cavalry come raging down from the hilltop like a scarlet avalanche. One thousand two hundred heavy horses carrying men in red iron, their lances a limbless forest against the sky, and that terrible, barbaric battle-hymn roaring down with them.

They sped into a gallop, their lines separating out, and the wicked lances came down from the vertical. The Merduk skirmishers took one look at that looming juggernaut, and began to run.

The first rank of the Cathedrallers rode them down, spearing them through their spines and galloping on. Half a dozen of the horsemen went down, their mounts tripping on the broken ground, but they closed the gaps and kept coming. The main Merduk formations below frantically tried to change their facings to meet this new, unlocked-for enemy clad in their own armour but glowing red as fresh blood and singing in some barbaric tongue. A regiment of *Hraibadar* arquebusiers stood to fire a volley, but the approaching maelstrom was too much for some of them to bear, and they ran also. Their formation was scrambled, even as the first rank of the Cathedrallers smashed into them.

The big horses rode down the Merduks as though they were a line of rabbits, and the terrible lances of the riders speared scores in the first clash. Horses went down, cartwheeling, screaming, crushing friend and foe alike, but the charge's momentum was too powerful to stop. They rode on, and behind them came the second rank, and the third, and the fourth. More horses falling, brought down by the corpses underfoot, their riders flung through the air to be trampled by the ranks behind them. Corfe lost sixty men in the first thirty seconds, but the Merduks died by the shrieking hundred.

The entire Merduk right wing recoiled, the Cathedrallers ploughing through it in a cataclysm of slaughter. The Merduks were crushed together so tightly that men in the centre of the press could not even raise their arms, and scores were trampled to death in Torunnan mud. The entire enemy battle-line shuddered backwards as officers tried to pull their men out of the disaster and reorganize them. But the Cathedrallers kept coming. Most of their lances were lost or broken now, and the tribesmen had swept out their swords and were cutting down the enemy like scythemen harvesting corn. Nothing could withstand the sheer impact of those hundreds of tons of flesh and muscle and steel, but they were slowing down. The sheer numbers of the enemy were bringing the charge to a halt, and while the horsemen had speared and hacked and crushed a path into the very heart of the Merduk right wing, they were now becoming surrounded as reserve regiments were rushed up around them.

Corfe could feel blood stiffening on his face. His horse's neck was black with it, and the Answerer was shining vermilion to the hilt. This was the first time since Ormann Dyke that he had met Merduks on the battlefield, and for a few minutes he had forgotten he was an officer, the commander of an army. He had ridden into the enemy with the fury of an avenging angel, screaming, his battlecry the wordless reiteration of his dead wife's name ringing through his mind like an agonizing accusation. Men had quailed before the naked murder on his face, and always in the charge he had been the foremost, desiring only to kill, forgetting strategy and tactics and the responsibilities of command. But now the battle-lust was fading, and he was seeing clearly again.

He pulled his mount out of the front line and looked around, panting, gauging the situation. He glimpsed the fresh enemy forces manoeuvring off to his left, and knew that his men had shot their bolt.

Cerne was still beside him, a bloody apparition of war, his eyes a maniacal glitter under his helm. "Stay by me," Corfe told him, and forged through the murderous press of men and horses off to the right.

Black-clad infantry here, pikes outlined against the sky. His men had broken though to the Fimbrian line. Something tugged at Corfe's shoulder, and he instantly raised his sword to strike but found Joshelin at his side. The veteran Fimbrian had a look in his eyes not unlike that in Cerne's, and a wild gaiety about him.

"I'll get them to pull back," he shouted over the road. "I'll talk to them. They'll take it from me. But you have to get your men up the hill, or they'll be overwhelmed!"

Corfe nodded. Joshelin gave him a crisp Fimbrian salute, and then rode off into the heart of his countrymen's lines.

This was the hardest part, the worst manoeuvre to undertake in war – a fighting withdrawal. Did the Fimbrians have enough left in them to cover it? And where was Martellus?

"Colonel!" a voice shouted, and Corfe wheeled round.

Joshelin was there, leading his horse, and with him a red-sashed moustached Fimbrian.

"I am Marshall Barbius," the man said. "How many are you?"

"Thirteen hundreds."

"That's all? You've made quite a dent."

Corfe leaned over in the saddle. He had received a heavy slash from a Merduk tulwar which had not penetrated his armour but which nonetheless was stiffening his entire torso. He hissed with pain as he shook the marshal's hand.

"You must get your men out," he told him. "Where is Martellus? I will save as many of you as I can."

"Martellus is dead," Barbius told him without emotion. "My right is encircled and the centre too closely engaged to break away. But I have given orders for the left wing to follow you out. We will cover your retreat."

"How?"

"Why, by attacking, of course."

The man was serious. Corfe did not know whether to admire or despise him.

"You must escape with me," he told Barbius, but the marshal shook his head. "My place is here. What is your name?"

"Corfe Cear-Inaf."

"Then look after my men, Corfe. Joshelin, you go with him."

"Sir —"

"Obey orders, soldier. You must go now, Colonel. I will not be able to hold them for long."

Corfe nodded. "God go with you," he said, knowing Barbius would not survive. The marshal turned without another word and strode back to his embattled line. Joshelin passed a hand over his face, eyes closed.

"Sound me the *Retreat*," Corfe ordered his trumpeter.

Cerne gaped at him a moment, and then put the horn to his lips and blew. High and clear over the clamour of war came the hunting call of the Cimbrics, this time announcing the kill. Corfe wondered how many of his men could hear it.

THE BATTLE OPENED out. The Merduk right wing, badly mauled by Corfe's charge, was reorganizing. Freed from its clutches for the moment was a motley formation of some six or seven thousand men, Torunnans and Fimbrians, who began to withdraw up the hill behind them, whilst what was left of the Cathedrallers formed a line to cover their retreat. Corfe kicked his exhausted horse into a canter and regained the hilltop, watching the battle unfold below.

A thousand surrounded Fimbrians out on the right were tying up ten times their number of the enemy and building a wall of dead around their pike square. Here on the left the western forces were in full retreat, the Torunnans running in a formless mob, the Fimbrians withdrawing in orderly fashion, by tercio. Their arquebusiers continued to fire aimed volleys at any of the enemy who ventured too close. But Corfe was concentrating on the centre, that howling, murderous chaos into which Barbius had disappeared. The Fimbrians there – hardly two thousand of them – dressed their lines, and began to advance.

Andruw joined him on the hilltop, reeking with blood, his horse earless where he had made too low a sword-swing. He did not speak, but sat and watched with Corfe as around the two of them the remnants of the Ormann Dyke garrison and Barbius's left wing streamed past.

"In the name of God," Andruw said in a shocked gasp as he saw the Fimbrians in the centre deliberately assault the main body of the Merduk host – thirty, forty thousand strong.

Their lines of pikes seemed inhuman, unstoppable. They actually pushed the enemy back, and began carving a swathe of slaughter deep in the Merduk centre. The enemy formations there recoiled from the machine-like efficiency of the Fimbrians. But it could not last. Already, the Merduks were flooding round the flanks and rear of the pikemen.

"Let's get out of here," Corfe said, his voice heavy and thick. "We can't waste the time they're buying us."

He kicked his horse into motion again. The animal could barely manage a trot. Around him his command was reforming. He saw Marsch there, and Morin haranguing the excited tribesmen, in some cases physically pulling at them to get them to retreat. They wanted to stay and fight, and Corfe could readily understand why. For a moment he wished that he, too, were down there in the valley with Barbius, making a glorious end. Easier to fight than to think. Better to fight than remember. But he had his job to do, and he had men depending on him. How many now? he wondered. How many left? He felt a weary disgust, but masked it as he always did. A black-garbed Fimbrian, his uniform in tatters under his armour, stood before him and saluted him.

"Yes?"

"Formio, sir, Barbius's adjutant. His orders are – were – to place myself and my men at your disposal. May I ask what your intentions are, sir?"

The Fimbrian was young, younger even than Corfe. He spoke stiffly, as if expecting to be given offence. Corfe found himself smiling at him.

"My intentions? My intentions, Formio, are to get us the hell out of here."

THIRTEEN

THEY HAD FORGOTTEN that he had been blinded. His ravaged face was a shock which rendered them dumb. He wore the simple brown robe of an Antillian, a single ring and a fine Saint's symbol of silver and black wood. A dozen Knights Militant, watchful, hard-faced men, ringed the walls of his chamber. There had been rumours of assassination attempts.

"Holy Father," Alembord said, bowing deep to kiss the ring, "those whom I told you of are here."

The High Pontiff Macrobius nodded and then spoke in a quavering voice, that of an old, tired man. "Strangers, introduce yourselves. And no ceremony, I beg. I hear your errand is most urgent."

Albrec it was who spoke up. Siward was eyeing balefully the surrounding Knights, and Avila seemed taken aback, almost disgruntled.

"Holiness, we are monks fleeing Charibon, under the protection of a Fimbrian soldier. Our names are unimportant, but what we bear may seal the fate of nations."

There was a long pause. Macrobius waited patiently, but Alembord snapped at last: "Well?"

"Forgive me, Monsignor, but what I have to say is for the Pontiff's ears alone."

"Merciful heavens, who exactly do you think you are? Holiness, let me take care of these upstarts. They are clearly eccentric adventurers, perhaps even in the pay of the Himerians. I will get the truth out of them."

Macrobius shook his head with the first touch of asperity they had seen in him.

"Step forward, young man – the one who spoke to me." Albrec did so. As he came close to the Pontiff he heard the slight metallic grate of swords being gently loosened in sheaths as the Knights tensed. He moved slowly and deliberately until he was two feet from the Pontiff's face.

And here Macrobius reached out and laid his hands on Albrec's features, his old fingers feather-light as he traced his eyes, cheeks, lips – and the gaping hole which had been his nose.

"Your voice... I thought there was something amiss. What happened, my son?"

"Frostbite, Holiness, in the Cimbrics. We would have died had the Fimbrians not found us. As it was, we did not come away untouched."

"A disfigurement can be a heavy trial," Macrobius said with his blind smile. "But cruelty to the flesh can also refine the spirit. I see more now than I ever did when I had two eyes and sat in a palace in Aekir. Tell me your errand."

Taking a breath, Albrec told him in a low tone of the ancient document he had found in the bowels of Charibon, a biography of the Blessed Ramusio written by one of his contemporaries, Honorius of Neyr. In it Honorius stated that Ramusio had not been assumed into heaven in the twilight of his life as the Church had taught for over four centuries, but had set off alone to proselytize among the heathen Merduks of the east and had become revered among them as Ahrimuz, the Prophet. The two great religions of the world, which had battled each other for centuries and piled up a million dead in their names, were the handiwork of one man. The Saint and the Prophet were one.

The expression of an eyeless man is hard to read. As Macrobius leaned back again Albrec could not be sure if he were shocked, angry, or merely bewildered.

"How do I know you are not an agent of Himerius, come here to sow the seeds of heresy and discord in the foundations of our New Church?" Macrobius asked gently.

Albrec sagged. "Holiness, I know it sounds like the merest madness, but I have the document here, and it is genuine. I know. I was a librarian in Charibon. This is the work of Honorius himself, written in the first century and hidden away by the Founding Fathers of the Church to suit their own ends. This is the truth, Holiness."

"These tidings, if they are indeed the truth, could tear up the world. I am an old blind man, Pontiff or no. Why should I act on your convictions? The world is in enough turmoil as it is."

"Holy Father," Albrec said hesitantly, "we met a man on the Western Road, a soldier who was going out to fight the Merduks, though he knew he was hopelessly outnumbered. He did not know if he would be coming back, but he went out anyway because it was his duty. And he knew you. He told us you were a good man, a humble one, and he bade me tell you to remember the retreat from Aekir."

"What was his name?" Macrobius asked, suddenly eager.

"Corfe, a colonel of cavalry."

Macrobius was silent for a long time, his face bent into his breast. A hush fell in the chamber, and Albrec wondered if he had fallen asleep. How could one tell, when he had no eyes or eyelids to shut? Finally, however, the Pontiff stirred. He rubbed his temples with his fingertips, raised his head, and said, "Monsignor Alembord!" in a voice that was startlingly clear and strong. Alembord actually flinched.

"Yes, Holiness?"

"Find suitable quarters for these travellers. They have journeyed a long way, bearing a heavy burden. And assemble the best scribes, scholars and copyists in the capital. I want them all gathered here tomorrow by noon, and quarters cleared in the palace for them also."

Alembord's mouth opened and closed like that of a landed fish for a few seconds, then he said, "It shall be done at once," and shot a look of pure hatred at Albrec. The little noseless monk felt a wave of relief flood over him, leaving him drained and exhausted.

"Corfe saved my life when it was not worth saving," Macrobius said quietly. "It was God's will that it be so, and it is God's will that you have come here to present me with this last task. What is your name?"

"Albrec, your Holiness."

"You shall be a bishop in the New Church, Albrec, and you are to have unhindered access to me any time you need it. Introduce your companions to me."

Albrec did so. "I knew your father," said Macrobius to Avila. "He was a rake and a spendthrift, but he had a heart as big as a mountain. He would never pay his tithes without a grumble, but no peasant on his lands ever wanted for anything. I honour his memory."

Avila kissed the Pontiff's ring, speechless.

"And I meet a Fimbrian at last," Macrobius went on. "You have my thanks, Siward of Gaderia, for preserving my brothers-in-faith. You have done the world as great a service as any ever performed on a battlefield. So it is true that a Fimbrian army marches to the aid of poor, embattled Torunna."

"It is true," Siward told him. "But only through the efforts of your friend Corfe will any of my people survive. Small thanks do we receive for shedding our blood on your battlefields."

"You have my thanks, for what it is worth."

Siward bowed, and managed to muster up some courtesy in return. "For myself, it is enough."

Macrobius nodded. "The audience is over. Monsignor Alembord will show you to your quarters. We will sup together tonight. Albrec, you shall sit by me and tell me what transpires in Charibon. It is time I concerned myself with the turning world again. For now, I must retire. I feel the need to pray as I never have before."

A young Inceptine came forward to help the Pontiff out of his chair and through a door in the rear of the chamber. The three travellers were left with Monsignor Alembord and the surrounding Knights.

"Your platitudes may have convinced *him*," Alembord told Albrec in a venomous whisper, "but I am not so simple. You had best watch your step, *Brother* Albrec."

THERE HAD BEEN rumours flying about the capital for the past two days, travelling faster than any courier. A great battle had been fought up north, it was said, and Martellus was destroyed. The Merduk light cavalry which of late had been patrolling almost to the very walls had withdrawn, and the land to the north was uneasily quiet, scouting parties reporting it utterly deserted by man and beast. What this tense hush presaged no one could say, but the wall sentries had been doubled on the orders of the King himself.

The gates of Torunn were closed, and Andruw and his men had to cajole and threaten for fully a quarter of an hour in the pouring rain before the guards would admit them to the city. Their horses clopped noisily though the gloom of the barbican with the gore of the North More battle still upon them, ten riders looking like warriors out of some primitive bloodstained myth.

The haptman of the gatehouse accosted them on the street below the walls, demanding to know their names and their errand. Andruw fixed him with a weary eye. "I bear dispatches for the High Command. Where do they meet these days?"

"The west wing of the palace," the haptman said. "Whose command are you with? I've never seen your like. That's Merduk armour your men wear."

"Very observant of you. I'm with Colonel Corfe Cear-Inaf's command. He's a day's march behind me with seven thousand men, two thousand of them Fimbrians."

The haptman's face lit up. "Is Martellus with him? Has he got through?"

"Martellus is dead; so is the Fimbrian marshal. The greater part of their armies lie slain up on the North More. Now are you satisfied?"

The officious haptman nodded, horrified. He stepped aside to let the sombre cavalcade pass.

Andruw was kept waiting half an hour in an antechamber despite the urgency of his errand. His normally sunny outlook was soured by grief and exhaustion. The North More had been a victory of sorts, he knew – Corfe had saved part of an army from destruction and was bringing it to the capital. But the rest, including men Andruw had served with along the Searil River, friends and comrades, had been wiped out. And he could not get out of his mind the vision of the Fimbrian pike phalanx advancing to its doom. It was the most admirable and terrible thing he had ever seen.

At last the door opened and he was admitted to the council room. A score of tall beeswax candles burned in sconces, and a trio of lit braziers glowed along one wall. A long table dominated the chamber. It was piled with maps and papers, quills and inkwells. At one end sat King Lofantyr in a fur cloak, his chin resting on one ring-glittering hand. A dozen other men were present also, some sitting, others standing, all in the resplendent finery of the Torunnan court. They looked up as Andruw entered, and he saw the distaste on more than one face as they took in his squalid condition. He bowed, the mud-stained dispatch Corfe had dashed off with a saddle for a desk clenched in one fist.

"Your Majesty, sirs, Haptman Andruw Cear-Adurhal, bearing dispatches from Colonel Corfe Cear-Inaf."

Andruw distinctly heard someone say "Who?" as he laid the dispatch before his monarch and retreated, bowing again. A series of chuckles rustled through the gathering.

"Is it true Martellus is dead?" Lofantyr said suddenly, quelling the buzz of talk that had arisen. He made no move to read the crumpled scroll.

"Yes, sire. We came too late. He and the Fimbrians were already heavily engaged."

"Fimbrians!" a voice barked. Andruw recognized the broad form of Colonel Menin, now a general, and the commander of Torunn's garrison.

"On whose orders did Colonel Cear-Inaf take his command north?" Lofantyr demanded querulously. Andruw blinked, shifting his feet.

"Why, on yours, sire. I saw the Royal seal myself."

Lofantyr's face twisted. He whispered something which might have been "*Damned* woman." And then: "Are you aware, Haptman, that your commanding officer was sent orders to turn over his command to Colonel Aras the morning your men left for the north?"

"No, sire. We received no such orders, but we did move out before dawn. Your courier must have missed us." *God almighty*, Andruw thought.

"And you arrived too late to save Martellus and his men, you say," Menin accused Andruw.

"We saved some five thousands, sir. They will be here in one, perhaps two days."

"Why were you late, Haptman? Was not this mission deserving of some urgency?"

Andruw flushed, remembering the breakneck forced

marches, the bone-numbing weariness of men and horses, tribesmen tumbling asleep from their saddles.

"No one could have gone any faster, General. We did our best. And" – his voice rose, and he looked Menin in the eye – "we were only thirteen hundreds, at the end of the day. Had Corfe been given more men, he might have saved the whole damned army, and Martellus might yet be alive to serve his country!"

"By God's blood, you insolent puppy!" General Menin raged. "Do you know who you are talking to, sir? Do you know?"

"Enough," the King said sharply. "Bickering amongst ourselves will lead us nowhere. I am sure that the full facts of this disaster will become known in time. Haptman, what in God's name are you wearing? And how do you come to present yourself before this council in such a state of filth? Have you no inkling of respect for your superiors?"

Andruw's blood was up, but he bit on his tongue to silence himself. He saw the drift of things. They needed a scapegoat, someone to off-load the burden of their own incompetence and cowardice upon. Corfe had not saved part of an army, he had lost the rest. They would twist the facts to suit themselves. *Lord God,* he thought. *They would wrangle at the very gates of Hell.*

"My apologies, sire. I thought my news warranted great haste. I am come straight from the field."

"Ay, but whose field, I wonder?" a voice said mockingly.

Andruw turned to see the dapper form of Colonel Aras. He bowed, very slightly. "Sir. I am happy to see you well after your... endeavours, in the south of the kingdom."

"I'm sure you are, Haptman. I brought thirty of your wounded savages north with me when I had finished thrashing the rebels there. Your commander really should take better care of his men. I'm sure I shall."

Andruw stared at him, and something in his eye made Aras cough and bury his nose in a wine goblet.

After that he was ignored, left to stand there in his bloody armour as the council debated the news he had brought. No one dismissed him, and he seemed to have been forgotten. His hauberk pressed down on his shoulders. The heat of the chamber seemed stifling after the chill air out of doors, and his head began to swim. Someone nudged him and he gave a start just as his knees had begun to buckle.

"Here, drink this, Haptman," a voice said, and a glass of dark liquid was pressed into his hand. He gulped it down, feeling the good wine warm his innards. His benefactor was a young officer in the blue of the artillery. He looked vaguely familiar. Perhaps they had been at gunnery school together. His mind was too fogged to remember.

"Come into a corner. They won't miss you."

He followed the officer to the far corner of the spacious chamber, and there set down his helm, unbuckled his sword baldric and with the other soldier's help levered off his breast and back plates. Feeling more nearly human, he accepted another glass. By this time there was a group of four or five other officers clustered about him, and the droning voices at the council table went on and on over their shoulders.

"What was it like?" the artilleryman asked him. "The battle, I mean. The city's been running with talk for days. They say you slew twenty thousand Merduks up there."

"This Corfe – what manner of man is he?" another asked.

"They say he is John Mogen come again," a third said in a low voice.

Andruw rubbed his eyes. He had never really sat back and considered Corfe before, the kind of man he was, the things he had done. But he saw something in the eyes of these young officers, something which startled him. It was a kind of awe, a reflected glory. At a time when all hope for the future was being ground down into the winter mud, and the once-great Torunnan military was decimated, cowering behind walls, this one man had raised an army out of thin air and with it had fought to a standstill the invincible Merduk horde.

"He's a man like any other," Andruw said at last. "The greatest friend I have."

"By God, I'd give my right arm to serve under him," one of the young men said earnestly. "He's the only officer we have who's *doing* anything."

"They say he's the Queen Dowager's bed mate," another said.

"*They* don't know what they're talking about," Andruw growled. "He's the best officer in the army, but those stuffed fools over there cannot see it. They pule and prate about precedent and decorum. They'll be huddled over a brazier arguing when the Merduks are setting light to the palace itself."

Some of the young officers looked over their shoulders nervously. The stuffed fools were barely ten yards away on the other side of the chamber.

"We'll stand siege here soon," the artilleryman said. "Then there will be glory enough for all."

"But no one to make songs about it once the walls are breached and your wives and sisters are carried off to Merduk harems," Andruw said savagely. "The enemy needs to be beaten in the field, and Corfe is the only man in the kingdom who might be able to do it."

"I fancy half the army are beginning to think so too," the artilleryman said in a whisper. "It's common knowledge that he beat the rebels down south single-handed, and Aras did nothing but a little mopping up. It doesn't do to say so, although –"

He broke off as Andruw was called back to the council table by his King.

"Be so good as to inform us of the strengths of the Merduk army your command encountered," the King said with a wave of his hand.

"At least forty thousand, sire, but our impressions were that it was but the van of the whole. More formations were coming up as we pulled out. I should not be surprised if the final number were double that."

A stir of talk, of disbelief, or rather an unwillingness to believe.

"And how badly mauled was the enemy by the battle?"

"We did not see the end of the Fimbrians, sire – we left them still fighting, though surrounded. I would wager the Merduk general has lost perhaps a quarter of his strength. Fimbrian pikemen die hard."

"You sound almost as though you admire these mercenaries."

"I never saw men die better, sire, not even at the dyke."

"Ah! So you were at the dyke. We had forgotten." Several officers in the room seemed to warm to Andruw somewhat. He received a few approving nods.

"Corfe was at the dyke also, sire. He led the defence of the eastern barbican."

"The first place to fall," Aras murmured.

Andruw stepped forward until he had Aras penned against the long table. "I should be very sorry, sir, to hear anyone impugn the good name of my commanding officer. I feel I would have to ask for satisfaction in such a case." His eyes blazed, and Aras looked away. "Of course, Haptman, of course..."

The King seemed to have missed the exchange. "Gentlemen," he said, "with the addition of these men salvaged from Martellus's command, we will have almost forty thousand available to defend the capital, though it means denuding our southern fiefs of troops. Thanks to the work of Colonel Aras, however, the rebellious provinces of the south are once again recalled to their ancient allegiance, and I think we need not fear for our rear in the struggle to come."

Aras graciously accepted the mutter of approbation from the assembled officers.

"All bridges over the River Torrin, right up to the mountains, have been destroyed. The geography of our beloved country favours the defender. Our rivers are our walls."

Like the Ostian and the Searil rivers, Andruw thought, *both of which had failed to hold back the Merduk advance.* Now that Northern Torunna had been evacuated, the Merduks might even send an army through the Torrin Gap and take Charibon if they chose, or cross the Torian Plains and assault Almark, even Perigraine. Those places were under the sway of the Himerian Church, however, and Andruw did not think that the men present would shed many tears if Charibon were sacked, or Almark – now rumoured to be Church-ruled – invaded. With the present religious schism dividing the Ramusian kingdoms, there could be no question of them presenting a united front to the invaders. Corfe was right: if the enemy were not crushed before Torunn, he would be able to send columns across half of Normannia. And if the Torunnan army allowed itself to be bottled up in the capital, besieged as Aekir had been besieged, then it would take itself out of the reckoning entirely. Almark and Perigraine were not great military powers. They could not withstand the Merduk and the troops of the Prophet would conquer the continent as far west as the Malvennor Mountains.

A palace courtier entered, interrupting Lofantyr's rosy predictions of Merduk disaster. He bent and whispered in the King's ear, and his sovereign shot up out of his seat, an outraged look on his face. "Tell her –" he began, but the doors of the chamber were thrown open, and the Queen Dowager entered with two of her ladies-in-waiting. Every man present bowed deeply, save for her son, who was furious.

"Lady, it is not appropriate that you be present here at this time," he grated.

"Nonsense, Lofantyr," his mother said with a winning smile, waving a folded fan. "I've sat in on meetings of the High Command all my life. Is that not true, General Menin?" Menin bowed again and murmured something incomprehensible.

"In any case, Lofantyr, you left something behind when you visited me in my apartments the other day. I wished to make sure you received it." She held out a scroll heavy with the scarlet wax of the Royal seal.

Lofantyr took it as gingerly as if he expected it to bite him. His eyes were narrow with suspicion. As he opened and read the document his face flushed red.

"From whence did this come?"

"Come now, my sovereign, it bears your own seal – one which I no longer possess. Pray read it out to this august company. I'm sure they are with child to hear the good news it contains."

"Another time, perhaps."

"*Read it!*" Her voice cracked like a gunshot, the authority in it making every man there wince. Lofantyr seemed to shrink.

"It... it is a general's commission, for one Corfe Cear-Inaf, confirming him second-in-command of Martellus's army or, if Martellus no longer lives, he is appointed sole commander."

Andruw thumped his gauntleted fist into his palm with delight, and behind him several of the junior officers cried "Bravo!" as if they were watching a play. The Queen Dowager glided over to Colonel Aras, who looked as though he had just swallowed a bolus of foul-tasting medicine. "I hope you are not too disappointed, Colonel. I know how much you looked forward to commanding those red-clad barbarians."

"No... no, not at all. Delighted, happy to..." He trailed off in confusion. Odelia's concentrated regard was hard to bear.

"This is a mistake," King Lofantyr managed, regaining his poise. "I sealed no such orders."

"And yet they exist. Countermanding them is tantamount to breaking one's word, my son. You are a busy man – you have merely misremembered that you issued them. I am sure the recollection will come to you. In time. Gentlemen; I will leave you to your high strategies. I, a poor, incompetent woman, am obviously out of my arena here. Haptman Cear-Adurhal, pray stop by my chambers before you return to your command."

Andruw bowed wordlessly, his face shining. The other men there followed suit as the poor, incompetent woman made a regal exit.

FOURTEEN

THEY MET HIM with a salvo of guns, Torunn's walls erupting in smoke and flame as the army came into view over the horizon. The exhausted men lifted their heads at the sound, and saw a thousand-strong guard of honour in rank on rank waiting to welcome them into the city. Corfe reined in, bemused, to regard the spectacle as his enlarged command continued to trudge past him. Torunnan sword-and-buckler men, arquebusiers and Fimbrian pikemen. His own Cathedrallers out on the wings and bringing up the rear.

Marsch and Ebro joined him.

"Why do they fire guns at us?" Marsch wanted to know. "Is it a warning?"

"It's a salute," Ebro informed him. "They're honouring us."

"About time someone did," another voice said as a fourth horseman joined them. This was Colonel Ranafast, the only officer of any rank to have survived from the dyke garrison. He was an emaciated-looking hawkish man who had commanded the dyke's cavalry, only a score of which were now left to him. He had known Corfe as an obscure ensign, Martellus's aide, but he showed no resentment at his former subordinate's elevation.

The streets of the capital were lined with people. Corfe could hear their cheers from here, a mile away. They had turned out the populace to welcome his men. For their sake, he was glad of it – their morale needed the boost – but for himself, he would sooner have curled up in a cloak and stolen some sleep out here in the mud. He knew that the pantomimes would begin again the moment he was in the capital, and his soul was sick at the thought.

"Riders approaching," Marsch said. "It is Andruw, I think. Yes, that is him. I know that smile of his."

Andruw halted before them, breathing hard, and threw Corfe a salute.

"Greetings, General. I have orders to show you and your officers to a special set of quarters in the palace. There's to be a banquet tonight in your honour."

"What the hell are you talking about, Andruw?" Corfe demanded. "And what is this *general* horseshit?"

"It's not a jest, Corfe. The Queen Dowager swung it for you. You're now commander of this lot." Andruw gestured at the long muddy column of men that was marching past. "She's a wonder, that woman. Remind me never to cross her. Bearded Lofantyr in his own council chamber, bold as you please. What a king she'd have made, had she been born a man!"

General. He had not really believed she would do it. General of a half-wrecked army. He could take little joy in it. A certain grim satisfaction perhaps, but that was all.

The Fimbrians were marching past now, and one detached himself to salute the group of riders.

"Colonel Corfe?" Formio, the Fimbrian adjutant, asked.

"General now, by the Saint!" Andruw chortled.

"Shut up, Andruw. Yes?"

"Are we to enter the city with your men? I shall understand if political ramifications dictate otherwise."

"What? No, by God, you'll march in along with the rest of us. I'll find quarters for every last one of you, in the palace itself if needs be. And if they refuse us, I'll damn well sack the place."

The men around Corfe fell silent. His anger subdued them. He had been like this ever since the battle.

"My thanks, General. And my congratulations on your promotion."

"What do you intend to do, Formio? You and your men."

"That is for you to decide."

"I don't follow you."

"The marshal's last order was to put ourselves at your disposal. Until I hear differently from the electorates, we are under your personal orders, not those of the Torunnan Crown. Good day, General." And the Fimbrian resumed his place in the long, disciplined column of pikemen.

"A good man," Marsch said approvingly. "These Fimbrians know their trade. It will be a fine thing to fight beside them again. They are strangely ignorant of horses, however."

"Corfe," Andruw said, "they're waiting for you down there. The Queen Dowager set this up: the salute, the triumphal entry, everything. If the population get behind you, then the King himself cannot touch you. It's all part of the game."

Corfe smiled at last. "A great game. Is that what it is? All right, Andruw, lead on. I'll wave and grin and look general-like, but at the end of it I want a bath, a flagon of good wine and a bed."

"Preferably with something in it," Ranafast said, with feeling.

At that, the group crackled with laughter, and they followed the marching line of their army down to the cheering crowds that awaited them.

THE CELEBRATORY NATURE of it stuck in Corfe's throat, though. The banquet that evening was attended by a mere six hundred guests – officers of the Torunnan army and their ladies, the nobility, rich men of no rank but with bottomless purses. It swept over him in a haze of candlelight and laughter. The wine was running freely, and the courses came and went in a blur of liveried attendants and silver trays. His own stomach was closed, and he was desperately tired, so he drank glass after glass of wine – the finest Gaderian – and sat in his court dress with the new silver general's braid at his shoulders.

It was a hollow feast. The King was not present, having pleaded some indisposition – hardly surprisingly – but Corfe sat at the right hand of the Queen Dowager as she managed small-talk with their neighbours and contrived to make Corfe feel part of conversations he contributed no word to. Everyone seemed intent on becoming roaring drunk and the din of the massed diners was unbelievable, though Corfe's own ears were still ringing from the thunder of the North More battle. His ribs, too, ached from the sword blow they had taken during the fighting.

Andruw was in tearing spirits, flirting outrageously with two pretty duke's daughters who sat opposite, and tossing back the good wine like a man unaware of what he was doing. Marsch was there also, utterly ill-at-ease and answering everyone in monosyllables. He seemed staring sober, though the sweat was streaming down his face and he had tugged his lace collar awry. Two seats down from him was Ensign Ebro, who was already drunk and leering and regaling his neighbours with gory tales of slaughtering Merduks. And the Fimbrian, Formio, sat like a mourner at a wake, drinking water, being carefully polite. The diners around him – a bluff Torunnan staff officer and a minor noble and their wives – were obviously plying him with questions. He did not seem particularly responsive. His eyes met Corfe's, and he nodded unsmilingly.

Martellus and the greater part of the Ormann Dyke garrison, the finest army left to the country, lay dead and unburied to the north. The wolves would be feasting on their bodies, a mid-winter windfall. Laid beside them, close as brothers, were three thousand of Formio's countrymen and his commander. And the city celebrated as though a victory had been won, a crisis averted. Corfe had never felt such a fraud in his life. But he was not an idealistic fool. Once he might have torn off this general's braid and raged at the crowd. Before Aekir, perhaps. But now he knew better. He had rank and he would use it. And he had a command with which something might yet be accomplished.

He thought he fathomed the frenzied gaiety of the assembled diners. It was a last fling, a defiance of the gathering dark. He had seen its like before. In Aekir, as the Merduks began to surround the city, many noblemen had staged banquets such as this, and seen out the night in torrents of wine, processions of dancing girls. And in the morning they had taken up their stations on the walls. What had Corfe done, the day the siege began? Oh, yes. That night was the last time he had slept in the same bed as his wife. The last time he had made love to her. After that there was no more time left. She had brought him his meals as he paced the battlements, snatched precious minutes with him. Until the end.

"You're drunk, Corfe!" Andruw cried gaily. "Lady" – this to the Queen Dowager – "you'd best keep one eye on the general. I know his fondness for wine."

He was indeed drunk. Silent, brooding drunk. There was no joy left for him in wine; it merely brought the pain of the past floating in front of his eyes, all new and raw and glistening again. He felt the Queen Dowager's knee press against his under the table. "Are you all right, General?" she whispered.

"Never better, lady," he told her. "A fine gathering, indeed. I must thank you for it – for everything."

He turned his head and met her eyes, those perilous green depths, like sunlight on a shallow sea. So beautiful, and she had done so much for him. Why? What payment would be required of him in the end?

"You must excuse me, lady. I am unwell," he said thickly. She did not seem surprised, and clapped her hands for the serving attendants. "The general is taken poorly. See him to his quarters."

HE RID HIMSELF of their ministrations as soon as he was out of the hall, and staggered on alone through the dimly lit palace, the sound of the banquet a golden roar behind him. His shoulder brushed the wall as he wove along. It was cold out here after the stuffiness of the close-packed crowd, and his head cleared a little. Why the hell had he drunk such a lot of the damned stuff? There was so much to do tomorrow, no time to nurse a blasted hangover.

His mind was too blurred to hear the soft footfalls behind him.

The parade ground before the palace. He stepped out into the star-bright night and stood looking up at the wheeling glitter of the sky. There were rows of massively designed buildings on both sides of the square, but most of their windows were dark. His men were quartered within, tribesmen and Torunnans and Fimbrians. No revelry there. They were too tired. They had seen too much. He would give them a few days to rest and refit, and then he would have to begin hammering these disparate elements into an organic whole, a close-knit organization.

Footsteps behind him, louder. He turned. "Andruw?"

And saw a dark shape lunging, the quicksilver flash of the knife. He twisted aside, and instead of slashing his throat it sliced open his right shoulder. The pain lit up his mind, burning away the wine fumes. He threw himself backwards as the blade came hissing towards his face, tripped and fell heavily on to his back. His attacker came at him again, and Corfe managed to plant a boot in his midriff and kick him away. He rolled, his cracked ribs screaming at him, his right arm weakening as the blood streamed out black in the starlight. But before he regained his feet another shape appeared. It piled silently into his attacker. There was a flurry of movement, too fast to follow in the darkness, and a grisly crack of bone. A body fell to the cobbles of the parade ground and the newcomer bent over him.

"General, are you much hurt?"

He was helped to his feet, his arm dangling stiff and useless. "Formio! By the Saint, that was timely. Let me have a look at the bastard."

They dragged the body inside and examined it. It wore a black woollen mask with slits for eyes and nose. Ripping it off they saw the swarthy face below, eyes wide with surprise. An easterner, perhaps Merduk. His neck was broken.

"I'll see the guard is turned out," the Fimbrian said. "There may be more of them. This man was a professional."

"How did you come to be here?" Corfe asked. He felt light-headed with loss of blood and the singing adrenalin of the struggle.

"I followed you. I am not a great lover of formal dinners either, and I wanted to talk..." He trailed off, seeming almost embarrassed.

"Lucky for me. He'd have cut my throat, else. An assassin, by God. The Sultan has a long arm."

"If it was the Sultan. Not all your enemies are beyond the walls. Come, we need to get that shoulder dressed."

THE INEVITABLE UPROAR as the guard turned out and the palace was scoured room by room for other assassins. The Queen

Dowager was informed and at once had Corfe conveyed to her personal apartments, but those at the banquet feasted on into the night, unaware of the goings-on.

"I should be at your side permanently," Odelia told Corfe as the wound in his shoulder closed under her hands and the faint ozone smell of the Dweomer filled the room. "That way you would get into less trouble. Where have you stowed the body?"

"Formio had it thrown into the river."

"A pity. I should like to have examined it. A Merduk, you say?"

"An easterner of some sort or other. Lady, I wish we had a dozen folk with your skills in the army. Our wounded would bless their names." Corfe moved his right arm experimentally and found it slightly stiff, but otherwise hale. A tiny scar remained, that was all, though the assassin's knife had laid bare the bone.

"You would have trouble finding them," she said. "The Dweomer-folk grow fewer every year. It is a decade since we even had a true mage at court here in Torunna. Golophin of Hebrion is the only one I know of who remains in the public eye. The rest have gone into hiding."

"But not you."

"I am a queen. Allowances are made for my... eccentricities." She kissed him on the lips and when she drew back he saw to his surprise that the amazing eyes were alight with tears which would not fall.

"Was it the Sultan's doing, you think?" he asked gruffly, looking away.

"Who is to know? The assassins are killers for hire, for all that they come from the east. Their employers can be Merduk or Ramusian. They must only be rich."

"As rich as a king, perhaps?"

"Perhaps. The world is a dangerous place for those whose star is on the rise. There are men in this country who would see it in ashes ere they would let a commoner save it."

"John Mogen was of low birth."

"Yes. Yes, he was. And he never let anyone forget it!" She smiled.

"You knew him well?"

"I knew him. You might say I sponsored him in much the same way as I am sponsoring you."

"So that is your role in the world. The raising up of generals."

"The redemption of this kingdom," she corrected him shortly, "by any means available."

"I am glad to have it explained to me," he said, with a terseness to match hers.

She rose to go. "I am a woman as well as a queen, though, Corfe. I sought military brilliance, and I found it. I do not seek to love or be loved, if that is what is worrying you."

"I am relieved to hear it," he said. And he cursed himself as she left the room with the hurt plain to see on her face.

FIFTEEN

"BY THE BEARD of the Prophet, who *were* they? Clad in our own armour, galloping out of nowhere and then disappearing again. Can anyone tell me, or are you all struck dumb?"

Aurungzeb the Golden, Conqueror of Aekir, Sultan of Ostrabar, raged at the huddle of advisors and officers who remained kneeling on the beautifully worked carpet before him. The walls of the great tent shuddered in the wind, and the dividing curtains billowed like rearing snakes.

"Well?"

A man in gorgeously lacquered iron half-armour spoke up. "We have spies out by the score at the moment, my Sultan. At this time, all we have are rumours picked up from captured infidels. They say this cavalry is something new, not even Torunnan. A band of mercenary savages from the Cimbric Mountains to the west led by a disgraced Torunnan officer. They are few though, very few, and we damaged them badly as they withdrew. They are not something we should be unduly concerned about, a... a unique phenomenon, a freak. It merely shows the desperation of the foe, when he must resort to hiring barbarians as well as the accursed Fimbrians."

"Well then." Aurungzeb appeared somewhat mollified. "It may be that you are correct, Shahr Johor. But I do not want any more surprises such as the last. Had it not been for those scarlet-clad fiends, we'd have destroyed the entire dyke garrison, and the Fimbrians as well."

"Our patrols have been redoubled, dread sovereign. All Torunnan forces are now within the walls of their capital. There is little doubt that they will stand siege there and then we will be free to send forces through the Torrin

Gap to Charibon, that nest of disbelief. Thus we will have destroyed both centres of the heinous Ramusian faith. The Ramusian Aekir is but a memory – soon it shall be so with Charibon and its black-robed priests."

Aurungzeb nodded, his eyes bright and thoughtful in his heavily bearded face. "Well said, Shahr Johor. Though they have a Pontiff in Torunn now also, the one we missed in Aekir; he is no friend to Charibon. Such is the squalid state of the Ramusians' faith that they fight amongst themselves even as the sons of the Prophet knock on their walls."

"It is God's will," Shahr Johor said, bowing his head. "And the Prophet's, may he live for ever."

An especially violent gust of wind made the entire massive fabric of the tent twitch and tremble. Aurungzeb's face darkened again. "This storm... Batak!"

A young man in a coral-coloured robe stepped out of the shadows. "My Sultan?"

"Can't you do anything about this cursed storm? We are losing time, and horses."

Batak spread his hands eloquently. "It is beyond my powers at present, lord. Weatherworking is an arcane discipline. Even my master –"

"Yes, yes. Orkh would have had this snow melted in a trice and the wind made gentle as an old man's fart. But Orkh is off chasing rainbows. See what you can do."

Batak bowed low and withdrew.

"That is all," Aurungzeb said. "I must commune with my God. You may all leave. Akran!" This to the tall, skeletal vizier who stood like a starved golem in one corner. "See I am not disturbed for one hour."

"Yes, lord. At once." The vizier banged his staff on the floor of the tent. Back in the palace it would have rung impressively against marble, but here it produced only a dull thump. Such were the indignities of following his Sultan into the field. The officers and ministers took the hint, rose, bowed and backed out of the tent into the baying blizzard outside, the vizier following with a resigned look on his face.

Aurungzeb stirred and glanced around. He looked now like a hirsute but mischievous boy.

"Ahara," he called softly. "Light of my heart, they are gone. Come out now, my little sweetmeat. Your master calls."

A slim shape, filmy with gauze, emerged from the curtained rear of the tent and knelt before him with head lowered. He raised her by the chin and peeled away the veil which hid her features. A pale face, grey eyes, dark lips touched with rouge. He wiped it off them. "You do not need paint, my sweet. Not you. Perfection brooks no improvement."

He clapped his large, hairy-knuckled hands. "Music, there! The slow dance from Kurasan!"

From an adjoining, closed-off portion of the tent came the sudden chimes and pluckings of musicians, somewhat ragged at first and then growing in speed and harmony.

"Dance for me. Dance for your weary master and make him forget the cares of the turning world."

Aurungzeb threw himself down on a pile of silken cushions and commenced to suck on a tall water-pipe whilst his concubine paused for a second, and then began to move as slowly as a willow in a summer breeze.

Heria's mind blanked out when she danced. She liked it. The exercise kept her supple and fit. It was the aftermath she did not care for, even now. Especially now. She had listened in on the report of Shahr Johor as she listened to everything that went on in the tent of the Sultan. Her command of the Merduk language was perfect, though she still pretended to have only a rudimentary grasp of it. She had hidden her grief at the news of the dyke's fall, and her heart had soared at the account of the recent battle and the last-minute intervention of the mysterious and terrible red horsemen. Debased and soiled though she might be, she was still Torunnan. The man whose life she had shared until the fall of Aekir had been a Torunnan soldier, and it was no more possible that she should forget it than that the sun should one day forget to set.

The pace of the dance quickened. Aurungzeb, intent on the whirling movement of her white limbs, puffed out smoke in swift little clouds. At last it ended, and Heria froze in position, arms above her head, breathing fast. The Sultan threw aside the stem of his water-pipe and rose.

"Here. To me."

She stood close to him. His beard tickled her nose. She was tall, and he had not far to bend to nuzzle the hollow of her collar bone. His hands twitched aside her gauzy coverings. "You are a queen among women," he murmured. "Magnificent." He stripped her naked whilst she stood unmoving. His fingers brushed her nipples, erect and painfully sensitive.

"My Sultan," she began hurriedly as his hands wandered down her body. She had been depilated, after the fashion of the harem, and her skin was smooth as alabaster. His fingers became more urgent. She forced herself not to flinch as they explored her.

"My Sultan, I am with child."

He went very still, straightened. His eyes glowed.

"Are you sure?"

"Yes, lord. A woman knows these things. The chamberlain of the harem confirms it."

"Name of the Prophet, a child. A son. And you danced before me!" He was outraged, furious. He raised a hand to strike and then thought better of it. Instead he brought it down to rest on her taut belly. "My child – my son. I have never had a son that lived. Miserable girls, yes, but this – this shall be a boy."

"It may not be, my lord."

"It must be! He was conceived in war, at a time of victory. All the omens are favourable. I shall have Batak examine you. He shall see. An heir, at long last! You must dance no more. You must keep to your bed. Ah, my flower of the west! I knew your coming would be luck to me! I shall make you first wife, if it is a boy – it will be a boy." He started to laugh, and crushed her in a bearish embrace, releasing her an instant later. "No, no – no more of that. Like porcelain you shall be treated, like the rarest glass. Put on your clothes! I must have the eunuchs find something more fitting for the mother of my son, not these damn slave-girl silks. And maids – you shall have servants and a pavilion of your own –" He stopped. He felt her over as if she were some rare and delicate vase that might be shattered in a moment. "How long? How far grown is he?"

"Not far, lord. Two months, perhaps."

"Two months! My son's heart has been beating these two months! I shall burn a waggonload of incense. Prayers shall be said in every temple of the east. Ha, ha, ha! A son!"

A son, Heria thought. Yes, it would be a boy – she knew that, somehow. What would her Corfe have thought of that? She bearing a son to some eastern tyrant, a child of rape. Corfe had always wanted children.

The tears burned her eyes. "You weep, my dove, my precious beauty?" Aurungzeb asked with concern.

"I weep with joy, my lord, that I have the honour of bearing the Sultan's child."

Why was she still alive? Why had she not found some way to end herself? But she knew the answer. Human nature can bear many things, unimaginable things. The body eats, sleeps, excretes and lives, even while the mind prays for oblivion. And in time the mind adapts itself, and the insupportable becomes the everyday. Heria wanted to live, and she wanted her child to be born. It was his son, but it would be hers also, something of her own. She would love it as though it were Corfe's, and her life might yet become worth something after all. She hoped that her husband's ghost would understand.

SIXTEEN

URBINO, DUKE OF Imerdon, was a tall, lean, cadaverous man with the look of an ascetic about him. He dressed habitually in black, and had done so since the death of his wife twenty-three years earlier. He was the most powerful nobleman in Hebrion, besides the King himself, but he was entirely unrelated – by blood at least – to the Royal house of Hibrusids. Imerdon had once been an outlying fief of the Fimbrian Electorate of Amarlaine, but the Fimbrians had relinquished their claims upon it decades ago, after the last battle of the Habrir River (which they had won). Few knew precisely why the Fimbrians had given up the duchy – the cities of Pontifidad and Himerio, all the land right up to the Merimer River – but it was rumoured that one of their then-endless civil wars had necessitated the removal of the garrison and its deployment elsewhere. The commander of the retreating garrison had not been able to resist giving the Hebrians a bloody nose one last time, hence the senseless battle of the Habrir.

The native nobility of the duchy had sworn fealty to the Hebrian monarch, whose kingdom was well-nigh doubled by Imerdon's acquisition, and successive rulers of the province had intermarried with the Royal house. But though the Duke of Imerdon and his family were well respected, and indeed immensely powerful, they tended to be seen as outsiders, foreigners. Imerdon's folk were of the same stock as those of Hebrion proper, but the long Fimbrian domination – almost five centuries – had rendered them slightly different from their western cousins. Many of them dressed in black for preference, like the men of the electorates, and they were generally a more disciplined and religious people who looked upon the excesses of gaudy old Abrusio with fascinated distaste. Their duke had remained aloof from the horrific war that had wrecked the kingdom's capital city, though he had given free passage to the Himerian Knights Militant as they fled the country after their defeat. It was said that though he followed his king into heresy, considering it his duty, he did so reluctantly, and his sympathies lay yet with the Himerian Church.

The duke now sat in a covered carriage in upper Abrusio, not far from the Royal palace. If he pulled back the leather curtains of the vehicle he could count the cannonballs still embedded in the walls.

"My lord," one of his retainers said outside the curtain. "The lady is here."

"Help her in then," the duke said.

The lady Jemilla climbed in beside him. He thumped the roof of the carriage with one bony beringed fist, and they trundled off.

"I hope I see you well, lady," he said courteously.

"I am blooming, thank you, sir," she replied. A few minutes of silence, as if each waited for the other to speak, until at last the duke said: "I take it your mission was successful."

"Completely. I delivered the petition yesterday. The Astaran woman and the mage are no doubt pondering its implications even as we speak."

Urbino nodded, his face expressionless. Jemilla was dressed in sober grey, the garb of a respectable noble matron, and no hint of paint or rouge had touched her face. She knew that different tactics were called for in dealing with the austere Duke of Imerdon. One hint of impropriety or wantonness, and he would drop her like a dead rat.

The duke appeared ill-at-ease, uncomfortable. He was obviously not fond of clandestine assignations and midnight conspiracies, and yet he was the key and cornerstone of all Jemilla's schemes, and his signature at the head of the petition she had delivered to Isolla one of her greatest coups. If this man, this cold-livered, utterly respectable aristocrat, acknowledged the validity of her claims, then the rest would follow suit. Duke Urbino was famous for his fastidiousness, his dislike of intrigue. Only his sense of duty and honour had prompted him to meet Jemilla, and a rising unease with regard to the condition of the monarchy in Hebrion. And she had convinced him. Abeleyn was incapable of ruling, was barely alive. And the government of the country had been usurped by three commoners, one of whom was a wizard. And she bore the King's heir. If the kingdom were not to become some outrageous oligarchy headed by men of low blood, then it was up to him, the most powerful nobleman remaining in Hebrion, to do something. His fellow lords agreed, and their letters had been arriving on his table for the past sennight. Jemilla had been very busy since her escape from semi-imprisonment in the palace. She had met the head of almost every noble house in Hebrion.

They were cowed, of course, terrified at the thought of sharing the fate of Sastro di Carrera and Astolvo di Sequero. Abeleyn's kingship had been restored in a welter of fire and blood, the Carreras and the Sequeros rendered impotent by the slaughter of their retainers and the execution of their leaders. If anything further was to be done, it had to be done constitutionally. Where the sword had failed, the pen might yet succeed.

"This council of nobles we have envisioned, it makes me uneasy, I have to say," Urbino said. "There is a certain lack of precedent... The traditional platform of the nobles is the House Conclave, held yearly in this city, with the King as chairman and arbiter. I do not like something which smacks so of... *innovation*."

"The King, my lord, is in no condition to chair anything," Jemilla told him, "and the House Conclave is legally unable to debate any motion not tabled by the King himself." A blue-blooded talking-shop was what that outmoded institution represented. Jemilla wanted something different, something with teeth.

"I see. And since the King cannot or will not appear, we are justified in setting up an entirely new institution to deal with this unique situation... Still –"

"The other noble families have already indicated their support, lord," Jemilla broke in swiftly. "But they await your word, as the foremost among them. They will not move without you." *Play on his pride*, she thought. *It's his one vice – vanity. The cold-blooded old lizard.*

Urbino did in fact seem visibly gratified by her words. "I cannot pretend you are mistaken," he said with a trace of

smugness. "Do you think it wise, however, to convene this
– this council in Abrusio itself?"

"Why not? It shows we have no fear of the King's forces,
it brings the issues we are debating out into the open, and if
the King should, by the grace of God, recover, then we will
be at hand to bear witness and rejoice."

Urbino looked thoughtful. "If what you tell me of his
injuries is accurate, then I fear there will be no recovery, not
even with that Dweomer-crow Golophin lurking around."
He sighed. "He was an able young man. Impulsive maybe,
hot-headed at times, and sadly lacking in piety, but a worthy
ruler for all that."

"Indeed," said Jemilla with the right mixture of regret
and sorrow. "But the good of the kingdom cannot be
neglected, despite our grief and our devotion to its nominal
head. The house of the Hibrusids, lord, is virtually extinct.
Abeleyn's reluctance to marry was a clever instrument of
policy, but it has redounded against him in the end."

"The Astaran princess –" Urbino began.

"– is becoming a visiting dignitary, no more. She should,
naturally, be accorded the respect due to her rank, but to suggest
that her one-time betrothal to our dying sovereign renders her
the right to govern this kingdom is absurd. Hebrion would
become nothing more than a satellite of Astarac. Besides, she
is a woman of low wit and mean understanding – I have met
her, as you know – and she is hardly able to govern her own
servants, let alone a powerful nation."

"Of course, of course..." Urbino trailed off.

What a dithering, vacillating old fool he is, Jemilla
thought, *for all his blue blood. Great God, would that I
had been a man!*

"And the Hibrusid house is not truly extinct," she went
on smoothly. "I bear in my womb, my lord, the last scion of
Abeleyn's line. What the kingdom needs is a strong caretaker
who will watch over this unhappy realm until my son enters
his majority. I cannot think of a more honourable task, or
a more prestigious role. And may I say, confidentially, that
the heads of the noble families with whom I have already
been in contact seem to be in unanimity. There is only one
obvious candidate for the position."

Urbino's chin had sunk on to his breast, but there was a light in his eye. She knew he was weighing up the risks to his own person on the one hand, and the dazzling prospect of the regency on the other. And the risks could be minimized if they proceeded as she planned. A proper show of loyalty to the Crown. Public and decorous proceedings open to all. Once the true nature of the King's condition became widely known, the commoners would clamour for someone to fill Abeleyn's shoes. A kingdom without a king – unthinkable!

"It may be that I have a certain standing," Urbino conceded, "but it is also possible that I am not the closest in... blood, to the monarch."

"That is true," Jemilla admitted in her turn. The fact was that if it came to blood, he was not close at all. "But according to my enquiries there are only two other candidates for the position with better claims of blood, and who have not been tainted by the late rebellion. One is the eldest Sequero boy, son of the executed Astolvo, and the other is Lord Murad of Galiapeno, the King's cousin."

"Well, what of their claims?" Urbino demanded somewhat petulantly, no doubt envisioning the loss of the regency.

Jemilla let him squirm for a second before replying. "Both men are dead, or as good as. They were members of an ill-fated naval expedition into the west. Nothing has been heard of them in over six months, and we can safely assume that they are out of the running." A momentary pang as she thought of Richard Hawkwood, also lost in the west. A man she thought she might once have loved, though a commoner. His child in her womb, not Abeleyn's, but she was the only person living who knew.

"This is not a race, lady," Urbino snapped, but he looked relieved.

"Of course, my lord. Forgive me. I am only a woman, and these matters confuse my mind. The fairer sex can in no way fully understand the dictates and glories of honour, that goes without saying." *And thank God for it*, she thought.

The duke bowed his head as if in gracious forbearance. She could have killed him, then and there, for his pompous stupidity. But it was also why she had chosen him.

"So," the duke went on more affably. "When will this council convene, and where?"

"This very week, on St. Milo's day – he is the patron of rulers – and it shall be in the halls of the old Inceptine monastery. They have been empty since the end of the rebellion, and it will be a long time, I fear, before Hebrion has another prelate or another religious order to steer her in spiritual affairs. It is fitting that the council convene there, and the adjoining abbey will be convenient for those who wish to seek counsel in prayer. Though to be frank, my lord, I need some help refurbishing the place. It suffered grievously during the final assaults."

"I shall have my steward send you a score of domestics," Urbino said. His thin face darkened. "They say that is where he was struck down, you know, just outside the abbey walls."

"Do they? They say so many things. Now, my lord, I must test your forbearance with a further request. In order that this council be conducted with proper pomp and ceremony, and its participants welcomed with the dignity becoming their stations, I am afraid that certain sums are required. The other lords have agreed to contribute to a central fund which I have begun to administer through a trusted friend, Antonio Feramond. I hesitate to ask, but –"

"Think no more on it. My money man will call on you tomorrow and make out a writ for any sum you deem necessary. We cannot stint when it comes to upholding the dignity of our offices."

"Indeed not. I am greatly indebted to you, my lord, as all Hebrion one day will be. It is inspiring to see that there are still men of resolution and decision in this realm. I honour you for it." *Blind fool.* Perhaps a third of the collected monies would go towards prettifying the prelatial palace and laying in a larder of dainties and a cellar of wine for these highbred buffoons. The remainder would be distributed in bribes across the city. A significant sum would ensure the cheering presence of a crowd of citizens to welcome the assembled nobles to Abrusio and the rest would persuade several officers in the city garrison to look the other way. It was how life operated in this venal world. Antonio Feramond was Jemilla's steward, and she held enough secrets over his head to warrant his unswerving devotion to her. He was also an extortionist and money-lender of some repute in what was left of the lower city, and had a gang of verminous thugs at his beck and call. If anyone knew which palms to grease it was he.

"And now, my lord, I am afraid I must leave you," Jemilla told Urbino with a proper show of deference. "I have errands to run on my own behalf. You would not believe the price of silk in the bazaars these days, what with the war in the east."

"You are still living in the palace, I trust?"

"In the guest wing, my lord."

"Pray send my greetings and best wishes to the lady Isolla and the Mage Golophin. One must remain civilized in these matters, mustn't one?"

Civilized, she repeated to herself as her barouche sped her away. *The spectacle of the recent blood-letting has gelded the lot of them. And they call themselves men!*

Weakness she despised in all things and all people, but especially in those hypocrites who professed to be strong. Men of power whose spines were made of willow-wand. She idly went over in her mind the men she had found to be different. Those whom she might have respected. Abeleyn, yes, once he had grown a little. And Richard, her lost mariner. They were both gone, but there was a third. Golophin. He, she thought, could well be the most formidable of the three. A worthy adversary.

Naturally enough, she did not take her fellow woman, the lady Isolla, into account.

ACROSS THE BREADTH of the Old World, the wide kingdoms of the Ramusians. Beleaguered Torunn bristled with troops like the fortress it had become, and the city was deep in snow. The blizzards had whirled farther down into the lowlands than they had in decades, and rime lay even on the shores of the Kardian Sea.

Afternoon in Hebrion was dark evening here. Albrec, Avila and the High Pontiff (or one of them), Macrobius, sat around one end of a massive rectangular hardwood table littered with papers. Fine candles burned by the dozen to illuminate their reading matter. Down at the far end of the table were gathered half a dozen other clerics, most in Antillian brown, but two – Monsignor Alembord and Osmer of Rone – in the black of Inceptines. The room was silent as they prayed together. Finally Macrobius raised his head.

"Mercadius of Orfor, I ask you again: are you sure?"

An old gnomish Antillian monk started. Before him on the table was the battered, stained and bloodied document which Albrec and Avila had brought from Charibon. His hands trembled over it as though he were warming them at its pages.

"Holy Father, I say once more I am as sure as it is possible to be. It is Honorius's original hand, of that there is no doubt. We have nothing scribed by him here, but in Charibon once I saw an original of his *Revelations*. The hand is one and the same."

Albrec spoke up. "I too saw that copy. Mercadius is correct."

The glabrous face of Monsignor Alembord went even paler. "Holy Saint! But that does not confirm anything, surely. Honorius was mad. This document is the product of a mind unhinged."

"Have you read it?" Mercadius asked him.

"You know I have not!"

"Then I say to you, Monsignor Alembord, that this text was not written by a madman. It is measured, succinct and luminously clear. And intensely moving."

"You cannot expect me to believe that our own Blessed Saint and that abomination, the so-called Prophet Ahrimuz, are one and the same!"

"I wonder," Avila said lazily. "Has it ever occurred to you, Alembord? Ramusio, Ahrimuz. The names. There is a certain similarity, don't you think?"

Alembord was sweating. "Holy Father," he appealed to Macrobius, "I remained faithful to you when the usurper set himself up in Charibon. I never doubted, and still do not, that you are the one true head of the Church. But this gibberish – this vile identification of our faith's very founder with the evil one of the east – I cannot stomach. It is rank heresy, an affront to the Church and your holy office."

Macrobius was impassive. "It is said – by St. Bonneval, I believe – that the truth, when it is uttered, has a resonance not unlike that of a soundless bell. Those who can hear it recognize it at once, while for others there is only silence. I believe the document is genuine, and that, terrible though it may be, it tells the truth. God help us."

A stillness in the room as his words sank in. It was broken at last by Albrec – now a bishop, clad in the rich robes of one of the Church's hierarchy.

"This revelation is more important than the outcome of any war. The Merduks are our brothers-in-faith, and the hostility between them and the Ramusian race is founded on a lie."

"What must we do, then? Go out proselytizing among the enemy?" Avila asked lightly.

"Yes. That is precisely what we must do."

Shock was written over all their faces, save for that of the blind Pontiff. "Would you be a martyr, Albrec?" Avila asked.

The little monk retorted somewhat testily, "That is beside the point. This message is the nub of the matter. The Torunnan King must be informed at once, as must the Merduk Sultan."

"Sweet Saint's blood!" Osmer of Rone exclaimed. "You are serious."

"Of course I'm serious! Do you think it is mere chance that this revelation has come here, now, at this time? We may have an opportunity to halt the course of this awful war. It is the hand of God at work. There is no element of chance involved."

"The Merduks fight for the joy of conquest, not religion only," Osmer observed. "A common faith is not enough to settle all wars, as we Ramusians know only too well."

"Nevertheless, the attempt must be made."

"They'll crucify you on a gibbet as they did the Inceptines of Aekir," Alembord said. "Holy Father, if we assume that this is true, that our faith is founded on a lie, then at least let us keep it to ourselves for now. The Ramusian kingdoms are divided as it is. This message would cripple them utterly, and it will split down the middle the New Church itself. The only beneficiaries of such a course would be the Himerians."

"The Himerian Church, as it has been called, has a right to know also," Albrec told him. "An embassy must be sent to Charibon. This news will eventually be proclaimed from the roof tops, Brothers. The Blessed Saint himself would wish it so."

"The Blessed Saint, who died a Merduk prophet in some barbaric yurt city of the east," Osmer muttered. "Brothers, my very soul quakes, my faith flickers like a candle in the wind. What will the lowly and the uneducated of the Ramusian world make of such tidings? Maybe they will turn away from the Church altogether, seeing it as a hoarder and propagator of lies. And who could blame them?"

"This is the New Church," Albrec said implacably. "We have turned our face from the scheming and politicking of the old. Our job now is to tell the truth, no matter what the consequences."

"Noble words," Alembord sneered. "But the world is a messy place, Bishop Albrec. Ideals must yield to reality."

Albrec brought his fingerless fist thumping down on the table, startling them all. "Horseshit! It is attitudes such as that which have corrupted our faith and landed us in this quandary to begin with! It is no longer our purpose in this world to obfuscate and deal in semantics. We have had five centuries of it, and it has brought us to the brink of disaster."

"So we'll don the grey garb of the Friars Mendicant and preach the new message throughout the world, becoming an order of evangelists and missionaries, no less!" Alembord shouted back.

"Enough!" Macrobius broke in. "You forget yourselves. I will have decorum in my presence, is that clear?"

Hasty assent. They glimpsed for a moment the powerful authoritarian figure Macrobius had been before Aekir fell.

"I will talk to the king," the Pontiff went on. "Eventually. I will impress upon him the pre-eminent importance of our findings. Do not forget that we are here at the sufferance of the Torunnan sovereign and, high ideals or no, we must think carefully ere we cross his wishes. And I cannot believe he will look upon these revelations favourably. Albrec, Mercadius, you will continue your researches. I want every shred of evidence you can muster to support this work of

Honorius. Brothers, this thing goes out into the world soon, and once out it can never be recalled. Be aware always of the gravity of your knowledge. This is not a subject for gossip or idle speculation. The fate of the continent is in our hands – and I mean no exaggeration. The wrong thing said in a moment of carelessness could have the most severe consequences. I enjoin you all to silence whilst I meditate on my meeting with the King."

They bowed where they sat, and several made the Sign of the Saint at their breasts. This Pontiff was not the humble, vague man they had known hitherto. He sat upright and commanding in his seat, his head moving left and right. Had he possessed eyes, they would have been glaring at his fellow clerics.

"A Pontifical bull is the proper way to announce this thing, but I no longer have regiments of Knights Militant to ensure its swift dissemination among the kingdoms. We must rely on King Lofantyr for that, and I will not have him given information which is already extant in the tittle-tattle of the palace servitors. There must be discretion – for now. Albrec, your impulses do you credit, but Monsignor Alembord has a very valid point. If we are not to sow chaos among the faithful and fatally undermine the New Church, then we must be careful. So very careful..." Macrobius sagged. His brief assertion of authority seemed to have drained him. "I would that this cup had been passed to another, as I am sure you all do, but God in his wisdom has chosen us. We cannot change our fates. Brothers, join me in prayer now, and let us forget our differences. We must ask the Blessed Saint for his guidance."

The room went quiet as they joined hands in meditation. But there was no prayer in Albrec's mind. The Pontiff was wrong. This was not something to be announced by decree, to be carefully released to the faithful. It had to explode like some apocalyptic shell upon the world. And the Merduks – they had to be given their chance to accept or deny it also, and as soon as possible. If martyrdom lay along that road, then so be it, but it was the only road Albrec could see himself taking.

And at last he did pray, the tears running down his face.

SEVENTEEN

THE TALKING-SHOP IS open for business, Corfe thought
wearily.

The long table was almost obliterated by the scattered
papers upon it, and spread out over them was a large-scale
map of Northern Torunna, all the land from the capital up
to Aekir itself. Little wooden counters coloured either red
or blue were dotted about the map. Nearly all the blue were
crowded into the black square that represented Torunn,
whilst the reds were ranged over the region between the
River Torrin and the Searil. Ormann Dyke had a red
counter upon it. It pained Corfe to even look at it.

Men were sitting down both sides of the table, the King at
its head. To Lofantyr's right was General Menin, commander
of the Torunn garrison and the senior officer present. To
his left was Colonel Aras, pleased and self-important at
being seated so close to the King. Further down the table
was white-haired Passifal, the Quartermaster-General, and
a quartet of others whom Corfe had been introduced to at
the start of the meeting. The man in sober civilian clothing
was Count Fournier of Marn, head of Torunn's city council.
He looked like a clerk, a lover of quills and parchment and
footnotes. He was rumoured to be the Torunnan spymaster,
with a secret treasury to finance the comings and goings
of his faceless subordinates. Opposite him were two more
robust specimens: Colonel Rusio, commander of the artillery,
and Colonel Willem, head of cavalry. Their military titles
were largely traditional. In fact they were Menin's second-
and third-in-commands. Both were iron-grey, middle-aged
men with sixty years in the army between them, and court
rumour had it that both were as outraged as the King at the
upstart from Aekir's sudden promotion over their heads.

Seated to their left was a big, grey-bearded man dressed in oil-cured leather whose face was deeply tanned despite the season, his eyes mere blue glitters under lids which seemed perpetually half closed against a phantom gale. This was Berza, admiral of His Majesty's fleet. He was not a native Torunnan, having been born in Gabrion, that cradle of seafarers, but he had been twenty years in the Torunnan service and only a slightly odd accent betrayed his origins.

Corfe sat at the bottom of the table, flanked by Andruw – a colonel now, promoted on Corfe's own authority – the Fimbrian commander Formio, and Ranafast, once leader of Ormann Dyke's mounted arm. Marsch, whom Corfe had also promoted, should have been present, but he had begged off. There were too many things to do, and he had never been much of a one for talking. Besides, he had added, he served Corfe, not the King of Torunna. In his place sat Morin, obviously fascinated by this glimpse into the military politicking of Torunna. The tribesman had insisted on wearing his chainmail hauberk to the meeting, though he had been prevailed upon to leave his weapons behind. Clearly, he still distrusted all Torunnans, save for his general.

Two hours they had been here, listening to report after report, speculation piled upon speculation. They had heard lists of troops, equipment, horses, details of billeting, minor infractions of discipline, loss of weapons. And they had been saying nothing of any real use, Corfe thought. What was more, hardly a word had been said about the attempt on his life the previous night. The King had uttered some vague banalities about "that unfortunate incident," and there had been mutters around the table condemning the Merduks for resorting to such treacheries, but no discussion about palace security, or even speculation as to how the assassin had penetrated the palace. Clearly, it was not a subject the King wanted aired.

But now, finally, they were getting to more relevant matters. The deployment of the Merduk forces. Corfe's flagging interest waxed again.

"Intelligence suggests," Fournier was droning on, his voice as dry as his appearance suggested, "that the two main Merduk armies are in the process of combining. They are somewhere in this area" – he used a wooden pointer to indicate a position on the map some ten leagues north-east of the capital – "and their total strength is estimated at one hundred and fifty to two hundred thousand men. This, gentlemen, is after leaving one substantial detachment at the dyke, and another down on the coast to guard their supply base. Nalbenic transports are ferrying stores across the Kardian, building up a sizeable supply dump there – exactly where, we are not yet sure. They are provisioning for a siege, obviously. I would guess that within a week, perhaps two, we will have their van encamped within sight of the walls."

"Let them encamp all they like," General Menin growled. "They can't encircle the city, not so long as we control the river. And Berza here can see off any river-borne assault."

"What of our fleet, Admiral?" Lofantyr asked the sea-dog. "What is its condition?"

Berza had a voice as deep as a wine cask, coarsened to a bass burr by years of shouting orders over the wind. "At present, sire, the great ships are at anchor along the city wharves, taking on powder and shot. I have a squadron of lightly armed caravels down at the mouth of the Torrin, to warn us lest the Nalbeni try to fight their way upriver. Work on the two booms is almost complete. When they are ready, it will be virtually impossible for any vessel to force the passage of the Torrin."

"Excellent, Admiral."

"But sire," Berza went on, "I must put it to you again that the booms, whilst admirable for defence, curtail our own offensive movements. The Merduks cannot sail upriver, but equally the fleet cannot sail down to the sea. My ships will be little more than floating batteries once the city is besieged."

"And as such they will make a valuable contribution to Torunn's defences," the King said crisply. "Their broadsides will command the approaches to the walls, doubling our fire-power."

Berza subsided, but he seemed discontented.

Corfe could remain silent no longer. "Sire, with respect, would it not be better to keep our fleet free to manoeuvre? Count Fournier says the enemy is building a large supply dump on the coast. What if the fleet were to sally out and destroy it? The Merduks would have no choice but to retreat in order to preserve their lines of communication. We might throw them clear back to the Searil, and Torunn would be spared a siege."

The King looked intensely annoyed. "I quite understand your fear of sieges, General," he said. "Your record in such engagements is known to all. However, the strategy of the army and the fleet has already been decided upon. Your comments are noted."

If it's decided already, then why are we here? What are we talking about? Corfe wondered furiously. The gibe about sieges had cut deep. He was the only man of the Aekir garrison to have survived, and he had done so by running away, fleeing along the Western Road in company with the rest of the civilian refugees whilst Mogen's lieutenant, Sibastion Lejer, had led a last, hopeless stand west of the burning city. A senseless gesture. He might have brought eight or nine thousand men intact out of the wreck of Aekir, but he had chosen to die gloriously instead. Corfe did not admire a commander with a death wish. Not when it condemned the men under his command along with himself. Honour! This was war, not some vast tournament where points were awarded for quixotic gestures.

Admiral Berza met his eyes and made a small, hopeless gesture with one brown-skinned hand. So at least Corfe knew he was not alone in his thinking.

"With the addition of the forces that General Cear-Inaf recently brought into the capital," Fournier was saying, "we have some thirty-five thousand men available for Torunn's defence, not counting the sailors of the fleet. That is ample for our purposes. The Merduk armies will be broken before our walls. There will be no need to worry about supply bases then. Our main concerns will be the harrying of the defeated enemy, and the possibility of regaining Ormann Dyke. Aekir, I venture to say, sire, may well be lost for ever, but there is a good chance we can win back the land up to the Searil."

"We quite agree," the King said. "Now what concerns us today, gentlemen, is the organisation of a field army which might be sent out after the Merduks are repulsed from the walls. General Menin."

The corpulent general preened his magnificent moustache as he spoke. Perspiration gleamed on his bald scalp. "There are a few points which must be cleared up first, sire. The troops General Cear-Inaf commands must be integrated into the army, and that officer must be given a command more fitting his abilities." Menin did not look down the table. "Adjutant Formio, I assume your men are at our disposal."

The Fimbrian, dapper and composed in his sable uniform, frowned slightly. "That depends on what exactly you mean."

"What I mean? What I mean, sir, is that your command is now under the aegis of the Torunnan crown. That is what I mean!"

"I must disagree. My marshal's final orders were to place the command at the disposal of the officer who... came to our assistance. I take my orders from General Cear-Inaf, until I hear differently from my superiors in the electorates."

Admiral Berza barked with laughter whilst Menin's face grew purple. "Do you bandy words with me, sir? General Cear-Inaf is subject to the orders of the High Command, and the troops under him will be deployed as the High Command sees fit."

The Fimbrian was unperturbed. "We will not serve under anyone else," he said flatly.

The entire table, Corfe included, was taken aback by the statement. In the silence, Morin spoke up. "We tribesmen, also, will fight under no other." He smiled, happy to have added his mote of discord.

"God's blood, what is this?" Menin raged. "A God-damned mutiny?"

Old Ranafast, the hawk-faced survivor of the dyke's garrison, had a predatory grin on his face. "I fear it could well be so, General. You see, I think I may say the same for the remnants of my own comrades. As far as I can make out, this High Command was going to abandon us as a lost cause whilst it sat safe behind these walls. Had it not been for Corfe – acting entirely on his own initiative – I would not be here, nor would five thousand of Martellus's troops. The men are aware of this. They will not forget it."

No one spoke. Menin appeared decidedly uneasy, and

King Lofantyr was rubbing his chin with one hand, his gaze fixed on the papers before him.

"This... devotion is quite touching," he said at last. "And laudable, to a degree. But it is hardly conducive to good discipline. Soldiers cannot pick and choose their officers, especially in time of war. They must obey orders. Do you not agree, General Cear-Inaf?"

"Yes, of course, sire." Corfe knew what was coming, and he dreaded it. Lofantyr was not going to back away or smooth things over. The fool was going to assert the authority of the crown, and damn the consequences. His ego was too fragile to allow him to do otherwise.

"Then do as I say, General. Relinquish your command and submit yourself to the orders of your superiors."

There it was, naked as a blade. No room for compromise or face-saving. Corfe hesitated. He felt there was a fork in the road before him, and what he said next would set him irrevocably on one path or the other. There would be no turning back. Every man in the room was looking at him. They knew also.

"Sire," he said thickly, "I am your loyal subject – I always have been. I am yours to command." Lofantyr began to beam. "But I have a responsibility to my men also. They have followed me faithfully, faced fearful odds, and seen their comrades fall around them whilst they did my bidding. Sire, I cannot betray their trust."

"Obey my orders," Lofantyr whispered. His face had gone pale as bone.

"No."

Audible gasps around the table. Old Passifal, who had helped Corfe equip his men when no one else would, covered his face with his hands. Andruw, Formio and Morin were as rigid as statues, but Andruw's foot was tap-tap-tapping under the table as though it did not belong to him.

"*No?* You dare to say that word to your King?" Lofantyr seemed torn between outrage and something akin to puzzlement. "General, do you understand me aright? Do you comprehend what I am saying?"

"I do, sire. And I cannot comply."

"General Menin, explain to Cear-Inaf the meaning of the words 'duty' and 'fealty,' if you will." The King's voice was shaking. Menin looked as though he would rather have been left out of it. The colour was leaking from his cheeks.

"General, you have been given a direct order by your King," he said, his gruff voice almost soft. "Come now. Remember your duty."

His duty.

Duty had robbed him of his wife, his home, anything he had ever valued – even his honour. In return, he had been given the ability to inspire men, and lead them to victory. More than that: he had earned their trust. And he would not give that up. He would die first, because there was nothing else left for him in life.

"They are my men," he said. "And by God, no one but me will command them." And as he spoke, he realized that he had uttered a kind of inalienable truth. Something he would never compromise to the least degree.

"You are hereby stripped of your rank," the King said in a strangled voice. His eyes gleamed with outrage and a wild kind of triumph. "We formally expel you from the ranks of our officers. As a private soldier, you will be placed under arrest for high treason and await court martial at our pleasure."

Corfe made no answer. He could not speak.

"I think not," a voice said. The King spluttered. "What? Who – ?"

Andruw grinned madly. "Arrest him, sire, and you must arrest us all. The men won't stand for it, and I won't be able to answer for their actions."

"Your pitiful barbarian rabble!" Lofantyr shouted, outraged. "We'll slap them in irons and send them back to the galleys whence they came!"

"If you do, you will have two thousand Fimbrians storming this palace within the hour," Formio said calmly.

The men at the King's end of the table were stunned. "I – I don't believe you," Lofantyr managed.

"My race has never been known for idle boasting, my lord King. You have my word on it."

"By God," the King hissed, "I'll have your heads on pikes before the day is out, you treacherous dogs. Guards! *Guards!*"

Admiral Berza leaned across his neighbour and grasped the King's wrist. "Sire," he said earnestly, "do not do this thing."

The doors of the chamber burst open and a dozen Torunnan troopers rushed in, swords drawn.

"Arrest these men!" the King screamed, tugging his hand free of Berza's grip and gesturing wildly with it.

The guards paused. Around the table were the highest ranking officers and officials in the kingdom. They were all silent. At last General Menin said: "Return to your posts. The King is taken poorly." And when they stood, unsure, he barked like a parade-ground sergeant-major. "*Obey my orders, damn it!*"

They left. The doors closed.

"Sweet blood of the Blessed Saint!" the King exclaimed, leaping to his feet. "A conspiracy!"

"Shut up and sit down!" Menin yelled in the same voice. He might have been addressing a wayward recruit. Beside him, Colonel Aras was aghast, though the others present seemed more embarrassed than anything else.

Lofantyr sat down. He looked as though he might burst into tears.

"Forgive me, sire," Menin said in a lower voice. His once ruddy face was the colour of parchment, as if he was realizing what he had just done. "This has gone quite far enough. I do not want the rank-and-file privy to our... disagreements. I am thinking of your dignity, the standing of the crown itself, and the good of the army. We cannot precipitate a war amongst ourselves, not at this time." Sweat set his bald pate gleaming. "I am sure General Cear-Inaf will agree." He looked at Corfe, and his eyes were pleading.

"I agree, yes," Corfe said. His heart was thumping as though he were in the midst of battle. "Men say things in the heat of the moment which they would never otherwise contemplate. I must apologize, sire, for both myself and my officers."

There was a long unbearable silence. The King's breathing steadied. He cleared his throat. "Your apologies are accepted." He sounded as hoarse as a crow. "We are unwell, and will retire. General Menin, you will conduct the meeting in our absence."

He rose, and staggered like a drunken man. They all stood, and bowed as he wove his way to the door.

"Guards!" Menin called. "See the King to his chamber, and fetch the Royal physician to him. He is – he is unwell."

The door closed, and they resumed their seats. None of them could meet one another's eyes. They were like children who have caught their father in adultery.

"Thank you, General," Corfe said finally.

Menin glared at his subordinate. "What else was I to do? Condone a civil war? The lad is young, unsure of himself. And we shamed him."

The lad was scarcely younger than Corfe, but no one pointed this out.

"Been hidden behind his mother's skirts too long," Admiral Berza said bluntly. "You did right, Menin. It's common knowledge that General Cear-Inaf's troops could wipe the floor with the rest of the army combined."

Menin cleared his throat thunderously. "Gentlemen, we have business still to attend to here, matters which cannot be postponed. The deployment of the army –"

"Hold on a moment, Martin," Berza said, addressing General Menin by his rarely heard first name. "First I suggest we take advantage of His Majesty's... indisposition to air a few things. There's too much damned intrigue and bad feeling around this fucking table, and I'm well-nigh sick of it."

"Admiral!" Count Fournier exclaimed, shocked. "Remember where you are."

"Where I am? I'm in a meeting convened to discuss our response to a military invasion of our country, and for hours I've been forced to listen to a stream of administrative piddle and procedural horseshit. According to the King, all we have to do is sit with our thumbs up our arses and the enemy will obediently march into the muzzles of our guns. That, gentlemen, is a surrender of the initiative which could prove fatal to our cause."

"For a foreigner and a commoner, you are remarkably patriotic, Admiral," Fournier sneered.

Berza turned in his seat. His broad whiskered face was suffused with blood, but he spoke casually. "Why you insignificant blue-veined son of a bitch, I've bled for Torunna more times than you've taken it up the arse from that painted pansy you call an aide."

Fournier's face went chalk-white.

"Call me out if you dare, you self-important little prick."
The Admiral grinned maliciously. Corfe had to nudge
Andruw, who was trying desperately not to let his mirth
become audible.

"Gentlemen, gentlemen," General Menin said. "Enough
of this. Admiral Berza, you will apologize to the Count."

"In Hell I will."

"You will ask his pardon or you will be expelled from
this meeting and suspended from command."

"For what? Telling the truth?"

"Johann –" Menin growled.

"All right, all right. I apologize to the worthy gentleman
for calling him a prick, and for insinuating that he is an
unnatural bugger with a taste for pretty young men. Will
that suffice?"

"It'll have to, I suppose. Count Fournier?"

"The good of my country comes before any personal
antipathies," Fournier said, with a definite emphasis on
the "my."

"Indeed. Now, gentlemen, the army," Menin went on. "We
are, it seems, committed to a... defensive posture, but that does
not mean we cannot sortie out in force. It would be a pity to let
the foe entrench and camp in peace before the walls. General
Cear-Inaf, according to the battle plan the King and I have
drawn up, your command – it was to have gone to Colonel
Aras, of course, but circumstances change – will be our chief
sortie force, since it has a significant proportion of heavy
cavalry. Your men will be re-billeted within easy distance of
the north gate and will hold themselves in a state of readiness
should a sortie be called for. In the general engagement that
will no doubt follow the Merduk repulse from the walls, your
men will form the centre reserve of the army, and as such will
remain to the rear until called upon. I hope that is clear."

Exceedingly clear. Corfe and Andruw glanced at one
another. They would bleed before the walls, wear the
Merduks down; and if the decisive battle were finally fought,
they would be safely in the rear. "All the work and none of
the glory," Andruw muttered. "Things don't change."

"Perfectly clear, sir," Corfe said aloud.

"Is this strategy yours or the King's, Martin?" the irrepressible Berza asked.

"It – it originated with His Majesty, but I have had my hand in it as well."

"In other words he thought it up, and you had to make the best of it."

"Admiral..." Menin glowered warningly. Berza held up a hand.

"No, no, I quite understand. He is our King, but the poor fellow doesn't know one end of a pike from the other. We are outnumbered – what? Five, six to one? – it makes sense that we rely on walls to equal the odds. But no army ever won a war by letting itself become besieged, Martin, you know that as well as I. We cannot win that way. It will be Aekir over again."

A gloom hung over the chamber, oppressing everyone. It was Formio who broke the silence. "Numbers mean nothing," he said. "It is the quality of the men that counts. And the leadership which directs them."

"Fimbrian wisdom has always come cheap," Fournier retorted. "If platitudes won wars there would never be any losers." Formio shrugged.

Finally, reluctantly, Menin cleared his throat and in an oddly savage tone of voice he said, "General Cear-Inaf, you were at Aekir, and again at Ormann Dyke. Perhaps" – it evidently pained Menin to say it – "perhaps you could give us the benefit of your – ah, *unique*, experience."

All eyes were on him again, but there was not so much of hostility in them now. *They are afraid,* Corfe thought. *They are finally facing the truth of things.*

"Aekir was stronger than Torunn, and we had John Mogen – but Aekir fell," he said harshly. "Ormann Dyke was stronger than Aekir, and we had Martellus – but the dyke fell also. If Torunn is besieged, it will fall, and with it the rest of the kingdom. And if Torunna goes under, then so will Perigraine and Almark. That is reality, not speculation."

"Then what would you have us do?" Menin asked quietly.

"Take to the field with the men we have. It is the last thing the enemy expects. And we must do it at once, try to defeat the foe piecemeal before the two Merduk armies have fully integrated. Shahr Baraz lost many of his best men before the dyke and much of the remaining enemy strength will be the peasant levy, the *Minhraib*. We seek them out, hit them hard, and the odds will be substantially reduced. The Merduk always encamp the *Minhraib* separately from the *Ferinai* and the *Hraibadar* – the elite troops. I would undertake to lead out two thirds of the garrison and take on the *Minhraib*. At the same time, Admiral Berza should assault this coastal supply base of theirs and destroy it, then put the fleet to patrolling the Kardian so that there will be no more amphibious flanking manoeuvres such as the one which lost us the dyke. With the bulk of his levies destroyed or scattered, his supply lines threatened and the weather worsening, I think Aurungzeb will be forced to withdraw."

"There is almost a foot of snow out there," Colonel Aras pointed out. "Would you have us seek battle in a blizzard?"

"Yes. It will help hide our numbers, and increase confusion. And the foe will not be expecting it."

Silence again. General Menin was studying Corfe's face as if he thought he might read the future from it. "You take a lot upon yourself, General," he said.

"You asked me for my opinion. I gave it."

"Foolhardy madness," Count Fournier decided.

"I agree," Aras said. "Attack a foe many times our strength in the middle of a snowstorm? It is a recipe for disaster. And the King will never consent to it."

"His mother would," Berza rumbled. "But she has more balls than most of us here."

"It may have escaped your notice, General Cear-Inaf," Menin said, "but I am the senior officer here, not you. If this strategy were agreed upon, I would command." Corfe said nothing.

"Enough then," Menin continued. "I must speak to the King. Gentlemen, this meeting is at an end. We will reconvene when His Majesty is... recovered and I have put this new strategy to him. I am sure you all have a lot to do."

"Shall I leave off work on the river booms?" Berza demanded.

"For the moment, yes. We may as well keep our options open. Gentlemen, good day." Menin rose, and everyone else with him. The assembled officers collected their papers and made for the door. Corfe and his group of subordinates remained behind whilst their superiors exited.

Admiral Berza came over and clapped Corfe on the shoulder.

"You spoke up well. I'd have done the same, had they tried to take me away from my ships. But they hate you now, you know. They can't stand having the error of their ways pointed out to them. Even Martin Menin, and he's a good friend."

Corfe managed a smile. "I know."

"Aye. In some ways, palace corridors are the deadliest battlefields of all. But from what I hear, you're quite the hero to the common soldiers. Keep their loyalty, and you may just survive." Berza winked, and then left in his turn.

EIGHTEEN

ALL MORNING THE brightly liveried cavalcades had been trekking into the city. Crowds of commoners turned out to cheer them as they trotted and trundled across the blackened lower city and began following the paved expanse of the Royal way into Upper Abrusio and the twin towering edifices of the palace and the monastery.

They were magnificently turned out, the horses richly caparisoned, the closed carriages gay with paint and banners, the gonfalons and fanions of the noble houses of the kingdom snapping and flaming out overhead like brilliantly plumaged birds. Their procession stretched for the better part of a mile, from the east gate clear across to the foot of Abrusio Hill. Above them, the abbey and the monastery of the Inceptines were hung with flags in welcome, patches of newly mortared stone bright against their weathered old walls. In the courtyard before the abbey, ranks of servitors waited and a dozen trumpeters stood ready to blare out a salute when the nobles drew near.

Jemilla sat watching from an open carriage, well wrapped up against the flurries of sleet that were rattling in from the Hebros. Beside her sat her steward, Antonio Feramond. He was red-nosed and sniffling and had his collar turned up against the raw wind.

"There – there, do you see? That bloodless, pompous old fool. There he sits, the very picture of the gracious host, looking like the cat who caught the mouse."

Jemilla spat. She was talking of Urbino, Duke of Imerdon, who sat on a patient white destrier at the entrance to the great courtyard, ready to welcome his fellow nobles to the council.

Well, one could not have everything. Those with an inkling of intelligence would know who had brought this about. But it galled Jemilla that she was to have no part in the proceedings until Urbino produced her and the child she bore like a cony from a conjuror's hat. She would act the dutiful noblewoman, grieving for the King who had been her lover, whilst behind the scenes she would pull the strings that made Urbino dance.

"The venison was brought in this morning, was it not?" she demanded of the miserable Antonio.

"Yes, madam. A score of plump does, well hung, too. But had I known these blue-bloods were going to flood the city with their retainers I'd have ordered a dozen more."

"Don't worry about the hangers-on. Bread, beer and cheese is good enough for them."

"At least we did not pay for the wine. That saved us a pretty penny," Antonio said smugly. Though the monastery and abbey had been looted in the aftermath of the late war, the Inceptine cellars had escaped damage. There was enough wine in them to float a fleet of carracks. Antonio had also made himself a pretty penny by selling a few tuns of it to an enterprising Macassian ship's captain. He thought this was his secret, and Jemilla did not intend to disabuse him of the fact until she deemed it useful to do so.

"How stand our funds at the moment?" she asked him.

"We have fifteen hundred and twelve gold crowns left over, madam. The duke was very generous. We'll make a profit from the affair, never fear."

Short-sighted fool. He thought in terms of profit and loss, while Jemilla's eye was set much higher. One day soon she'd have the entire Hebrian treasury at her disposal. Let them have their pomp and panoply, for now.

A commotion at the western side of the courtyard drew her attention. A knot of riders trotting into view.

"Who in the world – ?"

Foremost among them was a noble lady riding sidesaddle. She was hooded and cloaked against the inclement weather, but Jemilla knew her at once. That Astaran bitch, Isolla. What did she think she was doing here? And beside her a man in a broad-brimmed hat that buckled and tugged in the wind. He wore a patch over one eye and seemed a mere skeleton under his fur-trimmed riding robes. Jemilla's mouth opened as she recognized Golophin. Behind the pair were four heavily armed knights bearing the livery of Astarac, and then four more in the colours of Hebrion. The group of riders joined Duke Urbino in the centre of the square. Even from this distance, Jemilla could see that the duke was taken aback. Golophin swept off his hat and bowed in the saddle, his head as bald as an eggshell. Isolla offered the bemused duke her hand to kiss.

"Madam," Antonio began. "Who – ?"

"Shut up, you fool. Let me think."

The head of the nobles' procession entered the square, and there was a deafening flourish of trumpets. Isolla and Urbino greeted the arriving noblemen together, the Astaran princess throwing back her hood to reveal an intricately braided head of auburn hair set with diamond-headed pins.

Jemilla had been outmanoeuvred, upstaged. But as she turned the thing over in her mind she realized that it did not matter. The council would run its course, a regency would be voted into existence. Let the odd pair have their triumph; it would mean little enough in the end.

THE COUNCIL ASSEMBLED in what had once been the refectory of the monastery. The broken windows had been replaced – though plain glass was now installed where once there had been ancient and beautiful stained-glass windows – and the huge chamber had been swept clean, the walls replastered and the banners of the nobles hung along the massively beamed vault of the ceiling. Two fireplaces, each large enough to accommodate a spit-turned bullock, had been cleaned out and blazed with welcome flame. The long refectory table had survived and stood where it always had. Crafted of iron-hard teak from Calmar, the only marks it bore of the recent fighting were a few arquebus balls buried deep in the timber. High-backed chairs, ornate as small thrones, were ranged along it, and the nobility of the kingdom took its seats amid a buzz and hubbub of animated talk, whilst serving attendants set decanters of wine and platters of sweetmeats at intervals along the table and lit the dozens of thick beeswax candles which stood in clusters everywhere.

Along the walls, scribes sat at little desks prepared to take down every word spoken by the assembled dignitaries, and a trio of brawny servitors manhandled extra chairs to accommodate the unexpected additions to the throng. The seating had been nicely arranged in order of precedence and rank, but the arrival of Isolla and Golophin had thrown these out and things were being hastily rejuggled. The larger throne at the table's head would remain empty, of course, to represent the absent King and, a princess being as lofty in rank as a duke, Isolla would be sitting opposite Urbino in the next two places. Golophin declared himself happy with a well-padded chair by the fire. He had a decanter and glass brought to him there and sat sipping and watching the crowd with evident enjoyment.

It took an hour for the notables to finish greeting each other, find their places and assume their seats. During that time Jemilla appeared and had another comfortable chair brought in so that she could sit opposite Golophin at the fire. He offered her wine but she demurred graciously, citing her pregnancy. They sat staring into the flames, for all the world like an old married couple, whilst the clamour died around them into an orderly silence.

A grey-clad Friar Mendicant appeared by the empty King's place, and raised his hands.

"My lords, noble lady, a moment of prayer, if you please, for our poor afflicted King. May he soon recover his senses and rule over us with the justice and compassion that was his wont."

Those present bowed their heads. Golophin leaned forward and whispered to Jemilla:

"Your idea, I suppose."

"You won't object to a prayer for the King's health, surely, Golophin."

"Poor and afflicted. I'll bet you just wish."

The cleric withdrew. Duke Urbino stood up. For a second he seemed at a loss for words. Then he met Jemilla's eye, and his spine seemed to stiffen.

"Gentlemen, my worthy cousins, gracious lady, we are gathered here on a mission of paramount importance for the future of the kingdom of Hebrion..."

"A good choice," Golophin told Jemilla. "Respectable, but dense. No doubt you've got him close to thinking he's his own man."

"Any man who thinks he's his own man is a fool. Even you, Golophin. You hold fast to Abeleyn although he's as good as a corpse. Why not give your loyalty to his son? What principles would that compromise? He would wish it so, were he alive."

"He is alive. He is alive and my King. And he is my friend."

"If he were dead – truly dead – would you recognize his son as the heir to the throne?"

Golophin was silent a long time whilst the Duke of Imerdon rambled on in his portentous, pompous way and the rest of the assembly listened with grave attention to his platitudes.

"If it were his son," he said finally.

Jemilla felt a cold hand about her heart. "You need not concern yourself on that score. Abeleyn himself was convinced. Besides, there have been no others in my bed."

"Palace guards do not count, then."

"I had to gain my freedom. I used the only tool I had." It seemed suddenly very warm here by the fire with the old wizard's bird-bright eye intent upon her.

Golophin's eye left her as he drank more wine. Jemilla's face did not show the relief she felt. *This man must go*, she thought. *He is too knowing, too damned shrewd by half. I can fool the rest, but not him – not for ever.*

"Do not trouble to talk to me of the King's heir, lady," the wizard said, wiping his mouth. "We know who will rule in Hebrion if that prating fool up there is appointed Regent, or if your brat is finally brought into the world and survives to his majority. If it is indeed Abeleyn's child in your belly, then I would be the first to recognize the infant's claims, but I would sooner stick my head in a she-wolf's den than let you have any say in the child's rearing."

"It is well that we understand each other," she said.

"Yes. Honesty is often refreshing, don't you find? Have a taste of this superb wine. You look somewhat peaked, and one glass will not hurt the child any."

He poured her some, and they both raised their glasses, looked at each other, and clinked the glasses together.

"To the King," Golophin said.

"To the King. And his heir."

"WELL?" GOLOPHIN ASKED Isolla. "What did you make of it?"

They were in the King's private chambers, sharing a late supper of pheasant stuffed with truffles and basil – one of Golophin's favourites. The weather had worsened, and hail rattled at the tall windows.

"The Hebrian nobility is even more long-winded than that of Astarac," Isolla replied. "They must have talked for seven or eight hours, and they barely got beyond introductions."

"They're feeling their way. Our presence unsettled them. After Jemilla left I made a point of ostentatiously taking down their names. Let them fear a pogrom. It will concentrate their minds wonderfully."

"That Jemilla; you were talking to her for a long time. One might have thought you were old friends."

"Let us say that we understand one another. In many ways she is an admirable woman. She might have made Abeleyn a worthy queen, were she not so... ambitious."

"She'd rather be king."

Golophin laughed. "There you have hit the nail on the head. But she is not of the calibre of Odelia of Torunna, another scheming and ambitious woman. Jemilla wants to rule, and damn the consequences. She would lay the kingdom waste if it would put her on a throne."

"Is she that highly born? I was not aware."

"Oh, no. She is a noblewoman, and she married well, but her blood is not of such a vintage that it would ever enable her to rule constitutionally, even if she had been a man. But she has brains. She will rule through others."

"Urbino of Imerdon."

"Quite."

"How are you going to stop them, Golophin? They'll begin discussing the regency tomorrow."

"We can't stop them, lady," Golophin said quietly.

Isolla was startled. "So what are we to do?"

The old wizard sat back from the table and laid aside his napkin. "Jemilla has planned well. In the absence of the King, a quorum of the nobility is allowed to make decisions of state. It has precedent, my legal minds tell me. The decrees of the council will have the full force of law."

"But we have the army and the fleet behind us."

"What would you have me do, lady? Stage a coup? Rovero and Mercado would never agree to it. The city has suffered enough, and it would make us no better than Jemilla. No. There is another way, though. Only one thing can take the wind out of their sails now."

"And that is?"

"The King himself."

"Then we are finished. That's impossible. Isn't it, Golophin?"

"I – I'm not entirely sure. I must do some reading on the matter. I will tell you later. Later tonight, perhaps. Could you meet me in the King's bedchamber by, say, the fifth hour of the night?"

"Of course. Have your powers come back, then?"

The old mage grimaced. "They are not a migrating flock, Isolla. They do not flyaway and return overnight. There is some recuperation, certainly. Whether it will be enough is another matter."

"Do you think you could heal him? It would be the answer to everything."

"Not quite everything, but it would make life... better, yes."

Isolla regarded her companion closely. Although he was still rail-thin, his face did not have quite the skull-like look about it which had so startled her at their first meeting. She wondered what had happened to his eye. She had not asked, and Golophin had ventured no explanation. It wept tears of black blood from under the patch sometimes, and he carried a stained handkerchief to blot them away.

"My thanks for the fowl, lady," he said. "I must retire to my books for a while." He rose. There had never been any ceremony between them after the first few days.

"Are you – are you in pain, Golophin?"

His quirkish smile, warm and yet gently mocking. "Aren't we all, in this unhappy world? Until later, Isolla."

GOLOPHIN HAD A tower out in the hills, a discreet run-down place where he could attend to his researches in peace. Once he might have spirited himself there in a matter of moments, but nowadays it took two hours on a fast-stepping mule. The door, invisible to the naked eye, opened on a word of command and he wearily climbed the circling steps to the uppermost room. From there he could look out of the wide bay windows across twenty leagues of Hebrion, a kingdom asleep under the stars, the sea a faint glimmer on the horizon, and to his right the black bulk of the Hebros Mountains blotting out the sky. The witching hour, some called it. Dweomer worked best at night, which did nothing for the reputations of those who practised it. Something to do with the interfering energy of the sun, perhaps. There had been a paper presented to the guild about it a few years back, he remembered. Who – ? Ah yes, Bardolin, his former apprentice.

And where are you now, Bard? Golophin wondered. *Did you ever find that land in the west, or are your bones fifty fathoms deep in green water?*

He closed his remaining eye. Mindrhyming was one of his disciplines, and the one least affected by all that had come to pass lately. He let his thoughts drift free, gossamer thin, frail as shadow, and sent them drifting over the sea. They touched upon a few hard-working night fishermen in a winter ketch, flicked around the massive, formless intelligence of a whale, and ranged farther yet, out into the empty seas of the west.

No good. His power was still ragged and convalescent. It could not focus or observe with any accuracy. Even when he had been whole, his gyrfalcon familiar had always been necessary for that. He began to withdraw, to call back his glimmering mindscrap.

Who might you be?

He staggered physically. Something like the glare of a bonfire passed over him, the massive, all-seeing regard of an immensely powerful mind.

Ah, there I have you. Hebrion! Now there is synchronicity in action. Not many of you left, are there? The continent is dark as a grave. They have almost done us all to death.

Golophin was frozen, a specimen turned this way and that for inspection. He tried to send a probing feeler towards the mind that held him, but it was rebuffed. Amusement.

Not yet, not yet! You'll know me soon enough. What are you doing scanning the empty west this night? Ah, I see. He lives, you know. He is not happy, but he will come to it in time. I have great plans for your friend Bardolin.

And then a feeble spark of someone else, hurled across the darkling ocean.

Golophin! Help me, in the name of God –

And nothing. Golophin fell to his knees. Something huge and dark seemed to blot out the stars beyond the tower window for an instant, and then it was gone and the cold night air was empty and silent.

"Lord God," he croaked. He spun a cantrip to light up the midnight room, but it guttered and flared out in seconds. He knelt in the darkness, gasping, until finally he mustered the strength to fumble for flint and tinder and light a candle. His hands were shaking and he skinned a knuckle with the flint.

And it smote him.

A bolt of mind energy so intense that it manifested physically. He was tossed across the room. The power crackled through him, contorting his limbs, ripping a shriek out of his throat. He rose in the air and the chamber grew bright as day as the excess poured out of him in a discharge like the effulgence of a captured sun. He blazed like a torch for ten seconds, writhing in an extremity of pain he had never before experienced or imagined. His robes burned away to ash and the candle was shrivelled into a pool of steaming wax. The heavy wood furniture of the room smouldered.

Then it left him, and he fell with a crack of bones to the floor.

NINETEEN

THE COPYISTS HAD finished ahead of time, and the fruit of their round-the-clock labours sat on the table amid a jumbled pile of other gear. Albrec had had it bound in oilskin against the wet, but it was small enough to fit into the bosom of his robe if need be.

He ran his hands over his things again. Fur-lined boots, socks that stank of mutton fat, a pair of thick woollen habits, mittens, a heavy cloak and hood, and the capacious valise with the extra straps he had had a leatherworker add. Some store of dried and smoked food, a full wineskin, flint and tinder in a cork-lined metal box, and a bearskin bag that he was somehow supposed to sleep in. And the book, the precious copy of the even more precious original which he had carried from Charibon.

He dressed in the bulky winter travelling clothes, stuffed his valise with the rest and pulled the straps over his shoulder. *Done,* he thought. *The baggage is ready, but is the resolve?*

Torunn's streets were quiet as he left the palace. The succession of blizzards which had been battering the city of late had stalled, and there was icy stillness in their place, the creak of solid ice underfoot. But the stars were veiled in thick cloud, the night sky heavy with the promise of more snow.

Albrec negotiated three separate sets of sentries without incident, passing as a Pontifical courier, and crunched through the freezing snow towards the north gate. They opened the postern for him, though one soldier wanted to hold the little monk until he could call on an officer for confirmation of Albrec's errand. But another, looking at the monk's ravaged face, prevailed upon his comrade to forbear.

"There's no harm in him," he said. "Go with God, Father, and for the Saint's sake watch out for those fucking Merduk cavalry, begging your pardon."

Albrec blessed the unsure group of gate guards, and moments later heard the deep boom as the heavy postern was shut behind him. He made the Sign of the Saint, sniffed the frigid night air through the twin holes which had been a nose, and began trudging north through the snow. Towards the winter camps of the enemy.

FROM THE HEIGHT of the palace Corfe could clearly see the tiny shape forging off into the hills, black against the snow. What poor soul might that be? he wondered. A courier without a horse? Unlikely. He considered sending down to the gate guards to find out, but thought better of it. He closed the balcony screen instead, and stepped back into the firelit dimness of the Queen Dowager's bedchamber.

"Well, General," Odelia said softly, "here we are."

"Here we are," he agreed.

She was in scarlet velvet beaded with pearls, a net of them in her golden hair. The green eyes seemed to have a light of their own in the darkened room.

"Won't you come and sit with me, at least?"

He joined her at the fire. Mulled wine here, untouched, a silver tray of cloying pastries.

"How is your shoulder?" she enquired.

"Good as new."

"I'm glad. The kingdom has need of that arm. No word on the investigation into the... incident?"

His mouth curved into a sardonic smile. "What investigation?"

"Quite. It was my son, you know."

Corfe gaped. "My God. You're sure?"

"Quite sure. He is learning, but not fast enough. His spies do not rival mine yet. The assassin was not one of the true brotherhood, but a sellsword from Ridawan. An apprentice. As well for you, I suppose, though even an adept of the Brotherhood of the Knife would have had trouble with both you and that Fimbrian acolyte of yours."

Corfe frowned, and she laughed. "Corfe, you have this rare gift with men. There's not a soldier in the garrison would not give an arm to ride by your side. Even that Fimbrian martinet is not immune. Do you think he'd have put the remnants of his men at the disposal of Menin or Aras, had they been his rescuers? Think again. And then his absurd offer to storm the palace. You have become a power in the world, General. From now on you will attract followers as a candle does moths."

"You are well-informed," Corfe told her.

"I make it my business to be, as you well know. The King has decided to adopt your suggested strategy, by the way."

"Has he?" Hope leapt in Corfe's heart.

"Yes, but only because Menin put it forward as his own. Lofantyr will be leading the army, and he and Menin will do their best to keep you out of any great victory."

"I don't care. As long as we win. That's all that matters."

She shook her head in mock wonder. "Such altruism! Even Mogen was not so selfless. Have you no lust for glory?"

He had asked that question himself once, when Ebro was worried about the odds they faced. He could answer it honestly now.

"No, lady. I have seen glory enough to turn my stomach."

"Have you, indeed?" The marvellous eyes looking him up and down, forever gauging him. Then she rose, and stretched like a girl before him. "Well, you'll receive your orders in the morning, and the army will march the day after tomorrow. Right into the maw of another blizzard, no doubt." Her tone was off-hand, but he sensed a tenseness in her. The taut, velvet-clad abdomen was inches from his face. She set her hands on his shoulders, and it seemed the most natural thing in the world for him to encircle the slim waist with his arms, and lay his head on her, burying his face in the warm velvet. Her fingers ruffled his hair like those of a mother.

"My poor Corfe. You will never revel in your glory, will you?"

"It's bought with too much blood."

She knelt and kissed him on the lips. In a second, they seemed somehow to catch fire from one another. He tugged the gown down her shoulders and it fell to her hips, gripped it harder and rent the material so that it flowed down her thighs. A little explosion of dislodged pearls, her warm skin under his hands. She was entirely nude underneath the gown. He fumbled with his breeches, but she made a kind of sign in the air with her hand which left a momentary glimmer behind, and at once he was naked also. He laughed.

"The Dweomer certainly has its uses."

Afterwards they lay before the fire on a tangled mat of their discarded clothing. She rested her head on his chest whilst he stroked the small of her back, the delicate bumps of her spine. As always, the sadness hit him, the desolation of loss as he recalled Heria, and the times they had been like this. But for once he fought the feeling. He was tired of seeing only the shadow cast by every light. He esteemed this woman – there was no need to feel guilty about that. He *would* not feel guilty.

She raised her head and touched the tears on his face. "Time heals," she said gently. "A cliché, but true."

"I know. It seems endless, though. I don't want to forget her, yet I must."

"Not forget, Corfe. But she must not become a ghost to haunt you, either." She paused. "Tell me about her."

He found it incredibly hard to speak. His throat ached. His voice when it finally came out sounded harsh as a raven's.

"There is not much to tell. She was the daughter of a silk merchant in the city – Aekir, I mean – and she ran the business for him. As the junior officer of my regiment, I was colour-bearer, responsible for our banners, which were of silk, like the Merduks'. They needed replacing, so I was sent to this merchant's house, and there she was."

"And there she was," Odelia repeated quietly. "She never came out of Aekir, then?"

"No. I looked for her after the walls were overrun, deserted my post to try and find her, but our home was already behind the Merduk lines and that part of the city was burning. I was caught up in the flood of refugees, borne along the Western Road. I wanted to die, but did my best to live. I don't know why. I just hope it was quick, for her. I have pictures in my mind..." He could speak no longer.

His body had become rigid in Odelia's arms. She felt the bottled-up sobs quiver through his frame, but he made not a sound and when she looked at his face at last she saw that he was dry-eyed again. There was a glitter in those eyes that chilled her, a light of pure hatred. But it faded, and he smiled at the concern on her face.

"I am glad of this," he said haltingly. "I am glad of you, lady. Time heals, perhaps, but you do also." And he pulled her closer.

She finally admitted it to herself. She was in love with him. The knowledge shook her, rendered her abruptly unsure of herself. She found herself hating the memory of his dead wife, envying a ghost for its hold on him. All her life, she had schemed and plotted and fucked to further her ambitions, to safeguard this kingdom. And she realized now that she would walk away from it – palace, kingdom, velvet robes and all – if he asked her to. She felt dizzied with fear and exhilaration in equal measure.

"Is there hope for us?" she asked him.

"I think so. If we hit them hard enough, quickly enough, and Berza's fleet does its job down on the coast, they must withdraw. We will have won time, and a little space. But even so, it will not be over. Come spring, we will see the decisive battle."

It was not what she had meant, but she was glad he had misunderstood her. It was near dawn, and he had come quite far enough for one night.

Dawn in Torunna was the sixth hour of the long winter night in Hebrion. Isolla paced the Royal bedchamber impatiently. Golophin was late, which was unlike him. If she opened the screens and peered out of the balcony she would be able to see the lights and merrymaking that had been going on throughout the night in the former monastery on the hilltop opposite the palace. A ball was being thrown there for the assembled nobility. It had been no great wrench on her part to turn down her invitation, but the faint, tinny clamour of the music penetrated even this room and intruded on her thoughts, irritating. She was beginning to doubt her role in this, and even found herself thinking nostalgically of the Astaran court, and especially her brother, Mark. What was she to do, send him a letter saying "I want to come home," for all the world like a child sent away to a strange school? Her pride would never let her recover. So she paced the room with her long, mannish stride, and thought.

The click of the secret doorway stopped her dead. The section of wall slid inwards, and Golophin appeared. He smiled at her. "My apologies for being late, lady."

"It doesn't matter." There was something different about him. Something –

"Golophin!" she cried. "Your eye, it's healed."

He raised a hand to his face. "So it is."

"Have you recovered your powers?"

He stood before her. He had changed. His bones had fleshed out and he stood somehow taller. He looked twenty years younger than when she had last seen him, scant hours ago. But something was amiss. She could have sworn that he was confused – no, more than that. He was *frightened*.

"Golophin, are you all right?"

"I suppose I am. Very much so. I am wholly restored, Isolla." Bale-fire clicked into life above his head, lighting the gloomy room. At the same time, every unlit candle in the chamber suddenly fizzled into flame.

"But that's wonderful!" Isolla exclaimed.

The old wizard shrugged. "It is. It is, indeed."

"What's wrong? You should be overjoyed. You will be able to heal the King. Our troubles are over."

"*I don't know how it happened!*" he shouted, shocking her.

"You don't? But... how is that possible?"

"I don't know, lady, and my ignorance is driving me mad. Something happened to me this night, but I can remember nothing of it."

"It's like a miracle."

"I don't believe in them," he said darkly. "Enough. This is not the time or place." He rubbed his eyes. "I must to work at once, if this damn council of theirs is to be thwarted. They'll be voting on the regency tomorrow afternoon. Forgive me my bluntness, lady. I am somewhat out of order."

"It doesn't matter. Just heal him."

He nodded and sighed as if exhausted, though he was fairly crackling with energy. Even the wattles below his chin had tightened and disappeared. She longed to pose question after question, but remained mute. They repaired to the King's bedside. Golophin looked down on the unconscious, mutilated form, and seemed to calm. He glanced around. "What have we here to work with? Not a lot. We are in too much haste." He stroked the heavy wood of the bedposts. "It will do for now, I suppose." He turned to Isolla, "Lady, I need you to hold the King's hands. Whatever you see, whatever he does, you must not let them go. Am I clear?"

"Perfectly," she lied.

"Very well. Then let us draw up some chairs and begin." She took Abeleyn's hands. They were hot and feverish, but the King's face was as still as that of a wax image. The sheets, though changed daily, were soaked with sweat. The King seemed to be burning away like a hearth of coals with a bellows feeding them.

Golophin closed his eyes and sat as motionless as his King. Nothing happened. A quarter of an hour went by. Isolla longed to change her posture, stretch her neck, but she dared not move. She had been prepared for lightnings, thunder, a blaze of theurgy or a chattering of summoned demons – *something*. But there was only the stifling room, the weird flicker of the bale-fire, the wizard's composed face.

And then the creak of wood. She started as the bed began to tremble and shake. The canopy overhead billowed like a ship's sail. It cracked and flapped, the heavy drapes whipping her across the face, and then the whole thing took off and tumbled end over end across the room.

The bedposts, thick carved baulks of timber as wide as her thigh, began shrinking. She gaped at them. They were disappearing from the top down. It was like watching the hugely accelerated work of termites. They had been taller than a man – now they were dwindling foot by foot as she watched.

At the same time, the sheet covering Abeleyn shifted and moved. Isolla stifled a cry as something began to grow under there. It was the stumps of the King's legs. They were lengthening, pushing up their covering. She glanced at the wizard. His face had not changed, but sweat had set it ashine and his eyes were rolling frantically behind their closed lids.

Two feet poked out at the end of the sheet that covered the King's body. Isolla jumped in horror. They were human, perfectly shaped down to the very toenails, but they were made of dark wood. And they twitched with life.

The King groaned, and for the first time the wizard spoke.

"Abeleyn," he said quietly but, low though his voice was, it made the very furniture in the room shake.

"Abeleyn. My King."

The man in the bed growled like a beast. His hands, hitherto limp, clenched tightly upon Isolla's, squeezing out the blood until her fingers were white. She bit her lip on the pain, determined not to cry out.

Then the King's body arched up in the bed, his wooden heels drumming on the mattress, his spine bent back like a fully drawn bow. His sweating hands were slipping free. In panic, Isolla threw herself on top of him. Convulsions battered her up and down. One hard knee came up and stove in a rib. The King shrieked, and she wept with the pain.

The convulsions died, and he was quiet again. Isolla's face was buried in his neck. She could not move. His hands loosed their awful grip and disengaged gently from hers.

"What in the world?" the King said.

She raised her head, peered into his face. His eyes were open, and he smiled at her, looking utterly bewildered and at the same time amused.

"Issy Long-nose," he said, and laughed. "What *are* you doing?"

TWENTY

ALL MORNING, THE army had been marching out of the
north gate of Torunn. The line of men and horses and
ox-drawn field artillery and baggage waggons and pack
mules seemed endless. They had trodden the new snow
down into the mud and carved a dark line across the hills
north of the capital. On the flanks of the column patrolled
restless squadrons of heavy Torunnan cuirassiers. The
column's head was already out of sight three miles away.
Over thirty thousand men were on the march, the last field
army left in the kingdom.

"There is a grandeur in war," Andruw said, blowing on his
mittened hands. His metal gauntlets hung at his saddle bow.

"I never thought there were so many Torunnans in the
world," Marsch admitted. "If we had known, we might not
have fought you for so long."

"Numbers aren't everything," Corfe said.

"Any sign of our lot yet?" Andruw asked.

They were sitting on their horses on a knoll half a mile
from the north gate. They had been here an hour already,
and still the stream of men went on.

"Shouldn't be long now," Corfe said. "Here comes the
main baggage train. We're behind that."

A convoy of tall, heavy waggons drawn by mules and
oxen. The baggage train held the spare ammunition and
rations. Corfe had been given the job of guarding it, and
the rear of the army. When the battle occurred, he and his
men would be spectators rather than participants. Unless
something went badly wrong.

"The best troops in the army, and we're guarding the
waggons," Andruw said disgustedly. "What a prick that
Menin is."

Corfe disagreed. "He did what he could. It's a miracle he persuaded the King to march out and fight at all. And besides" – he grinned at Andruw – "the rear is the post of honour. If the army's beaten, then it's we who have to cover the retreat."

"Post of honour my –"

"Here they come," Marsch interrupted.

Corfe's command began marching out of the gate behind the last of the waggons. The thousand-strong scarlet-armoured Cathedrallers were unmistakable, their stark banner flapping in the cold wind. Behind them came the black-clad, pike-wielding Fimbrians, marching in perfect time – two thousand of them, with Formio at their head. And finally, the last survivors of Ormann Dyke, five thousand arquebusiers and sword-and-buckler men under Ranafast. The command formed a column almost a mile long.

How would they fight together? There was a strong bond between them, Corfe knew. It came from the North More battle, when they had faced annihilation together. And they collectively despised the garrison soldiers of Torunn, most of whom had never fought in a single pitched battle. But they were certainly a disparate bunch. Wild mountain tribesmen, Fimbrian professionals and Torunnan veterans. They had had a chance to recover from their ordeal at the North More, and were rested, refitted and their morale was superb. If things went well, they would hardly need to fire a shot in the forthcoming contest. Corfe hoped it would be so, much though he would have liked to wield this new instrument of his in battle.

"Snow's starting again," Andruw noted gloomily. "God's teeth, will this winter never end? Bloody unnatural time of the year to be campaigning."

"Let's join the column," Corfe said, and the three riders cantered down the slope, kicking up a cloud of snow which the wind bore away like smoke behind them.

THE ARMY MARCHED a mere six miles that first day, the endless procession of men halting and starting again, the waggons getting stuck in the mud that lay beneath the snow, the heavy guns losing wheels, mules going lame. Corfe's men finally halted for the night three hours after the head of the column had pitched their tents. As far as the eye could see, the wink of campfires stretched over the hills and lit the sky from afar. It was good to be in the field again. Things were always simpler here.

Or so he thought. While he was at the horse-lines with Marsch and Morin inspecting some lamed mounts, a courier brought him a message from the High Command. There was to be a strategy meeting that evening in the Royal tent, and his presence was required.

Resigned, he made his way through the vast firelit camp. Everywhere, men sat around their campfires heating their rations and drying their boots. A few flurries of snow had fallen during the day and it was getting colder. The mud was starting to harden underfoot, and the snow crunched.

The King's tent was a massive leather affair with half a dozen shivering sentries posted about it, their armour beginning to glister with frost. On his own authority, Corfe ordered them to build themselves a fire.

Inside the tent three braziers were glowing merrily. The King was there, dressed plainly in the leather gambeson that soldiers wore under their armour. With him were Count Fournier, General Menin, Colonels Aras and Rusio and seven or eight more junior officers whom Corfe did not recognize. Colonel Willem had been left in command of the five thousand or so men who remained in the capital.

"Ah, so we are all here. At last," the King said as Corfe came in. Lofantyr looked as though he had not slept in a week. There were grey hollows under his eyes and new lines of strain about his mouth. "Very well, Fournier, proceed." The King sat himself down in a canvas camp chair. Everyone else had to stand.

Fournier, rather ridiculous in antique half-armour that had not a scratch on it, cleared his throat and toyed unceasingly with a wooden pointer.

"Our scouts have just returned, sire, and they report that the enemy is in three camps. The largest is some four leagues to the north-west. They estimate there are some eighty to ninety thousand men within it. It is not fortified, and they have horse herds picketed around its perimeter and patrols of light cavalry as well as the regular sentries." Fournier cleared his throat again. "The second camp is a league to the east of the first. The scouts estimate that it holds some fifty thousand, including *Ferinai* heavy cavalry and many arquebusiers. It is fortified with a ditch and palisade. The third is farther yet to the north, perhaps another league from the first two. Within it are the elephants, many more cavalry and the main baggage train. It is believed that the Sultan himself is in this third camp, and his – his harem. Another forty or fifty thousand."

"Why does he split up his army so?" someone muttered.

"Flexibility," Corfe said. "If one camp is attacked, the attacker will find columns from the other two on his flanks."

Menin frowned at Corfe. "The general idea was that we would attack their main camp and remain immune to assaults from the other two. But we had not bargained for the camps being so close together. Suddenly this campaign looks a lot riskier than it did."

"You can still do it, if the assault is swift and powerful enough. To rouse the men of a large encampment, get them into battle-line and then march them a league will take at least two to three hours. In that time, given a little luck, we could cripple the *Minhraib* contingent of the Merduk army – the bulk of its troops. We would then be in a position to deal with the other two armies as they came up, or we could withdraw. In any case, it would be wise to detach strong formations to the flanks, in case we're still heavily engaged when the Merduk reinforcements come up."

"Yes. Yes, of course," Menin said. "My thought exactly..." He trailed off, appearing old and apprehensive.

"Ninety thousand men in that first camp," someone said dubiously. "That's three times our strength. Who says they'll be an easy target?"

"Their camp is unfortified," Corfe pointed out. "They'll be keeping warm in their tents. Plus, they are nothing more than the peasant levy of Ostrabar, conscripts without firearms. So long as we retain the element of surprise, they should not prove too much trouble."

"I am relieved to hear it," the King said. He looked with obvious dislike at his youngest general. "You seem to have an answer for everything, General Cear-Inaf. I see we no longer have need of strategy conferences. All we need do is consult you."

A series of titters throughout the tent. Corfe was impassive. He merely bowed to his monarch. "My apologies, sire, if I overstep my station. I worry only about the good of the army."

"Of course." The King stood up. "Gentlemen, regard this plan here. Fournier, will you oblige us, please?"

The count unrolled a page of parchment with a pattern of diagrams drawn upon it. They gathered closer to look.

"This is how the army will go into battle. General Menin, kindly explain."

"Yes, sire. Gentlemen, we shall be in four distinct commands. In the centre will be the main body, eighteen thousand men under His Majesty, myself and Colonel Rusio. Within this formation will be the field artillery – thirty guns under you, Rusio – and the cuirassiers – three thousand horsemen. His Majesty will lead the heavy horse personally.

"On the right flank of the main body will be a smaller formation, a flank guard to deal with the possibility of a Merduk assault from that quarter. This will be under Colonel Aras, and will number some five thousand, primarily arquebusiers. To the rear will be General Cear-Inaf's command, eight thousand men. These constitute our only reserve, and will also have the task of guarding the baggage train. Am I clear, gentlemen?"

"What about the left flank?" Corfe asked. "It's up in the air."

"We do not feel that the left flank is particularly threatened," the King told him. "The only threat from that quarter is from the baggage and headquarters camp of the enemy. We feel that the Merduk Sultan will not detach troops which are guarding his person until he knows exactly what the situation is. By that time we will have withdrawn. No, the only real threat is on the right, from the camp of the *Hraibadar* and the *Ferinai*. Aras, you have the position of honour. Hold it well."

"I will indeed, sire, to the last man, if needs be."

Corfe opened his mouth to protest, and then thought better of it. There was a possibility that the King was right, but he did not like it. Nor did he think it wise to have the heavy cavalry in the centre, where their mobility would be reduced and they would face the prospect of a charge into a tented camp: no job for horsemen. It would do no good to point it out, though.

"We move out in the morning," the King went on. "Two days' march will bring us to the environs of the enemy. We will go into battle-line somewhere out of view from their camp, and sweep down on them in one grand charge at dawn. As General Cear-Inaf has said, numbers will be less important in the confusion. We have an impenetrable screen of cavalry about us, so the enemy should remain unaware of our intentions until it is too late. We hit them hard, and then withdraw. Admiral Berza's fleet will be attacking their coastal bases at around about the same time. After this double-pronged attack, the Sultan will have to retreat to the Searil, and Ormann Dyke is almost indefensible if one is attacking from the south. We will have delivered Northern Torunna from the enemy. Gentlemen, are there any questions?"

"This battle will go down in history, sire!" Aras exclaimed. "We are lucky to have the chance to participate in it."

The King inclined his head graciously. Even Menin looked a little impatient at Aras's toadying.

"You are dismissed, gentlemen," the King said. We will meet again the night before the battle commences to finalize things. Until then, fare you well."

The assembled officers exited, bowing. General Menin caught Corfe outside the tent flap and grasped his arm. In a low voice he said, "A word with you, if you please, General."

They strolled through the camp together. Menin's face was a study in night-dark and firelight. He seemed deeply troubled.

"This is not to be bruited about," he said in a subdued tone. "But if I do not live through the battle, I wish you to take command of the army and lead the withdrawal."

Corfe froze in his tracks. "Are you serious?"

The older man produced a sealed scroll. "Here it is in writing. The King will object, of course, but there will be little time for objections. His first choice after me for the command is Aras, and he has already been promoted beyond his abilities. This army must survive, whatever happens. Get these men back to Torunn, Corfe."

Corfe took the scroll. "You pick an odd time to finally show confidence in me," he said, not without bitterness.

"The time for politics is past. The country needs a soldier to lead it now."

"You will survive, Menin. This is unnecessary."

"No, General. My death lies there to the north. I know I shall not be coming back. But you make sure that this army does!" He gripped Corfe's forearm with bruising force. His face was stark and livid. There was fear on it, but not for himself, Corfe was certain.

"I'll do what I can, if it should prove necessary," Corfe said haltingly.

"Thank you. And Corfe, your men may be in the rear, but they will have the hardest job in the days ahead, make no mistake about it." And he walked away without further ceremony.

"HERE," ANDRUW SAID, offering him the wineskin. "You look as though you could use a snort. What did they do, overwhelm you with their strategic brilliance?"

Corfe squeezed a stream of acrid army wine into his mouth. "Lord, Andruw, I needed that."

Seated about the campfire were most of his senior officers. He had asked them to await his return from the conference. They looked at him expectantly. In addition to Andruw, Marsch was there, and Morin beside him. Formio stood warming his hands at the flames next to Ranafast, and Ebro had paused in the process of whittling a stick to stare at his commanding officer. In the shadows beyond were many others. Corfe thought he saw Joshelin, the Fimbrian veteran, and Cerne, his trumpeter. His very heart warmed at the sight of them, doing away with some of the chill generated by Menin's words. With the loyalty of men such as these, he felt he could accomplish almost anything.

"We pitch into them in two days, lads," he said at last. "Ebro, give me your stick. Gather round, everyone. Here's how we're going to do it."

TWENTY-ONE

DAWN OVER NORTHERN Torunna. In the Merduk camps the sentries were being changed and men were stirring the embers of their campfires in preparation for breakfast. Along the horse-lines, thousands of animals were champing on hay and oats and generating a steam of damp warmth into the frigid air. Supply waggons came and went in sluggish convoys. Over the tented cities of the Merduks a haze of smoke and vapour rose skywards, visible for many miles despite the low cloud. The conical tents sprawled for hundreds of acres, and streets had been laid down between their rows, fashioned of corduroyed logs. Women and children were visible, and there were market places and bazaars in the midst of the encampments where the canny traders that followed the armies had set up their stalls. The three vast winter camps of the Merduks were as peaceful looking as military settlements could possibly be. It was commonly known that the cowardly Torunnans were lurking behind the walls of their capital, preparing for the inevitable siege. There were no enemy formations for leagues around, apart from a few isolated bodies of cavalry. In a week or two the tent cities would be broken up and the armies would be on the move again, but for now the soldiers of the Sultan were more preoccupied with the problems of keeping warm and dry and well fed in the barbarous Torunnan winter.

Shahr Indun Johor, senior khedive of the Sultan's forces, had his headquarters tent in the midst of the encampments of the *Hraibadar* and the *Ferinai*, the elite of the army. Rank had its privileges, and he was dozing with his head between the breasts of his favourite concubine when his subadar, or head staff officer, poked his head around the heavy curtains of the tent.

"Shahr Johor." And again when there was no answer: "Shahr Johor!"

He stirred, a young, lean man, dark and quick as an otter. "What? What is it, Buraz?"

"It may be nothing, my Khedive. Some of the perimeter guards report gunfire coming from the west."

"I'll be a moment. See my horse is saddled." Shahr Johor threw aside his grumbling concubine and hauled on his breeches and tunic. He wrapped a sash about his middle, thrust a poniard in the folds and pulled on his heavy knee-high riding boots. Then he kissed his scented bed partner. "Later, my dove," he murmured, and strode out of the tent into the raw half-light of dawn.

Buraz awaited him with two saddled horses, their breaths steaming in the cold. The two officers mounted and cantered off to the perimeter of the vast camp, scattering soldiers and camp followers as they clattered along the timbered road. He sat in the saddle, breathing hard, staring at the empty horizon. It was still so gloomy that he could see the glare of the *Minhraib*'s campfires against the cloudy sky, three miles away. Thin flakes of snow had begun to fall, and there was more in the lowering nimbus overhead.

"I hear nothing. Who reported this?"

A *Hraibadar* sergeant stepped forward, a veteran with a hard, seamed face and black eyes. "I did, my Khedive. It comes and goes. If you wait, you have my word, you will hear it."

They sat still, listening, whilst behind them the great camp and its tens of thousands of occupants came to life in the growing light. And at last Shahr Johor caught it. A distant, intermittent thunder rolling in from the west, the fainter crackle of what might have been volley fire.

"Artillery," Buraz said.

"Yes. And massed arquebusiers. There is a battle going on out there, Buraz."

"It may be only a raid, a skirmish."

They both listened again. The *Hraibadar* sergeant angrily called for silence and around the two officers hundreds of men stopped what they were doing and paused, listening also.

The faraway thunder intensified. Everyone could hear it now. It seemed to echo off the face of the very hills.

"That is no skirmish," Shahr Johor said. "It is a full-scale engagement, Buraz. The Unbelievers have attacked the *Minhraib* camp."

"Would they dare?" his subordinate asked incredulously.

"It would seem so. Get me a trumpeter. Sound the alarm. I want the army ready to move immediately. And send a courier off to the Sultan in the northern camp. We will chastise these infidels for their impertinence. I shall come down on their flank with the *Ferinai*. You follow with the infantry. Make haste, Buraz!"

THE *MINHRAIB* CAMP was a rough square, a mile and a half to a side. It lay on a gently undulating plain criss-crossed with small watercourses and dotted with copses of alder and willow where the ground was wet. To the east of it a small range of hills rose to perhaps four or five hundred feet, and on these heights a smaller camp of perhaps a thousand men had been pitched to dominate the ground below and safeguard communications with the other Merduk camp to the east. The main encampment was a huge sea of tents bisected by muddy roads, with corrals for the pack animals to the north. Southwest of it, on a slight rise, was a long string of scattered woods, perhaps two miles from the first lines of tents. In these woods, the Torunnan army shook out from column into line of battle.

THREE GREAT FORMATIONS of men emerged from the woods as the sky lightened steadily above their heads. They were late. The approach to the enemy was meant to be made under cover of the pre-dawn darkness, but it had, inevitably, taken longer than expected to reform thirty thousand men in the dark, and now they had two flat and open miles to march at the quick-time before they would come to blows with the Merduks.

Out in front of the main body, batteries of galloper guns under Colonel Rusio had dashed ahead and were unlimbering a mile from the enemy lines. Soon the little six-pounders were barking and smoking furiously, generating bloody chaos in the camp, flattening tents, shattering men.

Behind them the King's formation, eighteen thousand strong, advanced at the double. The battle-line was on average six ranks deep, and it stretched for almost two miles, a dark, bristling, clanging apocalypse of heavily armoured men and horses. The earth shook under their feet, and in the centre the heavy sable-clad cuirassiers were ranged under the banners of the King and his noble bodyguard.

Off to the east, perhaps a mile from the main body, Colonel Aras's five thousand were advancing also, their target the small Merduk camp on the hills. They were to take the camp, and hold the heights against the arrival of any enemy reinforcements. Aras's men were lightly armoured, swift moving, and they trailed streamers of smoke from the slow-match of their arquebusiers, making it look as though they were burning a path across the land as they came.

And behind the main fighting line, another formation. Seven thousand foot and a thousand horse – Corfe's men, in a deep body only some two thirds of a mile long. He was stationed on the left of his line with the Cathedrallers, the Fimbrians were on the right, ten deep, and his dyke veterans were in the centre. Behind them, in the woods, were the hundreds of waggons that comprised the baggage train. Field surgeons and their assistants were busy amid the vehicles setting out their instruments, and crowds of waggoneers were frantically unpacking crates of shot, barrels of gunpowder. Scores of light galloper carts stood in their midst, ready to start ferrying forward ammunition and ferrying back casualties to the rear aid stations. A thousand men worked busily there, and Corfe had also left behind two hundred arquebusiers in case small bodies of the enemy should break through the front lines.

He halted his command when it was a mile from the Merduk camp. The roar of the artillery had begun to intensify. He could see the frenzied activity in the midst of the tented city, officers trying to get clotted crowds of men into battle-line only to have the artillery blow them apart as soon as they had dressed their ranks. The main Torunnan line advanced inexorably to the dull thunder of the infantry drums and a braying of army bugles. It looked as though nothing on earth would be able to stop it. Corfe felt a moment of pure, savage exultation, a fierce, dizzying joy at the sight of the advancing Torunnan army. If there was any glory in war, it was in spectacles such as this, neat lines of men advancing like chess pieces on the gameboard of the world. Once you took a closer look the glory died, and there was only the scarlet carnage, the agonizing misery of men dying and being maimed in their thousands.

The King's formation was passing through the galloper batteries now. The squat guns fired only on a flat trajectory and thus were masked by their own troops as the advance continued. The gunners leaned on their pieces and cheered as their comrades passed by. Had they no further orders? Corfe scowled. Thirty guns left sitting idle. It was an incompetent oversight, and technically he outranked Colonel Rusio, the artillery commander. He reached in his saddlebag for pencil and paper, scrawled a message and sent it off to the idle batteries. A few minutes later, the gunners began limbering their pieces and withdrawing up the slope towards Corfe's command. He could see Rusio in their midst, shouting orders, helmless. The grey-haired officer looked furious. Too bad. Corfe would find him something better to do than sit on his hands for the remainder of the battle.

Farther away on the plain, the main Torunnan formation had halted a scant two hundred yards from the Merduk camp, and the entire battle-line erupted with smoke as the massed arquebusiers let off a volley. A second later, the stuttering crackle of it could be heard. Then there was a huge, formless roar as the line charged, eighteen thousand men shouting their heads off as they slammed into the Merduk camp at a run.

Corfe could see the wedge of three thousand heavy cavalry, the King's banner at its head, forging ahead of the rest. Horses going down already, no doubt tripping on downed tents and guy-ropes. The disorganized unfortunates of the *Minhraib* had no chance. They presented a ragged line, which disintegrated into a howling mob, then a crowd of fleeing individuals. In minutes, the Torunnans had smashed deep into the enemy encampment and were carrying all before them. But now their own lines had become splintered and disorganized. The fighting inside the complex of tents degenerated into a massive free-for-all, and in the thick of it the King and his cuirassiers rampaged like dreadful animated engines of slaughter. *Lofantyr has courage*, Corfe thought. *You have to give him that.*

Corfe looked at the right, where another, smaller struggle had begun on the eastern hills. Aras had his men advancing in a perfect line, firing as they went. The Merduks in the hill camp, outnumbered five to one, nevertheless rushed down to meet them. They had few or no firearms and so had to try and engage at close quarters. They were cut down in windrows by exact volleys, and the survivors, a beaten rabble, fled the field. Aras advanced his men up to the hilltops and arranged them for defence.

"I hope he digs in," Corfe muttered. He felt uneasy about the small size of Aras's force. Soon they would have to cover the withdrawal of the King's formation, and if the enemy came in any strength from the east they would have a hard time of it.

"Colonel Rusio reporting, *as ordered*," a voice spat. Corfe turned. Rusio and his guns had reached his position. The older officer was glaring at him, but there was no time to massage his ego.

"Take your guns over to Aras's position and make ready to repel an attack on the hills, Colonel," Corfe said briskly. "How much ammunition is left in your limbers?"

"Ten rounds per gun."

"Then I suggest you send galloper carts back to the baggage for resupply. You'll need every round you can muster in a little while."

"With respect, sir, we seem to be driving them beautifully. I was given no such orders in my briefing. I don't see why –"

"Do as you're damn well told!" Corfe snapped, his patience fraying. "This is an army, not a debating chamber. Go!"

Rusio, Corfe's elder by thirty years, glared venomously again, then spun his horse off without another word and began bellowing at his gun teams. Thirty guns, each pulled by eight horses, pounded off eastwards.

The Merduk camp was wreathed in a pall of smoke. Flames glowed sullenly at its base and tiny black figures flickered in mobs like throngs of ants. *It will be utter chaos in there*, Corfe thought, *as bad for the attackers as the defenders*. But chaos favoured the smaller army. It was easier to control eighteen thousand in that toiling hell than ninety thousand. So far, so good.

It was full daylight now, a dull morning low with cloud, the snow showers coming and going. The trained warhorses of the Cathedrallers were restless and sweating despite the cold; they could smell the stink of battle, and their blood was up. The men were much the same, and the ranks of horsemen buzzed with talk. In the centre of Corfe's line the dyke veterans had their arquebuses primed and ready, laid on the Y-shaped gunrests they had stabbed into the ground before them. And on the far right the black-armoured Fimbrians stood like raven statues, their pikes at the vertical.

Andruw cantered over and doffed his helm. "What's our job in all this, Corfe?" he asked. "To make notes?" He had to shout to be heard over the titanic din of battle.

"Hold your water, Andruw. This thing is only just begun."

Andruw joined his general in staring out at the left of the battlefield, to the west of the Merduk camp. Men were streaming away there, fleeing enemy trying to escape the murderous hell within the tent lines, tercios of Torunnans firing at their backs as they ran. But beyond them there was only a huge stretch of empty hill and moorland, completely deserted.

"You think they'll hit the left?" Andruw asked.

"Wouldn't you? We're killing conscripts at the moment. The professionals have yet to arrive. Aras will hold on the right I think, what with Rusio's guns and the terrain. But the left is another thing entirely. We have nothing there, Andruw, nothing. If the Sultan makes even a cursory reconnaissance, he'll realize that and he'll come roaring down on us there."

"And then?"

"And then – well, we'll have a fight on our hands."

"That's why you've kept us so far back. You think we'll have to move up to support the left."

"I hope not, but it's as well to be prepared."

"Aye. At any rate, the King is doing his job. Another hour and he'll have wiped half the Merduk army off the map."

"Getting into the fight is one thing, getting out is something else."

"Do I detect a note of envy, Corfe?" Andruw grinned.

"It's a glorious charge, but I wish he'd stop and take stock for a minute. The army is hopelessly disorganized in there. It'll take hours to reform them and withdraw." Corfe smiled. "All right, maybe I envy him his glory a little."

"Give him his due, he took them in there like a veteran. I'd best get back to my wing. Cheer up, Corfe! We're making history, after all." And he galloped off.

Corfe sat his restive horse another half an hour. The fighting in the *Minhraib* camp went on unabated, though it had spilled out on to the plain beyond the tents. He could see Torunnan arquebusiers and cuirassiers fighting intermingled, banners flashing bright through the smoke. Beyond the camp a great cloud of men took shape as the *Minhraib* abandoned the tent lines and strove to reform in the open ground to the north-west. Twenty, thirty thousand of them dressing their ranks unmolested whilst the Torunnans were embroiled in the terrible struggle within the camp. The enemy had taken huge losses, but he had the numbers to sustain them and he was bringing some order out of chaos at last. It was time to get out. The Merduk reinforcements would be on the march by now.

A courier emerged from the cauldron, beating his half-dead horse up the slope towards Corfe's line. Corfe cantered out to meet him. The man was a cuirassier. His mount was slashed in half a dozen places and his armour was a pitted mass of dents and scrapes. He saluted.

"Beg pardon, sir –" He fought for breath. "But the King, the King –"

"Take your time, trooper," Corfe said gently. "Cerne! Give this man some water."

His trumpeter handed the man his waterskin and the courier squirted half a pint into his smoke-parched mouth. He wiped his lips.

"Sir, the King wants your men in the camp right away. The enemy is fleeing before him but his own men are exhausted. He wants you to take up the pursuit. You must bring the entire reserve into the enemy camp and finish the buggers off – begging your pardon, sir."

Corfe blinked. "The King, you say?"

"Yes, sir, at once, sir. He says we'll bag the whole lot if only you make haste."

Just then a heavy fusillade of gun and artillery fire broke out on the right. Aras's men had opened up on an unseen enemy below them. Corfe called for Andruw.

"Have a courier sent to Aras. I want to know the strengths and dispositions of the enemy he's firing at, and his best estimate as to how long he can hold them. And Andruw, tell Marsch to take a squadron out on the left a mile or two. I want advance warning if they start coming in on us from there." Andruw saluted and sped off towards the ranks. Corfe fished out his pencil and grubby paper again and used the thigh-guard of his armour as a desk.

"What's your name, soldier?" he asked the battered courier.

"Holman, sir."

"Well, Holman, take a look at the land beyond the Merduk camp, to the north. What do you see?"

"Why, General, it's an army, another Merduk army forming. Looks like it's going to attack our lads in the tents!"

"It's not another army, it's the one you've been fighting, but so far you've only tackled the half of it. The other half has withdrawn and has been reorganizing for the better part of an hour. Soon, it'll be ready to charge back into its camp and retake it. And now Merduk reinforcements have arrived on the right, also. You must tell the King that his position is untenable. I cannot reinforce him – he must withdraw at once. And I want you to take this to General Menin first, Holman. It's absolutely vital this message gets through. The army *must* withdraw, or it will be destroyed. Do you understand me, soldier?"

Holman was wide-eyed. "Yes, General."

"My command will cover the retreat for as long as we can, but the main body has to fall back at once."

"Yes, sir." Holman was eager and appalled. Down in the hellish melee of the Merduk camp no one had noticed the Merduk thousands beyond preparing for a counter-attack. Corfe did not envy the young man his errand. The King would explode, but Menin would probably see sense.

Holman thundered off, his tired mount rolling like a ship on a heavy swell. At the same time Marsch and his squadron set off north-westwards to keep an eye on the left flank. Corfe slammed one gauntleted fist into another. To sit here, doing nothing, galled him beyond measure. He half wished he were a junior officer again, doing as he was told, in the thick of it.

The courier from Aras, a tribesman whose mount was blowing foam, stamping and snorting. He handed his general a scrap of paper, saluted awkwardly and rejoined the ranks.

6-8000 to my front, all cavalry – the Ferinai I believe. A body of infantry visible several miles behind. Artillery keeping them at a distance for now. They are massing for general assault. Can hold another hour or two, not more.
Aras.

"Lord God," Corfe said softly. The Merduk khedive had been quick off the mark.

He kicked his mount into motion and cantered along the battle-line until he reached the Fimbrians. His men cheered as he passed and he waved a hand absently at them, his mind turning furiously.

"Formio? Where are you?"

"Here, General." The slim Fimbrian officer stepped out from the midst of his men. Like them, he bore a pike. Only the sash about his middle differentiated him from a private soldier.

"Take your men out to the hills in the east and reinforce Colonel Aras. He's up against heavy cavalry – your pikes will keep them at bay. You have to buy us time, Formio. You must hold that position until you hear otherwise from me. Is that clear?"

"Perfectly, General."

"Good luck."

A series of shouted commands, a bugle call, and the Fimbrians moved into march column and stepped off as smoothly as a great machine, every component perfect. Corfe hated splitting his command, but Aras would not be able to hold for long enough by himself. He felt like a man trying frantically to repair a leak in a dyke, but every time he plugged a hole in one place, the water erupted out of another.

Andruw joined him again. "I have a feeling there's hot work approaching," he said, almost merry. Action always did that to him.

"They'll hit the left next," Corfe told him. "And if they hit it hard, I'll have to commit the rest of the command. There are no more reserves."

"You think we've bitten off more than we can swallow?"

Corfe did not answer. He could feel time slipping away minute by minute as though it were his lifeblood ebbing from his veins. And with the passing of that time, the army's chances of survival grew ever slimmer.

TWENTY-TWO

AURUNGZEB HAD NOT ridden a horse any distance for longer
than he cared to admit. His thighs were chafing and his
buttocks felt like a pair of purple bruises. But he sat straight
in the saddle, mindful of his station, and ignored the snow
thickening in his beard.

"Blood of the Prophet!" he exclaimed, exasperated.
"Can't they move any faster?"

Shahr Harran, his second khedive, sat a horse with more
obvious ease beside him. "It takes time, Highness, to get
an army on the march. These things always appear slow at
first, but the Torunnans will be embroiled for hours yet. Our
scouts report that they are fighting square in the midst of
the *Minhraib* camp – they have their heavy cavalry engaged
right among the tents, the fools. They will not escape us,
never fear. And their left flank is still unguarded."

"What of those damned red-armoured horsemen
everyone is so terrified of? Where are they?"

"To the enemy rear, my Sultan, in reserve. And they
number scarcely a thousand. We are sending in twenty
thousand Nalbenic horse-archers on their left and Shahr
Johor should be assaulting their right with the *Ferinai* any
time now. The Torunnans cannot escape. We will destroy
their army utterly, and it is the last field army their kingdom
can possibly muster."

"Oh, hold the damn thing straight, can't you?" the Sultan
barked. This to the unfortunates who were striving to shield
their lord from the spitting snow with a huge parasol, but
the wind was wagging it like a kite above Aurungzeb's head.
"I am sure you are right, Shahr Harran; it is just that lately I
have had my khedives assure me of Torunnan annihilation
many times, and always the accursed Ramusians seem to be

able to salvage their armies with some last-minute trick. It must not happen this time."

"It will not. It cannot," Shahr Harran assured him.

The two riders were surrounded by hundreds of others in silvered mail – the Sultan's personal bodyguard. Beyond them a steady stream of lightly armoured cavalry trotted past endlessly. These were unarmoured, though well wrapped up against the cold. Their horses were light, high-stepping, delicate-looking creatures built for speed. The riders were dark men as fine boned as their steeds, armed with bows and with quivers of black-fletched arrows hanging from their pommels.

"Where is my intrepid infidel?" Aurungzeb asked in a lighter tone. "I must hear what he thinks of this array."

A small, dark figure on a mule rode to Aurungzeb's side. He was dressed in the habit of a Ramusian monk and his face was hideously disfigured.

"Sultan?"

"Ah, priest. How does it feel to look upon the might of Ostrabar, and know it shall soon accomplish the spiritual liberation of your benighted nation? Speak freely. I value the nonsense you spout. It reminds me how hopelessly misled you Ramusians are."

Albrec smiled strangely. "Not only the Ramusians, Sultan, but your own people too. Both peoples worship the same God and venerate the same man as his messenger. It is the pity of the world that you war on each other over an ancient misunderstanding. A lie. One day both Merduk and Ramusian will have to come to terms with this."

"Why you arrogant little –" Shahr Harran sputtered, but Aurungzeb held up a hand that flashed with rings.

"Now, Khedive, this maniac came to us in good faith, to show us the error of our ways. He is as good a jester as I have ever had." The Sultan laughed loudly. "Priest, you have spirit. It is a shame you are mad. Keep up your insane pronouncements and you may even live to see the spring, if you do not endeavour to escape first." And he laughed again.

Albrec bowed in the saddle. His feet had been lashed to his stirrups and the mule was connected by a leading rein to a nearby warrior's destrier. Escape was a possibility so

remote as to be laughable. But he did not want to escape.
He would not have chosen to be anywhere else. His ravaged
face was impassive as he watched the mighty army that
coursed endlessly past – and this, he had learned, was only
one third of the whole, and not the greatest third at that.
His heart twisted in his breast at the thought of the slaughter
that would soon begin. Torunna could never hope to win
this awful war through force of arms alone. His mission
among the Merduks was more important than ever.

They had beaten him, the night he staggered into their
camp on the wings of the storm, and he had almost been
slain out of hand. But some officer had been intrigued by
his appearance, thinking him perhaps a turncoat who
might have useful information, and he had been sent to the
Sultan's camp, and beaten again. At last the Sultan himself
had been curious to see this strange traveller. Aurungzeb
spoke Normannic well enough to need no interpreter. Albrec
wondered who had taught him – some captured Ramusian
or other, he supposed. The Sultan had been first astonished
and then intensely amused when Albrec had told him of his
mission: to convince the Merduk peoples that their Prophet
was one and the same as the Ramusian's Blessed Saint. He
had called in a pair of mullahs – learned Merduk clerics –
and Albrec had debated with them all night, leaving them
as astonished as the Sultan. For Albrec had read every scrap
he could find about the Merduks and their history, both at
Charibon and then in the smaller library in Torunn. He knew
Aurungzeb's pedigree and clan history better than the Sultan
did himself, and the monarch had been oddly flattered by the
knowledge. He had kept Albrec in light chains in the Royal
pavilion, for all the world like a performing bear, and when
the army's officers assembled for conferences, Albrec had
been there and was told to stand up and do his party piece
for the amusement of his captors.

Many of the men he had spoken before had not been
amused, however. What the Sultan considered a diverting
madman, others deemed a blasphemer worthy of a
lingering death. And still others said nothing, but looked
troubled and confused as Albrec told of the Blessed
Ramusio's coming into the eastern lands beyond the Jafrar,

his teachings, his transformation into the Prophet who had enlightened the eastern tribes and brought to an end their petty internecine warfare, moulding them into the mighty hosts which threatened the world today.

There had been a woman present on one of these occasions, one of the Sultan's wives, dressed as richly as a queen, veiled, silent. Her eyes had never left Albrec's face as the little monk had gone through his sermon. The light-coloured eyes of a westerner. There was a despair in them, a sense of loss which wrenched at his heart. He seemed to remember seeing the same look in someone else's eyes once, but he could not for the life of him remember whose.

The distant roar of battle jerked his mind back to the present. The Sultan was talking to him again.

"So do you know who this general is who leads these red-clad horsemen, priest? My spies tell me nothing of use. I know that the Torunnan King is no phoenix, and his High Command are a bunch of old women, and yet against all expectations they have come out to fight us. Someone among them is a true warrior at least."

"I know little more than you, Sultan. I have met this general you speak of, though."

Aurungzeb twisted in the saddle, eyes alight with interest. "You have? What manner of man is he?"

"It was a brief meeting. He is –" Suddenly Albrec remembered. That look he had seen in a woman's eyes, above a veil. Now he knew who it reminded him of. "He is a singular man. There is a sadness to him, I think." He recalled the hard grey eyes of the officer named Corfe he had encountered outside Torunn, the line of scarlet, barbaric cavalry behind him, passing by like something out of legend.

"A sadness! What a fellow you are, priest. By all accounts he is their best general since Mogen, and a raging fury in the saddle. I should like to meet him. Perhaps I will order him to be kept alive after we have broken his army." And Aurungzeb chuckled to himself. "Listen to me! I am becoming like Shahr Baraz, chivalrous towards enemies."

"Magnanimity becomes a great ruler, Sultan," Albrec told him. "Only lesser men indulge their cruelty."

"What is that, one of your Saint's platitudes?"

"No. It is a saying of your Prophet."

ANOTHER COURIER, THE snow freezing on his shoulders and matting his horse's mane. "I come from Marsch," he said, and pointed westwards to reinforce the statement.

"Well?" Corfe demanded.

"Many, many horsemen coming. Small horses, men with bows."

"How many? How far?"

The courier wrinkled his tattooed face. "Marsch tell me," he said, "as many as the King's army, or more, coming from the north-west. In one hour they will be here." His face relaxed. He was obviously relieved to have got it out without mishap.

"Men with bows," Andruw said thoughtfully. "Horse-archers. That'll be the Nalbenic contingent. And if they have as many as the King commands..."

"Eighteen, twenty thousand," Corfe said tonelessly.

"Damn it, Corfe, we're finished then. Menin and the King have started to reorganize down in the camp, but there's no way they can get their men out in an hour."

"Then we'll have to take them on ourselves," Corfe said flatly.

Andruw managed a rueful grin. "I know we're good at beating the odds, but don't you think we're pushing what luck we have left? We don't even have the Fimbrians now. Just the Cathedrallers and Ranafast's men. Six thousand."

"We've no choice. They have to be thrown back before they can come in on our left. If they do that, the entire army will be surrounded."

"How?" Andruw asked simply.

Corfe kicked his mount forward a few yards. He had learned many things about the nature of war in the last few months. It was like any other field of human endeavour: often appearance was as important as reality. And guile more important than brute strength.

Charge horse-archers with his heavy cavalry? Suicide. The enemy would simply fall back, shooting as they retreated.

They would wear his men down with arrow fire and never let them come to grips. He had to pin them in place somehow, and then hit them hard at close quarters where the weight and armour of his men would make up for their lack of numbers. Fight fire with fire, he realized. Fire with fire. And he had five thousand veteran arquebusiers from Ormann Dyke under his command.

He scanned the huge battlefield before him. Down in the wreckage of the *Minhraib* camp the fighting was still going on, but it seemed to have abated somewhat. Both armies were trying to reorganize and he could see crowds of Torunnan troops being dressed back into disciplined lines. Fully half the tents in the vast camp seemed to have been flattened, and fires were burning everywhere, smoke hanging in great sodden grey banks. Beyond the camp, the *Minhraib* survivors had almost completed their own rebuilt battle-line. They would counter-attack soon. But that was not his problem right now. One thing at a time.

Over to the east, Aras and the Fimbrians were struggling to contain the Merduk flanking column. Formio had mingled his pikemen with Aras's arquebusiers and Rusio's guns. The position was enveloped in a pall of smoke which the flickering stabs of gunfire lit up red and yellow, but the westerners were holding. Corfe knew that Formio would not retreat a yard. The right flank was safe, for the time being.

So the left – the left was where disaster loomed most clearly. How to cripple this new threat with the few men he had remaining to him...

It came to him all at once. Guile, not force. And he knew exactly what he had to do. He jerked his horse round to face Andruw.

"We're moving out. I want Ranafast's men to lead the way, at the double. Andruw, you take the Cathedrallers off to their left. I'll explain as we go along."

TWENTY-THREE

A VAST CAVALCADE of horsemen, numerous as a locust swarm. There was no order in their ranks and as they trotted along they jostled one another and expanded and contracted with every dip in the terrain. They had a frontage of half a mile, but as they advanced the rear ranks broke into a canter and began to move up to left and right, extending that yard by yard. By the time they had come within sight of the *Minhraib* camp and the battle that was tapering off there, they had expanded into a great arc, a shallow new-moon sickle which stretched almost half a league from tip to tip and whose coming seemed to make the frozen earth quake and quiver below their hooves. Twenty thousand of Nalbeni's finest men, come here in alliance with the Sultanate of Ostrabar to close the trap on the enemy and grind the Torunnans into the snow.

Corfe watched them from the trees, and could not help but feel a kind of admiration. They were a magnificent sight. In these days of cannon and gunpowder they were like something out of the barbaric past, but he knew that their powerful compound bows had virtually the range of an arquebus, and were easier to reload. They had teeth in plenty.

Behind him, hidden in the line of trees which extended all the way to the rear of the Torunnan line, his Cathedrallers waited with growing impatience. The Nalbenic horsemen would sweep past them on their way to take the King's forces in the flank. He in turn would attack them in the rear, and hit them hard. But first they had to be halted. They had to meet the anvil before the hammer could fall.

And the anvil was in place, awaiting their arrival.

Clouds and spumes of powdery snow were blowing across the slopes of the hills. The sky had lightened a little, but the day had become much colder and Corfe's breath was wreathing a white filigree about the front of his helm. The blowing snow would cover the fume of four thousand coils of burning match. Ranafast and his men, in two ranks over a mile long, lying out there somewhere in the snow, waiting. Corfe's anvil.

He had found them a long reverse slope where they could lie hidden until the last moment, and the blowing snow had quickly broken up the stark blackness of their uniforms. It would be cold out there on the hard ground with the rime blowing in their faces, but they would have warm work soon enough. How long had the fighting been going on? It seemed to have lasted for ever, and yet Corfe's sword had not yet cleared its scabbard. That was part of the price of command: ordering other men to die while you watched.

Not for much longer, by God. Soon the enemy –

A huge tearing sound, like heavy fabric being ripped. Off to the right a wall of smoke rose. Ranafast's men had fired.

Corfe sat up in the saddle. His horse was dancing under him. He drew out Mogen's sword and held it upright. He could feel the eyes of his men on him in anticipation of the signal. It was like sitting with one's back to a bulging dam, waiting for it to burst.

The lead ranks of the Nalbenic horsemen looked as though they had simultaneously hit a tripwire. Ranafast had fired at point-blank range – less than a hundred yards. As Corfe watched, the second rank fired. He could faintly hear the commands in the brief moments between volleys: "Ready your pieces! Prime your pieces! Give fire!"

The enemy had been halted as if they had slammed into a stone wall. They milled there for a few deadly minutes with the heavy lead bullets snicking and ripping and slamming into them. Horses screaming, rearing, kicking, tumbling to the snow, men jerking as the heavy balls impacted, flying out of the saddle, shrieking, grasping at bloody holes. The press of animals was so great that the riders who were being decimated at the front could not retreat from the murderous fire. Showers of arrows were fired, but Ranafast's men were lying down and presented a minuscule target. The thousands of horsemen in the fore of the Nalbenic host were caught there like a beetle on a pin, the victim of their own numbers. In the space of a hundred heartbeats a veritable wall of writhing bodies built up

– hundreds, thousands of them. It was one of the most ghastly things Corfe had ever seen. With a flash of intuition he realized he was looking at the death of cavalry – of all cavalry.

But it was not enough. The work had to be completed. The Nalbenic formation was beginning to become more fluid. They were backing away, rear ranks streaming in retreat so the wretches at the front could get clear of the withering barrage. Soon they would open out, find the ends of Ranafast's line and envelop him. They had to be packed together again, forced back upon the anvil.

Corfe brought down Mogen's sabre. "*Charge!*"

The hammer fell.

THE KING OF Torunna wiped the soot from his face and, grimacing, realized that his gauntlet had been dripping with blood. He was trembling with fatigue and his armour seemed twice its normal weight. He was mounted on his third horse of the day, his ankle so badly twisted by the headlong fall of the first that he could no longer walk. His crowned helm had given him an almighty headache and below it the sweat ran in streams. His throat was dry as sand, and his voice had become a croak.

Around him the remains of his three thousand cuirassiers clustered. Two thirds of them were dead or too injured to lift a sword, and nine tenths of them were afoot. They had been in the forefront of the attack all morning and had performed wonders. He was proud of them – he was secretly proud of himself. His first battle, his first charge, and he had acquitted himself as a king should, he thought.

The rest of the army was reforming, crowds of men being harangued into line by their surviving officers. The *Minhraib* had withdrawn for the moment, and the camp was his, what was left of it. It was a dreary, smoking wasteland strewn with mounded corpses, collapsed tents and dead horses, shrouded in smoke. Here and there the wounded writhed and wailed, but there were not many of those. No quarter had been asked or given, and when a man on either side fell helpless he would find his throat cut soon after. There was a sputtering of arquebus fire where the perimeter tercios were still contending with the enemy out in the smoke, but for the most part the army had fallen back to reform and prepare for the final push. Now where were those damned reinforcements he had ordered?

Lofantyr could hear the glorious, sullen rumble of war continuing off to the right, where Aras and his men were fighting off the Merduk relief column. Nothing on the left as yet. Or was that arquebus fire he heard out there? No, it was too far away. An echo, no doubt. He had been right not to worry about the left flank. And they thought he was no strategist!

General Menin trudged wearily over, saluted. His sword arm was bloody to the elbow.

"Ah, General, what is the delay? Where is General Cear-Inaf and our reserve? The courier went out an hour ago."

An enormous clatter of musketry to their front, the roaring of a host of men in onset. The ranks of the Torunnans stiffened, and they strained to see through the murk and reek. Of the eighteen thousand the King had led into the camp, perhaps twelve thousand remained, but they had inflicted four or five times their own casualties on the enemy. Those twelve thousand were now arrayed in an untidy line a mile long. In some places the line was only two ranks deep, in others a veritable mob would gather, exhausted and injured men drawing together, taking reassurance out of the proximity of others. The army was spent, and it was hardly mid-afternoon on the longest day most of them had ever known.

"The courier returned a few minutes ago, sire."

"I see. And why did he not report to me?"

Menin leaned against the flank of the King's horse. He spoke quietly.

"Sire, Corfe is witholding the reserve. He fears for the left flank. Also, he informs me that the *Minhraib* are about to counter-attack." The general glanced northwards, to where the sound of battle was rising to a roar in the smoke. "In fact they may well be doing so already. He advises us to withdraw at once. I concur, and have already given the necessary orders."

"You have *what*? You exceed your authority, General. We are on the edge of a famous victory. One more push will see the day ours. We need Cear-Inaf's reserve here, now."

"Sire, listen to me. We have shot our bolt. According to General Cear-Inaf, thirty to forty thousand of the *Minhraib* have reformed on the northern edge of the camp and will be about our ears any minute. Aras is fighting for his life on the right, and Corfe must keep the reserve ready to face any new eventualities. We must fall back at once."

"By God, General –"

But his words were drowned. The clatter out in the smoke had risen to a crescendo, and men were appearing in ones and twos, running. Torunnan arquebusiers in confused flight, throwing away their weapons as they ran. And behind them the formless clamour of a great host of men, shouting.

"Too late," Menin said. "Here they come. Men! Prepare to repel an attack!"

The exhausted soldiers braced themselves.

"Sire, you should go to the rear," Menin urged Lofantyr. "I do not know if we can hold."

"What? Nonsense! I'll lead another charge. We'll see who –"

The western line erupted in a ragged volley as the lead elements of the enemy came thundering into view. Too soon – the Merduks were still out of range. But they were bowling forward, an unstoppable wave of armoured infantry under the bobbing horsetail standards. Tens of thousands of them.

The King's face paled at the sight. "My God! I did not think there were so many left," he croaked.

The two armies met in an appalling roar. It was hand-to-hand at once all down the line, the Torunnan arquebusiers unable to reload their weapons fast enough to keep the *Minhraib* at a distance.

Murderous, lunging chaos around the King as an entire enemy regiment homed in on the Royal standard. The more lightly armed Torunnans there were swept away by the fury of the Merduk onset, leaving the iron-clad cuirassiers standing alone like an island, swinging their heavy cavalry sabres to terrible effect. In moments the entire Torunnan battle-line had been thrown back. Menin and Lofantyr found themselves surrounded, cut off from the main body of the army.

Lofantyr's mind froze. He sat his terrified horse and watched as the Merduks flung themselves upon the ranks of his bodyguard with suicidal abandon. The heavily armoured knights were slaughtering their attackers, but they were being overwhelmed. Three or four of the enemy would throw themselves upon each armoured Torunnan, bear him down to the ground under their bodies, then rip off his helm and slit his throat.

"We are finished," Menin said.

Lofantyr read the words on his lips, though the din of battle suffocated the sound of his voice. Menin was smiling. Panic rose like a cloud in Lofantyr's throat. He would die? He, the King? It was impossible.

One of the enemy broke through the shrinking cuirassier cordon and dived at the King's horse. A tulwar glittered and the animal screamed as it was hamstrung. Menin decapitated the man, but the King was down. The warhorse crashed, kicking, on to its side, trapping Lofantyr's leg beneath it. He felt the bones wrench and shatter, and screamed, but his shriek was lost in the cacophony that surrounded him.

Menin was standing over him, hewing like a titan. Bodies were falling everywhere, men squirming in the snow and muck. An unbelievable tumult, a pitch of savagery and slaughter Lofantyr had not believed men could endure. He scrabbled feebly for the sword that had been his father's, a Royal heirloom, but it was gone. He felt no pain or fear, only a kind of crazed incredulity. He could not believe this was happening.

He saw four Merduks bring Menin down, the old general fighting to the last. They stabbed a poniard through one of his eyes and finally quelled his struggles. Where were the rest of the bodyguard? There was no line now, only a few knots of men in a sea of the enemy. The last of the cuirassiers were being torn down like bears beset by hounds.

Someone ripped off Lofantyr's helm. He found himself looking into a man's face. A young man, the eyes dark and wild, foam at the corners of the mouth. Lofantyr tried to raise an arm, but someone was standing on his wrist. He saw the knife and tried to protest, but then the swift-stabbing blade came down and his life was over.

TWENTY-FOUR

OF THE EIGHTEEN thousand Torunnans who had charged into the enemy camp that morning, perhaps half made it back out again. They withdrew doggedly, stubbornly, contesting every bloody foot of ground. The word of the King's death had not yet spread, and there was no panic despite the incessant fearsomeness of the *Minhraib* counter-attack. Field officers and junior officers took over, for the entire High Command lay dead upon the field, and brought their men out of the Merduk camp in a semblance of order. The *Minhraib* – once more disorganized, but this time by advance, not retreat – surged on regardless to the edge of what had been their encampment, and were astonished by the sight that met their eyes.

There on the high ground to their right, where they had been promised the Nalbenic cavalry would support them, they saw instead a steady unbroken line of five thousand grim Torunnan arquebusiers. And behind them in silent rank on rank were the dread figures of the red horsemen who had wreaked such havoc at the North More, their lances stark against the sky, their armour glinting like freshly spilled blood.

The Merduk advance died. The men of the *Minhraib* had been fighting since dawn. They had acquitted themselves well and they knew it, but nearly forty thousand of their number lay dead behind them, and thousands more were scattered and leaderless over the field. The unexpected sight of these fresh Torunnan forces unnerved them. Where had the Nalbeni disappeared to? They had been promised that their counter-attack would be supported on the Torunnan left.

As if in answer, a lone horseman came galloping out of the ranks of the scarlet riders. He brought his horse to within three hundred yards of the *Minhraib* host and there halted. In his hand he bore a horsetail standard which was surmounted by the likeness of a galley prow. It was the standard of a Nalbenic general. He stabbed the thing into the ground contemptuously, his destrier prancing and snorting, and as he did the cavalry on the hill behind him began to sing some weird, unearthly chant, a barbaric battle-paean, a song of victory. Then the horseman wheeled and cantered back the way he had come.

The song was taken up by the ranks of the Torunnan arquebusiers, and in their throats it became something else, a word which they were repeating as though it had some kind of indefinable power. Five thousand voices roared it out over and over again.

Corfe.

THE GUNFIRE DIED, and a tide of silence rolled over the tortured face of the hills. The winter afternoon was edging into a snow-flecked twilight. Two armies lay barely a league from one another, and between them sprawled the gutted wreck of what had once been a mighty encampment, the land about it littered with the dead. Two armies so badly mauled that as if by common agreement they ignored each other, and the shattered men which made them up strove to light fires and snatch some sleep upon the hard ground, hardly caring if the sun should ever rise on them again.

A single battered mule cart came trundling off the battlefield bearing a cloak-wrapped bundle. Besides its driver, four men on foot accompanied it. The four paused, doffed their helms and let it trundle into the Torunnan camp below, the wheels cracking the frozen snow like a salute of gunshots, whilst they stood amid the stiffened contortions of the dead and the first stars glimmered into life above their heads.

Corfe, Andruw, Marsch, Formio.

"Menin must have died defending him to the end," Andruw said. "That old bugger. He died well."

"He knew this day would be his last," Corfe said. "He told me so. He was a good man."

The foursome picked their way across the battlefield. There were other figures moving in the night, both Torunnan and Merduk. Men looking for lost comrades, brothers searching for the bodies of brothers. An unspoken truce reigned here as former enemies looked into the faces of the dead together.

Corfe halted and stared out at the falling darkness of the world. He was weary, more weary than he had ever been in his life before.

"How are your men, Formic?" he asked the Fimbrian.

"We lost only two hundred. Those *Ferinai* of theirs – they are soldiers indeed. I have never seen cavalry charge pikes like that, uphill, under artillery fire. Of course, they could not hope to break us, but they were willing enough."

"Nip and tuck, all the way," Andruw said. "Another quarter of an hour here or there, and we would have lost."

"We won, then?" Corfe asked the night air. "This is victory? Our King and all our nobility dead, a third of the men we brought out of Torunn lying stark upon the field? If this is victory, then it's too rich a dish for me."

"We survived," Marsch told him laconically. "That is a victory of sorts."

Corfe smiled. "I suppose so."

"What now?" Andruw asked. They looked at their general. Corfe stared up at the stars. They were winking bright and clean, untouchable, uncaring. The world went on. Life continued, even with so much death hedging it around.

"We still have a queen," he said at last. "And a country worth fighting for..."

His words sounded hollow, even to himself. He seemed to feel the fragile paper of Menin's final order crinkling in the breast of his armour. Torunna's last army, what was left of it, was his to command. That was something. These men – these friends here with him – that was something too.

"Let's get back to camp," he said. "God knows, there's enough to do."

EPILOGUE

THE DREGS OF the winter gale blew themselves out in the white-chopped turmoil of the Gulf of Hebrion. Over the Western Ocean the sun rose in a bloodshot, storm-racked glory of cloud, and at once the western sky seemed to catch fire from it, and the horizon kindled, brightening into saffron and green and blue, a majesty of morning.

And out of the west a ship came breasting the foam-tipped swells, scattering spindrift in rainbows of spray. Her sails were in tatters, her rigging flying free, and she bore the marks of storm and tempest all about her yards and hull, but she coursed on nevertheless, her wake straight as the flight of an arrow, her beakhead pointed towards the heart of Abrusio's harbour. The faded letters on her bow labelled her the *Gabrian Osprey*, and at her tiller there stood a gaunt man with a salt-grey beard, his clothes in rags, his skin burnt brown as mahogany by a foreign sun.

Richard Hawkwood had come home at last.

The

SECOND
EMPIRE

For John McLaughlin

PROLOGUE

THE MAKESHIFT TILLER bucked under their hands, bruising ribs. Hawkwood gripped it tighter to his battered chest along with the others, teeth set, his mind a flare of foul curses – a helpless fury that damned the wind, the ship, the sea itself, and the vast, uncaring world upon which they raced in mad career.

The wind backed a point – he could feel it spike into his right ear, heavy with chill rain. He unclenched his jaws long enough to shriek forward over the lashing gale.

"Brace the yards – it's backing round. Brace round that mainyard, God rot you!"

Other men appeared on the wave-swept deck, tottering out of their hiding places and staggering across the plunging waist of the carrack. They were in rags, some looking as though they might once have been soldiers, with the wreck of military uniforms still flapping around their torsos. They were clumsy and torpid in the bitter soaking spindrift, and looked as though they belonged in a sick-bed rather than on the deck of a storm-tossed ship.

From the depths of the pitching vessel a terrible growling roar echoed up, rising above the thrumming cacophony of the wind and the raging waves and the groaning rigging. It sounded like some huge, caged beast venting its viciousness upon the world. The men on deck paused in their manipulation of the sodden rigging, and some made the Sign of the Saint. For a second, sheer terror shone through the exhaustion that dulled their eyes. Then they went back to their work.

The men at the stern felt the heavings of the tiller ease a trifle as the yards were braced round to meet the changing wind. They had it abaft the larboard beam now, and the carrack was powering forward like a horse breasting deep snow. She was sailing under a reefed mainsail, no more. All the rest of her canvas billowed in strips from the yards, and where the mizzen-topmast had once been was only a splintered stump with the rags of shrouds flapping about it in black skeins.

Not so very far now, Hawkwood thought, and he turned to his three companions.

"She'll go easier now the wind's on the quarter." He had to shout to be heard over the storm. "But keep her thus. If it strengthens we'll have to run before it and be damned to navigation."

One of the men at the helm with him was a tall, lean, white-faced fellow with a terrible scar that distorted one side of his forehead and temple. The remnants of riding leathers clung to his back.

"We were damned long ago, Hawkwood, and our enterprise with us. Better to give it up now and let her sink with that abomination chained in the hold."

"He's my friend, Murad," Hawkwood spat at him. "And we are almost home."

"Almost home indeed – what will you do with him when we get there, make a watchdog of him?"

"He saved our lives before now –"

"Only because he's in league with those monsters from the west."

"– And his master, Golophin, will be able to cure him."

"We should throw him overboard."

"You do, and you can pilot this damned ship yourself, and see how far you get with her."

The two glared at one another with naked hatred, before Hawkwood turned and leant his weight against the trembling tiller with the others once more, keeping the carrack on her easterly. Pointing her towards home.

And in the hold below their feet, the beast howled in chorus with the storm.

26th Day of Miderialon, Year of the Saint 552.
Wind NNW, Backing. Heavy Gale. Course SSE under reefed Mainsail, running before the wind. Three feet of water in the well, pumps barely keeping pace with it.

Hawkwood paused. He had his knees braced against the heavy fixed table in the middle of the stern-cabin and the inkwell was curled up in his left fist, but even so he had to strain to remain in his seat. A heavy following sea, and the carrack was cranky for lack of ballast, the water in her hold moving with every pitch. At least with a stern wind they did not feel the lack of the mizzen so much.

As the ship's movement grew less violent, he resumed his writing.

Of the two hundred and sixty-six souls who left Abrusio harbour some seven and a half months ago, only eighteen remain. Poor Garolvo was washed overboard in the Middle Watch, may God have mercy on his soul.

Hawkwood paused a moment, shaking his head at the pity of it. To have survived the massacre in the west, all that horror, merely to be drowned when home waters were almost in sight.

We have been at sea almost three months, and by dead-reckoning I estimate our easting to be some fifteen hundred leagues, though we have travelled half as far as that again to the north. But the southerlies have failed us now, and we are being driven off our course once more. By cross-staff reckoning, our latitude is approximately that of Gabrion. The wind must keep backing round if it is to enable us to make landfall somewhere in Normannia itself. Our lives are in the Hand of God.

"The Hand of God," Hawkwood said quietly. Seawater dripped out of his beard onto the battered log and he blotted it hurriedly. The cabin was sloshing ankle-deep as was every other compartment in the ship. They had all forgotten long ago what it was like to be dry or have a full belly, and several of them had loose and rotting teeth, oozing scars which had healed ten years before; the symptoms of scurvy.

How had it come to this? What had so wrecked their proud and well-manned little flotilla? But he knew the answer, of course; knew it only too well. It kept him awake through the graveyard watch though his exhausted body craved oblivion. It growled and roared in the hold of his poor *Osprey*. It raved in the midnight spasms of Murad's nightmares.

He stoppered up the inkwell and folded the log away in its layers of oilskin. On the table before him was a flaccid wineskin, which he slung round his neck. Then he sloshed and staggered across the pitching cabin to the door in the far bulkhead and stepped over the storm-sill into the companionway beyond. It was dark here, as it was throughout every compartment in the ship. They had few candles left and only a precious pint or two of oil for the storm-lanterns. One of these hung swinging on a hook in the companionway, and Hawkwood took it and made his way forward to where a hatch in the deck led down into the hold. He hesitated there with the ship pitching and groaning around him and the seawater coursing round his ankles, then cursed aloud, and began to work the hatch-cover free. He lifted it off a yawning hole and gingerly lowered himself down the ladder there, into the blackness below.

At the ladder's foot he wedged himself into a corner and fumbled for the flint and steel in the bottom compartment of the storm-lantern. An aching, maddening time of striking spark after spark until one caught on the oil-soaked wick of the lantern and he was able to lower the thick glass that protected it and stand in a pool of yellow light.

The hold was eerily empty, home only to a dozen casks of rotting salt meat and noisome water that constituted the last of the crew's provisions. Water pouring everywhere, and the noise of his poor tormented *Osprey* an agonised symphony of creaks and moans, the sea roaring like a beast beyond the tortured hull. He laid a hand against the timbers of the ship and felt them work apart as she laboured in the gale-driven waves. Fragments of oakum floated about in the water around his feet – the seams were opening. No wonder the men on the pumps could make no headway. The ship was dying.

From below his feet came an animal howl that rivalled even the thundering bellow of the wind. Hawkwood flinched, and then stumbled forward to where another hatch led below to the bottom-most compartment of the ship, the bilge.

It was stinking down here. The *Osprey's* ballast had not been changed in a long time and the tropical heat of the Western Continent seemed to have lent it a particularly foul stench. But it was not the ballast alone that stank. There was another smell down here. It reminded Hawkwood of the beast's enclosure in a travelling circus – that musk-like reek of a great animal. He paused, his heart hammering within his ribs, and then made himself walk forward, crouching under the low beams here, the lantern swinging in a chaotic tumble of light and dark and sloshing liquid. The water was over his knees already.

Something ahead, moving in the liquid filth of the bilge. The rattle of metal clinking upon metal. It saw him and ceased its struggles. Yellow eyes gleamed in the dark. Hawkwood halted a scant two yards from where it lay chained to the very keelson of the carrack.

The beast blinked, and then, terrible out of that animal muzzle, came recognisable speech.

"Captain. How good of you to come."

Hawkwood's mouth was as dry as salt. "Hello, Bardolin," he said.

"Come to make sure the beast is still in his lair?"

"Something like that."

"Are we about to sink?"

"Not yet – not just yet, anyway."

The great wolf bared its fangs in what might have been a grin. "Well, we must be thankful."

"How much longer will you be like this?"

"I don't know – I am beginning to control it. This morning – was it morning? One cannot tell down here – I stayed human for almost half a watch. Two hours." A low growl came out of the beast's mouth, something like a moan.

"In the name of God, why do you not let Murad kill me?"

"Murad is mad. You are not – despite this – this thing that has happened to you. We were friends, Bardolin. You saved my life. When we get back to Hebrion I will take you to your master, Golophin. He will cure you." Even to himself, Hawkwood's word felt hollow. He had repeated them too many times.

"I do not think so. There is no cure for the Black Change."

"We'll see," Hawkwood said stubbornly. He noticed the lumps of salt meat which bobbed in the filthy water of the bilge. "Can't you eat?"

"I crave fresher meat. The beast wants blood. There is nothing I can do about it."

"Are you thirsty?"

"God, yes."

"All right." Hawkwood unslung the wineskin he had about his neck, tugged out the stopper, and hung the lantern on a hook in the hull. He half-crawled forward, trying not to retch at the stench which rose up all about him. The heat that the animal gave off was unearthly, unnatural. He had to force himself close to it and when the head tilted up he tipped the neck of the wineskin against its maw and let it drink, a black tongue licking every drop of moisture away.

"Thank you, Hawkwood," the wolf said. "Now let me try something."

There was a shimmer in the air, and something happened that Hawkwood's eyes could not quite follow. The black fur of the beast withered away and in seconds it was Bardolin the Mage who crouched there, naked and bearded, his body covered in salt-water sores.

"Good to have you back," Hawkwood said with a weak smile.

"It feels worse this way – I am weaker. In the name of God, Hawkwood, get some iron down here. One nick, and I am at peace."

"No." The chains that held Bardolin fast were of bronze, forged from the metal of one of the ship's falconets. They were roughly cast, and their edges had scored his flesh into bloody meat at the wrists and ankles, but every time he shifted in and out of beast form, the wounds healed somewhat. It was an interminable form of torture, Hawkwood knew, but there was no other way to secure the wolf when it returned.

"I'm sorry Bardolin... Has he been back?"

"Yes. He appears in the night-watches and sits where you

are now. He says I am his now – I will be his right hand one day. And Hawkwood, I find myself listening to him, believing him."

"Fight it. Don't forget who you are. Don't let the bastard win."

"How much longer – how far is there to go?"

"Not so far now. Another week or ten days perhaps. Less if the wind backs. This is only a passing squall – it'll soon blow itself out."

"I don't know if I can survive. It eats into my mind like a maggot – stay back, it comes again. Oh sweet Lord God –"

Bardolin screamed, and his body bucked and thrashed against the chains which held him down. His face seemed to explode outwards. The scream turned into an animal roar of rage and pain. As Hawkwood watched, horrified, his body bent and grew and cracked sickeningly. His skin sprouted fur and two horn-like ears thrust up from his skull. The wolf had returned. It howled in anguish and wrenched at its confining chains. Hawkwood backed away, shaken.

"Kill me – kill me and give me peace!" the wolf shrieked, and then the words dissolved into a manic bellowing. Hawkwood retrieved the storm lantern and retreated through the muck of the bilge, leaving Bardolin alone to fight the battle for his soul in the darkness of the ship's belly.

What God would allow the practice of such abominations upon the world he had made? What manner of man would inflict them upon another?

Unwillingly, his mind was drawn back to that terrible place of sorcery and slaughter and emerald jungle. The Western Continent. They had sought to claim a new world there, and had ended up fleeing in terror for their lives. He could remember every stifling, terror-racked hour of it. In the wave-wracked carcass of his once proud ship, he had it thrust vivid and unforgettable into his mind's eye once again.

PART ONE

RETURN *of the* MARINER

ONE

THEY HAD STUMBLED a mile, perhaps two, from the ash-laden air on the slopes of Undabane. Then they collapsed in on each other like a child's house of playing cards, what remained of their spirit spent. Their chests seemed somehow too narrow to take in the thick humidity of the air around them. They lay sprawled in the twilit ooze of the jungle floor while half-glimpsed animals and birds hooted and shrieked in the trees above, the very land itself mocking their failure. Heaving for breath, the sweat running down their faces and the insects a cloud before their eyes.

It was Hawkwood who recovered first. He was not injured, unlike Murad, and his wits had not been addled, unlike Bardolins'. He sat himself up in the stinking humus and the creeping parasitic life that infested it, and hid his face in his hands. For a moment he wished only to be dead and have done with it. Seventeen of them had left Fort Abeleius some twenty-four days before. Now he and his two companions were all that remained. This green world was too much for mortal men to bear, unless they were also some form of murderous travesty such as those which resided in the mountain. He shook his head at the memory of the slaughter there. Men skinned like rabbits, torn asunder, eviscerated, their innards churned through with the gold they had stolen. Masudi's head lying dark and glistening in the roadway, the moonlight shining in his dead eyes.

Hawkwood hauled himself to his feet. Bardolin had his head sunk between his knees and Murad lay on his back as still as a corpse, his awful wound laying bare the bone of his skull.

"Come. We have to get farther away. They'll catch us else."

"They don't want to catch us. Murad was right." It was

Bardolin. He did not raise his head, but his voice was clear, though thick with grief.

"We don't know that," Hawkwood snapped.

"*I* know that."

Murad opened his eyes. "What did I tell you, Captain? Birds of like feather." He chuckled hideously. "What dupes we poor soldiers and mariners have been, ferrying a crowd of witches and warlocks to their masters. Precious Bardolin will not be touched – not him. They're sending him back to his brethren with you as the ferryman. If anyone escaped, it was I. But then, to where have I escaped?"

He sat up, the movement starting a dark ooze of blood along his wound. The flies were already black about it. "Ah yes, deliverance. The blessed jungle. And we are only a few score leagues from the coast. Give it up, Hawkwood." He sank back with a groan and closed his eyes.

Hawkwood remained standing. "Maybe you're right. Me, I have a ship still – or had – and I'm going to get off this God-cursed country and get out to sea again. New Hebrion no less! If you've any shred of duty left under that mire of self pity you're wallowing in, Murad, then you'll realize we have to get back home, if only to warn them. You're a soldier and a nobleman. You still understand the concept of duty, do you not?"

The bloodshot eyes snapped open again. "Don't presume to lecture me, Captain. What are you but the sweeping of some Gabrionese gutter?"

Hawkwood smiled. "I'm lord of the gutter now, Murad, or had you forgotten? You ennobled me yourself, the same time you made yourself Governor of all this –" He swept out his arms to take in the ancient trees, the raucous jungle about them. Bitter laughter curdled in his throat. "Now get off your noble arse. We have to find some water. Bardolin, help me, and stop mooning around like the sky has just fallen in."

Amazingly, they obeyed him.

THEY CAMPED THAT night some five miles from the mountain, by the banks of a stream. After Hawkwood had browbeaten Bardolin into gathering firewood and bedding, he sat by

Murad and examined the nobleman's wounds. They were all gashed and scratched to some degree, but Murad's spectacular head injury was one of the ugliest Hawkwood had ever seen. The scalp had been ripped free of the skull and hung flapping by his left ear.

"I've a good sailmaker's needle in my pouch, and some thread," he told Murad. "It may not turn out too pretty, but I reckon I can get you battened down again. It'll smart some of course."

"No doubt," the nobleman drawled in something approaching his old manner. "Get on with it while there's still light."

"There's maggots in the flesh. I'll just clear them out first."

"No! Let them be. I've seen men worse cut up than this whose flesh went rotten for the lack of a few good maggots. Sew them in there, Hawkwood – they'll eat the dead meat."

"God almighty, Murad."

"Do it. Since you are determined that we are to survive, we may as well go through the motions. Where is that cursed wizard? Maybe he could make himself useful and magick up a bandage."

Bardolin appeared out of the gloom, a bundle of firewood in his arms. "He killed my familiar," he said quietly. "The Dweomer in me is crippled. He killed my familiar, Hawkwood."

"Who did?"

"Aruan. Their leader." He dropped his burden as though it burned. His eyes were dead as dry slate. "I will have a look, though, if you like. I may be able to do something."

"Stay away from me!" Murad shouted, shrinking from the mage. "You murderous dastard. If I were fit for it I'd break your skull. You were in league with them from the first."

"Just see if you can get a fire going, Bardolin," Hawkwood said wearily. "I'll patch him up myself. Later, we must talk."

The pop of the needle going through Murad's skin and cartilage was loud enough to make Hawkwood wince, but the nobleman never uttered a sound under the brutal surgery, only quivered sometimes like a horse trying to rid itself of a bothersome fly. By the time the mariner was done the daylight was about to disappear, and Bardolin's fire was a mote of yellow brightness on the black jungle floor. Hawkwood surveyed his handiwork critically.

"You're no prettier than you were, that's certain," he said at last.

Murad flashed his deaths-head grin. The thread crawled along his temple like a line of marching ants, and under the skin the maggots could be seen squirming.

They drank water from the stream and lay on the brush that Bardolin had gathered to serve as beds while around them the darkness became absolute. The insects fed off them without respite but they were too weary to care, and their stomachs were closed. It was Hawkwood who pinched himself awake.

"Did they really let us go, you think? Or are they waiting for nightfall to spring on us?"

"They could have sprung on us fifty times before now," Murad said quietly. We have not exactly been swift, or careful in our flight. No, for what it's worth, we're away. Maybe they're going to let the jungle finish the job. Maybe they could not bring themselves to kill a fellow sorcerer. Or there may be another reason we're alive. Ask the wizard! He's the one has been closeted with their leader."

They both looked at Bardolin. "Well?" Hawkwood said at last. "We've a right to know, I think. Tell us, Bardolin. Tell us exactly what happened to you."

The mage kept his eyes fixed on the fire. There was a long silence while his two companions stared steadily at him.

"I am not entirely sure myself," he said at last. "The imp was brought to the top of the pyramid in the middle of the city – Gosa, he was a shape-shifter –"

"You surprise me," Murad snorted.

"I met their leader, a man named Aruan. He said he had been high in the Thaumaturgist's Guild of Garmidalan in Astarac a long time ago. In the time of the Pontiff Willardius."

Murad frowned. "Willardius? Why, he's been dead these four hundred years and more."

"I know. This Aruan claims to be virtually immortal. It is something to do with the Dweomer of this land. There was a great and sophisticated civilization here in the west at one time, but it was destroyed in a huge natural cataclysm. The mages here had powers hardly dreamed of back on the Old World. But there was another difference..."

"Well?" Murad demanded.

"I believe they were all shifters as well as mages. An entire society of them."

"God's blood," Hawkwood breathed. "I thought that was not possible."

"So did I. It is unheard of, and yet we have seen it ourselves."

Murad looked thoughtful. "You are quite sure, Bardolin?"

"I wish I were not, believe me. But there is another thing. According to this Aruan, there are hundreds of his agents already in Normannia, doing his bidding."

"The gold," Hawkwood rasped. "Normannic crowns. There was enough of it back there to bribe a king, to hire an army."

"So he has ambitions, this shifter-wizard of yours," Murad sneered. "And how exactly do you fit into them, Bardolin?"

"I don't know, Murad. The Blessed Saint help me, I don't know."

We will meet again, you and I, and when we do you will know me as your lord, and as your friend. The parting words of Aruan burned themselves across Bardolin's brain. He would never reveal them to anyone. He was his own man, and always would be despite the foulness he now felt at work within him.

"One thing I do know," he went on, "They are not content to remain here, these shifter-mages. They are going to return to Normannia. Everything I was told confirms it. I believe Aruan intends to make himself a power in the world. In fact he has already begun."

"If he can make a werewolf of an Inceptine then his words are not idle," Hawkwood muttered, remembering their outward voyage, and Ortelius, who had spread such terror throughout the ship.

"A race of were-mages," Murad said. "A man who claims to be centuries old. A network of shifters spread across Normannia spending his gold, running his errands. I would say you were crazed, had I not seen the things I have on this continent. The place is a veritable hell on earth. Hawkwood is right. We must get back to the ship, return to Hebrion, and inform the King. The Old World must be warned. We will root out these monsters from our midst, and then return here with a fleet and an army, and wipe them from the face of the earth. They are not so formidable – a taste of iron and they fall dead. We will see what five thousand Hebrian arquebusiers cannot do here, by God."

For once, Hawkwood found himself wholly in agreement with the gaunt noblemen. Bardolin looked troubled, however.

"What's wrong now?" he asked the wizard. "You don't approve of this Aruan's ambitions, do you?"

"Of course not. But it was a Purge of the Dweomer-folk which drove him and his kind here in the first place. I know what Murad's proposal will lead to, Hawkwood. A vast, continent-wide purge of my people such has never been seen before. They will be slaughtered in their thousands, the innocent along with the guilty. We will drive all of Normannia's mages into Aruan's arms. That is exactly what he wants. And his agents will not be so easy to uncover, at any rate. They could be anyone – even the nobility. We will persecute the innocent while the guilty bide their time."

"The plain soldiers of the world will take their chances," Murad retorted. "There is no place on this earth for your kind anymore, Bardolin. They are an abomination. Their end has been coming for a long time now – this is only hastening the inevitable."

"You are right there, at least," the wizard murmured.

"Whose side are you on?" Hawkwood asked the mage.

Bardolin looked angry. "I don't know what you mean."

"I mean that Murad is right. There is a time coming, Bardolin, when it will be your Dweomer-folk ranged against all the ordinary people of the world, and you will have to either abet their destruction, or stand with them against us. That is what I mean."

"It will not – it must not come to that," the mage protested.

Hawkwood was about to go on when Murad halted him with a curt gesture.

"Enough. Look around you. The odds are that we will never have to worry about such things, and we'll leave our bones to fester here in the jungle. Wizard, I'll offer you a truce. We three must help each other if any of us is ever to get back to the coast. The debates of high policy can wait until we are back aboard ship. Agreed?"

"Agreed," Bardolin said, his mouth a bitter line in his face.

"Excellent." The irony in Murad's voice was palpable. "Now, Captain, you are our resident navigator. Can you point us in the right direction tomorrow?"

"Perhaps. If I can get a look at the sun before the clouds start building up. There is a better way though. We must make an inventory. Empty your pouches – I must see what we have to work with."

They tore a broad leaf from a nearby bush and upon it they placed the contents of their pockets and pouches, squinting in the firelight. Bardolin and Hawkwood both had waterproofed tinderboxes with flint and steel and little coils of dry wool inside. The wizard also had a bronze pocket-knife and a pewter spoon. Murad had a broken iron knife-blade some five inches long, a tiny collapsible tin cup and a cork water-bottle still hanging from his belt by its straps. Hawkwood had his needle, a ball of tough yarn, a lead arquebus bullet and a fish-hook of carved bone. All of them had broken pieces of ship's biscuit lining their pockets and Murad a small lump of dried pork which was hard as wood and inedible.

"A meagre enough store, by God," the nobleman said. "Well Hawkwood, what wonders can you work with it?"

"I can make a compass, I think, and we can do some fishing and hunting if we have to also. I was shipwrecked when I was a boy in the Malacars, and we had little more than this upon us when we were washed up. We can use the yarn as fishing line, weight it with the bullet and bait it with the pork. The blade we can tie to a stave for a spear. There's fruit all around us too. We won't starve, but it's a time-consuming business, foraging for food, even in the jungle. We'd best be prepared to tighten our belts if we're to get back to the coast before the spring."

"The spring!" Murad exclaimed. "Great God, we may have to eat our boots, but we'll be back at the fort before that!"

"We were almost a month coming here, Murad, and we travelled along a road for much of the way. The journey back will be harder. Maybe they did allow us to escape, but I still don't want to frequent their highways." He remembered the heat and stink of the great werewolf lying beside him in the brush, back inside the mountain –

Would I harm you, Captain, the navigator, the steerer of ships? I think not. I think not.

– and shuddered at the memory.

THEY STOOD WATCHES that first night, taking it in turns to feed the fire and stare out at the black wall of the rainforest. When they were not on guard they slept fitfully. Bardolin lay awake most of the night, exhausted but afraid to sleep, afraid to find out what might be lurking in his dreams.

Aruan had made a lycanthrope of him.

So the Archmage had said. Bardolin had had sexual relations with Kersik, the girl who had guided them to Undabane. And then she had fed him a portion of her kill – that was the process. That was the rite that engendered the disease.

He almost thought he could feel the Black Disease working in him, a physical process changing body and soul with every heartbeat. Should he tell the others? They distrusted him already. What was going to happen to him – what manner of thing was he to become?

He considered just walking off and becoming lost to the jungle – or even returning to Undi like some prodigal son. But he had always been stubborn, proud and stiff-necked. He would resist this thing, battle it for as long as there was any remnant of Bardolin son of Carnolan left in him. He had been a soldier once: he would fight to the very end.

Thus he thought as he sat his watch, and fed the fire while the other two slept. Hawkwood had given him a task; he was to rub the iron needle with wool from one of the tinderboxes. It made little sense to Bardolin, but at least it was something to help keep sleep at bay.

To one side, Murad moaned in his slumber, and once to his shock Bardolin thought he heard the nobleman gasp out Griella's name. The base-born lover Murad had taken aboard ship who had turned out to be a shifter herself. What unholy manner of union had those two shared? Not rape, not love freely given either. A kind of mutual degradation which wrought violence upon their sensibilities and yet somehow left them wanting more.

And Bardolin, the old man, he had been envious of them.

He sat and excoriated himself for a thousand failings, the regrets of an ageing man without home or family. In the black night the darkness of his mood deepened. Why had Aruan let him go? What was his fate to be? Ah, to Hell with the endless questions.

He spun himself a little cantrip, a glede of werelight which flickered and sputtered weakly. In sudden fear he sent it bobbing around the limits of the firelight, banishing shadows for a few fleeting seconds. It wheeled like an ecstatic firefly and then went out. Too soon. Too weak. He felt like a man who has lost a limb and yet feels pain in phantom fingers. He drank some water from Murad's bottle, eyes smarting with grief and tiredness. He was too old for this. He should have an apprentice, someone to help bear the load of a greybeard's worries. Like young Orquil perhaps, whom they had sent to the fire back in Abrusio.

What about me, Bardolin. Will I do?

He started. Sleep had almost taken him. For a moment he had half-seen another person sitting on the other side of the fire. A young girl with heavy bronze-coloured hair. The night air had invaded his head. He brutally knuckled his aching eye-sockets and resumed his solitary vigil, impatiently awaiting the dawn.

THEY WERE ON their feet with the first faint light of the sun through the canopy. Water from the stream and a few broken crumbs of biscuit constituted breakfast, and then they looked over Hawkwood's shoulder as he set the needle floating on a leaf in Murad's tin cup. It twisted strangely on the water therein, and then steadied. The mariner nodded with grim satisfaction.

"That's your compass?" Murad asked incredulously. "A common needle?"

"Any iron can be given the ability to turn to the north," he was told. "I don't know why or how, but it works. We march south-east today. Murad, I want you to look out for a likely spear-shaft. Myself, I reckon I might have a go at making a bow. Give me your knife, Bardolin. We'll have to blaze trees to keep our bearing. All right? Then lets go."

Rather nonplussed, Hawkwood's two companions fell into step behind him, and the trio was on its way.

They tramped steadily until noon, when it began to cloud over in preparation for the almost daily downpour. By that time Murad had his iron knife-blade tied onto a stout shaft some six feet long, and Hawkwood was laden with a selection of slender sticks and one stave as thick as three fingers. They were famished, pocked with countless bites, scored and gashed and dripping with leeches. And Murad was finding it difficult to keep the pace Hawkwood set. The mariner and the mage would often have to pause in their tracks and wait for him to catch up. But when Hawkwood suggested a break, the nobleman only snarled at him.

In the shelter of an enormous dead tree they waited out the bruising rain as it began thundering down in torrents from the canopy overhead. The ground they sat on quickly became a sucking mire, and the force of the downpour made it difficult to breathe. Hawkwood bent his chin into his breast to create a space, a pocket of air, and in that second it filled with mosquitoes which he drew in helplessly as he breathed, and spat and coughed out again.

The deluge finally ended as abruptly as it had begun, and for a few minutes afterwards they sat in the mud and gurgling water which the forest floor had become, sodden, weary, frail with hunger. Murad was barely conscious, and Hawkwood could feel the burning heat of his body as the nobleman leaned against him.

They laboured to their feet without speaking, staggering like ancients. A coral-bright snake whipped through the puddles at their feet, and with a cry Murad seemed to come alive. He stabbed his new spear at the ground and transfixed the thrashing reptile just behind the head. It twined itself about the spear in its last agony, and Murad smiled.

"Gentlemen," he said, "dinner is served."

TWO

HAPTMAN HERNAN SEQUERO surveyed the squalid extent of his little kingdom and pursed his lips in disapproval. He rap-rap-rapped his knuckles lightly on the hardwood table, ignoring the bead of sweat that was hovering from one eyebrow.

"It's not good enough," he said. We'll never be self-sufficent here if these damned people keep on dying. They're supposed to be blasted magicians, after all – can't they magick up something?"

The men around him cleared their throats, shifted on their feet or looked away. Only one made any attempt to reply. A florid, golden-haired young man with an ensign's bar at his collar.

"There are three herbalists among the colonists sir. They're doing their best, but the plants here are unfamiliar to them. It is a process of trial and error."

"And in the meantime the cemetery becomes our most thriving venture ashore," Sequero retorted dryly. "Very well, one cannot argue with nature I suppose, but it is vexing. When Lord – when his Excellency returns he will not be pleased. Not at all."

Again, the uneasy shuffling of feet, brief shared glances.

There were three men standing about the table besides Sequero, all in the leather harness of the Hebrian soldiery. They were in one of the tall watchtowers which stood at each corner of the palisaded fort. Up here, it was possible to catch a breath of air off the ocean, and in fact to see their ship, the *Gabrian Osprey*, as it rode at anchor scarcely half a mile away, the horizon beyond it a far blur of sea and sky at the edge of sight.

Closer to, the view was less inspiring. Peppering the two acres or so within the palisade were dozens of rude huts, some little better than piled up mounds of brush. The only substantial building was the Governor's Residence, a large timber structure which was half villa and half blockhouse.

A deep ditch bisected the fort and served the community as a sewer, running off into the jungle. It was bridged in several places with felled trees, and the ground around it was a foul-smelling swamp swarming with mosquitoes. They had dug wells, but these were all brackish, so they continued to take their water from the clear stream Murad had discovered on the first day. One corner of the fort was corralled off and within it resided the surviving horses. Another few days would see it empty. When the last beasts had died they would be salted down and eaten, like the others.

"Fit for neither man nor beast," Sequero muttered, brow dark as he thought of the once magnificent creatures he had brought from Hebrion, the cream of his father's studs. Even the sheep did not do well here. Were it not for the wild pigs and deer which hunting-parties brought out of the jungle every few days they would be gnawing on roots and berries by now.

"How many today then?" he asked.

"Two," di Souza told him. "Miriam di –"

"I don't need to know their names!" Sequero snapped. "That leaves us with, what? Eighty-odd? Still plenty. Thank God the soldiers and sailors are made of sterner stuff. Sergeant Berrino, how are the men?"

"Bearing up well sir. A good move to let them doff their armour, if I might say so. And Garolvo's party brought in three boars this morning."

"Excellent. A good man, that Garolvo. He must be the best shot we have. Gentlemen, we are in a hellish place, but it belongs to our King now and we must make the best of it. Make no mistake, there will be promotions when the Governor returns from his expedition. Fort Abeleius not be much to look at now, but in a few years there will be a city here, with church-bells, taverns and all the trappings of civilization."

His listeners were dutifully attentive to his words, but he could almost taste their scepticism. They had been ashore two and a half months now, and Sequero knew well that the Governor was popularly believed to be long dead, or lost somewhere in the teeming jungle. He and his party had been away too long, and with his absence the discontent and fear within the fort was growing week by week. Increasingly, both soldiers and civilians were of the opinion that nothing would ever come of this precarious foothold upon the continent, and the Dweomer-folk were ready to brave even the pyres that awaited in Abrusio rather than suffer the death by disease and malnutrition that was claiming so many of them. At times Sequero felt as though he was swimming against an irresistible tide of sullen resentment which would one day overwhelm him.

"Ensign di Souza, how many of the ship's guns have we ashore now?"

"Six great culverins and a pair of light sakers sir, all sited to command the approaches. That sailor, Velasca, he wants to complain to you personally about it. He says the guns are the property of Captain Hawkwood and should remain with the ship."

"Let him put it in writing," said Sequero, who like all the old school of noblemen could not read. "Gentlemen, you are dismissed. All but you, di Souza. I want a word. Sergeant Berrino, you may distribute a ration of wine tonight. The men deserve it – they have worked hard."

Berrino, a middle-aged man with a closed, thuggish face, brightened. "Why thank you sir –"

"That is all. Leave us now."

The two soldiers clambered down the ladder that was affixed to one leg of the watchtower, leaving Sequero and di Souza alone in their eyrie.

"Do have some wine, Valdan," Sequero said easily, and gestured to the bulging skin that hung from a nearby peg.

"Thank you sir." Di Souza squirted a goodly measure of the blood-warm liquid down his throat and wiped his mouth on the back of his hand. They had been equals in rank, these two young men, until landfall here in the west. Murad had then promoted Hernan Sequero to haptman, making him military commander of the little colony. The choice had been inevitable; di Souza was noble only by adoption, whereas Sequero was from one of the high families of the kingdom, as close by blood to the Royal house as Murad himself. The fact that he was illiterate and did not know one end of an arquebus from another was neither here nor there.

"The Governor's party has been away almost eleven weeks," Sequero told his subordinate. "Within another week or two they should return, with God's grace. In all that time we here have been cowering behind our stockade as if we were under siege. That has to change. I have seen nothing in this country which warrants this absurd defensive posture. Tomorrow I will order the colonists to start marking out plots of land in the jungle. We'll slash and burn, clear a few acres and see if we can't get some crops planted. If things work out, then some of the colonists can be ejected from the fort and can start building homes on their own plots of land. Valdan, I want you to register all the heads of household among them, and map out their plots. They will hold them as tenants of the Hebriate Crown. We must start thinking of some form of tithe, of course, and you will organize a system of patrols... You wish to say something, Ensign?"

"Only that Lord Murad's orders were to remain within the fort sir. He said nothing about clearing farms."

"Quite true. But he has been away a lot longer than he originally anticipated, and we must all show a little initiative now and then. Besides, the fort is overcrowded and rapidly becoming unhealthy. And these damned mariners must do their share. How many soldiers do we have fit for duty?"

"Besides ourselves, eighteen. Hawkwood's second-in-command, Velasca, has a dozen sailors out surveying the coast in two of the longboats. He's also been salvaging timbers and iron from the wreck of the caravel that foundered on the reef. There are a score more still busy making salt and preserving meat and suchlike. For the return voyage. And four of them are in the fort, instructing some of our men in the firing of the big guns."

"Yes. They like to set themselves apart, these sailors. Well, that must change also. Tell Velasca I want a dozen of his men, with firearms, to join our soldiers and place themselves under sergeant Berrino. We need more men on the stockade."

"Yes sir. Anything else?" Di Souza's face was completely neutral.

"No. Yes – you will dine with me tonight in the Residence, I trust."

"Thank you, sir." Di Souza saluted and left via the creaking ladder. When he had gone, Sequero wiped the sweat from his face and allowed himself a mouthful of wine.

He was not yet sure if this place were an opportunity for advancement or the graveyard of his ambitions. Had he stayed in Hebrion he might be a regimental commander by now – his blood demanded no less. On the other hand, that very blood might have been considered a little too blue for the King's liking, hence his presence here, in this Godforsaken so-called colony. Still, if anyone had ambition, it was his superior, Lord Murad. That one would not have taken part in such a reckless scheme if he had not seen some kind of advantage in it for himself. Better here than at court then. In the field, superior officers had a habit of dying. At court there was only the age-old manoeuvring for power and rank, none of it counting for much in the presence of a strong king. And Abeleyn was a strong king, for all his youth. Sequero liked him, though he thought him too informal, too ready to lend an ear to his social inferiors.

Was Murad dead? It seemed hard to believe – the man had always seemed to be constructed equally out of sinew and pure will. But it had been a long time – a very long time. For the first time in his life, Sequero was unsure of himself. He knew the soldiers were close to mutiny, believing the colony to be cursed, and without Murad's authority to hold them in check...

A clattering of boots on the ladder, and a red-faced soldier appeared at the lip of the watchtower.

"Begging your pardon sir, but it's my turn on sentry. Ensign di Souza told me to come on up."

"Very well. I was just finished." What was the man's name? Sequero couldn't remember and felt vaguely irritated with himself. What did it matter? He was just another stinking trooper.

"See you keep your eyes open – Ulbio." There. He had remembered after all.

Ulbio saluted smartly. "Yes sir." And remained the picture of attentive duty as his commander lowered himself down from the watchtower. When Sequero had disappeared he spat over the side. *Fucking nobles*, he thought. *None of them give a damn about their men.*

THE GOVERNOR'S RESIDENCE was the only edifice with any pretensions to architecture within the colony. Loopholed for defence like the strongpoint it was, it nonetheless had a long veranda upon which it was almost pleasant to sit and dine of an evening. The wood of the great trees about the fort was incredibly hard and fine-grained, but it made admirable furniture. The sailors had set up a pedal-powered lathe of sorts, and that evening Sequero and his guests were able to eat off a fine long table with beautifully turned legs. There was still crystal and silver to eat off and drink from, and tall candles to light the flushed faces of the diners and attract the night-time moths. Were it not for the cloying heat and the raucous jungle they might have been back in Hebrion on some nobleman's estate.

The gathering was not a large one. Besides Sequero and di Souza there were only three other diners. These were Osmo of Fulk, a fat, greasy and sycophantic wine merchant whose personal store of Gaderian meant it politic to invite him, Astiban of Pontifidad, a tall, grey man with a mournful face who in Abrusio had been a professional herbalist and an amateur naturalist, and finally Fredric Arminir, who hailed originally from Almark, of all places, and who was reputed to be a smuggler.

None of the three men were actual wizards, so far as Sequero knew, but they all possessed the Dweomer in varying degrees, else they would not be here. He felt a childish urge to make them perform in some way, to do some trick or feat, and he was absurdly gratified when the stout Osmo set weird blue werelights burning at the far corners of the veranda. The insects crowded around them and sizzled to death in their hundreds, whilst the diners were able to eat and drink without continually slapping the vermin from around their faces.

"Something I picked up in Macassar," Osmo explained casually. "The climate there is similar in many ways."

"And you, Astiban," Sequero said. "Being a naturalist, I assume you are rapt with wonder at the wealth of creatures that crawl and flit about us on this Continent."

"There is much that is unfamiliar, it is true, Lord Sequero. With Ensign di Souza's permission I have accompanied some of the hunting parties out into the jungle. I have seen tracks there belonging to creatures not seen in any Bestiary of the Old World. On my own initiative, I explored the ground beyond our stockade for several hundred yards out into the forest. These tracks approach the fort, and mill about, and then retreat again. It is a pattern I have found a hundred times."

"What are they doing, coming to have a look at us?" Fredric asked, amused.

"Yes. I think so. I think we are being closely watched, but by what exactly, I cannot say."

"Are you assigning a rationality to these unknown beasts?" Sequero asked, surprised.

"I do not know if I would go that far. But I am glad we have a stout palisade in place, and soldiers to man it. When the Governor returns from his expedition I am sure he will have learned much of this continent, which may clarify my findings."

The man sounds like a lecturing professor, Sequero thought irritably. But at least he seemed to think that the Governor would actually return. From the sidelong glances that Fredric and Osmo exchanged, it seemed they did not share his confidence.

Aloud, Sequero said "We are pioneers. For us the risks are outweighed by the rewards."

"A pioneer you may be, my lord," Astiban said, "but we are refugees. For us, it was a place on Captain Hawkwood's ships, or an appointment with the pyre."

"Quite. Well, we are all here now, and must make the best of it."

A solitary gunshot cracked heavily through the thick night air, making them all start in their seats. Di Souza rose. "Sir, with your permission –"

"Yes, yes, Valdan, go and see. Another sentry firing at shadows, I presume."

Then there was a great crashing boom that ripped the darkness apart, and the flash of a cannon firing from the palisade. Men were shouting out there in the darkness. Di Souza pelted off, snatching his sword from where it hung at the front of the veranda and disappearing. Deliberately, Sequero sipped his wine before his wide-eyed guests. "Gentlemen, I am afraid our dinner may well be cut short."

Some unknown beast was bellowing in rage, and there was a flurry of shots, little saffron sparkles. Torches were being lit along the stockade, and someone began beating the ship's bell that was their signal for a full alarm. Sequero rose and buckled on his sword-belt.

"You had best go to your families and make sure they are safe, but I want every able-bodied man on the palisade as soon as possible. Go now."

He finished the last of the Gaderian in his glass as the three men hurried off. It would have been a pity to waste it. There was a regular battle going on out there. He set down the empty glass and strolled off the veranda towards the firing. Behind him, Osmo's blue werelights sputtered and went out.

THREE

"WHAT IS IT?" Hawkwood asked, waking to find Bardolin standing listening to the night-time jungle.

"Something – some noise far off, towards the coast. I almost thought it was a cannon firing."

Hawkwood was wide awake in an instant and on his feet beside the wizard. "I knew we were close, but I didn't think –"

"Hush – there it is again."

This time they both heard it. "That's a cannon all right," Hawkwood breathed. "One of my culverins. Perhaps they brought them ashore. God's blood, Bardolin, it can't be more than a few miles away. We're almost home."

"*Home*," Bardolin repeated thoughtfully. "But why are they firing cannon in the middle of the night, Hawkwood? Tell me that. I don't think it means good news."

They both sat down by the fire again. On the other side of the flames Murad lay like a corpse, mouth open, his face rippled with scar-tissue.

"We'll find out tomorrow," Hawkwood said. "A few more miles, and it's finished. We'll board the *Osprey* and get the hell out of this stinking country. Breathe clean sea air again, feel the wind on our faces. Think of that, Bardolin. Think of it."

The far-off gunfire continued for perhaps an hour, including one well-spaced salvo that sounded exactly like a ship's broadside. After that, there was silence again, but by that time Hawkwood had set up his primitive compass and taken a bearing on the sound, so that in the morning they could march straight towards it. Then he fell asleep, exhausted.

Bardolin remained awake. They had long since given up keeping any kind of sentry, but as the weeks had drawn on he had found himself needing less and less sleep.

Their journey had been incredibly hard – indeed, it had come close to killing them. They had been transformed by it into matt-haired, sunken-eyed fanatics, whose only mission in life was to keep walking, who revered Hawkwood's home-made compass as though it were the holiest relic, who scrabbled for every scrap of anything resembling food and wolfed it down like animals. All the patina of civilization had been scraped away by day after day of back-breaking toil, and the filth and heat of the rainforest. Many times, they had decided they could go no further, and had become resigned to the idea of death – even inured to it. But odd things had saved them at those critical moments. The discovery of a stream of pure water, finding a freshly killed forest deer, or a medicinal herb which Hawkwood had recognised from his travels in Macassar. Somehow they had lurched from one lucky windfall to another, all the time keeping to the bearing that Hawkwood set for them every morning. And they were going to survive. Bardolin knew that – he had for a long time. But now he also knew why.

When the darkest hour of each night came upon him he lay alone by the fire and fought the disease that was working in him, but each time it progressed a little farther before it receded again.

It came upon him once more this night – it felt like a blessed breath of cold air stealing over him, a chill invigoration which flooded strength into his wasted frame. And then his sight changed, so that he was beginning to see things he normally could not. Murad's heart beating like a bright, trapped bird in his chest. The veins of blood which nestled in his forearms pulsing like threads of liquid light.

Bardolin felt his very bones begin to creak, as if they were desperately trying to burst into some new configuration. His tongue circled up and down his teeth, and they had become different; the inside of his mouth felt hot as an oven, and he had to open it and pant for air. When he did, his tongue lolled out over his lower lip and the sweat rolled off it.

He raised his hands to his eyes and found that his palms had become black and rough. Joints clicked and reclicked. His hearing grew so acute it was almost unbearable, and yet madly fascinating. He could hear and see a whole universe of life twittering in the rainforest around him.

This was it, the most seductive time. When the Change felt like a welcome relief, the chance to metamorphosize into something bigger, better, in which life could be tasted so much more keenly and all his old man's aches and weaknesses could be forgotten.

At one instant he writhed there, perfectly suspended between the desire to let the Change have its way and his own stubborn refusal to give in. Then he had beaten it again, and lay there as weak as a newborn kitten, the jungle a black wall about him.

"Bravo," the voice said. "I have never seen anyone fight the Black Disease with such pugnacious determination before. You have my admiration, Bardolin. Even if your struggle is misguided, and futile in the end."

Bardolin raised his exhausted face. "I have not seen you in a while, Aruan. Been busy?"

"In a manner of speaking, yes. You heard the gunfire. You can guess what it means. The ship is intact, though – of that I made sure. My only worry was that the survivors would sail away before you reach the coast tomorrow, so I have whistled up a landward wind, which will keep them anchored if they do not want to be run aground."

"How very thoughtful."

"I think of everything. Do you think you would have made it this far without my help? Though that mariner of yours is certainly ingenious – and indomitable. I like him. He reminds me of myself when I was young. You are lucky in your friends, Bardolin. I never was."

"My heart bleeds for you."

Aruan leaned over the fire so that the flames carved a molten mask out of his features. "It will, one day. I will leave you now. Keep fighting it if you will, Bardolin, but you harm yourself by doing so. I believe I will summon someone who may be able to clarify your thinking. There. It is done. Fare well. When I see you again you shall have the wide ocean under you." And he disappeared.

Bardolin drank thirstily from the wooden water-bottle, sucking at the neck until it was empty. When he felt the cool fingers massage his knotted neck, he closed his eyes and sighed.

"Griella, what did he do to you?"

The girl leaned down and kissed his cheek from behind. "He gave me life, what else?"

"No-one can raise the dead. Only God can do that."

The girl knelt before him. She was perhaps fifteen years old and possessed of a heavy helmet of bronze-coloured hair which shone rich as gold in the firelight. Her features were elfin, fine, and she hardly reached Bardolin's breastbone when standing straight.

She was a werewolf, and she had died months ago – before they had even set foot on the Western Continent. What monstrous wizardry had raised her from the ranks of the dead, Bardolin could not imagine and preferred not to guess at. She had appeared several times during their awful journey back from Undabane, and each time her coming had been a comfort and a torment to him – as Aruan had no doubt meant it to be. For Bardolin had come to love her on their westward voyage, though that love filled him with twisted guilt.

"If you only let it happen, Bardolin, I could be with you always," she said. "We have the same nature now, and it is not such a bad thing, the Black Change. He is not a good man, I know, but he is not evil, either, and most of the time he speaks the truth."

"Oh, Griella," Bardolin groaned. She was the same and not the same. An instinct told him she was some consummate simulacrum, a created thing, like the imps Bardolin had grown as familiars. But that did not make her face any less dear to him.

"He says I can be your apprentice, once you accept your lot. You told me once, Bardolin, that shifters cannot also become mages. Well, you were wrong. How about that? I can be your pupil. You will teach me magic, and I will teach you of the Black Change."

He gaze strayed towards where Murad lay in twitching sleep across the fire.

"What about him?" Bardolin asked.

She looked confused, then almost frightened. "I remember things. Bad things. There was a fire. Murad did things... No – I can't see it." She raised a hand to her face, let it drop, pawed at her mouth, her eyes suddenly empty. In the next moment, she had winked out of sight with the same preternatural swiftness as Aruan.

"Child, child," Bardolin said mournfully. She was indeed some form of familiar, a creature brought life through the Dweomer. And he felt a furious rage at Aruan for such a perversion. The games he played, with people's lives and the very forces of nature. No man could do such things and be wholly sane.

IN THE MORNING Hawkwood and Bardolin told Murad of the gunfire in the night. He seemed neither surprised nor overjoyed by the news. Instead he sat thoughtfully, picking at the scar which distorted one side of his head.

"When the firing ended it meant that the fort has either beaten off the attack or has been overrun."

No-one said anything. They were all thinking of the fantastic creatures that had butchered their comrades in Undi. A massed assault by such travesties would be hard for any group of men to withstand, especially since they could only be permanently slain by the touch of iron.

"Let's go," Murad said, rising like some emaciated scarecrow. "We'll find out soon enough."

By mid-morning they had glimpsed a line of high ground rising off to their right, broken heights jutting through the emerald jungle like decaying teeth. Hawkwood stopped to study it and then called to the others excitedly. "Look – you know what that is? It's Circle Ridge: *Heyeran Spinero*. My God, we've only a mile or two to go!"

It was almost three months since they had set out, and they were finally back at that stretch of coastline they had explored in the first days of the landing. They went more cautiously now. After all this time, they were almost reluctant to admit any hope into their hearts.

They found the first body close by the clear stream from which the settlement drew its water. A middle-aged woman, by her dress, though she had been so badly mauled it was hard to tell. Ants and beetles were already at work upon the carcass in their thousands, and it stank in the morning heat.

Even Murad seemed somewhat shaken. The three men did not look at one another, but continued on their way. Here was the slope they had toiled up on the first day – now a churned-up mire. Things had been discarded in the mud. A powder-horn, a scrap of leather gambeson, a rent piece of linen shirt. And under the bushes at the side of the clearing, two more bodies. These also were civilians. One was headless. Their intestines coiled like greasy, fly-spotted ropes in the grass.

They trudged down the slope with their hearts hammering in their breasts, and finally the rainforest rolled back, and they were stumbling over hewn tree-stumps, a cleared space. Before them, the sagging and skewed posts of the stockade stood deserted, and there was a stink of burning in the air, the reek of corruption. Beyond the clearing, they could glimpse the sea through the trees.

"Hello!" Murad shouted, his voice cracking with strain. "Anyone here?"

The gates of the stockade had been smashed flat. A litter of bodies were scattered here, an arquebus trodden into the mud. Blood standing in puddles with a cloud of midges above every one.

"Lòrd God," Hawkwood said. Murad covered his eyes.

Fort Abeleius was a charnel-house. The Governor's residence had burned to the ground and was still smouldering. Remnants and wreckage from other huts and buildings were scattered about in broken, splintered piles. And there were bodies and parts of bodies everywhere, scores of them.

Bardolin turned aside and vomited.

Hawkwood was holding the back of his hand to his nose. "I must see if the ship survived. I pray to God –" He took off at a run, stumbling over corpses, leaping broken lumber, and disappeared in the direction of the beach beyond the clearing.

Murad was turning over the bodies like a ghoul prowling a graveyard, nodding to himself, making a study of the whole ghastly spectacle.

The stockade was overrun from the north first," he said. "That split our people in two. Some made a stand by the gate, but most I think fell back to the Governor's residence..." He shambled over that way himself, and picked his way through the burnt ruins of the place that he was to have administered his colony from.

"Here's Sequero. I know him by the badge on his tunic. Yes – they all crammed in here" – he kicked aside a charred bone – "and when they had held out for a while, some fool's match set light to the thatch, or perhaps the powder took light. They might have held out through the night otherwise. It was quick. All so quick. Every one of them. Lord God."

Murad sank to his knees amid the wreckage and the burnt bodies and set the heels of his hands in his eyes. "We are in Hell, Bardolin. We have found it here on earth."

Bardolin knew better, but said nothing. He felt enough of a turncoat already. There had been over a hundred and forty people here in the Fort. Aruan had said the ship would survive – who manned it now?

"Let's go down to the sea," he said to Murad, taking the nobleman by the elbow. "Perhaps the ship is still there."

Murad came with him in a kind of grieved daze. Together they picked their way across the desolation, gagging on the smell of the dead, and then plunged into the forest once more. But there was that salt tang to the air, and the rush of waves breaking somewhere ahead, a sound from a previous world.

The white blaze of the beach blinded them, and the horizon-wide sea seemed too vast to take in all at once. They had become used to the fetid confines of the rainforest, and it was pure exhilaration to be able to see a horizon again, a huge arc of blue sky. A wind blew off the sea into their hot faces. A landward wind, just as Aruan had promised.

"Glory be," Bardolin breathed.

The *Gabrian Osprey* stood at anchor perhaps half a mile from the shore. She looked intact, and wholly deserted – until Bardolin glimpsed some movement on her forecastle. A man waving. And then he caught sight of the head bobbing in the waves halfway out to the ship. Hawkwood was swimming out to her, pausing in his stroke every so often to wave to whatever crew remained and shout himself hoarse. Bardolin and Murad watched until he reached the carrack and clung to the wales on her side, too weak to pull himself up the tumblehome. A group of men appeared at the ship's rail. Some were sailors, a couple wore the leather vests of soldiers. They hauled Hawkwood up the ship's side, and Bardolin saw one of them embrace his captain.

Murad had sunk down upon the sand. "Well, Mage," he said in something resembling his old manner. "At least one of us is happy. It is time to leave, I think. We have outstayed our welcome in this country. Thus ends New Hebrion."

But Bardolin knew that this was not the end of something. Whatever it was, it had only just begun.

FOUR

THE KING WAS dead, his body lying stark and still on a great bier in the nave of Torunn's cathedral. The entire kingdom was in mourning, all public buildings decked out in sable drapes, all banners at half-mast. Lofantyr had not reached thirty, and he left no heir behind him.

THE TIREDNESS BUZZED through Corfe's brain. He stood in shining half-armour at the dead king's head, leaning on an archaic greatsword and inhaling sweet incense and the muddy smoke of the candles that burned all around. At the King's feet stood Andruw in like pose, head bent in solemn grief. Corfe saw his mouth writhe in the suppression of a yawn under the heavy helmet, and he had to fight not to smile.

The cathedral was thronged with a great murmuring crowd of damp-smelling people. They knelt on the pews or on the flagged floor and queued in their hundreds to have a chance to say goodbye to their monarch. Unending lines of them. They were not grieving so much as awed by the solemnity, the austere splendour of the dead King's lying-in-state. Lofantyr had not ruled long enough to become loved, and was a name, no more. A figurehead in the ordered system of the world.

Outside it sounded as though a heavy sea were beating against the hoary old walls of the cathedral. Another crowd, less tractable. The surf-roar of their voices was ominous, frightening even. A quarter of a million people had gathered in the great square beyond the cathedral gates. No-one was quite sure why – probably they did not truly know themselves. The common people were confused. Palace bulletins stated that the recent battle had been a victory for Torunnan arms. But why then was their king dead and eight thousand of their menfolk lying stark and cold upon the winter field? They felt themselves duped, and were angry. Any spark would set them off.

And yet, Corfe thought, *I am expected to take my turn standing ceremonial guard over a dead man, when I am now commander in chief of a shattered army. Tradition. Its wheels turn on tirelessly even in a time like this.*

But it gave him a space to think, if nothing else. Two days since the great battle of the Torunnan Plain. *The King's Battle* they were already calling it. Odd how people always thought it so important that a battle should have a name. It gave some strange coherence to what was, after all, a chaotic, slaughterous nightmare. Historians needed things neater, it seemed.

Twenty-seven thousand men left to defend the capital – the last army. Torunna had squandered her soldiers with sickening prodigality. An entire field army destroyed in the sack of Aekir. Another decimated in the fall of Ormann Dyke. And even this remaining force had lost nearly a third of its number in the latest round of bloodletting. But the Merduks – how many had they lost? A hundred thousand in the assaults on Aekir, it was now reckoned. Thirty thousand more in front of the Dyke. And another forty thousand in the King's Battle. How could a single people absorb losses on that scale? Numberless though the hordes of the east might be, Corfe could not believe that they were unaffected by such awful arithmetic. They would hesitate before committing themselves to another advance, another round of killing. That was his hope, the basis for all his half-formed plans. He needed time.

Corfe and Andruw were relieved at last, their place taken with grim parade-ground formality by Colonels Rusio and Willem. Corfe caught the cold glance of Willem as he marched away towards the back of the cathedral. Hatred there, resentment at the elevation of an upstart to the highest military command in the west. Well, that was not unexpected, but it would complicate things. Things were always complicated, even when it came to that most basic of human activities, the killing of one's fellow man.

CORFE WAS RELIEVED of his armour by a small regiment of palace servitors in the General's Suite of the palace. His new quarters were a cavernous cluster of marble-cold rooms within which he felt both uncomfortable and absurd. But the general could no longer be allowed to mess with his men, drink beer in the common refectories, or pick the mud off his own boots. The Queen Dowager – now Torunna's monarch and sole remaining vestige of royalty – had insisted that Corfe assume the trappings of his rank.

It is a long time, Corfe thought to himself, *since I shared cold turnip with a blind man on the retreat from Aekir. Another world.*

A discreet footman caught his eye and coughed. "General, a simple repast has been set out for you in your dining chamber. I suggest you avail yourself of it while it is still hot. Our cook –"

"I'll eat later. Have the palace Steward sent to me at once, and some writing materials. And the two scribes who attended me last night. And pass the word for Colonel Andruw Cear-Adurhal."

The footman blinked, crinkling the white powder on his temples. *Where in the name of God did that fashion begin?* Corfe wondered distractedly.

"All shall be as you wish, of course. But General, the palace Steward, the Honourable Gabriel Venuzzi, is answerable only to the Monarch of Torunna. He is not under your aegis, if you will forgive me. He is a person of some considerable importance in the household, and were I to convey so – so peremptory a summons, he might take it ill. If you will allow me, I, as senior footman of the household, should be able to answer any questions you might have about the running of the palace and the behaviour expected of all who dwell within it, as guests or otherwise." This last sentence had inserted within it a sneer so delicate it almost passed Corfe by. He frowned, turned a cold eye upon the powdered fellow. "What's your name?"

The footman bowed "Damian Devella, General."

"Well, Damian, let's get a few things straight. In future, you and all your associate servitors will wipe that white shit off your faces when you attend me. You're not ladies' maids, nor yet pantomime performers. And you will send for this Venuzzi fellow. Now. Clear it with Her Majesty if you must, but get his powdered backside in this room within the quarter-hour, or by God I'll have you and your whole prancing crew conscripted into the army, and we'll see if there's even six inches of backbone hidden under all that velvet and lace. Do you understand me?"

Devella's mouth opened, closed. "I – I – Yes, General."

"Good. Now fuck off."

Scribes, a writing desk, a decanter of wine, all appeared with remarkable speed. Corfe stepped out onto his balcony as, behind him, the dining chamber was transformed into an office of sorts and members of the household scurried about like ants whose nest had been poked with a stick.

Another raw day outside, sleet withering down from the Cimbric mountains. Corfe could see the vast crowd still milling about in Cathedral Square, their voices meshing into a shapeless buzz of noise. Half of them were Aekirian refugees, still without homes of their own or the prospect of any change in their wretchedness. That would change, if he could help it. They were his people too – he had been a refugee like them and could never forget it.

"What's afoot, General?" Andruw's cheery voice demanded. Corfe turned. His friend was dressed in old field fatigues and comfortable boots, but his Colonel's braid was bright and shining-new. It looked as though he had stitched it on himself. Some of the ice about Corfe's heart eased a little. It would be a black day indeed that saw Andruw out of humour.

"Just trying to get a few things done before the funeral," he told Andruw. "That crowd means business, even if they don't know it themselves yet. You brought the papers?"

"They're on the table. Lord, I'll need some sleep tonight. And some fresh air to blow away the smell of all that ink and paper. Stacks of it!"

"Think of it as ammunition. Ah – excuse me, Andruw."

A richly dressed man with an ebony staff of office had been admitted to the room by the footmen with all the pomp of an eastern potentate. He was very tall, very slim, and dark as a Merduk. A native of Kardikia or perhaps southern Astarac, Corfe guessed.

"Gabriel Venuzzi?"

The man bowed slightly, a mere nod of the head. "Indeed. You, I believe, are General Cear-Inaf."

"The very same. Now listen here, Gabriel, we have a problem on our hands and I believe you may be able to help me solve it."

"Indeed? I am glad to hear it. And what might be the nature of this problem, General? Her Majesty has requested me to give you any assistance in my power, and I of course must obey her commands to the letter."

"There's your problem, Gabriel. Down there." Corfe gestured at the view from the balcony. Venuzzi stepped over to the open doors, wincing slightly at the cold air coursing through them, and glanced out at the murmuring crowds below.

"I am afraid I don't quite understand you, General. I am not an officer of militia, merely the head administrator of the household. If you want the crowd cleared you should perhaps be addressing some of your junior officers. I do not deal with commoners."

His hauteur was almost impressive. Corfe smiled. "You do now."

"Forgive me my ignorance. I still do not follow you."

"That's all right, Gabriel. I don't mind explaining." Corfe lifted the sheaf of papers Andruw had brought in with him. The two of them had spent the early hours of the morning hunting them up in the storehouse of palace housekeeping records, a musty tomb-like warren dedicated to the storage of statistics.

"I have here records of all the foodstuffs kept in storage in the palace. Not only the palace in fact, but in Royal warehouses across the entire city and indeed the kingdom. Gabriel, my dear fellow, the household has squirrelled away hundreds of tons of wheat and corn and smoked meat and – and –"

"And stock-fish and hardtack and olive-oil and wine," Andruw added. "Don't forget the wine – eight hundred tuns of it, General."

"And I won't even mention the brandy and salt-pork and figs," Corfe finished, still smiling. "Now explain to me, Gabriel, why it is necessary to hoard these stupendous amounts of goods."

"I'd have thought it was obvious, General, even to you," Venuzzi drawled, not turning a hair. "They are Royal reserves, destined to supply the palace on an everyday basis, and also put aside in case of siege."

"All this, to keep the inhabitants of the palace well fed?" Corfe asked quietly.

"Why yes. Certain proprieties must be observed, even in times of war. We cannot" – and here Venuzzi's lean face broke into a knowing smirk – "we cannot expect the nobility to go hungry, after all. Think how it would look to the world."

"It is not a question of going hungry. It is a question of hoarding the means to feed tens of thousands when one has in fact only to supply the wants of a few hundred." There was a tone in Corfe's voice which made everyone in the room pause. His smile had disappeared.

Venuzzi retreated a step from that terrible stare. "General, I –"

"Hold your tongue. In case it had escaped your attention, we are at war, Venuzzi. I am issuing orders for the collection of all these hoarded stocks of food and their redistribution to all the refugees from Aekir, and anyone else in Torunn who has need of them. The orders will be posted up in public places this morning. These scribes have already made out fifty copies. I need your signature, I am told, before I can start the process."

"You shall not have it! This is outrageous!"

Corfe stepped closer to the Steward. "You will sign," he said in a voice so soft no-one else in the room heard, "or I will make a private soldier out of you, Venuzzi. I can do that, you know. I can conscript anyone I please."

"You're bluffing! You wouldn't dare."

"Try me."

A silence crackled in the room. Venuzzi's knuckles were bone white around his black staff of office. Finally he turned, bent over the desk, and seized a quill. His signature, long and scrawling, was scratched across the topmost set of orders.

"Thank you," Corfe said quietly.

The Steward shot him a look of pure vitriol. "The Queen shall know of this. You think I am friendless in this place? You know nothing. What are you but a backwoods upstart with mud still under your nails? You fool."

Then he turned on his heel and strode out of the room in a cloud of footmen. The great doors boomed shut behind him.

Andruw sighed. "Corfe, a diplomat you are not."

The general bent his head. "I know. I'm just a soldier. Nothing more." Then he caught his subordinate's eye. "You know, Andruw, there is a new cemetary outside the south gate. The Aekirians, they created it. There are over six thousand graves already. Many of them starved to death, the folk who rot in those graves. While we banqueted in the palace. So don't talk to me of diplomacy, not now – not ever again. Just see that those orders are posted up all over the city by noon. I'm off to have a look at the men."

Andruw watched him go without another word.

LATE THAT NIGHT in the capital a group of men met in the discreet upper room of a prosperous tavern. They wore nondescript riding clothes; long cloaks muddy with the filth of the streets and high boots. Some were armed with military sabres. They sat round a long candlelit tavern table marked with the rings of past carouses. A fire smoked and cracked in a grate behind them.

"It's intolerable, absolutely intolerable," one of the men said. A red-faced, grey-bearded fellow in his fifties. Colonel Rusio of the city garrison.

"They say he is the son of a peasant from down in Staed," another put in. "Aras – you were down there. Is it true, you think?

Colonel Aras, a good twenty years younger than anyone else in the room, looked uncomfortable and willing to please at the same time.

"I can't say for sure. All I know is he handles those demon tribesmen of his with definite ability. Sirs, you know he had the southern rebels crushed before I even arrived. I'm willing to admit that. Five hundred men! And Narfintyr had over three thousand, yet he stood not a chance."

"You almost sound as though you admire him, Colonel." A silken purr of a voice. Count Fournier, head of Torunna's Intelligence service, such as it was. He stroked his neat beard, as pointed as a spearhead, and watched his younger colleague intently.

"Perhaps – perhaps I do," Aras said, stumbling over the words. "In the King's Battle he stopped my position from being overrun when he sent me his Fimbrians. And then he threw back the Nalbeni horse-archers on the left, twenty thousand of them."

"*His* Fimbrians," Rusio muttered. "Lord above. He also sent you *my* guns, Aras, or had you forgotten?"

"I hope you are not prey to conflicting emotions in this matter, my dear Aras," Fournier said. "If so, you should not be here."

"I know where my loyalties lie," Aras said quickly. "To my own class, to the social order of the realm. To the ultimate welfare of the kingdom. I merely point out facts, is all."

"I am relieved to hear it," Fournier's voice rose. "Gentlemen, we are gathered here, as you well know, to discuss this – this phoenix which has appeared in our midst. He has military ability, yes. He has the patronage of our noble Queen, yes. But he is a commoner who prefers commanding savages and Fimbrians to his own countrymen and who is utterly lacking in any vestige of respect for the traditional values of this kingdom. Am I not right, Don Venuzzi?"

The palace steward nodded, his handsome face flushed with anger. "You've read the notices – they're all over the city. He is distributing the Royal reserves at this very moment, breaking open the warehouses and handing it out to every beggar in the street who has a hand to lift."

"Such largesse will win him many friends among the humbler elements of the population," one of the group said. A short, stocky individual this, with a black patch over one eye and a shaven pate. Colonel Willem, who had been commander of the troops left to garrison the capital when the army marched out to the King's Battle. "A shrewd move, indeed. He has brains, this fellow Corfe."

"Didn't you go to the Queen?" Fournier demanded of Venuzzi. "After all, it's her property he's giving away."

"Of course I did. But she is besotted with him, I tell you. I was told not to cross him."

"He must wield a mighty weapon besides that sword of Mogen's she gave him," Rusio grunted, and the men at the table sniggered, except for Fournier and Venuzzi, who both looked pained.

"She has what she has been hankering after for years," Fournier said icily. "Power in name as well as in fact. She is Torunna's ruler now, no longer the string-puller behind the throne but the occupant of the throne itself. And this Cear-Inaf fellow, he is the fist of the new regime. Mark my words, gentlemen, there are several of us at this table whose heads are about to roll."

"Perhaps literally," Rusio muttered. "Fournier, tell me, will they reopen the investigation into that assassination attempt?"

Fournier coloured. "I think not."

"It was you and the King, wasn't it?"

"What a monstrous accusation! Do you think I would stoop to –"

"Gentlemen, gentlemen," Willem interjected testily, "enough. We are allies here. There are to be no accusations or recriminations. We must answer this stark question – how do we rid Torunna of this parvenu?"

"Do we want to be rid of him at the moment?" Aras asked nervously. "After all, he is doing a good job of winning the war."

"Good Lord, Colonel," Rusio snapped. "I do believe you've fallen under this fellow's spell. What are you thinking? Winning the war? We left eight thousand dead on the field a few days ago, including our King. Winning the war, indeed!"

Aras did not reply. His face was white as bone.

"It must be legal, whatever else it is," Fournier said smoothly, gliding over the awkward little silence that followed. "And it must not jeapordise the security of the kingdom. We are, after all, in a fight for our very survival at the moment. It may be that Aras is right. This fellow Corfe has his uses – that cannot be denied. And if truth be told, I am not sure the troops would follow anyone else at the moment."

Rusio stirred at this but said nothing.

"So it behoves us to work with him for now. As long as he has the confidence of the Queen he is well-nigh untouchable, but no man is without his weak spots. Aras, you told us he lost his wife in Aekir."

"Yes. He never talks about it, but I have heard his friend Andruw mention it."

"Indeed. That is an avenue worth exploring. There is guilt there, obviously, hence his largesse to the scum of Aekir that we harbour in the capital. And you Aras, you must work to get closer to him. You obviously admire him, so that is a start. Remember, we are not out to destroy this fellow – we simply feel that he has been elevated beyond his station."

Aras nodded.

"And make sure you recall whose side you are on," Rusio growled. "It's one thing to admire the man, another to let him ride roughshod over the very institutions which bind this kingdom together." A murmur of agreement ran down the table. Willem spoke up.

"Another six hundred tribesmen from the Cimbrics arrived outside the city this evening, wanting to fight under him. Quartermaster Passifal is equipping them as we speak. I tell you, gentlemen, if we do not curb this young fellow he will set himself up as some form of military dictator. He does not even have to rely on the support of his own countrymen. What with those savages and his tame Fimbrians at his back, he has a power-base completely outside the normal chain of command. They won't serve under anyone else – we saw that at the last planning conference the King chaired, here in the capital. And now he's stirring up the rabble who fled from Aekir when he should be shipping them south, dispersing them. There's a pattern to it all. It's my belief he aims at the throne itself."

"It is disturbing," Fournier agreed. "Perhaps – and this is only a vague suggestion, nothing more – perhaps we should be looking round for allies of our own outside the kingdom, a counterweight to this growing army of mercenaries he leads."

"Who?" Rusio asked bluntly.

Fournier paused, looked intently at the faces of the men round the table. Below them they could hear the buzz and hubbub of the tavern proper, but in the room now the loudest sound was the crackling of the fire.

"I have received in the last sennight a message brought by courier from Almark, gentlemen. That kingdom is, as you know, now on the frontier. The Merduks have sent exploratory columns to the Torrin gap. Reconnaisances, nothing more, but Almark is understandably alarmed."

"Almark is Himerian," Rusio pointed out. "And ruled directly by the Himerian Church now, I hear."

"True. The Prelate Marat is now Regent of the kingdom, but Marat is a practical man – and a powerful one now. If we agreed to certain… conditions, he would be willing to send us a host of Almarkan heavy cavalry in our hour of need."

"What conditions?" Willem asked.

"A recognition that there are grounds for doubting the true identity of the man who claims to be Macrobius."

Rusio barked with bitter laughter. "Is that all? Not possible, my dear Count. I know – I met Macrobius while he still dwelled in Aekir. The Pontiff we harbour here in Torunn is a travesty of that man, admittedly, but he is Macrobius. The Himerians are looking for a way to get their foot in the door, that's all. They failed with war and insurrection and now they'll try diplomacy. Priests! I'd get rid of the whole scheming crew if I had my way."

Fournier shrugged elegantly. "I merely inform you as to all the various options available. I, too, do not wish to see Almarkan troops in Torunna, but the very idea that they could be available is a useful bargaining tool. I shall brief the Queen on the initiative. It is as well for her to be aware of it." He said nothing of the other, more delicate initiative which had come his way of late. He was still unsure how to handle it himself.

"Do as you please. For myself, I'd sooner we were hauled out of this mess by other Torunnans, not heretical foriegners and plotting clerics."

"There are not many Torunnans left to do the hauling, Colonel. The once mighty Torunnan armies are a mere shadow of what they once were. If we do not respond, in some fashion at least, to this overture, then I would not be too sanguine about the safety of our own north-western frontier. Almark might just strike while the Merduks have our attention, and we would have foreign troops on

Torunnan soil in any case, except that we would not have invited them."

"Are you saying that we have no choice in the matter?"

"Perhaps. I will see what the Queen thinks. For all that she is a woman, she has as fine a mind as any of us here."

"We're getting away from the point of this meeting," Willem said impatiently.

"No, I don't think so," Fournier replied. He steepled his slender fingers and swept the table with hard eyes. "If we are trying to shift this Cear-Inaf from his current eminence, it may be best to use many smaller levers instead of one great one. That way the prime movers are more easily kept anonymous. More importantly, Cear-Inaf will find it harder to fight back."

"He's not ambitious," Aras blurted out. "I truly think he fights not for himself but for the country, and for his men."

"His lack of ambition has taken him far," Fournier said dryly. "Aras, you have met with him more often than any of us. What do you make of him?"

The young Colonel hesitated. "He's – he's strange. Not like most career soldiers. A bitter man, hard as marble. And yet the troops love him. They say he is John Mogen come again. There is even a rumour that he is Mogen's bastard son. It started when they saw him wielding Mogen's sword on the battlefield."

"Mogen," Rusio grunted. "Another upstart bedmate of the Queen."

"That's enough, Colonel," Fournier snapped. "General Menin, may God be good to his soul, obviously saw something in Cear-Inaf, else he would not have postumously promoted him."

"Martin Menin knew his death was near. It clouded his thinking," Rusio said heavily.

"Perhaps. We will never know. Do we have any inkling of our current Commander in Chief's plans for the future?"

"It will take time to reorganize and refit the army after the beating it took. The Merduks have withdrawn halfway to the Searil for the moment, so we have a breathing space. There is still no word from Berza and the fleet though. If they succeed in destroying the Merduk supply dumps on the Kardian, then we may be left alone until the spring."

"We have some time to work in then. That's good. Gentlemen, unless anyone has a further point to raise, I think this meeting is over. Venuzzi, I take it your people are all in place."

The steward nodded. "You shall know what he has for breakfast before he has it himself."

"Excellent," Fournier rose. "Gentlemen, good night. I suggest we do not all depart at once. Such things get noticed."

In ones and twos they took their leave, until only Aras and Willem were left. The older officer rose and set a hand on Aras's shoulder. "You have your doubts about our little conspiracy, do you not, Aras?"

"Perhaps. Is it wrong to wish for victory, no matter who leads us to it?"

"No. Not at all. But we are the leaders of our country. We must think beyond the present crisis, look to the future."

"Then we are becoming politicians rather than soldiers."

"For the moment. Don't be too hard on yourself. And do not forget whose side you are on. This Corfe is a shooting star, blazing bright today, forgotten tomorrow. We will all be here long after his gloryhunting has taken him to his grave." Willem slapped the younger man's shoulder, and left.

Aras remained alone in the empty room, listening to the late-night revellers below, the clatter of carts and waggons in the cobbled streets beyond. He was remembering. Remembering the sight of the Merduk heavy cavalry charging uphill into the maw of cannon, the Fimbrian pikes skewering screaming horses, men shrieking and snarling in a storm of slaughter. That was how the great issues of this world were ultimately decided; in a welter of killing. The man who could impose his own will upon the fuming chaos of battle would ultimately prevail. Before the King's Battle Aras had thought himself ambitious, a leader of men. He was no longer so sure. The responsibilities of command were too awesome.

"What will it be?" he said aloud to the firelight, the glowing candles.

Either way, he would end up betraying something.

FIVE

HIS WOODEN HEELS clicked on the floor like the castanets entertainers danced by. She had tried to make him don shoes, but he seemed fascinated by the sight of his timber toes tapping on marble. Many times, he sagged or slipped and she had to steady him. When she did, the pain speared into her ribs, making her breath come short. He had struck her there with his new knee as she held him down in the midst of Golophin's magicking. But there was no time for trivialities like that. Hebrion had a King again. With her help he was stalking and staggering up and down the Royal chambers like an unsteady lion pacing its cage.

And I have a husband, the thought came to her unbidden. *Or will have. A man half human, and the other half – what?*

"Unbelievable," King Abeleyn of Hebrion muttered. "Golophin has really surpassed himself this time. But why wood? Old Mercado got himself a silver face – couldn't I have been given limbs of steel or iron?"

"He was in a hurry," Isolla told him. "They vote on the regency today. There was nothing else available."

"Ah, yes. My noble cousins, flapping round me like gore-crows looking for a beakfull of the Royal carcass. What a shock it'll be when I walk in on the dastards! For I will walk in, Isolla. And in full mail too."

"Don't overdo things. We don't want you looking like an apparition."

Abeleyn grinned, the same grin that had quickened her heart as a girl. He was still boyish when he smiled, despite the grey of his hair and the scars on his face. "Golophin may have had to fix my legs, Issy, but the rest of me is still flesh and blood. How do you feel about marrying a carpenter's bench?"

"I'm not a romantic heroine in some ballad, Abeleyn.

Folk with our blood marry out of policy. I'll wear your ring, and both Astarac and Hebrion will be the better off for it."

"You haven't changed. Still the sober little girl with the world on her shoulders. Give us a kiss."

"Abeleyn!"

He tried to embrace her and pull her face towards his, but his wooden feet slipped on the stone floor and he went down with a clack and crash, pulling her with him. They landed in a billow of her brocade and silks, and Abeleyn roared with laughter. He kept his grip, and kissed her full on the mouth, one hand cradling the hollow of her neck. She felt the colour flame into her face as she pulled away.

"That put the roses into your cheeks!" he chortled. "By God Issy, you grew up well. That's a fine figure you've got lurking under those skirts."

"That's enough, my lord. You'll injure yourself. This is unbecoming."

"I'm alive, Isolla. Alive. Let me forget Royal dignity for a while and taste the world." His hand brushed her naked collarbone, drifted lower and caressed the swell of one breast where the stiff robe pushed it upwards. A jolt ran through her that dried up the words in her mouth. No-one had ever touched her in that way. She wanted it to stop. She wanted it to go on.

"Well sire, I see you are feeling better," a deep, musical voice said.

They disentangled themselves at once and Isolla helped the King to his feet. Golophin stood by the door with his arms folded, a crooked smile on his face.

"Golophin, you old goat," Abeleyn cried. "Your timing is as inept as ever."

"My apologies, lad. Isolla, get him to the bed. You've excited him enough for one morning."

Isolla had nothing to say. Abeleyn leaned heavily on her as she helped him back to the large four-poster. Only a two-poster now; the other two were grafted onto the King's stumps.

"My people have to see me," Abeleyn said earnestly. "I can't sit around in here like an ageing spinster – no offence, Isolla."

She tugged sharply at his hair, suddenly eleven years old again.

But he had changed that quickly. The boy disappeared. "Issy here has given me the bare bones of it. Now, you tell me, Golophin. It's written all over your face. What's been going on?" On his own visage as the humour faded, pain and exhaustion added an instant fifteen years to his age.

"You can probably guess." Golophin poured all three of them wine from the decanter by the King's bed and drained half his own glass in a single swallow.

"It's been only a few weeks, but your mistress Jemilla –"

"Ex-mistress," Abeleyn said quickly, glancing at Isolla. A warmth crept about her heart. She found herself taking the King's hand in her own. It was dry and hot but it returned her pressure.

"Ex-mistress," Golophin corrected himself. "She's proven herself quite the little intriguer. As we speak, a gathering of Hebrion's nobles gathers in the old Inceptine abbey and squabbles over the regency of the kingdom."

Abeleyn did not seem surprised, or even outraged. He said nothing for a moment. He was staring at his wooden legs. Finally he looked up. "Urbino, I'm thinking. The dry old fart. She'll find it easy to manage him, and he'll wield the most clout."

"Bravo, sire. He's the leading candidate."

"I knew Jemilla was ambitious, but I underrated her."

"A formidable woman," Golophin agreed.

"When is the vote?"

"This afternoon, at the sixth hour."

"Then it would seem I do not have much time. Golophin, call for a valet. I must have decent clothes. And a bath."

The old wizard approached his King, set a hand on the young man's shoulder. "Are you sure you are up to this lad? Even if Urbino is voted the regency today, all you have to do is make an appearance at any time, and he'll have to give it up. It might be better if you rested a while."

"No. Thousands of my people died to put me back on the throne. I'll not let one scheming bitch and her dried-up puppet take it from me. Get some people in here, Golophin. And I want to speak to Rovero and Mercado. We shall have a little military demonstration this afternoon I think. Time to put these bastard conspirators in their place."

Golophin bowed deeply. "At once, sire. Let me locate a couple of the more discreet palace servants. If we can keep your recovery quiet until this afternoon, then the impact will be all the greater." He left noiselessly.

Abeleyn sagged. "Give me a hand here, Isolla. Damn things weigh a ton."

She helped him arrange the wooden legs on the bed. He seemed to find it hard to keep his eyes off them.

"I never felt it," he said quietly. "Not a thing. Strange, that. A man has half his body ripped away and it does not even register. I can feel them now, though. They itch and smart like flesh and blood. Lord God, Isolla, what are you marrying?"

She hugged him close. It seemed amazingly natural to do so. "I am marrying a king, my lord. A very great king." Without thinking, she caressed his hair gently. It was silver-grey now, and when his face was in repose it made him look like some hale veteran of many wars.

He gripped her hand until the blood fled from it, his head bent into her shoulder. When he spoke again his voice was thick and harsh, too loud.

"Now where are those damn valets? The service has gone to Hell in this place."

ABRUSIO HAD ONCE been home to a quarter of a million people. A fifth of the population had died in the storming of the city, and tens of thousands more had packed up their belongings and left the capital for good. The trade which was the lifeblood of the great port had been reduced to a tithe of its former volume, and men were still working by the thousand to clear the battered wharves, repair bombarded warehouses and demolish those structures too broken to be restored. A wide swathe of the lower city had been reduced to a charred wasteland, and in this desolation thousands more were encamped like squatters under makeshift shelters.

But in the upper city the damage was less, and here, where the nobility of Hebrion had their great town houses, and the guilds of the city their halls, the only evidence of the recent fighting lay in the cannonballs which still pocked some

structures like black carbuncles, and the shallow craters in
the cobbled streets which had been filled with gravel.

And here, on the summit of one of the twin hills which
topped Abrusio, the old Inceptine monastery and abbey
glowered down on the Port-city. Within the huge refectory
of the Inceptine Order, the surviving aristocracy of the
kingdom were assembled in all their finery to vote upon the
very future of the kingdom.

THERE HAD BEEN a scurry of last minute deals and agreements,
of course, men shuffling and intriguing frantically to be part
of the new order that was approaching. But by and large
it had gone precisely as Jemilla had planned. Today, Duke
Urbino of Imerdon would be appointed Regent of Hebrion,
and the Lady Jemilla would be publicly proclaimed as the
mother of the crippled King's heir. She would be Queen in
everything but name. *What would Richard Hawkwood
have made of that?* she wondered, as the nobles convened
before her in their maddening, leisurely fashion, and
Urbino's face, for once wreathed in smiles, shone down the
great table at his fellow blue-bloods.

A crowd had gathered outside the abbey to await the
outcome of the Council. Jemilla's steward had bribed several
hundred of the city dregs to stand there and cheer when the
news was announced, and they had, in the manner of things,
been joined by a motley throng of some several thousand who
sensed the excitement in the air. Jemilla had also thoughtfully
arranged for fifty tuns of wine to be set up at various places
about the city so that the Regent's health might be drunk
when the criers went forth to spread the tidings about the
change of government. The wine ought to assuage any pangs
of uneasiness or lingering Royalist feeling left in the capital.
Nothing had been left to chance. This thing was here, now,
in her hand. What would she do first? Ah, that Astaran bitch,
Isolla. She'd be sent packing, for a start.

As the hubbub within the abbey died down and the
nobles took their places, it was possible to hear the clamour
of the crowds outside. It had risen sharply. They sounded as
though they were cheering. *Mindless fools,* Jemilla thought.

Their country is in ruins about their ears but splash them a measure of cheap wine and they'll make a holiday.

The nobles were finally assembled, and seated according to all the rivalries and nuances of rank. Duke Urbino rose in his space at the right hand of the King's empty chair. He looked as though he was trying not to grin, a phenomenon which sat oddly on his long, mournful face. The horsetrading which had occupied them day and night for the last several days was over. The outcome of the vote was already known to all, but the legal niceties had to be observed. In a few minutes he would be the *de facto* ruler of Hebrion, one of the great princes of the world.

"My dear cousins," Urbino began – and stopped.

The din of the crowds had risen to a roaring pitch of jubilation, but now they in turn were being drowned out be the booming thunder of artillery firing in sequence.

"What in the world?" Urbino demanded. He looked questioningly at Jemilla, but she could only frown and shake her head. No doing of hers.

The assembly listened in absolute silence. It sounded like a regular bombardment.

"My God, it's the Knights Militant – they've come back," some idiot gushed.

"Shut up!" another snapped.

They listened on. Urbino stood as though turned to wood, his head cocked to the sound of the guns. They were very close by – they must be firing from the battlements of the palace. But why? And then Jemilla realised, with a sickening plunge of spirit. It was a salute.

"Count the guns!" she cried, heedless of the shrill crack in her voice.

"That's nineteen now," one of the older nobles said. Hardio of Pontifidad, she remembered. A Royalist. His face was torn between hope and dismay.

The echoing rumble of the explosions finally died away, but the crowds were still cheering manically. Twenty eight guns. The salute for a reigning king. What in the world was going on?

"Maybe it's for the new Regent," someone said, but Hardio shook his head.

"That'd be twenty-two guns."

"Perhaps he's dead," one of the dullards suggested. "They always fire a salute on the death of a king."

"God forbid," Hardio rasped, but most of the men present looked relieved. It was Jemilla who spoke, her voice a lash of scorn.

"Don't be a fool. You hear the crowds? You think they'd be cheering the death of the King?" It was slipping way – she could feel it. Somehow Golophin and Isolla had stymied her. But how?

The question was soon answered. There was a deafening blare of horns outside and the clatter of many horses. A Royal fanfare was blown over and over. Beyond the great double doors of the refectory they could hear the tramp of feet marching in step. Then a sonorous boom as someone struck the doors fom the outside.

"Open in the name of the King!"

A group of timorous retainers belonging to Urbino's household stood there, unsure. They looked to their lord for orders, but he seemed lost in shock. It was Jemilla who rapped out – "Open the damn doors, then!"

They did so. Those inside the hall stood as one, scraping back their chairs on the old stone. Beyond the doors were two long files of Hebrian arquebusiers dressed in the rich blue of Royal livery. Banner-bearers stood, the Hibrusid gonfalons a silk shimmer above their heads. And at the head of them all, a tall figure in black half-armour, his face hidden by a closed helm upon which the Hebrian Crown gleamed in a spangle of gems and gold.

Wordlessly, the files of arquebusiers entered the room and lined the walls. Their match was lit and soon filled the chamber with the acrid reek of gunpowder. The solitary figure in the closed helm entered last, the banner-bearers closing the doors shut behind him. The assembled nobles stood as though turned to stone, until a hard voice snapped, "Kneel before your King." And the figure in black unhelmed. The aristocracy of Hebrion stared, gaped, and then did as they were bidden. The figure in the black armour was without a doubt Abeleyn IV, King of Hebrion and Imerdon.

He was taller than they remembered, and he looked old enough now to be the father of the young man they had once known. No trace of the boy-king remained. His eyes were like glitters of black frost as he surveyed the kneeling throng. Jemilla remained in her seat by the fire, too paralyzed to move, but he did not even glance at her. The chamber stank of fear as much as the burning match. He could have them all shot down, here and now, and no-one would be able to lift a finger.

Hardio and a few others who had been against the regency from the first were beaming. "Give you joy of your recovery, sire," the old nobleman said. "This is a glad day for the kingdom."

The severity on the seamed face of the King lifted somewhat: they glimpsed the youth of a few months past. "My thanks, Hardio. Noble cousins, you may rise."

A collective sigh, lost in the noise of the gathered aristocrats getting off their knees. They were to live, then.

"Now," the King went on quietly, "I believe you were gathered here to discuss matters of import that concern my realm." No-one missed the easy emphasis on the *my*, the momentary departure from the Royal *we*.

"We will – if you do not object – take our place at the head of this august gathering."

"By – by all means, sire," Urbino stammered. "And may I also congratulate you on recovering your health and faculties."

Abeleyn took the empty throne which headed the long table. His gait was odd – he walked on legs which seeemd too long for him, rolling slightly like a sailor on the deck of a pitching ship.

"I was not aware our faculties had ever been lost, Urbino," he said, and the coldness in his voice chilled the room. The nobles were once again aware of the lines of armed soldiers at their backs.

"But your concern is noted," the King continued. "It shall not be forgotten." And here Abeleyn's eyes swept the room, coming to rest at last on Jemilla.

"We trust we see you well, lady."

It took her a second to find her voice. "Very well, my lord."

"Excellent. But you should not be worrying yourself with the problems of state in your condition. You have our leave to go."

There was no choice for her, of course. She curtsied clumsily, and then left the room. The great doors boomed shut behind her, shutting her away from her ambitions and dreams. Jemilla kept her chin tilted high, oblivious to the roaring jubilation of the crowds outside, the grinning soldiers. Not until she had reached the privacy of her own apartments did she let the tears and the fury run unchecked.

"A VERY SATISFACTORY state of affairs," Himerius, High Pontiff of the Ramusian kingdoms of the west, said.

It was a day of brilliant sunshine which blazed off the snow-covered Narian Hills all around and glittered in blinding facets upon the peaks of the Cimbric Mountains to the east. Himerius stood foursquare against the bitter wind which billowed down from those grim heights, and when he exhaled the white smoke of his breath was shredded instantly away. Behind him, a group of monks in Inceptine black huddled within their habits and discreetly rubbed their hands together within voluminous sleeves in a futile effort to keep the blood in their fingers warm.

"Indeed, your Holiness," bluff, florid-cheeked Betanza said. "It could not have gone more smoothly. As we speak, Regent Marat is preparing an expeditionary force of some eight thousand men. They should be here in some fifteen days, if the weather holds."

"The couriers have gone out to Alstadt?"

"They went yesterday, under escort of a column of Knights. I would estimate that within three months we will have a fortified garrison in the Torrin Gap, ready to repel any Merduk reconnaisance, or to serve as a staging post for further endeavours."

"And what news from Vol Ephrir?"

"King Cadamost will accept a garrison on the Astaran border, but it must not be of Almarkan nationals. Knights Militant only – it is a question of national pride, you understand. Unfortunately, we do not currently have any Knights to spare."

"Almarkan troops are now the servants of the Church as much as the Knights Militant. If it will ease Perigraine's conscience the Almarkans can be clad in the livery of the Knights, but we must install our troops in southern Perigraine. Is that clear, Betanza?"

"Perfectly, Holiness. I shall see to it at once."

"Cadamost shall be made an honorary Presbyter of course. It is the least I can do. He is a faithful son of the Church, truly. But he cannot afford to think of Perigraine alone at a time like this. We must present a united front against the heretics. If Skarp-Hethin of Finnmark is willing to accept Almarkan garrisons, then Cadamost has no reason not to do likewise."

"Yes of course, your Holiness. It is merely a question of prestige. Skarp-Hethin is a Prince, and his principality has traditionally been closely allied with Almark. But Perigraine is a sovereign state. Some of the diplomatic niceties must be observed."

"Yes, yes. I am not a child, Betanza. Just get it done. I care not what hoops you have to jump through, but we must have the forces of the Church garrisoned throughout those kingdoms which acknowledge her spiritual supremacy. This is a time of crisis – I will not have the debacle of Hebrion repeated. We lost an entire kingdom to the heretics there because we had insufficient forces on the ground. That must never happen again."

"Yes, Holiness."

"If we are to strike back at the heretics then it can only be east through the Torrin Gap, and south into East Astarac... Still no word from Fimbria?"

"No, Holiness. Though rumour has it that the Fimbrian army sent east by the Electors was destroyed along with the Ormann Dyke garrison at the Battle of the North More."

"Rumour? We base our policy on rumours now?"

"It is difficult to obtain reliable information on the eastern war, Holiness. I have also heard that there has been a great battle close to the gates of Torunn itself, but of its outcome, we have no word."

"Have we no reliable scources in Torunn?"

"We have, yes, but with the Torunnan capital virtually under siege, it is a slow business getting their intelligence this far."

Himerius said nothing. His face was drawn and haggard in the harsh sunlight, but the eyes within it were bright as gledes. Over the past days he had displayed an astonishing reservoir of energy for a man of his years, working far into every night with shifts of scribes and scholars and Almarkan military officers. Privately, Betanza wondered how long he could keep it up. The Ramusian Church – or this version of it at any rate – had in a space of weeks been transformed into a great Empire which now encompassed not only Almark, but Finnmark, Perigraine, and half a dozen other minor principalities and duchies also. Cadamost of Perigraine, appalled by the carnage in the heretical states of Hebrion, Astarac and Torunna, had hastened to place his own kingdom under the protective wing of Charibon. *A loyal son of the Church indeed*, Betanza thought, *but one without any balls to speak of*.

Betanza himself regarded this sudden transformation of the Church with mixed feelings. He was Vicar-General of the Inceptine Order, the second most powerul figure in the Church hierarchy, but he found himself wondering about the accumulation of power that was taking place here. If Torunn had become the focus of resistance to the Merduk invasions, then Charibon was now the centre of a huge new power-bloc which stretched from the Malvennor Mountains in the west to the Cimbrics in the east, and even extended as far north as the Sultanate of Hardukh, not far from the foothills of the Northern Jafrar. Only Fimbria, in her heyday, had ever governed a tract of land so large, and the men who had had this awesome responsibility thrust so precipitately upon their shoulders were clerics, priests with no experience in governance. It made him uneasy. It also seemed not quite right to him that the head of the Ramusian faith in Normannia should spend twenty hours a day dictating orders for the levying of troops and the movement of armies. He had not joined the Church to become a general; he had done his soldiering in the lay world and wanted no more of it.

He looked up and out to where the savage peaks of the Cimbric mountains brooded, white and indomitable. The snow was blowing in great streaks and banners from their summits, as though the mountains were smoking. The world was on fire; the world he had known as a boy and a young man tottered on the brink of dissolution. *If only Aekir had not fallen*, he found himself thinking. *If only Macrobius had not been lost.*

Such thinking was absurd, of course, and dangerous. They had all to make the best of it. But why did he feel so afraid, so apprehensive of the future? Perhaps it was the change in Himerius. The Pontiff had always been a proud, vain man, capable of ruthless intrigue. But now it seemed that the ambition had left the faith behind. The man never *prayed* anymore. Could that be right, in the Head of the Church? And that odd light in his eyes occasionally, at night. It seemed otherworldly. Unsettling.

I am tired, Betanza thought. *I am tired, and I am older than I think I am. Why not step down, and walk the cloisters, contemplate the world beyond this one, and the God who created it? It is what I donned this habit to do, after all.*

But he knew the answer even as he asked the question. He would not stand down because he was afraid of whom Himerius might find to replace him. Already half the Church Hierarchy had been reshuffled – Escriban, Prelate of Perigraine was gone already. He had too independent a mind to sit easily with the New Order. Himerius had installed Pieter Goneril in his place, a non-entity who would do exactly as he was told. And Presbyter Quirion of the Knights Militant, as good a man who ever lifted a sword in the service of the Church, and a personal friend – he was gone now too, rotting in some little Almarkan border town. He had lost Hebrion to King Abeleyn, and over a thousand Knights besides. That could not be forgiven.

Charibon is become a Royal court, Betanza thought. *We are become nothing more than errand-runners for its black-clad monarch. And our faith? What has happened to it?*

He found it hard to admit to himself what nagged at him most, and caused him to wake up sweating in the middle of the cold nights. An old scrap of wandering prophesy dreamed up by a madman, but a madman who was nevertheless one of the Founding Fathers of the Church.

And the Beast shall come upon the earth in the days of the Second Empire of the world. And he shall rise up out of the west, the light in his eyes terrible to behold. With him shall come the Age of the Wolf, when brother will slay brother. And all men shall fall down and worship him.

Betanza had never been much of a reader before he set aside his Ducal robes and donned the black habit. In fact, strictly speaking, he had been illiterate. But he had learned his letters in his years with the Church, and now he found reading to be an occupation he loved. He had shelves of books in his chambers, among them certain tomes which, were they found in the possession of a novice, might just consign that novice to the pyre. He had begun collecting them after the strange murder of Commodius the Chief Librarian in the bowels of the great library of St. Garaso. There was a chill in his gut as he recalled the lines from the *Book of Honorius*. A madman's ravings or true prescience? No-one could say. And why had Commodius been murdered? Again, no-one knew. His investigations had led nowhere. The two monks who were the prime suspects had disappeared into the night. Oddly, Himerius had seemed unconcerned, more preoccupied with sealing off the catacombs below the library than with tracking down the murderers.

Lord God, it was cold! Would spring never come? What a terrible year.

Himerius had taken to roving the battlements of the cathedral trailed by a gaggle of scribes and subordinates. It helped him think, he said. That was why they were up here now, insects scurrying along the backbone of a slumbering stone giant, Charibon spread out below them like a toy city. The Sea of Tor was still frozen about its margins, and Betanza could see crowds of the local people out fishing on the ice. The winter had been hard on them, and harder still was the billeting in their homes of troops. Lines of soldiers marched into Charibon every day now, it seemed. The monastery city was becoming an armed camp.

Himerius strolled along the battlements dictating to his scribes. Betanza did not move, and only one cleric elected to remain with him. Old Rogien, head of the Pontifical household. His wrinkled face seemed almost transparent in the harsh light, the veins blue at his temples.

"Thinking, Brother?"

Betanza smiled. "I have much to ponder."

"Haven't we all? His Holiness is a man of phenomenal abilities."

"Phenomenal, yes."

"You sound a little disgruntled, Brother."

"Me?" Betanza glanced at the Pontiff's group. They were out of earshot. And he had known Rogien a long time. "Not disgruntled, Rogien. Apprehensive, perhaps."

"Ah. Well, in time of war, that is every man's right."

"We are not soldiers, though."

"Aren't we? We may not wear mail and wield swords, but we are warriors of a sort nonetheless."

"And Charibon is not a barracks for all the soldiery of Almark."

"But we are on the frontier now, Betanza. They say the Merduks have been sighted even on the eastern shores of the Sea of Tor itself. Charibon was sacked once, by the Cimbric tribes. Would you have it sacked again?"

Betanza grimaced. "You know very well that is not what I mean."

"Maybe I do," Rogien lowered his voice and drew close. "But you will not find me admitting it."

"Why not? Is free speech no longer allowed in Charibon?"

Rogien chuckled. "Come now Betanza – since when has free speech *ever* been allowed in Charibon?"

"You speak of heresy. I speak of policy," Betanza was not amused. But the older monk was unfazed.

"It is all the same these days – if you do not know that yet, then you have not been paying attention. Come now, Brother – you were a Duke, a man of power in the secular world. Are you so naïve? Relearn the skills which you used before you donned that habit. They will prove invaluable in the days to come."

"Damn it Rogien, I did not become a monk to become some monastic aristocrat."

"Oh please, Brother. You are a member of the most politicised religious order in the world – more than that, you are its head. Don't come the martyred ascetic to me. If you meant what you say you'd be in a grey habit and bare feet, preaching to the poor in some dung-heap town in Astarac."

Betanza could not reply. Rogien was right, of course. But it did not help.

"Come," he said, nodding to the receding backs of the Pontiff and his entourage. "We're being left behind."

"No, Brother," Rogien said coldly. "*You* are being left behind."

Six

THE OLD CONFERENCE chamber of the Torunnan High
Command was a cavernous place, the walls lined with
marble pillars, the fireplaces at each end large enough
for a grown man to stand upright within. The ceiling
arched up into a gloom of ancient rafters all hung with
banners and battle-flags whose bright colours had been
dimmed by age and smoke and dust – and the blood of the
men who had died carrying them in battle. The building
dated back to the Fimbrian Hegemony, but it had not
been used in years – King Lofantyr preferring to meet his
Generals in more congenial chambers within the palace.
But Queen Odelia, now ruler of Torunna, had reopened
the hall wherein John Mogen and Kaile Ormann had
once propounded their strategies. As the hierarchy of the
Torunnan army gathered within for their first conference
with the new Commander-in-Chief, the ghosts of those
past giants seemed to loom heavily out of the shadows.

The assembled officers were clad in their court dress:
blue for the artillery, black for infantry and deep burgundy
for the cavalry. They were an imposing crowd, though an
experienced commander might have noted that they were
all either very young or very old for their rank. Torunna's
most talented officers were all dead. John Mogen and
Sibastion Lejer at Aekir, Pieter Martellus at Ormann
Dyke, Martin Menin in the King's Battle. What remained
was the rump of a once great military machine. Torunna
had come to the end of the rope. There were no more
reserves to call up, and no-one expected the Fimbrians
to send another army to their rescue, not after the first
one had been decimated to little purpose up on the North
More. It was true that the Cimbric tribes were trickling

down out of the mountains to join them in ever increasing numbers, but none of the men present in that historic chamber thought much of the military abilities of those savages, for all that they had accomplished under General Cear-Inaf. They were a freakish anomaly, no more. Their presence at the King's funeral had been in bad taste, it was widely agreed, but the crowds had clamoured to see the famously exotic red horsemen stand guard in rank on scarlet rank as Lofantyr was laid to rest.

The chatter in the chamber was cut short as the general in question entered, and on his arm was the Queen herself. Odelia seated herself at the head of the long table that occupied the middle of the room and the rest of its occupants followed suit, some of them sharing quick, sceptical glances. A woman, at a war-council! A few of the more observant men there noted also the way the Monarch looked at her most recently promoted general, and decided that palace gossip might be in the right of it after all.

It was General Cear-Inaf who rose in his seat to bring the council to order. The Torunnan officers sat dutifully attentive. This man shouldered the burden of the kingdom's very survival. As importantly, he could make or break the career of any one of them.

"You all know me, or know of me," Corfe said. "I served under Mogen at Aekir, and fled my post when the city fell. I served at Ormann Dyke also – as did Andruw and Ranafast here. I commanded the forces that fought at the North More, and led the withdrawal after the King's Battle. Fate has seen fit to make me your commanding officer, and therefore, whatever your personal feelings, you will obey my orders as though they were the Word of God. That is how an army operates. I will always be open to suggestions and ideas from any one of you, and you may ask to see me in person at any time of the day or night. But my word in any military matter is final. Her Majesty has flattered me with her confidence in the running of this war, and I am to have an entirely free hand. But there will be no more arguments about seniority or precedence in the officer class. Promotion will from now on be won through merit alone, not through family connections or length of service. Are there any questions?"

No-one spoke. They had expected as much. A peasant who had risen through the ranks could hardly be expected to respect the values of tradition or social rank.

"Very good. Now, I have recieved in the last hour a message from Admiral Berza and the fleet, conveyed by despatch-galley. He informs me that he has located and destroyed two of the Merduk supply dumps on the shores of the Kardian Sea –"

A buzz of talk, quickly stilled as Corfe held up a hand.

"He writes that the Merduk casualties can be measured in the thousands, and he believes that he has sent perhaps three or four million of rations up in smoke. However, his own casualties were heavy. Of the marine landing parties, less than half survived, and he also lost two of his twenty-three great ships in the landings. At the time of writing, he has put to sea again to engage a Nalbenic fleet which is purportedly sailing north up the Kardian to secure the Merduk lines of communication. I have already sent him a set of orders which basically give him free rein. Berza is a capable man, and understands the sea better than any of us here. The fleet will therefore not be coming back upriver to the capital for the foreseeable future."

"But that leaves the line of the river wide open!" Colonel Rusio protested. "The Merduks will be able to cross at any spot they please and outflank us!"

"Correct. But intelligence suggests that the main Merduk field army has fallen back at least forty leagues from Torunn and is busy repairing the Western Road as far east as Aekir itself in order to maintain an alternative line of communication free from the depredations of our ships. I believe the enemy is too busy at present, gentlemen, to launch another assault. Andruw – if you please."

Corfe took his seat and Andruw rose in his turn. He looked a trifle nervous as the eyes of the High Command swivelled upon him, and cleared his throat whilst consulting a sheaf of papers in his hand.

"The main army has withdrawn, yes, but our scouting parties have reported that the Merduks are sending flying columns of a thousand or so up into the north-west, towards the Torrin Gap. They are obviously a reconnaissance-in-force, feeling out a way through the Gap to the Torian Plains beyond. Already, people fleeing these raids have made their way across the Searil and some have even come as far south as Torunn itself. The Merduk columns are sacking what towns and villages they find as they go, and we have unconfirmed reports that they are constructing a fortress or a series of fortresses up there, to use as staging posts for – for further advances. There may in fact be an entire Merduk army already operating in the north." Andruw sat down, obviously relieved to have gotten it out without a stumble.

"Bastards," someone murmured.

"Well there is obviously nothing we can do about that at the present," Colonel Rusio said impatiently. "We have to concentrate our efforts here in the capital. The army needs to be reorganised and refitted before it will be fit for further operations."

"Agreed," Corfe said, "but we cannot afford to take too long to do it. What we lack in numbers we must make up in audacity. I do not propose to sit tamely in Torunn whilst the Merduks ravage our country at will. They must be made to pay for every foot of Torunnan ground they try to occupy."

"Hear, hear," one of the younger officers said, and subsided quickly when his seniors turned a cold eye upon him.

"So," Corfe said heavily, "what I propose is that we send north a flying column of our own. My command suffered less severely than the main body of the army in the recent battle, plus I have just received an influx of new recruits. I intend to take it and clear northern Torunna of at least some of these raiders, then sweep back down towards the capital. It will be an intelligence-gathering operation as much as anything else. We need hard information on the enemy strength and dispositions in the north-west. Thus far we have been relying too heavily on the tales of refugees and couriers."

"I hope, General, that you are not impugning the professionalism of my officers," Count Fournier, head of Torunnan Military Intelligence, snapped.

"Not at all, Count. But they cannot work miracles, and besides, I still need most of them where they are – keeping an eye on the Merduk main body. A larger scale of operation is needed to clean up the north-west. My command will be able to brush aside most resistance up there and reassure the remaining population that we have not abandoned them. That has to be worth doing."

"A bold plan," Colonel Rusio drawled. "When do you intend to move, General – and who will be left in command here in the capital?"

"I shall ride out within the week. And you, Colonel, will be left in charge while I am away. The Queen has graciously approved my recommendation that you be promoted to general." Here, Corfe took up a sealed scroll which had been lying unobtrusively before him, and tossed it to the new general in question.

"Congratulations, Rusio."

Rusio's face was a picture in astonishment. "I have no words to express – that is to say... Your Majesty, you have my undying gratitude."

"Do not thank us," Odelia said crisply. "General Cear-Inaf has stated that you merit such a promotion and so we approved it. Make sure you fulfil our faith in you, General."

"Majesty, I – I will do all in my power to do so." Up and down the table, older officers such as Willem watched the exchange with narrowed eyes, and while several officers leaned over in their seats to shake Rusio's hand, others merely looked thoughtful.

"Your job, Rusio," Corfe went on, "is to get the main body of the army back in fighting trim. I expect to be away a month or so. By the time I get back I want it ready to march forth again."

Rusio merely nodded. He was clutching his commission as though he were afraid it might suddenly be wrenched away from him. His lifetime's ambition realised in a moment. The prospect seemed to have left him dazed.

"A month is not long to march an army up to the Thurians and back again, General," Count Fournier said. "It must be all of fifty leagues each way."

"Closer to seventy-five," Corfe retorted. "But we will not have to walk all the way. Colonel Passifal."

The Quartermaster General nodded. "There are a score of heavy grain lighters tied up at the wharves as we speak. Each of them could hold eight or nine hundred men with ease. With the wind coming off the sea, as it does for weeks at this time of year, they'll be able to make a fair pace upstream, despite the current. And they are equipped with heavy sweeps for when the wind fails. I have spoken to their crews: they usually make an average of four knots up the Torrin at this time of year. General Cear-Inaf's command could be up among the foothills in the space of five or six days."

"How very ingenious," Count Fournier murmured. "And if the Merduks assault whilst the general and the cream of our army is off on his river-outing? What then?"

Corfe stared at the thin, sharp-bearded nobleman, and smiled. "Then there will have been a failure of intelligence, my dear Count. Your agents keep sending back despatches insisting that the Merduks are even more disorganised than we are at present. Do you distrust the judgement of your own men?"

Fournier shrugged slightly. "I raise hypotheses is all, General. In war one must prepare for the unexpected."

"I quite agree. I shall remain in close contact with what transpires here in the capital, never fear. If the enemy assaults Torunn in my absence, Rusio will hold them at bay before the walls and I will pitch into their rear as soon as I can bring my command back south. Does that hypothesis satisfy you?"

Fournier inclined his head slightly but made no reply.

There were no further objections to Corfe's plan, but the meeting dragged on for another hour as the High Command wrestled with the logistic details of feeding a large army in a city already swollen with refugees. When at last they adjourned, the Queen kept her seat and ordered Corfe to do likewise. The last of the remaining officers left and Odelia sat watching her young general with her chin resting on one palm whilst he rose and began pacing the spacious chamber helplessly.

"It was a good move," she told Corfe. "And it was necessary. You have taken the wind out of their sails."

"It was a political move," Corfe snarled back. "I never thought I'd see the day I handed over an army to a man I distrust, merely to gain his loyalty – loyalty which should be freely given, in a time like this."

"You never thought you'd see the day when you'd be in a position to hand out armies," she shot back. "At this level, Corfe, the politics of command are as important as any charge into battle. Rusio was a figurehead for the discontented. Now you have brought him into your camp, and defused their intrigues – for a while at least."

"Will he be that grateful, then?"

"I know Rusio. He's been marking time in the Torunn garrison for twenty years. Today you handed him his heart's desire on a plate. If you fall, he will fall now too – he knows that. And besides, he is not such a pitiful creature as you suppose. Yes, he will be grateful, and loyal too I think."

"I just hope he has the ability."

"Who else is there? He's the best of a mediocre lot. Now rest your mind over it. The thing is done, and done well."

She rose with her skirts whispering around her, the tall lace ruff making her face into that of a doll – were it not for the magnificent green eyes that flashed therein. She took his arm, halted his restless pacing.

"You should rest more, let subordinates do some of the running for a change. You are no longer an ensign, nor yet a colonel. And you are exhausted."

He stared at her out of sunken eyes. "I can't. I couldn't even if I wanted to."

She kissed him on the lips, and for a moment he yielded and bent into her embrace. But then the febrile restlessness took him again and he broke away.

"God's blood, Corfe," she snapped, exasperated, "you can't save the world all by yourself!"

"I can try, by God."

They glared at one another with the tension crackling in the air between them, until both broke into smiles in the same instant. They had shared memories now, intimacies known only to each other. It made things both easier and harder.

"We are quite a team, you and I," the Queen said. "Given half a chance I think we might have conquered the world together."

"As it is I'll be happy if we can survive."

"Yes. Survival. Corfe, listen to me. Torunna is at the end of its strength – you know that as well as, or better than I. The people have buried a king and crowned a queen in the same week – the first Queen ever to rule alone in our history. We are swamped with the survivors of Aekir and a third of the realm lies under the boot of the invader whilst the capital itself is in the front line."

Corfe held her eyes, frowning. "So?"

She turned away and began pacing the room much as he had done, her hands clasped before her, rings flashing as her fingers twisted them.

"So hear me out now and do not speak until I am finished.

"My son was a weak man, Corfe. Not a bad man, but weak. He did not have the necessary qualities to rule well – not many men do. This kingdom needs a strong hand. I have the ability – we both know it – to give Torunna that strong hand. But I am a woman, and so every step I take is uphill. The only reason I am tolerated on the throne is because there are no other alternatives at present. The cream of Torunna's nobility died in the King's Battle around their monarch. In any case, Torunnans have never set as much store upon bloodlines as have the Hebrionese, say. But Count Fournier is quite capable of dreaming up some scheme to take power out of my hands and invest it in some form of committee."

Unable to help himself, Corfe interrupted. "That son of a bitch? He'd have to get through the entire army to do it."

Odelia smiled with genuine pleasure, but shook her head. "The army would have no say in the matter. But I am taking the long road to my destination. Corfe, Torunna needs a King – that is the long and the short of it.

"I want you to marry me and take the throne."

Thunderstruck, he sank down onto a chair. There was a long pause during which the Queen looked increasingly irritated.

"Don't look as me as if I'd just grown an extra head! Think about it rationally!"

He found his voice at last. "That's ridiculous."

She clawed the air, eyes blazing furiously. "Open up your blasted mind, Corfe. Forget about your fears and prejudices – I know how humble your origins are, and I care not a whit. You have the ability to be a great king – more importantly, a great warleader. You could pull the country through this war –"

"I can't be a king. Great God lady, I even feel uncomfortable in shoes!"

She threw back her head and laughed. "Then decree that everyone must wear boots – or go barefoot! Put the petty rubbish out of your mind for a moment, and think about what you could accomplish."

"No – no. I am no diplomat. I could not negotiate treaties or – or dance angels on the head of a pin –"

"But you would have a wife who could." And here her voice was soft, her face grave as a mourner's.

"I would be there, Corfe, to handle the court niceties and the damn protocol. And you – you would have the army wholly your own."

"No – I don't understand. We are already there, aren't we? I have the army, you have the throne. Why change things?"

She leaned close. "Because it could be that others will change them for us. You may have won over Rusio today, but you pushed the rest of them even further into a corner. And that is when men are at their most dangerous. Corfe, there is no legal precedent in this kingdom for a queen to rule alone, and thus no legal basis."

"There's no law forbidding it, is there?" he asked stubbornly.

"I don't know – no-one does for sure. I have clerks rifling through the Court Archives as we speak, hoping to turn something up. The death of the King has shocked all the office-seekers for the moment – they glimpsed the cliff upon which this kingdom teeters. But sooner or later the shock will wear off, and my position will be challenged. And if they manage to curb my powers even slightly, there is a good chance they will be able to take the army away from you."

"So there it is."

"So there it is. You see now the sense of what I am suggesting? As King you would be untouchable."

He jumped to his feet, stalked across the room with his mind in a maelstrom. Himself a king – absurd, utterly absurd. He would be a laughing-stock. Torunna would be the joke of the world. It was impossible. He reeled away from even the contemplation of it.

And marriage to this woman. Oddly, that disturbed him more than the idea of the Crown. He turned and looked at her, to find that she was standing before the fire, staring into the flames as though waiting for something. The firelight made her seem younger, though she was old enough to be Corfe's mother. That old.

"Would it be so terrible to be married to me?" she asked quietly, and the insight of her question made Corfe start. She was a witch, after all. Could she read minds as well as everything else?

"Not so terrible," he lied.

"It would be a marriage of convenience," she said, her voice growing hard. "You would no longer have to come to my bed – I am beyond child-bearing age, so there would be no question of an heir. I do not ask you for love, Corfe. That is a thing for the poets. We are talking about a route to power, nothing more." And she turned her back on him, leaned her hands on the mantle as a man might.

Again, that pain in his heart when he looked at her, and imagined the golden hair turned raven, the green eyes grey. Ah, Heria. Lord God, I miss you.

He did not want to hurt this formidable yet vulnerable woman. He did not love her – doubted if he would ever love her or any other woman again. And yet he liked her, very much. More than that, he respected her.

He strode over to the fireplace, stood behind the Queen and placed his hands on hers so that they were standing one within the other. She leaned back into his body and their fingers intertwined, the ornate rings on hers digging into his flesh. Pain, yes. But he did not mind. Nothing good came without pain in this life. He knew that now.

"I would have you as a wife," he said, and in that moment he believed he meant it. "But the Kingship is too lofty a prize for me. I am not the stuff of royalty."

Odelia turned and embraced him, and when she drew

back she looked strangely jubilant, as though she had won something.

"Time will tell," was all she said.

FIFTY LEAGUES FROM where Corfe and his Queen stood, the new winter camps of the Merduk army were almost complete. Tens of thousands of men were toiling here, as they had toiled ceaselessly in the days since the King's Battle. Their redeployment – it was not a withdrawal, or a retreat – entailed a massive labour. They had felled a fair-sized forest to raise a series of stockades that stretched for miles. They had dug ditches and set up thickets of abatis out to the west, all covered by dug-in batteries of artillery. They had erected tall watch-towers, created roads of corduroyed logs and set up their tents within the new defences. A veritable city had sprung up on the plains west of Ormann Dyke, the new roads leading to it thronged with troops coming and going, supply-waggons, artillery limbers, fast-moving couriers, and trudging gangs of Torunnan slaves serving as forced labour. Farther east, nestled within yet more lines of field-fortifications, a vast supply-depot had been set up, and boxes, sacks and barrels of food and ammunition were piled in lines half a mile long and twenty feet high. Crates of blankets and spare uniforms and tents were stacked to one side by the thousand. Waggons plied the bumpy log roads between the depot and the camps continuously, keeping the front-line troops fed and clothed. Perhaps ten square miles of the Torunnan countryside had been thus transformed into the largest and most populous armed camp in the world. Alhough Aurungzeb, Sultan of Ostrabar, was commander-in-chief of this mighty host, it now included large contingents from the Sultanates of Nalbeni, Ibnir and Kashdan. The Merduk states had set aside their differences and were finally combining to settle the issue with the Ramusians once and for all. They aimed now at nothing less than the conquest of all Normannia as far as the Malvennors, and had decided to stop there only because of the dread name of Fimbria.

Aurungzeb himself and his household were not in the winter camps, but had relocated to Ormann Dyke in order to pass the cold weeks of waiting more comfortably. Ostrabar's Sultan stood this day on the tower from which Martellus the Lion had once watched the Merduk assaults break upon the Dyke's impregnable defences, and silken Merduk banners now flew above the long walls that Kaile Ormann had reared up centuries before.

"Shahr Johor," Aurungzeb boomed.

One of the gaggle of soldiers and courtiers who hovered nearby stepped forward. "My Sultan?"

"Do you know how many of our men died trying to take this fortress?"

"No, Highness, but I can find out –"

"It was a question, not an order. Almost thirty thousand, Shahr Johor. And in the end, we never took it, we only outflanked it and forced its evacuation. It is the greatest fortress in the world, it is said. And you know what?"

Shahr Johor swallowed, seeing the flush creep into his Sultan's swarthy cheeks. "What, Highness?"

But the explosion did not happen. Instead, Aurungzeb spoke in a low, reasonable tone. "It is utterly useless to us."

"Yes, Highness."

"The Fimbrians, curse their names, constructed it that way. Approaching it from the east, it is unconquerable. But if you by some chance happen to capture it intact, then it is worthless. All the defences face east. From the west, it is indefensible. Very clever, those Fimbrian engineers must have been."

The courtiers and soldiers waited, wondering if this strange calm were the herald of an unprecedented rage. But when Aurungzeb turned to face them he looked thoughtful.

"I want this fortress destroyed."

Shahr Indun Johor blinked, "Highness?"

"Are you deaf? Level it. I want the Dyke filled in, I want the walls cast down and the tower broken. I want Ormann Dyke wiped off the face of the earth. And when that is accomplished, you shall create another fortress, on the *east* bank of the river, facing west. If by some freakish chance the Ramusians ever manage to push back our armies, then we shall halt them here, on the Searil. And we shall bleed them white as they did us. And Aekir, my new capital – it shall be safe. Golden Aurungabar, greatest city of the world. See to it, Shahr Johor. Gather together our engineers. I want a set of plans drawn up for me to see by tonight. And a model. Yes, a scale model of how it will look, Ormann Dyke obliterated, and this new fortress in its place. I must think of a name..."

Shahr Johor bowed, unnoticed, and left the summit of the tower to do his master's bidding. The courtiers who remained looked at one another. Never before had they heard their Royal master speak of anything save advances and victories, and now here he was planning for defeat. What had happened?

A flabby, glabrous palace eunuch piped up. "My Sultan, do you truly believe that the accursed unbelievers could ever push our glorious armies back to the Searil? Surely, they are in their death throes. We shall soon be feasting in the palace of Torunn."

Aurungzeb stared moodily out at the ancient fortress below him. "I wish I had your optimism, Serrim. This general of the red horsemen. My spies tell me that he is now commander-in-chief of all the Torunnan forces. He and his damned scarlet cavalry have saved the Torunnans from destruction twice now..."

"Who is this man, lord? Do we know? Perhaps our agents –"

Aurungzeb snorted with mirth. "He is, by all accounts, a hard man to kill."

Then his mood soured again. "Leave me, all of you. No – Ahara, you will remain." He broke into halting Normannic. "Ramusian – you stay here also." And in Merduk again: "The rest of you, get out of my sight."

The tower cleared of people, leaving two figures behind. One was a small man in a black habit whose wrists were bound with silver chains. The other was a slim, silk-clad woman whose face was hidden behind a jewelled veil. Aurungzeb beckoned the woman over, the thunder on his brow lifting a little. He twitched aside her veil and caressed a pale cheek.

"Heart of my heart," he murmured. "How does it go with you and my son?"

Heria stroked her abdomen. The bulge was visible now. "We are well my lord. Batak has used his arts to examine the child. It is a healthy boy. In five months, he shall be born." She spoke in the Merduk tongue.

Aurungzeb beamed, encircled Heria's shoulders with one massive arm and sighed with contentment.

"How I love to hear you use our speech. It must become your own, now. The lessons will continue – that tutor has earned his pay." He lowered his voice. "I shall make you my Queen, Ahara. You are a follower of the Prophet now, and you shall be the mother of a sultan one day. My heir cannot have a mere concubine for a dam. Would you like that? Would you like to be a Merduk queen?" And here Aurungzeb set his huge hands on her shoulders and scrutinised her face.

Heria met his eyes. "This is my world, now. You are my lord, the father of my child. There is nothing else. I will be a queen if you wish it. I am yours to do with as you will."

Aurungzeb smiled slowly. "You speak the truth. But you are no slave to me – not any more. A wife you shall be as well as a queen. We will live in Aurungabar, and our union shall be a symbol." Here the Sultan turned and raised his voice so that the black-garbed man behind them might hear.

"The meeting of two peoples, priest. Would you like that? This way the Ramusians who remain east of the Torrin will see that I am not the monster they – and you – believe me to be."

Albrec shuffled forward, more chains clinking invisibly under his habit. "I think it is a worthy idea. I never thought you were a monster, Sultan. I know now that you are not. In the end, a truly great ruler does what is best for his people, not what pleases himself. You are beginning to realise that."

Aurungzeb seemed taken aback by the priest's bluntness. he forced a laugh. "Beard of the Prophet, you are a fearless little madman, I'll give you that. You and your people have courage – Shahr Baraz always told me so. I thought him a sentimental old fool, but I see now he was right."

Heria regarded Aurungzeb with some wonder. She had never before heard him speak of Ramusians with anything resembling moderation. Were the court rumours true then? Was Aurungzeb tiring of war?

He caught her glance, and stepped away towards the parapet.

There was a pause. Finally Heria mustered the resolve to speak. "My lord, do you really believe this new general of the Ramusians is so dangerous?"

"Dangerous? His army is a broken rabble, his country is now led by a woman. Dangerous!" But the words rang hollow somehow.

"Come here, Ahara. Beside me."

She joined him. Albrec stood forgotten behind them.

Together they could look down from the dizzying height of the tower to the battered walls of the fortress and the River Searil beyond, now crossed by the new wooden bridges that the engineers had been working on for weeks. On the far side of the river was the great desolation of craters and rubble that had once been the eastern barbican of the fortress. The Ramusian garrison had packed it with gunpowder and destroyed it just as it fell into the hands of the Merduks.

"Look up on the hills to the east, Ahara. What do you see there?"

"Waggons, my lord, dozens of them. And hundreds of men digging."

"They are digging a mass grave to hold our dead." Aurungzeb's face seemed to slump. "Every time we fight the Torunnans, another must be dug."

"Can it go on much longer, lord? So much killing."

He did not reply at once. He seemed tired – exhausted even. "Ask the holy madman behind you. He has all the answers, it seems."

Albrec clinked forward until he too stood on the lip of the parapet. "All wars end," he said quietly. "But it takes more courage to bring them to a close than it does to start them."

"Platitudes," Aurungzeb said disgustedly.

"Your Prophet, Sultan, did not believe in war. He counselled all men to live as brothers."

"As did your Saint," Aurungzeb countered.

"True. They had much in common, the Prophet and the Saint."

"Listen, priest –" the Sultan began heatedly, but just then there was a clatter of boots on the stairway and a soldier appeared on the parapet, panting. He fell to his knees as Aurungzeb glared.

"Highness, forgive me, but despatches have arrived from our forces in the north. Shahr Johor said you were to be informed immediately. Our men have reached the Torrin Gap, Highness. The way to Charibon is open!"

The trouble on Aurungzeb's brow evaporated. "I'll come at once," and as the soldier leapt up, he followed him off the tower without a backward glance, his stride as energetic as that of a boy. Heria and Albrec were left behind, momentarily forgotten.

"You are from Aekir?" the little priest asked her at once.

"I was married to a soldier of the garrison, and captured in the sack of the city."

"I am sorry. I thought – I am not sure what I thought."

"Why did you come here, Father – to the Merduks?"

"I had a message I wished them to hear."

"They don't seem to be listening."

Albrec shrugged. "Oh, I don't know. I feel the tide is turning. I think he is beginning to listen, or at least to doubt, Ahara."

"My name is Heria Cear-Inaf. I am still Ramusian, no matter who they make me pray to."

"Cear-Inaf." Albrec knew that name. Somewhere he had heard it before. Where?

"What is it?"

"Nothing – no, nothing." It was somehow important he remember, but as was the way with these things, the more he thought about it, the farther it receded.

"The other Sultanates are tiring of the war," Heria said quickly. "Especially Nalbeni – they lost ten thousand men in the last battle, and there are rumours that their fleet is being beaten in the Kardian by Torunnan ships. The army is going hungry because its supply-lines are overstretched, and the levy, the *Minhraib*, they are discontented and want to get back to their farms. If the Torunnans could win one more battle, I think Aurungzeb would sue for peace."

"Why are you telling me this, Heria?"

She looked around as if they might be overheard. "There is not much time. The eunuchs will come for me soon. He has forgotten about us for a moment, but not for long. You must escape back to Torunn, Father. You have to let them know these things. That new general there – they're all afraid of what he might do next, but it must be quick, whatever it is. He must hit them before they recover their nerve."

Albrec felt a chill about his heart. He remembered meeting the leader of a long column of scarlet-armoured horsemen marching out of Torunn. His eyes, as grey as those of the woman who now stood before him.

Who are you?

Corfe Cear-Inaf, Colonel in the Torunnan army.

"Sweet blood of the Saint," Albrec breathed, his face gone white as paper.

"What is it?" Heria demanded. "What's wrong?"

"Lady, you are to come down to the harem at once," a high voice said. They spun round to see the eunuch, Serrim, flanked by a pair of soldiers. "And that Ramusian – he is to go back to his cell."

Heria replaced her veil, her eyes meeting Albrec's in one last, earnest appeal. Then she bowed her head and followed the eunuch away obediently. The Merduk soldiers seized the little priest and shoved him roughly towards the stairs, but he was hardly aware of them.

Coincidence, of course, it had to be. But it was not a common name. And more than that, the look in the eyes of them both. That awful despair.

Lord God, he thought. *Could it be so? The pity of it.*

SEVEN

THE RIVERFRONT OF Torunn was packed with crowds to see them off, so much so that General Rusio had deemed it necessary to station five tercios of troops there to keep the people back from the gangplanks. The last of the horses had been led blindfolded aboard the boats and the great hatches in the sides of the vessels closed up, then re-pitched and caulked while they wallowed at the quays. Corfe, Andruw and Formio stood now alone on the quayside whilst the caulkers climbed back down the tumblehome of the transports and the watermen began the heavy business of unmooring.

General Rusio stepped forward out of the knot of senior officers who had come to see Corfe off. He held out a hand. "Good luck to you then, sir." His face was set, as if he expected to be insulted in some way. But Corfe merely shook the proffered hand warmly. "Look after this place while I'm away, Rusio," he said. "And keep me informed. You have the details of our march, but we may have to cut corners here and there. Multiple couriers."

"Yes sir. I'll send the first out in three days, as arranged."

"Lords and ladies," a thick-necked waterman called out, "if'n you don't want to swim upriver you'd best climb aboard." And he spat into the river for emphasis.

Corfe waved a hand at him, and turned back to Rusio. "Keep the patrols out," he said. "By the time I get back I want to know where every Merduk regiment has so much as dug a latrine."

"I won't let you down, General," Rusio said soberly.

"No – I don't believe you will. All right – Andruw, Formio, you heard the man. Time to join the navy."

The trio hauled themselves up one of the high-sided vessels with the help of manropes that had been installed especially for landsmen. They climbed over the bulwark and stood breathing heavily on the deck of the freighter which Corfe jokingly referred to as his flagship.

"All aboard?" the captain roared out from the little poop at the stern of the vessel.

"Aye sir!"

"Cast off fore and aft. Set topsails and outer jib. Helmsman, two points to larboard as soon as she's under weigh."

"Two points. Aye sir."

A great booming, flapping shadow as the topsails were loosed by the men on the yards high above. The offshore breeze took the sails and bellied them out. The freighter accelerated palpably under Corfe's feet and began to score a white wake through the water. All around them, the other vessels in the convoy were making sail also, and they made a brave sight as they took to the middle of the wide river. The Torrin was almost half a mile in width here at the capital, crossed by two ancient stone bridges whose middle spans were ramps of wood which could be raised by windlass for the passage of ships. They were approaching the first one now, the Minantyr Bridge. As Corfe watched with something approaching wonder, the wooden spans creaked into motion and began rising in the air. Gangs of bridge-raisers were kept permanently employed and worked in shifts day and night to ensure the smooth passage of trade up and down the Torrin. Corfe had always known this, but he had never before been part of it, and as the heavy freighter moved into the shadow of the looming Minantyr Bridge he gawped all about him, for all the world like a country peasant come to see the sights of the city for a day.

They passed through the gurgling, dripping gloom under the raised bridge and emerged into pale winter sunlight again. Their captain, a tall, thin man who nevertheless had a voice of brass, yelled out at his crew. "Unfurl the spanker – look sharp now. Ben Phrenias, I see you. Get up on that goddamned yard."

Andruw and Formio were staring around themselves with something of Corfe's wonder. Neither had ever set foot on a boat before and they had thought that the transports which were to take them upriver would be glorified barges. But the grain freighters, though of shallow draught, displaced over a thousand tons each. They were square-rigged, with a sail plan similar to that of a brigantine, and seemed to all intensive purposes to be great ocean-going ships. To a landsman, at any rate. They had a crew of two dozen or so, though their own captain, Mirio, confessed that they were short-handed. Some of his men had jumped ship and refused to take their vessel north into what was widely seen as enemy-held territory now. As it was, all the ship-owners had been well-paid out of the shrinking Torunnan Treasury, and some of the soldiers constituting the cargo of the sixteen craft Corfe had hired would be able to haul on a rope as well as any waterman.

Inside these sixteen large vessels were eight thousand men and two thousand horses and mules. Corfe was bringing north all his Cathedrallers – some fifteen hundred now, with the recent reinforcements – plus Formio's Fimbrians and all the Dyke veterans who had served under him at the King's Battle. It was, he gauged, a force formidable enough to cope with any enemy formation except the main body of the Merduk army itself. He intended to alight from the freighters far up the Torrin, and then thunder back down to the capital slaughtering every Merduk he chanced across, and delivering north-western Torunna from the invaders – for a while, at least. Awful stories had been trickling south to Torunn in the past few days, tales of rape and mass executions. These things were part and parcel of every war, but there was a grim pattern to the reports: the Merduks seemed intent on depopulating the entire region. It was an important area strategically also, in that it bordered on the Torrin Gap, the gateway to Normannia west of the Cimbrics. The enemy could not be allowed to force the passage of the Gap with impunity.

And the last reason for the expedition. Corfe had to get out of Torunn, away from the court and the High Command, or he thought he would go quietly insane.

Marsch appeared out of one of the wide hatches in the deck of the freighter. He looked careworn and uneasy. It had taken some cajoling to get the tribesmen aboard the ships: such a means of transport was entirely inimical to them, and they feared for the welfare of their horses. Those who remained out of Corfe's original five hundred had been galley-slaves, and they associated ships with their degradation. The others had never before set eyes on anything afloat larger than a rowboat, and the cavernous holds they were now incarcerated within amazed and unsettled them.

Corfe could see that the big tribesman was averting his eyes from the riverbank that coursed smoothly past on the starboard side of the vessel. He gave an impression of deep distaste for everything maritime, yet he had greeted the news of their waterborne expedition without a murmur.

"The horses are calming down," he said as he approached his commander. "It stinks down there." His face was haunted, as if the smell brought back old memories of being chained to an oar with the lash scoring his back.

"It won't be for long," Corfe assured him. "Four or five days at most."

"Bad grazing up north," Marsch continued. "I am hoping we have enough forage with us. Mules carry it, but eat it too."

"Cheer up, Marsch," Andruw said, as irrepressible as ever. "It's better than kicking our heels back in the city. And I for one would rather sit here like a lord and watch the world drift past than slog it up through the hills to the north."

Marsch did not look convinced. "We'll need one, two days to get the horses back into condition when they leave the" – his lips curled around the word – "the *boats*."

"Don't let Mirio hear you calling his beloved *Seahorse* a boat," Andruw laughed, "or he's liable to turn us all ashore. These sailors – your pardon – these *watermen*, are a trifle touchy about their charges, like an old man with a young wife."

That brought a grin to all their faces. Corfe detached himself from the banter and made his way aft to where Mirio was standing taking a stint at the helm. The river-captain nodded unsmilingly at him. "We're making three knots, General. Not as fast as I would have hoped, but we'll get you there."

"Thank you, Captain. You mustn't mind my men. They're new to the river, and to ships."

"Aye, well I'll not pretend that I wouldn't prefer to be shipping a hold full of grain instead of a bunch of seasick soldiers and screaming horses, but we must take what comes, I suppose. There – we're past the last of the river-batteries, and the Royal naval yards."

Corfe looked out towards the eastern bank. The shore – the river was big enough to warrant that name for its banks – was some two cables away. The walls of Torunn came right down to the riverside here, protected by a series of squat towers which hid countless heavy cannon. Jutting out into the Torrin itself were dozens of jetties and wharves, most of them empty, but a few busy with men unloading the small riverboats that plied back and forth across the river here. And sliding behind them now he could glimpse the Royal naval yards of Torunna. Two great ships – tall, ocean-going carracks – were in dry-dock there, their sides propped up by heavy beams and hundreds of men swarming over them in a confusion of wood and rope.

"How far is it to the sea?" Corfe asked, peering aft over the taffrail. Behind the *Seahorse* the remainder of the expedition's vessels were in line astern, the foam flying from their bows as they fought upstream against the curent.

"Some five leagues," Mirio told him. "In times of storm the Torrin is brackish here, and sometimes ships are blown clear up the estuary from the Kardian."

"So close? I had no idea." Corfe had always thought of Torrin as a city divided by a river. Now he realized that it was a port on the fringe of a sea. That was something to remember. He must talk to Berza when the admiral returned to Torunn with the fleet. If the Merduks could transport armies by sea, then so could he.

The wind freshened through the day, and Mirio was able to report with visible satisfaction that they were making five knots. The capital had long disappeared, and now the transports were moving through the heavily populated country to its west. Farmers here reared cattle, planted crops and fished from the river in equal measure. But while the southern shore seemed prosperous and untouched by war, many houses and hamlets to the north were obviously deserted. Corfe saw livestock running wild, barn doors yawning emptily, and in a few places, the blackened shells of burnt villages off on the horizon.

The freighters always moored for the night – the risk of running into a sandbank in the dark was too great. Their practice was to moor the bows to stout trees onshore and drop a light anchor from the stern to keep the vessels from being swept into the bank by the current. The men could not be disembarked en masse, but on Marsch's insistence Corfe saw to it that a few of the horses and mules were brought ashore in shifts all night and exercised up and down the riverbank. It was also an effective way of posting mobile sentries, and the duty was popular with the men, who found their squalid quarters in the depths of the freighters less than congenial.

FOUR DAYS WENT by. The Torrin arced in a great curve until it began to flow almost directly north to south, and then it turned north-west towards its headwaters in the Thurian Mountains. They could see the Thurians on the northern horizon now, still blanketed by snow. And to their left, or to larboard, the stern white peaks of the Cimbrics reared up, their heads lost in grey cloud. There were no more farms on the riverbank now – this region had been sparsely settled even before the war. Now it seemed utterly deserted, a wilderness hemmed in by frowning mountains and bisected by the surging course of the young river.

The Torrin was barely two cables wide here, and occasionally during the fourth day they had all felt the keel of the heavily laden freighter scrape on sunken sand-bars. In addition, the current had become stronger and they averaged barely two knots. On the morning of the fifth day Corfe finally decided to leave the ships behind, to the obvious relief of both soldiers and watermen, and the sixteen huge craft spent an anxious morning edging and nudging their way to the eastern bank, before dropping every anchor they possessed in order to hold fast against the efforts of the river to shove them downstream.

What followed was a prolonged nightmare of mud and water and thrashing, cursing men and panicky animals. Each of the freighters possessed floating jetties which could be winched over the side to provide a fairly stable pathway to the shore, but they had not been designed for the offloading of two thousand horses and mules. The animals were hoisted out of the holds by tackles to the yardarms and set down wild-eyed and struggling upon the pitching jetties, with predictable results. By the time the last mule and man was ashore, and the army's supplies were piled in long rows on dry land, it was far into the night. Two men had drowned and six horses had been lost, but Corfe counted himself lucky not to have lost more. The eastern bank was a sucking quagmire of mud and horse-shit for almost a mile, and the troops were hollow-eyed ghosts staggering with weariness. But they were ashore, essentially intact, having covered over eighty leagues in five days. Corfe decreed that the following day would be one of rest for men and animals alike. The army bivouacked a mile from the river-bank, gathered firewood, set out sentries, and then as one, eight thousand men fell into a dreamless sleep.

THE LAST OF the horses had been settled down for the night and the campfires were scattered all about the dark earth like some poor counterfeit of the stars overhead. The ground was hard as stone underfoot, which would make for easy marching, but the cold was difficult to keep at bay with a single blanket, even with one's feet in the very embers of the fire. Strangely, Corfe felt less tired than at any time since the King's Battle, for all that he had snatched barely four hours sleep a night on the voyage upriver. It was the freedom of being out in the field with his own command. No more conferences or councils or scribbling scribes, just a host of exhausted, chilled men and animals encamped in the frozen wilds of the north.

The men had meshed together well. They had fought shoulder-to-shoulder in the King's Battle, guzzled beer together in the taverns of Torunn, and endured the unpleasantness of the river-journey north. Now they were a single entity. Cimbric tribesmen, Fimbrian pikemen, Torunnan arquebusiers. There were still rivalries of course, but they were healthy ones. Corfe sat by the campfire and watched them sleep uncomplainingly upon the hard earth, their threadbare uniforms sodden with mud – and realized that he loved them all.

Andruw picked his way through the fires towards him, then dug into his saddlebags. He handed his general a wooden flask.

"Have a snort, Corfe. It'll keep the cold out. Compliments of Captain Mirio."

Corfe unstoppered the neck and had a good swallow. The stuff seemed to burn his mouth, and blazed a fiery path all the way down his gullet. His eyes watered and he found himself gasping for air.

"I swear Andruw, you'll go blind one of these days."

"Not me. I've the constitution of a horse."

"And about as much sense. What about the powder?"

Andruw looked back across the camp. "We lost six barrels, and another eight are wet through. God knows when we'll have a chance to dry them."

"Damn. That eats into our reserves. Well, we've enough to fight a couple of good-sized engagements, but I want Ranafast's men made aware that they can't go firing it off like it's free."

"No problem."

Two more figures came picking their way out of the flickering dark towards them. When they drew closer Corfe saw that it was the unlikely duo of Marsch and Formio. Formio looked as slight as an adolescent beside the bulk of the towering tribesman, his once dapper sable uniform now a harlequin chequer of mud. Marsch was clad in a greasy leather gambeson. He looked happier than he had for days.

"What is this, a meeting of the High Command?" Andruw asked derisively. "Here you two – have some of this. Privileges of rank."

Formio and Marsch winced over the rough grain liquor much as Corfe had done. "Well, gentlemen?" their commanding officer asked.

"We found those stores that were lost overboard," Formio said, wiping his mouth. "They had come up against a sandbank two miles downstream."

"Good, we need all the match we can get. Marsch?"

The big tribesman threw the wooden flask back to Andruw. "Our horses are in a better way than I thought. That exercise when we were in the boats – that was a good thing. Two days, we need, to" – he hesitated, groping for the word – "to restore them. Some would not eat on the boats and are weak."

Corfe nodded. "Very well. Two days – but no more. Marsch, in the morning I want you and Morin to saddle up a squadron of the fittest horses and begin a reconnaisance of the area, out to five miles. If you are seen by a small body of the enemy, hunt them down. If you find a large formation, get straight back here. Clear?"

Marsch's face lifted in a rare smile. "Very clear. It shall be so."

Andruw was still gulping out of Mirio's flask. He sat, or rather half-fell on his saddle and stared owlishly into the campfire, leaning one elbow on the pommel.

"Are you all right?" Corfe asked him.

"In the pink." His gaiety had disappeared. "Tired, though. Lord, how those boats did stink! I'm glad I'm a cavalryman and not a sailor."

Marsch and Corfe reclined by the fire also. "Makes a good pillow, a war-saddle does," Andruw told them, giving his own a thump. "Not so good as a woman's breast though."

"I thought you were an artilleryman, not a horse-soldier," Corfe baited him. "Forgetting your roots, Andruw?"

"Me? Never. I'm just on extended loan. Sit down, Formio, for God's sake. You stand there like a graven image. Don't Fimbrians get tired?"

The young Fimbrian officer raised an eyebrow and did as he was bidden. He shook his head when Andruw offered the wooden flask to him once again. Andruw shrugged and took another swig. Marsch, Formio and Corfe exchanged glances.

"Do you remember the early days at the Dyke, Corfe? When they came roaring down from the hills and my guns boomed out, battery after battery? What a sight. What happened to those gunners of mine, I wonder? They were good men. I suppose their bones lie up around the ruins of the Dyke now, in the wreckage of the guns."

Corfe stared into the fire. The artillerymen of Ormann Dyke, Ranafast had told them, had been part of the thousand-man rearguard that had covered Martellus's evacuation of the fortress. None of them had escaped.

A curlew called out, spearing through the night as though lost in the dark. They heard a horse neighing off along the Cathedraller lines, but apart from that the only sounds were the wind in the grass and the crackling of the campfire. Corfe thought of his own men, the ones he had commanded in Aekir. They were a long time dead now. He found it hard to even remember their faces – there had been so many other faces under his command since then.

"Soldiers die – that is what they do," Formio said unexpectedly. "They do not expect to fall, and so they keep going. But in the end that is what happens. Men who have no hope of life, they either cease to fight, or they fight like heroes. No-one knows why, it is the way of things."

"A Fimbrian philosopher," Andruw said, but smiled to take some of the mockery out of his words. Then his face grew sombre again.

"I was born up here, in the north. This is the country of my family, has been for generations. I had a sister, Vanya, and a little brother. God alone knows where they are now. Dead, or in some Merduk labour camp I expect." He tilted up the bottle again, found it was empty, and tossed it into the fire. "I wonder sometimes, Corfe, if at the end of all this there will be anything left of our world worth saving."

Corfe set a hand on his shoulder, his eyes burning. "I'm sorry Andruw."

Andruw laughed, a strangled travesty of mirth. His own eyes were bright and glittering in the flame-light. "All these little tragedies. No matter. I hadn't seen them in years. The life of a soldier, you know? But now that we are up here, I can't help wondering about them." He turned to the Fimbrian who sat silently beside him. "You see, Formio, soldiers are people too. We are all someone's son, even you Fimbrians."

"Even we Fimbrians? I am relieved to hear it."

Formio's mild rejoinder made them all laugh. Andruw clapped the sable-clad officer on the back. "I thought you were all a bunch of warrior monks who dine on gunpowder and shit bullets. Have you family back in the Electorates, Formio?"

"I have a mother, and a – a girl."

"A girl! A female Fimbrian – just think of that. I reckon I'd wear my sword to bed. What's she like, Formio? You're among friends now, be honest."

The black-clad officer hung his head, clearly embarrassed. "Her name is Merian." He hesitated, then reached into the breast of his tunic and pulled out a small wooden slat which split in two, like a slim book.

"This is – this is what she looks like."

They crowded around to look, like schoolboys. Formio held an exquisite miniature, a tiny painting of a blond-haired girl whose features were delicate as a deer's. Large, dark eyes and a high forehead. Andruw whistled appreciatively.

"Formio, you are a lucky dog."

The Fimbrian tucked the miniature away again. "We are to be married as soon – as soon as I get back."

None of them said anything. Corfe realized in that moment that none of them expected to survive. The knowledge should have shocked him, but it did not. Formio had been right in what he said about soldiers.

Andruw rose unsteadily to his feet. "Gentlemen, you must excuse me. I do believe I'm going to spew."

He staggered, and Corfe and Marsch jumped up, grasped his arms, and propelled him into the shadows, where he bent double and retched noisily. Finally he straightened, eyes streaming. "Must be getting old," he croaked.

"You?" Corfe said. "You'll never be old, Andruw." And an instant later he wished he had never said such an unlucky thing.

EIGHT

GOLOPHIN WIPED THE sweat from his face with an already damp cloth and got up from the workbench with a groan. He padded over to the window and threw open the heavy shutters to let the quicksilver radiance of a moonlit night pour into the tower chamber. From the height whereon he stood, he could see the whole dark immensity of south-western Hebrion below, asleep under the stars. The amber glow of Abrusio lit up the horizon, the moon shining liquid and brilliant upon the waves of the Great Western Ocean out to the very brim of the world beyond. He sniffed the air like an old hound, and closed his eyes. The night had changed. A warmer breeze always came in off the sea at this time of the year, like a promise of spring. At long last, this winter was ending. At one time he had thought it never would.

But Abeleyn was King again, Jemilla had been foiled, and Hebrion was, finally, at peace. Time perhaps to begin wondering about the fate of the rest of the world again. A caravel from Candelaria had put into Abrusio only the day before with a cargo of wine and cinnamon, and it had brought with it news of the eastern war. The Torunnan King had been slain before the very gates of his capital, it was said, and the Merduks were now advancing through the Torrin Gap. *Young Lofantyr dead*, Golophin thought. *He had hardly even begun to be a king.* His mother would take the throne now, but that might create more problems than it solved. Golophin did not give much for Torunna's chances, with a woman on the throne – albeit a capable one – the Merduks to one side, and the Himerians to the other.

Closer to home, the Himerian Church was fast consolidating its hold over a vast swathe of the continent. That polite ninny, Cadamost, had invited Church forces into Perigraine with no thought as to how he might ever get them out again. What would the world look like in another five years? Perhaps he was getting too old to care.

He stretched and returned to the workbench. Upon it a series of large glass demi-johns with wide necks sat shining in the light of a single candle. They were all full of liquid, and in one a dark shape quivered and occasionally tapped on the glass which imprisoned it. He laid a hand on the side of the jar. "Soon, little one, soon," he crooned. And the dark shape settled down again.

"Another familiar?" a voice asked from the window. Golophin did not turn round.

"Yes."

"You Old World wizards, you depend on them too much. I think sometimes you hatch them out for companionship as much as anything else."

"Perhaps. They have definite uses though, for those of us who are not quite so... adept as you."

"You underestimate yourself, Golophin. There are other ways of extending the Dweomer."

"But I do not wish to use them." Golophin turned around at last. Standing silver in the moonlight by the window was a huge animal, an eldritch wolf standing on its hind legs, its neck as thick as that of a bull. Two yellow lights blinked above its muzzle.

"Why this form? Are you trying to impress me?"

The wolf laughed, and in the space of a heartbeat there was a man standing in its place, a tall, hawk-faced man in archaic robes.

"Is this better?"

"Much."

"I commend you on your coolness, Golophin. You do not even seem taken aback. Are you not at least a little curious about who I am and what I am doing here?"

"I am curious about many things. I do not believe you come from anywhere in the world I know. Your powers are... impressive, to say the least. I assume you are here to enlighten me in some fashion. If you were going to kill me or enslave me you could have done so by now, but instead you restored my powers. And thus I await your explanations."

"Well said! You are a man after my own heart." The strange shape-shifter walked across the chamber to the fireplace, where he stood warming his hands. He looked around at the hundreds of books which lined the circular walls of the room, noted one, and took it down to leaf through.

"This is an old one. No doubt much of it is discredited now. But when I wrote it I thought the ideas would last forever. Man's foolish pride, eh?" He tossed the aged volume over to Golophin. *The Elements of Gramarye* by Aruan of Garmidalan. It was hand-written and illuminated, composed and copied in the second century.

"You can touch things – you are not a simulacrum," Golophin said steadily, quelling the sudden tremble in his hands.

"Yes. Translocation, I call it. I can cross the world, Golophin, in the blink of an eye. I am thinking of announcing it as a new Discipline. It is a wearying business, though. Do you happen to have any wine?"

"I have Fimbrian brandy."

"Even better."

Golophin set down the book. There was an engraving of its author on the cover. The same man – Lord above, it was the same man. But he would have to be at least four centuries old.

"I think I also need a drink," he said as he poured out two generous measures of the fragrant spirit from the decanter he kept filled by the fire. He handed one to his guest and Aruan – if it truly could be he – nodded appreciatively, swirled the liquid around in the wide-necked glass, and sipped it with gusto.

"My thanks, Brother Mage."

"You would seem to have discovered something even more startling than this *Translocation* of yours. The secret of eternal youth, no less."

"Not quite, but I am close."

"You are from the uttermost west, the place Bardolin disappeared to. Aren't you?"

"Ah, your friend Bardolin! Now there is a true talent. Golophin, he does not even begin to appreciate the potential he harbours. But I am educating him. When you see him again – and you will soon – you may be in for a surprise. And to answer your question – yes, I come from the west."

Golophin needed the warmth of the kindly spirit in his throat. He gulped it down as though it were beer.

"Why did you restore my powers, Aruan – if that is who you are."

"You were a fellow mage in need. Why not? I must apologise for the... abrupt nature of the restoration. I trust you did not find it too wearing."

It had been the most agonising experience Golophin had ever known, but he said nothing. He was afraid. The Dweomer stank in this man, like some pungent meat left to rot in a tropical clime. The potency he sensed before him was an almost physical sensation. He had never dreamed anyone could be so powerful. And so he was afraid – but absolutely fascinated too. He had so many questions he did not know where to begin.

"Why are you here?" he asked at last.

"A good idea – start out with the most obvious one. Let us just say that I am on a grand tour of the continent, catching up on things. I have so much to see, and so little time! But also, I have always had a liking for Hebrion. Do you know, Golophin, that there are more of the Dweomer-folk here in this kingdom than in any other? Less, since the purges orchestrated by the Mother Church of course, but still, an impressive number. Torunna is almost wholly deserted by our people now, Almark never had many to begin with – too close to Charibon. And in Fimbria there was some kind of mind-set which seemed to militate against our Folk from the earliest times. One could hypothesise endlessly on the whys and wherefores, but I have come to believe that there is something in the very bones of the earth which causes Dweomer-folk to be born, an anomaly which is more common is some locations than others. Were your parents mages?"

"No. My father was an official in the Merchant's Guild."

"There – you see? It is not heredity. There is some other factor at work. We are freaks of nature, Golophin, and have been persecuted as such for all of recorded history. But that will change."

"What of Bardolin? What have you done with him?"

"As I said, I have begun to unlock his powers. It is a painful procedure – such things have never been easy – but in the end he will thank me for it."

"So he is still alive, somewhere out in the west. Are the myths true then – there is actually a Western Continent?"

"The myths are true. I had a hand in creating some of them. Golophin, in the west we have an entire world of our own, a society founded on the Dweomer. There is something back there in the very air we breathe –"

"There are more of you then."

"I am the only one of the original Founders who survived thus far. But there are others who came later. We are few, growing fewer. That is why I have returned to the Old World. We need new blood, new ideas. And we intend to bring with us a few ideas of our own."

"Bring with you? So you mages from the west are all intent upon returning to Normannia."

"One day, yes. That is our hope. My work at present is the preparation of the world for our coming. You see now why I am here? We will need friendly voices raised on our behalf in every kingdom, else our arrival might result in panic, even violence. All we wish, Brother Mage, is to come home."

A sudden thought shook Golophin. "One moment – the wolf-image. That was a simulacrum, yes?"

Aruan grinned. "I wondered when that question would come up. No, it was not. I am a shifter, a sufferer of the Black Disease, though I no longer see it as an affliction."

"That is impossible. A mage cannot also be a lycanthrope."

"Bardolin thought so also. He knows better now. I am a master of all Seven Disciplines, and I am busy creating more. What I am here tonight to ask, Golophin, is whether you will join us."

"Join you? I'm not sure I understand."

"I think you do. Soon I will no longer be a furtive night-visitor, but a power in the world. I want you to be my colleague. I can raise you very high, Golophin. You would no longer be the servant of a king, but a veritable king yourself."

"Some might think your ambitions a little too wide-ranging. How are you going to manage all this?"

"Time will tell. But it is going to happen – the lines are being drawn all over the continent, though not many are aware of them yet. Will you join us, Golophin? I would consider it an honour to have a man such as you in our camp. Not merely a powerful mage, but a keen mind used to the intricacies and intrigues of power. What do you say?"

"You are very eloquent, Aruan, but vague. Do you fear to tell me too much?"

Aruan shrugged. "You must take some things on trust, that is true. But I cannot relate to you the details of a plan which is still incomplete. For now, it would be enough if you could at least consider yourself our friend."

The lean old wizard stared at his visitor. Aruan's face was angular and autocratic, and there was a cruelty lurking there in the eyes. Not a kindly, nor yet a generous countenance. But Golophin sensed that in this at least, he was speaking the truth. Imagine – an entirely new world out there beyond the endless Ocean, a society of mages living without fear of the pyre. It was a staggering concept, one that sent a whole golden series of speculations racing through Golophin's mind. And they wanted to come back here, to the Old World. What could be wrong with finding a home for such – such castaways? The knowledge they must have gathered through the centuries, working in peace and without fear! The ancient wizard had a point – how many more decades or centuries of perscution could the Dweomer-folk withstand before they were wiped out altogether? At some point they had to stand up together and halt it, turn around the prejudices of men and demand acceptance for themselves. It was a glittering idea, one which for a second made Golophin's heart soar with hope. If it were only possible!

And yet, and yet – there was something deeply disturbing here. This Aruan, for all his surface charm, had a beast inside him. Golophin could not forget that one, desperate mind-scream he had heard Bardolin give thousands of leagues away.

Golophin! Help me in the name of God –

The terror in that cry. What had engendered it?

"Well?" Aruan asked. "What do you say?"

"All right. Consider me friendly to your cause. But I will not divulge any of the secrets or strategies of the Hebrian Crown. I have other loyalties too."

"That is enough for me. I thank you, Golophin." And Aruan held out a hand.

But Golophin refused to shake it. Instead he turned and refilled his glass. "I suggest you leave now. I have to be on my way back to the city very soon. But –" he paused. "I wish to speak with you again. I possess an inquisitive mind, and there is so much I would know."

"By all means. I look forward to it. But before I go, I will show my goodwill with a little gift..."

Before Golophin could move, Aruan had swooped forward like a great dark raptor. His hand came down upon Golophin's forehead and seemed fixed there, as though the fingers had been driven like nails through the skull. Golophin's glass dropped out of his hand and shattered on the stone floor. His eyes rolled up to show the whites and he bared his teeth in a helpless snarl.

Moisture beaded Aruan's face in a cold sheen. "This is a great gift," he said in a low voice. "And a genuine one. You have a subtle mind, my friend. I want it intact. I want loyalty freely given. There." He stepped back. Golophin fell to his knees, the breath a harsh gargle in his throat.

"You will have to experiment a little before you can use it properly," Aruan told him. "But that inquisitive mind of yours will find it a fascinating tool. Just do not try to cross the Ocean with it in search of your friend Bardolin. I cannot allow that yet. Fare thee well, Golophin. For now." And he was gone.

Panting, Golophin laboured to his feet. His head was ringing as though someone had been tolling a bell in his ears for hours. He felt drunk, clumsy, but there was a weird sense of well-being burning through him.

And there – the knowledge was there, accessible. It opened out before him in a blaze of newfound power and possibilities.

Aruan had given him the Discipline of Translocation.

NINE

WILD-EYED, FILTHY AND exhausted, the prisoners were herded
in by Marsch's patrol like so many cattle. There were
perhaps a dozen of them. Corfe was called to the van of the
army by a beaming Cathedraller to inspect them. He halted
the long column and cantered forward. Marsch greeted him
with a nod.

The prisoners sank to the cold ground. Their arms had
been bound to their sides and some of them had blood on
their faces. Marsch's troopers were all leading extra horses
with Merduk harness. Compact, fine-boned beasts with the
small ears and large eyes of the eastern breeds.

"Where did you find them?" Corfe asked the big
tribesman.

"Five leagues north of here. They are stragglers from a
larger force of maybe a thousand cavalry. They had been
in a town." Here Marsch's voice grew savage. "They
had burned the town. The main body had waggons full
of women among them, and herds of sheep and cattle.
These" – he jerked his head towards the gasping, prostrate
Merduks – "were busy when we caught them."

"Busy?"

Again, the savagry in Marsch's voice. "They had a
woman. She was dead before we moved in. They were
taking turns."

The Merduks cowered on the ground as the Torunnans
and tribesmen gathered about them glared.

"Kill the fuckers," Andruw said in a hiss which was
wholly unlike him.

"No," Corfe said. "We interrogate them first."

"Kill them now," another soldier said. One of Ranafast's
Torunnans.

"Get back in ranks!" Corfe roared. "By God, you'll obey orders or you'll leave this army and I'll have you march back to Torunn on your own. Get back there!"

The muttering knot of men moved apart.

"There were over a score of them," Marsch went on as though nothing had happened. "We slew eight or nine, took these men as they were pulling on their breeches. I thought it would be useful to have them alive."

"You did right," Corfe told him. "Marsch, you will escort them down the column to Formio. Have the Fimbrians take charge of them."

"Yes, General."

"You saw only this one body of the enemy?"

"No. There were others – raiding parties, maybe two or three hundred each. They swarm over the land like locusts."

"You weren't seen?"

"No. We were careful. And our armour is Merduk. We smeared it with mud to hide the colour and rode up to them like friends. That is why we caught them all. None escaped."

"It was well done. These raiding bands, are they all cavalry?"

"Most of them. Some are infantry like those in the big camp at the King's Battle. All have arquebuses or pistols though."

"I see. Now take them down to Formio. When we halt for the night I want them brought to me – in one piece, you understand?" This was for the benefit of the glowering Torunnans, who were standing in perfect rank but whose knuckles were white on their weapons.

"It shall be so." Then Marsch displayed a rare jet of anger and outrage.

"They are not soldiers, these things. They are animals. They are brave only when they attack women or unarmed men. When we charged them some threw down their weapons and cried like children. They are of no account." Contempt dripped from his voice. But then he rode close to Corfe and spoke quietly to his general so that none of the other soldiers overheard.

"And some of them are not Merduk – they look like men of the west, like us. Or like Torunnans."

Corfe nodded. "I know. Take them away now, Marsch."

ALL THE REST of the day, as the army continued its slow march north, the prisoners were cowering in Corfe's mind. Andruw was grim and silent at his side. They had passed half a dozen hamlets in the course of the past two days. Some had been burnt to the ground, others seemed eerily untouched. All were deserted but for a few decaying corpses, so maimed by the weather and the animals that it was impossible to tell even what sex they were. The land around them seemed ransacked and desolate, and the mood of the entire army was turning ugly. They had all fought Merduks before, met them in open battle and striven against them face to face. But it was a different thing to see one's own country laid waste out of sheer wanton brutality. Corfe had seen it before, around Aekir, but it was new to most of the others.

Andruw, who knew this part of the world only too well, was directing the course of their march. The plan was to circle round in a great horseshoe until they were trekking back south again. The Cathedrallers would provide a mobile screen to hide their movements and keep them informed as to the proximity of the enemy. When they encountered any sizeable force the main body of the army would be brought up, put into battle-line, and hurled forward. But so far they had not encountered any enemy formation of a size which warranted the deployment of the entire army, and the men were becoming frustrated and angry. It was four days now since they had left the boats behind, and while the Cathedrallers had been skirmishing constantly, the infantry had yet to even see a live Merduk – apart from these prisoners Marsch had just brought in. Corfe felt as though he were striving to manage a huge pack of slavering hounds eager to slip the leash and run wild. The Torunnans especially were determined to exact some payment for the despoliation of their country.

They camped that night in the lee of a large pine wood. The horses and mules were hobbled on its edge and the men were able to trudge inside and light their first campfires in two days, the flames hidden by the thick depths of the trees. Eight thousand men required a large campsite, some twelve acres or more, but the wood was able to accommodate them all with ease.

Once the fires were lit, rations handed out, and the sentries posted, Formio and four sombre Fimbrians brought the Merduk prisoners to Corfe's fire. The Merduks were shoved into line with the dark trees towering around them like watchful giants. All about them, the quiet talk and rustling of men setting out their bedrolls ceased, and hundreds of Corfe's troopers edged closer to listen. Andruw was there, and Ranafast and Marsch and Ebro – all the senior officers of the army. They had not been summoned, but Corfe could not turn them away. He realized suddenly that if it came down to it, he trusted the discipline of his own Cathedrallers and the Fimbrians more than he did that of his fellow countrymen. This night they were not Torunnan professional soldiers, but angry, outraged men who needed something to vent their rage upon. He wondered, if it came to it, whether he would be able to stop them degenerating into some kind of lynch mob.

He walked up and down the line of prisoners in silence. Some met his eyes, some stared at the ground. Yes, Marsch had been right – at least four of them had the fair skin and blue eyes of westerners. They were no doubt part of the *Minhraib* of Ostrabar, the peasant levy. Ostrabar had once been *Ostiber*, a Ramusian kingdom. The grandfathers of these soldiers had fought the Merduks as Corfe's Torunnans were fighting them now, but these men had been born subjects of the Sultan, worshippers of the Prophet, their Ramusian heritage forgotten. Or almost forgotten.

"Who among you speaks Normannic?" Corfe snapped.

A short man raised his head. "I do, your honour. Felipio of Artakhan."

Felipio – even the name was Ramusian. Corfe tried to stop his own anger and hatred from clouding his thinking. He fought to keep his voice reasonable.

"Very well, Felipio. The name of your regiment if you please, and your mission here in the north-west of my country."

Felipio licked dry lips, looking round at the hate-filled faces that surrounded him. "We are from the sixty-eighth regiment of pistoleers your honour," he said. "We were infantry, part of the levy before the fall of the Dyke. Then they gave us horses and matchlocks and sent us out to scout the north clear up to the Torrin Gap."

"Scouting is it?" a voice snarled from the blackness under the trees, and there was a general murmur.

"Be silent!" Corfe cried. "By God, you men will hold your tongues this night. Colonel Cear-Adurhal, you will take ten men and secure this area from further interruption. This is not a God-damned court-martial, nor yet a debating chamber."

Andruw did as he was ordered without a word. In minutes he had armed men stationed about the prisoners with their swords drawn.

"Go on, Felipio," Corfe said.

The prisoner studied his feet and continued in a mumble. "There is not much more to tell, your honour. Our Subhadar, Shahr Artap, he commanded the regiment, gave us a speech telling us that this was Merduk country now, and we were to do as we pleased..." Sweat broke out on Felipio's forehead and rolled down his face in great shining beads of stress and terror.

"Go on," Corfe repeated.

"Please, your honour, I can't –"

Andruw stepped forward out of nowhere and smashed the man across the face with a mailed fist, bursting open his nose like a plum and ripping the flesh from one cheekbone.

"You will obey the general's orders," he said, his voice an alien growl which Corfe did not even recognize.

"That's enough, Andruw. Step back."

Andruw looked at him. There were tears flaming in his eyes. "Yes, sir," he said, and retreated into the shadows.

A murmuring from the men all around. The night air crackled with suppressed violence. The firelight revealed a wall of faces which had gathered around despite Corfe's orders. Naked steel gleamed out of the dark. Corfe met Formio's eyes, and held the Fimbrian's gaze for a few seconds. Formio nodded fractionally and walked away into the trees.

"On your feet, Felipio."

The squat Merduk rose unsteadily, his face a swollen, scarlet mess through which bone gleamed. One eye was already closed.

"How far north did your regiment go – clear up to the Gap?"

Felipio nodded drunkenly.

"Are there any other Merduk forces up there – is it true your people are building forts up there?"

Felipio did not answer. He seemed half-conscious. Corfe watched him for a moment, then moved down the line of prisoners to the next fair-skinned one.

"Your name." This one was little more than a boy. He had pissed in his pants and his face was streaked with tears and snot. Not too young to rape, though. Corfe seized him by the hair and drew him upright.

"Name."

"Don't kill me – please don't kill me. They made me do it. They took me off the farm. I have a wife at home –" he started sobbing. Corfe reined in an urge to strike him, to let loose his own fury and hatred and beat his stupid young face into a bloody morass of flesh and broken bone. He lowered his voice and whispered in the blubbering boy's ear.

"Talk to me, or I will hand you over to *them*," and he gestured to the press of silent men around them.

"There are other regiments up north," the boy bleated. "Four or five of them. They are building a big camp, walls and ditches. Another big army is coming north – they are going to – to the monkish place by the shores of the sea. That's all I know, I swear it!"

Corfe released him and he sagged, hiccuping and crying. So the Merduks were going to launch an expedition against Charibon, and they were fortifying the Gap. Something worth knowing, at last. He turned away, deep in thought. As he did, a large group of men advanced out of the shadows, the wall of faces dissolving into a crowd which surged forward.

"We'll take care of them from here, General."

"Get back in ranks!" His bellow made them pause, but one stepped forward and shook his head. "General, we'd follow you to Hell and back, but a man has his limits. Some of us have lost families and homes to these animals. You have to leave the scum to us now."

At once another knot of figures appeared, with Formio at their head. Sable-clad Fimbrians with their swords drawn. Cimbric tribesmen in their scarlet armour. They positioned themselves with swift efficency about Corfe and the Merduks as though they were a bodyguard. Formio and Marsch stood at Corfe's shoulders like brothers.

"The general gave you an order," Formio said evenly. "Your job is to obey. You are soldiers, not a mob of civilians."

The two bands of armed men faced each other squarely for several moments. Corfe could not speak. If they began to fight one another he knew that the army was doomed, irrevocably split between Fimbrian and Torunnan and tribesman. His authority over them all hung by a straw.

"All right, lads," Andruw said breezily, materializing like a ghost from the surrounding trees. "That's enough. If we start into them, then we're no better than they are. They're criminals, no more. And besides, are you willing to see the day when a Torunnan officer is obeyed by Fimbrians and mountain savages, and not by his own countrymen? Where's your pride? Varian – I know you – I saw you on the battlements at the Dyke. You did your duty then. Do it now. Do as the general says, lads. Back to your bivouacs."

The Torunnans shifted on their feet, looking both embarrassed and sullen. Corfe moved forward to speak to their ringleader, Varian. Thank God Andruw had remembered his name.

"I too lost a home, and family, Varian," he said quietly. "All of us here have suffered, in one way or another."

Varian's eyes were hot blazes of grief. "I had a wife," he croaked, hardly audible. "I had a daughter."

Corfe gripped his shoulder. "Don't do anything that would offend their memory."

The trooper coughed, wiped his eyes roughly. "Yes, sir. I'm sorry. we're bloody fools, all of us."

"So are all men, Varian. But we were husbands and fathers and brothers once. Save the hatred for a battlefield. These animals are not worthy of it. Now go and get some sleep."

Corfe raised his voice. "All of you, back to your lines. There is nothing more to do here, nothing more to see."

Reluctantly, the throng broke up and began dispersing. Corfe felt the relief wash over him in a tepid wave as they obeyed him. They were still his to command, thanks to Formio and Andruw. They were still an army, and not a mob.

IN THE MIDDLE watch of the night he did the rounds of the camp as he always did, exchanging a few words with the sentries, looking in on the horses. He took his own mount, an equable bay gelding, from the horse-lines and rode it bareback out of the wood and up to the summit of a small knoll that lay to the east of the camp. Another horseman was there ahead of him, outlined against the stars. Andruw, staring out upon a sleeping Torunna. Corfe reined in beside him, and they sat their horses in silence, watching.

On the vast dark expanse of the night-bound earth they could see distant lights, throbbing like glow-worms. Even as Corfe watched, another sprang up out on the edge of the horizon.

"They're burning the towns along the Searil," Andruw said laconically.

Corfe studied the distant flames and wondered what scenes of horror and carnage they signified. He remembered Aekir's fall, the panic of the crowds, the inferno of the packed streets, and wiped his face with one hand.

"I'm sorry I lost my head back there for a time," Andruw said tonelessly. "It won't happen again." And the anger and despair ate through the numbness in his voice as he spoke again. "God's blood, Corfe, will it ever end? Why do they do these things? What kind of people are they?"

"I don't know Andruw, I truly don't. We've been fighting these folk for generations, and still we know nothing about them – and they know as little about us, I suspect. Two peoples who have never even tried to understand one another, but who are simply intent on wiping each other out."

"I've heard that in the west, in Gabrion and Hebrion, the Sea-Merduks trade and take ship with Ramusian captains as though there were no barriers between them. They sail ships together and start businesses in partnership with each other. Why is it so different here?"

"Because this is the frontier, Andruw. This is where the wheel meets the road.

"I stood ceremonial guard in Aekir once, at a dinner John Mogen was giving to his captains before the siege. I think that if anyone had some understanding of the Merduks, he did. I think he even admired them. He said that men must always move towards the sunset. They follow it as surely as swallows flit south in wintertime.

"Originally the Merduks were chieftains of the steppes beyond the Jafrar, but they followed the sun and crossed the mountains, and were halted by the walls and pikes of the Fimbrians. The Fimbrians contained them: we cannot. That is the simple truth. If we are not to fight one another into annihilation, then one day we shall have to broker a peace, and make a compromise with them. Either that, or we will be swept into the mountains, and end our days the leaders of roving homeless tribesmen, like Marsch and his people."

"I must talk to Marsch. That mountain savage bit – I have to tell him –"

"He knows, Andruw. He knows."

Andruw nodded. "I suppose so." He seemed to find it hard to find the words he wanted. Corfe could sense the struggle in him as he sat his horse and picked at its mane.

"They shamed us back there, Formio and Marsch and their men. There they were, foreigners and mercenaries, and they stood by you while your own people were almost ready to push you out of the way. Those men were at the Dyke with us – they saw us there. A few even served under you in the Barbican. There's no talk around their campfires tonight. They have failed you – and themselves."

"No," Corfe said quickly. They are just men who have been pushed too far. I think none the worse of them for it. And this army is not made up of Fimbrians and Torunnans and the tribesmen. Not any more. They're my men now, all of them. They've fought together and they've died together. There is no need to talk of shame, not to me."

Andruw grimaced. "Maybe... You know Corfe, I was ready to slit the throats of those prisoners back there. I would have done it without a qualm and slept like a baby afterwards. I never really hated before, not truly. In a way it was all some huge kind of game. But now this – this is different. The refugees from Aekir, they were just faces, but these hills – I skylarked in them when I was a boy. The people up here are my own people, not just because they are Torunnan – that's a name. But because I know how they live and where. Varian back there, he hasn't seen his wife and child in almost a year, and he doesn't know if they're alive or dead. And there are many more like him throughout the troops that came from the Dyke. They sent their families out of the fortress at the start, back here, to the north, or to the towns around Torunn. They thought the war would never come this far. Well, they were wrong. We all were."

"Yes," Corfe said, "we were."

"Are we all doomed, you think – madmen fighting the inevitable?"

"I don't know. I don't care, either, Andruw. All I know is how to fight – it's all I've ever known. Perhaps one day it will be possible to come to some kind of terms with the Merduks. I hope so, for the sake of Varian and his family and thousands like them. If it does not prove so, however, I will fight the bastards until the day I die, and then my ghost will plague their dreams."

Andruw laughed, and Corfe realised how much he had missed that sound of late.

"I'll just bet it will. Merduk mothers will frighten children yet unborn with tales of the terrible Corfe and his red-clad fiends."

"I hope so." Corfe smiled.

"You think that snot-nosed boy was telling the truth about the army marching on Charibon?"

"Possibly. It could be misinformation, but I doubt it. No, I think it's time the army went hunting. The quickest road to the Gap from Ormann Dyke lies two days march east of here. Tomorrow that's where we're going, with the Cathedrallers out in front under you and Marsch."

"Any guesses on the size of the army we're looking for?"

"Small enough for us to take on, I should think. The Sultan still believes all the Torunnan military to be penned up in Torunn, licking their wounds, and Charibon has never been well defended. We may be outnumbered, but not by much, I hope."

"We can't stay out too long – we carry only enough rations for another three weeks."

"We'll go on half-rations if we have to. I will not allow them to send an army through the Gap. I've no more love for the Ravens of Charibon than the next man, but I'm damned if I'll let the Merduks waltz all over Normannia like they owned it already. Besides, I have this feeling, Andruw. I think that the enemy is slowing down. We've blunted their edge. If they find they have to fight for every yard of Torunnan soil, then they may end up content with less of it."

"An open battle will do the men good."

"This is war we're talking about, Andruw. A battle that will kill and maim great numbers of the men."

"You know what I mean, Corfe. They need to taste blood again. Hell, so do I."

"All right, I take your point." Corfe turned his horse around with a nudge of his knee. "Time to get some sleep."

"I think I'll say here and think awhile," Andruw said.

"Don't think too much, Andruw. It doesn't do any good. Believe me, I know." And Corfe kicked his mount into a canter, leaving Andruw to stare after him.

ALBREC'S CELL WAS sparse and cold, but not unbearably so. To a monk who had suffered through a Ramusian novitiate it seemed perfectly adequate. He had a bed with a straw pallet which was surprisingly free of vermin, a small table and rickety chair and even a stub of candle and a tinderbox. There was one small window, heavily barred and set so high up in the wall that he had no chance of ever seeing out of it, but at least it provided a modicum of light.

He shared his cell with sundry spiders and an emaciated rat whose hunger had made it desperate. It had nibbled at Albrec's ears in the first nights he had been here, but now he knew to set aside for it some morsel of the food which was shoved through a slot in the door every day, and it had come to await the approaching steps of the turnkey more eagerly than he. The food was not appetizing – black bread and old cheese and sometimes a bowl of cold soup with lumps of gristle bobbing in it – but Albrec had never been much of an epicure. Besides, he had much to occupy his mind.

Every so often his solitary reveries were interrupted by a summons from the Sultan, and he would be hauled out of the cell, to the grief and bewilderment of the rat, and taken to the spacious chambers within which Aurungzeb had set up his household. The eunuchs would fetter him ceremoniously – more for effect than anything else, he thought – and he would stand in a discreet corner awaiting the pleasure of the Sultan. Sometimes he was left forgotten for hours, and was able to watch and listen in avid fascination to the workings of the Merduk court. Sometimes Aurungzeb was dining with senior army officers, or learned mullahs, and Albrec would be called upon to debate with them and expound his theory on the common origin of the Saint and the Prophet. The Sultan, it seemed, like to shock his guests with the little infidel. Not only were Albrec's words – often translated by the western concubine, Heria – inflammatory and blasphemous, but his appearance was agreeably bizarre. He was a court jester, but he knew that his words and theories shook some of the men who listened to them. Several of the mullahs had demanded he be executed at once, but others had argued with him as one might with a learned adversary – a spectacle that Aurungzeb seemed to find hugely entertaining.

He thought about Avila sometimes, and about Macrobius, and could not help but wonder how things were in the Torunnan capital. But for some reason he thought mostly about the cavalry officer he had once briefly encountered outside the walls of Torunn. Corfe Cear-Inaf, now the Commander-in-Chief of all the Torunnan armies. The Sultan seemed obsessed by him, though to the Merduks he was known only as the leader of the Scarlet Cavalry. They had not yet learned his name. Albrec gained the impression that the Merduk army in general existed in a state of constant apprehension, awaiting the descent of the terrible red horsemen upon them. Hence the current emphasis on fortification.

And Heria, the Sultan's chief concubine, pregnant by him and soon to become his Queen – she could very well be this Corfe Cear-Inaf's lost wife. Albrec locked that knowledge deep within himself and resolved never to divulge it to anyone. It would wreck too many lives – it might even tip the balance of the war. Let this Torunnan general remain nameless.

And yet – and yet the despair in her eyes was so painful to behold. Might she not take some comfort from the fact that her husband was alive and well? On this matter Albrec was torn. He was afraid he might inflict further pain on someone who had already suffered so much. What good would it do her anyway? The situation was like some ethics problem set for him during his novitiate. The choice between two courses of action, both ambiguous in their outcome, but one somehow more spiritually correct than the other. Except here he held in his hands the power to make or break lives.

A clamour of keys and clicking locks at his door announced another summons. The rat glanced once at him and bolted for its hole. It was not mealtime. Albrec sat on the edge of his bed. It was very late – unusual for him to be wanted at this hour.

But when the door swung open it was not the familiar figure of the turnkey who stood there, but a Merduk mullah – a richly dressed man with a beard as broad as a spade – and the cloaked and veiled figure of a woman. They entered his cell without a word and shut the door behind them.

The woman doffed her veil for a brief second to let him see her face. It was Heria. The mullah sat down upon Albrec's solitary chair without ceremony. His face was familiar – Albrec had spoken to him before at a dinner.

"Mehr Jirah," the mullah said. And in heavily accented Normannic: "We talk four – five days –" he looked appealingly at Heria.

"You and Mehr Jirah spoke together last week," she said smoothly. "He wished to speak to you again, in private. The guards have been bribed, but we do not have much time, and his Normannic is sparse, so I will interpret."

"By all means," Albrec said. "I appreciate his visiting me."

The mullah spoke in his own tongue now, and after a moment's thought Heria translated. Albrec thought he sensed a smile behind the veil.

"First he asks if you are a madman."

Albrec chuckled. "You know the answer to that, lady. Some have labeled me an eccentric, though."

Again, the speech in Merduk, her interpretation of it.

"He is an elder in the *Hraib* of the Kurasin in the Sultanate of Danrimir. He wants to know if your claims about the Prophet are mere devilment, or if they are based on any kind of evidence."

Albrec's heart quickened. "I told him when we spoke before that they are based on an ancient document which I believe to be genuine. I would not make such claims if I did not believe in my soul that they are true. A man's beliefs are not something to make a jest out of."

When this was translated Mehr Jirah nodded approvingly. He seemed then to hesitate for a long while, his head bent upon his breast. One hand stroked his voluminous beard. At last he sighed and made a long speech in Merduk. When he had finished Heria stared at him, then collected herself and rendered it into Normannic in a voice filled with wonder.

"The Kurasin are an old tribe, one of the oldest of all the Merduk *Hraib*. They had the privilege of being the first of the eastern peoples to hear the preachings of the Prophet Ahrimuz, almost five centuries ago. They hold a tradition that the Prophet crossed the Jafrar Mountains from the west, alone, on a mule, and that he was a pale-skinned man who did not speak their tongue but whose holiness and learning were self-evident. He dwelled with the Kurasin for five years, before travelling on northwards to the lands of the Kambak *Hraib*. In this way the true faith came to the Merduk peoples. Through this one man they deemed a Prophet sent by God, who came out of the west."

Albrec and the mullah looked at one another as Heria finished translating. In the Merduk cleric's eyes was a mixture of fear and confusion, but Albrec felt uplifted.

"So he believes me, then."

Merduk and Normannic. A long, halting speech by Mehr Jirah. Heria spoke more swiftly now. "He is not sure. But he has studied some of the books which were saved from the library of Gadorian Hagus in Aekir. Many of the sayings of both St. Ramusio and the Prophet Ahrimuz are the same, down to the very parables they used to illustrate their teachings. Perhaps the two men knew each other, or Ramusio was a student of Ahrimuz –"

"They were one and the same. He knows that. I can see it in his eyes."

When this was translated there was a long silence. Mehr Jirah looked deeply troubled. He spoke in a low voice without looking at Albrec.

"He says you speak the truth. But what would you have him do about it?"

"This truth is worth more than our lives. It must be declared publicly, whatever the consequences. The Prophet said that a man's soul suffers a kind of death every time he tells a lie. There have been five centuries of them – it is enough."

"And your people, the Ramusians, will they wish to hear the truth also?"

"They are beginning to hear it. The head of my faith in Torunn, Macrobius, he believes it. It is only a matter of time before men begin to accept it. This war must end – Merduks and Ramusians are brothers-in-faith and should not be slaying one another. Their God is the same God, and his messenger was a single man who enlightened us all."

Mehr Jirah rose. "He will think upon your words. He will think about what to do next."

"Do not think too long," Albrec said, rising also.

"We must go now." The Merduk opened the cell door. As he was about to leave he turned and spoke one last time.

"Why were we chosen to do this thing, do you think?"

"I do not know. I only know that we were, and that we must not shirk the task God has assigned us. To do so would be the worst blasphemy we could commit. A man who spends his life in the service of a lie, knowing it to be a lie, is offensive to the eyes of God."

Mehr Jirah paused in the doorway, and then nodded as Heria interpreted Albrec's words. A moment later he was gone.

"Will he do anything?" Albrec asked her.

"Yes, though I don't know what. He is a man of genuine piety, Merduk or no. He is the only one out of all of them who does not despise me. I'm not sure why."

Perhaps he knows quality when he sees it, Albrec found himself thinking. And out of his throat the words came tumbling as though without conscious volition.

"Your husband in Aekir – was his first name Corfe?"

Heria went very still. "How do you know that?"

A rattle of metal up the corridor beyond Albrec's cell. Men talking, the sound of boots on stone. But Heria did not move.

"How do you know that?" she repeated.

"I have met him. He is still alive. Heria" – the words rushed out of him as someone outside shouted harshly in Merduk – "he is alive. He commands all the armies of Torunna. He is the man who leads the red horsemen."

The knowledge had almost a physical heft as it left him and entered her. He believed for an instant that she would fall to the floor. She flinched as if he had struck her, sagged against the door.

The turnkey appeared on the threshold. He looked terrified, and plucked at Heria's sleeve whilst jabbering in Merduk. She shook him off

"Are you sure?" she asked Albrec.

He did not want to say it, for some reason, but he told the truth. "Yes."

A soldier appeared at the door, a Merduk officer. He pulled Heria away, looking both exasperated and frightened. The door was slammed shut, the keys clicking the lock into place again. Albrec slumped down on the bed and covered his face with his hands. *Blessed Saint*, he thought, *what have I done?*

TEN

IT WAS SPRING when they first sighted the Hebros Mountains
on the horizon, and Hawkwood bent his head at the tiller and
let the tears come silently for a while, and around him others
of the crew were more vocal, loudly thanking God for their
deliverance, or sobbing like children. Even Murad was not
unmoved. He actually shook Hawkwood's hand. "You are a
master-mariner indeed, Captain, to make such a landfall."

Hebrion loomed up steadily out of the dawn haze, the
mountains tinted pink as the sun took them. They had
weathered North Cape five days ago, beat before a passing
storm in the Gulf of Hebrion, and were now sailing up
Abrusio's great trefoil-shaped bay with a perfect south-west
breeze on the larboard quarter. They had been away almost
eight months, and the brave *Osprey* was sinking under
them at last, every able-bodied man taking a shift at the
pumps, but the water almost over the orlop. Bardolin had
had to be rechained in the master's cabin or he would have
drowned in the bilge.

Fair winds almost all the way, and apart from the one
squall which had almost sunk them, they had had a swift
passage, and the accuracy of their landfall was indeed
nothing short of miraculous. Hawkwood was burnt dark
as mahogany by the sun, and he stood at the tiller in rags,
his beard and unkempt hair frosted by salt and sea-wind,
his eyes blue flashes, startling in so swarthy a face. With the
aid of his cross-staff, the accumulated lore of a lifetime at
sea, and a string of good luck, he had brought the *Osprey*
home at last after one of the longest voyages of recorded
history. And surely one of the most disastrous.

The seventeen survivors of the expedition at liberty stood
on deck and stared as the carrack wheeled smoothly round

to north-north-east and the familiar shoreline slid past on the larboard side. There was still snow on the Hebros, but only a light dusting of it, and the sun was warm on their naked backs – not the punishing hothouse heat of the west, but a refreshing spring warmth. They could see Abrusio's heights rising up out of the haze ahead, and one of the soldiers cried out, pointing at the little flotilla of fishing yawls off the port beam as though they were some great marvel.

Abrusio, and they saw now the ruined expanses of the lower cty, the devastation of the docks, and the frantic rebuilding work that was going on there, thousands of men at work on miles of scaffolding. Hawkwood and Murad looked at one another. They had missed a war – or some great natural disaster – in their time away, it seemed. What other surprises were waiting for them in the old port-city?

"Back topsails!" Hawkwood cried as the *Osprey* slid through the sparsely populated wharves, all of which seemed damaged in some way or other. The Inner Roads were almost deserted of vessels, though the Hebrian Naval yards were crammed full of warships, most of which were under repair.

"Stand ready with the bow-line there!"

The carrack slowed as the sails were backed and spilled their wind. Half a dozen men stood at the beakhead, ready to leap ashore with the heavy mooring ropes and make them fast to the bollards there. A small crowd had gathered on the quayside. Men were shading their eyes and pointing at the battered ship, some arguing with each other and shaking their heads. Hawkwood smiled. There was a slight jar as the *Osprey* came up against the rope buffers at the lip of the wharves.

"Tie her off lads – we're home!"

Men leapt overboard and made the ship fast. Then they embraced each other, laughing, weeping, jumping up and down like a crowd of bronzed ragamuffins gone mad.

"Your Excellency," Hawkwood said with heavy irony, "I have brought you home."

The nobleman stared at him, and smiled. "*Excellency* no more. My title expired with the colony, as did yours, master Hawkwood. You will die a commoner after all."

Hawkwood spat over the carrack's side. "I can live with that. Now get your aristocratic backside off my ship."

Nothing in Murad's eyes – no shared comradeship, no sense of achievement, nothing. He turned away without another word and walked off the ship. The *Osprey* was so low in the water that one no longer had much of a climb down from the ship's rail to the wharf. Murad continued walking, a grotesque, tatterdemalion figure that drew a battery of stares from the crowd that was gathering. None of them dared accost him though, despite their consuming curiosity. The last Hawkwood saw of him he was negotiating the burnt expanse of what had been the lower city, his face set towards the heights whereon Hebrion's Royal palace loomed up out of the dawn haze.

Done with him at last, Hawkwood thought, and thanked God for it – for a whole host of things.

"Is that the *Gabrian Osprey* – is that really her?" someone shouted out from the buzzing throng on the wharf.

"Aye – it's her. Come home from the edge of the world."

"Ricardo! Ricardo Hawkwood! Glory be to God!"

A short, dark man in rich but soiled garments of blue and yellow pushed through the crowd. He wore the chain of a harbour-master. "Richard! Ha ha ha! I don't believe it. Back from a watery grave."

Hawkwood climbed over the ship's rail, and staggered as the unmoving stone of the wharf met his feet. It seemed to be gently rising and falling under him.

"Galliardo," he said with a smile, and the short man clasped his hand and shook it as though he meant to wring it off. There were tears in his eyes.

"I had a mass said for you these six months past," Galliardo was saying. "Oh God, Richard, what has happened to you?"

The press of bodies about Hawkwood seemed almost unbearable. Half the dock workers in the area seemed to have gathered about the *Osprey* to look and wonder and hear her story. Hawkwood blinked away his joy at landfall, tried to make himself think.

"Did you find it, Richard?" Galliardo was babbling. "Is there indeed a continent out in the west?"

"Yes, yes there is, and it can rot there as far as I'm concerned. Listen, Galliardo, she's about to sink at her moorings. Every seam in her has sprung. I need men to man her pumps and caulkers to stop her holes, and I need them now."

"You shall have them. There's not a mariner or carpenter in the city would not give his arm to have the privilege of working on her."

"And there's another thing." Hawkwood lowered his voice. "I have a – a cargo I need offloaded with some discretion. It has to go to the upper city, to the palace."

Galliardo's eyes were shining with cupidity. "Ah, Richard, I knew it. You've made your fortune out there in the west. A million in gold, I'll bet it is."

"No no – nothing like that. It's a... a rare beast, brought back for the King's entertainment."

"And worth a fortune, I'll wager."

Hawkwood gave up. "Yes Galliardo. It's priceless."

Then the harbour-master's face grew sombre. "You don't know what happened here in Abrusio – you haven't heard, have you?"

"No," Hawkwood said wearily. "Listen, you can tell me over a flagon of beer."

Galliardo laid a hand on his arm. "Richard – I have to tell you. Your wife Estrella, she is dead."

That brought him up short. Slender, carping little Estrella. He'd hardly thought about her in half a year.

"How?" he asked. No grief there, only a kind of puzzled pity.

"In the fires, when they torched the lower city. During the war. They say fifty thousand died at that time. It was Hell on earth."

"No," Hawkwood said. "I have seen Hell on earth, and it is not here. Now get me a gang of caulkers, Galliardo, before the *Osprey* settles where she stands."

"I'll have them here in half a glass, don't worry. Listen, join me in the *Dolphin* as soon as you can. I keep a back room there, now, since the house went."

"Yours too? Lord, Galliardo, has no-one any good news for me?"

"Precious little, my friend. But tidings of your return will be a tonic for the whole port. Now come – let me buy you that beer."

"Let me fetch my log and rutter first."

Hawkwood reboarded the carrack and made his way along the familiar companionway to the stern cabin. Bardolin sprawled there, a filthy mass of sores and scars, his eyes dull gleams in a tangle of beard and hair. Blood crusted his chains, and he stank like a cage in a zoo.

"Home at last, eh, Captain?" he whispered.

"I'll be back soon, Bardolin, with some helpers. We'll get you to Golophin by tonight. He lodges in the palace, doesn't he?"

Bardolin stirred. "No, don't take me to the palace. Golophin has a tower out in the foothills. It's where he carries out his researches. That's where you must take me. I know the way; it's where I served most of my apprenticeship."

"If you say so."

"Thank you, Captain, for everything. At one time all I wished for was death. I have had time to think. I begin to see now that there may be some value in living after all."

"That's the spirit. Hang on here, Bardolin. I'll be back soon." Hawkwood tentatively laid a hand on the chained man's shoulder, then left.

"You have a worthy friend there, Bardolin," Griella said. She materialised before him like a ghost.

"Yes. He is a good man, Richard Hawkwood."

"And he was right – it is worth going on. Life is worth living."

"I know. I see that now."

"And the disease you live with – it is not an affliction, either. Do you see that?"

Bardolin lifted his head and stared at her. "I believe I do, Griella. Perhaps your master has a point."

"You are my master now, Bardolin," she said, and kissed him on his cracked lips.

MURAD'S TOWN HOUSE had survived the war intact but for a few shot-holes in the thick masonry of the walls. When the heavy door was finally opened under his furious knocking the gatekeeper took one look at him and slammed it shut in his face again. Murad broke into a paroxysm of rage, hammering on the door and screaming at the top of his lungs. At last the postern door opened to one side, and two stout kitchen-lads came out, cracking their knuckles. "No beggars, and no madmen allowed at this house. Listen you –"

Murad left them both groaning and semi-conscious in the street and strode through the open postern, pushing aside sundry servants and bellowing for his steward. The kitchen staff scattered like a flock of geese before a fox, the women yelling that there was a maniac loose in the house. When the steward finally arrived, a cleaver in his hand, Murad pinioned him and stared into his eyes. "Do you know me, Glarus of Garmidalan? Your father is a gamekeeper on my estates. Your mother was my father's housekeeper for twenty years."

"Holy God." Glarus faltered. And he fell to his knees. "Forgive me, lord – we thought you were long dead. And you have – you have changed so –"

Murad's febrile strength seemed to gutter out. He sagged against the heavy kitchen table, releasing the man. The cleaver clanged to the floor. "I am home now. Run me a bath, and have my valet sent to me. And that wench there" – he pointed to a cowering girl with flour on her hands – "have her sent at once to the master bedroom. I want wine and bread and cheese and roasted chicken. And apples. And I want them all laid up there within half a glass. And a message sent to the palace, requesting an audience. Do you hear me?"

"Half a glass?" Glarus asked timidly. Murad laughed.

"I am become a naval creature after all. Ten minutes will do, Glarus. God's blood, it is good to be home!"

TWO HOURS LATER, he was admiring himself in the full-length mirror of the master bedroom, and the weeping kitchen-maid was being led away with a blanket about her shoulders. His beard and hair had been neatly trimmed and he wore a doublet of black velvet edged with silver lace. It hung on him like a sack, and he had to don breeches instead of hose, for his legs were too thin to be revealed without ridicule. His valet helped him slide the baldric of his rapier over his shoulder, and then he sipped wine and watched the stranger in the mirror preen himself. He had never been a handsome man, though there had always been something about him which the fair sex had found not unattractive. But now he was an emaciated, scarred scarecrow with a brown face in which a lipless mouth curled in a perpetual sneer. Governor of New Hebrion. His Excellency. Discoverer of the New World.

"The carriage is ready in the courtyard, my lord," Glarus ventured from the door.

"I'll be there in a moment."

It was barely mid-morning. Only a few hours ago he had been a beggar on a sinking ship with the scum of the earth for company. Now he was a lord again, with servants at his beck and call, a carriage waiting, a king ready to receive him. Some part of the world had been put back to rights, at least. Some natural order restored.

He went down to the carriage and stared about himself avidly as it negotiated the narrow cobbled streets on the way to the palace. Not too much evidence of destruction in this part of the city, at least. It was good of Abeleyn to see him so promptly, but then the monarch was probably afire with curiosity. Important that Murad's own version of events in the west was the first the King heard. So much was open to misinterpretation.

Glarus had told Murad of the war, the ruin of the city and king's illness, while he had pounded his seed into the rump of the whimpering maid. A lot had been happening, seemingly, while he and his companions had been trekking through that endless jungle and eating beetles in order to survive. Murad could not help but feel that the world he had come back to had become an alien place. But the Sequeros were destroyed now, as were the Carreras. That meant that he, Lord Murad of Galiapeno, was now almost certainly closest by blood to the throne itself. It was an ill wind which blew nobody any good. He smiled to himself. War was good for something after all.

The King received him in the palace gardens, amid the chittering of cicadas and the rustling of cypresses. A year before, Murad had sat here with him and first proposed the expedition to the west. It was no longer the same world. They were no longer the same men of that summer morning.

The King had aged in a year. His dark hair was brindled with grey now, and he bore scars on his face even as Murad did. He was taller than he had been, Murad was convinced, and he walked with an awkward gait, the legacy of the wounds he had suffered in the storming of the city. He smiled as his kinsman approached, though the lean nobleman had not missed the initial shock on his face, quickly mastered.

"Cousin, it is good to see you."

They embraced, then each held the other at arm's length and studied the other man's face.

"It's a hard journey you've been on," Abeleyn said.

"I might say the same of you, sire."

The King nodded. "I expected word from you sooner. Did you find it, Murad, your Western Continent?"

Murad sat down beside the King on the stone bench that stood sun-warmed in the garden. "Yes, I found it."

"And was it worth the trip?"

For a second, Murad could not speak. Pictures in his mind. The great cone of Undabane rising out of the jungle. The slaughter of his men there. The jungle journey. The pitiful wreck of Fort Abeleius. Bardolin howling in the hold of the ship in nights of wind. He shut his eyes.

"The expedition was a failure, sire. We were lucky to escape with our lives, those of us who did. It was – it was a nightmare."

"Tell me."

And he did. Everything from the moment of weighing anchor in Abrusio harbour all those months ago, through to mooring the ship again that very morning. He told Abeleyn virtually everything; but he did not mention Griella, or what Bardolin had become. And Hawkwood's part in the tale was kept to a minimum. The survivors had pulled through thanks to the determination and courage of Lord Murad of Galiapeno, who had never despaired, even in the blackest of moments.

The birds sang their homage to the morning, and Murad could smell juniper and lavender on the breeze. His story seemed like some cautionary tale told around a sailor's

fireside, not something which could actually have happened.
It was a bad dream which at last he had woken from, and
he was in the sunlit reality of his own world again.

"Have you breakfasted?" the King asked at last when
Murad was done.

"Yes. But I could do so again. I threw up most of this
morning's."

"Then come with me. I also have a tale to tell, though no
doubt you've heard a part of it already."

The King rose with an audible creaking of wood, and the
pair of them left the garden together, the birds singing their
hearts out all around them.

THE MESSAGE WAS brought to Golophin in the palace by a
breathless boy straight from the waterfront. He had eluded
every footman and guard in the place and was bursting
with news. The *Gabrian Osprey* had returned at last, and
her captain was having some precious form of supercargo
sent to his tower in the hills. It would be there around mid-
afternoon. Captain Hawkwood would like to meet with him
this evening, if it was convenient, and discuss the shipment.
The whole dockside was in a high state of excitement. The
surviving crewmembers of the *Osprey* were being feted in
every tavern that still existed in the lower city, and they
were telling tales of strange lands, stranger beasts, and
rivers of gold!

Golophin gave the boy a silver crown for his pains and
halted in his tracks. He had been on the way to see the King,
but he had an idea he knew what Hawkwood's cargo was.
Instead, he snapped to an eavesdropping palace attendant
that he wanted his mule saddled up at once, and then
repaired to his apartments in the palace to gather up some
books and herbs that he thought he might need.

Isolla found him there, packing with calm haste. "We
were meant to be meeting with the King fully ten minutes
ago, Golophin."

"Give the lad my apologies, Isolla. Something has come up.
I must leave for my tower at once. I may be gone a few days."

"But haven't you heard the news? Some lord who went

off to find the Western Continent has come back. He's to be the star of a levee this afternoon."

"I had heard," Golophin said with a smile. "Lord Murad is known to me. But a friend of mine is – is in trouble. I am the only one who can help him."

"He must be a close friend," Isolla said, obviously curious. She had not thought Golophin close to anyone except perhaps the King himself.

"He was a pupil of mine at a time."

A page-boy knocked and poked his head around the door. "The mule is saddled and ready, sir."

"Thank you." Golophin slung his packed leather bag over one thin shoulder, clapped his broad-brimmed hat on his pate, and kissed Isolla hurriedly. "Watch over him while I'm away, lady."

"Yes, of course. But, Golophin –"

And he was gone. Isolla could have stamped her foot with frustration and curiosity. Then again, why not indulge herself? Much though she liked Golophin, she sometimes found his air of world-weary superiority infuriating.

She would miss the levee, and the explorer's tales, but something told her that Golophin's urgent errant was tied into the arrival of this ship from the west.

Isolla strode off to her chambers. She needed to change into clothes more suitable for riding.

ELEVEN

THE ARMY WOKE up in the black hour before the dawn, and in the frigid darkness men stumbled and cursed and blew on numbed fingers as they strapped on their armour and gnawed dry biscuit. Corfe shared a mug of wine with Marsch and Anrdruw while the trio stood and watched the host of men about them come to life.

"Remember to keep sending back couriers," Corfe said through teeth clenched against the cold. "I don't care if there's nothing to report – at least they'll keep me updated on your location. And don't for God's sake pitch into anything large before the main body comes up."

"No problem," Andruw said. "And I won't teach your grandmother how to suck eggs, either."

"Fair enough." The truth was that Corfe hated to send the Cathedrallers off under someone else's command – even if it were Andruw. He was beginning to realize that his elevated rank entailed sacrifice as well as opportunity. He shook Marsch's and Andruw's hands and watched them disappear into the pre-dawn gloom towards the horse-lines. A few minutes later the Cathedrallers began to saddle up, and within half an hour they were riding out in a long, silent column, the sunrise just beginning to lighten the lowering cloud on the horizon before them.

By mid-morning the remainder of the army, some six and a half thousand men in all, was strung out in a column half a league long whose head pointed almost due east. In the van rode Corfe, surrounded by the fifteen or so cuirassiers who were all that remained of Ormann Dyke's cavalry regiment. His trumpeter, Cerne, had insisted on remaining with him, and Andruw had ceremoniously left behind a further half-dozen of the tribesmen as a kind of bodyguard. Behind this little band of horsemen marched five hundred Torunnan arquebusiers, followed by Formio's two thousand Fimbrians, and then another group of three thousand arquebusiers under Ranafast. After them came the mule train of some six hundred plodding, bad-tempered, heavily laden animals, and finally a rearguard of almost a thousand more Torunnans.

For the first few miles of their advance they could actually glimpse the Cathedrallers off close to the horizon: a black smudge in an otherwise grey and drear landscape. But towards mid-morning the country began to rise in long, stony ridges across the line of march, which slowed their progress and obscured their view of the terrain to the east. By noon the cloud had broken up and there were wide swathes of sunlight come rushing across the land, let slip by fast-moving mare's-tails high above their heads. At the eastern limit of sight, they could all see black bars rising straight into the air and leaning over as they were taken by the high altitude winds. The smoke from the towns aflame along the Searil River. The infantry stared at the smoke as they marched, and the winding column of men toiled along in simmering silence.

Camp was made that night in the shelter of a tall ridge. Sentries paced its summit and Corfe allowed the men to light fires, since the high ground hid them from the east and south. It was bitterly cold, and the sky had cleared entirely so that above their heads was a vast blaze of stars, the larger winking red and blue.

A courier came in from Andruw at midnight, having been five hours on the road. The Cathedrallers were bivouacked in a fireless camp some four leagues south-west of the river. They had destroyed three roving bands of Merduk scavengers at no loss to themselves, and were now turning south-east, parallel with the Searil. There was a large town named Berrona there which seemed not to have been sacked yet, but from the increasing numbers of the enemy that Andruw was encountering, he thought that their main body must not be too far away, and Berrona would be too plump a target for the Merduks to pass by.

Corfe sat by his campfire for a few minutes whilst the courier snatched a hasty meal and some of the cuirassiers rubbed down his horse for him and saddled up another to take him back.

Squinting in the firelight, Corfe scrawled a reply. Andruw was to scout out the environs of Berrona with one or two squadrons only, keeping the rest of his men out of sight. The main body would force-march to his location in the morning – Corfe estimated it was some thirty-five miles away, which would be a hard day's going, but his men would manage it. Then they would await the turn of events.

If the army was to return to Torunn in any kind of fighting condition, then this was the only chance Corfe had to bring a large Merduk force to battle. Another two days, three at most, and they would have to head for home, or start cutting rations even past the meagre amount they were subsisting on at present. And that would almost certainly mean that the horses would start to fail, something which Corfe could not afford to let happen.

The weary courier was sent on his way again. He would reach Andruw just before dawn, with luck, having ridden seventy miles in a single night. How he found his way in a region wholly unknown to him, over rough ground, in the dark, was a mystery to Corfe. He and Andruw had taken a series of maps north with them, only to discover that they were years out of date. Northern Torunna, in the shadow of the Thurians, had always been a wilder place than the south of the kingdom. It had few roads and fewer towns, but strategically it was as vital as the lines of the Searil and Torrin rivers. One day, when he had the time, Corfe would do something about that. He would make of the Torrin Gap a fortress and build good roads clear down to the capital for the passage of armies. The Torunnans hitherto had relied too much on what the Fimbrians had left behind them. Ormann Dyke, Aekir, Torunn itself and the roads that connected them – they were all legacies of the long-vanished Empire. It was time the Torunnans built a few things of their own.

The army was on the march again before dawn. Corfe and his Cathedraller bodyguards rode ahead of the main body, leaving old Ranafast in charge behind them. They passed isolated farmsteads that had been burned out by Merduk marauders and once came across a lonely church which had inexplicably been spared the flames, but within which the enemy had obviously stabled their horses for some considerable time. The charred remains of two men were bound to a stake in the churchyard, the blackened stumps of their legs ending in a mound of dead embers and ash. Corfe had them buried and rode on.

They halted at noon to rest the horses and wait for the infantry to come up. Corfe gnawed salt beef and bit off chunks of hard army biscuit while ceaselessly searching the eastern horizon for signs of life. Around him the tribesmen talked quietly in their own tongue to each other and their horses.

A solitary horseman appeared in the distance and the talk ceased. He was riding at full, reckless gallop, yanking up his mount's head when it stumbled on loose rock, bent low in the saddle to extract every ounce of speed out of the beast. A Cathedraller, his armour winking like freshly spilt gore. Corfe waved at him and he changed course. A few minutes later he had come to a staggering halt in front of them, his horse spraying foam from its mouth, nostrils flared and pink, sides heaving. He leapt off his steed and proffered a despatch-case, gasping.

"Ondruw – he send me –"

"Good man. Cerne – give him some water. See to his horse and get him a fresh one." Corfe turned away and shook out the scroll of tattered paper Andruw had scrawled his despatch upon.

Merduk main body sighted three leagues south of Berrona. Some fifteen thousand men, plus two thousand cavalry out to their front. All lightly armed. My position half a league north of the town, but am withdrawing another league to the north to avoid discovery. Looks like they intend to enter Berrona this afternoon. Citizens still unaware of either us or the Merduks. How soon can you come up?

    Andruw Cear-Adurhal,
    Colonel Commanding

Corfe could sense the desperate plea in Andruw's words. He wanted to save the town from the horror of a Merduk sack. But men can only march so fast. It would be nightfall before the army was reunited again, and Corfe did not intend to launch the men into a night attack after a thirty-five mile march, against a superior foe. What was more, he could not even afford to let Andruw warn the townsfolk of the approaching catastrophe – that would give away the fact that there was a Torunnan army in the region, and when his men came up in the morning they would find the Merduks ready for them.

No – it was impossible. Berrona would have to take its chances.

There had been a time when he might have done it, when he had less braid on his shoulders and there was not much more at stake than his own life. But if he crippled this army of his now, Torunna would be finished. He scribbled out a reply to Andruw with his face set and pale.

Hold your new position. Do not engage the enemy under any circumstances. Infantry will be with you tonight. We will assault in the morning.
Corfe Cear-Inaf
Commander-in-Chief

There. It gave Corfe a sick feeling in his stomach to hand the return despatch to the courier, and as the man set off again he almost thought better of it and recalled him. But it was too late. The tribesman was already a receding speck soon lost to view. It was done. He had just consigned the citizens of Berrona to a night of hell.

"What are we to do with the prisoners?" Ranafast asked as the endless column of trudging men filed past.

The infantry had come up, and after the briefest of rests was on the move again. The sun was already westering, and they still had a long way to go to effect the rendezvous with Andruw and the Cathedrallers. But not a single man had dropped out, Ranafast and Formio had informed Corfe. The news that they were about to pitch into the Merduk raiders had filled the troops with fresh energy, and they stepped out with a will.

"Let them go," Corfe said. "They're nothing but a damned nuisance."

Ranafast stared at him, dark eyes glittering over a hawk nose and an iron-grey beard which looked as though it had been filed to a point.

"I can have the men take care of them," he said.

"No. Just set them free. But I want to talk to them first."

"Sir, I have to protest –"

"I won't make the men into murderers, Ranafast. We start slaughtering prisoners out of hand, and we're no better than they are. The men will have plenty of chances to kill themselves a Merduk tomorrow, in open battle. Now have the prisoners sent to me."

"I hope you know what you're doing, General," Ranafast said.

The captives were a miserable looking bunch, guarded by a couple of Fimbrians who regarded their charges with detached contempt. They cowered before Corfe as though he were their executioner. Part of him was longing to order their deaths. He held no illusions about what they had been doing up here in the north, but at the same time he was thinking of the peasant army he had slaughtered down at Staed. Narfinyr's tenants, small farmers forced to take up arms for a lord they barely knew and who regarded them as expendable chattel. It had sickened Corfe, the slaughter of such poor ignorant wretches, and these Merduks were the same. They had been conscripted into the Sultan's army, leaving families and farms behind. Some of them did not even possess Merduk blood. He would kill men like these in their nameless thousands in the days and months to come, but that was the unavoidable consequence of war. He would not stain his conscience with their cold-blooded murder. He had enough blood on his hands already.

"You are free to go," he told them. "On the condition that you do not rejoin the Merduk army, but instead try to find your way home to your families. I know you did not join this war by choice, but because you were forced to. So be on your way in peace."

The men gaped, then looked at one another, jabbering in Merduk and Normannic. They were incredulous, too astonished to be happy. Some reached out to touch his stirruped feet and he backed his horse away from them.

"Go now. And don't come back to Torunna ever again. If you do, I promise that you will die here."

"Thank you your honour!" the man Corfe recognized as the battered Felipio shouted out. Then the Merduks broke away, and as a group began running towards the long shadows of the Thurian Mountains in the north, as if trying to get away before Corfe changed his mind. The marching Torunnans watched them go, some of them spitting in disgust at the sight, but not a man protested.

Corfe turned to Ranafast, who still sat his horse nearby.

"Am I a bloody fool, Ranafast – am I going soft?"

The veteran smiled. "Maybe, lad. Maybe you are just becoming something of a politician. You know damn well those bastards are going to try and rejoin their comrades – they've nowhere else to go. But if they make it, the news that the Torunnans treat their prisoners well will spread like a wildfire in high summer. If the Merduk levy thinks it will receive quarter when it lays down its arms, then it may not fight quite so hard."

"That's what I was hoping, I suppose, though I'm still not convinced of it. But I've come to a conclusion Ranafast – that we can't win this war through force alone. We need a little guile also."

"Aye, we do. Doesn't taste too good in the mouth though, does it?" And Ranafast wheeled his horse away to rejoin the army column. Corfe sat his own mount and watched the freed Merduks running madly up into the foothills until they were mere dots against snow-worn bulk of the Thurian Mountains on the horizon before them. For a crazed, indecipherable moment, he almost wished he were running with them.

CATHEDRALLER SCOUTS GUIDED them in that night. The weather had deteriorated into a face-stinging drizzle which was flung at them by winds off the mountains, but the wind would at least muffle the sound of their marching feet and clinking equipment. The men had their heads down and were dragging their feet by that time, and in the blustery darkness half a dozen pack-mules had somehow broken free from their handlers and been lost, but in the main the army was intact, the column a little ragged perhaps, but still whole. Andruw had found a level campsite some five miles north of the town. There was a stream running through it, a boon to both horses and men, but as the weary soldiers filed into the bivouac their heads lifted and they peered intently at the southern horizon. There was an orange glow flickering in the sky there. Berrona was burning.

Andruw greeted Corfe unsmilingly, his face a pale blur under his helm marked only by two black holes for eyes and a slot for a mouth.

"Their cavalry entered the town several hours ago," he said. They took the men off to the south. Now they're having a little fun with the women."

Corfe rode up close until their knees were touching. He set a hand on Andruw's shoulder.

"We can't do it – not tonight. The men are done up. We'll hit them at dawn, Andruw."

Andruw nodded. "I know. We must be sensible about it." His voice was cracking with strain.

"Have you scouted out the main body?"

They're still bivouacked to the south. Their camp is full of the loot and women from half a dozen different towns. These lads have been having a fine old time of it up here in the north. It must seem like a kind of holiday for them."

"It ends tomorrow morning with the dawn, I promise you. Now get the officers together. I want you to tell us all you know about the dispositions of these bastards."

Andruw nodded and started to move his horse away. Then he halted.

"Corfe?"

"Yes?"

"Promise me something else."

Andruw's voice was thick with grief but it was too dark for Corfe to read his face. "Go on."

"Promise me that tomorrow we will take no prisoners."

The wind and the subdued clamour of an army settling down for the night filled the silence that stretched between them. Politics, strategy, his talk with Ranafast; they rose like a cloud in Corfe's mind. But smouldering there under all the rationalizations were his own anger, and his friend's grief. When Corfe finally responded, his voice was as raw as Andruw's had been.

"All right, then. Tomorrow there will be no quarter. I promise you."

TWELVE

THE TOWN OF Berrona had always been an unremarkable place, tucked away on the north-western border of Torunna, not far from the headwaters of the Searil River. Some six thousand people dwelt there in the shadow of the western Thurians, their only link with Torunna proper a single dirt road which snaked away to the south across the foothills. With the fall of Ormann Dyke, they were now technically behind the Merduk lines, but thus far in this winter of carnage and destruction they had remained untouched. They were too far out of the way, closer to Aekir than to Torunn, and cradled by the long outthrust spurs of the Thurian mountains so that the war had passed them by and was a matter of tall tales and rumours, no more. A few of the survivors of Aekir's fall had somehow made their way there and had been welcomed, holding forth to packed audiences in the inns of the town and chilling the listeners with tales of war and atrocity. *Get out of here*, the Aekirians said. *Cross the Torrin river while there is still time.* But the townsfolk, though they shuddered appropriately at the stories of horror the refugees had to tell, could not believe that the war would touch them. *We are too out of the way*, they said. *Why would the Merduks want to come this far north when the armies are fighting way down on the plains about the capital? We will sit the war out and see what happens.*

The Aekirians – shocked, broken travesties of the prosperous city-dwellers they had once been – merely shook their heads. And though they were invited to stay with genuine compassion by the folk of Berrona, they refused, and resumed their weary flight west towards the shrinking Torunnan frontier.

But the people of the town were proved right, it seemed. As midwinter passed and the new year grew older they were indeed forgotten and left undisturbed. They hunted in the hills as they had always done in the dark months, and bored fishing holes in the ice that crusted the Searil, and ate into their stores of pickles and dried meat and fish and fruit. And the world left them alone.

"HORSES, ARJA – LOOK! Men on horses!"

The girl straightened, pressing her fists into the hollow of her back as though an old woman, though she was not yet fifteen. She shaded her eyes against the glare of sunlight on snow and peered out across the white hills to where her younger brother was pointing with quivering excitement.

"You're imagining again, Narfi. I can't see a thing." She bent to knot the rawhide rope about the firewood she had gathered, dark hair falling about her face. But her brother Narfi tugged at her sleeve, his head hardly reaching to her elbow.

"Look now! I'll bet you can see them now! Anyone could."

Sighing, she slapped his hand away and stared again. A dark bristle of movement, like a spined snake off in the distance. They were so far away it was impossible to tell if they were even moving. But they were definitely men on horses, a long column of them riding half in shadow, half in sunlight as the scudding winter clouds came and went before the wind. Even as she watched, Arja saw the fleeting sparkle as the sun glittered off a line of metal accoutrements. Lance-points, helmets, breastplates.

"I see them," she said lightly. "I see them now."

"Soldiers, Arja. Are they ours, you think? Would they let me up on a horse?"

Arja abandoned the firewood and grasped her brother's arm roughly. "We have to get home."

"No! I want to watch. I want to wait for them!"

"Shut up Narfi! What if they're Merduks?"

At the word *Merduks* her brother's round face clouded. "Dada said they wouldn't come here," he said faintly.

His sister dragged him away. When she glanced back over her shoulder she could see that they were bigger now. The dark snake had broken up into hundreds of little figures, all glittering in long lines. And farther away – back where the cloud and the distance rendered all things hazy, she thought she saw more of them. It looked like the line of a faraway forest undulating along the slopes and hollows of the hill. An army. She had never seen one before but she knew instantly what it was. A big army. She gulped for air, prayers flitting through her head like a tumble of summer swallows. They would ride on past. No-one ever came to Berrona. They would pass by. But she had to tell her father.

THAT AFTERNOON THE column of horsemen rode into the town as though they were triumphal warriors returning home. There were hundreds of them, perhaps even thousands, all mounted on tall bay horses and clad in outlandish armour, their lance-points gay with silk streamers and a pair of matchlock pistols at the pommel of every saddle. The silent townsfolk lined the streets and some of the riders waved as they rode past, or blew kisses to the more comely of the women. They came to a halt in front of the town hall and there the leading riders dismounted. The town headsman was waiting for them on the steps of the hall, pale as snow but resolute. One of the more gorgeously caparisoned horsemen doffed his helm to reveal a brown smiling face, his eyes as dark as sloes.

"I bring greetings in the name of Aurungzeb my Sultan, and the Prophet Ahrimuz, may he live forever," he cried in a clear, young voice. His Normannic was perfect, only a slight accent betraying its origins.

"Ries Millian, town headsman," the white-faced figure on the steps said, his voice wavering with strain. "Welcome to the town of Berrona."

"Thank you. Now please have all the people in this town assemble in the square here. I have an announcement to make."

Millian hesitated, but only for a moment. "What is it you wish of us?" he asked.

"You will find out. Now do as I say." The Merduk officer turned and rapped out a series of commands to his men in their own language. The column of horsemen split up. Some two hundred remained in the square before the town hall whilst the rest splintered into groups of one or two dozen and set off down the side-streets, the hooves of their horses rising a clattering din off the cobbles.

The headsman was conferring with other men of the town in whispers. At last he stepped forward. "I cannot do as you say until I know what you intend to do with us," he said bravely, the men behind him nodding at his words.

The Merduk officer smiled, and without a word he drew his tulwar. A flash of steel in the thin winter sunlight, and Ries Millian was on his knees, choking, his hands striving in vain to close up his gaping windpipe. Blood on the cobbles, squirts and gouts of it steaming like soup. The headsman fell on his side, twitched, lay still. In the crowd a woman shrieked and rushed forward onto the body. The Merduk officer gestured impatiently and two of his men lifted her away, still shrieking. In full view of the packed square, they stripped her, cutting the clothes from her body with their swords and slicing flesh from her limbs as they did so. When she was naked, they bent her over, and one thrust his scimitar up between her legs with a grunt, until only the hilt of the weapon was visible. The woman went silent, collapsed, and slid off the end of the blade. The Merduks grinned and laughed. He who had killed her sniffed his bloody sword and made a face. They laughed again. The Merduk officer wiped his tulwar off on the headman's carcass and turned to the paralyzed huddle of men Millian had been conferring with.

"Do as I say. Get everyone here in the square. Now."

THE DAY DREW on into an early winter evening, but for the folk of Berrona it seemed that it would never end.

The Merduks had cleared out the town house by house, stabling their horses in the humbler dwellings. The menfolk had been separated from the women and children and marched away south over the hills by several hundred of the invaders. Then there had been the sound of gunfire, crackling out into the cold air endlessly. It had gone on for hours, but none of the women could or would agree on what it meant. A few of the local shepherds had been dragged in by the invaders, bloody and terrified. They said that there was a huge Merduk army encamped out in the pastures to the south of the town, but few of the people believed them or had time to consider the ramifications of such a phenomenon. Their own tragedy filled their minds to overflowing.

Arja had seen some women dragged off into empty houses by groups of the laughing soldiers. There had been screams, and later the Merduks had emerged restrapping their armour, smiling, talking lazily in that horrible language they had. One woman, Frieda the blacksmith's wife who was held to be the prettiest in the town, had been stripped and forced to serve wine to the Merduk officers as they lounged in the headman's house. Her husband they had searched out and trussed up in a corner so that he was forced to watch as they finally raped her one by one. In the end they had killed her. But they blinded and castrated the blacksmith before leaving him a moaning heap on the floor. No-one had dared help him, and he had bled to death beside the violated corpse of his wife. Vanya knew this because some of the other women had been treated in the same manner as Frieda and then released. They had seen it happen.

Perhaps fifty of the women of the town had been herded up and were now in the town hall. They were the young, the pretty, the well-shaped. Outside, night was drawing in and the Merduks had lit bonfires in the streets, piling them high with furniture from the empty houses. They were sacking the town, looting anything of value and destroying what they could not carry away. Many buildings had been burned to the ground already, and it was rumoured the Merduks had locked most of the old people inside them first.

Arja had not seen her father since the men had been taken away. Her brother, though barely eight years old, had been taken along with him. Now she was alone with a crowd of women and girls, imprisoned in the dark. A few of the women were sobbing quietly, but most were silent. Occasionally there were whispered conversations, most of them consisting of speculation on the fate of their husbands and fathers and brothers.

"They are dead," one woman hissed. "All dead. And soon we will be too."

"No no," another said frantically. "They have taken away the men to work for them. Why would they kill their labourers? The men are digging defences out beyond the town. Why kill those who can work for you? It makes no sense."

This straw of hope seemed to cheer many of the women. "It is war," they said. "Terrible things happen, but there has to be a sense to it all. Soldiers have their orders. So we are under the Merduks now – they have to eat too. We will adjust. We can be useful to them."

A scraping and thudding as the double-doors of the town hall were opened. It was full night outside, but the saffron light of the bonfires flickered in and the sky was orange and red with distant flames as the outskirts of the town blazed. The women could see the black silhouettes of many men outlined by the flames. Some held flasks and bottles, others naked swords. There was no talk of usefulness now.

Some screamed, some were dully passive. The Merduk troopers walked among them looking into their faces and running their hands up and down their bodies as though testing the mettle of an auctioned horse. When they found what they wanted they took the woman by the wrist or the hair and dragged her outside. When half the women had been taken, the doors were closed again and those who remained huddled in a corner embracing each other, bereft of speech.

Shrieks in the night. Men laughing. Arja cowered with the rest, her mind a white furious blank. Every sensation seemed to be dragged out, as in some hideous dream. She could not believe that this day had happened, these things. It was all utterly beyond anything she had ever known or imagined before, a window into another world she had not known could exist. Was this what war was like, then?

What seemed like hours passed, though they had no way of telling the passage of time, and their estimation of what constituted hours and minutes seemed to have been skewed and twisted until all frames of reference were useless in this new universe.

The screams died away. No-one slept. They sat with their arms about one another and stared at the black door, awaiting its opening.

And at last the clumps and scrapes as their turn came and the portals of the town hall swung wide once more. Arja was almost relieved. She felt that she had been stretched so taut in the black time of waiting that soon she must snap like a green stick bent too far.

The selection procedure was swifter this time. A shadow which reeked of sweat and beer and urine seized Arja's arm and drew her outside into the hellish light of the bonfires. There were waggons parked in the square now, filled brim-full of naked women who hid their faces with their hair. Some had blood matting them. A few bodies, contorted out of all humanity, sprawled upon the cobbles with their innards piled like glistening heaps of mashed berries around them. In one of the bonfires what looked like the trunk of a small tree burned, but the sickening stink of its burning was not that of charring wood.

Arja's captor plucked at her clothes. He was a small man, and to her surprise he was not dark-skinned or dark-eyed. He looked like a Torunnan and when he spoke it was in good Normannic.

"Take them off. Quickly."

She did as she was bidden. All over the square women were undressing whilst a crowd of several hundred men watched. When she had stripped down to her undershirt she could go no further. The numbness was eaten through and she felt a moment of pure, incapacitating panic. The Torunnan-looking Merduk chuckled, swigged from a bottle, and then ripped her undershirt from her back so that she stood naked before him.

Some of his comrades gathered with him, eating her up with their eyes. When she tried to cover herself with her hands they slapped them away. They were laughing, drunk. Some had their breeches unbuttoned and their members lolled and shone wetly in the firelight. Again, the panic beating great dark wings about Arja's head. Again, a sense of the unreality of it all.

The soldiers spoke together in the Merduk tongue, as easy and unforced as men who have met in an inn after a long day's work. Two of them grabbed her by the arms. Two more forced her knees apart. And then the little Torunnan-like trooper took his bottle and thrust it up between Arja's thighs.

She screamed at the agony of it, struggled impotently in the grasp of the four soldiers who held her. The small trooper worked the bottle up and down. When he pulled it out at last the glass was red and shining. He winked at his fellows and then took a long draught from the bloody neck, smacking his lips theatrically.

They bent her over a pile of broken furniture, splintered wood piercing her breasts and belly. Then one mounted her from behind and began thrusting into her torn insides. There was only the pain, the blooming firelight, the hands grasping her so tightly her hands were numb. Something soft was pushed against her lips and she pulled her head back from the smell but her hair was grasped and a voice spoke in Normannic: *open up*. She took the thing into her mouth and it grew large and rigid and was pushed back down her throat until she gagged. They thrust into her from both directions. Warm liquid cascaded down her naked back and the men cursed and laughed. Liquid pulsed into her mouth, salty and foul. The thing in there softened again and slid out between her lips. She vomited, the taste of her bile somehow cleaner, though it scalded her lips and tongue.

The hands released her and she slumped onto the hard cobbles. They were cold and wet beneath her. *It is over*, she thought. *It is done*.

Then another knot of soldiers strode up, pushing aside the first group, and she was seized upright once again.

THE DAWN AIR was full of the smell of burning, the blue winter horizon smudged with smoke. The mobs of horsemen took their time to rub down their mounts, assemble in the square, and root in their saddlebags for breakfast. Finally a series of orders were shouted out and the troopers mounted. Their horses were burdened with wineskins, flapping chickens, bolts of cloth and clinking sacks. Their officers were already outside the town, on a hill to the south. With them were a gaggle of splendidly accoutred senior commanders from the Merduk main body, their banner-bearers holding up bravely flapping silk flags in the freshening wind.

Finally the heavily burdened cavalry formed up and filed out of the gutted wreck of Berrona. Some were sullen and heavy-headed. A few were nodding in the saddle, and yet others seemed to be still drunk with the excesses of the night. They pointed their horse's noses to the south, where less than two miles away a great Merduk camp sprawled across the land. They rode with the rising sun an orange blaze in their left eyes and the town still smouldering behind them. Near the rear of their meandering and straggling column half a dozen waggons trundled and jolted along, drawn by mules, cart-horses and plodding oxen. A conglomeration of naked, bleeding and sodden humanity crouched in the waggons, silent as statues. Around them some of the soldiers of the Sultan, light at heart, began singing to welcome the dawn of the new day.

Arja had her head bent into her knees to shut out the world. She and the other women of the town – those who had survived – huddled together for warmth and comfort in the beds of the waggons. Some of them were sobbing soundlessly, but most were dry-eyed and seemed almost to be elsewhere, their minds far away. Thus it hardly registered upon them when the Merduks stopped singing.

The waggon halted. Men were shouting. Arja lifted her head.

The Merduk column had coalesced into a formless crowd of mounted men who milled about in disorder. What was happening? Some of the Merduks were throwing their garnered loot from their saddles in panic. Others were fumbling for the matchlocks at their pommels. Officers were yelling, frantic.

Then Arja saw what had caused the transformation. On the hillside behind the burnt-out wreck of Berrona a long line of men had appeared, thousands of them. They were still a mile away, but they were coming on at a run. Black-clad soldiers, some carrying guns, others with shouldered pikes. They advanced with the drilled remorselessness of some terrible machine.

"The army is here!" one of the women called out gladly. "The Torunnans have come!" A nearby Merduk trooper hacked her furiously about the head with his scimitar and she toppled over the side of the waggon.

A few minutes of chaos as the Merduks hovered, indecisive. Then the whole body of cavalry took off to the south in a muck-churning, frenzied gallop. The waggons were left behind along with a litter of discarded plunder.

It was painful to regain interest in the world, almost like coming alive again in some agonizing wrench of rebirth. Arja raised herself to her bloody knees the better to see what was happening. Tears coursed down her face.

The ground under the wheels of the waggons seemed to shake with a subterranean thunder. It was both a noise and a physical sensation. The Torunnans were by-passing the burnt-out streets of the town, their formation dividing neatly and with no loss of speed. But they would never catch up with the fleeing Merduk cavalry – they were all on foot. Arja felt a hot blaze of pure hatred flare up in her heart. The Merduks would get away. They had killed her father and her brother but they would get away.

The thunder in the ground grew more intense – it was an audible roar now, as though a furious river were coursing under the stones and heather of the hills –

– and then they burst into view with all the sudden fury of an apocalypse. A great mass of cavalry erupted in a long line from behind a ridge to the south, at right-angles to the fleeing Merduks. Arja heard a horn-call ring out clear and free above the awesome rumble of the horses. The riders were all armoured in scarlet, and singing as they came.

The Merduks looked over their right shoulders, and even at this distance, Arja could see the naked terror on their faces. They kicked their mounts madly, tossing away booty, weapons, even helmets. But they were not fast enough.

The red horsemen ploughed into the mob of Merduk cavalry like a vermillion thunderbolt. She saw dozens of the lighter enemy horses actually hurled end over end by the impact. A thrashing Merduk trooper was lifted high into the air on the end of a lance. The enemy seemed to simply melt away. The red tide engulfed them, annihilating hundreds of men in the space of heartbeats. Only a few dozen Merduks broke free of the murderous scrum of men and horses, to continue their manic flight south towards their main camp. More were running about on foot, screaming, but the heavily armoured scarlet cavalry hunted them down like rabbits, spearing them as they ran, or trampling them underfoot. Then there was another horn-call and at once the horsemen broke off the pursuit and began to reform in a neat line. A black and crimson banner billowed above their heads, some device she could not quite make out. The whole engagement had taken not more than three or four minutes.

The Torunnan infantry were running past the waggons now, panting men with the sweat pouring down their faces and their eyes glittering like glass. They kept their line as though connected by invisible chains, and as they ran a great animal growl seemed to be coming from their throats. One man hurriedly seized Arja's hand as he passed by, and kissed it, before running on. Others were weeping as they ran, but all kept their ranks. The smoke from their lit match hung in the air after they had passed, like some acrid perfume of war. As they reached the ranks of the cavalry ahead, the horsemen split swiftly in two and took up position on their flanks. Then the united formation advanced again, at a fast march this time, and began eating up the ground between them and the Merduk camp with the calm inexorability of a tidal wave.

It seemed to Arja in that moment one of the most glorious things she had ever seen.

THIRTEEN

THE CEREMONY WAS a simple one, as befitted the steppes where it had ultimately originated. It took place in the open air, with the Thurians providing a magnificent backdrop of white peaks on the northern horizon. The ruins of Ormann Dyke's Long Walls glowered nearby like ancient monuments, and the Searil river rushed foaming to the west.

Two thousand Merduk cavalry, caparisoned in all the finery they possessed, surrounded an isolated quartet of figures, making three parts of a hollow square about them. On the fourth side a special dais had been constructed and canopied with translucent silk. The wind twisted and turned the fine material like smoke, giving glimpses of the Royal concubines seated on scarlet and gold cushions within, the eunuchs standing to their rear like pale statues. A host of gaudy figures clustered around the foot of the dais, fleeting flashes of winter sunlight sparkling off an emperor's ransom in gems and precious metals. To the rear of the surrounding cavalry, a dozen elephants stood, painted out of all recognition, hung with silk and brocade and embellished with gold and leather harness. On their backs were wide kettle-drums and a band of Merduk musicians gripping horns and pipes. As the ceremony began, the kettle-drums rumbled out with a sound like a distant barrage of artillery, or thunder in the mountains. Then there was silence but for the wind hissing over the hills of northern Torunna.

Mehr Jirah stood before Aurungzeb, Sultan of Ostrabar, and Ahara, his concubine. The Sultan held the reins of a magnificent warhorse in his right hand and a worn and ancient-looking scimitar in his left. He was dressed in the plain leather and furs of an ancient steppe chieftain. Ahara was clad as soberly as Aurungzeb, in a long woollen cloak and a linen veil.

Mehr Jirah cried out loudly in the Merduk tongue, and the two thousand cavalry clashed their lances against their shields and roared out in affirmation. Yes, they would accept this union, and they would gladly recognize this woman as their Sultan's First Wife. Their Queen.

Then Aurungzeb put the reins of his warhorse in Ahara's hand, and set the scimitar which had been his grandfather's at her feet. She stepped over it lightly, and the whole host cheered, the musicians on the backs of the elephants blasting out a cacophony of noise. Mehr Jirah offered a bowl of mare's-milk to the couple and they sipped from it in turn, then kissed. And it was done. Aurungzeb the Sultan of Ostrabar had a new wife; with a child growing in her belly who would one day be the legitimate heir to the throne.

THEY HAD CLEARED a new set of apartments for her in the tower of Ormann Dyke. Their windows looked east over the Searil River towards Aekir and the Merduk lands beyond. She sat at the window for a long time whilst a small army of maids and eunuchs hurried back and forth lighting braziers, moving furniture, setting out arrays of sweetmeats and wines. Finally she became aware that someone stood behind her, watching. She turned from the view out the window, still dressed in the sombre steppe-costume in which she had been married, and found Serrim the chief eunuch standing there, and beside him a tall Merduk in leather riding-breeches, a silk tunic and a wide sash about his middle with a knife thrust into it. He was weather-worn and gaunt, his beard as hoary as sea-salt. His eyes were grey like her own but he was staring out the window over her shoulder and did not meet her appraisal. He looked to be in his sixties but his carriage was that of a much younger man.

"Well?" Heria asked. Serrim had been a bully when she was a mere concubine. Now that she had been catapulted into the Merduk nobility he had quickly become a sycophant. She disliked him the more for it.

"Lady, His Majesty has sent Shahr Baraz to you to be your personal attendant."

The lean Merduk hauled his gaze from the window and met her eyes for the first time. He bowed without a word.

"My attendant? I have plenty of those already." Shahr Baraz looked as though he belonged on a horse with a sword in his hand, not in a lady's chambers.

"He is to be your – your bodyguard, and is to attend you at all times."

"My bodyguard," Heria said wonderingly. And then something stirred from her memory. "Was it not Shahr Baraz who commanded the army which took Aekir? I thought he was an old man – and – and no longer with us."

"This is the illustrious khedive's son, lady."

"I see. Leave us, Serrim."

"Lady, I –"

"Leave us. All of you. I want the chamber cleared. You can finish your work here later."

A procession of maids left the room at once. The eunuch padded off with them, looking thoroughly discontented. Heria felt a brief moment of intense satisfaction, and then the cloud came down again.

"Would you like some wine, Shahr Baraz?"

"No lady. I do not indulge."

"I see. So you are my bodyguard. Who do you intend to protect me from?"

"From whomsoever would wish to harm you."

She switched to Normannic. "And can you understand this tongue?"

The Merduk hesitated. A muscle twitched in his jaw. There was a long, livid scar there that ran from one cheek into his beard.

"Some words I know," he replied in the same language.

"Do you understand this, then – that I believe you are nothing more than a spy set here by the Sultan to keep watch over me and report my every move?"

"I am not a spy," Shahr Baraz said heatedly.

"Then why would the Sultan place the capable son of such an illustrious father in such a menial position?"

His grey eyes had flared into life. His Normannic was perfect as he replied. "To punish me."

"Why would he want to punish you?"

"Because I am my father's son, and he thinks my father failed him before this fortress."

"Your father is dead, then?"

"No – I don't know. He disappeared into the mountains rather than return to court to be – to answer for his actions."

She switched back to Merduk. "Your Normannic is better than you think."

"I am no spy," he repeated. "Even the Sultan would not ask me to be that. My family have served the house of Ostrabar for generations. I will not fail the Sultan's trust – nor yours, lady. I swear it. And besides" – here a glint of humour pierced his sternness – "the harem is full of spies already. The Sultan has little need of another."

She actually found herself liking him. "Have you family of your own?"

"A wife and two daughters. They are in Orkhan."

Hostages for his good behaviour, no doubt. "Thank you, Shahr Baraz. Now please leave me."

But he stood his ground stubbornly. "I am to remain with you at all times."

"All times?" she asked with one raised eyebrow. Shahr Baraz flushed.

"Within the bounds of propriety, yes."

She felt a pang of pure despair, and abandoned the game. "All right." The prison walls were still intact then. She might be able to order about a flock of flunkeys, but her position was essentially unchanged. She had been a fool to think otherwise.

Heria turned to regard the view from the lofty window once more. The pain was there, of course, but she kept it at bay, skirted around it as a man might avoid a bottomless quagmire in his travels. Somewhere over the horizon in the east the ruins of Aekir stood, and somewhere in those ashes were the remains of another life. But the man with whom she had shared that life was still alive. Still alive. Where was Corfe now, her one and only husband? Strange, and terrible that the knowledge he still lived and walked and breathed upon the earth was a source only of agony. She could take no joy in it, and she scourged herself for that. She bore another man's child, a man who now called her wife. She had been ennobled by the union, but would live out what remained of her life behind the bars of a jewelled cage. While her Corfe was alive – out there somewhere. And leading the fight against the world she now inhabited.

She wanted to die.

But would not. She had a son in her belly. Not Corfe's child, but something that was precious all the same – something that was hers. For the child, she would stay alive – and she might even be able to do something to aid Corfe and the Torunnans, to help those who had once been her own people.

But the pain of it; the sheer, raw torment.

"Shahr Baraz," she said without turning round.

"Lady?"

"I need – I need a friend, Shahr Baraz." The tears scalded her eyes. She could not see. Her voice throbbed with a beat like the sob of a swan's wing in flight.

A hand touched the top of her head gently, resting there only for a second before being withdrawn. It was the first touch of genuine kindness she had received for a very long time, and it broke some wall within her soul. She bowed her head and wept bitterly. When she had collected herself she found Shahr Baraz on one knee before her. His fingers tapped her lightly on the forearm.

"A Merduk queen is not supposed to weep," he said, but his voice was gentle. He smiled.

"I have been Queen for only a morning. Perhaps I will get used to it."

"Dry your eyes lady. The kohl is running down your face. Here." He wiped the streaked paint from her cheeks with his thumb. Her veil fell away.

"A man who touches one of the Sultan's women will have his hands cut off," she reminded him.

"I will not tell if you do not."

"Agreed." She collected herself. "You must forgive me. The excitement of the morning..."

"One of my daughters is about your age," Shahr Baraz said. "I pray she will never have to suffer as I believe you have. I would rather she lived out her days in a felt hut with a man she loved than –" He stopped, then straightened.

"I will have your maids sent in, lady, so that you may repair yourself. It is inappropriate that I should be here alone with you, even if I am an old man. The Sultan would not approve."

"No. If you want to do something for me, then have the little Ramusian monk sent here. I wish to speak with him. He is imprisoned in the lower levels of the tower."

"I am not sure that –"

"Please, Shahr Baraz."

He nodded. "You are a queen, after all." Then he bowed, and left her.

A queen, she thought. *So is that what I am now?* She remembered the hell of Aekir at its fall, the Merduk soldier who had raped her with the light of the burning city a writhing inferno in his eyes. The terrible journey north in the waggons, John Mogen's Torunnans trudging beside them with their necks in capture-yokes. Men crucified by the thousand, babies tossed out in the snow to die. All those memories. They made part of her mind into a screaming wilderness which she had walled off to keep from going mad.

She was alone in the room. For a blessed moment she was alone. No gossiping maids or spying eunuchs. No gaggle of concubines intriguing endlessly and bitching about petty slights and imagined neglects. She could stand at the window and look at at what had once been her own country, and feel herself free. Her name was Heria Cear-Inaf, and she was no queen, only the lowly daughter of a silk merchant, and her heart was still her own to bestow where she pleased.

"Beard of the Prophet – what does this mean – are you sitting here alone? God's teeth, this will not do – where is that scoundrel Baraz? I'll have him flogged."

The Sultan of Ostraber strode into the Chamber like a gale, accompanied by a knot of his staff officers. He was dripping with jewels and gold once more, and a rich, fur-lined cloak whirled about him like a cloud. Silver tassels winked on the pointed toes of his boots.

Heria refastened her veil hurriedly.

"Shahr Baraz is off running an errand for me, my lord. Do not blame him. I wanted to see if he were truly mine to command."

Aurungzeb boomed with laughter. He bristled a kiss through her thin veil that bruised her lips. "Well done, wife! That family needs humbling – they take too much of the world's troubles upon themselves. Have you tumbled to my jest then? The officer's quarters are buzzing with it. A Baraz as a lady's maid! Keep him on the tips of his toes – it will do him good. But you are still in your bridal gown! Get those ancient rags off your back – tradition is all well and fine, but we cannot have my First Wife looking like a beggar off the steppe. Where are your attendants? I'll kick Serrim's fat arse next time I see him."

"They are preparing my wardrobe," Heria lied. "I sent them all off to do it – they are so slow."

"Yes, yes – you must be firm with them you know. Have a few of them flogged, and they'll start to jump right smartly." Aurungzeb embraced her. The top of her head came barely to his chin, though she was tall for a woman.

"Ah, those beautiful bones. I do not know how I shall keep myself from them 'til the babe is born." He nuzzled her hair, beaming.

"I must be off, my Queen. Shahr Johor – hunt out those damn maids. My wife sits here alone like a mourner. And get the furniture sent up – the things from Aekir we had shipped." Aurungzeb looked around the room. It had been part of Pieter Martellus's chambers in the days when the Dyke had been Torunnan, and was as bare as a barracks.

"Poor surroundings for a woman. We'll have to prettify the place a little. I may just let this tower stand, as a monument. Better than a tent out in the field though. I must be off. We are to dine together later, Ahara – I have invited all the ambassadors. We are having lobsters sent up from the coast. Have you ever tasted a lobster? Ah, here is Shahr Baraz – what do you mean by leaving the Queen alone?"

Shahr Baraz stood in the doorway. His face was expressionless. "My apologies, Sultan. It will not happen again."

"That's all right, Baraz – she's been playing with you, I think, my western doe." And in an aside to Heria: "He looks so much like his terrible old father, and he's just as stiff-necked. Keep him on the hop, my love – that's the way. Well, I must be off. Wear the blue today – the stuff the Nalbeni sent us – it sets off your eyes." And he was gone, striding out of the room with his aides struggling to keep up, his voice booming down the corridor beyond.

By THE TIME Albrec had been brought to the new Queen's chambers she had cast aside her sombre marriage garments and was swathed head to toe in sky-blue silk. A circlet of silver sat upon her veiled head and her eyes were as striking as paint could make them. She reclined on a low divan whilst around her half a dozen maids perched on cushions. A tall Merduk of advanced years whom Albrec had never seen at the court before stood straight as a spear by the door. The room's austere stone walls had been hung with embroidered curtains and bright tapestries. Incense smouldered in a golden burner and several braziers gave off a comfortable warmth, the charcoal within their filigreed sides bright red. Three little girls kept the coals glowing with discreet wheezes of their tiny bellows. The contrast between the delicate sumptuousness of the chamber and the disfigured poverty of the little monk could not have been greater.

Albrec bowed at a nudge from Serrim, the eunuch.

"Your Majesty, I believe I am to congratulate you on your wedding."

The Merduk Queen took a moment to respond.

"Be seated, Father. Rokzanne, some wine for our guest."

Albrec was brought a footstool to perch himself upon and a silver goblet of the thin, acrid liquid the Merduks chose to call wine. He did not take his eyes from the Queen's veiled face.

"I would have received you with less ceremony," Heria said lightly, "but Serrim here insisted that I begin to, to comport myself as befitting my newly exalted rank."

Albrec cast his eyes about the chamber, a cross between a barracks and a brothel. "Admirable," he muttered.

"Yes – come, let me show you the view from the balcony." Heria rose and extended a hand to the little monk. He rose awkwardly off his low stool and took her fingers in what remained of his own hand. The women in the chamber whispered and murmured.

She led him out onto the balcony and they stood there with the fresh wind in their faces, looking down upon the ruin of the great fortress. Already the Long Walls were demolished, and thousands of soldiers were working to dismantle their remnants and float the cyclopean granite blocks on flatboats across the Searil. The foundations for another fortress were being laid there on the east bank of the river. The tower in which Heria and Albrec stood would soon be all that remained of Kaile Ormann's great work. Even the Dyke itself was to be dammed up and filled in through the labour of thousands of Torunnan slaves. The minor fortifications on the island would be rebuilt, and where the Long Walls had stood would be a Barbican. Aurungzeb was constructing a mirror-image of the ancient fortress, to face west instead of east.

"Tell me about him, Father," Heria murmured. "Tell me everything you know. Quickly."

The maids and eunuchs were watching them. Albrec kept his voice so low the wind rendered it almost inaudible.

"I have heard it said that he is John Mogen come again. He sits high in the favour of the Torunnan Queen – it was no doubt she who made him Commander-in-Chief. This happened after I left the capital. He fought here, at the Dyke, and in the south. Even the Fimbrians obey him."

"Tell me how he looks now, Father."

Albrec studied her face. It was white and set above the veil, like carved ivory. With the heavy paint on her eyelids she looked as though she were wearing a mask.

"Heria, do not torment yourself."

"Tell me."

Albrec thought back to that brief encounter on the road to Torunn. It seemed a very long time ago now. "He has pain written on his face – and in his eyes. There is a hardness about him." *He is a killer*, Albrec thought. *One of those men who find they have an aptitude for it, as others can sculpt statues or make music.* But he said nothing of this to Heria.

The Merduk Queen remained very still, the cold wind lifting her veil up like smoke. "Thank you, Father."

"Will you not come in from the balcony now, lady?" the eunuch's high-pitched voice piped behind them. "It becomes cold."

"Yes Serrim. We will come in now. I was just showing Brother Albrec the beginnings of our Sultan's new fortress. He expressed a wish to see it." And to Albrec in a quick, hunted aside: "I must get you out of here, back to Torunn. We must help him win this war. But you must never tell him what I have become. His wife is dead. Do you hear me? *She is dead.*"

Albrec nodded dumbly, and followed her back into the scented warmth of the room behind.

FOURTEEN

IT WAS RAINING as the long column of weary men and horses filed through the east gate, and they churned the road into a quagmire of shin-deep mud as they came. An exhausted army, straggling back over the hills to the north for miles – an army that had in its midst a motley convoy of several hundred waggons and carts, all brimming over with silent, huddled civilians, some with oilcloths pulled over their heads, others sitting numbly under the rain. Almost every waggon had a cluster of filthy footsoldiers about it, fighting its wheels free of the sucking muck. The entire spectacle looked like some strange quasi-military exodus.

Corfe, Andruw, Marsch and Formio stood by and watched while the army and its charges filed through the gate of the Torunnan capital. The guards on the city walls had come out in their thousands to watch the melancholy procession, and they were soon joined by many of the citizens so that the battlements were packed with bobbing heads. No-one cheered – no-one was sure if the army was returning in defeat or victory.

"How many altogether, do you think?" Andruw asked.

Corfe wiped the ubiquitous rain out of his eyes. "Five, six thousand."

"I reckon they took another two or three away with them," Andruw said.

"I know, Andruw, I know. But these, at least, are safe now. And that army was crippled before we gave up the pursuit. We have delivered the north from them, for the time being at least."

"They are like a dog which cannot be trained," Formio said. "It lunges forward, you rap it on the muzzle and it draws back. But it keeps lunging forward again."

"Yes – persistent bastards, I'll give them that," Andruw said with a twisted smile.

The army had virtually destroyed the Merduk force they had encountered outside Berrona, charging down on them while they were still frantically trying to form up outside their camp. But once they had been broken and hurled back inside the campsite the battle had degenerated into a murderous free-for-all. For inside the tents had been thousands of brutalised Torunnan women; inhabitants of the surrounding towns gathered together for the pleasure of the Merduk troops. Ranafast's Torunnans had run wild after the discovery, slaying every Merduk in sight. Corfe estimated the enemy dead at over eleven thousand.

But while the army had been embroiled in the butchery within the camp, several thousand of the enemy had managed to flee intact, and they had taken with them a large body of captives. Corfe's men had been too spent to follow them far, and snow had begun to drive down on the wings of a bitter wind off the mountains. The pursuit had been abandoned, and after digging four hundred graves for their own dead the army had reformed for the long march south. The waggons had slowed them down, and they had shared out their rations with the rescued prisoners. With the result that not a man of the army had eaten in the last three days, and half the Cathedrallers were now on foot. As their overworked mounts had collapsed, they had been carved up and eaten by the famished soldiers. Six hundred good warhorses were now mere jumbles of bones on the road behind them. But the campaign had been successful, Corfe reminded himself. They had done what he had set out to do. It was simply that he could take no joy in it.

"Beer," Andruw said with feeling. "A big, frothing mug of the stuff. And a wedge of cheese so big you could stop a door with it. And an apple."

"And fresh-baked bread," Marsch added. "With honey. Anything but meat. I will not eat meat again for a month. And I would sooner starve than eat another horse."

Corfe thought of the Queen's chambers, a bath full of steaming water and a roaring fire. He had not taken his boots off in a week and his feet felt like swollen masses of sodden meat. The leather straps of his armour were green with mould and the steel itself was a rusted saffron wherever the red paint had chipped away. Only the blade of John Mogen's sword was still bright and untarnished. He had Merduk blood under his nails.

"The men need a rest," he said. "The whole army needs refitting – and we'll have to send south for more horses. I wonder how Rusio has been getting on while we've been away."

"I'll wager his backside has not been far from a fire the whole time," Andruw retorted. "Send out some of those paper-collar garrison soldiers next time, Corfe – remind them what it's like to feel the rain in their face."

"Maybe I will, Andruw. Maybe I will. For now, I want you three to go on inside the city. Make sure that the men are well bedded down – no bullshit from any quartermasters. I want to see them all drunk by nightfall. They deserve it."

"There's an order easily obeyed." Andruw grinned. "Marsch, Formio, you heard the man. We have work to do."

"What about you, General?" Formio asked.

"I think I'll stand here a while and watch the army march in."

"Come on Corfe – get in out of the rain," Andruw cajoled. "They won't march any faster with you standing here."

"No – you three go on ahead. I want to think."

Andruw clapped him on the shoulder. "Don't philosophise too long – you may find all the beer drunk by the time you walk through the gate."

Andruw and Marsch mounted their emaciated horses and set off to join the column, but Formio lingered a moment.

"We did all we could, General," he said quietly.

"I know. It's just that it never feels as though it's enough."

The Fimbrian nodded. "For what it is worth, my men are content to serve under you. It seems that Torunna can produce soldiers too."

Corfe found himself smiling. "Go on – see to your troops, Formio. And thank you." He realised that he had just been given the greatest professional compliment of his life.

Formio set off in the wake of Marsch and Andruw without another word.

CORFE STOOD ALONE until the rearguard came into sight almost an hour later. Then he mounted his own horse and trotted down to join them. Two hundred Cathedrallers under Ebro and Morin, thir steed's noses drooping inches from the ground.

"What's the story, Haptman?" he asked.

Ebro saluted. The pompous young officer Corfe had first met the previous year was now an experienced leader of men with the eyes of a veteran. He had come a long way.

"Five more horses in the last two miles," Ebro told him. "Another day and I reckon we'd all be afoot."

"No sign of the enemy?"

Ebro shook his head. "General, I do believe they're all halfway back to Orkhan by now. We put the fear of God into them."

"That was the idea. Good work, Ebro."

The scarlet-armoured horsemen filed past in a muddy stream. Some of them looked up as they passed their commander and nodded or raised a hand. Many had shrivelled Merduk heads dangling from their pommels. Corfe wondered how few of his original galley slaves were left now. He sat his horse until they had all passed by and then finally entered the east gate himself, the last man in the army to do so. The heavy wooden and iron doors boomed shut behind him.

IT WAS VERY late by the time he finally entered his chambers. He had visited the wounded in the military hospitals, racking his brains to try and address every man by his name, singling out those whom he had seen in battle and reminding them of their courage. He had gripped the bony fist of one wounded Cimbric tribesman as the man died then and there, in front of him. All those days in the open, eating horseflesh, rattling in agony in the back of a springless waggon, only to lose the fight when placed at last in a warm bed with clean blankets. The tribesman had died saying Corfe's name, understanding no word of Normannic.

Then there had been the dwindling horse-lines, seeing to it that the surviving mounts were well looked after, and then a half-dozen meetings with various quartermasters to ensure that the freed prisoners Corfe had brought south were being looked after. Most of them had been billeted with the civilian population. And at the last there had been a swift beer with Andruw, Marsch, Formio, Ranafast and Ebro, standing in a rowdy barracks and gulping down the tepid stuff by the pint, the six of them clinking their jugs together like men at a party whilst around them the soldiers did the same, most of them naked, having cast off their filthy clothes and rusted armour. Corfe had left his officers to their drinking and had staggered off towards the palace, both glad and reluctant to leave the warmth and comradeship of the barracks.

It seemed a crowd of people were waiting for him when he finally arrived, all bobbing and bowing and eager to lay hands on him. For once he was happy to have a crowd of flunkeys around, unbuckling straps, pulling off his boots, bringing him a warm woollen robe. They had built up a blazing fire in the hearth and closed the shutters on the pouring rain beyond the balcony. They brought in ewers of steaming water and trays of food and drink. They would have washed him too, if he had let them. He ordered them out and performed that task himself, but was too tired to use the towels that had been left out, and so sat alone watching the flames with his bare feet stretched out to the hearth, a puddle of water on the flagged stone of the floor below him. His skin was white and wrinkled and there was still dead men's blood under his nails, but he did not care. He was too weary even to pick at the tray of delicacies they had set out for him, but poured himself some wine and gulped it down in order to warm his innards. So good to be alone, to have silence and no immediate decisions to make. To just feel the kindly wine warm him and hear the rain rattling at the window.

"Hail, the conquering hero," a voice said. "So you are back."

He did not turn round. "I'm back."

The Torunnan Queen came into the firelight. He had not even heard her enter the room.

"You look exhausted."

Odelia was dressed in a simple linen gown, and her hair hung loose around her shoulders, shining in the firelight. She looked like a young woman ready for bed.

"I waited up for you," she said, "but they said you were somewhere in the city, with the army."

"I had things to do."

"I'm sure you had. You have been nearly six weeks away. Could you not have found time to visit your Queen and tell her about the campaign?"

"I was going to leave it until the morning. I'm meeting the High Command at dawn."

Odelia pulled a chair up beside him. "So tell me now, plainly, without all the military technicalities."

He stared at the flame-light which the wine had trapped, scarlet, in his glass. It was as though a little heart struggled to beat in there.

"We found a Merduk army near Berrona, close to the Searil, and destroyed it. They had been ravaging the whole country up around there. They took the women and murdered all the men. The entire region is littered with corpses, depopulated. A wilderness. The march back to Torunn was... difficult. The waggons slowed us down and we went short on food. Half the horses are gone, but our casualties were very light, considering. I believe the Torrin Gap is secure again, at least for a while."

"Well, that is news indeed. I congratulate you, Corfe. Your band of heroes has done it again. How many Merduks did they kill this time?"

He thought of the unbelievable slaughter within the Merduk camp, all order lost, men squirming for their lives in the thick mud, shrieking. Ranafast's Torunnans had captured two hundred of the enemy as they tumbled out of their tents and then cut the throats of every last one. No quarter. No prisoners.

"What news here, in the capital?" he asked, ignoring her question.

"Berza's fleet has defeated the Nalbenic ships in an action off the Kardikian coast. There will be no more shipborne supplies for Aurungzeb's armies. Fournier's spies tell us that the Sultan has found himself a wife. He demolished Ormann

Dyke and married her in the ruins. She is rumoured to be a Ramusian."

Corfe stirred. "Ormann Dyke is –"

"No more. yes. Kaile Ormann's walls have been cast down, and the Merduks are busy rearing up another fortress on the east bank of the river. It would seem they intend to stay."

"It could be a good sign – a signal that the Sultan is beginning to think defensively."

"I am glad to hear it."

"This wife of his – why should he marry a Ramusian? He has a whole harem of Merduk princesses to bed, or so I had always heard."

"She is supposed to be a great beauty, that is all we know."

"Maybe she'll have an influence on him."

"Perhaps. I would not put too much store in the wiles of women! They are overrated."

"Coming from you, your Majesty, that is hard to credit."
She leaned forward and kissed him. "I am different."

"That I believe."

"Come to bed, Corfe. I have missed you."

"In a moment. I want to feel my feet again, and remember what a chair feels like under my arse."

She laughed, throwing her head back, and in that moment he loved her. He shunted the feeling aside, swamped by guilt, confusion, even a kind of shame. He did not love her. He would not.

"Fournier has been busy in my absence, I take it."

"Oh yes. By the way – did you ever meet a little deformed monk named Albrec?"

Corfe frowned. "I don't think so. No – wait. Yes, once, outside Torunn. He had no nose."

"That's the one. Macrobius has told me that the little fellow went out to preach to the Merduks."

"There is a fool for every season I suppose. What did they do, crucify him?"

"No. He is now something of a fixture in the Merduk court, pontificating about the Brotherhood of Man and such."

"We seem very well informed about the doings of the Merduk court."

"That is what I have been leading up to. Fournier has planted a spy there, God knows how. He may be a weaselly treasonous dastard, but he knows his business. Even I am not allowed to know our agent's name. Twice now in the past month a Merduk deserter has come to the gates with a despatch hidden on him."

"He uses Merduks – a man for every message? He'll be caught soon. You can't keep that kind of thing secret for long. I take it there is no way to get a message to this agent?"

Odelia shrugged. "I fail to see how even Fournier can do that."

"What about your... abilities? Your –"

"My witchery?" The Queen laughed again. "They run a different road, Corfe. Do you know anything of the Seven Disciplines?"

"I've heard of them, that's all."

"A true mage must master four of the seven. I know only two – Cantrimy and True Theurgy. I may be one step better than a common hedge-witch, but I am no wizard."

"I see. Then I would like to talk to these so-called Merduk deserters."

"So would I. There is something odd going on at the Merduk court. But Fournier has hidden them away as though they were a miser's hoard. He may even have disposed of them already."

"You are the Queen – order him to produce them, or the despatches they carried, at least."

"That would offend him, and then we might lose his co-operation entirely."

Corfe's eyes narrowed and a light kindled in them, red from the hearth-glow. When he looked like that, you could see the violence graven in him. Odelia felt herself shiver, as though someone had walked over her grave.

"You mean to tell me," Corfe said softly, "that this blue-blooded son of a bitch will deliberately withhold information which could be vital to the conduct of this war, simply out of a fit of pique?"

"He is not one of your soldiers, Corfe. He is a noble, and must be handled with care."

"*Nobles.*" His voice was still soft, but the tone of it set the hair rising on the back of her neck. "I have never yet seen one who was worth so much as a bucket of warm spit. These deserters, or whatever they are, their knowledge of what goes on in the Merduk camps could be priceless to us."

"You cannot touch Fournier," Odelia snapped. "He is of the nobility. You cannot sweep aside the entire bedrock of a kingdom's fabric just like that. Leave him to me."

"All right then; if the kingdom's fabric is so important I will leave him alone."

What would he be like as a king? Odelia wondered. *Am I mad to consider it? He has so much anger in him. He might save Torunna, and then tear it apart afterwards. If only he could be healed.*

She set a hand on his brow. "What are you doing?" he demanded, still angry.

"Stealing your mind – what do you think? Now be quiet."

Very well – do it. Take that plunge. She was no mind-rhymer, but she was a healer of sorts, and she loved him. That opened the door for her. She stepped through it with a fearful sort of determination.

It was like hearing distant thunder, a baying recklessness of baffled hurt and fury. She dove past scenes of slaughter, ecstasies of boundless murder. Corfe's trade, his vocation, was the killing of his fellow man, and he was good at it – but he did not enjoy it. That gave her a vast sense of relief. His soul was not that of a bloodthirsty barbarian, but it was savage nonetheless. He was possessed of a deep self-loathing, a desire for redemption that surprised and touched her.

There – that was Aekir, burning like the end of the world. Go back further, to before all that. And there was an ordinary young man with kinder eyes and less iron certainty in his heart. Wholly different, it seemed, and unexceptional.

She realised then that he must not be healed – not by her. His suffering had made him what he was, had forged a man out of the boy and rendered him steel-hard. She found herself both in awe of him and pitying his pain. There was nothing to be done here. Nothing.

She came out again, unwilling to look at the happiness there had been before Aekir, the fleeting images of the raven-haired girl who had been and would always be his only love. But the youth who had married the silk-merchant's daughter was no more. Only the general remained. Yes, he could be King. He could be a very great king, one that later centuries would spin legends around. But he would never be truly at ease with himself – and that was the mainspring, the thing that drove him to greatness.

She sat back in her chair and rubbed her eyes, feeling old and alone.

"Well?" he asked.

"Well, nothing. You are a muddle-headed peasant who needs to get drunk more often."

His smile warmed her. There would never be passion there, not for her, but he esteemed her nonetheless. That would have to be enough.

"I think your magicks are overrated," he said.

"Magic often is. I am off to bed. I am an old woman who needs her rest."

He took her hand. "No. Sit with me a while, and we will go together."

She actually felt herself blushing, and was glad of the dimness of the room. "Very well, then. Let us sit here by the fire and pretend."

"Pretend what?"

"That there are no wars, no armies. Just the rain on the window, the wine in your glass."

"I'll drink to that."

And they sat there hand in hand as the fire burned low, as content with their common silence, it seemed, as some long-married couple at the end of a long day's labour.

IT HAS BECOME *a bizarre habit for an old man,* Betanza thought, *this night-time pacing of wintry cloisters. I am getting strange in my twilight years.*

Charibon's cathedral bells had tolled the middle of the night away, and the cloisters were deserted except for his black-robed shape walking up and down, the very picture of a troubled soul. He did this most nights of late, marching his doubts into the flagstones until he was weary enough to finally tumble into dreamless sleep. And then dragging himself awake in time for matins, with the sun still lost over the dark horizon.

The old need less sleep than the young anyway, he told himself. *They are that much more familiar with the concept of their own mortality.*

There had been a thaw, and now instead of snow it was a chill black rain that was pouring down out of the Cimbrics, flattening the swell on the Sea of Tor and rattling on the stone shingles of the monastary city. It was moving slowly east, washing down the Torian plains and beating on the western foothills of the Thurians. In the morning it would be frowning over northern Torunna, where Corfe's army was still a long day's march away from their beds.

Betanza paused in his endless pacing. There was a solitary figure standing in the cloister ahead of him, looking beyond the pillars to the sodden lawn they enclosed and the black starless wedge of sky above it. A tall figure in a monk's habit. Another eccentric, it seemed.

As he drew close the man turned, and Betanza made out a beak of a nose and high forehead under the cowl. A hint of bristling eyebrows.

"God be with you," the man said.

"And with you," the Vicar-General replied politely. He would have walked on, not wanting to interrupt the solitary cleric's devotions, but the other spoke again, stalling him.

"Would you be Betanza by any chance, head of the Inceptine Order?"

"I would." Impossible to make out the colour of the monk's habit in the darkness, but the material of it was rich and unadorned.

"Ah, I have heard of you, Father. At one time you were a Duke of Astarac I believe."

His curiosity stirred, Betanza looked more closely at the other man. "Indeed. And you are?"

"My name is Aruan. I am a visitor from the west, come seeking counsel in these turbulent times."

The man had the accent of Astarac, but there was an archaic strangeness to his dialect. He spoke, Betanza thought, like a character from some old history or romance.

There were so many clerics from so many different parts of the world in Charibon at present, however. Only yesterday a delegation had arrived from Fimbria, of all places, with an escort of forty sable-clad pikemen.

"What part of Astarac do you hail from?" he asked.

"I was originally from Garmidalan, but I have not lived there for many years. Ah – listen, Betanza. Do you hear it?"

Betanza cocked his head, and over the hissing rain there came, faint but clear, a far-off melancholy howl. It was amplified by another, and then another.

"Wolves," he said. "They scavenge right into the very streets of the city at this time of year."

Aruan smiled oddly under his hood. "Yes, I'll warrant they do."

"Well, I must be getting on. I will leave you to your meditations, Aruan." And Betanza continued his interrupted walk. Something about the stranger unsettled him, and he did not care to be addressed in such a familiar fashion. But he was not in the mood to make an issue of it. He buried his cold hands in his sleeves and paced out the flagstones round the cloister once more, the familiar dilemmas doing the rounds of his mind –

– and he stopped short. The man Aruan was in front of him once again.

Startled, he actually retreated a step from the dark figure. "How did you –"

"Forgive me. I am very light on my feet, and you were lost in thought. If you could perhaps spare me some of your time, Betanza, there are things I would like to discuss with you."

"See me in the morning. Now get out of my way," Betanza blustered.

"That is a pity. Such a pity." And something preternatural began to occur before Betanza's astonished eyes. The black shape of Aruan bulked out and grew taller, the hem of his habit lifting off the ground. Two yellow lights blinked on like candles under its cowl, and there was the sound of heavy cloth tearing. Betanza made the Sign of the Saint and backed away, struck dumb by the transformation.

"You are a capable man," a voice said, and it was no longer recognisable as wholly human. "It is such a shame. I like independent thinkers. But you do not have the abilities or the vulnerabilities I seek. Forgive me, Betanza."

A werewolf towered there, the habit shrugged aside in rented fragments. Its ears spiked out like horns from the massive skull. Betanza turned to run but it caught him, lifting him into the air as though he were a child. Then it bit once, deep into the bone and cartilege of his neck, nameless things popping under its fangs. Betanza spasmed manically and fell limp as a rag, his eyes bulging sightlessly. He was set down gently upon the blood-spattered flagstones of the cloister, a puddle of black robes with a white, agonised face staring out of them.

Beyond the monastery, the wolves howled sadly in the rain.

FIFTEEN

"AM I A fool? Do I look like a fool to you?" the Sultan of Ostrabar roared. "Do you expect me to believe that a host of fifteen thousand men constitutes a reconnaisance patrol? Beard of the beloved Prophet, I am surrounded by imbeciles! What is this – some game of your own, Shahr Johor? Tell me how this could have happened – and explain why I was not informed!"

The lofty conference chamber within which Pieter Martellus had once planned the defence of Ormann Dyke was silent. The assembled Merduk officers kept their faces carefully blank. Shahr Indun Johor, Commander-in-Chief of the Merduk army, cleared his throat. A fine sheen of sweat varnished his handsome face.

"Majesty, I –"

"No elaborations or justifications now. I want the truth!"

"I may have exceeded my orders, it is true. But I was told to conduct a reconnaissance in force of the Torrin Gap, and if practicable establish a garrison there to cut communications between Torunna and Almark."

"You are parroting the very text of my written orders. Very good! Now explain to me how they were disobeyed."

"Majesty, I did not disobey them – truly. But resistance was so minimal up there that I thought the time ripe to establish a firm foothold. That is – that is what the army of Khedive Arzamir was to accomplish. None of our patrols reported the presence of regular Torunnan troops. Not one! Still less those accursed red horsemen and their Fimbrian allies. So I – I exceeded my orders. I told Arzamir that if resistance did not stiffen he was push on and try for Charibon. It was a mistake, I know." Shahr Johor drew himself up as if awaiting a blow. "I take full responsibility.

I gambled, and I lost. And we are ten thousand men the poorer for it. I have no excuses."

The room was very still. It might have been populated by a crowd of armoured statues. On the riverbanks below they could hear a Merduk subadar haranguing his troops, and beyond that, the regular clink of a thousand hammers as the last remnants of the Long Walls were demolished stone by stone.

Aurungzeb seemed to slump, the rage which had ballooned his frame leaking out of him. He ground his teeth audibly and hissed, "What manner of man is he? Is he a magician? Can he read our minds? I would give half my kingdom to have his head on a spear. Batak!"

There was a leathery flapping sound, and a pigeon-sized homunculus swooped down from the rafters to land on the table in the middle of the room. Several of the officers present backed away from it; others wrinkled up their noses in disgust. The tiny creature folded its wings, cocked its head to one side, and spoke with the voice of a full-grown man.

"My Sultan?"

"Damn it Batak – cannot you be here in person? How much longer must you hole up in that tower of yours with your abominations?"

"My researches are almost complete, my lord. How may I be of service?"

"Earn the gold that has been showered upon you. Rid me of this Torunnan general."

The homunculus picked up a discarded quill from the table, nibbled on it, and then cast it away, spitting like a cat. The glow which infested its eyes wavered, then grew strong again.

"What you ask is no light thing, my Sultan. The Assassins –"

"Have declined my offer. Apparently one of their number has been lost in Torunn already, and they have no wish to hazard more. No – you are the wizard, the great master of magic. Your late master Orkh had every confidence in you, else he would not have made you Court Mage after him. Now fulfil his confidence. I want this man dead, and soon. The final assault on Torunna will begin within weeks. I want this paladin of theirs cold in the ground ere it begins."

"I will see what I can do my lord." The glow in the homunculus's eyes went out. It glared at the men who surrounded it, baring its miniature fangs. Then it took off, the wind from its wings sending papers flying from the table. It bobbed in mid-air for a moment, and then flew out of the open windows and disappeared.

"Such creatures are inherently evil, and should not be utilised by a follower of the Prophet," a voice said harshly. Aurungzeb turned. It was Mehr Jirah, and beside him was Aurungzeb's Queen, Ahara, a vision of veiled midnight-blue silk. To their rear stood the austere figure of Shahr Baraz. Silent attendants closed the doors again behind the trio.

"In time of war, all means must be utilised," the Sultan mumbled uncomfortably. "Is there something we can help you with, Mehr Jirah? This is a closed indaba of the High Command. There is no place for mullahs here. And Ahara, my Queen, what brings you here at this time? We are a gathering of men. Women – even queens – do not appear at such gatherings. It is not fitting."

Ahara remained silent, but looked at her companion.

"We wish to speak with you, my Sultan," Mehr Jirah said, "both of us. Our matter, however, is of the greatest importance, not something to be blurted out in haste – thus it can wait until the indaba has run its course."

His calm certainty appeared to subdue Aurungzeb. He seemed about to speak, but thought better of it, and turned back to the table, one hand toying with the hilt of the curved dagger he wore tucked into his belt-sash.

"We were nearly done, at any rate. Shahr Johor, you made a grave error of judgement, but I can see what led you to it. For that reason I am willing to be clement. I will give you one more chance, and one only. Tell me of your plans for the final campaign. A swift outline, if you please. I can see that Mehr Jirah and my Queen are impatient." This last was said with obvious curiosity.

The Merduk khedive unrolled a large map on the table and weighted down its corners with inkwells. "The planning is already far advanced, Majesty, and is completely unaffected by our losses in the north. As you know, we have had to bring forward the date of our advance due to the loss of the seaborne supply line –"

"Nalbenic bombasts. They swore they could sweep the sea of Torunnan ships, and what happens? They lose half their fleet and keep the other half cowering in port."

"Quite. Our logistics are now slightly more precarious than I could wish, which means that –"

"Which means that this is our last throw."

"Yes, Majesty. This is likely to be the last chance we will have to take the Torunnan capital. We simply do not have the resources, or the men, to continue this campaign for another year."

There was a long, almost reverent silence in the chamber at these words. They had all known this, of course, but to have it stated so baldly, and in the presence of the Sultan, brought it home to them. The Ramusians might view the Sultan's forces as illimitable, but the men around the table knew better. Too many troops had died in the heavy fighting since the fall of the Dyke, and their lines of supply had been whittled down to a single major road; a slender thread for the fate of any army to hang upon. The reconstruction of a Merduk Ormann Dyke now seemed foresight, not pessimism, but for the victors of Aekir, it was a bitter pill to swallow.

Finally Aurungzeb broke the stillness, heavily. "Go on, Shahr Johor."

The young Merduk khedive picked up a dry quill and began pointing at the unrolled map. Depicted upon it in some detail was the region between the Torrin river and the southern Thurians. Once a fertile and peaceful land, it had become the cockpit for the entire western war.

"The main army will advance in a body, here, down the line of the Western Road. In it will be the *Minhraib*, the *Hraibadar*, our new arquebusier regiments, the elephants, artillery and siege train – some hundred thousand men all told. This force will pitch into any enemy body it meets, and pin it. At the same time, the *Ferinai* and our mounted pistoleers, plus the remnants of the Nalbenic horse-archers; twenty-five thousand men in all, will set off to the north and advance separately."

"That second force you mention is is entirely cavalry," Aurungzeb pointed out.

"Yes, Majesty. They must be completely mobile, and swift-moving. Their mission is twofold. Firstly, they will protect the northern flank of the main body, in case the red horsemen and their allies are still at large in that area. If this proves to be unnecessary – and I believe it will – they will wait until the main body has engaged the Torunnan army, and then come down upon the enemy flank or rear. They will be the hammer to our anvil."

"Why do you believe this enemy force in the north is no longer in the field?"

"They freed a large quantity of female captives that our troops had rounded up. I am certain that they will escort these back to the Torunnan capital. It was, I believe, only due to the presence of these captives that any of Khedive Arzamir's army escaped intact at all."

"Hammer and anvil," Aurungzeb murmured. "I like it."

"It's how he caught the Nalbeni in the Torunn battle," one of the other officers said, an older man with a scarred face.

"Who?"

"This Torunnan general, Majesty. He halted them with arquebusiers and then threw his cavalry at their flanks. Decimated them. If it worked against troops as fleet as horse-archers I'll wager it will against Torunnan infantry."

"I am glad to see we are learning lessons from the behaviour of the enemy," Arungzeb said wryly, but his brow was thunderous. "Very well. Shahr Johor, when will the army move out?"

"Within two weeks, Majesty."

"What if this vaunted general of theirs does not come out to meet us, but stands siege in Torunn? What then?"

"He will come out my Sultan. It is in his nature. It is said he lost his wife in Aekir, and it has taught him to hate us. All his strategies, even the defensive ones, are based on the tactical offensive. These scarlet-armoured cavalry of his excel in it. He will come out."

"I hope you are right. We would win a siege, no doubt of that, but then the war would drag through the summer, perhaps later. The *Minhraib* must be returned to Ostrabar in time for the harvest."

"By harvest-time, your Majesty, you shall be using the throne of Torunna as a footstool. I stake my life upon it."

"You have, Shahr Johor – believe me, you have. This is very well. I like this plan. The Torunnan army numbers no more than thirty thousand. If we can pin them down in the open and launch the *Ferinai* into their rear, I cannot see how they will survive. If Batak's magicks do not put paid to him first, I shall have this Torunnan general in a capture yoke. I will walk him to Orkhan, where he will be crucified," Aurungzeb chuckled. "Having said that, if he meets his fate upon the field of battle, I shall not be unduly displeased."

A rustle of laughter flitted about the room.

"That will do for now. You will all leave, but for Mehr Jirah and his urgent errand. Ahara, my sweet, seat yourself. Shahr Baraz, are you a complete boor? Find my Queen a chair."

The Merduk officers filed out, bowing in turn to Aurungzeb and Ahara. The door clicked shut behind them.

"Well, Mehr Jirah – what is so urgent that you must enter an indaba unannounced, and though I am not one to prate about protocol, why is my Queen at your side?"

"Forgive me, Sultan. But when something momentous occurs which impinges upon the very faith of our people and the manner of their Belief, then I deem it necessary to bring it to your attention at once."

"You intrigue – and alarm – me. Go on."

"You recall the Ramusian monk who has come to us from Torunn."

"That madman – what about him?"

"Sultan, I believe he is not mad." Mehr Jirah's face grew stern and he rose to his full height as though bracing himself. "I believe he speaks the truth."

Aurungzeb blinked. "What? What are you telling me?"

"I have been conducting researches in all our archives for the last two months, and I have had access – which you so graciously granted – to all the documents that were saved from the ecclesiastical and historical sections of the great library in Aekir. They tally with a tradition that my own *Hraib* hold to be true. In short, the Prophet Ahrimuz, blessed be his name, came to us out of the west, and it now seems certain that he was none other than the western Saint Ramusio –"

"Mehr Jirah!"

"Sultan, the Saint and the Prophet are the same person. Our religion and that of the westerners are products of one mind, worshipping the same God, and venerating the same man as His emissary."

Aurungzeb sank down upon a chair. His swarthy face had gone pale. "Mehr Jirah, you are mistaken," he barked hoarsely. "The idea is absurd."

"I wish it were, truly. This knowledge has shaken me to the very core. The little monk whom we deemed a madman is in fact a scholar of profound learning, and a man of great faith. He did not come to us out of a whim – he came to tell us the truth, and he bore with him the copy of an ancient document which confirms it, having fled with it from Charibon itself. The Ramusian Church has suppressed this knowledge for centuries, but God has seen fit to pass it on to us."

There was a pause. Finally Aurungzeb spoke, unwillingly it seemed.

"Ahara – what part have you in this?"

"I acted as interpreter for Mehr Jirah in his conversations with the monk Albrec, my lord. I am able to confirm what Mehr Jirah says."

"Do you not think, Sultan," the mullah continued, "that it is a strange twist of fate which has brought a western queen and a Ramusian scholar to you at this time? I see the Hand of God at work. His word has been corrupted and hidden for long enough. Now is the time to finally let it see the light of day."

Aurungzeb's eyes flashed. He rose, and began pacing about the room like a restlss bear. "This is all a trick – some ruse of the Ramusians to divide us and mislead us in the very hour of our final victory. My Queen – she was once a Ramusian, I can see how she was taken in, wishing to reconcile the faith of her past and the true faith which she has had the fortune to be reborn into. But you, Mehr Jirah – you are a Holy man, a man of learning and shrewdness. How can you bring yourself to believe such lies – such a blasphemous falsehood?"

"I know the truth when I hear it," Mehr Jirah retorted icily. "I am not a fool, nor yet some manner of wishful thinker. I have spent my life pondering the words of the Prophet and reviling the teachings of the western imposter-saint. Imagine my shock when I look more closely at these teachings, and find in some cases the same phrases uttered by Ramusio and Ahrimuz, blessed be his name, the same parables – even the mannerisms of the two men are the same! If this is a Ramusian trick, then it is one that was conceived centuries ago. Besides, the Ramusian texts I studied antedated the arrival of our own Prophet. Ahrimuz was there – before he ever crossed the Jafrar and taught the Merduk peoples, he was there, in Normannia, and he was a westerner. His name, my Sultan, was Ramusio."

Aurungzeb was managing to look both frightened and furious at the same time.

"Who else knows of this discovery of yours?"

"I have taken the liberty of gathering together the mullahs of several of the closest *Hraib*. They all agree with me – albeit reluctantly. Our concern now is in what manner we should disseminate this knowledge among the tribes and Sultanates."

"All ths was done without my knowledge. On whose authority –"

Mehr Jirah thumped a fist on the table, making the map of Torunna quiver. "I am not answerable to you or anyone else on this earth for my actions or the dictates of my conscience! I am answerable to God alone. We do not ask your permission to do what we know to be right, Sultan – we are merely keeping you informed. We will not sit on the truth – as the Ramusians have for the past five centuries. Their current version of their faith is a stench in the very nostrils of God. Would you genuinely have me commit the same blasphemy?"

Aurungzeb seemed to shrink. He pulled himself up a chair and sat down heavily. "This will affect the outlook of the army – you realise that. Some of the *Minhraib* are unwilling to fight as it is. If it gets out that the Ramusians are some kind of – of co-religionists, why then–"

"I prefer to think of them as brothers-in-faith," Mehr Jirah interrupted grimly. "According to the Prophet, it is a heinous crime to attack one whose beliefs are the same as one's own. Eventually, Sultan, we may have to see the Ramusians as such. They may be riven with discord, but they all revere the same Prophet as we do."

"Belief in the same God has not stopped men from killing one another – it never will. Take a close look at your brothers-in-faith, Mehr Jirah. They are busy cutting one another's throats as we speak. In Hebrion and Astarac – and even Torunna – they have been fighting civil wars incessantly, even while we hammer at their eastern frontier."

"I am not naïve, Sultan. I know the war cannot be halted in its tracks. But all I ask is that when the time comes to make peace – as it will – you keep in your mind what you have been told here."

"I will do so, Mehr Jirah. You have my word on it. When we have taken Torunn I will be merciful. There will be no sack, I assure you."

Mehr Jirah looked long and hard at his Sultan for several tense seconds, and then bowed. "I can ask no more. And now, with your permission, I will leave –"

"Are you still intent on disseminating this news among the troops, Mehr Jirah?"

"Not quite yet. There are many points of doctrine which remain to be clarified. I would ask you one favour though, my Sultan."

"Ask away."

"I would like the little Ramusian monk released into my custody. I tire of skulking round this fortress's dungeons."

"By all means, Mehr Jirah. You shall have your little maniac if you please. Tell Akran I said he was to be freed. Now you may leave me. Shahr Baraz – you also."

"Sultan, my lady –"

"Can do without her shadow for five minutes. Escort Mehr Jirah out will you? Your mistress will be with you presently."

Mehr Jirah and Shahr Baraz both bowed, and departed. Heria had risen to her feet, but Aurungzeb held up a hand. "No, please, my dear. Sit down. There is no ceremony between a sultan and his queen when they are alone together."

As she resumed her seat he padded close until he hulked above her like a hill. He was smiling. Then one hairy-knuckled hand swooped down and ripped off her veil. The fingers grasped her jaw, their pressure pursing up her lips like a rose. When Aurungzeb spoke it was in a low, soft purr, like that of a murmuring lover.

"If you ever, ever do anything like this again behind my back, I will have you sent to a field-brothel. Do you understand me, Ahara?"

She nodded dumbly.

"You are my Queen, but only because you have my son in your belly. You will be treated with respect because of him, and because of me – but that is all. Do not think that your beauty, intoxicating though it is, will ever make a fool of me. Do I make myself clear? Am I transparent enough for you?"

Again, the silent nod.

"Very good." He kissed the blood-red lips. As his hand released her face it flushed pink, save for the white finger-marks.

"You will come to my bed tonight. You may be with child, but there are ways and means around that. Now put on your veil and return to your chambers."

WHEN HERIA HAD returned to her suite in the austere old tower, she let her maids disrobe her passively, sitting upon her dressing-stool like a sculpture. Her evening robes donned, she dismissed them all and sat alone for a long time, utterly still. At last there was a knock at the door.

"My lady," Shahr Baraz said. "Are you all right?"

She closed her eyes for a moment, and then said calmly: "Do come in, Shahr Baraz."

The old Merduk looked concerned. "His displeasure is like a gale of wind, lady – soon over, soon forgotten. Do not let it trouble you."

She smiled at that. "What do you think of Mehr Jirah's findings?"

"I am surprised no-one else has noticed such things in the five centuries Merduk and Ramusian have co-existed."

"Perhaps they have. Perhaps the knowledge was always buried again. It will not be this time, though."

"Lady, I am not sure if you wish to set us all at each other's throats, or if you are genuinely crusading for the truth. Frankly, it worries me."

"I want the war to end. Is that so bad? I want no more men killed or women raped or children orphaned. If that is treason, then I am a traitor to the very marrow of my bones."

"The Ramusians also do their share of killing," Shahr Baraz said wryly.

"Which is why the monk Albrec must be released and allowed to return to Torunn. They are sitting on this information there as they would like to do here."

"Men will always kill each other."

"I know. But they at least can stop pretending to do it in the name of God."

"There is that, I suppose. I would say this to you, though: do not push Aurungzeb too far."

"I thought he was a gale of wind."

"He is, when he is crossed in what he thinks is a small thing, but he did not become Sultan by sitting on his hands. If anything threatens the foundation of his power, he will annihilate it without regret or remorse."

"Including me."

"Including you."

"Thank you for your frankness, Shahr Baraz. It's strange – since coming to live among the Merduks I have met more honest men than I ever did in my life before. There is you, Mehr Jirah, and the monk, Albrec."

"Three men are not so many. Were folk so dishonest in Aekir then?" Shahr Baraz asked with a smile.

Her face clouded. She looked away.

"I'm sorry lady. I did not mean to –"

"It's nothing. Nothing at all. I will get used to it in time. People can grow accustomed to all manner of things."

There was a pause. "I will be outside the door if you need me for anything, lady," Shahr Baraz said at last. He bowed and left the room, when what he wanted to do was take her in his arms. As he resumed his post outside her door he scourged himself for his weakness, his absurdity.

She was too fine to be a Merduk brood-mare, and yet he thought there could be a core of pure steel behind those lovely eyes. That fellow she had loved in Aekir, who had been her husband – he must have been a man indeed. She deserved no less.

SIXTEEN

BARDOLIN SQUATTED ON the stone floor and rubbed his wrists thoughtfully. The sores had dried up and healed in a matter of moments. The only evidence of his suffering that remained were the silver scars on his skin. He felt his shaven chin and chuckled with wonder.

"My God, I am a man again."

"You were never anything else," Golophin said shortly from his chair by the fire. Have yourself some wine, Bard. But go easy. Your stomach will not be used to it."

Bardolin straightened and rose from the floor with some difficulty, grimacing. "I'm not yet used to standing upright, either. It's been three months since I was able to stretch my limbs. God, my throat is as dry as sand. I have not talked so much in a year, Golophin. It is good to get it all out at last. It helps the healing. Even your magicks cannot restore me wholly in a moment."

"And your magicks, Bardolin; what of them? You should have recovered from the loss of your familiar by now. What about your own Disciplines? Are they still there, or has the Change stifled them?"

Bardolin said nothing. He sipped his wine carefully and eyed the pile of junk at one side of the circular tower room. His chains lay there, with his blood and filth still encrusted upon them. And the splintered fragments of the crate they had transported him here within. Six brawny longshoremen terrified out of their wits as the thing within the crate roared and snarled at them and beat against the walls of its wooden prison. They had tumbled the crate off the end of their waggon and then urged the frightened horses into a gallop, fleeing the lonely tower with all the speed they could whip out of the beasts.

"It comes and goes without any reason or rhyme," he said finally. "As every day passes it grows more uncontrollable. The Wolf I mean."

"That will pass. In time you and the beast will mesh together more fully, and you will be able to change form at will. I have seen it before."

"I'm glad one of us is an expert," Bardolin said tartly.

Golophin studied his friend and former pupil for a while in silence. He had become a gaunt shade of a man, the bones of his face standing out under the skin, his eyes sunk in deep orbits, the flesh around them dark as the skin of a grape. His head had been shaven down to the scalp to rid him of the vermin that infested it, and it gave him the air of a sinister convict. The wholesome, hale-looking soldier-mage Golophin had once known seemed to have fled without a trace.

"You touched my mind once," the old mage said quietly. "I was scanning the west on the chance I might find some trace of you, and I heard you cry out for help."

Bardolin stared into the fire. "We were at sea, I think. I felt you. But then he came along and broke the connection."

"He is a remarkable man, if man is indeed the word."

"I don't know what he is, Golophin. Something new, as I am. His immortality has something to do with the Black Change, as has his power. I am beginning to fathom it all. Here in the Old World we always thought that a shifter could not master any of the other six Disciplines – the Beast disrupted some necessary harmony in the soul. But now I think differently. The Beast, once mastered, can lead one to the most intimate understanding of the Dweomer possible. A shifter is in essence a conjured animal, a creature owing its existence entirely to some force outside the normal laws of the universe. When a man becomes a lycanthrope, he becomes, if you like, a thing of pure magic, and if he has the will, then it is all there waiting for him. All that power."

"You almost sound as though you accept your fate."

"Hawkwood brought me here thinking you could cure me. We both know you cannot. And perhaps I do not want to be cured anymore, Golophin – have you thought of that? This Aruan is incredibly powerful. I could be too. All I need is time, time to think and research."

"This tower and everything in it is at your disposal, Bard, you know that."

"Thank you."

"But I have one question. When you unlock this new reservoir of power, if you ever do, what will you do with it? Aruan is intent on establishing himself here in the Old World; perhaps not tomorrow or this month or even this year, but soon. He intends some kind of sorcerous hegemony. He's been working towards it for centuries, from what you tell me. When that day comes, then it will be all the ordinary Kings and soldiers of the world versus him and his kind. Our kind. Where do the lines get drawn?"

Bardolin would not look at him. "I don't know. He has a point, don't you think? For centuries we've been persecuted, tortured, murdered because of the gift we were born with. It is time it was stopped. The Dweomer-folk have a right to live in peace –"

"I agree. But starting a war is not the way to secure that right. It will make the ordinary folk of the world more fearful of us than ever."

"It is time the ordinary folk of the world were made to regret their blind bigotry," Bardolin snarled, and there was such genuine menace in his voice that Golophin, startled, could think of nothing more to say.

HAWKWOOD HAD NOT ridden a horse for longer than he could remember. Luckily, the animal he had hired seemed to know more about it than he did. He bumped along in a state of weary discomfort, his destination visible as a grey finger of stone shimmering in the spring haze above the hills to the north. There was another rider on the road ahead; a woman, by the looks of things. Her mount was lame. Even as he watched, she dismounted and began studying its hooves one by one. He drew level and reined in, some battered old remnant of courtesy surfacing.

"Can I help?"

The woman was well-dressed, a tall, plain girl in her late twenties with a long nose and a wondrous head of fiery hair that caught the sunshine.

"I doubt it." And she went back to examining her horse.

His appearance was against him, Hawkwood knew. Though he had bathed and changed and suffered a haircut at the hands of Domna Ponera, Galliardo's formidable wife, he still looked like some spruced up vagabond.

"Have you far to go?" he tried again.

"He's thrown a shoe. God's blood. Is there a smithy hereabouts?"

"I don't know. Where are you heading for?"

The girl straightened. "Not far – yonder tower." She gave Hawkwood a swift, unimpressed appraisal. "I have a pistol here. You'll find easier pickings elsewhere."

Hawkwood laughed. "I'll bet I would. It so happens I also am going to the tower. You know the Mage Golophin then?"

"Perhaps." She looked him over with more curiosity now. He liked the frankness of her stare, the strength he saw in her features. Not much beauty there, in the conventional sense, but definite character. "My name is Hawkwood," he said.

"I am Isolla." She seemed relieved when her name elicited no reaction from him. "I suppose we may as well travel the rest of the way together – it's not so far. Is Golophin expecting you?"

"Yes. And you?"

A slight hesitation. "Yes. You may as well dismount, instead of staring down at me."

"You can ride my horse if you like."

"No – I only ride side-saddle anyway."

So she was well-born. He could have guessed that from her clothes. Her accent intrigued him though – it was of Astarac.

"You know Golophin well?" he asked her as they walked side by side leading their mounts.

"Well enough. And you?"

"Only by reputation. He is looking after a sick friend of mine."

"Are you all right? You have a strange gait."

"I have not ridden a horse in a long time. Or walked upon solid earth for that matter."

"What, do you possess wings that take you everywhere?"

"No – a ship. She put in only this morning."

He saw a light dawn in her eyes. She looked him up and down again, this time with some wonder. "Richard Hawkwood the mariner – of course. I am a dunce. Your name is all over the city."

"The very same." He waited for her to give some fuller account of herself, but in vain. They strolled together companionably enough after that, the miles flitting by with little more conversation. For some reason Hawkwood was almost disappointed when they finally knocked on the door of Golophin's tower. There was something about this Isolla that finally made him feel as though he had come home.

I've been at sea too long, he told himself.

"CURIOSITY," GOLOPHIN SAID, annoyed. "In a man it is a virtue, leading to enlightenment. In a woman it is a vice, leading to mischief." He looked at Isolla disapprovingly, but she seemed unabashed.

"There's a saying dreamed up by a man. I am not some gossiping lady's maid, Golophin."

"You should not be behaving like one then. Ah, Captain Hawkwood, I thank you for delivering our Princess safe and sound, since she was pig-headed enough to come out here."

"Princess?" Hawkwood asked her. Some absurd little hope died within him.

"It's not important," she said uncomfortably.

"You are looking at the next Queen of Hebrion, no less," Golophin said. "As if the world needed another queen. Make yourself useful, Isolla – pour us all some wine. There's a jug of it cooling in the study."

She left the room, undismayed by the old wizard's disapproval. And indeed, as soon as she had left the room a smile spread across his face.

"She should have been a man," he said with obvious affection.

Hawkwood disagreed, but kept his opinion to himself.

"So, Captain, we meet at last. I am glad you came."

"Where's Bardolin?"

"Asleep, for now. It will speed his healing."

"Is he – has he –"

"The Beast is dormant for now. I have been able to help him control it."

"You can cure him, then."

"No – no-one can. But I can help him manage it. He has been telling me of your voyage. A veritable nightmare."

"Yes. It was."

"Not many could have survived it."

Hawkwood went to the window. It looked out from the tower's great height over southern Hebrion, the land green and serene under the sun, the sea a sparkle on the horizon.

"I think we were meant to survive it – Bardolin was, anyway. They allowed us to escape. I sometimes wonder if they even guided our course on the voyage home. Bardolin told you of them, I suppose. A race of monstrosities. He thinks some of them are in Normannia already, and more are coming. They have plans for us, the wizards of the west."

"Well, we are forewarned at least – thanks to you. What are your own plans now, Captain?"

The question took Hawkwood by surprise. "I hadn't thought about it. Lord, I've only been back on dry land a day. So much has happened. My wife died in Abrusio, my house is gone. All I have left is my ship, and she is in a sorry state. I suppose I was thinking of going to the King, to see if he had anything for me." He realised how that sounded, and flushed.

"You have earned something, that much is true," Golophin reassured him gently. "I am sure Abeleyn will not be remiss in recognising that. Your expedition may have been a failure, but it has also been a valuable source of information. Tell me, what think you of Lord Murad?"

"I think he's unhinged. Oh, not in a foaming-at-the-mouth kind of way. But something has gone awry in his head. It was the west that did it."

"And the girl-shifter, Griella."

"Bardolin told you of that? Yes, perhaps. That was a queer thing. He felt something for her, and she for him, but it harmed them both."

Isolla came back with pewter mugs of chilled wine. "Your Majesty," Hawkwood said as he took his, eyes dancing.

She frowned. "Not yet."

"Not for several weeks," Golophin grinned. "I think she grows impatient."

"With you, yes. Sometimes you are like a little boy, Golophin."

"Is that so? Abeleyn always thought of me as an old woman. I am a man for all seasons it seems."

Hawkwood dragged his gaze away from Isolla and set aside his tankard after the merest sip. "I'll be going. I just wanted to make sure all was well with Bardolin."

"I'll speak to the King on your behalf, Captain. We'll see you are recompensed for your losses, and your achievement," Golophin promised.

"That won't be necessary," Hawkwood said with stiff pride. "Look after Bardolin; he's a good man, no matter what that bastard wizard turned him into. I can look after myself. Goodbye Golophin." He bowed slightly. "Lady," and left.

"A proud man for a commoner," Isolla said.

"He is not a common man," Golophin retorted. "I was a fool to phrase it so. He deserves recognition for what he did, but he'll turn his back on it if he thinks it smacks of charity. And meanwhile Lord Murad is no doubt standing on his hind legs as we speak, relating the marvels of his expedition and reaping as much of the credit as he can. It's a filthy world, Isolla."

"It could be worse," she told him. He glanced at her, and laughed.

"Ah, what it is to be in love." Which made her blush to the roots of her hair.

"You'll make him a grand wife, if our stiff-necked captain doesn't steal you away first."

"What? What are you saying?"

"Never mind. Hebrion has her King again, and will soon have a worthy queen. The country needs a rest from war and intrigue for a while. So do I. I intend to immure myself here with Bardolin, and lose myself in pure research. I have neglected that lately – too much of politics in the way. You and Abeleyn can run the kingdom admirably between you without my help. Just be sure to keep an eye on Murad, and that harpy, Jemilla."

"She's finished at court – none of the nobles will give her the time of day now."

"Don't be too sure. She still bears a king's child who, although illegitimate, will always be older than any you have."

"We had best hope she has a girl then."

"Indeed. Now get back to the palace Isolla. There is a man there who has need of you."

She kissed the old wizard on the cheek. In Hebrion she had found a husband, and a man who had become like a father. Golophin was right – the worst was over now, surely. The country would have its rest.

PART TWO

DEATH *of a* SOLDIER

Soon a great warrior
Will tower over the land
And you will see the ground
Strewn with severed heads.
The clamour of blue swords
Will echo in the hills;
The dew of blood
Will lace the limbs of men.

– Njal's Saga

DANRIMIR

SOUTHERN JAFRAR MOUNTAINS

OSTRABAR

THURIAN MOUNTAINS

ORKHAN

OSTIAN RIVER

THURIAN PASSES

AURUNGABAR

EASTERN (RIMNIR) ROAD

WESTERN ROAD

KARDIKIA

COASTAL ROAD

SEARUL RIVER

KHEDI ANWAR

RIVER TORRIN

KARDIAN GULF

TORUNNA

KARDIAN SEA

N

TORUNN

LEAGUES

0   15   30

ROUTE OF
MERDUK ARMIES

SEVENTEEN

THE PONTIFICAL PALACE of Macrobius had once been an Inceptine abbey, and was now bursting at the seams with all manner of clerics and office-seekers, armed guards and inky-fingered clerks. Their numbers were augmented now by richly dressed Torunnan soldiers, a bodyguard fit for a queen. And in their midst, like a scarlet spearhead, eight Cathedrallers in all their barbaric glory. The military tailors had quickly run up some crimson surcoats for them – it would not do for them to tramp into the Pontiff's presence in their battered armour – and though they were, sartorially speaking, smarter than they had ever been before, their tattooed faces and long hair set them apart.

Queen Odelia and her senior general had come to call upon Macrobius, and they must needs be received with all the pomp and ceremony that embattled Torunn could muster. Two thrones had been set up – that reserved for the Queen noticeably less ornate than Macrobius's – and to one side there was a stark black chair for her sable-clad general.

Corfe was far and away the most sombre-looking member of the cavalcade that had made its way through Torunn's packed streets to the Pontifical palace, but it was he who elicited the most excitement from the gathered crowds. They cheered him to the echo, and some of the more effusive pushed through the cordon of troops to touch his stirruped boot or even stroke the flank of his restive destrier. Andruw, who rode at his side, thought it all immensely funny, but for himself, he felt like a fraud. They called him "the deliverer of his country," but that country was a hell of a long way from being delivered yet, he thought.

The cavalcade dismounted in the main square of the abbey, the balconies surrounding them lined with cheering monks and priests – a weird and somewhat comical sight. Then Corfe took his Queen's arm, and to a flourish of trumpets they were ushered into the great reception hall of the palace, running the gauntlet of a throng of clapping notables. These were most of what remained of Torunna's nobility, and their greeting was markedly less enthusiastic than that of the crowds beyond the abbey walls. They eyed the tattooed tribesmen with distaste, the black-clad general with wonder and dislike, and the ageing Queen with guarded disapproval. Corfe's face was stiff as wood as he stood before the Pontifical dais and looked once more on the blind old man who was the spiritual leader of half the western world.

Monsignor Alembord had barely cleared his throat to announce the eminent visitors in his stately fashion when Macrobius cut him short by hobbling down from the dais and reaching out blindly.

"Corfe."

Corfe took the searching hand. It felt as dry as an autumn leaf in his grasp, frail as thistledown. He looked at the ravaged face and remembered the long cold nights on the Western Road on the retreat from Aekir.

"Holiness. I am here."

The great chamber fell into silence, Alembord's proclamation strangling into a muted cough. All eyes swivelled to the general and the Pontiff.

Macrobius smiled. "It has been a long time, General."

"Yes. It has."

"I told you once your star had not yet stopped rising. I was right. You have come a long way from Aekir, my friend. On a long, hard road."

"We both have," Corfe said. His throat burned. The sight of Macrobius's face brought back memories from another world, another time. The old man gripped his shoulder. "Sit beside me now, and tell me of your travels. We shall have more than burnt turnip to share this time."

The chair which had been set aside for Corfe was hurriedly moved closer to the Pontifical throne and the trio took their seats after Macrobius had greeted the Queen with rather more formality. Musicians began to play, and the crowd in the hall broke into a loud surf of conversation. Andruw remained standing at the foot of the dais with the Cathedraller bodyguards and found himself next to a young man of about his own age in the robes of an Inceptine.

"What cheer, Father," he said brightly.

"What cheer *your grace*, soldier. I'm a bishop, you know."

Andruw looked him up and down. "What shall I do – kiss your ring?"

Avila laughed, and took two brimming glasses of wine from an attendant who passed by with a tray. "You can kiss my clerical backside if you want. But have a drink first. These levees are liquid occasions, and I hear you've been working up quite a thirst in the north, you and your scarlet barbarians."

"I didn't know they made bishops so young these days."

"Or colonels either, for that matter. I came here from Charibon with – with a friend of mine."

"Wait – I know you, I think. Didn't we run into you and your friend? You were with a couple of Fimbrians on the Northern Road a few months back. Corfe stopped and talked to you."

"You have a good memory."

"Your friend – he was the one without a nose. Where's he today, keeping out of the way of the high and mighty?"

"I... I don't know where he is. I tell you what though, we'll drink to him. A toast to Albrec. Albrec the mad, may God be good to him."

And they clinked their glasses together, before gulping down the good wine.

"WE HAVE REASON to believe he is still alive, this errant Bishop of yours," Odelia said, "and what is more, he is moving freely in the Merduk court, spreading his message. As far as we know, the Merduk mullahs are debating this message even now."

Macrobius nodded. "I knew he would succeed. He has the same aura of destiny about him as I sensed in Corfe here. Well, mayhap it is better this way. The thing is taken out of our hands after all. I see no option now but to broadcast the news abroad here in Torunna also. The time for discussion and debate is past – we must begin spreading the word of the new faith."

"Quite a revelation, this new faith of yours," Corfe said quietly. Odelia had finally told him what was engendering the rancorous argument in the Pontifical palace. He had been as astonished as anyone, but had tended to think of it as a Church affair. Now that the Merduks were purportedly engaged in the same debate, that gave it a different colour entirely. There might be military ramifications.

The Pontiff, the Queen and the general were closeted in Macrobius's private quarters at the end of a long, tiring day much given over to speech and spectacle. The whole occasion had been a complete success, Odelia had been keen to point out. Her coronation had been ratified by the New Church's approval, and everyone had seen the Pontiff greet Corfe like a long-lost friend. Anyone seeking to destabilise the new order would think twice now they had seen the rapturous welcome given to them by the crowds, and the apparent amity between the Crown and the Church.

"If the Merduks take this Albrec's message to heart, will it affect their conduct of the war?" Odelia asked.

"I do not know," the Pontiff told her. "There are men of conscience among the Merduk nation, we have always known that. But men of conscience do not often have the influence necessary to halt wars."

"I agree," Corfe put in. "The Sultan will keep fighting. Everything points to the fact that this campaign is meant to be the climax of the entire war. He means to take Torunn before the autumn, and he will not let the mullahs get in his way – not now. But if we can survive through to the summer, it may be that a negotiated end to the war will be more feasible."

"An end to the war," Odelia said. "My God, could that be possible? A final end to it all?"

"I spoke to Fournier yesterday. He is as insufferably arrogant as always, but when I persevered he deigned to tell me that the Merduk armies are completely overstretched, with desertions rising daily. If this next assault fails, he cannot see how the Sultan will continue the war. The *Minhraib* campaigned right through last year's harvest. If they do so a second year running, then Ostrabar will face famine. This is Aurungzeb's last throw."

"I had no idea," Odelia said. "I don't think of them as men with crops and families. To me they are more like – like cockroaches. Kill one and a dozen more appear. So there is hope at last – a light at the tunnel's end."

"There is hope," Corfe said heavily. "But as I say, he is betting everything on this last assault. We could be facing as many as a hundred and fifty thousand enemy in the field."

"Should we not then stay behind these walls and stand siege? We could hold out for months – well past harvest."

"If we did that he could send the *Minhraib* home and contain us with a smaller force. No – we need to make him commit every man he has – we have to push him to the limit. To do that, we will have to take to the field and challenge him openly."

"Corfe," Macrobius said gently, "the odds you speak of seem almost hopeless."

"I know, I know. But victory for us is a different thing from the kind of victory the Merduks need. If we can smash up their army somewhat – blunt this last assault – and yet keep Torunn from undergoing a siege – then we will have won. I believe we can do that, but I need some advantage, some chance to even things up a little. I haven't found it yet, but I will."

"I pray to God you do," Macrobius said. His eyeless face was sunken and gaunt, vivid testimony to what Merduks would do in the hour of their victory.

"If this happens – if you manage to halt this juggernaut of theirs – what then?" Odelia asked. "How much can we expect to regain, or lose by a negotiated peace?"

"Ormann Dyke is gone forever," Corfe said flatly. "That is something we must get used to. So is Aekir. If the kingdom can be partitioned down the line of the Searil, then we will have to count ourselves fortunate. It all depends on how well the army does in the field. We'll be buying back our country with Torunnan blood, literally. But my job is to kill Merduks, not to bargain with them. I leave that to Fournier and his ilk – I have no taste or aptitude for it."

You will acquire one, though, I will see to that, Odelia thought. And out loud she said: "When, then, will the army take to the field?"

Corfe sat silently for what seemed a long time, until the Queen began to chafe with impatience. Macrobius seemed serene.

"I need upwards of nine hundred warhorses, to replace our losses and mount the new recruits that are still coming in," Corfe said finally. "Then there are the logistical details to work out with Passifal and the Quartermaster's department. This will be no mere raid – when we leave Torunn this time we must be prepared to stay out for weeks, if not months. To that end the Western Road must be repaired and cleared, depots set up. And I mean to conscript every able-bodied man in the kingdom, whatever his station in life."

Odelia's mouth opened in shock. "You cannot do that!"

"Why not? The laws are on the statute-books – theoretically they are in force already, except for the fact that they have never actually been enforced."

"Even John Mogen did not try to enforce them – wisely. He knew the nobles would have his head on a spear if he ever even contemplated such a thing."

"He did not have to do it at Aekir. Every man in the city willingly lent a hand in the defence, even if it was only to carry ammunition and plug breaches."

"That was different. That was a siege."

Corfe's fist came hurtling down onto the table with a crash that astonished both the Queen and the Pontiff. "There will be no exceptions. If I conscript, then I can leave an appropriate garrison in the city and still take out a sizeable field army. The nobles in the south of the kingdom all have private armies – I know that only too well. It is time these privately raised forces shared in the defence of the kingdom as a whole. Today I had orders written up commanding all these blue-bloods to bring their armed retainers in person to the capital. If my calculations are correct, the local Lords alone could add another fifteen thousand men to the defence."

"You do not have the authority –" Odelia began heatedly.

"Don't I? I am Commander-in-Chief of all Torunna's military. Lawyers may quibble over it, but I see every armed man in the kingdom as part of that military. They can issue writs against me all they like once the war is over, but for now I will have their men, and if they refuse, by God I'll hang them."

There was naked murder on his face. Odelia looked away. She had never believed she could be afraid of any man, but the savagery that scoured his spirit leapt out of his eyes like some eldritch fire. It unnerved her. For how many men had those eyes been their last sight on earth? She sometimes thought she had no idea what he was truly capable of, for all that she loved him.

"All right then," she said. "You shall have your conscription. I will put my name to your orders, but I warn you, Corfe, you are making powerful enemies."

"The only enemies I am concerned with are those encamped to the east. I piss on the rest of them. Sorry, Father."

Macrobius smiled weakly. "Her Majesty is right, Corfe. Even John Mogen did not take on the nobility."

"I need men, Father. Their precious titles will not be worth much if there is no kingdom left to lord them about in. Let it be on my head alone."

"Don't say such things," Odelia said with a shiver. "It's bad luck."

Corfe shrugged. "I don't much believe in luck anymore, lady. Men make their own, if it exists at all. I intend to take an army of forty thousand men out of this city in less than two sennights, and it will be tactics and logistics which decides their fate, not luck."

"Let us hope," Macrobius said, touching Corfe lightly on the wrist, "that faith has something to do with it also."

"When men have faith in themselves, Father," Corfe said doggedly, "they do not need to have faith in anything else."

ALBREC AND MEHR Jirah met in a room within Ormann Dyke's great tower, not far from the Queen's apartments. It was the third hour of the night and no-one was abroad in the vast building except a few yawning sentries. But below the tower thousands of men worked through the night by the light of bonfires. On both banks of the Searil river they swarmed like ants, demolishing in the west and rebuilding in the east. The night-black river was crowded with heavy barges and lighters full to the gunwale with lumber, stone, and weary working-parties, and at the makeshift docks that had been constructed on both sides of the river, scores of elephants waited patiently in harness, their mahouts dozing on their necks. The Sultan had decreed that the reconstruction of Ormann Dyke would be complete before the summer, and at its completion it would be renamed *Khedi Anwar*, the Fortress of the River.

The chamber in which Albrec and Mehr Jirah sat was windowless, a dusty storeroom which was half full of all manner of junk. Fragments of chainmail, the links rusted into an orange mass. Broken sabre-blades, mouldering Torunnan uniforms, even a box of mouldy hardtack much gnawed by mice. The two clerics, having nodded to each other, stood waiting, neither able to speak the other's tongue. At last they were startled by the swift entry of Queen Ahara and Shahr Baraz. The Queen was got up like a veiled Merduk maid, and Shahr Baraz was dressed as a common soldier.

"We do not have much time," the Queen said. "The eunuchs will miss me in another quarter-hour or less. Albrec, you are leaving for Torunn tonight. Shahr Baraz has horses and two of his own retainers waiting below. They will escort you to within sight of the capital."

"Lady," Albrec said, "I am not sure —"

"There is no time for discussion. Shahr Baraz has procured you a pass that will see you past the pickets. You must preach your message in Torunna as you have here. Mehr Jirah agrees with us in this. Your life is in danger as long as you remain at Ormann Dyke."

Albrec bowed wordlessly. When he straightened, he shook the hands of Mehr Jirah and Shahr Baraz. "Whatever else I have found among the Merduks," he said thickly, "I have found two good men." Heria translated the brief sentence and the two Merduks looked away. Shahr Baraz produced a leather bag with dun coloured clothing poking out of its neck.

"Wear these," he said in Normannic. "They are clothes

of a Merduk mullah. A Holy man. May – may the God of Victories watch over you." Then he looked at Heria, nodded and left. Mehr Jirah followed without another word.

"I can still preach here too, Lady," Albrec said gently.

"No. Go back to him. Give him this." She handed the little monk a despatch scroll with a military seal. "They are plans for the forthcoming campaign. But do not tell you who gave them to you, Father."

Albrec took the scroll gingerly. "I seem to make a habit of bearing fateful documents. Was there no other way you could get this to Torunn? I am not much of a courier."

"Two men we have sent out already," Heria said in a low voice. "Merduk soldiers with Ramusian blood in them – Shahr Baraz's retainers. But we do not know if they got through."

Albrec looked at her wonderingly. "So he is in on it too? How did you persuade him?"

"He said his father would have done it. The Shahr Baraz who took Aekir would not have condoned a war fought in the way Aurungzeb fights it today. And besides, my Shahr Baraz is a pious man. He thinks now the war should stop, since the Ramusians are brothers-in-faith. Mehr Jirah and many of the mullahs think likewise."

"Come with me, Heria," Albrec said impulsively. "Come back to your people – to your husband."

She shook her head, the grey eyes bright with tears above the veil. "It is too late for me now. And besides, they would miss me within the hour. We would be hunted down. No, Father, go back alone. Help him save my people."

"Then at least let me tell him you are alive."

"No! I am dead now, do you hear? I am not fit to be Corfe's wife anymore. This is my world now, here. I must make the best of it I can."

Albrec took her hand and kissed it. "The Merduks have a worthy queen then."

She turned away. "I must go now. Take the stairs at the bottom of the passage outside. They lead out to the west courtyard. Your escort awaits you there. You will have several hours start – they won't miss you until after dawn. Go now, Father. Get that scroll to Corfe."

Albrec bowed, his eyes stinging with pity for her, and then did as he was bidden.

THE SUN WAS failing. A stiff easterly breeze had winnowed all the dark anvil-headed clouds from the sky. As the day died into a wilderness of silence, there was a little crossroads some twelve leagues north of Torunn, upon the Western Road, which sat deserted in the last bloom of the ruddy sunset. An empty hamlet stood there at the meeting of the ways, and on the gables of the abandoned houses ravens perched, fat from the pickings of war. The name of the place was Armagedir, which in the language of the Cimbric tribes meant *Journey's End*. As the sunset settled low into darker hues of violet and aquamarine in the early starlight, so the forsaken houses sank into shadow, their peace undisturbed, for now, by the sight or sound of any living man.

EIGHTEEN

ALL DAY THEY had been trooping into the city, a motley procession of armed men in livery all the colours of the rainbow. Some were armed with nothing more than halberds and scythes on long poles, others were splendidly equipped with arquebuses and sabres. Most were on foot, but several hundred rode prancing warhorses in half armour and had silk pennons whipping from their lance-heads.

Corfe, General Rusio and and Quartermaster Passifal stood on the catwalk of the southern barbican and watched them troop in. As the long serried column trailed to an end, a compact group of five hundred Cathedraller cavalry came up behind them, Andruw at their head. As the tribesmen passed through the gateway below Andruw saluted and winked, then was lost to view in a cavernous clatter of hooves as he and his men entered the city.

"That's the last contingent will make it this week, General," Passifal said. He was consulting a damp sheaf of papers. "Gavriar of Rone has promised three hundred men, but they'll be a long time on the road, and the Duke of Gebrar, old Saranfyr, he's put his name down for four hundred more, but it's a hundred and forty leagues from Gebrar if it's a mile. We'll be lucky to see them inside of a month."

"How many do we have then?" Corfe asked.

"All told, some six thousand retainers, plus another five thousand conscripts – most of them folk from Aekir."

"Not as many as we had hoped," Rusio grumbled.

"No," Corfe told him. "But it's a damn sight better than nothing at all. I can leave six or seven thousand men to garrison the city and still march out with – what? Thirty-six or seven thousand."

"Some of these retainers the lords sent are nothing more than unschooled peasants," Rusio said, leaning on a merlon. "In many cases they've sent us squads of village idiots and petty criminals, the dregs of their demesnes."

"All they have to do is stand on the battlements and wave a pike," Corfe said. "Rusio, I want you to take five hundred veterans and start training up the more incapable. Some of the contingents, though, can be drafted straight into the regular army."

"What about their fancy dress?" Passifal asked, mouth twitching. Many of the lords had clad their retainers in all manner of garish heraldry.

"It won't look so fancy after a few days in the mud, I'll warrant."

"And the Lords themselves?" Rusio inquired. "We've half a dozen keen young noblemen who are set on leading their fathers' pet armies into battle."

"Rate them all as ensigns, and put capable sergeants under them."

"Their daddies may not like that, nor the young scrubs themselves."

"I don't give a stuff what they think. I won't hand men over to untried officers to be squandered. This is war, not some kind of parlour game. If there are any complaints, have them forwarded to the Queen."

"Yes, General."

Feet on the catwalk behind them, and Andruw appeared, his helm swinging from one hand. "Well, that's the last of them," he said. "The rest are hiding in the woods or the foothills."

"Did you have any trouble?" Corfe asked him.

"Are you serious? Once they saw the dreaded scarlet horsemen they'd have handed over their daughters if we'd asked. And I very nearly did, mark you. Poor stuff, though, most of 'em. They might be all right standing atop a wall Corfe, but I wouldn't march them out of here. They'd go to pieces in the field."

"What about the retainers?"

"Oh, they're better equipped than the regulars are, but they've no notion of drill at any level higher than a tercio. I'd rate them baggage guards or suchlike."

"My thoughts exactly. Thanks, Andruw. Now, what about these horses?"

"I have a hundred of the men under Marsch and Ebro escorting the herd as we speak. They'll be here in three or four days."

"How many did you manage to scrape up?"

"Fifteen hundred – but only a third of those are true destriers. Some of them are no better than cart-horses, others are three year olds, barely broken."

"They'll have to do. The Cathedrallers are the only heavy cavalry we have. If we mount every man we can muster up some..."

"I make it a little over two thousand," Passifal said, consulting his papers again. "Another batch of tribesmen arrived this morning. Felimbri I think, nearly two hundred of them on little scrub ponies."

"Thanks, Colonel."

"If this goes on, half the damn Torunnan army will be savages or Fimbrians," Rusio said tartly.

"And it would be none the worse for that, General," Corfe retorted. "Very well. Now, how are the work-gangs proceeding on the Western Road..."

The little knot of men stood on the windswept battlements of the barbican and went through the headings on Passifal's lists one by one. The lists were endless, and the days too short to tackle half their concerns, but little by little the army was being prepared for the campaign ahead. The last campaign, perhaps. That was what they all hoped. In the meantime billets had to be found for the new recruits, willing and unwilling, horses had to be broken in and trained in addition to men, the baggage train had to be inventoried and stocked with anything thirty-odd thousand soldiers might need for a protracted stay in a veritable wilderness, and the road itself, which would bear their feet in so few days time, had to be repaired lest they find themselves bogged down in mud within sight of the city. Nothing could be left to chance, not this time. It was the last throw of the dice for the Torunnans. If it failed, then there was nothing left to stand between the kingdom and the horror of a Merduk occupation.

CORFE HAD BEEN invited to dine that night at the town house of Count Fournier. He did not truly have the time to spare for leisurely dinners, but the invitation had intrigued him, so he dressed in court sable and went, despite Andruw's jocular warning to watch what he ate. Fournier's house was more of a mansion, with an arch in one wing wide enough to admit a coach and four. It stood in the fashionable western half of the city, within sight of the palace itself, and to the rear it had extensive gardens which ran down to the river. On the bank of the Torrin there was a small summer-house and it was to this that Corfe was led by a crop-headed page as soon as he had left his horse with another young stable-boy. Fournier met him with a smile and an outstretched hand. The summer-house had more glass in it than Corfe had ever seen before, outside of a cathedral. It was lit by candle-lanterns, and a table within had been set for two. To one side the mighty Torrin gurgled and plopped in the darkness, its bank obscured by a line of willows. As Corfe looked around, something detached itself from one of the willows and flapped away with a beat of leathery wings. A bat of some sort.

"No escort or entourage, General?" Fournier asked with raised eyebrow. "You keep little state for a man of such elevated rank."

"I thought I'd be discreet. Besides, the Cathedrallers are mobbed every time they ride through the streets."

"Ah, yes, I should have thought. Have a seat. Have some wine. My cook has been working wonders tonight. Some bass from the estuary I believe, and wild pigeon."

Silver glittering in the candlelight upon a spotless white tablecloth. Crystal goblets brimming with wine, a gold-chased decanter, and a small crowd of footmen, not one yet in his thirties. Fournier noted Corfe's appraising glances and said shortly, "I like to be surrounded by youth. It helps keep my – my energy levels high. Ah – Marion, the first course, if you please."

Some kind of fish. Corfe ate it automatically, his plate cleared by the time Fournier had had three mouthfuls. The nobleman laughed. "You are not in the field now, General. You should savour my cook's work. He is an easterner, as a matter of fact, a convert from Calmar. I believe in his youth he might have been a corsair, but one should not enquire too thoroughly into the antecedents of genius, should one?"

Corfe said nothing. Fournier seemed to be enjoying himself, as if he possessed some secret knowledge which he was savouring with even more gusto than he did the food.

The plates were taken away, another course came and went. Fournier talked inconsequentially of gastronomic matters, the decline in Torunn's fishing fleet, the proper way to dress a carp. Corfe drank wine sparingly and uttered the odd monosyllable. Finally the cloth was drawn and the two men were left with a dish of nuts and a decanter of brandy. The servants left, and for a while the only sound was the quiet night music of the river close-by.

"You have shown commendable patience, General," Fournier said, sipping the good Fimbrian spirit. "I had expected an outburst of some sort ere the main course arrived."

"I know."

"Forgive me. I like to play my little games. Why are you here? What's afoot on this, the eve of great events? I will tell you, as a reward for your forbearance."

Fournier reached under his chair and set upon the table a bloodstained scroll of paper. Upon it was a broken seal, but enough of the wax remained for Corfe to make out the crossed scimitars of Ostrabar's military. Despite himself, he sat up straight in his chair.

"Do have a walnut, General. They complement the brandy so well." Fournier broke one open with a pair of ivory handled nutcrackers. There was blood on the nutcrackers also.

"Make your point, Fournier," Corfe said. "I do not have any more time to waste."

Fournier's voice changed – the bantering tone fled to be replaced by cold steel. "My agents made a capture today of some interest to us all. A Merduk mullah with two companions, out riding alone. The mullah was a strange little fellow with a mutilated face and no fingers on one hand. He spoke perfect Normannic, with the accent of Almark, and claimed to be one Bishop Albrec, fresh from the delights of the Merduk court."

Corfe said nothing, but the candlelight made two little hellish fires of his eyes.

"Our adventurous cleric was bearing this scroll on him – he took quite a deal of persuasion to give it up, I might add. After further persuasion he revealed that he had been charged with delivery of it to you, my dear General. You alone, and in person. Now, we have an agent in the enemy camp, that you already know. But would you believe that until tonight I did not know the identity of that agent? Strange, but true. Now I know everything there is to know, General. Or almost everything. Perhaps you could explain to me why exactly you are receiving despatches from someone at the very heart of the Merduk court?"

"I have no idea what you're talking about, Fournier. Now what is in this scroll?"

"That is of no matter for the moment. However, there is the rather alarming prospect of the Torunnan Commander-in-Chief being in clandestine communication with the enemy High Command. That, my dear Corfe Cear-Inaf, is treason, in anyone's book."

"Don't be absurd, Fournier. It's come from this agent of yours you've been preening yourself over for weeks. What's in the damned scroll? And what have you done with this Albrec?"

"All in good time, General. You see, the interesting thing is that the scroll did not come from any agent of mine. It came, as my little mishapen bishop finally admitted, direct from the hands of the Merduk Queen herself. Perhaps you could explain this."

Corfe blinked, startled. "I have no idea –"

"Colonel Willem," said Fournier, raising his voice a fraction. And out of the darkness a group of men instantly appeared. The candles lit up the length of their drawn swords.

A shaven-headed man with a patch over one eye stepped into the summer-house. Willem, one of Corfe's senior officers. Behind him was young Colonel Aras. Willem had a horse-pistol cocked and ready, the match already smouldering on the lock.

"Place General Cear-Inaf under arrest. You will take him to my offices down by the waterfront and hold him there."

"With pleasure, Count," Willem said, grinning to show broad gap-ridden teeth. "Get up, traitor."

Corfe remained in his seat. The amazement fled out of his mind in a moment. Suddenly many things had become clear. He took in the faces of the newcomers with a quick glance. All strangers to him but for Willem and Aras. They were not even in army uniform. He turned to Fournier, keeping his voice as casual as he could.

"Why not just have me shot now?"

"It's obvious, I would have thought. The mob would never wear it – you're their darling, General. We must discredit you before we hang you."

"You'll never convince the Queen," Corfe told him.

"Her opinion is as immaterial as her rule is unconstitutional. The line of the Fantyrs is at an end. Torunna must look elsewhere for her rulers."

"I'll wager she'll not have to look far."

Fournier smiled. "Willem, get this upstart peasant out of my sight."

THEY HAD A closed carriage waiting in the courtyard. Corfe was manacled and locked inside. Aras shared it with him, another pistol cocked and pointed at his breast, whilst Willem and the others rode pillion. The carriage lurched and bumped through the sleeping capital, for it was late now – some time past the middle night, Corfe guessed. His mind was racing but he felt curiously calm. It was all in the open at last. No more intrigue – only naked force would work now.

He looked Aras in the eye. "When I saw you hold your ground in the King's Battle I never would have believed you could be a part of something like this."

Aras said nothing. The carriage interior was lit by a single fluttering candle-lantern and it was hard to see the expression on his face.

"This will mean civil war, Aras. The army will not stand for it. And the Merduks will be handed the kingdom on a plate. That is what he intends – to be Governor of a Merduk province."

Again, silence but for the rumbling of the iron-bound wheels and the horse's hooves on the cobbles.

"For God's sake, man – can't you see where your duty lies?"

The carriage stopped. The door was unbolted and opened from without and Corfe was hauled outside. He could smell dead fish in the air, pitch and seaweed. They were down near the southern docks, on the edge of the estuary. Lightless buildings bulked up against the sky, and he could see the masts of ships outlined before the stars. He offered no resistance as they manhandled him; Willem wanted him dead at once, that was plain. Corfe would not give him an excuse to fire.

Swinging lanterns scattering broken light on the wet cobbles. Men in armour, arquebuses, pikes. The soldiers were all in strange liveries – part of the conscripted retainers that Corfe had brought into the capital. They had foxed him there. He had brought the enemy into the city himself. That was the reason for their confidence.

Inside. Someone boxing him on the ear for no reason. Down stone stairs with water running down the walls. Torchlight guttering here, a noisome stink that turned his stomach.

"Hold him," Willem's voice said, and men pinioned him. The one-eyed colonel sized him up in the unsteady torchlight.

"Caught you by surprise, didn't we? You thought it was all signed, sealed and delivered. Well, you thought wrong. You little guttersnipe –" and he brought the butt of his pistol down on Corfe's temple.

Corfe staggered, and at the second blow the world darkened and his legs went out from under him. He struggled, but the men about him held him fast as Willem rained blow after blow down on his head. No pain, just a succession of explosions in his brain. Like a battery of culverins going off one by one. Somehow he remained conscious. His blood dappled the flags of the floor, gummed shut his eyes and nose. He heard his own breathing as though from a great distance, as stertorous as that of a dying consumptive.

Keys clinking, and then he was flung into a black cell, and the door clanged shut behind him. The footsteps outside retreated, laughter retreating with them.

His head felt like it belonged to someone else. The lights were sparkling through it like a twilit battle, and the tight manacles were already puffing up his hands. The floor was sodden and stinking.

Corfe sat up, and the pain began to seep in under the shock of it all. His ears were ringing, his mouth full of blood. He retched, heaving out a mess of bile onto the filthy floor.

"Who is that?" a voice asked in the darkness, an odd voice, something wrong with it.

"Who wants to know?" he rasped.

"My name is Albrec. I'm a monk."

He fought for breath. "We meet again, then. My name is Corfe. I'm a soldier." And then the blackness of the cell folded over his mind, and his face hit the floor.

BY DAWN THE arrests had begun. Willem and his men went round in squads. Andruw and Marsch were picked up first, along with Morin, Ebro and Ranafast. Then Quartermaster Passifal and General Rusio were roused out of their beds and led away in chains. The Cathedrallers' barracks were surrounded by three thousand arquebusiers under Colonel Willem, while Colonel Aras led twenty more tercios to confine Formio's Fimbrians. An order was issued to the army in general, directing it to stay in barracks, and a curfew was imposed upon the entire city. Lastly, Fournier himself took fifty men and marched them into the palace, demanding admittance to the Queen's chambers. Odelia was placed under guard – for her own protection, naturally – and the palace was sealed off.

By noon the waterfront dungeons were crammed full with almost the entire Torunnan High Command, and the brightly clad retainers whom Andruw had mocked were in control of three quarters of the city. The Cathedrallers had made an abortive breakout attempt, but Willem's arquebusiers had shot them down in scores. The Fimbrians had as yet made no move except to fortify their barracks with a series of makeshift barricades. They had little or no ammunition for their few arquebuses however, and their pikes would be almost worthless in street fighting. They were contained, for the moment. Fournier was confident they would accept some form of terms and was content to leave them be. As the afternoon wore round, however, he had batteries of heavy artillery wheeled into position around both them and the Cathedrallers, and Colonel Willem took some twelve thousand of the Torunnan regulars out of the city to the north. They had been told that a Merduk raiding party was closing in on the city and their Commander-in-Chief had ordered them to intercept it. Once they had left Torunn, however, Willem led them off to the east, towards the coast, where they would be safely out of the way. The rest of the regulars, leaderless and bewildered, remained in barracks, while around them the populace were kept off the streets by armed patrols, and rumours of Merduk infiltrators were circulated to keep them cowed. Thus, with a judicious mixture of bluff, guile, and armed force did Fournier tighten his grip upon the capital.

He made his headquarters in the chambers of the High Command in a wing of the palace, and by the early evening the place was abuzz with couriers coming and going, officers recieving new appointments and confused soldiers standing guard. After a frugal meal he dismissed everyone from the room and sat at the long table in the chair which King Lofantyr had once occupied, toying with the oiled point of his beard. When the clap of wings sounded at the window he did not turn round, nor did he seem startled when a homunculus landed before him amid the papers and maps and inkwells. The little creature folded its wings and cocked its head to one side.

"I must congratulate you," the beast said in a man's voice. "The operation proceeded even more smoothly than we had hoped."

"That was the easy part. Maintaining the facade for the next week will be harder. I trust you are keeping your master well informed."

"Of course. And he is mightily pleased. He wants Cear-Inaf kept alive, so that he may dispose of him at his leisure when he enters the city."

"And the Queen? What of her? She cannot live, you know that."

"Indeed. But Aurungzeb has this strange aversion to the execution of royalty. He feels that kind of thing puts odd ideas in men's minds."

"It may be that she will simply disappear then – she may escape and never be heard of again."

"I think that would be best."

"When does your master's army move?"

"It has begun to march already. In less than a week, my dear Count, you will be the new Governor of Torunna, answerable only to the Sultan himself. The war will be over."

"The war will be over," Fournier repeated thoughtfully. "Cear-Inaf is an upstart and a fool. He has done well, but even his much-vaunted generalship could not prevail against a hundred and fifty thousands. What I have done is spare Torunna a catastrophic defeat. I have saved thousands of lives."

"Indubitably." Was it his imagination, or was there a sardonic sneer to the voice which issued out of the homunculus?

"Go now," he said sharply. "Tell your master I will hold Torunn for him. When the army arrives, the gates shall be thrown open, and I shall see to it that the regulars are deployed elsewhere. There will be no resistance."

"What of Cear-Inaf's personal troops? Those tribesmen and the Fimbrians, not to mention the veterans from the Dyke?"

"They are contained. They will be entirely neutralised within the next few days."

The homunculus gathered itself up for flight, spreading its bat-like wings. "I certainly hope so, my dear Count. For your sake." Then the creature paused in the act of springing into the air. "By the way, we have heard rumours that there is an agent of yours at work in the court. Is this true?"

"That is a rumour, nothing more. All my attempts to insert an agent close to Aurungzeb have failed. You may congratulate him on his security."

"Thank you. The homunculus will return in two days, to monitor your progress. Until then Count, fare well." And the thing took off at last, and flapped its way out of the open window. Fournier watched it go, and when it had disappeared he took a handkerchief from his pocket and wiped the sweat out of his moustache.

WHEN CORFE WOKE he thought that the nightmare which had plagued his unconsciousness was still about him, cackling in the darkness. He raised a hand to his face and felt agony shoot through his wrists as its chained fellow came with it. His hands were swollen to the point of uselessness. Another day in these manacles and he would lose them. His face, when he touched it gingerly, felt as though it did not belong to him – it was some misshapen caricature his fingers found strange to the touch. Despite himself, he groaned aloud.

"Corfe?" a voice said. "Are you awake?"

"Yes."

"What have they done? I've heard shooting."

"They're trying to take over the city by now, I should think."

"They've been bringing in other prisoners all morning. Dozens of them. I hear the doors."

Corfe found it hard to keep his thoughts together. His mind seemed wrapped in wool. "Fournier caught you," he said muzzily.

"Yes, on the way in. I had two companions – Merduks. He killed them after the torture. They would not speak." There was a sound like a sob. "I'm so sorry. I could not bear it."

"The scroll. What was in it?"

"The entire Merduk campaign-plan, and order of battle."

Corfe struggled to clear his mind, collect his thoughts. He fought against the urge to lay his head in the foul-smelling muck of the floor and go to sleep.

"The Merduk Queen – he said it was from her. Is that true?"

There was a silence. Finally Albrec said "Yes."

"Why? Why would she do such a thing?"

"She is – she is a Ramusian, from Aekir. She wanted revenge."

"I honour her for it."

"Yes, though nothing will come of it now. What is Fournier going to do?"

"I think he means to surrender the city to the Merduks. He has done some deal. I have been an arrogant fool, such a fool."

Quiet descended upon the interior of the cell. Water was gurgling away somewhere, and they could hear the rush of the sewers below.

The sewers.

"Father," Corfe said with sudden energy. "Go over the floor of this place. There must be a drain somewhere, a grating or something."

"Corfe –"

"*Do it!*"

They began searching around in the fetid darkness with their hands, their fingers squelching into nameless things. Once, Corfe's fastened upon the wriggling wetness of a rat. He listened for the sound of the water, and finally found it, and tore heaps of rotting straw from around the grating. His half-numb fingers searched out its dimensions – eighteen inches square, no more.

A yank on the metal of the bars, but it would not budge. It was firmly set in mortar. he searched his pockets with fevered haste, and found there a folded clasp knife. Willem had taken his poniard, but had been too busy pistol-whipping him to search his pockets.

"Bastards," Corfe spat in triumph. He unfolded the knife with his clumsy hands and began scraping at the mortar that held the grating fast. It was already crumbling in places, loosened by the wetness of the floor. He levered up clods and splinters of the stuff., stabbing with the little knife. There was a crack, and the point broke off. He hardly paused, but worked on in the smothering darkness by touch. Every so often the coruscating lights in his head came back, and he had to pause and fight the dizzying sickness they brought. It took hours – or what seemed like hours – but at the end of that time he had picked out every trace of the mortar from around the grating. He put the broken knife carefully back in his pocket. Something warm and liquid was trickling down his temples. Sweat or blood, he knew not.

"Over here, Father. Help me."

Albrec bumped into him. "I have only one good hand."

"No matter. Three are better than two. Get a hold here." He positioned the monk's fingers for him. "Now, after three, pull like a good 'un."

They heaved until Corfe thought his head would burst. A slight shift, a tiny grating sound, no more. He collapsed onto his side on the floor.

Several minutes passed, and then they tried again. This time Corfe was sure one corner of the grating had shifted, and when he felt over it he found that it was raised above the level of the floor flags some half an inch.

A strange, unearthly time of blinding pain and intense physical struggle, all in pitch blackness. They tugged on one corner of the grating after another, their fingers slipping on slime. Finally Corfe was able to get the chain of his manacles under one corner and pull back, feeling as though his hands were about to be wrenched off at the wrists.

A squeal of scraped metal, and he fell over on his back, the heavy grating jerking free to smash into his kneecap with dazzling pain. He lay on his back, gasping for air. "We – we did it, Father."

They rested and listened in the blackness. No jailer approached, no alarm was raised.

"Are we going to go down there?" Albrec asked at last.

"We're on the waterfront. The sewers here all lead straight into the river. It shouldn't be far – not more than a hundred yards. Come now, Father Albrec. I'll have you breathing clean air inside of fifteen minutes. I'll go first."

The sound of rushing water seemed very loud as Corfe squeezed himself into the drain. He retched once at the smell, but nothing came up. His stomach had long since rid itself of the last vestiges of Fournier's dinner.

His legs were dangling in a current of icy liquid. He felt a moment of black panic at the idea of venturing down there. What if there was no room to breathe? what if –

His grip on the lip of the drain slipped and he scraped down through the short shaft and splashed into the sewer below. The current took him and buffeted him against rough brick walls. His head was under water. He could not breathe, was not even sure which way was up. His lungs shrieked for air. The tunnel was less than a yard wide; he braced himself against it, shearing the skin from his knuckles and knees. A moment's gasp of air, and then he had slipped and was being hurtled along again. His head smacked against the tunnel wall. He felt like screaming.

And then was in mid-air, flying effortlessly before crashing into water again after a fall of several yards through nothingness. Clean, cold air. He was out. He was in the river, and it was night outside. The water was brackish here, this close to the estuary. He choked on it, struggled frantically to keep his head up, his manacled hands flailing. The current was taking him downstream, out to sea. But there was a willow here, leaning low over the water. He grasped at a trailing limb, missed, was slashed in the face by another and caught hold of a third, his grip slicing down the leaves. He pulled himself up it as though on a rope, and found mud under his feet. He waded ashore, shuddering with cold, and took a second to collect himself. Then he remembered Albrec, and floundered about on the muddy bank until he had found a long stick, all the while watching the surface of the racing river. He waited then for a long time, but saw nothing. It was too cold to remain. Either Albrec had drowned, or he had remained in the cell. He could not wait any longer. The lights of Torunn were bright and yellow and the city wall towered like a monolith barely two hundred yards away. Corfe had been washed ashore on a little patch of wasteland just within the city perimeter, not far from the southern barbican. It was too exposed here. He had to move on.

There were reed-beds here at the riverside, filled with old rubbish and stinking with the effluent of the sewers. He crept along in them as quietly as he could, and then stopped. Something was crashing about in front of him. A man.

"Lord God," a voice whispered. "Oh, Lord –"

"Albrec!"

"Corfe?"

He moved forward again. The monk was caught in thigh-deep mud and looked like some glistening swamp-denizen. Corfe hauled him out and then they lay there in the reeds for a while, utterly spent. Above them the clear sky was ablaze with stars from one horizon to the next.

"Come," Corfe said at last. "We have to get away. We'll die here else."

Wordlessly, Albrec staggered to his feet and the two of them staggered off together like a pair of mud-daubed drunks.

"Where are we going?" the monk asked.

"To the only man of importance I think Fournier will have left alone. Your master, Macrobius."

"What about the army?"

"Fournier will have it under control somehow. And he'll have neutralised all my officers. Maybe the Queen, too. I have to get these damned manacles off before my hands die. How much shooting did you hear when you were in there?"

"A lot of volleys. But they lasted a few minutes, not more."

"There's been no major battle then. They must have my men bottled up somehow. The Merduks are probably on the march already. Hurry, Albrec! We don't have time to waste."

NINETEEN

As THE LADIES-IN-WAITING quaked, terrified, the Queen twitched and snarled in her chair, the whites of her eyes flickering under closed lids. She had been like this for almost two hours, and they longed to cry out to someone for help, a doctor or apothecary to be sent. But ancient Grania, who had been at the palace longer than any of the rest and whose dark eyes were unclouded by any vestige of senility, told them to hush their useless mouths and pretend nothing untoward was happening, else the guards posted outside might take it into their heads to come in. So the little flock of ladies embroidered and knitted with absent fervour, stabbing fingertips with monotonous regularity while brimming over with hiccuping little sobs for the predicament they had all found themselves in: and Grania glanced towards heaven and helped herself to the wine.

None of them noticed when the black furred shape with ruby eyes crept back into the chamber through the smoke hood and took up its accustomed place in the centre of a huge web that quivered sootily in the shadows of the great rafters. The Queen sighed, and sagged in her chair. Then she rubbed her eyes and stood up, putting a hand to the hollow of her back. For several seconds she looked what she was; a tired woman in her sixth decade. As the ladies-in-waiting chattered around her she took the goblet of wine that the silent Grania offered and drained it at a draught.

"I am getting to old for this sort of thing," she said to the aged woman who had once been her wet-nurse.

"We all are," the crone retorted dryly. And to the brightly plumaged chatterers about her she snapped: "Oh, shut up, all of you."

"No," Odelia said. "Keep talking – that is an order. Let

the guards hear us gossiping away. Were we too silent, they would be the more suspicious."

"How bad is it?" Grania asked her Queen, as the surrounding women talked desperately now of the weather, the price of silk – all the while trying to spare an ear for the Queen's words.

"Bad enough. They have massacred many of his Cathedrallers. The poor fools charged massed arquebusiers with nothing more than sabres."

"And his Fimbrians?"

"Strangely supine. But something tells me that their commander, Formio, is not letting the grass grow under his feet. The rest of the city is under curfew. Fournier has installed himself in the east wing – so sure of himself is he that he has only fifty or sixty men around him. The rest patrol the city. There are fires down by the dockyards, but I don't know what they signify. Arach's vision is limited, and sometimes hard to decipher."

"Sit, lady. You are exhausted."

"How can I sit?" Odelia exploded. "I do not even know if he is alive or dead!" She passed a hand over her face. "Pardon me. I am tired. I was blind: I should have forseen this."

"No-one else did," Grania said bluntly. "Do not torment yourself because you are no soothsayer."

The Queen sank back down upon her chair. "He cannot be dead, Grania. He must not be dead." And she buried her face in her hands and wept.

IT WAS A long, weary way from the waterfront to the Pontifical palace, and it took Corfe and Albrec most of the remainder of the night to traverse it. Fournier's patrols were easy to dodge – they spent as much time gawking at the wonders of the great city as they did keeping an eye out for curfew-breakers. They were, when it came down to it, untutored men of the country awed by the size and sprawl of the capital. Eavesdropping on their conversations as they trooped past, Corfe realised that they did not even know why they were here, except that it was some kind of emergency engendered by the Merduk War.

Halted at the gates of the abbey by watchful Knights

Militant, Corfe and Albrec were eyed with astonished disbelief when they demanded to see Macrobius. They were still fettered, and liberally plastered with mud and sewer filth. But something in Corfe's eye made one of the gate-guards dash off at once to fetch Monsignor Alembord. The portly Inceptine looked none too pleased to be dragged out in the middle of the night but there was no denying that he recognised the bedraggled pair straight away. They were ushered inside the gates amid much whispering and brought to a little reception-chamber where Corfe demanded a blacksmith or armourer to cut off their manacles. Alembord waddled away, looking thoroughly confused. He was almost entirely unaware of the coup that had taken place: Fournier's men had left the abbey alone, as Corfe had suspected they would.

The yawning armourer arrived soon after with a wooden box full of the tools of his trade. The fetters were cut from the two prisoner's wrists, and Corfe had to clench his teeth against the agony of returning circulation in his hands. They were swollen to twice their normal size and where the iron had encircled his wrists, deep slices had been carved out of the puffed flesh. He let them bleed freely, hoping it would wash some of the filth out of them.

Basins of clean, hot water, and fresh clothes were found for the two men. The clothes turned out to be spare Inceptine habits, and thus it was dressed as a monk that Corfe finally found himself ushered into Macrobius's private suite. It still wanted an hour until dawn.

Private though the suite might nominally be, it was crowded with anxious clerics and alarmed Knights Militant. They and Macrobius listened in grim silence as Corfe related the events of the night, Albrec narrating his own part in the story. As he and Corfe had agreed, however, no mention was made of the spy at the Merduk court.

When they had finished, Macrobius, who had listened without a word, said simply: "What would you have me do?"

"How many armed men can the abbey muster?" Corfe asked.

"Monsignor Alembord?"

"Some sixty to seventy, Holiness."

"Good," Corfe said. "Then you must sally at dawn with all of them, and go to the City Square. Call a meeting, raise the rooftops – create a commotion that will get people out onto the streets. Fournier does not have enough men to clamp down on the entire city, and he will not be able to cow the population if they can be raised against him. Get the people onto the streets, Holiness."

"And you, Corfe, what will you do?"

"I'm going to try and get through to my men. If you can make enough of a commotion, Fournier will have to take troops away from their containment, and then there will be a good chance I can break them out. After that, he will be defeated, I promise you."

"What of the Merduks?" Alembord asked with round eyes.

"I am assuming they are on the move even as we speak. If they force-march, they can be here in four or five days at most. That does not give us much time. This thing must be crushed by tomorrow at the latest if we are to take the field in time."

"Very well," Macrobius said, his chin outthrust. "It shall be as you say. "Monsignor Alembord, rouse out the entire abbey. I want everyone in their best habits, the Knights in full armour and mounted, with every flag and pennon they can find. We shall make a spectacle of it, give Fournier something to distract his mind. See to it at once."

As the unfortunate Alembord hurried away, Macrobius turned back to Corfe. "How do you intend to get through to your men?"

"With your permission, Holiness, I will retain the disguise I've been given. I will be a cleric desiring only to offer spiritual succour to the beleaguered soldiers. For that reason, I will go to Formio's Fimbrians first. The idea of a priest offering comfort to my Cathedrallers would not stand up."

"And will you go alone?"

"Yes. Albrec here is too easily recognisable, even by these bumpkins from the south. He will have to remain here in the abbey."

"And what about the Queen, Corfe?"

"She, also, will have to be left to her own devices for a while. For now it is soldiers I need, not monarchs."

Count Fournier's beard had been tugged from its usual fine point into a bristling mess. He paced the room like a restless cat while his senior officers stared woodenly at him.

"Escaped? Escaped? How can you be telling me this? The one man above all who must be contained, and you tell me he is now at large. Exactly how could this have happened?"

Gabriel Venuzzi's handsome face was sallow as a whitewashed wall. "It seems he managed to lever up a grating and make his way into the sewers, Count. He and that noseless monk who was incarcerated with him."

"That is another thing – I specifically said that all the prisoners were to be confined separately."

"There are not enough cells in the waterfront dungeons. By my last estimate, we have almost four-score prisoners down there. Some of them are even three to a cell now. Every officer above the rank of ensign is being picked up. Perhaps we could relax the rules a little."

"No! We must cut off the head if the body is not to crush us. Every man on the lists must be arrested. Start using the common gaols if you have to, but take every name on the list!"

"It shall be as you say."

"What of the Queen?"

"Still confined to her chambers."

"Have the guards look in on her every few minutes."

"Count Fournier!" Venuzzi was shocked. "She is the Queen – do you expect common soldiers to tramp in and out of her chambers like gawking sightseers?"

"Do as I say, damn it. I don't have time for your lace-edged court niceties now, Venuzzi. Our heads will all be on the block if this does not come off. How in the world could he have got away? Where would he go? To his men, obviously. But how to get through the lines? By subterfuge, naturally. Venuzzi, inform all our officers that no-one – *no-one* is to be allowed through the lines to the Fimbrians or the Cathedrallers. Do you understand me, Venuzzi? Not so much as a damned mouse."

"I am not an imbecile, Count."

"I thought that also until you let Cear-Inaf slip away – now get out and set about your errands."

Venuzzi left, his formerly livid face now flushed and furious. Fournier turned to a beefy figure who lounged by the door. "Sardinac, get some more men up here in the palace, and some artillery pieces."

The man called Sardinac straightened. "We don't have too many artillerists to spare, Count. These are hired retainers we're working with, remember; not Torunnan regulars."

"Don't I know it. Take some of the guns which they have deployed about the Fimbrian quarter. And send another courier in to treat with that ass Formio. His position is hopeless, it's not his fight, safe-conduct out of the city – the same as the last one."

Sardinac bowed, and exited in Venuzzi's wake.

Fournier wiped his brow with a scented handkerchief. He was surrounded by fools, that was the problem. Such a beautiful plan, but it had to work in all things or it would work in none. There was so little margin for error.

His restless feet took him out onto the balcony. You could see a corner of the City Square from here. It was like glimpsing a slice of some odd carnival. He could see Knights Militant bedecked with banners, richly robed priests – and a milling crowd of several thousand of the city lowly who had braved the curfew to see what was going on. That also had to be contained. His men were like butter scraped across too much bread. Who would have thought Macrobius would issue out of his lair and get up on his hind legs to preach, the old fool?

There was a lit brazier in the room, the charcoal red and grey with heat. Fournier went to the table, unlocked a small chest, and took out a battered scroll with the broken seal of the Merduk Military upon it. He studied it for a moment, thoughtfully, and seemed about to consign it to the brazier, but then thought better of it. He tucked it into the breast of his doublet, and patted it with one manicured hand.

"SERGEANT! WE'VE A priest here wants to go and talk to the Fimbrians," the young soldier said. "That's all right, ain't it?"

The sergeant, a corpulent veteran of many tavern brawls, marched ponderously over to the barricade where the black-robed Inceptine stood surrounded by half a dozen nervous young men with the slow-match smouldering balefully on the clamps of their arquebuses. He drew a sabre.

"New orders, Fintan, lad. No-one to go through the lines. Courier arrived just this minute. Father, your time has been wasted. You might want to say a prayer for us though – out here facing those damned Fimbrians."

"By all means, my son." The priest, his face hidden in the cowl of his habit, raised his hands in the Sign of the Saint. As he did, the wide sleeves of his raiment fell back to reveal badly cut wrists. The soldiers had bowed their heads to receive his blessing, but they snapped upright when a clear young voice shouted out: "Sergeant! Bring that man to me at once!"

Colonel Aras was standing outside a nearby grain warehouse surrounded by a crowd of other officers and couriers. He stalked forward. "The priest! Grab that priest and bring him here!"

The Inceptine tensed as he found the barrels of six arquebuses levelled at him. The sergeant looked him up and down quizzically.

"Looks like someone else is in need of a prayer, Father."

"It seems so, Sergeant," the priest said. "Be careful of those Fimbrians. They collect the ears of their enemies, I've heard."

"Bring him into my quarters, Sergeant, and be quick about it!" Aras barked, white-faced. "Enough chatter."

The Inceptine was escorted past the crowd of staring soldiers and into the cavernous interior of the warehouse. There was a little office within, divided off from the rest of the building. They left him there. Some young noblemen were bent over a map. They straightened and nodded at him, looking a trifle bewildered. Aras ordered the room emptied.

"You can throw back your hood now, General," he said when they had gone.

Corfe did as he was told. "I congratulate you, Aras. You have quick eyes."

The two men looked at one another in silence for a long moment, until Aras stirred, and reached for a decanter. "Some wine?"

"Thank you."

They drank, each watching the other.

"What now?" Corfe said. "Will you turn me over to your master – and the kingdom over to the Merduks? Or will you remember your duty?"

Aras flopped down onto a chair. "You have no idea what this has cost me," he whispered.

"To do what? Betray your country?"

The younger man sprang to his feet again, his face outraged. But it leaked out of him like water from a punctured skin. He stared into his wine.

"You were wrong," he said quietly. "Wrong to go about things the way you did. The great men of a kingdom cannot be trampled upon – they will not wear it."

"And in the end their own prestige is worth more to them than the kingdom. You know me, Aras. If a man has ability I could care less whether he's a duke or a beggar. Look at Rusio – I made him a general though he was one of my bitterest enemies. But Fournier – he is motivated by more than wounded pride, you must know that. He has his heart set on ruling Torunna, even if it is only as a pawn of the Merduks. You are all – all of you – merely his tools, to be used and discarded."

"He's going to negotiate a peace, and end the war with honour," Aras said.

"He is going to capitulate unconditionally, and feed off the carcass that the Merduks leave behind."

Aras turned away. "What would you have me do?" he murmured. "Betray him?"

"A traitor cannot be betrayed. These Fimbrians you are besieging – they served under you in battle. They held their line at your orders, and died where they stood because you asked them to. They are your comrades, not your enemies. When did Fournier ever set his shoulder beside yours, or face a battle-line with you? Give it up, Aras – do the honourable thing. Order your men to stand down and let me save this city of ours."

Aras said nothing for a long time. When he spoke again it was in a loud voice. "Haptman Vennor!"

A young man in the livery of one of the southern Lords put his head around the door. "Colonel?"

"The men are to stack arms and stand down. This priest here is to be escorted through our lines to the Fimbrian barracks. Dismantle the barricades. It is over."

Haptman Vennor gaped at him. "Sir – on whose authority –"

"Obey my orders now, damn it! I command here, now do as I say!"

The startled officer saluted and withdrew.

"Thank you," Corfe said quietly.

"I hope you will speak up for me at my court martial, sir," Aras said.

"Court martial?" Corfe laughed. "Aras my dear fellow, I need you in the ranks. As soon was we have this little mess sorted out, we have a meeting with the Merduk army to arrange. I cannot afford to lose an officer with your experience." He held out a hand. Aras hesitated, and then shook it warmly. "I won't let you down, sir – not again. I am your man until death."

Corfe smiled. "I think I knew that already, or part of me did – else I would have bolted as soon as you recognised me."

"What do you want me to do with these mercenaries?"

"They will remain under your command for now. Mercenaries or not, they are still Torunnans. As soon as Formio and his men have shaken out, we'll march on the palace together."

ODELIA STOOD ON the balcony and watched the smoke of war drift over the tortured city. Out by the north gate there were crackles of volley-fire rolling still, and the waterfront was a mass of fire above which the smoke toiled in billowing thunderheads. The masts of great ships stood stark and angular against the flames. Some of them had had their moorings cut to save them from the inferno and were now drifting helplessly down the estuary towards the sea.

Nearer at hand, the deafening roar of the artillery salvoes had subsided at last, to be replaced by a chaotic storm of gunfire and the massed roaring of men fighting for their lives. The Fimbrians were storming the palace, and terrified valets and maids had come running to her chambers to huddle in panic-stricken crowds, like rabbits fleeing a wildfire. And Corfe was alive. He and Formio were retaking the palace room by gutted room. Fournier had lost the gamble, and would soon surrender his life as well. It warmed her to think on it.

The doors burst open and a knot of grimy soldiers burst into the room, making the maids scream and cower. Behind them came Count Fournier himself, along with Gabriel Venuzzi and a gaggle of the southern nobles' sons who had marched into the city scant days before with such pomp and heraldry. They were all smoke-blackened or bloodstained now, with frightened eyes and drawn swords. Fournier, however, was as dapper as always – in fact he seemed to have taken special care with his toilet, and was dressed in midnight blue with black hose and a silver-hilted rapier. He held a handkerchief to his nose against the powder-smoke that eddied through the entire palace, but when he saw the Queen he pocketed it with a flourish and then bowed deeply.

"Your Majesty."

"My dear Count. What could possibly bring you here at this time?"

A crash of gunfire drowned out his reply and he frowned, irritated. "Your pardon, Majesty. I thought it the merest good manners to come and make my farewells."

"Are you leaving us then, Count?"

Fournier smiled. "Sadly, yes. But my journey is not a long one."

The roar of battle seemed to be raging just down the corridor. Fournier's companions took off towards it, yelling – except for Gabriel Venuzzi, who collapsed upon the floor and began sobbing loudly.

"Before I go," Fournier went on, "there is something I would like to give you – a parting gift which I hope will be of some little use to the – ah, the new Torunna which will no doubt come into existence after my departure."

He reached into the breast of his doublet and pulled out a tattered scroll. It was bloodstained and ragged, with a broken seal upon it.

"You see, lady, despite what you may think, I never wanted harm to come to this kingdom – I simply could not see any way to save it except my own. Others may save it – that is quite possible – but in doing so they will also destroy it. If you do not see what I mean already, I am sure you will one day."

Odelia took the scroll with a slight inclination of her

head. "I will see you hanged, Count. And your head I will post above the city gate."

Fournier smiled. "I am sorry to disappoint you, Majesty, but I am a nobleman of the old school, who will take his leave of the world in the manner he sees fit. Excuse me."

He walked over to a table in the corner which had decanters of wine and brandy set upon it, ignoring the crash and roar of the fighting raging a few doors down. Pouring himself a goblet of wine, he sprinkled a white powder into the glass from a screw of paper he had palmed. Then he tossed off the liquid with one swift gulp.

"Gaderian – as good a vintage to finish with as any, I suppose." He bowed perfectly. When he had straightened, Odelia could see the sudden sweat on his forehead. He took one step towards her, and then folded over, and toppled to the floor.

Odelia went to him and, despite herself, she knelt and cradled his head in her hand.

"You are a traitor, Fournier," she said gently, "but you never lacked courage."

Fournier smiled up at her.

"He is a man of blood and iron, lady. He will never make you happy." Then his eyes rolled back, and he died.

Odelia shut the dead eyelids, frowning. The firing down the passageway reached a crescendo, and there was the clash of steel on steel, men shrieking, orders half-lost in the chaos. Then a voice she knew thundered out: "Cease fire! Cease fire there! You – drop your weapons. Formio, round them up. Andruw, come with me."

An eerie quiet fell, and then booted feet were marching up the corridor, crashing on marble. Through the door came Corfe and Andruw, with a bodyguard of Fimbrians and wild-eyed Cathedrallers. Corfe's face was badly bruised and black with powder. The Queen rose, letting Fournier's head thump to the floor.

"Good day, General," she said, aching with the need to run to him, embrace him.

"I trust I see you well, lady?" Corfe replied, his eyes scanning the room. Coming to rest on Fournier they narrowed. "The Count made good his escape, I see."

"Yes, just this moment."

"Lucky for him. I'd have impaled the traitor, had I taken him alive. Lads, check the next suite. That yokel down there says there's no more but we can't be too sure." Andruw and the other soldiers tramped off purposefully. Corfe noticed the bedraggled heap of the weeping Venuzzi and kicked him out of his way.

"The city is secure, Majesty," he said. "A force has been sent out to bring in the head of Colonel Willem. He is holed up to the east with some of the regulars."

"What of the other conspirators?" the Queen asked.

"We shot them as we found them. Which reminds me." Corfe drew John Mogen's sword. There was a flash as swift as lightning, a sickening crunch, and Gabriel Venuzzi's head spun end over end, attached to the body only by a ribbon of spouting arterial blood. The ladies-in-waiting shrieked; one fainted. Odelia curled her lip.

"Was that necessary?"

Corfe looked at her with no whit of softness in his eyes. "He had eighty of my men shot. He's lucky to have died quickly." He wiped his sword on Venuzzi's body.

Odelia turned her back on him and walked away from the puddle of gore on the floor. "Clean up that mess," she snapped at one of the maids.

The view out the window again. Fully a quarter of the city was burning, most of it down by the river. But the gunfire had stopped. Macrobius was still preaching in the City Square, as he had been doing since dawn. What was he talking about, she wondered absently.

Corfe joined her. One eye was swollen almost shut and he had black bruises on his cheekbones and jaw. He looked like a prize-fighter who had lost his bout.

"Well, you have delivered the city, General," Odelia said, angry with him for all manner of reasons she could not name. "I congratulate you. Now all you have to do is save us from the Merduks." Was it possible that Fournier's last words had registered with something in her? That disgusting murder in cold blood – right in front of her eyes! What kind of man was he anyway?

"Marsch is dead," Corfe said quietly.

"What?"

"He was killed while leading the breakout attempt."

She turned to him then and saw the tears coursing down his cheeks, though his face was set hard as marble.

"Oh Corfe, I'm so sorry." She took him into her arms and for a moment he yielded, buried his face in the hollow of her shoulder. But then he pulled away, wiped his eyes with his fingers. "I must go now. There's a lot to do, and not much time."

She turned to watch him go. He left the room blindly, tramping through Venuzzi's gore and leaving a trail of bloody footprints behind him.

TORUNN'S BRIEF BUT bloody agony ended at last as the regular army stamped out the last embers of the abortive coup. The fires were brought under control, thousands of the capital's citizens mobilised to form bucket-chains. Safely perched on a cherry tree in the heights of the palace gardens, the homunculus watched the spectacle with unblinking eyes. As darkness fell, it took off again and flapped northwards.

That night, on the topmost battlements of Ormann Dyke's remaining tower, Aurungzeb, Sultan of Ostrabar, hammered his fist down on the unyielding stone of the ancient battlement.

"Who is sovereign here? Who commands? Shahr-Johor, you may be my khedive, but you are not irreplaceable. I have indulged your whims once before, and forgiven you for the failure which resulted. You will now indulge me!"

"But, Highness," Shahr Johor protested, "to change a battle-plan when the army is only days away from contact with the enemy is – is foolhardy."

"What did you say?"

Hopelessly, Shahr Johor pinched the bridge of his nose. "Your pardon, my Sultan. I am a little tired."

"Yes, you are. Get yourself some sleep ere the great fight begins. Or you will be of no use to anyone." Aurungzeb's voice lost its harsh edge. "I am not a complete child in military matters, Shahr Johor, and what I am suggesting is not a complete rewriting of the plan, merely a minor revision."

Shahr Johor nodded, too weary to protest further.

"Batak failed to have this Torunnan commander-in-chief neutralised. That traitor Fournier failed to deliver Torunn to me without a fight. Batak tells me that the coup has already been stamped out – in the space of a single day! There has been too much intrigue – and all of it a mere waste of time. Enough of it. Brute force is all that will destroy the Torunnans now – that, and a good battle-plan. I have made a study of your intentions." Here, Aurungzeb's voice fell, became more reasonable. "Your plan is fine – I have no quarrel with it. All I am asking is that you strengthen this flank-march of yours. Take ten thousand of the *Hraibadar* from the main body and send them along with the cavalry."

"I don't understand your sudden desire to change the plan, Highness," Shahr Johor said stubbornly.

"There has been a lot of coming and going between here and Torunn. I suspect" – Aurungzeb lowered his voice further – "I suspect that we may have a traitor in our midst."

Shahr Johor snapped upright. "Are you sure?"

Aurungzeb flapped one massive hand. "I am not *sure*, but it is as well to be suspicious. That mad monk escaped from here with the connivance of someone at the court – and who knows what information he might have in his addled pate. Make the change, Shahr Johor. Do as I wish. I shall not meddle further in your handling of this battle."

"Very well, my Sultan. I bow to your superior wisdom. The flank-march we planned will be augmented – and with the best shock-infantry we possess. And no-one shall know of it but you and I, until the very day they set out."

"You relieve my mind, Shahr Johor. This may well be the deciding battle of the war. Nothing about its conduct must be left to chance. Mehr Jirah has half the army convinced that the western Saint is also our Prophet, and the *Minhraib*, curse them, are simple enough to believe that it means an end to war with the Ramusians. It may be that this is the last great levy Ostrabar will ever be able to mobilise."

"I won't fail you, Highness," Shahr Johor said fervently. "The Unbelievers will be struck as though by a thunderbolt. In a few days, not more, you will sit in Torunn and receive the homage of the Torunnan Queen. And this much-vaunted general of theirs shall be but a memory."

TWENTY

THERE HAD BEEN no time for councils-of-war, debates on strategy, or any of the last minute wrangles so beloved of High Commands since man had first started waging organised war. Before the fires which raged down on the waterfront of Torunn had even stopped smouldering, the army was on the move. Corfe was leading thirty-five thousand men out of the Capital, and leaving four thousand behind to garrison it. Some of the men in both the garrison and the field army had lately been in arms against each other, but now that it was the Merduk they were to fight against, their former allegiances were forgotten. Care had to be taken, however, to keep the Cathedrallers away from the conscripts. The tribesmen had taken Marsch's death hard, and were not inclined to forgive or forget in a hurry.

Andruw commanded the Cathedrallers now, with Ebro as his second-in-command. Formio led the Fimbrians, as always, and Ranafast the Dyke veterans. The main body of the Torunnan regulars were under General Rusio, with Aras as his second, and the newly arrived conscripts had been scattered throughout the veteran tercios, two or three to a company. Back in Torunn, the garrison had been left under the personal command of the Queen herself, which had raised more than a few eyebrows. But Corfe simply did not have the officers to spare. Many had died as they were broken out of the dungeons. In any case, if the field army were destroyed, Torunn would have no chance.

It was not the best-equipped force that Torunna had ever sent out into battle. Most of the conscripts did not even possess uniforms, and some were still unfamiliar with their weapons, though Corfe had weeded out the most unhandy and reserved them for the garrison. In addition, the baggage train was a somewhat haphazard affair, as many of the supplies destined to be carried by it had gone up in smoke along with the riverfront warehouses. So the men were marching forth with rations for a week, no more, and two hundred of the Cathedrallers were serving as heavy infantry for lack of horses. But tucked away in Corfe's saddlebags was something he hoped would tip the scales in their favour: the Merduk battle-plan which Albrec had brought away from Ormann Dyke, and which the Queen had had translated. He knew what part of the enemy army was going where, and even though their advance had been brought forward, he thought they would stick to their original plan – for it is no light thing to redesign the accepted strategy of a large army, especially when that army is already on the march.

Without that information, Corfe privately believed that there would have been little or no hope for his men, and in his mind he blessed Aurungzeb's nameless Ramusian Queen.

No CHEERS TO see them off, but the walls were thickly crowded with Torunn's population all the same. There was a headlong sense of urgency about the city. So much had happened in such a short space of time that the departure of the army for the decisive battle seemed but one more notable event among many. No time for farewells, either. The regulars had an appointment to keep, and they marched out of the city gates knowing they were already late for it.

The army tramped eighteen miles that first day, and when the lead elements started to lay out their bivouacs the rearguard was still a league behind them. As was his wont, Corfe found himself a nearby knoll and sat his horse there, watching them all trudge into camp. He was not seeing them, though. He was thinking of an ex-slave who had once sworn allegiance to him with the chains of the galleys still on his wrists. A savage from the Cimbrics who had become his friend.

Andruw and Formio joined him, the Fimbrian actually mounted on a quiet mare. The trio exchanged sombre salutes and then sat and watched as the first campfires were lit below, until there was a constellation of them rivalling the brilliance of the first stars.

The darkness deepened. The trio sat their horses without sharing a word, but all glad of one another's company. Then Andruw twisted in the saddle and peered north. "Corfe, Formio – look there."

On the horizon, a ruddy glow, like that of a burning town. Except that there were no towns for many leagues in that direction.

"It's their campfires," Corfe realised. "Like the lights of a city. That's the enemy, gentlemen."

They studied the phenomenon. It was, in its way, as awe-inspiring as the Northern Lights which could be seen in winter from the foothills of the Thurians.

"It doesn't seem as though it could be the work of man, somehow," Formio said.

"When there's enough of them, men can do just about anything," Andruw told him. "And they're capable of anything." His voice fell into something approaching a whisper. "But I've never known or heard of them fighting a war like this one. There has never been a pause in it, from the first assaults on Aekir until now. Ormann Dyke, the North More, the King's Battle, Berrona, and then the battle for the city itself. There's no end to it – all in the space of a year."

"Is that all it's been?" Corfe wondered. "One year? And yet the whole world has changed."

They were all thinking of Marsch, though no-one mentioned his name.

"Sound *Officer's Call* as soon as the rearguard is bedded down," Corfe said at last. "We'll meet here. I have something to show you all."

"Going to pull a rabbit out of a hat, Corfe?" Andruw asked lightly.

"Something like that."

They saluted and left him. Corfe dismounted, hobbled and unsaddled his horse, and let it graze. Then he sat on a mossy boulder and watched the northern horizon, where the Merduk host was lighting up a Torunnan sky. One single year, and the deaths of untold thousands. He had begun it as a junior officer, obscure but happy. And he had ended it commander of Torunna's last army, his heart as black and empty as a withered apple. All in that one year.

FORMIO HELD A lantern over the map and the assembled officers kept down its corners with the toes of their boots. They crowded round the circle of light as though straining to warm themselves at a fire. Corfe pointed out features with a broken stick.

"We are here, and the enemy is... there, or thereabouts. You've seen the light of their camp for yourselves – I reckon they're less than half a day's march away. They number a hundred and twenty-five thousand, one fifth of them cavalry. The Merduk khedive, Shahr Johor, is going to send all this cavalry out on a flank march to the north, to come in on our left flank when we've engaged the main body, and roll us up. Hammer and anvil – simple, but effective. His cavalry consist of *Ferinai*, horse-archers, and mounted infantry who've been taken out of the *Minhraib* and armed with horse-pistols. The *Ferinai* are the core of the force – if we cripple them, the rest will crumble. They number only some eight thousand – they lost a third of their men in the King's Battle, attacking Aras and Formio."

"And I suppose you can tell us what they're going to have for breakfast in the morning," Andruw said with a raised eyebrow. "General, we seem remarkably well-informed as to the enemy's composition and intentions."

"That is because I have managed to get hold of a copy of their battle-plan, Colonel," Corfe said with a smile.

That raised a ripple of astonishment among the assembled officers. "Sir," Aras began, "how –"

Corfe held up a hand. "It's enough that we possess it. Don't trouble yourselves about how we came by it. I intend to detach the commands of Colonel Cear-Adurhal and Adjutant Formio to deal with this flank-march. Attached to them will be Ranafast's arquebusiers. This combined force will be under the overall command of Colonel Cear-Adurhal. It should be able to see the enemy cavalry off."

"Of course – they'll only be outnumbered three-to-one," someone murmured.

"The *Ferinai* will be in the van – Andruw, if you can cripple them, the rest will fold too. I have it on good authority that the *Minhraib* – over a third of the Merduk army – have no stomach for this fight. The Sultan will be keeping them in reserve to the rear. There's a good chance they'll remain skulking there if they see things going badly.

"This is the line of the main body's advance" – he traced it out on the map with his stick – "as you can see, they're using the Western Road. What I intend to do is to take our own regulars up, and if we can, pitch into them whilst they're still in march-column; that way we'll deal with them piecemeal."

"Where do you think we'll contact them?" Rusio asked.

"About here, at this crossroads." Corfe peered more closely at the map. "Roughly where this little hamlet lies. Armagedir."

He straightened. "Andruw, Formio and Ranafast – your task will be to rout the Merduk cavalry and then come in on the enemy flank, much as they were intending to do with us. On the success or failure of that manoeuvre the fate of the battle will hinge. Gentlemen, I can't emphasise enough that we must rely on speed. There can be no foul-ups, no delays. What we lack in numbers, we must make up for in – in –"

"Alacrity?" Aras suggested.

"Aye. That's the word. When we attack, we must follow up every enemy retreat, and give them no chance to reform. If they manage to bring their numbers to bear, then they'll swamp us. Those of you who were at Berrona will remember how we pitched into them while they were still struggling to get their boots on. We must do the same here – we cannot allow them a moment to take stock. This fact must be instilled all the way down the chain of command. Do I make myself clear?"

There was a collective murmur of assent.

"Good. I don't have to point out to you that we have little in the way of reserves –"

"As usual," someone said, and there was a rustle of laughter. Corfe smiled.

"That's right. The line must not break. If it does, then it's all over – for us, for your families, for our country. There will be no second chance."

The faces grew sober again as this sank in. Corfe studied them all. Andruw, Formio, Ranafast, Rusio, Aras, Morin, Ebro and a dozen others. How many fewer would there be after this battle, which he meant to make the last? For once, he felt the burden of their lives and deaths heavy on his conscience. He was sure of one thing though. They were not fighting so that after the war, lords in gilt carriages could dictate the running of their country. If they accomplished this feat, if they saved Torunna, then there would be many things that needed changed in this country. And they would have earned the right to make those changes.

"Very well, gentlemen, *Reveille* is two hours before dawn. Andruw, Formio and Ranafast; you know your orders. General Rusio, in the morning the main body will shake out straight into battle-line, and advance in that fashion. Mounted pickets out in front."

Rusio nodded. Like the others, he was white-faced and determined. "When do you reckon we'll run into them, sir?"

Corfe studied the map again. In his mind's eye he saw the armies on the march, on a collision course. Like two short-sighted titans bent on violence.

"I reckon we'll hit them just before noon," he said.

Rusio nodded. "I wish you joy of the encounter, sir."

"Thank you. Gentlemen, you know speech-making isn't my bent. I don't have to inspire you with rhetoric or inflame your spirits. We're professionals, at the end of the day, and we have a job ahead of us that cannot be shirked. Now go to your commands. I want your junior officers briefed, and then you can get some sleep. Good luck, to all of you."

"May God be with us," someone said. Then they saluted him and filed away one by one. At last only Andruw remained. There was none of his accustomed levity on his face.

"You're giving me the army, Corfe. Our army."

"I know. They're the best we've got, and they've been given the hardest job."

Andruw shook his head. "It should be you leading them, then. Where are you going to be – stuck in the main body with all the other footslogging regulars? Babysitting Rusio?"

"I need to keep an eye on him. He's capable, but he's got no imagination."

"I'm not up to it, Corfe."

"Yes, you are. You're the best man I have."

They faced each other squarely, without speaking. Then Andruw put out his hand. Corfe clasped it firmly. In the next instant they were embracing like brothers.

"You take care, out there tomorrow," Corfe said roughly.

"Look for me in the afternoon. I'll be coming out of the west, yelling like a cat with its tail afire." Then Andruw punched him playfully on the stomach, and turned away. Corfe watched him retreating into the night, until he had disappeared into the fire and shadows of the sleeping army. He never saw Andruw alive again.

HE DID THE rounds of the camp himself that night, as he always did, having quiet words with the sentries, nodding to those soldiers who were lying staring at the stars, unable to sleep. Sharing gulps of wine with them, or old jokes. Once even a song.

For the first time in a long while, it was not cold. The men slept on grass, not in squelching mud, and the breeze that ruffled the campfires was not bitter. Corfe could almost believe that spring was on its way at last, this long winter of the world finally releasing its grip on the cold earth. He had never been a pious man, but he found he was silently reiterating a formless sort of prayer as he walked between the crowded campfires and watched his men gathering strength for the ordeal of the day to come. Though killing was his business, the one thing in which he excelled, he prayed for it to end.

ON THE TOPMOST tower of Torunn's Royal palace, four people stood in the black hour before the dawn, and waited for the day to begin. Odelia, Queen of Torunn; Macrobius the Pontiff; and Bishops Albrec and Avila.

When at last the sky lightened from black to cobalt blue to a storm-delicate green, the boiling saffron ball of the sun soared up out of the east in a fierce conflagration of colour, as though the scattered clouds on the world's horizon had all caught light and were being consumed by the heat of some vast, silent furnace that burned furiously at the edge of the earth. The foursome stood there as the morning light grew and waxed and took over a flawless sky, and the city came to life at their feet, oblivious. They watched the thousands of people who climbed the walls and stood waiting on the battlements, the packed crowds hushed in all the public squares. The very church bells were stilled.

And finally, faint over the hills to the north, there came the long, distant thunder of the guns, like a rumour from a darker world. The last battle had begun.

TWENTY-ONE

THE FINAL CLASH between Merduk and Ramusian on the continent of Normannia took place on the nineteenth day of Forialon, in the Year of the Saint 552.

The Merduks had a screen of light cavalry out to their front. These Corfe dispersed by sending forward a line of arquebusiers, who brought down half a dozen of the enemy with a swift volley. The rest fled to warn their comrades of the approaching cataclysm. The Torunnan advance continued, lines of skirmishers out to flanks and front, the main body of the infantry sweating and toiling to maintain the brutal pace Corfe had set. The line grew ragged, and sergeants shouted themselves hoarse at the men to keep their dressing, but Corfe was not worried about a few untidy ranks here and there. Speed was the thing. The Merduks had been warned, now, and would be struggling to redeploy their forces from vulnerable march-column into battle-line. But that would take time, as did all manoeuvres involving large numbers of men. Had he possessed more cavalry, he might have sent forward a mounted screen of his own, strong enough to wipe out the Merduk pickets and take their main body totally by surprise – but there was no point wishing for the moon. The Cathedrallers had been needed on the flank, and there were simply no more horsemen to be had.

He turned to Cerne, who with seven other tribesmen had remained with him as a sort of unofficial bodyguard.

"Sound the *Double-March*."

The tribesman put his horn to his lips, closed his eyes and blew the intricate yet instantly recognisable call. Up and down the three mile line, other trumpeters took it up. The Torunnans picked up their feet and began to run.

Over a slight rise in the ground they jogged, panting. Corfe cantered ahead of the struggling army, and there it was. Perhaps half a mile away, the mighty Merduk host was halted. Its battlefront was as yet less than a mile wide, but men were sprinting into position on both flanks, striving to lengthen it before the Torunnans struck. Back to the rear of the line, a mad chaos of milling men and guns and elephants and baggage waggons stretched for as far as the eye could see. At a crossroads to the left rear of the Merduk line, the hamlet of Armagedir stood forlornly, swamped by a tide of hell-bent humanity. There were tall banners flying amid the houses – the Merduk general seemed to have taken it as his command-post.

They had chosen their ground well. The line was set upon a low hill, just enough to blunt the momentum of an infantry charge. There was a long, narrow row of trees to their rear which some long-dead farmer had planted as a wind-break. Corfe could see a second rank falling into position there. The Merduk khedive had been startled by the unlooked-for appearance of the Torunnans, but he was collecting his wits with commendable speed.

Corfe looked west, to the moorland which rolled featurelessly to the horizon. Andruw was out there somewhere, hunting the Merduk cavalry. It would be a few hours yet before he could be expected to arrive. If he arrived at all, Corfe told himself quickly, as if to forestall bad luck.

The army was running past him now, and his restive horse danced and snorted as the great crowd of men passed by. He thought he could feel the very vibration of all those tens of thousands of booted feet through his saddle. He heard his name shouted by short-of-breath voices. Equipment rattling, the smell of match already lit, the stench of many bodies engaged in hard labour. A distilled essence of men about to plunge into war.

Then the thumping of hooves on the upland turf, and Rusio had reined in beside him accompanied by a gaggle of staff-officers.

"We've got them, General! We're going to knock them flying!" he chortled.

"Get your horse batteries out to the front, Rusio. I want

them unlimbered and firing before the infantry go in. First rank halts and gives them a volley: the other ranks keep going. You know the drill – see to it!"

Rusio's grin faded. He saluted and sped off.

Galloping six-horse teams now pulled ahead of the infantry, each towing a six-pounder. The artillery unlimbered with practised speed and their crews began loading frantically. Then the first lanyard was pulled, the first shell went arcing out of a cannon muzzle – you could actually follow it if you possessed quick eyes – and crashed into scarlet ruin in the ranks of the deploying Merduks. A damn good shot, even at such close range. The cannon-barrels were depressed almost to the horizontal, so close were the gunners to the enemy.

Twenty-four guns were deployed now, and they began barking out in sequence, the heavy weapons leaping back as they went off. *Those gunners know their trade all right,* Corfe thought approvingly.

Almost all the first salvo was long; instead of hitting the Merduk front line it landed in the rear elements, sowing chaos and slaughter – but that was just as good. The gunners had orders to elevate their pieces to maximum once their own infantry passed them by, and keep lobbing shells on an arc into the Merduk rear. That would disrupt the arrival of any reinforcements.

Four salvoes, and then the infantry was running past the guns. They were in a line a league long and four ranks deep; a frontage of one yard per man – and despite his quip the night before, Corfe had kept back some three thousand veterans as a last-ditch reserve, in case disaster struck somewhere. These three thousand were in field-column, and formed up beside him now as he sat his horse surrounded by his bodyguard and a dozen couriers.

The first Torunnan rank halted, brought their arquebuses into the shoulder, and then fired. Six thousand weapons going off at once. Corfe heard the tearing crackle of it a second after he had watched the smoke billow out of the line. The enemy host was virtually hidden by a cliff of grey-white fumes. The other three Torunnan lines charged through the first and disappeared into the reek of powder-smoke, a formless roar issuing from their throats as they went. It would be like a vision of Hell in there as they came to close quarters with the enemy.

That was it: the army was committed now, and had caught the Merduks before they had properly deployed. The first part of his plan had worked.

ANDRUW REINED IN his horse and held up a hand. Behind him the long column of men halted. He turned to Ebro. "Hear that?"

They listened. "Artillery," Ebro said. "They've engaged."

"Damn, that was quick." Andruw frowned. "Trumpeter, sound *Battle-Line*. Morin, take a squadron out to the north. Find me these bastards, and find them quick."

"It shall be so," the tribesman grinned. He shouted in Cimbric, and a group of Cathedrallers peeled off and pelted away after him northwards.

"We should have run across them by now," Andruw fretted. "What are they doing, hiding down rabbit holes? They must be making slower time than we'd thought. Courier – to me."

A young ensign pranced up, unarmoured and mounted on a long-limbed gelding. His eyes were bright as those of an excited child. "Sir!"

"Go to General Cear-Inaf. Tell him we still have not located the enemy cavalry, and our arrival on the battlefield may be delayed. Ask him if our orders stand. And make it quick!"

The courier saluted smartly and galloped off, clods of turf flying in the wake of his eager horse.

"Twenty-five thousand horsemen," Andruw said irritably. "And we can't find hide nor hair of them."

"They'll turn up," Ebro said confidently. Andruw glared at him, and realised how easy it was to be confident when there was a superior around to make the hardest decisions. Then, "Listen," he said again.

Arquebus fire now, a rolling clatter of it to the south of them.

"The infantry has gotten stuck in," he said. "That's it – they can't break off now. They're in it up to their ears. Where the hell is that damned enemy cavalry?"

CORFE SAT HIS horse and watched the battle rage before him like some awesome spectacle laid on for his entertainment. He hated this – watching men dying from a distance with his sword still in its scabbard. It was one of the burdens of high rank he thought he would never get used to.

What would he be doing if he were the Merduk khedive? The first instinct would be to shore up the sagging line. The Torunnans had pushed it clear back to the row of trees, but there the Merduks seemed to have rallied, as men often will about some linear feature in the terrain. Their losses had been horrific in those first few minutes of carnage, but they had the numbers to absorb them. No – if the khedive was second-rate, he would send reinforcements to the line, but if he were any good, he would tell the men there to hang on, and send fresh regiments out on the flanks, seeking to encircle the outnumbered Torunnans. But which flank? He had his cavalry out on his right somewhere, so the odds were it would be the left. Yes, he would build up on his left flank.

Corfe turned to the waiting veterans who stood leaning their elbows on their gun-rests and watching.

"Colonel Passifal!"

The white-haired Quartermaster saluted. "Sir?"

"Take your command out on our right, double-quick. Don't commit them until you see the enemy feeling round the end of our line. When you do, hit them hard, but don't join our centre. Keep your men mobile. Do you understand?"

"Aye sir. You reckon that's where they'll strike next?"

"It's what I would do. Good luck, Passifal."

The unearthly din of a great battle. Unless it had been experienced, it was impossible to describe. Heavy guns, small-arms, men shouting to encourage themselves or intimidate others. Men screaming in agony – a noise unlike any other. It all coalesced into a stupendous barrage of sound which stressed the senses to the point of overload. And when one was in the middle of it – right in the belly of that murderous madness – it could invade the mind, spurring men on to inexplicable heroism or craven cowardice. Laying bare the very core of the soul. Until it had been experienced, no man could predict how he would react to it.

Passifal's troops doubling off, a dark stain on the land.

En masse, soldiers seen from a distance looked like nothing so much as some huge, bristling caterpillar slithering over the face of the earth. Men in the centre of a formation like that would see nothing but the back of the man in front of them. They would be treading on heels, cursing, praying, the sweat stinging their eyes. The heroic balladeers knew nothing of real war, not as it was waged in this age of the world. It was a job of work: sheer hard drudgery punctuated by brief episodes of unbelievable violence and abject terror.

There – Corfe felt a moment of intense satisfaction as fresh Merduk regiments arrived to extend the line on the right, just as he had thought they would. They were getting into position when Passifal's column slammed into them, all the weight of that tight-packed body of men. The Merduks were sent flying, transformed from a military formation into a mob in the time it took for a man to peel an apple. Passifal reformed his own men into a supported battle-line, and they began firing, breaking up attempts by the enemy to rally. He might be a Quartermaster, but he still knew his trade.

Corfe looked back at the centre. Hard to make out what was going on in there, but Rusio still seemed to be advancing. That was the thing – to keep the pressure on, to deny the enemy time to think. So far it was working well. But men can only fight for so long.

He turned his face towards the deserted moors in the north. Where was Andruw? What was going on out there?

"I FIND THEM, Ondruw – I find them!" Morin crowed, his horse blowing and fuming under him, sides dank with sweat.

"Where?"

Morin struggled to think in Torunnan units of distance. "One and a part of a league east of here, in long –" he grasped for the word, face screwed up in concentration.

"Line?" Like we are now?"

The tribesman shook his head furiously.

"Column, Morin – are they in column, like along a road?"

Morin's face cleared. "Column – that is the word. But they have their *Ferinai* out to front, in – in line. And they have men on foot – infantry – coming up behind."

Formio came trotting up on his long-suffering mare. He had taken to horseback for the sake of speed, but he clearly did not relish it any more than she did. "What's afoot, Andruw?"

"Morin sighted them, thank God," Andruw breathed. "That was good work. Spread the word, Formio. We're going to pitch into 'em as we are. Cathedrallers on the right, Fimbrians in the middle, Ranafast's lads to the rear." Then he hesitated. "Morin – did you say infantry?"

"Yes, men on foot with guns. Behind the horsemen."

Formio's face remained impassive, but he rode up close to Andruw and spoke close to his ear. "No-one said anything about infantry. I thought it was just cavalry we were facing."

"It's probably just a baggage guard or suchlike. No need to worry about them. The main thing is, we've located them at last. If I have to, I'll face the arquebusiers about, and we'll make a big square. Let them try charging Fimbrian pike and Torunnan shot, and see where it gets them."

Formio stared at him a moment, and then nodded. "I see what you mean. But we have to destroy them, not just hold our own."

It was Andruw's turn to pause. "All right. I'll hold the Cathedrallers back. When the time is ready, they'll charge, and roll them up. We'll hammer them, Formio, don't worry."

"Very well, then. Let's hammer them." But Formio looked troubled.

The army redeployed towards the east. The Fimbrians led the advance while the Cathedrallers covered the flanks and the Torunnan arquebusiers brought up the rear. Just over seven and a half thousand men in all, they could hear the distant clamour of the battle raging around Armagedir, and marched over the upland moors with a will, eager to come to grips with the foe.

Thirty-five thousand Merduk troops awaited them.

BACK AT ARMAGEDIR, the morning was wearing away, and the Torunnan advance had stalled. Rusio's men had been halted in their tracks by sheer weight of enemy numbers. The line of trees had changed hands half a dozen times in the last hour and was thick with the dead of both armies. The battle here was fast degenerating into a bloody stalemate, and unlike the Merduk khedive, Corfe did not have fresh troops to feed into the grinder. He could hold his own for another hour, perhaps even two, but at the end of that time the army would be exhausted. And the Merduk khedive had fully one third of his own forces as yet uncommitted to the battle. They were forming up behind Armagedir, molested only by stray rounds from the Torunnan artillery. Something had to be done to smash through his line, or those thirty thousand fresh troops would be coming around Corfe's flank in the next half hour.

Where the hell was Andruw? He ought to at least be on his way by now.

Corfe made up his mind and called over a courier. He scribbled out a message while giving it verbally at the same time.

"Go to the artillery commander – Nonius. Have him limber up his guns and move them forward, into our own battle-line. He is to unlimber there in the middle of our infantry and give the enemy every charge of canister he possesses. When that happens, Rusio is to advance. He is to push forward to the crossroads and take Armagedir. Repeat it."

The courier did so, white-faced.

"Good. Take this note to Nonius first, and then to General Rusio. Tell Rusio that Passifal's men will support his right flank. He is to break the Merduk line. Do you hear me? He is to break it. Here. Now go."

The courier seized the note and took off at a tearing gallop.

Something had happened to Andruw, out in the moors. Corfe could feel it. Something had gone wrong.

Then another courier thundered in, this one's horse about to founder under him. He had come from the north. Corfe's heart leapt.

"Compliments of Colonel Cear-Adurhal, sir –" the man gasped. "He has still – still not found the enemy. Wants to know if his orders stand."

"How long ago did you leave him?" Corfe asked sharply.

"An hour, maybe. He is a league away. No sign of the enemy out there, sir."

"God's blood," Corfe hissed. What was going on?

"Tell him to keep looking. No – wait. It'll take you an hour to get back to him. If he hasn't found anything by then, he's to come here and attack the Merduk right – throw in everything he's got."

"Everything he's got – yes, sir."

"Get yourself a fresh horse now, and get going."

Corfe tried to shake off the apprehension that was flooding through him. He kicked his horse into motion and cantered southwards, to where Passifal's men were standing ready out on the right. They were the only reserve he had, and he was about to throw them into the battle. He could think of nothing else to do.

ANDRUW'S COMMAND CHARGED full-tilt into the enemy with a shouted roar that seemed to flatten the very grass. The *Ferinai*, the elite of Merduk armies, came to meet them, eight thousand men on heavy horses dressed in armour identical to that worn by the Cathedrallers. And the tribesmen spurred their own mounts into a headlong gallop, drawing ahead of the Fimbrians and Torunnans.

There was a tangible shock as the two bodies of cavalry met. Horses were shrieking, some knocked clear off their feet by the impact. Men were thrown through the air to be trampled by the huge horde of milling beasts. Lances snapped off and swords were drawn. There was a rising clatter, like a preternatural blacksmith's shop gone wild, as troopers of both sides hammered at their steel-clad adversaries. The struggle became a thousand little hand-to-hand combats as the formations ground to a halt and a fierce melee developed. The Cathedrallers were pushed back, hopelessly outnumbered though fighting like maniacs. But then the Fimbrians came up, their pike-points levelled. They smashed a swathe through the halted enemy cavalry , their flanks and rear protected by Ranafast's arquebusiers. The combined formation was as compact as a clenched fist, and seemed unstoppable. Andruw led the Cathedrallers back out of the battle-line, and reformed them in the rear. Many of them were on foot: others had dismounted comrades clinging on behind them or were dragged out by the grasp of a stirrup. Andruw had lost his helmet in the whirling press of men and horses, and seemed infected by a wild gaiety. He joined in the cheer when the *Ferinai* fell back, their retreat turning into something resembling a rout as the implacable Fimbrians followed up. The plan was working after all.

Then there was a staggering volley of arquebus fire that seemed to go on for ever. The Fimbrians collapsed by the hundred as a storm of bullets mowed them down, clicking through their armour with a sound oddly like hail on a tin roof. They faltered, their front ranks collapsing, men stumbling backwards on their fellows with the heavy bullets blasting chunks out of their bodies, cutting their feet out from under them, snapping pike-shafts in two. The advance ground to a halt, its furthest limit marked by a tide-line of contorted bodies, in places two or three deep.

To the rear of the *Ferinai* had been a huge host of infantry, ten thousand of them at least. They had lain down in the rough upland grass and the wiry heather, and the retreating Merduk cavalry had passed over them. Then when the pikemen had approached, they had risen to their feet and fired at point-blank range. It was the same tactic Corfe had used on the Nalbenic cavalry in the King's Battle. Andruw stared at the carnage in the Fimbrian ranks with horror. The Merduks had formed up in five lines, and when one line fired it lay down again so that the one behind it could discharge the next volley. It was continuous, murderous, and the Fimbrians were being decimated.

Andruw struggled to think. What would Corfe do? His own instinct was to lead the Cathedrallers in a wild charge, but that would accomplish nothing. No – something else.

Ranafast cantered up. "Andruw – they're on our flanks. The bastards have horse-archers on our flanks."

Andruw tore his eyes away from the death of the Fimbrians to the surrounding hills. Sure enough, massed formations of cavalry were moving to right and left on the high ground about them. In a few minutes his command would be surrounded.

"God Almighty," he breathed. What could he do? The whole thing was falling to pieces in front of his eyes.

Hard to think in the rising chaos. Ranafast was staring at him expectantly.

"Take your arquebusiers, and keep those horse-archers clear of our flanks and rear. We're pulling out."

Ranafast was astonished. "Pulling out? Saint's blood, Andruw, the Fimbrians are being cut to pieces and the enemy is all over us. How the hell do we pull out? They'll follow up and break us."

But it was becoming clear in Andruw's mind now. The initial panic had faded away, leaving calm certainty in its place.

"No – it'll be all right. Get a courier to Formio. Tell him to get his men the hell out of there as soon as he can. He must break off contact. As he does, I'll lead the Cathedrallers in. We'll keep the enemy occupied long enough for you and Formio to shoot your way clear. I'm making you second-in-command now, Ranafast. Get as many of your and Formio's men out as you can. Take them to Corfe."

Ranafast was white-faced. "And you? You've no chance, Andruw."

"It'll take a mounted charge to make an impact in there. Besides, the Fimbrians are spent, and your lot are needed to keep the horse-archers at bay. It'll have to be the tribesmen."

"Let me lead them in," Ranafast pleaded.

"No – it's on my head, all this mess. I must do what I can to remedy it. Get back to Corfe for God's sake. Leave another rearguard on the way if you have to – but get there with as many as you can and pile into the enemy flank. He can't hold them unless you do."

They shook hands. "What shall I tell him?" Ranafast asked.

"Tell him – Tell him he made a cavalryman out of me at last. Good bye, Ranafast."

Andruw spun his horse around and galloped off to join the Cathedrallers. Ranafast watched him go, one lone figure in the middle of all that murderous turmoil. Then he collected himself and started bellowing orders at his own officers.

THE FIMBRIANS WITHDREW, crouching like men bent against a rainstorm, their pikes bristling impotently. As they did, the *Hraibadar* arquebusiers confronting them gave a great shout, elated at having made a Fimbrian phalanx retreat. They began to edge forward, first in ones and twos, then by companies and tercios, gathering courage as they became convinced that the enemy retreat was not a feint. Their carefully dressed lines became mixed up, and they began firing at will instead of in organised volleys.

An awesome thunder of hooves, and then the Cathedrallers appeared on one flank; a great mass of them at full, reckless gallop, the tribesmen singing their shrill battle-paean. Andruw was at their head, yelling with the best of them. The *Hraibadar* ranks seemed to give a visible shiver, like the twitch of a horse under a fly, just as the moment of impact.

And the heavy cavalry plunged straight into them. Fifteen hundred horsemen at top speed, the destriers trained not to flinch from impact. Ranafast watched them strike from his own position in the middle of the Dyke veterans. The *Hraibadar* line buckled and broke. He saw one massive warhorse turn end over end through the air. Its fellows trampled the enemy infantry as though they were corn. He felt a surge of hope. By God, Andruw was going to do it. He was going to make it.

But there were ten thousand of the *Hraibadar*, and while the tribesmen had sent reeling fully one third of the Merduk regiments, the remainder were pulling back in good order, redeploying for a counter-attack. The success of the charge was temporary only, as Andruw had known it would be. But it had opened a gap in the encirclement, a gap that Ranafast's own men were widening, blasting well-aimed volleys into the harassing horse-archers. The Fimbrians had completely disengaged now, and were surrounded by Torunnan arquebusiers. The formation resembled nothing so much as a great densely-packed square. Lucky the enemy had no artillery – the massed ranks would have made a perfect target. Ranafast bellowed the order, and the square began to move southwards, towards Armagedir, sweeping the Nalbenic light cavalry out of its way as a rhino might toss aside a troublesome terrier. Behind it, the Cathedrallers fought on in a mire of slaughter, surrounded now, but battling on without hope or quarter.

A knot of Fimbrians were carrying something towards Ranafast. A body. The Torunnan dismounted as they approached. It was Formio. He had been shot in the shoulder and stomach and his lips were blue, but his eyes were unclouded.

"We've broken free," he said. There was blood on his teeth. "I suggest we counter-attack, Ranafast. Andruw –"

"Andruw's orders were to keep going and to join with Corfe," Ranafast said, his voice harsh as that of an old raven. Not Formio too. "I intend to obey him. There is nothing we can do for the tribesmen now. We must make the most of the time they've bought us."

Formio stared at him, then bent forward and coughed up a gout of dark gore which splashed his punctured breast-plate. Some inhuman reserve of strength enabled him to straighten again in the arms of his men and look the Torunnan in the eye.

"We can't –"

"We must, Formio," Ranafast said gently. "Corfe is fighting the main battle – this is only a sideshow. We must."

Formio closed his eyes, nodded silently. One of his men wiped the blood from his mouth, then looked up.

"He's almost gone, Colonel." The Fimbrian's visage was a set mask.

"Bring him with us. I won't leave him here to become carrion." Then Ranafast turned away, his own face a bitter gnarl of grief.

THE TORUNNAN INFANTRY had lunged forward once more, clawing for the ground under them yard by bloody yard. Rusio's troops now occupied the line of trees which had been the rallying-point for the enemy. Out on the left, Aras had his standard planted in the hamlet of Armagedir itself, and fifteen tercios had grouped themselves around it and were holding against twenty times their number. The thatch on the roofs of the houses there was burning, so that all Corfe could glimpse were minute red flashes of gunfire crackling in clusters and lines, sometimes the glint of armour through the dense smoke.

Nonius was moving his guns forward with the infantry, but it was slow work. Many of the horses had been killed, and the gunners were manhandling the heavy pieces over broken ground strewn with corpses. The Merduk artillery was still embroiled in the hopeless tangle of men and equipment which backed up the Western Road for fully five miles to their rear.

The insane roar of the battle went on without pause, a barrage of the very senses. Along a three mile stretch of upland moor the two opposing lines of close-packed men strove to annihilate one another. They fought for possession of a line of trees, a burnt-out cluster of houses, a muddy stretch of road. Every little feature in the terrain took on a greater significance when men struggled to kill each other upon it. Untold thousands littered the field of battle already, and thousands more had become pitiful maimed wrecks of humanity that swore and screamed and tried to drag themselves out of the holocaust.

Over on the right, Passifal had fully committed his men to the line. That was it – the bottom of the barrel. Corfe had nothing left to throw into the contest. And on the Merduk right, opposite Aras's hard-pressed tercios, the enemy was massing for a great counter-attack. When the Merduk general was ready he would launch some thirty thousand fresh men into the battle there, and it would all be over.

Strangely, Corfe found the knowledge almost liberating. It was finished at last. He had done his best, and it had not been good enough, but at least now there was nothing more to worry about. Something had happened to Andruw, that was clear. The last two couriers that Corfe had sent out seemed to have been swallowed up by the very hills. It was as though all those men had simply disappeared.

There – large formations moving through the smoke, pointed towards Armagedir. The Merduk general had finally launched the counter-attack. Aras was about to be crushed. Corfe looked about himself. He had with him his eight Cathedraller bodyguards, and another ten youthful ensigns who acted as aides and couriers. Not much of a reinforcement, but better than nothing.

He turned to one of the young officers.

"Arrian, go to General Rusio. Tell him he is to hold the line at all hazards, and if he deems it practicable, he is to advance. Tell him I am joining Colonel Aras's men. They are about to be hit by the enemy counter-attack. Go now."

The young officer saluted smartly and galloped off. Corfe watched him go, wondering if he had ever been that earnest. He missed his friends. He missed Andruw and Formio. Marsch and the Cathedrallers. It was not the same, fighting without them. And he realised with a flash of insight or intuition that it would never be the same again. That time was over now.

Corfe kicked his horse savagely in the belly and it half-reared. He did not fear death, he feared failure. And he had failed. There was nothing more to be afraid of.

He drew Mogen's sword for the first time that day and turned to Cerne, his trumpeter. "Follow me."

Then the group of riders took off after him as he rode full tilt up the hillside, into the smoking hell of Armagedir.

HUNDREDS OF MEN lay wounded to the rear of the line here, making it hard for the horses to pick their way over them. The fuming roar of the battle was unbelievable, astonishing. Corfe had never before known its like, not even in the most furious assaults upon Ormann Dyke. It was as though both armies knew that this was the deciding contest of the century-old war. For one side complete victory beckoned; for the other, annihilation. The Torunnans would not retreat because, like Corfe, they had ceased to be afraid of anything except the consequences of failure. So they died where they stood, fighting it out with gunstocks and sabres when their ammunition ran out, struggling like savages with anything that came to hand, even the very stones at their feet. They were dying hard, and for the first time in a long while, Corfe felt proud to be one of them.

His own party dismounted as they approached the ruins of the hamlet around which Aras's men had made their stand. The ground was too choked with bodies for the horses to be ridden further, and even the war-hardened destriers were becoming terrified by the din.

Aras's command stood at bay like an island in a sea of Merduks. The enemy had poured around its left flank and was pushing into the right, where it connected with the main body of the Torunnan army. They were trying to pinch off the beleaguered tercios from Rusio's forces, isolate and destroy them. But their assaults on the hamlet itself broke like waves on a sea-cliff. Aras's troops stood and fought in the ruins of Armagedir as though it were the last fortress of the western world. And in a way it was.

The Torunnans looked up as Corfe and his entourage pushed their way through the choked ranks, and he heard his name called out again and again. There was even a momentary cheer. At last he found his way to the sable standard under which Aras and his staff officers clustered. The young colonel brightened at the sight of his commander-in-chief, and saluted with alacrity. "Good to see you sir. We were beginning to wonder if the rest of the army had forgotten about us."

Corfe shook his hand. "Consider yourself a general now, Aras. You've earned it."

Even under grime and powder-smoke he could see the younger man flush with pleasure. He felt something of a fraud, knowing Aras would not live long enough to enjoy his promotion.

"Your orders, General?" Aras asked, still beaming. "I daresay our flank-march will be arriving any time now."

Corfe did not have to lower his voice to avoid being overheard; the raging chaos of the battle was like a great curtain.

"I believe our flank march may have run into trouble, Aras. It's possible you will not be reinforced. We must hold on here to the end. To the end, do you understand me?"

Aras stared at him, the dismay naked across his face for a second. Then he collected himself, and managed a strangled laugh. "At least I'll die a general. Don't worry sir – these men aren't going anywhere. They know their duty, as do I."

Corfe gripped his shoulder. "I know," he said in almost a whisper.

"Sir!" one of the staff-officers shouted. "They're coming in – a whole wave of them!"

The Merduk counter-attack rolled into Armagedir like some unstoppable juggernaut. It was met with a furious crescendo of arquebus fire which obliterated the leading rank – and then it was hand to hand all down the line. The Torunnan perimeter shrank under that savage assault, the men crowded back onto the blazing buildings of the hamlet they defended. And there they halted. Corfe shoved his way to the forefront of the line and was able to forget strategy, politics, all the worries of a high ranking officer. He found himself battling for his life like the lowliest ranker, his Cathedraller bodyguards ranged about him and singing as they slew. The little knot of scarlet-armoured men seemed to draw the enemy as a candle will moths at twilight. They were more heavily armoured than their Torunnan comrades, and stood like a wedge of red-hot iron while the lightly armed warriors of the *Minhraib* crashed in on them to be hewn down one after another. Armagedir became cut off from the rest of the army as the Merduks swamped the Torunnan left wing. It became a murderous cauldron of insane violence within which men fought and killed without thought of self preservation or hope of rescue. It was the end, the apocalypse. Corfe saw men dying with their teeth locked in an enemy's throat, others strangling each other, snarling like animals, eyes empty of reason. The *Minhraib* threw themselves on the Cathedrallers like dogs mobbing a bear, three and four at a time sacrificing themselves to bring down one steel-clad tribesman and cut his throat on the blood-sodden ground. Corfe swung and hacked in a berserk rage, sword-blows clanging off his armour, one ringing hollow on his helm, exploding his bruised face with stars of agony. Something stabbed him through the thigh and he fell to his knees, bellowing, Mogen's sword dealing slaughter left and right. He was on the ground, buffeted by a massive scrum of bodies, trampled by booted feet. He fought himself upright, the sword-blows raining down on him. Aras and Cerne were at his shoulders, helping him up. Then a blade exploded out of Cerne's eye, and he toppled without a sound. The detonation of an arquebus scorched Corfe's hand. He stabbed out blindly, felt flesh and bone give way under the *Answerer's* wicked edge. Someone hacked at his neck, and his sight exploded with stars and spangled darkness. He went down again.

A sunlit hillside above Aekir in some age of the world long past, and he was sat on crackling bracken with Heria by his side, sharing wine. His wife's smile rent his heart.

Andruw laughing amid the roar of guns, a delight in life lighting up his face and making it into that of a boy.

Barbius's Fimbrians advancing to their deaths in terrible glory at the North More.

Berrona burning low on a far horizon.

A smoky hut in which his mother wept quietly and his father stared at the earthen floor as Corfe told him he was going for a soldier.

Dappled sunlight on the Torrin River as he splashed and swam there, one long summer afternoon.

And the roar and blare of many trumpets, the beat of heavy drums rising even over the clamour of war. The press of bodies about him eased. He was hauled to his feet and found himself looking through a film of blood at Aras's slashed face.

"Andruw has come!" he was shouting. "The Fimbrians have struck the Merduk flank!"

And raising his heavy head he saw the pikes outlined against the fuming sky, and all about him the men of Armagedir were cheering as the Merduks poured away in absolute panic. The Dyke veterans were lined on a hillside to the north, blasting out volley after volley into the close-packed throng of the enemy. And the Fimbrians were cutting them down like corn, advancing as relentlessly as if they meant to sweep every Merduk off the edge of the world.

Corfe bent his head and wept.

TWENTY-TWO

THE LEVEE HAD gone very well, Murad thought. Half the kingdom's remaining nobility seemed to have been present, and they had listened, agog, as Murad had told one and all of his experiences in the west. It was good of the King to have allowed him to do it – it announced that the Lord of Galiapeno had returned indeed, and what was more, enjoyed the Royal favour. But it had also been a draining experience.

Traveller's tales. Is that all they thought he had to tell? Empty-headed fools.

The King had limped down from his throne and was now mingling with his subjects. He had a genius for gestures like that, Murad thought, though it was hardly fitting, not so soon after these same men who were now fawning about him had been conspiring to take the throne away from him.

If it were I wearing that crown, Murad thought, *I'd have executed every last one of them.*

His head was swimming a little. He had been able to keep down nothing but wine since stepping off the ship. *I am back in my own world*, he thought. *And what a little world it is. Time to retire.* He craved a dreamless slumber, something that would restore the weariness of his very soul. Oblivion, without the bloody pictures that haunted his sleep.

"Lord Murad," a woman's voice said. "How very honoured I am to meet you."

She was a striking, dark-haired lady with intelligent eyes and a low-cut bodice. She was also very pregnant. Murad bowed. "I am flattered. Might I ask –"

"I am the lady Jemilla. I have a feeling you probably know of me already."

He did indeed. Abeleyn had told him everything. So this was the woman who bore the King's child, who had tried to set up a regency. Murad's interest quickened. She was a beauty, no doubt of that. Why was she at liberty? Abeleyn was so damned soft. She ought to be hidden away somewhere, and the brat strangled when it was born.

"I believe," she went on, fluttering her fan under her chin, "that you now enjoy the happy distinction of being the man closest by blood to the King himself."

"I am," Murad said, and smiled. It would be nice to bed her. It was obvious what she was doing; fishing for a new puppet to play against the king.

"It is so hot in here, lady," he said. "Would you care to take a turn with me outside in the gardens?"

She took his arm. Her eyes had suddenly lost their coy look. "What woman could refuse such a gallant adventurer?"

SHE GASPED AND squealed and moaned as he thrust into her, pulling her hips towards him with fistfuls of her dress. Murad clenched his teeth as he spent himself within, gave her one last savage thrust, and pulled away with the sweat running down his face. Jemilla sank to her side in the deeper shadows under the tree. Twilight was fast sinking into darkness and her face was a mere livid blur. The gardens were alive with evensong all around them, and he could still hear the buzz and laughter of the chattering guests in the Reception Hall. Murad refastened his breeches and leaned on one elbow in the resinous-smelling dimness under the cypress.

"You have a direct way of approaching things," he told Jemilla.

"It saves time."

"I agree. You have hopes for your child, obviously, but what exactly is your fascination with me? I am no young girl's dream. And I have been away from court a long time."

"Precisely. You are not tainted by the events which have been transpiring in Abrusio – your hands are clean. We could be useful to one another," Jemilla said calmly.

Murad brushed the dead leaves from his shoulders. "I could be useful to you, you mean. Lady, your name is mud at court. The King tolerates you out of some outdated chivalric impulse. Your child, when it is born, will be shunted off to some backwater estate in the Hebros, and you with it. What can you offer me, aside from the occasional roll in the grass?"

She leaned closer. Her hand slid down his belly and over the brim of his breeches. He flinched minutely as her hot fingers gripped his flaccid member.

"Marry me," she said.

"What?" Murad actually chuckled.

"I could not then be shunted off, as you put it. And my son's claims would be all the stronger." Her hand started to work up and down on him. He began to harden again in her grasp.

"This may be true – but what do I get out of it, I ask again?"

"You become the legal guardian of the King's heir. If something were to happen to the King after my son is born, he would be too young to be crowned. And you would be Regent automatically."

"Regicide? Is that your game?" He wrenched her hand out of his breeches. "Lady, if something were to happen to the King, I would be next in line anyway, have you thought of that? I would have no need to play uncle to your bastard."

"You may be the King's cousin, but you are not of the Hibrusid house. You might find some difficulty persuading the rest of the nobles that your claim is pre-eminent. With myself as your wife, the King's only son as your legal ward, your position would be unassailable. Call yourself Regent if you would – you would be King in everything but name."

"And what would you be – a dutiful little wife? I'd sooner share my bed with a viper."

She sat up, and shrugged. Her bodice had come down and her heavy, dark-nippled breasts were bare. She took his hand and set it upon one of them, squeezed his fingers in on the ripe softness.

"Think on it a while," she said, her voice a low purr. "Abeleyn is a travesty of a man held together by sorcery alone. He will not make old bones."

"I may be many things," Murad said, "but I am not yet a traitor."

"Think on it," she repeated, and rose to her feet, tugging up her dress, shaking grass out of her hair.

"By the way, your ship was piloted by one Richard Hawkwood, was it not?"

"Yes. So?"

Her voice changed. She lost some of her assured poise. "How is he? I have a lady's maid who wishes to know."

"A lady's maid with a yen for a mariner? He's well enough, I suppose. Like me, he survived. There is not much more to be said."

"I see." She became her assured self again, and bent forward to kiss Murad's scarred forehead. "Think on my offer. I am staying in the west wing – the guest apartments. You can visit me there when you like. Come and talk to me. I am lonely there." She brushed one delicate finger along the scar that convulsed the skin of his temple, then turned and walked away across the garden towards the lights of the palace, her fan fluttering all the way.

Murad watched her go. A peculiar hunger arose within him. There was something about the lady Jemilla that challenged his pride. He liked that. Her schemes were dangerous daydreams – but he would visit her, of that he was sure. He would make her squeal, by God.

He left the shadow of the tree and looked up at the first stars come gleaming in the spring sky. *Abrusio*. He was home at last. And all that murderous nightmare he had left behind him could be forgotten. His venture had been a failure, but it had taught him many things. He had information now that could one day prove useful.

Tomorrow he would visit the city barracks and see about getting back his old command. And he needed a new horse – something bad-tempered and spirited from the Feramuno studs. Something he would enjoy breaking down.

There were many things he was going to enjoy breaking down. Murad lifted his face and laughed aloud into the starlit sky. It was good to be alive.

EPILOGUE

SPRING, IT SEEMED, had come at last. There was a freshness to the air, and primroses had come out in bright lines about the margins of the Western Road. Corfe stood on the summit of the tower and watched the light tumble cloud-patterned over the hills. If he turned his head, he could see the sea glimmering on the world's horizon. A world at peace.

"I thought I would find you here," a woman's voice said. She touched him lightly on the arm, her long skirts whispering around her. She wore a crown.

An aged woman. She looked old enough to be his grandmother, and yet she was about to become his wife.

"It looks so quiet now," he said, still staring out at the empty hills beyond the city walls. "As if it had all been a dream."

"Or a nightmare," Odelia retorted.

He said nothing. The great burial mounds of Armagedir were too far away for him to see, but he knew he would always feel them there, somewhere at his shoulder. Andruw lay in one of them, and Morin and Cerne and Ebro and Ranafast and Rusio – and ten thousand other faceless men who had died at his bidding. They were one monument he would never be able to forget.

"It's time, Corfe," Torunna's Queen said gently.

"I know."

If he looked east, towards the sea, he would find a large, ornate encampment pitched there, gay with the silk pennons and horsetail standards of the Merduks. The enemy had come calling in the aftermath of defeat, not exactly cap in hand, but with a certain strained humility all the same. Corfe had given leave for the Merduk Sultan and a suitable escort to pitch their tents within sight of the city walls. His representatives had been permitted into the city this very morning, entering in peace the place they had squandered so much blood to take. They wanted to witness the crowning of Torunna's new King, the man with whom they would be treating in the days to come. It was all too bizarre for words. Andruw would have found it immensely funny.

Corfe blinked away the heat in his eyes. It was hard, harder than he could have imagined.

"He died well," Odelia said gently, "the way he would have wished. They all did."

Corfe nodded. He, too, would have been happy to die that day, knowing the battle was won.

"There is still the peace," Odelia said with that disquieting insight of hers. "It remains to be achieved. What you do today is part of that."

"I know. I'm not sure it is the way I would have chosen though."

"It is the best way," she said, pressing his arm. "Trust me, Corfe."

He limped away from the parapet with her hand still on his arm, turning back towards the city below. From this height, Torunn looked like some fairy-tale metropolis. The streets were packed with people – it was said a quarter of a million had gathered in the city square – and every house seemed to be flying some flag or banner. The citizens crowded upper-floor windows like tiers of house-martins, and Torunnan regulars in full dress were stationed at every corner.

"Let's get it over with," Corfe said.

FORMIO HAD DRAWN up an honour-guard of pike-stiff Fimbrians in the courtyard of the palace, and as Corfe and Odelia appeared they snapped to attention like automatons. The Fimbrian adjutant saluted his commander with a rare smile, one arm still in a sling. He looked pale and somewhat ethereal, but had insisted on leaving his sick-bed for this day. The chill in Corfe warmed a little. Aras was there too, the great scar in his face nearly healed – the Queen had worked tirelessly in the aftermath of Armagedir, saving countless lives, and wearing herself down to a shadow in the process. "Give you joy, sir," Aras ventured.

"Thank you, General."

Corfe and Odelia climbed into the open bardouche that awaited them, and set off out of the palace flanked by fifty mounted Cathedrallers – all that had survived. As soon as they appeared at the palace gates a great roar went up from the waiting crowds. They trundled through the cobbled streets with the Cathedrallers raising a clattering din of hooves about them and the people cheering madly. The air was full of blossoms that spectators were scattering from the windows overhead.

"Wave, Corfe," Odelia said out of the corner of her mouth. "They're your people. They are what you won the war for."

The cavalcade halted before the steps of the city cathedral and there they got out in a cloud of footmen, dignitaries and whirling blossom. There was a salute of massed trumpets. They paused on the stone steps, Odelia smiling and nodding graciously at the Merduk ambassador, one Mehr Jirah, Corfe giving him a cold glance before they walked on, page-boys lifting the Queen's train and the hem of Corfe's long cloak.

And into the cathedral, its pews stuffed to overflowing with what nobility the kingdom still possessed, their numbers augmented by the great and the good of Torunna. Corfe's eye was caught by Admiral Berza, near the aisle. The old admiral winked at him as he passed by, his face as stiff as wood. There was Passifal's white head, among the assembled military. Corfe recognised no-one else. He limped up the aisle, staring straight ahead, expressionless.

Up at the altar Macrobius himself stood ready, smiling his blind smile. He was flanked by Bishops Albrec and Avila, who each bore velvet cushions. On one rested the crown of Torunna. On the other was a pair of plain gold wedding rings. One led to the other: both were deemed necessary for the well-being of the country.

Corfe and the Queen came to a halt before the Pontiff. As they did, Albrec caught Corfe's eye – he seemed strangely troubled. For a moment Corfe thought the little cleric was about to speak, but he thought better of it. The moment passed.

Another blare of trumpets. Incense, heady as powdersmoke, writhing in ribbons within the shafted sunlight of the high windows. The stained glass threw down a maelstrom of colour upon the flagstones, dimming the serried candleflames, raising painful glitters off the gold and gems that sparkled everywhere, even on Corfe's clothing.

Pictures pelting through his mind like rain. His first marriage, in a small chapel near Aekir's south gate. Heria had held a posy of primroses. It had been spring, as it was today. They had been married two years when the siege began.

Sitting in the mud under a wrecked ox-waggon on the Western Road with this same man who was about to crown him, gnawing on a half-raw turnip and wiping the rain out of his eyes.

Sharing a skin of wine with Marsch and Andruw on the battlements of Hedeby, after their first battle together. Drunk with victory and the comradeship that had enriched it, momentarily believing that all things were possible.

"Yes, I will," he answered when Macrobius asked him the question. And he had the cold gold slipped upon his finger. Odelia looking into his eyes, the years all come crowding into her face at last. When he set the other ring in place she clenched her fist around it as if to prevent it ever slipping off. Her kiss was dry and chaste as a mother's. A few moments later the crown was set upon his head. It was surprisingly light, nothing like the weight of a helm. It might have been made of tinsel and feathers for all Corfe felt it.

When he straightened, the sunlight caught the precious metals of his crown and set it aflame, and all the bells of Torunn's cathedral began tolling at once in peal after jubilant peal, and outside he could hear the massed crowds of people who were now his subjects set up a mighty roar.

And it was done. He had a wife once more, and Torunna a King.

THE MERDUK AMBASSADOR was first in line at the levee that afternoon. Corfe and his Queen received him in the huge audience hall of the palace, flanked by guards and palace functionaries. The new Steward was present – none other than Colonel Passifal, appointed by Royal decree. He stood to one side of the trio of thrones looking uncomfortable but oddly determined. General Aras, also present, had been elevated to Commander-in-Chief of the army, with Formio as a de facto second-in-command. The Fimbrian was Corfe's first choice, but as Odelia had made very clear, even a king had to think twice before placing the national army under the command of a foreigner.

Corfe needed familiar faces about him, and they were becoming increasingly hard to find. The third throne on the dais was occupied by another one, that of Macrobius. Standing beside him was Albrec, and a gnomish old cleric named Mercadius, who could speak fluent Merduk. The strange thing was, Corfe shared a history with almost all of those present. He had fought side by side with Aras, Formio and Passifal. He had saved Macrobius's life. He had escaped from Fournier's dungeons with Albrec. The war had cost him his wife, and the best comrades he had ever known, but had it not been for the war, he would never have known the friendship of men like these, like Andruw and Marsch, and he would have been the poorer for it.

Mehr Jirah entered the audience chamber without ceremony, flanked only by a pair of Merduk clerics who looked surprisingly similar to Ramusian monks, albeit without tonsures. Mercadius of Orfor translated his speech into Normannic for the assembled listeners.

"These are the words I was bade to say to the King of Torunna by my master, the Sultan of Ostrabar:

"'We send greetings to Torunna's new King, and congratulate him on his unexpected elevation. Truly, God has been kind to him. We will suffer ourselves to speak to him now as one soldier to another, in terms as plain as we can make them. The slaughter of our young men has gone on long enough. We have carpeted the world with the bodies of our dead, and in the name of God and his Prophet, we offer the new Torunnan King this chance to end the killing. In our generosity we will withhold the wrath of our mighty armies, and suffer the kingdom of Torunna to survive, if King Corfe will merely acknowledge the suzerainty of Aurungzeb the Great, Sultan of Ostrabar, conqueror of Aekir and Ormann Dyke. He has to but bend his knee to us, and this war will come to an end, and we shall have peace between our peoples for all time. What says Torunna's Monarch?'"

There was an angry stir from the assembled Torunnans as Mercadius translated the words, and Aras took a step forward, his hand going to where his sword should have been. But no-one bore arms in the Audience Chamber save the King alone. Corfe stood up, eyes flashing.

"Mehr Jirah, you are known to some of us here. I have been told you are a man of integrity and honour, and so I ask you to remember that what I say now is not directed at you or the faith you profess – a faith we now know to be almost the same as our own. This is to Aurungzeb, your lord.

"Tell him that Torunna will never submit to him, not if he brings ten times the armies he possesses in front of her walls. At Armagedir he tried to destroy us, and we defeated him. If we have to, we will defeat him again. We will never surrender, not if we must fight to the last man hiding in the hills. We will fight him until the world cracks open at Doomsday.

"Peace we would have, yes, but only if he takes his beaten armies and leaves Torunna's soil forever. If he does not, I swear by my God that I will drive him out. His people will never know a moment of rest while I live. If it takes twenty years, I will throw him back beyond the Ostian river. I will slay every Merduk man, woman and child who falls into my hands. I will burn his cities and salt his soil. I will make of his kingdom a howling wilderness, and wipe the very memory of Ostrabar and its Sultan from the face of the world."

A great cheer erupted in the chamber. Mehr Jirah looked shocked for a moment, but quickly regained his dignified poise.

"That is our answer. Take it back to your master, and make it clear to him that there will be no second chance. I am King here now, and I will not hesitate to mobilise every able man in my kingdom to back my words. He no longer fights an army, but an entire people. This is his choice, now and only now – peace, or a war that will last another hundred years. Tell him to think carefully. His decision will alter the very fate of the world for him and all those who come after him. Now you may go."

Mehr Jirah bowed. He nodded at Albrec, and then turned on his heel and left. Corfe took his seat once more. "Passifal, our next supplicant, if you please." He had to raise his voice to make himself heard over the surf of talk in the hall.

Odelia leaned over the arm of her throne and whispered fiercely in his ear.

"Are you out of your mind? Have you no notion of diplomacy at all? We had a chance to halt the war – now you are set on starting it again."

"No. I may be no diplomat, but I have some military insight. He can't fight on. We've beaten him, and he has to be told that. And I didn't fight Armagedir so that I could place my neck in a Merduk yoke. He thinks he knows what war is – he has no idea. If he is stupid and proud enough to keep fighting now, *I will show him how war can be waged.*"

There was such contained ferocity about Corfe as he spoke that Odelia's retort died in her throat. At that moment she realised that she had overreached herself. She had thought that Corfe, once King, would be content to lead armies and fight wars, while she negotiated the treaties and dictated policy. She knew better now. Not only would he rule, and rule in all things, but other rulers would want to deal with him and him alone, not with his ageing Queen. It was he who had won the war, after all. It was he whom the common people mobbed in the streets and cheered at every opportunity. Even her own attendants looked first to him now.

She uttered a bitter little laugh that was lost in the next fanfare. All her life she had ruled through men. Now one had come to power through her, and reduced her to a cipher.

AURUNGZEB RECEIVED MEHR Jirah in silence. In the sumptuous ostentation of his tent he had Corfe's words relayed to him by the mullah and listened patiently as his officers and aides expressed outrage at the Ramusian's insolence. His Queen sat beside him, also silent. He took her cold hand, thinking of his son in her belly, and what world he might be born into. He had the makings of it here, at this moment. And for the first time in his life he was afraid.

"Batak," he said at last. "That little beast of your flits about the Torunnan palace day and night. What say you in this matter?"

The mage pondered a moment. "I think his words, my Sultan, are not empty. This man is not a braggart. He does what he says."

"We have all realised that by now, I think," Aurungzeb said wryly. "Shahr Baraz?"

The old Merduk shrugged. "He's the best soldier they've ever produced. I believe he and my father would have had much in common."

"Is there no-one around me who can give me some wisdom in their counsel?" Aurungzeb snapped. "I am surrounded by platitude-mouthing old women! Where is Shahr Johor?"

The occupants of the tent looked at one another. Finally Akran, the chamberlain, ventured, "You – ah – you had him executed this morning, Majesty."

"What? Oh, yes of course. Well, that was inevitable. He should have died with his men at Armagedir. Blood of God, what happened there? How did he do it? We should have won!"

"We did, at least, destroy those accursed red horsemen, Majesty," Serrim the eunuch offered.

"Yes, those scarlet fiends. And we slew ten thousand more of his army, did we not? He must be as severely crippled as we are! How does he come to be making threats? What manner of maniac is he? Does he know nothing of the niceties of negotiation?"

The gathering of attendants, advisors and officials said nothing. In the quiet they could hear the crowds of Torunn still cheering, less than half a league away. The noise grated on Aurungzeb's nerves. Why did they cheer him? He had led so many of their sons and fathers to their deaths, and yet they loved him for it. The Torunnans – there was a collective madness about them. They were a people unhinged. How did one deal with that? When Aurungzeb spoke again the petulance in his voice was like that of a child refused a treat.

"I asked him for safe conduct, the reception of an ambassador – *I opened negotiations with the bastard!* Now he must give something in return. Isn't that right, Batak?"

"Undoubtedly, sire. But remember that he is reputed to be nothing more than a common soldier, a peasant. He has no idea of protocol, or the basic courtesies that exist between monarchs. The conventions of diplomacy are beyond him – he speaks the language of the barrack-room only."

"That may be no bad thing," Shahr Baraz rumbled. "At least if he gives his word on a thing, you can be sure he'll keep it."

"Don't prate to me about the virtues of soldiers," Aurungzeb growled. "They are over-rated."

No-one spoke for a time. The members of the court had never seen their Sultan so unsure, so needful of advice. He had always been one to follow his own counsel, even if it meant flying in the face of facts.

"The war must end," Mehr Jirah said. "Of that there is no question. Thirty thousand of our men died at Armagedir. Our army can fight no more."

"Then neither can his!"

"I think it can, Sultan. The Torunnans are not striving for conquest, but for survival. They will never give up, especially with this man leading them. Armagedir was the last chance we had to win the war at a stroke – every one of our soldiers knows it. They also know now that this is no longer a Holy War. The Ramusians are not infidels, but co-believers in the Prophet –"

"That's you and your damn preachings have done that," Aurungzeb raged.

"Would you deny the tenets of your own faith?" Mehr Jirah asked, unintimidated.

"No – no, of course not. All right then. It seems I have no choice. We will remain in negotiation. Mehr Jirah, Batak, Shahr Baraz, the three of you will go to Torunn in the morning and offer to broker a treaty. But no backsliding mind! God knows I have grovelled enough for one day. Ahara – you were once a Ramusian. What say you? Are they right in this thing? Will this new soldier-king fight us to the end?"

Heria did not look at him. She placed a hand on her swollen abdomen. "You will have a son soon, my lord. I would like him to grow up in peace. Yes, this man will never give in. He – Father Albrec told me that he had too much iron in him. But he is a good man at heart. A decent man. He will keep his word, once given."

"Perhaps," Aurungzeb grunted. "I must say, I have a perverse hankering to meet him, face to face. Perhaps if we sign a treaty we may pay him a state visit." And he laughed harshly. "The times are changing, indeed."

No-one noticed how white Heria's face had gone – the veil was good for that much at least.

THE WAR BETWEEN the Merduks and the Ramusians had begun so long ago that no-one except the historians was sure in what year the two peoples had first come to blows. But everyone now knew when it had ended. In the first year of the reign of King Corfe, the same year the Fantyr dynasty had ceased to be.

And five and a half centuries after the coming of the Blessed Saint who had also been the Prophet, the dual nature of Ramusio was finally recognised, and the two great religions he had founded came together and admitted their common origin. All this was written into the Treaty of Armagedir, a document it took soldiers and scholars several weeks to hammer out in a spacious tent erected half way between the walls of Torunn and the Merduk encampment especially for that purpose.

The Merduks agreed to make the Searil River the border of their new domain. Khedi Anwar, which had once been Ormann Dyke, became the westernmost of their settlements, and Aekir was renamed Aurungabar, and designated the Ostrabarian capital. The cathedral of Carcasson was transformed into the Temple of Pir-Sar, and both Merduks and Ramusians were to be allowed to worship there, since it had been made holy by the founder of both their faiths. Those Aekirian refugees who wished to return to their former home were free to do so without fear of molestation, and the monarchs of Torunna and

Ostrabar exchanged ambassadors and set up embassies in each other's capitals.

But much of that was still in the future. For now, the gates of Torunn were thrown open for the Treaty-signing ceremonies, and the war-weary city made ready to receive a visit from the man who had tried to conquer it. For Corfe, it all had the surreal quality of a dream. He and Aurungzeb had negotiated through intermediaries, the Sultan considering it beneath his dignity to haggle over the clauses of a treaty in person. Today he would see the face of – perhaps even shake the hand of – the man he had striven so long to destroy. And his mysterious Ramusian Queen, whose contribution to the winning of the war only Corfe and Albrec knew of. Corfe wondered how the history-books would view the event. He had come to realise that the facts, and history's perception of them, were two very different things.

He stood in his dressing chamber with the spring sunshine flooding in a glorious stream through the tall windows, whilst half a dozen valets stood by, disconsolate. They held in their arms a bewildering array of garments dripping with gems, gold lace and fur trimmings. Corfe had refused them all, and stood in the plain black of a Torunnan infantryman. He wore no crown, but had been persuaded to place on his head an ancient circlet of silver that Fimbrian Marshals had once worn at the court of the Electors. Albrec, of all people, had dug it up for him out of some dusty palace coffer. It had once belonged to Kaile Ormann himself, which Corfe thought rather fitting.

Trumpets ringing out down by the city gates, heralding the approach of the Sultan's cavalcade. It seemed to Corfe he had heard more damned trumpets blown in the past few weeks than he had heard in all his life upon battlefields. Torunn had become one vast carnival of late, the people celebrating victory, peace, a new King – one thing after another. And now this, the last of the state occasions that Corfe intended to preside over for a long time.

He'd like to take Formio and Aras out into the hills and go hunting for a while, sleep out under the stars again, stare into a campfire and drink rough army wine. The past year had been a hellish time, but it had possessed its moments of sweetness too. Or perhaps he was merely a damned nostalgic fool, destined to become a dissatisfied old man for whom all glory was in the past. Now, there was a concept. The very idea made him smile. But as one of the more courageous of the valets stepped forward for the third time with the ermine-trimmed robe the smile twisted into a frown.

"For the last time, no. Now get the hell out of here, all of you."

"Sire, the Queen insisted –"

"Bugger off."

"My lord, that is hardly the language a king is expected to use," Odelia said, sweeping into the room with a pair of maids behind her.

He limped about to meet her eyes. Despite all her ministrations, he suspected that his Armagedir wound had marked him permanently. He would be lame for the rest of his life. Well, many had come out of the war with worse souvenirs.

"I always thought that Kings could use what language they chose," he said lightly. Odelia kissed him on the cheek, then drew back to survey his plain attire with mock despair.

"The Sultan will mistake you for a common soldier, if you're not careful."

"He made that mistake before. I doubt he will again."

Odelia laughed, something she had begun to do more often of late. The bright sunlight was not kind to the lines on her face. Whatever magicks she had once applied to maintain her youthful appearance had all been used up on the wounded of the army. Her newfound age still perturbed him sometimes. So he took her hand and kissed it.

"Are they at the walls yet?"

"Just entering the barbican. Perched upon a column of elephants, if you please. It looks like a travelling circus is coming to town."

"Well then, lady, let us go down and greet the clowns."

Her hand came up and touched his temple briefly. "You have gone grey, Corfe. I never noticed before."

"That was Armagedir. It made an old man of me."

"In that case, you will not mind taking an old woman's arm. Come. We have a dais set out for us all hung with lilies and primroses, and they're beginning to wilt in the sun. It's height has been carefully calculated – just high enough to make Aurungzeb look like a supplicant, yet not so high that he can feel insulted."

"Ah, the subtleties of diplomacy."

"And of carpentry."

The crowd gave a massive roar as they appeared side by side and climbed into a carriage that would transport them to the dais just beyond the palace gates. Once there, Odelia had a final, critical look at the arrangements, and they sat down upon the waiting thrones. Behind them Mercadius stood, blinking like an owl in the sunlight and looking half asleep on his feet: he was to interpret the proceedings. A dozen Cathedrallers, their armour freshly painted and shining, stood about the sides of the dais like scarlet statuary.

Corfe found himself looking down a wide avenue from which the crowds were held back by two lines of Torunnan regulars. The noise was deafening and the sun surprisingly hot. Odelia's hand was cold as he gripped it, however. It felt insubstantial as straw within his own strong fingers.

Albrec mounted the dais, his face dark with some unknown worry. He bowed to his King and Queen. "Your pardon, Majesties. I would count it an honour if you allowed me to be present at this time. I will stay out of the way."

Odelia looked as though she was about to refuse, but Corfe waved him closer. "By all means, Father. After all, you're better acquainted with the Merduk royalty than we are." Why did the little monk look so troubled? He was wiping sweat off his face with one sleeve.

"Albrec, are you all right?" Corfe asked him quietly.

"Corfe, I must –"

And here the damnable trumpets began sounding out again. A swaying line of palanquin-bearing elephants approached, painted and draped and bejewelled until they seemed like beasts out of some gaudy legend. Atop the lead animal, which had been painted white, Corfe could make out the broad, turbaned shape of the man who must be Aurungzeb, and beside him under the tasselled canopy, the slighter shadow of his Queen.

The playacting part of it was scheduled to last no more than a few minutes. In the audience hall of the palace, two copies of the treaty waited to be signed – that was the real business of the day. Then there would be a banquet, and some entertainments or other that Odelia had dreamed up, and it would be done. Aurungzeb would not be staying in Torunn overnight, treaty or no treaty.

Formio and Aras appeared at the foot of the dais. Corfe had thought it only fair that they be here for this moment. The two had become fast friends despite all the odds. The Aras Corfe knew now was a long way from the pompous young man he had first encountered at Staed. What was it Andruw had said? *All piss and vinegar* – yes, that was it. And Corfe smiled. *I hope you can see this, Andruw. You made it happen, you and those damned tribesmen.*

So many ghosts.

The lead elephant halted, and then went to its knees as smoothly as a well-trained lap-dog. Silk-clad attendants appeared and helped the Sultan and his Queen out of the high palanquin. A knot of people, as bright as silk butterflies, fussed around the couple. Corfe looked at Odelia. She nodded, and they both rose to their feet to greet their guests.

The Sultan was a tall man, topping Corfe by half a head. The fine breadth of his shoulders was marred somewhat by the paunch that had begin to develop under the sash belting his middle. He had a huge beard, as broad as a besom, and his snow-white turban was set with a ruby brooch. The eyes under the turban's brim were alight with intelligence and irritation. Clearly, he did not like the fact that, thanks to the dais, Corfe and Odelia were looking down on him.

Of Aurungzeb's Queen, Corfe could make out little, except that she was heavily pregnant. She was clad in blue silk, the colour of which Corfe immediately liked. It reminded him of his first wife's eyes. Her face above the veil had been garishly painted, the eyebrows drawn out with stibium, kohl smeared across the lids. She did not look up at the dais, but kept her gaze fixed resolutely on the ground. Directly behind her stood an old Merduk with a formidable face and direct glance. He looked like an over-protective father.

The Sultan's chamberlain had appeared at one side to announce his master's appearance, but Aurungzeb did not wait for the diplomatic niceties to begin. Instead he clambered up onto the dais itself – which caused Corfe's Cathedraller bodyguard to half-draw their swords. Corfe held up a hand, and they relaxed.

The Sultan loomed over him. "So, you are the man I have been fighting," he said, his Normannic surprisingly good.

"I am the man."

They stared at one another in frank, mutual curiosity. Finally Aurungzeb grinned. "I thought you would be taller."

They both laughed, and incredibly, Corfe found himself liking the man.

"I see you have your mad little priest here as well – except that he is not mad, of course. Brother Albrec, you have turned our world upside-down. I hope you are pleased with yourself."

Albrec bowed wordlessly. The Sultan nodded to Odelia. "Lady, I hope you are good – well. Yes, that is the word." He took Odelia's hand and kissed it, then scrutinised the nearest Cathedraller, who was watching him warily.

"I thought we had killed them all," he said affably.

Corfe's face darkened. "Not all of them."

"You must be running short of *Ferinai* armour for them by now. I can perhaps send you a few hundred sets."

"There is no need," Odelia said smoothly. "We captured several hundred more at Armagedir."

It was the Sultan's turn to frown. But not for long. "My manners have deserted me. Let me introduce my Queen. Ahara – Shahr Baraz – help her up here. That's it."

The old, severe-looking Merduk helped the Merduk Queen up on the dais. All around the little tableau of figures, the crowds had gone quiet, and were watching events unfold as if it were some passion play laid on for their entertainment.

"Ahara was from Aekir," the Sultan explained. "Now she will soon give me a son. The next Sultan of Ostrabar will have Ramusian blood in him. For that reason at least, it is good that this long war finally comes to an end."

Albrec laid a hand on Corfe's shoulder, surprising him. The little monk was staring intently at him. Half amused, half puzzled, he took the Merduk Queen's hand to kiss, raised it to his lips. "Lady –"

Her eyes were full of tears. Corfe hesitated, wondering what was wrong, and in that instant, he knew her.

He knew her.

Albrec's grip on his shoulder tightened bruisingly.

"It may be that one day our children will even play together," Aurungzeb went on, oblivious. He seemed to enjoy showing off his command of Normannic. "Imagine how we will be able to improve our respective kingdoms, if there is no war to fight, no frontier to maintain. I forsee a new era with the signing of this treaty. Today is a famous day."

So much, in one terrible moment. A whole host of impulses come roaring at him, only to be beaten back. His life shipwrecked beyond hope or happiness. Albrec's grip on his shoulder anchoring him to reality in a world which had suddenly gone insane.

Her eyes had not changed, despite the paint that had been applied about them. Perhaps there was a wisdom in them now which had not been there before. Her fingers clasped his hand as they hovered below his lips, a gentle pressure, no more.

Something broke, deep within him.

Corfe shut his eyes, and kissed the hand of the woman who had been his wife. He held her fingers one moment more, and then released them, and straightened.

"I hope I see you well, lady," he said, his voice as harsh and thick as a raven's croak.

"I am well enough, my lord," she replied.

One second longer they had looking at one another, and then the madness of the world came flooding back in on them, and the day must be seen through, and the thing they had come here for must be done. Had to be done.

"Are you all right?" Odelia whispered to Corfe as they led the Merduk Royal couple down from the dais to the open carriages that awaited.

He nodded, grey in the face. Albrec had to help him into the carriage; he was unsteady as an old man.

The crowds found their voices at last, and began to cheer their King as the carriages trundled the short distance to the open doors of the great audience hall, where rank after rank of Fimbrian pikemen were drawn up alongside Torunnan regulars and a small, vermilion line of Cathedrallers. Aras and Formio rode alongside the carriage.

"Wave, Corfe," Odelia said to him. "This is supposed to be a glad day. The war is over, remember."

But he did not wave. He stared out at that sea of cheering people, and thought he saw faces he knew in the crowd. Andruw and Marsch. Ebro, Cerne, Ranafast, Martellus. And at the last he saw Heria, the woman who had once been his wife, with that heartbreaking smile of hers, one corner of her mouth quirking upwards.

He closed his eyes. She had joined the faces of the dead at last.

SHIPS
from the
WEST

For Peter Talbot

PROLOGUE

YEAR OF THE SAINT 561

RICHARD HAWKWOOD HAULED himself out of the gutter whence the crowds had deposited him, and viciously shoved his way through the cheering throng, stamping on feet, elbowing right and left and glaring wildly at all who met his eye.

Cattle. Goddamned cattle.

He found a backwater of sorts, an eddy of calm in the lee of a tall house, and there paused to catch his breath. The cheering was deafening, and en masse, the humble folk of Abrusio were none too fragrant. He wiped sweat from his eyelids. The crowd erupted into a roar and now from the cobbled roadway there came the clatter of hooves. A blast of trumpets and the cadence of booted feet marching in time. Hawkwood ran his fingers through his beard. God's blood, but he needed a drink.

Some enthusiastic fools were throwing rose-petals from upper windows. Hawkwood could just glimpse the open barouche through the crowds, the glint of silver on the grey head within, and beside it a brief blaze of glorious russet hair shot through with amber beads. That was it. The soldiers tramped on in the raucous heat, the barouche trundled away, and the crowd's frenzy winked out like a pinched candle-flame. The broad street seemed to unclench itself as men and women dispersed, and the usual street-cries of Abrusio's lower city began again. Hawkwood felt for his purse – still there, although as withered as an old woman's dugs. A lonely pair of coins twisted and clinked under his fingers. Enough for a bottle of the Narboskim at any rate. He was due at the Helmsman soon. They knew him there. He wiped his mouth and set off, a spare, haggard figure in a longshoreman's jerkin and sailor's breeks, his face nut-brown above the grizzled beard. He was forty-eight years old.

"Seventeen years," Milo, the innkeeper said. "Who'd have thought he'd last so long? God bless him, I say."

A rumble of slurred but cheerful assent from the men gathered about the Helmsman's tables. Hawkwood sipped his brandy in silence. Was it really that long? The years winked past so quickly now, and yet this time he had on his hands here, in places like this – the present – it seemed to stretch out unendingly. Bleary voices, dust dancing in the sunlight. The glare of the day fettered in the burning heart of a wineglass.

Abeleyn IV, son of Bleyn, king of Hebrion by the Grace of God. Where had Hawkwood been the day the boy-king was crowned? Ah, of course. At sea. Those had been the years of the Macassar Run, when he and Julius Albak and Billerand and Haukal had made a tidy sum in the Malacars. He remembered sailing into Rovenan of the Corsairs as bold as brass, all the guns run out and the slow-match smoking about the deck. The tense haggling, giving way to a roaring good-fellowship when the Corsairs had finally agreed upon their percentage. Honourable men, in their own way.

That, Hawkwood told himself, had been living, the only true life for a man. The heave and creak of a living ship under one's feet, answerable to no-one, with the whole wide world to roam.

Except that he longer had that hankering to roam. The life of a mariner had lost much of its shine in the past decade; something he found hard to admit, even to himself, but which he knew to be true. Like an amputated limb which had finally ceased its phantom itching.

Which reminded him why he was here. He swallowed back the foul brandy and poured himself some more, wincing. Narboskim gut-rot. The first thing he would do after – after today, would be to buy a bottle of Fimbrian.

What to do with the money? It could be a tidy sum. Maybe he'd ask Galliardo about investing it. Or maybe he'd just buy himself a brisk, well-found cutter, and take off to the Levangore. Or join the damned Corsairs, why not?

He knew he would do none of these things. It was a bitter gift of middle-age, self-knowledge. It withered away the damn fool dreams and ambitions of youth, leaving so-called wisdom in its wake. To a soul tired of making mistakes it sometimes seemed to close every door and shutter every window in the mind's eye. Hawkwood gazed into his glass and smiled. *I am become a sodden philosopher*, he thought, the brandy loosening up his brain at last.

"Hawkwood? It is Captain Hawkwood, is it not?" A plump, sweaty hand thrust itself into Hawkwood's vision. He shook it automatically, grimacing at the slimy perspiration that sucked at his palm.

"That's me. You, I take it are Grobus."

A fat man sat down opposite him. He reeked of perfume, and gold rings dragged down his earlobes. A yard behind him stood another, this one broad-shouldered and thuggish, watchful.

"You've no need of a bodyguard here, Grobus. No-one who asks for me has any trouble."

"One cannot be too careful." The fat man clicked his fingers at the frowning innkeeper. "A bottle of Candelarian there, my man, and two glasses. Clean ones, mind." He dabbed his temples with a lace handkerchief.

"Well, Captain, I believe we may come to an arrangement. I have spoken to my partner and we have hit upon a suitable sum." A coil of paper was produced from Grobus's sleeve. "I trust you will find it satisfactory."

Hawkwood looked at the number written thereon, and his face did not change.

"You're in jest, of course."

"Oh no – I assure you. This is a fair price. After all –"

"It might be a fair price for a worm-eaten row-boat, not for a high-seas carrack."

"If you will allow me, Captain, I must point out that the *Osprey* has been nowhere near the high seas for some eight years now. Her entire hull is bored through and through with teredo, and most of her masts and yards are long since gone. We are talking of a harbour-hulk here, a mere shell of a ship."

"What do you intend to do with her?" Hawkwood

asked, staring into his glass again. He sounded tired. The coil of paper he left untouched on the table between them.

"There is nothing for it but the breaker's yard. Her interior timbers are still whole, her ribs, knees and suchlike sound as a bell. But she is not worth refitting. The navy yard has already expressed an interest."

Hawkwood raised his head, but his eyes were blank and sightless. The innkeeper arrived with the Candelarian, popped the cork and poured two goblets of the fine wine. The wine of ships, as it was known. Grobus sipped at his, watching Hawkwood with a mixture of wariness and puzzlement.

"That ship has sailed beyond the knowledge of geographers," Hawkwood said at last. "She has dropped anchor in lands hitherto unknown to man. I will not have her broken up."

Grobus pinched wine from his upper lip. "If you will forgive me, Captain, you do not have any choice. A multitude of heroic myths may surround the *Osprey* and yourself, but myth does not plump out a flaccid purse – or fill a wineglass for that matter. You already owe a fortune in harbour fees; even Galliardo di Ponera cannot help you with them any more. If you accept my offer you will clear your debts and have a little left over for your – for your retirement. It is a fair offer I am making, and –"

"Your offer is refused," Hawkwood said abruptly, rising. "I am sorry to have wasted your time, Grobus. As of this moment, the *Osprey* is no longer for sale."

"Captain, you must see sense –"

But Hawkwood was already striding out of the inn, the bottle of Candelarian swinging from one hand.

A MULTITUDE OF *heroic myths*. Is that what they were? For Hawkwood they were the stuff of shrieking nightmare, images which the passing of ten years had hardly dulled.

A slug from the neck of the bottle. He closed his eyes gratefully for the warmth of it. My, how the world had changed – some things, anyway.

His *Osprey* was moored fore and aft to anchored buoys in the Outer Roads. It was a fair pull in a skiff, but at least here he was alone, and the motion of the swell was like a lullaby. Those familiar stinks of tar and salt and wood and sea-water. But his ship was a mastless hulk, her yards sold off one by one and year by year to pay for her mooring-rent. A stake in a freighting venture some five years before had swallowed up what savings Hawkwood had possessed, and Murad had done the rest.

He thought of the times on that terrible journey in the west when he had stood guard over Murad in the night. How easy murder would have been back then. But now the scarred nobleman moved in a different world, one of the great of the land, and Hawkwood was nothing but dust at his feet.

Seagulls scrabbling on the deck above his head. They had covered it with guano too hard and deep to be cleared away. Hawkwood looked out the wide windows of the stern-cabin within which he sat – these at least he had not sold – and stared landwards at Abrusio rising up out of the sea, shrouded in her own smog, garlanded with the masts of ships, crowned by fortresses and palaces. He raised the bottle to her, the old whore, and drank some more, setting his feet on the heavy fixed table and clinking aside the rusted, broad-bladed hangar thereon. He kept it here for the rats – they grew fractious and impertinent sometimes – and also for the odd ship-stripper who might have the stamina to scull out this far. Not that there was much left to strip.

That scrabbling again on the deck above. Hawkwood glared at it irritably but another swallow of the good wine eased his nerves. The sun was going down, turning the swell into a saffron blaze. He watched the slow progress of a merchant caravel, square-rigged, as it sailed close-hauled into the Inner Roads with the breeze – what there was of it – hard on the starboard bow. They'd be half the night putting into port at that rate. Why hadn't the fool sent up his lateen yards?

Steps on the companionway. Hawkwood started, set down the bottle, reached clumsily for the sword, but by then the cabin door was already open, and a cloaked figure in a broad-brimmed hat was stepping over the storm-sill.

"Hello, Captain."

"Who in the hell are you?"

"We met a few times, years ago now." The hat was doffed, revealing an entirely bald head, two dark, humane eyes set in an ivory-pale face. "And you came to my tower once, to help a mutual friend."

Hawkwood sank back in his chair. "Golophin, of course. I know you now. The years have been kind. You look younger than when I last saw you."

One beetling eyebrow raised fractionally. "Indeed. Ah, Candelarian; may I?"

"If you don't mind sharing the neck of a bottle with a commoner."

Golophin took a practised swig. "Excellent. I am glad to see your circumstances are not reduced in every respect, Captain."

"You sailed out here? I heard no boat hook on."

"I got here under my own power, you might say."

"Well, there's a stool by the bulkhead behind you. You'll get a crick in your neck if you stoop like that much longer."

"My thanks. The bowels of ships were never built with gangling wretches like myself in mind."

They sat passing the bottle back and forth companionably enough, staring out at the death of the day and the caravel's slow progress towards the Inner Roads. Abrusio came to twinkling life before them, until at last it was a looming shadow lit by a half million yellow lights, and the stars were shamed into insignificance.

The lees of the wine at last. Hawkwood kissed the side of the bottle and tossed it in a corner to clink with its empty fellows. Golophin had lit a pale clay pipe and was puffing it with evident enjoyment. At last he thumbed down the bowl and broke the silence.

"You seem a remarkably incurious man, Captain, if I may say so."

Hawkwood stared out the stern-windows as before. "Curiosity as a quality is overrated."

"I agree, though it can lead to the uncovering of useful knowledge, on occasion. You are bankrupt, I hear, or within a stone's cast of it."

"Port gossip travels far."

"This ship is something of a maritime curiosity –"

"As am I."

"Yes. I had no idea of the hatred Lord Murad bears for you, though you may not believe that. He has been busy, these last few years."

Hawkwood turned at last. He was a black silhouette against the brighter water shifting behind him, and the last red rays of the sun had touched the waves with blood.

"Remarkably busy."

"You should not have refused the reward the King offered. Had you taken it, Murad's malignance would have been hampered at least. But instead he has had free rein these last ten years to make sure that your every venture fails. If one must have powerful enemies, Captain, one should not spurn powerful friends."

"Golophin, you did not come here to offer me half-baked truisms or oldwive's wisdom. What do you want?"

The wizard laughed and studied the blackened leaf in his pipe. "Fair enough. I want you to enter the King's service."

Taken aback, Hawkwood asked, "Why?"

"Because kings need friends too, and you are too valuable a man to let crawl into the neck of a bottle."

"How very altruistic of you," Hawkwood snarled, but his anger seemed somehow hollow.

"Not at all. Hebrion, whether you choose to admit it or no, is in your debt, as is the King. And you helped a friend of mine at one time, which sets me in your debt also."

"The world would be a better place if I had not bothered."

"Perhaps." There was a pause. At last Hawkwood said quietly:

"He was my friend too."

The light had gone, and now the cabin was in darkness save for a slight phosphorescence from the water beyond the stern-windows.

"I am not the man I was, Golophin," Hawkwood whispered. "I am become afraid of the sea."

"We are none of us what we were, but you are still the master-mariner who brought his ship back from the greatest voyage in recorded history. It is not the sea you fear,

Richard, but the things you found dwelling on the other side of it. Those things are here, now; you are one of a select few who have encountered them and lived. Hebrion has need of you."

A strangled laugh. "I am a withered stick for Hebrion to lean on, to be sure. What service had you and the King in mind – Royal Doorkeeper, or Master of the Royal Rowboat, perhaps?"

"We want you to design ships for the Hebrian navy, along the lines of the *Osprey* here. Fast, weatherly ships which can carry many guns. New sail-plans and new yards."

Hawkwood was speechless for a while. "Why now?" he asked at last. "What has happened?"

"Yesterday the Archmage Aruan, whom you and I know, was proclaimed Vicar-General of the Inceptine Order here in Normannia. His first act in office was to announce the creation of a new Military Order. Though it is not generally known, I have been able to find out that this new body is to be composed entirely of mages and shifters. He calls them the Hounds of God."

"Saint in Heaven."

"What we want you to do, Captain, is to help prepare Hebrion for war."

"What war is that?"

"One which is to be fought very soon; not this year, perhaps, but within the next few. A battle for mastery of this continent. No man will be unaffected by it, nor will any man be able to ignore it."

"Unless he drinks himself to death first."

Golophin nodded sombrely. "There is that."

"So I am to help you prepare for some great struggle with the warlocks and werewolves of the world. And in return –"

"In return you will attain a high position in the navy, and at court, I promise you."

"What of Murad? He won't like my... elevation."

"Murad will do as he's told."

"And his wife?"

"What of her?"

"Nothing. No matter. I will do it, Golophin. For this I'll crawl out of that bottle."

The wizard's grin shone in the gloom of the cabin. "I knew you would. How very fortunate that Grobus offered so paltry a price today. We will have need of the *Gabrian Osprey*. She is to be the prototype for a new fleet."

"You knew of that – you had a hand –"

"Damn right."

Nothing changes, Hawkwood thought. *The nobility have sudden need of you, so they pluck you out of the gutter, peer at the disappointed little life they pinch twisting between their fingers, and set it down on their great gaming board where it can be put to use. Well, this pawn has its own rules.*

"It's dark as pitch in here. Let me light a lantern." Hawkwood fumbled for his tinderbox and after striking flint and steel a dozen times was able to coax into life a ship's lantern which still had some oil in its well. The thick glass was cracked, but that was of no moment. Its yellow kindly light illuminated the creviced features of the wizard opposite and blacked out the sea astern.

"So may I expect you at the gate of Admiral's Tower tomorrow morning?" Golophin asked. Hawkwood nodded assent.

"Excellent." The mage tossed a small doeskin bag on the table that clinked heavily. "An advance on your wages. You might want to outfit yourself with a new wardrobe. Quarters will be arranged in the Tower."

"Will be arranged, or have been arranged?"

Golophin rose and donned his hat. "Until tomorrow then, Captain," and he held out a hand.

Hawkwood shook it, rising in turn. His face was a stiff mask. Golophin turned to go, and then halted. "It is no bad thing when personal inclination and the dictates of policy go together, Captain. We need you, it is true, but I for one am glad to have you besides. The court is full of well-bred snakes. The King has need of one or two honest men around him too."

He left, stooping as he entered the companionway. Hawkwood listened to him stride forward to the waist, and then there was that scrabbling seagull on deck again, and then silence.

LATER, HE LAY on his oars a cable's-length from the *Osprey* and watched her burn. Somehow the ship reclaimed some of her old beauty as the flames swept up from her decks and roared bright and blazing into the night sky. The fire reflected wet and shining from his eyes and he sat watching until she had burned down to the waterline and the sea began rushing in to quench the inferno. A hissing of steam, and then a murmuring gurgle as what was left of her hull turned over and sank beneath the waves. Hawkwood wiped his face in the choppy darkness.

He'd build their damn navy, and jump through whatever hoops they put in front of him – it was a way of surviving, after all. But his brave ship would never become a mere blueprint in some naval surveyor's office.

He picked up his oars, and began the long haul back to shore.

PART ONE

The FALL *of* HEBRION

He uncovers the deeps out of darkness,
and brings great darkness to light.
He makes nations great, and he destroys them;
He enlarges nations, and leads them away.
He takes away understanding from the chiefs
of the people of the earth,
And makes them wander in a pathless waste.

– Job ch. 12, v. 23-24

ONE

THE KNOT OF riders pummelled along the sea-cliffs in a billow of tawny dust. Young men on tall horses, they came to a thundering halt scant inches from the edge and sat their snorting mounts, laughing and slapping dust from their clothes. The sun, bright as a cymbal, beat down on the sky-blue sea far below and made the glitter of the horizon too bright for the eye to bear. It caused the sere mountains behind the riders to ripple and shimmer like a vision.

Cantering up to join the horsemen came another, but this was an older man, his dress sombre, and his beard gunmetal grey. His mount came to a sober halt and he wiped sweat from his temples.

"You'll break your damn fool necks if you're not careful. Don't you know the rock is rotten there at the edge?"

Most of the younger men eased their horses away from the fearsome drop sheepishly, but one remained in place, a broad-shouldered youth with pale blue eyes and hair black as a raven's feather. His mount was a handsome grey gelding that stood prick-eared and attentive between his knees.

"Bevan, where would I be without you? I suppose mother told you to follow us."

"She did, small wonder. Now get away from the edge, Bleyn. Make an old man happy."

Bleyn smiled and backed the grey from the brink of the sea-cliff one yard, two. Then he dismounted in a motion as easy as the flow of water, patted the neck of the sweating horse and slapped dust from his riding leathers. On foot he was shorter than one would have guessed, with a powerfully built torso set square on a pair of stout legs. The physique of a longshoreman, topped by the incongruously fine-boned face of an aristocrat.

"We came to see if we could catch a glimpse of the fleet," he said, somewhat contrite.

"Then look to the headland there – Grios Point. They'll be coming into view any time now, with this breeze. They weighed anchor in the middle of the night."

The other riders dismounted also, hobbled their horses and unhooked wineskins from their saddles.

"What's it all about anyway, Bevan?" one of them asked. "Stuck out here in the provinces, we're always the last to know."

"It's a huge pirate fleet, I hear," another said. "Up from the Macassars looking for blood and plunder."

"I don't know about pirates," Bevan said slowly, "but I do know that your father, Bleyn, had to call up all the retainers on the estate and tear off to Abrusio with them in tow. It's a general levy, and we haven't seen one of those in... oh, sixteen, seventeen years, now."

"He's not my father," Bleyn said quickly, his fine-boned face flushing dark.

Bevan looked at him. "Now listen –"

"There they are!" one of the others shouted excitedly. "Just coming round the point."

They all stared, silent now. The cicadas clicked endlessly in the heat around them, but there was a breeze off the barren mountains at their backs.

Around the rocky headland, over a league away. Coming into view was what resembled a flock of far-off birds perched on the waves. It was the brightness of the sails that was striking at first; the heavy swell partially hid their hulls. Tall men o' war with the scarlet pennants of Hebrion snapping from their mainmasts. Twelve, fifteen, twenty great ships in line of battle, smashing aside the waves and forging out to sea with the wind on their starboard beam and their sails bright as a swan's wing.

"It's the entire western fleet," Bevan murmured. "Now what in the world?"

He turned to Bleyn, who was shading his eyes with one hand and peering intently seawards.

"They're beautiful," the young man said, awed. "They truly are."

"Ten thousand men you're looking at there, lad. The greatest navy in the world. Your – Lord Murad will be aboard, and no doubt half the Galiapeno retainers, puking their guts out, I'll be bound."

"Lucky bastards," Bleyn breathed. "And here we are like a bunch of widows at a ball, watching them go."

"What is it all for – is it a war we haven't heard of?" one of the others asked, perplexed.

"Damned if I know," Bevan rasped. "It's something big, to draw out the entire fleet like that."

"Maybe it's the Himerians and the Knights Militant, come invading at last," one of the younger ones squeaked.

"They'd come through the Hebros passes, fool. They've no ships worth speaking of."

"The Sea-Merduks, then."

"We've been at peace with them these forty years or more."

"Well, there's something out there. You don't send a fleet out to sea for the fun of it."

"Mother will know," Bleyn said abruptly. He turned and remounted the tall grey in one fluid movement. "I'm going home. Bevan – you stay with this lot – you'll slow me down." The gelding pranced like a sprightly ghost below him, snorting.

"Now you just wait a moment –" Bevan began, but he was already gone, leaving only a zephyr of dust behind.

LADY JEMILLA WAS a striking woman with hair still as dark as her son's. Only in bright sunlight could the grey be seen threading it through, like silver veining the face of a mine. She had been a famous beauty in her youth, and it was rumoured that the King himself had at one time honoured her with his attentions; but she was now the dutiful well-bred wife of Hebrion's High Chamberlain, Lord Murad of Galiapeno, and had been for almost fifteen years. The colourful escapades that had enlivened her youth were now all but forgotten at court, and Bleyn knew nothing of them.

Murad's fiefdom, tucked away on the Galapen Peninsula south-west of Abrusio, was something of a backwater, and the high manse which had housed his family for generations was an austere fortress-like edifice built out of cold Hebros stone. In the heat of high summer it still retained an echo of winter chill and there was a low fire burning in the cavernous hearth of Jemilla's apartments. She was running over the household's accounts at her desk, whilst beside her an open window afforded a view of the sun-baked olive-groves of her husband's estates like some brightly-lit fragment of a sunnier world.

The clamour of her son's arrival was unmistakable. She smiled, losing ten years in an instant, and knuckled her small fists into the hollow of her back as she arched, cat-like, from the desk.

The door opened and a grinning footman appeared. "Lady –"

"Let him in, Dominan."

"Yes, lady."

Bleyn blew in like a gale, reeking of horse and sweat and warm leather. He embraced his mother, and she kissed him on the lips. "What is it this time?"

"Ships – a million ships – well, a great fleet, at any rate. They passed by Grios Point this morning. Bevan tells me that Murad is aboard, with the retainers he took to Abrusio last month. What's afoot, mother? What great events are sailing us by this time?" Bleyn collapsed onto a nearby couch, shedding dust and horsehair over its antique velvet.

"He is Lord Murad to you, Bleyn," Jemilla said tartly. "Even a son must not be too familiar when his father is of the High Nobility."

"He's not my father." An automatic snap of petulance.

Jemilla leaned forward wearily, lowering her voice in turn. "To the world he is. Now, these ships –"

"But we know better, mother. Why pretend?"

"If you want to keep your head on your shoulders, then to you he must be father also. Prate to your friends all you want; I have them watched. But in front of strangers, you will swallow this pill with a smile. Understand me now, Bleyn. I am tired explaining."

"I am tired pretending. I am almost seventeen, mother – a man in my own right."

"When you cease pretending, this man you have suddenly become will no longer have a life to be tired of, I promise you. Abeleyn will not tolerate a cuckoo, not yet, for all that that Astaran whore has a womb as barren as a salted field."

"I don't understand. Surely even a bastard heir is better than no heir at all."

"It comes of the Civil War. He wants everything absolutely clear. A legitimate King's heir, with whom no-one can quibble. He is not yet fifty, and she is younger. And they have that sorcerer Golophin weaving his spells, coaxing his seed into her year by year."

"And all for nothing."

Yes. Be patient, Bleyn. He will come to his senses in the end, and realise as you say, that a bastard is better than nothing." Jemilla smiled as she said this, and her smile was not altogether pleasant. She saw how it wounded him. Well and good – it was something he would have to get used to.

She ruffled his dust-caked hair. "What is this about a fleet of ships then?"

He was sullen, slow to answer, but she could see the curiosity burning away the sulk.

"The whole battle-fleet, Bevan says. What's going on, mother? What war have we missed?"

Now it was she who paused. "I – don't know."

"You must know. He tells you everything."

"He does not. I know little more than you do – all the households have been turned out, and there has been a grand alliance signed, the likes of which has not been seen since the days of the First Empire. Hebrion, Astarac –"

"– Gabrion, Torunna and the Sea-Merduks. Yes, mother, that has been old news for months now. So the Himerians are finally invading, is that it? But they have no fleet worth speaking of. And Bevan said our ships were westbound. What's out there but empty ocean?"

"What indeed? A host of rumours and legends perhaps. A myth about to be made flesh."

"And now you talk in riddles again – cannot you ever give me a straight answer?"

"Hold your tongue," Jemilla snapped. "You're barely seventeen summers old in the way of the world, and you think you can bandy words with me and belittle your – your father? Whelp."

He subsided, glowering.

In a softer tone she went on. "There are legends of a land out in the uttermost west, a New World that remains undiscovered and uninhabited. They are the stuff of children's bedtime stories here in Hebrion, and have been for centuries. But what if the children's tales were true? What if there was indeed a vast, unknown continent out there in the west? And what if I told you that Hebrian ships had already been there, Hebrian feet had trodden those uncharted strands?"

"I would say, 'Bravo for Hebrian enterprise,' but what has this to do with the armada I saw this morning?"

"There's been talk at court, Bleyn, and even here I have caught the gist of it. Hebrion is about to face the threat of invasion it would seem."

"So it is the Himerians!"

"No. It is something else. Something from the west."

"The west? Why – A-ha! – you mean there really is some new empire out beyond the sea? Mother, this is amazing news! How can you sit there so calm? What marvellous times we live in!" Bleyn leapt up and began striding back and forth across the chamber, slapping the palms of his hands together in his excitement. His mother watched him dourly. Still a boy, with a boy's enthusiasms, and a boy's ignorance. She had thought to have done better. Perhaps if his father had truly been Abeleyn – or Murad – he would have been different, but this pup was the progeny of Richard Hawkwood, a man Jemilla might once, ironically enough, have actually loved – the only man she might once have loved – but a commoner, and thus useless to her life and her ambitions. *Still*, she thought, *one must work with the tools one is given. And he is my son, after all. I am his mother. And I do love him – there is no gainsaying that.*

"Not an empire," she corrected him. "Or at least, not yet. Whatever it is that has arisen out there, it seems to have been connected to events here, in Normannia, for untold centuries. How, I am not sure, but the Himerians are part of it, and the Second Empire somehow within its control."

"You are very vague, mother," said Bleyn with some circumspection.

"It is all I know. Few men anywhere know more except Lord Murad, and the King, and Golophin his wizard."

And Richard Hawkwood, the thought came unbidden to her. He too would know everything, having captained that unhappy voyage all those years ago. The greatest feat of maritime navigation in history, it was said, but the Crown had clamped down on all mention of it in subsequent years. The initial interest – nay, hysteria – had faded within a year. No log-books were published, no survivor ever hawked his story in street-sold handbills. It was as though it had never happened.

Her husband it was who had seen to that. Murad forgot nothing, forgave nothing. The man was obsessed with ruining Richard Hawkwood – why, Jemilla could not fathom. Something had happened to them out there in the west, something horrible. It was as if Murad were trying to expunge it from his soul. And if he could not, then he would bury every reminder of it he could.

If he ever found out that Bleyn were actually the mariner's *son*... Jemilla's face grew cold at the thought.

So Hawkwood had gained nothing from his great voyage, once the initial run of banquets and audiences had run their course. It had been a nine-day's wonder, quickly forgotten. Even the King, she thought, had been happy to have it that way. What had happened out there, to destroy their expedition and so blight their lives?

And what was coming from that terrible place now that warranted such preparations? Alliances, shipbuilding programs, fortification projects – in the last five years Hebrion and her allies had been preparing for a vast struggle with the unknown. And now, it had begun. She could sense it as surely as if it were some noisome reek brought on the back of the wind.

Bleyn was watching her. "How can you sit here like this, mother – so uninterested? You're a woman, I know, but not like any other woman I know –"

"You know so many then?"

"I know other noblewomen. You are a hawk amongst pigeons."

She laughed. Perhaps he was not so much of a boy as she had thought. "I keep my place, Bleyn, as I must. Lord Murad is not a man to cross lightly, as you know, and he prefers that you and I stay away from court. The King prefers it that way also – we are a skeleton long hidden in the back of a closet. We must be patient, is all."

"I am a man now. I can sit a horse as well as any trooper, and I'm the best fencer in all of Galiapeno. I should be out there on those ships, or at least commanding a tercio in the city garrison. My blood demands it. It would demand it even were I Murad's son and not the King's."

"Yes, it would."

"What kind of education do you think I get out here in the country? I know nothing of court or of the other nobility –"

"That's enough, Bleyn. I can only counsel patience. Your time will come."

Bleyn's voice rose. "It will come when at last I am a doddering greybeard and my youth has been poured out on the stones of this damned backwater!" He stormed out of the chamber, his shoulder thumping the doorframe as he went. The dust of his passage hung in the air after him. Jemilla could smell it. Dust. All that was left of sixteen years of her life. She had aimed high once – too high – and this semi-imprisonment had been her punishment, Murad her jailer. She was lucky to be alive. But Bleyn was right. It was time to chance another cast, perhaps, before sixteen more years passed in the arid dust and sunlight of this damned backwater.

TWO

THE FIRST PRIMROSES were out, and new bracken was curling up in gothic green shoots through the massed needles of the pinewoods. That smell in the wind – of pine-resin and new grass and growing things; a clean sharpness from which the chill was finally departing, to be replaced by something new.

The horses had caught the flavour of the air and were prancing and nipping at each other like colts. The two riders ahead of the main party let them have their heads, and were soon galloping full tilt along the flank of one of the great upland fells which formed this part of the world. When their mounts were blowing and steaming, they reined them in again, and continued at an amble.

"Hydrax is coming on well," the man said. "It seems you have a talent there, after all."

His companion, a girl or young woman, curled her lip. "I should think so. Shamarq says that if I spend any more time on horseback I'll be bow-legged. But who would notice in court dress anyway?"

The man laughed, and they rode on in companionable silence, the horses picking their way through the tough gnarls of hill-heather. Once the girl pointed wordlessly skywards, to where a solitary raptor soared in the north. The man followed her finger and nodded.

Half a mile behind them a straggling band of some forty riders followed doggedly. Some were richly dressed ladies, others armoured cavalrymen. One bore a silk banner which whipped and twisted in the wind so that its device was impossible to make out. Many led heavily-laden pack-mules that clanked as they walked.

The man turned in the saddle. "We'd best let them catch up. They're not all centaurs like you."

"I know. Briseis rides like a frog on a griddle. And Gebbia is not much better."

"They're ladies-in-waiting, Mirren, not horse-troopers. I'll wager they sew and cook a good deal better than they ride. Well, sew at any rate."

That curl of the lip again. The man smiled. He was a broad-shouldered fellow in middle age, his once dark hair grey at the temples, giving him the look of a grizzled badger. Old scars marked his weather-beaten face and his eyes were deep-hollowed, grey as a winter sea, and there was a coldness to them that softened only when he looked upon the girl at his side. He sat his mount with the consummate ease of a born horseman, and his clothing, though well-made, was plain and unadorned. It was also black, dark as a panther's pelt with nothing to relieve it.

The girl at his side, in contrast, was dressed in bright brocade, heavily worked with pearls and gems, with a lace ruff at her white throat and a finely woven linen and wire head-dress atop her yellow hair. She sat her horse like a young queen. Her elegance was marred, however, by the battered old riding cloak she had thrown over her shoulders. It was a soldier's cloak, and had seen hard service, though it had been lovingly repaired many times. Peeping out from under its folds there appeared for a moment the wizened face of a marmoset. It sniffed the bracing air, shuddered, and withdrew once more.

"Must we go back, father?" the girl asked her sombrely clad companion. "It's been such fun."

Her father, the King of Torunna, set his warm hand atop her fingers on the reins.

"The best things," he said quietly, "are better not savoured too long." And there came into his cold eyes a shadow that held no hope of spring. Seeing it, she took his hand and kissed it.

"I know. Duty calls once more. But I'd rather be out here like this than warm in the greatest palace of the world."

He nodded. "So would I."

The thud and snuffle and chatter of the party behind them as they caught up, and Corfe turned his horse to greet them.

"Felorin, I believe we may begin to make our way back to the city. Turn this cavalcade around, and warn the steward. We will make camp one hour before sunset. I trust you to find a suitable site. Ladies, I commend your forbearance. This last night in tents, and tomorrow you shall be in the comfort of the palace. I entrust you to the care of my bodyguard. Felorin, the princess and I will catch you up in a few hours. I have somewhere I wish to go."

"Alone, sire?" the rider called Felorin asked. He was a slender whip of a man whose handsome face was a swirl of scarlet tattoos. He wore a black surcoat with vermilion trimming, and a cavalry sabre bounced at his thigh.

"Alone. Don't worry, Felorin. I still know my way about this part of the world."

"But the wolves, sire –"

"We have fleet horses. Now stop clucking at me and go seek out tonight's campsite."

Felorin saluted, looking discontented and concerned, and then turned his horse about and sped off to the rear of the little column. The cavalcade, turning about, made a clanking, braying, confusing circus of soldiers, ladies and servants, restive mules, mincing palfreys. Corfe turned to his daughter.

"Come, Mirren," and led her off into the hills at a fast canter.

THE CLOUDS BROKE open above their heads, and flooding out of the blueness came bright sunlight which kindled the flanks of the fells and made of them a tawny and russet pelt running with tumbled shadow. Mirren followed her father as he pounded along what appeared to be an old, overgrown track nestled in the encroaching heather. The horse's hooves thudded on hard, moss-green gravel instead of soggy peat, and they picked up speed. The track ran straight as an arrow into the east; in summer it would be well-nigh invisible beneath the bracken.

Corfe slowed to a walk and his daughter wrestled her own mount to a similar pace beside him. Despite her youth her horse, Hydrax, was a solid bay fully as large as her father's black gelding. A martingale curbed some of his wilder head-tossing, but he was still prancing mischievously under her.

"That bugger will have you off one of these days," Corfe said.

"I know. But he loves me. It's high spirits is all. Father, what's all the mystery? Where are we going? And what is this old road we're on?"

"You've not much notion of history – or geography – despite those tutors we gathered from the four corners of the world. I take it you know where we are?"

"Of course," Mirren said scornfully. "This is Barossa."

"Yes. *The Place of Bones*, in Old Normannic. It was not always named so. This is the old Western Road, which once ran from Torunn clear to what was Aekir."

"Aurungabar," his daughter corrected him.

"Yes, by way of Ormann Dyke…"

"Khedi Anwar."

"The very same. This was the spine of Torunna once upon a time, this old track. The Kingsway runs to the north-west, some twelve leagues, but it's barely fifteen years old. Before Torunna even existed, before this region was known as Barossa, it was the easternmost province of the old Empire. The Fimbrians built this road we trot upon, as they built most things that have endured in the world. It's forgotten now, such are men's memories, but once it was the highway of armies, the route of fleeing peoples."

"You – you came along this way from Aurungabar when you were just a common soldier," Mirren ventured, with a timidity quite unlike her.

"Yes," Corfe said. "Yes, I did. Almost eighteen years ago, now." He remembered the mud, the cold rain, and the hordes of broken people, the bodies lying by the hundred at the side of the road.

"The world is different now, thank God. Up along the Kingsway they've cleared the woods and burnt off the heather and planted farms in the very face of the hills. There are towns there where before it was wilderness. And here, where the towns used to be before the War came, the land has been given back to nature, and the wolves roam unmolested. History turns things on their heads. Perhaps it is no bad thing. And there, up ahead – can you see the ruins?"

A long ridgeline rose ahead of them, a dark spatter of trees marking its crest. And at its northern end could be seen broken walls of low stone, like blackened teeth jutting up from the earth. But closer to, there rose up from the flatter land a tumulus, too symmetrical to be of nature. Atop it a stone cairn stood stark against the sky. The birdsong which had been brash and cheery about them all morning had suddenly stilled. "What is this place?" Mirren asked in a whisper.

Corfe did not answer, but rode on to the very foot of the tall mound. Here he dismounted, and gave Mirren his hand as she followed suit. The marmoset reappeared and swarmed up to her shoulder, its tail curling about her neck like a scarf.

There were stone flags set in the grass, and the pair climbed up them until they stood before the cairn on the summit. It was some five feet high, and a granite slab had been set upon its top. There were words chiselled into the dark stone.

Here lie we, Torunna's dead,
Whose lives once bought a nation liberty.

Mirren's mouth opened. "Is this –"

"The ruins you see were once a hamlet named Armagedir," Corfe said quietly.

"And the mound –"

"A grave-barrow. We gathered all those whom we could find, and interred them here. I have many friends in this place, Mirren."

She took his hand. "Does anyone else come here any more?"

"Formio and Aras and I, once every year. Apart from that, it is left to the wolves and the kites and the ravens. Since the mound was raised, this world of ours has moved on at a pace I would never once have believed possible. But it exists in its present form only because of the men whose bones moulder underneath our feet. That is something you, as my daughter, must never forget, even if others do."

Mirren made as if to speak, but Corfe silenced her with a gesture. "Wait."

Arrowing out of the west there came a single bird, a falcon or hawk of some kind. It circled their heads once, and plummeted towards them. The marmoset shrieked, and Mirren soothed it with a caress. The bird, a large gyrfalcon, alighted on the grass mere feet away, and spent a few seconds rearranging its pinion-feathers before opening its hooked beak and speaking in the low mellifluous voice of a grown man.

"Your Majesty. We are well-met."

"Golophin. What tidings from the west?"

The bird cocked its head to one side to bring one inhuman yellow eye to bear. "The combined fleet put to sea three days ago. They are cruising in the area of North Cape and have a squadron out keeping watch on the western approaches to the Brenn Isles. Nothing as yet."

"But you're sure the enemy is at sea."

"Oh yes. We've had a picket-line of galliots cruising beyond the Hebrionese for four months. In the last sennight every one of them has disappeared. And a fair portion of the northern herrin fleet has failed to make it back to port, and yet the weather has been fine and clear. There's something out there, all right."

"What of your raptor's eyes?"

A pause, as if the bird were distracted or Golophin was considering his words. "My familiar is based here – in Torunna – for the moment, your Majesty, to keep whole the link between east and west."

"Charibon, then. What news?"

"Ah. There I have something a little more tangible. The Himerian armies are breaking up winter quarters as I speak. They will be on the march within a fortnight, I would hazard, or as soon as the Torrin Gap is free of the last drifts. The Thurian Line is awash with marching men."

"It has begun, then," Corfe breathed. "After all this time, the curtain has risen."

"I believe so, sire."

"What of the Fimbrians?"

"No word as yet. They are playing a waiting game. The Pact of Neyr may have broadcast their neutrality to the world, but they will have to climb down from their fence sooner or later."

"If this yet-unseen fleet manages to make landfall it could well make up their minds for them."

"And it will also mean a two-front war."

"Yes of course."

"I trust, sire, that all your preparations are in hand?"

"The principal field army awaits only my word to march, and General Aras has the northern garrison on alert at Gaderion. You will let me know as soon as anything happens?"

"Of course, sire. May I convey to you the compliments and greetings of your Royal cousin Abeleyn of Hebrion? And now I must go."

The bird's wings exploded into a flurry of feathers and it took off like a loosed clothyard, soaring up into the spring blue. Corfe watched it go, frowning.

"So that was Golophin – or his familiar at least," Mirren said, eyes bright. "The great Hebrian mage. I've heard so much about him."

"Yes. He's a good man, though his years are beginning to tell on him now. He took it hard, his apprentice going the way he did."

"Ah, the Presbyter of the Knights. Is it true he is a werewolf as well as a mage?"

Corfe looked at his daughter closely. "Someone has been listening at keyholes."

Mirren flushed. "It is common folklore, no more."

"Then you will know that our world is threatened by an unholy trinity. Himerius the Anti-Pontiff, Aruan the Sorcerer, now Vicar-General of the Inceptine Order, and Bardolin, another Archmage, who is Presbyter of the Knights Militant. And yes, this Bardolin is rumoured to be a shifter. He was Golophin's friend, and brightest pupil. Now he is Aruan's creature, body and soul. And Aruan is the greatest of the three, for all that he has the lesser rank in the eyes of the world."

"They say that Aruan is an immortal, the last survivor of an ancient race of men who arose in the west, but who destroyed themselves in ages past with dabbling in black sorcery," Mirren whispered.

"*They* say a great deal, but for once there is a nubbin of truth under all the tall tales. This Aruan came out of nowhere scarcely six years ago now, landing at Alsten Island with a few followers in strange looking ships. Himerius at once recognised him as some kind of messianic prodigy and admitted him to the highest circles of power. He claims to be some form of harbinger of a better age of the world. He is immensely old, that we know, but as for the lost race of conjurors – well, that's a myth, I'm sure. In any case, he has the armies of Perigraine and Almark and half a dozen other principalities to call upon, as well as the Orders of the Knights Militant and the mysterious Hounds. The Second Empire, as this unholy combine is known, is a fact of our waking world –"

"The Fimbrians," Mirren interrupted. "What will they do?"

"Ah, there's the rub. Which way will the Electorates jump? They've been hankering after a rekindling of their hegemony ever since the fall of Aekir, but this new Thearchy has stymied them. I'm not sure. We will be fighting for the self-determination of all the Ramusian kingdoms, and that is not something the Fimbrians would particularly like to see. On the other hand, they do not want to watch the Himerians become invincible, either. I reckon they'll wait it out until we and Charibon have exhausted ourselves, and then step in like hyaenas to pick over the bones."

"I've never known a war," Mirren said quietly. She stroked the marmoset which perched on her shoulder. "What is it like, father?"

Corfe stared out over the barren swells of the upland moors. Sixteen years ago, this quiet emptiness had been the epicentre of a roaring holocaust. If he tried, he was sure he would hear the thunder of the cannon echoing still, as it echoed always in the dark, hungry spaces of his mind.

"War is a step over the threshold of Hell," he said at last. "I pray you never experience it first hand."

"But you were a great general – you commanded armies – you were a conqueror."

Corfe looked down at her coldly. "I was fighting for survival. There's a difference."

She was undaunted. "And this next war – it also is about survival, is it not?"

"Yes. Yes it is. We have not sought this battle; it has been thrust upon us – remember that." His voice was sombre as that of a mourner.

But the hunger and the darkness within him were crowing and cackling with glee.

THREE

"THE BIRDS," SAID Abeleyn. "They follow the ships."

Over the fleet hung a cloud of raucous gulls, thousands of them. They wheeled and swooped madly and their unending shrieks hurt the air, carrying over even the creak of timber, the smash of keel striking water, the groan of rope and yard.

"Scavengers," Admiral Rovero called out from the quarterdeck below. "But it's strange, is it not, to see them so far out from land."

"I have never seen it before. The odd one, yes, but not flocks like these," Hawkwood told him.

All down the four levels of the spar-deck – forecastle, waist, quarterdeck, poop – soldiers and sailors were staring upwards, past the cracking, bellied sails, the straining yards, the bewildering complexities of the rigging. The gulls circled tirelessly, screaming.

Below them the flagship shouldered aside the swell with a beautiful easy motion. The *Pontifidad* was a tall man o' war of twelve hundred tons with seven hundred men on board, and eighty long guns which were now bowsed up tight against the closed portlids like captured beasts straining for their liberty. A floating battery of immense destructive power, she was the largest warship in the western world, the pride of the Hebrian navy.

And she may not be enough, Abeleyn thought. *She and all her mighty consorts, the assembled might of four nations. What are men and ships compared to –*

"Sail ho!" the lookout yelled down from the maintopgallant yard. "A caravel coming out of the eye of the wind, fine on the larboard beam."

"Our reconnaissance returns," Hawkwood said. "With what news I wonder?"

The knot of men stood on the poop deck of the *Pontifidad* and awaited the approaching ship calmly. Two days before a small squadron had been sent out to the west to reconnoitre while the fleet beat up round the headland now safely astern.

Admiral Rovero called up to the lookout from the quarterdeck. "How many sail there?"

"Still just the one, sir. She's got a foretopsail carried away and I see braces on her flying loose."

Abeleyn and Hawkwood looked at one another.

"What do you think, Captain?" Abeleyn asked.

Hawkwood rubbed a hand through the peppery tangle of his beard. "I think the squadron may well have found what it was looking for."

"My thoughts also."

Admiral Rovero thumped up the companionway to the poop and saluted his monarch. "Sire, there's no-one to be seen on her deck. It smells bad to me. Permission to beat to quarters."

"Granted, Rovero. Captain Hawkwood, I believe we should signal the allied contingents. Enemy to nor'-west. Clear for action."

"Aye sir."

OVER SEVERAL SQUARE miles of ocean, the fleet came to urgent, scurrying life. Fifty-three great Ships and dozens of smaller carracks and caravels were travelling north-east with the breeze broad on their larboard beam. The solitary caravel, a small vessel gauging no more than a hundred tons, ran headlong before the wind towards their gaping broadsides.

The fleet was in a rough arrowhead formation. The point was formed of Hebrian ships, the largest contingent. The left barb belonged to the Gabrionese, eleven lean, well-manned vessels with crews of superb seamen. The right barb consisted of the Astarans; larger ships, but less experienced crews. And the shank of the arrowhead was made up of the Sea-Merduks. Their vessels were lighter, as were their guns, but they were crowded with arquebusiers and buckler-men.

All told, over thirty thousand men rode the waves this bright spring morning, fifty leagues off the west coast of Hebrion. It was the greatest conglomeration of naval power the world had yet seen, and its assembling had been the patient work of years. Ten days now they had been cruising westwards together, having rendezvoused off the Hebrian coast a fortnight since. All for this one day, this moment in time. This bright spring morning on the swells of the Western Ocean.

The stink of slow-match drifted up to Abeleyn from the gun-deck, along with the sweat of the sailors as they hauled the great guns outboard so that their muzzles protruded from the ship's sides like blunt spikes. Above him, in the tops, soldiers were loading the wicked little two-pounder swivels, ramming loads down the barrels of their arquebuses, hauling up buckets of seawater to fight the inevitable fires that would catch in the sails.

The caravel was less than three cables away now, and careering directly for the flagship. There was no-one at her tiller, but her course was unerring.

"I don't like this. That's a dead ship with a live helm," Rovero said. "Sire, permission to blow her out of the water."

Abeleyn paused in thought, and for a moment could have sworn that the regard of all those hundreds of sailors and soldiers and marines was fastened upon him alone. At last he said: "Granted, Admiral."

The signal-pennants went up, and moments later the massed ordinance of the fleet began to thunder out, awesome as the wrath of God.

The caravel disappeared in a murderous storm of spuming water. Hawkwood saw timbers flying high in the air, a mast lurch and topple enmeshed in rigging. Cannonballs fell short and overshot, but enough were on target to smash the little vessel to kindling. When it reappeared it was a dismasted hulk, low in the water and surrounded by debris. The gulls shrieked overhead as the smoke and roar of the broadsides died away.

"I hope to God we were right," Admiral Rovero murmured.

"Look at her decks!" someone yelled from the masthead.

Men crowded the ship's rail, impatient for the powder-smoke to clear. The knot of officers on the poop were higher up, and thus saw it before the sailors in the waist.

Cockroaches? Hawkwood thought. *My God.*

As the caravel settled, black, shining things were clambering up out of her hatches and taking to the sea, for all the world like some aquatic swarm of beetles. A horrified buzz ran through the ship as the men glimpsed them.

"Back to your stations!" Hawkwood roared. "This is a King's ship, not a pleasure-yacht! Bosun – start that man by the cathead."

The beetle-figures tried to clasp onto the wreckage of the caravel, but it was in its death-throes, circling stern-first down into a foaming grave and sucking most of them down with it. Soon there was nothing left on the surface of the sea but a few bobbing fragments of wreckage.

A yelp of pain as the Bosun brought a knotted rope's end down on some unfortunate's back. The men returned to their battle-stations, but their whispering could be heard like a low surf from the poop.

"They captured our squadron, and obviously are aware of our location," Admiral Rovero said.

Whatever they *are*, Abeleyn thought. But he nodded in agreement. "That is what we wanted, after all. We cannot cruise indefinitely. The enemy must come to us." He turned to Hawkwood, and lowered his voice. "Captain, the things in that ship. Have you –"

"No sire. We saw nothing like that in the west."

As Hawkwood spoke there was the sudden flap and crack of wilting canvas overhead. They looked up to see the sails go limp as the wind died. For a few moments it was so silent on board that the only noise seemed to be the rasping of the sea past the cutwater. Then that faded too.

The very waves became still. In the space of half a glass the entire fleet was wallowing in a clock-calm, its formation scrambling as the ships began to box the compass. The descent of the stillness was astonishing

"What in the world?" King Abeleyn said. "Captain, this cannot be right."

"It's not natural," Hawkwood told him. "There's sorcery at play here – weather-working."

The ship's bell rang out, and seconds later those of the other ships in the fleet followed suit as their quartermasters collected their wits. The sound was somehow desolate in the midst of that vast, dead ocean. Seven bells. It was barely mid-afternoon. The sea was a vast blue mirror, as even and unruffled as the flawless sky above it. The fleet resembled nothing so much as a chaotic, bristling city somehow set afloat upon the ocean, and for all its teeming might, it was dwarfed into insignificance by the vastness of the element which surrounded it. The gulls had disappeared.

THE PRETERNATURAL CALM lasted into the evening, when a mist began to creep up on the fleet from the west. Faint as spider-silk at first, it swiftly thickened into a deep fog laden with moisture, blotting out the stars, the young moon, even the mast-lanterns of all but neighbouring ships. Into the night the conches blew, arquebuses were fired at stated intervals, and lookouts posted fore and aft shouted their enquiries into the blank grey wall. It was deemed unwise to put off in smallcraft in such a fog, and so the fleet drifted with flaccid sails, and crews spent anxious hours at the rail with long poles, lest they be needed to ward off a collision. All order was lost, and ships of Astarac became entangled with ships of Gabrion, and slim Merduk vessels were thumped and dunted by great Hebrian galleons.

THE KINGS OF Hebrion and Astarac, along with Admiral Rovero and Captain Hawkwood met in the Great Cabin of the *Pontifidad* just after eight bells had struck the end of the last dog-watch. King Mark had set out for the flagship to confer with his Royal cousin just after the fog had descended, and had been several hours in a cutter, rowed from ship to ship until he found his goal. His face was pasty and ill-looking despite the motionless sea.

The setting was a magnificent one, the curving, gilded sweep of the stern-windows glittering in the light of overhead lanterns slung in gimbals, and two eighteen-pounder culverins bowsed up snug to their ports forward. The long table that ran athwartships was covered in charts, wineglasses, and a decanter. The liquid within the latter was as level as if it sat upon dry land.

"The men are becoming tired," Hawkwood said. "We've had them at quarters for nigh on six hours – the last watch has missed its turn below-decks –"

"The enemy is very close, somewhere out in the fog," Rovero said harshly. "They have to be. They'll come at us ere the dawn. The men must remain at their posts."

A momentary silence. They sipped their wine and listened to the melancholy calls of the lookouts, the far-off crack of an arquebus. Hawkwood had never known a crew so quiet – usually there was a hum of talk, a splurge of laughter, ribaldry or profanity to be heard, even as far aft as this – but the ship's company waited on deck in the dew-laden darkness with scarcely a word, their eyes wide as they watched the wall of fog swirl formlessly before them.

"And who – or what – exactly are the enemy?" King Mark asked. "Those things in the caravel were not human, or did not appear so. Nor did they seem to be shifters like those encountered by the captain here on his expedition."

The table looked at Hawkwood. He could only shrug. "I am as much in the dark as anyone sire. It's a fair number of years since that voyage. Who knows what they have been doing there in that time, what travesties they have been hatching?"

A knock on the cabin door, and a marine stepped in. "Lord Murad, sire. Desires an audience." The marine's face was chalky with fear.

Hawkwood and Rovero shared a swift look, but then Murad was with them, bowing prettily to his king. "I hope I see you well, sire." To their surprise his voice shook as he spoke. Water droplets beaded his face.

"You do. How was the haul to the flagship, cousin? The night is as thick as soup."

"My coxswain hailed every ship in turn until we found the *Pontifidad*. He is as hoarse as a crow and I am dew-soaked and salt-crusted. We followed in the wake of King Mark, it seems. Your Majesty, forgive me" – this to Mark of Astarac, who sat watching wordlessly – "Duke Frobishir of Gabrion has also been looking for the flagship, I am told. He must be still out there in the fog. A man could be rowed around all night and finish where he started, it is so thick. But I am forgetting my manners. Admiral Rovero, my compliments – and here of course is my old comrade and shipmate, Captain Hawkwood. It has been a while, Captain, since we exchanged more than a nod at court."

Hawkwood nodded, face closed.

Murad had put on some flesh since returning from his ill-starred voyage to the Western Continent. He would never be plump, but there was a certain sleekness to him now which made his scarred, wedge-shaped face less sinister than it once had been. Neither would he ever be handsome in any conventional sense, but his eyes were deep-set coal-gleams which missed nothing and which gazed often, it was said, on the naked forms of other men's wives. This despite his marriage to the celebrated beauty Lady Jemilla. Hawkwood met those obsidian eyes and felt the mocking challenge within them. The two men were bitter enemies, the mariner's elevation of the past few years seemingly adding an even keener edge to Murad's hatred, but they kept up a civilised enough pretence in front of the King.

Murad's initial discomfiture had fled. "I have brought you a gift, sire, something which I think we may all find intriguing, and, dare I say it, educational. With your permission –" He raised his voice to a shout. "Varian! Have it brought in here!"

There was a commotion in the companionway beyond the stern-cabin, men swearing and bumping. The door opened to admit four burly sailors dragging a large hessian sack which bulged heavily. They dropped it on the deck of the Great Cabin, knuckled their foreheads to the astonished company within, and then left with a strange, hunted haste.

The thing stank, of stagnant seawater, and some other, nameless reek which Hawkwood could not identify, though it seemed hauntingly familiar. The men in the cabin rose to their feet to peer as Murad pulled back the mouth of the sack.

Something black and gleaming lay bundled within.

The nobleman took his poniard and ripped open the hessian with a flourish. Spilling out onto the cabin floor was what seemed at first glance to be a jumbled set of black armour. But the stink that poured out of it set them all to coughing and reaching for handkerchiefs.

"God Almighty," Abeleyn exclaimed.

"Not God, sire," Murad said grimly. "Nothing to do with God at all."

"How did you snare it?" demanded Hawkwood.

"We trolled for it with a net one of the crew had, in the wake of the caravel's sinking. We brought up others – all dead, like this – but threw them back and kept this as the finest specimen." There was surly triumph in Murad's voice.

"At least they drown, then, like normal beasts," Rovero said. "What in the Saint's name is that stuff? It's not metal."

"It's horn." Abeleyn, less ginger than the rest, had knelt beside the carcass and was examining it closely, tapping it with the pommel of his dagger. "Heavy, though. Too heavy to float. Look at the pincers there at the end of the arms! Like a giant lobster. And the spikes on the feet would pierce wood. Captain, help me here."

Together the mariner and the King grasped a segment of plate that might be said to be the helm of the creature. They tugged and grunted, and there was a sharp crack, followed by a nauseating sucking sound. The helm-part came free, and the smell it released set them all to coughing. Hawkwood controlled his heaves first.

"It's a man, then, after all."

A contorted ebony face with snarling yellow teeth, the lips drawn back, the eyes a pale amber colour. It was a study in bone and sinew and bulging tendon, an anatomist's model.

"A man," King Mark of Astarac said, rather doubtfully.

"If they're men, then they can be beaten by other men," said Abeleyn. "Take heart, my friends. Rovero, let this news be passed onto the crew at once – it's ordinary men in strange armour we face, not soulless demons."

"Aye, sire." Rovero gave the corpse a last, dubious stare, and left the cabin.

Hawkwood, Abeleyn, Murad and Mark were left to gaze at the dripping carrion at their feet.

"It's like no kind of man I've ever seen before," Hawkwood said. "Not even in Punt are their skins so black. And see the corner teeth? Sharp as a hound's. They've been filed, I believe. Some of the Corsairs do the same to render themselves more fearsome-looking."

"Those eyes," Abeleyn muttered. "He burns in Hell

now, this fellow. You can see it in the eyes. He knew where he was going."

They stood in an uncomfortable silence, the agony in the dead man's face holding them all.

"He may be a man, but something dreadful has been done to him all the same," Mark said in almost a whisper. "These sorcerers... Will their lord Aruan be here in person, you think?"

Abeleyn shook his head. "Golophin tells me he is still in Charibon, marshalling his forces."

"This fleet of theirs –"

"Is very close now. It may only have been sighted once or twice in the last ten years, but it exists. Small ships, it is said, lateen-rigged and bluff-bowed. Scores of them. They appear out of mists like this. They've been raiding the Brenn Isles these two years past and more, taking the children and disappearing as they came. Odd-looking ships with high castles to fore and aft."

"Like the cogs of ancient times," Hawkwood put in.

"Yes, I suppose so. But my point is that they are built for boarding. Our long guns can – can keep them at bay..." The King's voice fell and they all looked at one another as the same thought struck them at once. In this fog, long guns next to useless, and an enemy ship might drift close enough to board before anyone had any notion of her.

"If our sails are empty, then theirs are also," Hawkwood said. "I've not heard tell they have any galleys, and even the most skilled of Weather-workers can affect only an area of ocean – he cannot choose to propel individual ships. They're boxing the compass just like us – and these things here" – he nudged the corpse with his foot – "they can't swim, it seems, which is another blessing."

Abeleyn slapped him on the shoulder. "You hearten me, Captain. It is the good sense of mariners we need now, not the paranoia of politicians. You may rejoin the admiral on deck. We shall be up presently."

Dismissed, Hawkwood left the cabin, but not before trading chill glances with Murad.

Abeleyn flicked the hessian over the snarling dead face on the deck and poured himself a long glass of wine. "I should like to keep this thing as a specimen for Golophin to examine when he next visits us, but I fear the crew would not be overly enthusiastic at the notion. And the stink!" he drained his glass.

"Mark, Murad, no formality, now. I want advice as the" – he raised his empty glass ironically – "supreme commander of our little expedition. We have enough supplies for another month's cruising, and then we must put about for Abrusio. If we are not attacked tonight, then –"

"We're not going anywhere as long as this calm lasts," Murad interrupted him harshly. "Sire, while we are helpless and blind in this airless fog, it may be that the enemy is sailing past us in clear skies, and is intent on invading a kingdom stripped of its most able defenders."

"Golophin has six thousand men garrisoned in Abrusio, and another ten scattered up and down the coast," Abeleyn snapped.

"But they are not the best men, and he is no soldier, but a mage. Who's to know how his weathercock loyalties may swing if he sees this thing going against us?"

"Don't go doubting Golophin's loyalty to me, cousin. Without him this alliance would never have been possible."

"All the same, sire," Murad answered him, unabashed, "I'd as soon as seen a soldier in command back in Hebrion. General Mercado –"

"Is dead these ten years. I see where you are going with this, kinsman, and the answer is no. You remain with the fleet. I need you here."

Murad bowed. "Cousin, forgive me."

"There is nothing to forgive. And I do not believe we will be bypassed by the enemy."

"Why not, sire?"

King Mark of Astarac spoke up in the act of filling his own glass. His face had regained some of its colour. "Because there are too many ripe royal apples in this basket to let it go by unplucked. Isn't that so, Abeleyn? We're dangling out here like the worm on the end of a hook."

"Something like that, cousin."

"Hence the pomp and circumstance that attended our departure," Mark said wryly. "Bar an engraved invitation, we have done everything we could to persuade the enemy to rendezvous with us. Abeleyn, I salute your cleverness. I just hope we have not been too clever by half. When is Golophin due to drop in again?"

"In the morning."

"You can't summon him in any way?"

"No. His familiar is with Corfe, in the east."

"A pity. For all your doubts, Murad, I for one would feel a lot happier with the old boy around. If nothing else, he might blow away this accursed mist, or whistle up a wind."

"Sire, you speak sense," Murad said, with what passed for humility with him. "If the enemy has any intelligence at all of our comings and goings, then he will attack tonight, while the elements are still in his favour. I must get back to my ship."

"Don't bump into anything in the dark," Abeleyn told him, shaking his hand.

"If I do, it had best not be allergic to steel. Your majesties, excuse me, and may God go with you."

"God," said Abeleyn after he had left. "What has God to do with it anymore?" He refilled the wineglasses, and emptied his own at a single draught.

THE NIGHT PASSED, the stars wheeled uncaring and unseen beyond the shroud of fog that held the fleet captive.

Unforgivably, Hawkwood had nodded off. He jerked upright with a start, a sense of urgent knowledge burning in his mind. As his eyes focused he took in the steady glow of the lamp, motionless in its gimbals, the blur of the chart on the table before him resolving itself into the familiar coastal line of Hebrion, the shining dividers lying where they had dropped from his limp fingers. He had been dozing for a few minutes, no more, but something had happened in that time. He could feel it.

And he looked up, to see he was not alone in the cabin.

A darkness there in the corner, beyond the reach of the light. It was crouched under the low ship-timbers. For an instant he thought he saw two lights wink once, and then the darkness coalesced into the silhouette of a man. Above his head eight bells rang out, announcing the end of the middle watch. It was four hours after midnight, and dawn was racing towards him over the Hebros Mountains far to the east. It would arrive in the space of half a watch. But here on the Western Ocean, night reigned still.

"Richard. It is good to see you again."

Hawkwood tilted the lamp and saw, standing in the corner of the cabin, the robed figure of Bardolin. He shot to his feet, letting the lamp swing free and career back and forth to create shadowed chaos out of the cabin. He lurched forward, and in a moment had grasped Bardolin's powerful shoulders, bruising the flesh under the black robes. A wild grin split his face, and the mage answered it. They embraced, laughing – and the next instant Hawkwood drew back again as if a snake had lunged at him. The smile fled.

"What are you come here for?" His hand went to his hip, but he had unslung his baldric, and the cutlass hung on the back of his chair.

"It's been a long time, Captain," Bardolin said. As he advanced into the light, Hawkwood retreated. The mage held up a hand. "Please, Richard, grant me a moment – no calling out or foolishness. What has it been, fifteen years?"

"Something like that."

"I remember Griella and I searching the docks of old Abrusio for the *Osprey* that morning" – a spasm of pain ran across his face – "and the brandy I shared with Billerand."

"What happened to you, Bardolin? What did they do to you?"

The mage smiled.

"How the world has changed under our feet. I should never have gone into the west with you, Hawkwood. Better to have burned in Hebrion. But that's all empty regret now. We cannot unmake the past, and we cannot wish ourselves other than we are."

Hawkwood's hammering heart slowed a little. His hand edged towards the hilt of the cutlass. "You'd best do it and have done, then."

"I'm not here to kill you, you damned fool. I'm here to offer you life." Suddenly he was the old Bardolin again; the dreamy menace retreated. "I owe you that at least – of them all, you were the only one who was a friend to me."

"And Golophin."

"Yes – him too. But that's another matter entirely. Hawkwood, grab yourself a longboat or a rowboat or whatever passes for a small insignificant craft among you mariners, and get into it. Push off from this floating argosy and her consorts, and scull out into the empty ocean if you want to see the dawn."

"What's going to happen?"

"You're all dead men, and your ships are already sunk. Believe me, for the love of God. You have to get clear of this fleet."

"Tell me, Bardolin."

But the strange detachment had returned. It did not seem to Hawkwood that it was truly Bardolin who smiled now.

"Tell you what? For the sake of old friendship, I have done my best to warn you. You were always a stubborn fool, Captain. I wish you luck, or if that fails, a quick and painless end."

He faded like the light of a candle when the sun brightens behind it, but Hawkwood saw the agony behind his eyes ere he disappeared. Then was alone in the cabin, and the sweat was running down his back in streams.

He heard the gunfire and the shrieking up on deck, and knew that whatever Bardolin had tried to warn him about had begun.

FOUR

Snow lay bright and indomitable on the peaks of the Cimbrics, and beyond their blinding majesty the sky was blue as a kingfisher's back. But spring was in the air, even as high up as this, and the margins of the Sea of Tor were ringed with only a mash of undulating pancake-ice which opened and closed silently around the bows and sterns of the fishing-boats that plied its waters.

In Charibon the last yard-long icicles had fallen from the eaves of the cathedral and the lead of the roof was steaming in the sunlight. The monks could be heard singing Sext. When they were done they would troop out in sombre lines to the great refectories of the monastery-city for their midday meal, and when they had eaten they would repair to the scriptoriums or the library or the vegetable and herb-gardens or the smithies to continue the work which they offered up to God along with their songs. These rituals had remained unchanged for centuries, and were the cornerstones of monastic life. But Charibon itself, seat of the Pontiff and tabernacle of western learning, had changed utterly since the Schism of eighteen years before.

It had always been home to a large military presence, for here were the barracks and training-grounds of the Knights Militant, the Church's secular arm. But now it seemed that the austere old city had exploded into an untidy welter of recent building, with vast swathes of the surrounding plain now covered with lines of wooden huts and turf-walled tents, and linking them a raw new set of gravel-bedded roads spider-webbing out in all directions. West to Almark they went, north to Finnmark, south to Perigraine, and east to the Torrin Gap, where the Cimbrics and the tall Thurians halted, leaving an empty space against the sky, a funnel through which invading armies had poured for millennia.

And on the parade-grounds the armies mustered, bristling masses of armoured men. Some on horseback with tall lances and pennons crackling in the wind, others on foot with shouldered pikes, or arquebuses, and others manhandling the carriages of long-muzzled field-guns, waving rammers and linstocks and sponges and leading trains of mules drawing rattling limbers and caissons. The song of the monks in their quiet cloisters was drowned out by the cadenced tramp of booted feet and the low thunder of ten thousand horses. The flags of a dozen kingdoms, duchies and principalities flapped over their ranks: Almark, Perigraine, Gardiac, Finnmark, Fulk, Candelaria, Touron, Tarber. Charibon was now the abode of armies, and the seat of Empire.

THE FIMBRIAN EMBASSY had been billeted in the old Pontifical palace which overlooked the library of Saint Garaso and the Inceptine Cloisters. Twelve men in trailworn sable, they had tramped at their fearsome pace across the Malvennor Mountains, over the Narian hills and down onto the plains of Tor to consult with the Pontiff Himerius in Charibon. They had marched for miles amid the tented and log-hewn city which had sprung up around the monastery, noting with a professional eye the armouries and smithies and horse-lines, the camp-discipline of the huge host dwelling there, and the endless lines of supply waggons that came and went to the rich farmlands of the south and west, all under tribute now. Almark and Perigraine were no longer counted among the Monarchies of the Five Kingdoms. Himerian Presbyters ruled them, priestly autocrats answerable only to the High Pontiff himself, and King Cadamost had shaved his head and become an Inceptine novice.

It was twelve years since the Fimbrian Electors had signed the Pact of Neyr with the Second Empire, wherein they had professed complete neutrality in the doings of the continent outside their borders. They had sent an army east to aid Torunna against the Merduk, only to see half of it destroyed and the other half desert to the command of the new Torunnan King. This had brought to an abrupt halt their dreams of rekindling some form of imperial power in Normannia, and to add insult to injury they had in subsequent years seen a steady trickle of their best soldiers desert and take ship for the east, where they had joined the Tercios of King Corfe and his renegade Fimbrian general, Formio. The Torunnan victories of sixteen years before had shaken the Electorates, who had long been accustomed to viewing all other western powers as inferior in military professionalism to themselves. But the heterogeneous army which Corfe had led to such savage victories against the Merduk had given them much food for thought. The Torunnans were now the most renowned soldiers in the world – at least as long as they were led by their present King. And they were now part of this Grand Alliance which encompassed Hebrion, Astarac, Gabrion, and even Ostrabar. Set against this confederation was the might of the Second Empire. At the court of the Electors it had long been decided that Fimbria would swallow her pride, bide her time and await the collision of these two titans. After the dust had cleared, then that would be the time for Fimbria to reassert her old claims on the continent, and not before – no matter how this neutrality might frustrate and even anger the common soldiers of the army, who were burning to reclaim their reputation as the conquerors of the west. But times were changing with a rapidity bewildering to those who had grown up with the twin certainties of the indivisible Holy Church and the menace of the heathen east, and Fimbria had decided to review her policies, and take stock of the new order of the world.

"I make it at least thirty thousands of infantry, and ten of cavalry," Grall said, consulting the varicoloured counters which littered the table.

Justus turned from the window and his view of Charibon's faithful streaming out of the cathedral into the square below. Almost all the clerics he saw were in black. One or two in Antillian brown here and there, but for the most part the Inceptines seemed to have virtually subsumed every other religious order in the world. In this half of the continent at any rate.

"There are other camps," he told his companion. "Further to the east, towards the Gap. They have fortresses there in the foothills of the Thurians. Their entire strength may be half as much again."

"And that's not counting their garrisons," a third raven-clad Fimbrian put in from his post by the fire. "Our intelligence indicates that they have large contingents in Vol Ephrir and Alstadt, and even as far west as Fulk."

"Hardly surprising," Grall said. "They have the resources of half the continent to draw upon, and then there are these *others*…" With an impatient gesture, he began scooping the counters into a leather pouch, scowling.

"It is mainly these others that we are here to find out about," Justus told him. "Armies of men, we can prepare for. But if half the rumours are true –"

"If half the rumours are true then the Second Empire has both God and the Devil on its side," Grall chuckled. "I daresay it is mostly a case of tall tales and skilful rumour-handling."

The Fimbrian at the fire was shorter, and older than the other two. His hair was a cropped silver, and his face was as hard and seamed as wood. Only his eyes gave him away – they flashed now like cerulean gemstones. "There is more to it than that. There are strange things happening in Charibon; there have been ever since this Aruan appeared out of nowhere five, six years go and waltzed into the Vicar-Generalship as though it had been specially set aside for him."

"Do you think the stories about him are true then, Briannon?" Grall asked. There was a mocking edge to his voice.

"The world is full of strange things. This man has opened the doors of the Himerian Church to all the sorcerers and witches of the Five Kingdoms, reversing the ecclesiastical policies of generations, and they have come flocking to him as though he were Ramusio himself. Why would he do this? Where has he come from? And what manner of man is he? That is what we are here to find out. Now, before the storm-clouds break and it is too late."

A knock on the door of the chamber, and a man who might have been brother to any of those within peered inside and said, "it's time, sir. They're expecting us in a few moments."

"Very well," Briannon answered. He repaired to a side chamber for a few minutes, and when he returned some of the worst of the grime had been slapped off his uniform, and he wore a scarlet sash about his middle.

"No circlet?" Grall asked wryly. He and Justus had buckled on short swords of iron and wiped some of the mud off their boots, but aside from that they looked much as they had when they had marched into Charibon the night before.

"No. As we agreed, I am Marshal Briannon here – no relation to the Elector who happens to share my name."

THE PONTIFICAL RECEPTION Hall had been built to overawe. It resembled the nave of a cathedral. Every supplicant who sought an audience with the High Pontiff must needs tramp a long, intimidating path down its length towards the high dais at the end, his every move flanked by alcoves in the massive walls – every one of which held the figure of a Knight Militant in full armour, standing like a graven statue, but following everything with his eyes.

At the far end, Himerius sat on a tall throne, and on each side of him stood his Vicar-General, and the Presbyter of the Knights. Other monks were black shadows in the background, murmuring and scraping quills across parchment. Although it was a bright spring day outside, and sunlight flooded in through the tall windows butting the vaulted roof of the building, braziers were burning around the dais, and elaborately carved wooden screens had been drawn around, so it seemed that Himerius and his advisors were cloaked in shadow and flame-light, and difficult to make out after the dazzling length of the hall.

The twelve Fimbrians marched sombrely towards this darkness. Their swords had been left in the antechamber and their hands were empty, but they somehow seemed more formidable than the heavily armoured Knights whom they passed by.

They came to a cadenced halt before the dais, and were enveloped in the shadow that surrounded Himerius.

Grall was listening to the opening exchanges with one part of his mind, but more of it was studying the men he saw before him. Himerius was old – in his late seventies now – and his frame seemed withered and lost in the rich robes that clad it. But his eyes were bright as a raptor's, his ivory face still retaining a haggard vitality.

To his right stood a tall man in Inceptine black, with the chain of the Vicariate around his neck. He was monk-bald, but had the air about him of a great nobleman. A hawk nose that put even Himerius's to shame, and thick, sprawling eyebrows over deep orbits within which the eyes were mere glints. He looked somehow foreign, as though he came from the east; it was the high cruelty of the cheekbones, perhaps. There was about him an air of command that impressed even Grall.

This was Aruan of Garmidalan, the Vicar-General of the Inceptine Order, and, some said, the true head of the Himerian Church. The power behind the throne at any rate, and an object of mystery and speculation throughout all the Normannic kingdoms.

To Himerius's left stood a different pot of fish entirely. A broad-shouldered, shaven-headed soldier in half armour with a broken nose and the scar of long helm-wearing on his forehead. In his sixties, perhaps, he looked as hale and formidable as any Fimbrian drill-sergeant Grall had ever known. But there was intelligence in his eyes, and when Grall met them he felt he was being gauged and, as the eyes moved on, dismissed again. This man had seen battle, spilled blood. The violence in him could almost be smelled. Bardolin of Carreirida, Presbyter of the Knights Militant – another enigma. He had been a mage, apprentice to the great Golophin of Hebrion, but had turned against his master and now completed the Triumvirate of powers here in Charibon.

"– Always a pleasure to see the representatives of the Electorates here in Charibon. We trust that your quarters agree with you, and that there will be time during your visit to discuss the many and varied subjects of importance which now concern both our fiefdoms. The Grand Alliance, as it styles itself, has been for years a warlike and threatening presence on our shared continent, and it borders both our states, yet of late its posturing has become more substantial, and we must needs consult together, I believe, as to how its ambitions may be curtailed." This was Himerius, his old voice surprisingly clear and resonant under the massive beams of the hall.

"The restraint shown by the Electorates has been admirable, considering the many hostile acts committed against it by the Alliance, but we feel here at Charibon, the seat of the true faith, that it is perhaps time that Fimbria and the Empire made common cause against these aggressors. The world is divided irrevocably. To our sorrow, our advisors tell us that war may not be long in coming, despite all our efforts to prevent it. The anti-Pontiff Albrec the Faceless and his benefactor, the murderous usurper Corfe of Torunna, not to mention the despicable despoilers of the Holy City of Aekir, are all massing troops on our eastern borders. While in the west, Hebrion, Gabrion and Astarac – also in league with the Merduk – blockade our coasts and strangle trade. We pray therefore, Marshal Briannon, that your embassy is come here today to make common cause with us in this approaching struggle – one that will, with God's Blessing, wipe the heresy of Albrec from our shores forever, and bring to an end the disgusting spectacle of Merduk and Ramusian worshipping together – in the same temple, at the same altar – as it is said they do in the iniquitous sink that is Torunn."

Grall blinked in surprise. As diplomatic statements went, this one was as subtle as an onager's kick. He wanted to glance at Briannon, to see how the Elector had received this speech – nay, this demand – but faced his front rigidly, and kept his face as blank as wood.

"Your Holiness makes many valuable points," Briannon replied, his voice hard as basalt after Himerius's music. "Too many, in fact, to be addressed adequately standing here. As you know, no Fimbrian embassy is ever despatched lightly, and our presence here is evidence enough that we, also, share your concerns about the current state of affairs on our borders and yours. I will divulge to you that I stand here with the authority to make or break any treaty hitherto entered into by the Electorates. The Treaty of Neyr, guaranteeing Fimbrian neutrality in any war in which the Second Empire might become involved, has served us well over these last twelve years. But times are changing. I rejoice that you and I are of one mind in this respect, Holiness."

Himerius actually smiled. "Shall we adjourn for dinner then, my dear Marshal, and afterwards, perhaps we can meet more informally and begin to explore the new possibilities that this current state of affairs has brought to light?"

Briannon bowed slightly. "I am at your Holiness's disposal."

"I HAD THOUGHT Himerius to be a wily negotiator," Justus said. "He as much as stated we are either for or against him, the old buzzard."

"They were not his words," Briannon told him. "Himerius is a mere figurehead. We are dealing with this Aruan, no other, and he is confident enough of his strength that he thinks to lay down the law to the Electorates."

"What will it be, then?" Grall asked impatiently. "Are we to throw in our lot with these sorcerers and priests?"

Briannon stared at him coldly. "We will do whatever is best for our people, no matter if we have to lay down with the Devil to do it." The trio of sombrely clad men tramped back to their quarters in silence after that. Grall found himself thinking of his cousin, Silus, who had deserted to Torunna not three weeks before. *To serve under a soldier*, he had said bitterly. The only real soldier left in the west.

WHEN THE GREAT doors had boomed shut on the Fimbrians' retreating backs the trio of figures on the dais seemed to become animated.

"We were too obvious," Himerius said discontentedly. "Master, these Fimbrians have the stiffest necks of any men alive. One has to handle them with care, courtesy, flattery."

"They tolerate these things – they do not appreciate them," Aruan said. "And they are men like any other, fearful of what the future may bring. Our friend Briannon is in fact the same Briannon who is Elector of Neyr, and should the Fimbrians ever set aside their internal differences and decide to raise up an emperor again, then he will be the man clad in imperial purple. He is not here for the exercise. I believe they will sign the new treaty. We will have Fimbrian Pike within our ranks yet, I promise you. Not for a while, perhaps, but once Hebrion and Astarac fall, they will see which way the wind is blowing."

"They don't like us," Bardolin said. "They would prefer to serve under King Corfe – a fighting man."

"They would prefer to serve under no-one but themselves. However, their rank and file will obey orders – it's what they're good at, after all." Aruan smiled. "My dear Bardolin, you have been very promiscuous in your comings and goings of late. I sometimes regret letting you into the mysteries of the Eighth Discipline. Do I detect a note of sympathy for this soldier-king?"

Bardolin met Aruan's hawkish gaze without flinching. "He's the greatest general of the age. The Fimbrian rank and file may obey their orders in the main, but over the past fifteen years thousands of them have flocked to his banner. *The Orphans*, they call themselves, and they are fanatics. I've met them in the field, and they are a fearsome thing to contend against."

"Ah, the Torrin Gap battle," Aruan mused. "But that was a small affair – and almost ten years ago. We have our own brand of fanatics now, Bardolin, and they laugh at pikes no matter who wields them. Children? *Am I not right?*"

At this the monks who stood in the shadows raised their heads, and as their cowls slipped back there were revealed the slavering muzzles of beasts. These opened their maws and howled and yammered, and then crawled forward to fawn at the feet of Aruan, their yellow eyes bright as the flickering flames of the braziers.

FIVE

THE SOUND CAME first, a noise like the massed thudding of a thousand heartbeats. The ship's company roused itself from the exhausted torpor into which it had fallen and stood on deck, staring fearfully into the fog. Their officers were no wiser. King Abeleyn stood on the poop in a golden swirling soup gilded by the huge stern lanterns of the *Pontifidad*. Along the gangways of the waist, marines were replenishing their slow-match, which had burned down to stubs, and all about the forecastle, waist and quarterdeck the gun-crews wiped their faces, spat on their hands and exchanged wordless looks. The beating noise was all around, and growing louder as they stood. Dawn would come in an hour, but something else was coming first.

Admiral Rovero had ordered the swivel-men to remain in the tops, though up there they were on self-contained little islands adrift in an impenetrable grey sea. There was confused shouting from above now, within the fog, and the sudden, shattering bark of the wicked little swivel-guns firing in a formless barrage. Pieces of rope and shards of timber fell to the deck, shot off the yards.

"It's begun," Abeleyn said.

"Sergeant Miro!" Rovero bellowed. "Take a section up the shrouds and see what's going on up there." And in a lower tone. "You, master-at-arms – go get Captain Hawkwood."

The firing intensified. Miro and his men abandoned their arquebuses and took to the shrouds, disappearing into the fog. All along the packed decks of the ship the crew looked upwards in fearful wonder as the fog began to spin in wild eddies and the shouting turned to screaming. A warm rain began to fall on their faces and a wordles cry went up from the decks as they realised it was raining blood. Then one, two, three – half a dozen bodies were falling down out of the fog, smashing off spars, bouncing from ropes, and thumping in scarlet ruin amid their shipmates below, or splashing overboard into the black sea. The volleyed gunfire sputtered out into a staccato confusion of single shots. Men on the spar-decks ducked and dodged as even more dreadful debris rained down from the invisible tops: limbs, entrails, heads, warm spatters of blood. And all the while over the gunfire and the wails of the dying, that drumbeat-murmur overhead.

Ashen faced and panting, Hawkwood joined Abeleyn and Mark on the poop.

"What in Hell's going on?"

No-one answered him. The firing from the tops had all but died, but the shrieking went on, and now men were appearing out of the fog overhead, pouring down the rigging, sliding down backstays so swiftly as to burn the flesh from their hands. It was Abeleyn who first snapped out of the dreamlike paralysis that seemed to have seized all the men on deck.

"Marines there – fire a volley into the tops. Ensign Gerrolvo, get a grip of your men, for God's sake! All hands, all hands prepare for boarding! Sergeant-at-arms, issue cutlasses."

The spell was broken. Given orders to carry out that made sense of the nightmare, the men responded with alacrity. A ragged salvo of arquebus fire was directed towards the swirling mists into which the masts disappeared ten feet above everyone's heads, and the rest of the mariners raced to the arms barrels to seize close-combat weapons, since it was clear the great guns were useless against whatever was attacking the ship.

On the poop beside Abeleyn, Hawkwood drew his own cutlass and fought the sickening panic that was rising up his throat like a cloud. Almost he mentioned Bardolin's visitation to the Hebrian King, but then bit back his words. *You're all dead men.* It was probably too late now anyway.

Admiral Rovero was in the waist, thrusting men to their stations, kicking aside the mutilated corpses which littered the deck. He grasped one mad-eyed marine whose arm looked as though it had been chewed short at the wrist. The man stood grasping his stump and watching the arteries spurt as if they belonged to someone else.

"Miro, you got up to the maintop, didn't you? What in the name of God is happening up there?"

"Demons," Miro said wildly. "Yellow-eyed fiends. They have wings, admiral. There's no-one left alive up there."

The man was in deep shock. Rovero shook him angrily, baffled. "Get below to the sickbay. You there – Grode – help him down the hatch. Stand to your weapons, you whoresons. Remember who you are!"

All around them in the wall of mist it was possible to see the red darting flashes of small-arms fire, and seconds later to hear the muted crackle of distant volleys through a far surf of shouting – the other ships of the fleet were enduring a similar assault.

A knot of bodyguards, Hebrian and Astaran, joined Abeleyn, Mark and Hawkwood at the taffrail with drawn swords. They were in half-armour with open helms, glaring about in bewildered determination. Something swooped out of the fog above them, was lit up saffron as it wheeled into the light of the stern-lanterns, and smashed full-tilt into their ranks. The men were sent sprawling like skittles. One was knocked over the ship's rail and splashed into the sea below without a sound. His armour would sink him like a stone. Hawkwood, in the midst of the tumbling, chaotic flailing of arms and legs and impotently swinging blades glimpsed a winged shape, featherless as a snake – wickedly swiping claws, a long bald tail like that of a monstrous rat – and then it was gone again, the fog spinning circles in the draughts stirred by its wingbeats.

All the length of the ship, men were fighting off this attack from above. Scores, hundreds of the creatures where diving down out of the fog, raking mariners and marines to shreds with their wicked talons, and then disappearing again. The masters-at-arms were manning the quarterdeck swivels and indiscriminately blasting the air with wicked showers of metal. Ropes and lines sliced apart by shrapnel came hissing down on the struggling men below; falling blocks and tackle cracking open skulls and adding to the mayhem. Hawkwood saw what must have been the main topgallant yard – thirty feet of stout wood frapped with iron – come searing down like a comet trailing all its attendant rigging and tackle. It speared through the deck and disappeared below, dragging with it two gunners who had been caught up with its lines. The splintered wood of the deck tore their bodies to pieces as they were yanked through it.

"They're breaking up the ship from the masts down," he cried. "We must get men back up into the tops or they'll cripple her."

He ran forward towards the quarterdeck-ladder. Behind him, the two Kings were helping their heavily armoured bodyguards to their feet. Another one of the winged creatures swept low and Hawkwood swiped at it with his iron cutlass, hacking off one of the great talons. It crashed full into the taffrail in a stinking flap of beating bone and leathery wings. The six-foot stern-lantern above it shuddered at the impact, tottered, and fell to the deck in an explosion of flame, burning oil spraying everywhere. King Mark of Astarac was engulfed and transformed into a blazing torch, the bodyguards beside him likewise drenched, roasting inside their armour. Some threw themselves overboard. The King tried to bat out the flames but they rushed hungrily up his body, blackening his skin, withering his hair away, melting his clothes. Dazed, and on fire himself, Hawkwood saw Astarac's monarch rip the flesh from his own face in his agony. Abeleyn was trying to smother the blaze with his cloak, but it caught too. One of the Hebrian bodyguards pulled his King away and lay on his body, smiting the flames which had caught in his sleeves and hair. Hawkwood rolled across the deck and beat to death the burning droplets on his own clothing. "Fire party!" he shouted. "Fire party aft!" The skin peeled off the back of his hands in perfect sheets and he stared at them, transfixed.

The stern of the ship was ablaze, the fire igniting the pitch in the deck-seams and catching in the tarred rigging of the mizzen backstays. When the heat reached the second stern-lantern, it exploded, spraying fiery oil as far as the quarterdeck. As the inferno took hold, it touched off the poop culverins and they detonated one after another, rearing back on their burning carriages. The spare powder charges stored beside them went up with a sound like a series of thunderous broadsides and blew great jagged holes in the superstructure of the *Pontifidad*, the massive timbers that formed the skeleton and ribs of the ship tossed like twigs into the air along with fragments of burning men. The ship groaned like a maimed beast and there was a great tearing crack as the mizzen gave way and toppled over, tearing free the shrouds and stays and crashing into ruin down the ship's larboard side. The great vessel began to list.

Hawkwood had been blasted clear of the burning poop by the powder-explosions. They had rendered him deaf, and thus the scene aboard was a surreal, soundless nightmare; a dream which seemed to be happening to someone else. He picked himself up out of a tangle of broken timber and piled cordage. All around him, men were fighting the fire with pitiful chains of buckets, or slashing and shooting at the swooping shadows overhead, or dragging their wounded comrades clear of the flames. There was utter confusion, but it had not yet bled into panic. That was something.

The King. Where was he?

Rovero, one side of his face a burnt bubbled ruin, had grabbed his arm and was shouting something, but Hawkwood could not make it out. He ducked as another one of the winged monstrosities dived low, and felt the wrench as Rovero was lifted free of the deck. He seized the admiral's hand, but toppled backwards as it came free. Rovero's decapitated torso tumbled like a rag across the deck. Hawkwood stared in horror.

Men were lifted struggling into the air and dropped with torn throats. A sergeant of marines was grappling fifteen feet off the deck, digging his fingers into his attacker's eyes while the bald wings flapped furiously about him. Sailors caught the hanging tails of their tormentors and dragged them down whilst their comrades hacked them to pieces. But there were hundreds of the beasts. They fastened like flies on the dead and the living alike, wreaking carnage with no thought of their own preservation.

Hawkwood experienced no fear, just a dazed series of decisions in his mind. He grabbed a steel marlin-spike from a fife-rail and stabbed with all his strength one of the winged creatures that was perched on the shattered deck, feeding off a shrieking marine. The beast reared backwards on top of him, the wings beating in a paroxysm of agony. He crawled out from under and knelt upon it, pinning the wings. A human face spat up at him, but the eyes were yellow as a cat's and it's fangs were as long as his fingers. Disgust and rage overmastered him. He punched the face with his raw fists until his knuckles cracked and broke, and the beast's glaring eyes were burst from their sockets.

There – there was Abeleyn. His bodyguards were dead or dying all around him and the King of Hebrion fought on alone, a curtain of flame behind him. Hawkwood staggered aft, no real notion of what he was to do in his mind, only a knowledge that he must get to the King, whatever happened.

A silent explosion staggered him – he felt the blast of hot air scorching his skin. He lurched to his feet. Some sounds were coming back, all overlaid with a shrill hissing that filled his head. The ship's wheel was on fire, and the binnacle. The chain of buckets had disappeared.

There was no order left now on board. Men were fighting their own private battles for survival and wielding anything that came to hand to beat off the enemy. No time to reload arquebuses; the marines were swinging them like clubs. Over the formless storm in his ears Hawkwood heard some shouting in despair, and saw them pointing. He turned.

Crawling over the ship's rails were hordes of the beetle-like warriors which had gone down in the caravel. Their pincers made short work of the boarding-netting and their spiked feet propelled them over the side with preternatural speed. Hawkwood peered over the ship's rail and saw that a mass of smallcraft was clustered there, and grapnels were being tossed aboard by the score. The *Pontifidad* gave a lurch to starboard which sent him sliding across the packed deck. A squirming mass of humanity went with him, men sliding off their feet and rolling in the remains of their shipmates. One sailor was pitched from the mainhatch square onto a baulk of broken timber that transfixed him. He writhed there in astonishment, grasping the bloody stave that now protruded from his belly, wound round with blue innards.

"On me!" Abeleyn cried. "To me, all of you! Repel boarders, damn you – stand fast!"

A knot of desperate men gathered about Abeleyn as the King took up position at the bulwark, setting a foot on it and swinging with his sword at the black shine of the enemy boarders. Men fought to their feet and clustered along the ship's side, ignoring the fire, their own wounds, the inevitable death of the ship beneath them. For a few moments they battled there, holding back the tide of enemy, Abeleyn's face transfigured in their midst, like that of a warrior saint out of legend. Then he went down.

Hawkwood did not see what became of him – he was too far away, in the midst of that maniac crowd of terrified men. The King's fall broke them. Resistance splintered, became a thing of individual survival, all higher aims forgotten. Their King was gone and, with him, the last of their hope.

Crowds of the beetle-warriors swarmed across the *Pontifidad* like cockroaches crawling over some great putrefying carcass. There was no escape for the survivors of the ship's company still on deck. They stampeded for the hatches. Hawkwood found himself in the midst of a crowd that bore him along towards the quarterdeck companionway. He fell to his knees, buffeted by the frenzied sailors, but elbowed a space and laboured upright. His numbed mind followed him down the companionway with the others, and at the foot of the companionway he paused, looking about him.

Battle-lanterns still burning in the tween decks, though they hung at an angle with the list of the ship. It was suffocatingly hot, and the smoke smarted his eyes, racked coughs out of his heaving chest. He opened the door that led to the officer's quarters aft, and was met by a hungry rush of flame that tightened the skin of his face and shrivelled his eyebrows. Nothing could live there. He slammed shut the smoking door, and headed forward with no thought in his mind except to escape the flames below and the carnage above.

He passed clots of wounded men who had dragged themselves down here to die, and slipped in their blood as the ship listed further. They must have holed her below the waterline somehow. Then the space between decks opened out into the middle gun-deck. Hawkwood found himself in a dark nightmare lit by battle-lanterns, crowded with panicked figures who were setting off the great guns in a disorderly broadside. They had something to fire at now, but their elevation was too high; the shot was passing over the hulls of the enemy craft grappled alongside. Hawkwood screamed at them to depress their pieces, and when they stared at him blankly he seized a handspike himself and wedged the nearest culverin up with a quoin so that the muzzle tilted downwards. It was loaded, and he stabbed the lighted match into the touch-hole with a savage joy. The gun jumped back with a roar, and beyond the port he glimpsed a spout of broken timbers.

But up through the gunport there squeezed now a glinting mass of the enemy, their pincers splintering wood. Hawkwood clubbed them back with the handspike, but they were squirming in through every port on the deck. Men left the guns and began fighting hand-to-hand, crouched under the low deck-beams. It looked like a battle fought far below the earth, in the subterranean chamber of a steaming mine.

Part of the deck about the mainhatch above their heads collapsed in a cataclysm of burning timber. It came down on the guncrews like a wooden avalanche. With it fell a mass of the glinting enemy. The beetle-warriors rolled like balls, righted themselves, and began laying about with hardly a pause. The awful pincers lopped off men's limbs and the black armour was impenetrable save at the joints. The guncrews fell back. Hawkwood tried to rally them, but his voice was lost in the tumult. Stooping under the deck-beams, he struggled forward again. Another hatch leading downwards. He followed it, borne along by a terrified mob of gunners with the same end in mind.

The orlop. They were below the waterline now, close to the hold.

I will die down here, Hawkwood thought. When a ship's crew was forced below the guns, she was finished.

There was water sloshing about his ankles. Somehow the enemy had holed the ship, attacking from the sea as well as the air. The *Pontifidad* was dying, and when she gave up the struggle against the pitiless waves she would take hundreds of trapped men with her. The pride of Hebrion, she had been. Hard to grasp that such a great vessel could be destroyed, and not by gunfire or storm, but by – by what?

His hands were agony to him now. Hawkwood staggered out of the way of the crowd coming down the hatch and fell to his side. The salt water scalded his burns. He crawled behind one of the great wooden knees of the ship supporting the deck-beams, and there halted. The water was rising fast.

The ship shook with a dull boom and the men below wailed helplessly, realising that their doom was not far off. There was a deafening, creaking roar, and then part of the very hull gave way. It burst inwards, admitting an explosion of spray. Hawkwood thought he saw a massive black snout in the midst of it for a second.

The water rose at an incredible rate, thundering in through a breach some eight feet wide. Men were clawing their way back up the hatches they had so lately fought to get down. The ship lurched further to starboard with a moan of overstressed timbers. Hawkwood slid towards the breach and was enveloped in foam. He went under, sucked into a storm of swirling seawater. Fighting to see, he found broken timbers under his nose, and beyond them, darkness. He clutched them with his skinless hands and fought against the push of the water, levering himself over them. Splinters raked his belly, his thighs. Then he was spinning freely in open water, a chaotic turbulence sucking him down. He struck out in the opposite direction, knowing that the ship was going down, and trying to bring him to the depths with it. Something struck him on the forehead and he lost ground. His lungs felt like cinder-filled bags about to explode. His torso convulsed with the need to suck in air, water, anything, but he fought against it, kicking upwards. His vision turned red. He bared his teeth, tasted blood in his mouth, but kept struggling.

At last his head burst clear of the water for a second. He exhaled and gulped a cupful of air, then was sucked under again.

Harder this time, the fight against the undertow. His arms and legs slowed. He looked up and saw light above him, but it was too far. His limbs stopped. He drifted slowly downwards, but still would not give up, would not breathe in though his body screamed for him to do so.

Damn you. Damn you!

Something became entangled with his legs. It caught there and spun him around, then began to tug him upwards again. A dark blob against the light, leather straps wrapped around his ankles. He was floating towards the surface feet first. He looked down past his wriggling fingers, down into the depths, and saw there a sight he would never forget.

Scores of men, dozens of other faces turned up to the light, some calm and otherworldly, others still fighting the sea like himself. They were suspended in the clear water below, trapped and dying. And behind them, the awesome dark bulk of the *Pontifidad* sliding towards the sea-bed like some tired submarine titan going to her rest. Broken, mastless, but still with one or two lights twinkling. She turned over and the last lights went out. Her black hulk slid soundlessly down into the deeper blackness beyond.

Hawkwood was still rising. He broke the surface and shouted the dead poison from his lungs. He flapped his weary legs free of the thing that had saved him, and found it was a leather-strapped wineskin, half-full of air. Grasping it in his arms he sobbed in great gouts of the cold air knowing only that he was alive, he had escaped. His ship was gone, and her crew had ridden her into the depths, but her captain remained. He felt a moment of overpowering shame.

Wind on his face. The mist was clearing, and the sun was riding up the morning sky. In the east it set light to a wrack of distant cloud and turned it into a tumbled melee of gold and scarlet and palest aquamarine. Hawkwood raised his head. There was a slight swell, and when it lifted him on its crest he saw he was surrounded by a horrible wreckage of bodies and parts of bodies, broken spars, limp cordage. To the west a bank of fog still lay stubbornly upon the water, but it was thinning moment by moment. Through it the ships of the enemy could be seen as a forested crowd of masts, and the early sunlight sparkled off milling hosts of armoured figures on their decks. Larger hulks, low in the water and bearing only the ragged stumps of their lower yards, drifted everywhere in and out of the fog, some burning, others appearing wholly lifeless and inert. And in the brilliant blue vault of the sky above a flock of the winged creatures was wheeling in a great spiral. Hawkwood watched as it descended, and lit upon a sinking galleon. Faint over the water came a series of shots.

Ships everywhere, looming like islands out of the mist. Hebrian galleons built to his own designs, Astaran carracks, Merduk xebecs, Gabrionese caravels. But all of them were dismasted, ablaze and sinking. The waves were thick with flotsam and jetsam, the wreckage of the greatest naval armament that history had ever seen. In the space of an hour it had been annihilated.

The *Pontifidad* had been at the forefront of the fleet, the tip of the arrow; and hence it had gone down some distance from the main body of ships. Hawkwood realised that he was drifting eastwards with the breeze, away from the lingering fog-banks and the terrible tangled mass of broken hulks to windward. Where they burned the water was still relatively calm; the weatherworking spell was fading last at its core. But here, scarcely half a sea-mile away, the wind was picking up. Hawkwood studied the sky and watched the clouds grow and darken in the west, heralding a storm. They were leaving nothing to chance, it seemed.

Had anyone else escaped from the flagship? Again, the choking sense of shame. Seven hundred men and two Kings. Lord God.

But he could not give up. He could not will himself to die – it was the same stubbornness that had kept him going all those years ago in the west. Without conscious volition he found himself scanning the pitching waves for something, anything, that might enable him to hold on to life a few hours longer.

Half a cable away a mass of wood rose and fell slowly on the swell. Deadeyes and the rags of shrouds clung to it still. Hawkwood realised it was what was left of the maintop. He struck out for it, leaving his wineskin, and for half a despairing hour fought the steeping waves with what was left of his strength. When he reached it he had not the strength to pull himself atop it, and so hung there, shivering and listless, his hands become rigid claws which no longer obeyed him. Above his head the clouds thickened, and on the wind he heard the screaming of gulls as they settled down to feast on the bounty of disaster, but he shut his eyes and hung on, no longer caring why.

AGONY IN HIS hands. He tried to cry out as they were constricted in a merciless grip, their blisters bursting, the charred skin flaying off. He was hauled out of the water, and fell with a thump to the sodden wood of the maintop wreckage. He lay there, awash, and a scream died in his salt-crusted mouth.

"It's all right, Richard. I have you."

He opened his eyes and saw only a shadow, limned black against the sky.

SIX

THE QUEEN'S CHAMBERS were a shadowed place. Despite the spring warmth of the air outside, there were fires burning in every massive hearth, and the ornate grilles that flanked each window were shut, letting in only a pale, mangled radiance that could barely compete with the blare of the firelight.

The ladies-in-waiting had all an attractive flushed look, and their low-cut gowns afforded an intriguing glimpse of the perspiration that gleamed in the hollows of their collar-bones. Corfe tugged at his own tight-fitting collar and dismissed them as they hovered around, curtseying. "Go on outside and get some air, for God's sake."

"Sire, we –"

"Go, ladies; I'll square it with your mistress."

More curtsies, and they whispered out, white hands flapping fan-like at their faces, long skirts hitched up as though they were tiptoeing through puddles. Corfe watched them go appreciatively, then collected himself.

"It's like a Macassian bath house in here!" he called. "What new fad is this, lady?"

His wife appeared from the inner bedchamber. She had a shawl wrapped about her shoulders and she leaned on an ivory cane.

"Nothing that need concern a loutish peasant up from the provinces for the day," she retorted, her voice dry and clear.

Corfe took her in his arms as carefully as though she were made of tinsel, and kissed her wrinkled forehead. It was marble-cold.

"Come, now. It's Forialon these two sennights past. There are primroses out along the side of the Kingsway. What's with this skulking in front of a fire?"

Odelia turned away. "So how was your jaunt up the road

of memory? I trust Mirren enjoyed it." She lowered herself into a well-stuffed chair by the fire, her blue-veined hands resting on top of her cane. As she did, a multi-legged, dark, furred ball skittered down the wall, climbed up her arm and nestled in the crook of her neck with a sound like a great cat's purr. A clutch of eyes shone like berries.

"It would do you good to take a jaunt yourself."

Odelia smiled. Her hair, once shining gold, had thinned and greyed, and her years sat heavily in the lines and folds of her face. Only her eyes seemed unchanged, green as a shallow sea in sunlight, and bright with life.

"I am old, Corfe. Let me be. You cannot fight time as though it were a contending army. I am old, and powerless. What gifts I possessed went into Mirren. I would have made her a boy if I could, but it was beyond me. The male line of Fantyr has come to an end. Mirren will make someone a grand queen one day, but Torunna must have a king to rule, always. We both know that only too well."

Corfe strode to a shuttered window and pulled back the heavy grilles, letting in the sun, and a cool breeze from off the Kardian in the east. He stared down at the sea of roofs below, the spires of the Pontifical palace down by the Square. The tower wherein he stood was two hundred feet high, but still he could catch the cacophony of sellers hawking their wares in the marketplace, the rattle of carts moving over cobbles, the braying of mules.

"We made slow going of it for the first few days," he said lightly. "It is incredible how quickly nature buries the works of man. The old Western Road has well-nigh disappeared."

"A very good point. Our job here is to prevent nature burying *our* works after we are gone."

"We've been over this," he said wearily.

"And will go over it again. Speaking of burying things, my time on this goodly earth is running out. I have months left, not years –"

"Don't talk like that, Odelia."

"And you must start to think of marrying again. It's all very well making these pilgrimages to the past, but the future bears looking at also. You need a male heir. Lord God, Corfe, look at the way the world is turning. Another conflict ripens at long last to bloody fruition, one whose climax could make the Merduk Wars look like a skirmish. The battles may have already begun, off Hebrion, or even before Gaderion. When you take to the field, all that is needed is one stray bullet to lose this war. Without you, this kingdom would be lost. Do not let what you have achieved turn to dust on your death."

"Oh, it's my death now? A fine conversation for a spring morning."

"You have sired no bastards – I know that – but I almost wish you had. Even an illegitimate male heir would be better than none."

"Mirren could rule this kingdom as well as any man, given time," Corfe said heatedly. Again, Odelia smiled.

"Corfe, the soldier-king, the iron general. Whose sun rises and sets on his only daughter. Do not let your love blind you, my dear. Can you see Mirren leading armies?"

He had no reply for that. She was right, of course. But the simple thought of remarrying ripped open the scars of old wounds deep in his soul. Aurungzeb, Sultan of Ostrabar had two children by – by his Queen, and several more by various concubines, it was said. Nasir, the only boy, was almost seventeen now, and Corfe had met him several times on state visits to Aurungabar. Black-haired, with sea-grey eyes – and the dark complexion of a Merduk. A son to be proud of. The girl was a couple of years younger, though she remained cloistered away in the manner of Merduk ladies.

Their mother, too, rarely left the confines of the harem these days. Corfe had not seen her in over sixteen years, but once upon a time, in a different world it seemed, she had been his wife, the love of his life. Yes, that old scar throbbed still. It would heal only when his heart stopped.

"You have a list, no doubt, of eligible successors."

"Yes. A short one, it must be said. There is a dearth of princesses at present."

He laughed, throwing his head back like a boy. "What does the world come to? So who is head of your list? Some pale Hebrian maiden? Or a dark-eyed matron of Astarac?"

"Her name is Aria. She is young, but of excellent lineage, and her father is someone we must needs bind to us with every tie we can at the present time."

"Abeleyn? Mark?" Corfe was puzzled.

"Aurungzeb, you fool. Aria is his only daughter by his Ramusian-born Queen, sister to his heir, and hence a princess of the Royal blood. Marry her, and you bind Torunna and Ostrabar together irrevocably. Sire children on her and –"

"No."

"What? I haven't finished. You must –"

"I said no. I will not marry this girl." He turned from the window and his face was bloodless as chalk. "Find another."

"I have already put out diplomatic feelers. Her father approves the match. Your issue would join the Royal houses of Ostrabar and Torunna for all time – our alliance would be rendered unbreakable."

"You did this without my permission?"

"I am still Torunna's Queen!" she lashed out, some of the old fire flashing from her marvellous eyes. "I do not need your permission every time I piss in a pot!"

"You need it for this," he said softly and his own eyes were winter-cold, hard as flint.

"What is your objection? The girl is young, admittedly, but then I'm not quite dead yet. She is a rare beauty by all accounts, the very image of her mother, and sweet-natured to boot."

"By God, you're well-informed."

"I make it my business to be." Her voice softened. "Corfe, I'm dying. Let me do this last thing for you, for the kingdom. I know I have not been much of a wife to you these last years –"

He strode from the window and knelt on one knee beside her chair. The skin of her face was gossamer thin under his hand. He felt that she might blow away in the breeze from the windows. "You've been a wife and more than a wife. You've been a friend and counsellor, and a great queen."

"Then grant me this last wish. Keep Torunna together. Marry this girl. Have a son – a whole clutch of sons. You also are mortal."

"What about Mirren?"

"She must marry young Nasir."

He shut his eyes. The old pain burned, deep in his chest. That one he had seen coming. But marry Heria's daughter – his own wife's child? Never.

He rose, his face like stone. "We will discuss this another time, lady."

"We are discussing it *now*."

"I think not." Turning on his heel he left the darkened chamber without a backward glance.

A COURTIER WAS waiting for him outside. "Sire, I've been instructed by Colonel Heyn to tell you that the couriers are in with despatches from Gaderion."

"Good. I'll meet them in the Bladehall. My compliments to the Colonel, and he is to join me there as soon as he can. The same message to General Formio and the rest of the High Command." The courtier saluted and fled.

Corfe's personal bodyguard, Felorin, caught up with him in the corridor as he strode along with his boots clinking on the polished stone. Not a word was spoken as the pair made their way through the Queen's wing to the palace proper. There were fewer courtiers than there had been in King Lofantyr's day, and they were clad in sober burgundy. When the King passed them they each saluted as soldiers would. Only the court ladies were as finely plumaged as they had ever been, and they collapsed delicately into curtsies as Corfe blew past. He nodded to them but never slowed his stride for an instant.

They crossed the audience hall, their footsteps echoing in its austere emptiness, and the palace passageways and chambers grew less grand, older-looking. There was more timber and less stone. When the Fimbrians had built the palace of Torunn it had been the seat of the Imperial Governor, who was also the general of a sizeable army. This part of the complex had originally been part of that army's barracks but until Corfe came to the throne had been used mainly as a series of storerooms. Corfe had restored it to its original purpose, and housed within it now were living quarters for five hundred men – the bodyguard of the King. These were volunteers from the army and elsewhere who had passed a rigorous training regimen designed by Corfe himself. Within their ranks served Fimbrians, Torunnans, Cimbric tribesmen, and even a sizeable element of Merduks. In garrison they dressed in sable and scarlet surcoats, the old *blood and bruises* that John Mogen's men had once worn. In the field they rode heavy warhorses – even the Fimbrians – and were armed with pistols and long sabres. Both they and their steeds were accustomed to wearing three-quarter armour, which Torunnan smiths had tempered so finely that it would turn even an arquebus ball. On the breastplate of every man's cuirass was a shallow spherical indentation where this had been put to the test.

"Where is Comillan today?" Corfe barked to Felorin.

"On the proving grounds, with the new batch."

"And Formio?"

"On his way in from Menin Field."

"We'll get there first, then. Run ahead, Felorin, and set up the Bladehall for a conference. Maps of the Torrin Gap, a clear sand-table and some brandy – you know the drill."

Felorin gave his monarch a strange look, though his tattooing rendered his expression hard to read at the best of times. "Brandy?"

"Yes, damn it. I could do with one. Now cut along."

Felorin took off at a run, whereas Corfe's pace slowed. Finally he halted, and propped himself by a windowsill which looked out on the proving grounds below, where a new set of recruits were being put through their paces. The glass was blurred with age, but he was able to make out the man-high wooden posts sunk in the ground, and the lines of sweating men who hacked at them with the arm-killing practice-swords whose blunt blades housed a core of lead. They had to strike defined spots at shoulder, waist and knee height on the right and then the left sides of the iron-hard old posts, and keep doing it until their palms blistered and the sweat ran in their eyes and their backs were raw masses of screaming muscle. Over thirty years before, Corfe had stood out there and hacked at those same posts while the drill-sergeants had shouted and jeered at him. Some things, at least, did not change.

The Bladehall was new, however. A long, vaulted, church-like building, Corfe had had it constructed after the Battle of the Torian Plains ten years before, close to the old quartermaster stores where he had once found five hundred sets of Merduk armour mouldering and used them to arm his first command. He disliked using the old conference chambers for staff meetings because they were in the palace, and curious courtiers and maids were always in and out. Though Odelia might remind him tartly that the older venue had been good enough for Kaile Ormann himself, Corfe felt a need to break with the past. He also wanted to create somewhere for the officers of the army to come together without the inevitable delays that entering the palace complex entailed. Deep down, he also welcomed any opportunity to get out of the palace himself, even now.

Still a peasant with mud under my nails, after all this time, he thought with sour satisfaction.

Along the walls of the Bladehall were ranged suits of antique armour and weapons, tapestries and paintings depicting past battles and wars won and lost. And near the massive timber beams that supported the roof were hung the war-banners and flags of generations of Torunnan armies. They had been found scattered in storerooms throughout the palace complex after Corfe had become King. Some were tattered and rotting, but others, crafted of finest silk and laid aside with more care, were as whole as the day they had waved overhead on a shot-torn field.

Set into the walls were hundreds of scroll-pigeonholes, each of which held a map. On the upper galleries were shelves of books also: manuals, histories, treatises on tactics and strategy. Several sycophantic nobles had begged Corfe to write a general treatise on war years ago, but he had curtly refused. He might be a successful general, but he was no writer – and he would not dictate his clumsy sentences to a scribe so that some inky-fingered parasite might polish them up for public consumption afterwards.

Hung above the lintel of the huge fireplace at one end of the hall was John Mogen's sword, the Answerer. Corfe had carried it at the North More, at the King's Battle, and at Armagedir. A gift from the Queen, it had hung there with the firelight playing upon it for a decade now, for Torunna's King had not taken to the field in all that time.

There were large tables ringed with chairs set about the

floor of the lower Bladehall, and seated at these were several young men in Torunnan military uniform, trying hard to ignore the two muddy couriers who stood wearily to one side. Corfe encouraged his officers to come in here and read when they were off duty, or to study tactical problems on the long sand-table that stood in one of the side-chambers. Attendants were permanently on hand to serve food and drink in the small adjoining refectory, should that be required. In this way, among others, Corfe had tried to encourage the birth of a more truly professional officer class, one based on merit and not on birth or seniority. All officers were equal when they stepped over the threshold of the Bladehall, and even the most junior might speak freely. More importantly perhaps, the gratuities which army commanders had traditionally accepted in return for the granting of commissions had been stamped out. All would-be commanders started as lowly ensigns attached to an infantry tercio, and they sweated it out in the proving grounds the same as all other new recruits. Strange to say, once Corfe had instituted this reform, the proportion of gallant young blue-bloods joining the army had plummeted. He smiled at the thought.

There was as yet no formal military academy in Torunna, as existed in Fimbir, but it was something Corfe had been mulling over in his mind for several years. Though he was an almost absolute ruler, he still had to bear in mind the views of the important families of the kingdom. They would never dare to take the field against him again, but their opposition to many of his policies had been felt in subtler ways. They would see an academy of war as a means to build up a whole new hierarchy in the kingdom, based not on blood but on military merit. And they would be right.

The young men in the Bladehall ceased their reading. They stood up as Corfe entered and he returned their salutes. The two couriers doffed their helms.

"Your names?"

"Gell and Brinian, sir. Despatches from –"

"Yes I know. Give them here." Corfe was handed two leather cylinders. The same despatch would be in both. "Any problems on the road?"

"No, sir. Some wolves near Arboronn, but we outran them."

"When did you leave Gaderion?"

"Five days ago."

"Good work, lads. You look all in. Tell the cooks here to give you whatever you want, and change into some fresh clothes. I will need you back here later, but for now, get some rest." The couriers saluted and, gathering up their muddy cloaks, left for the refectory. Corfe turned to the other occupants of the hall, who had not moved.

"Brascian, Phelor, Grast." The three were standing together. At a table alone stood a dark young officer of medium height. Corfe frowned. "Ensign, forgive me. I do not recall your name."

The youngster stiffened further. "Ensign Baraz, your Majesty. We have not yet met."

"Officers simply call me *sir* in garrison. Are you part of the Ostrabarian Baraz family?"

"My mother's brother was Shahr Baraz the Queen's bodyguard, and my grandfather was the same Shahr Baraz who took Aurungabar, your – sir. I kept the Baraz name as I was the last male of the line."

"It was called Aekir, then. I do not know your uncle, but your grandfather was an able general, and a fine man, by all accounts." Corfe stared closely at Baraz. "How is it that you are become an ensign in the Torunnan army?"

"I volunteered, sir. General Formio inducted me himself, not three months ago."

When Corfe said nothing, Baraz spoke up again. "My family has been out of favour at the Ostrabarian court for many years. It is known all over the east that you will take loyal men of any race into your forces. I would like to try for the bodyguard, sir."

"You will have to gain some experience, then. Have you completed your provenance?"

"Yes sir. Last week."

"Then consider yourself attached to the general staff for the moment. We're short of interpreters."

"Sir, I would much prefer to be attached to a tercio."

"You'll follow orders, Ensign."

The young man seemed to sag minutely. "Yes, sir." Corfe kept his face grave.

"Very good. There's to be a conference of the staff here in a few minutes. You may sit in." He nodded to the other three officers who were still ramrod straight. "As may you gentlemen. It will do you good to see the wrangling of the staff, though you will of course say nothing of what you hear to anyone. Clear?" A chorus of *yes, sirs* and a bobbing of heads and hastily smothered grins.

MENIN FIELD WAS the name given to the new parade grounds which had been flattened out to the north of Torunn. They covered hundreds of acres, and allowed vast formations to be marched and counter-marched without terrain disordering the ranks. At their northern end, a tall plinth of solid stone stood dark and sombre; a monument to the war dead of the country. It towered over the drilling troops below like a watchful giant, and it was said that in times of trouble the shadows of past armies would gather about it in the night, ready to serve Torunna again.

General Formio raised his eyes from the courier-borne note to the knot of officers who sat their horses around him.

"I am wanted by the King; news from the north, it seems. Colonel Melf, you will take over the remainder of the exercise. Gribben's tercios are still a shambles. They will continue to drill until they can perform open order on the march without degenerating into a rabble. Gentlemen, carry on." He wheeled his horse away to a flurry of salutes.

Formio had years before bowed to necessity, and went mounted now like all other senior officers. He was Corfe's second-in-command in Torunn, and had been for so long now that people almost forgot he was a foreigner; a Fimbrian, no less. He had changed little since the Merduk Wars. His hair had gone grey at the temples and his old wounds ached in the winter, but otherwise he was as hale as he had been before Armagedir, from whose field he had been plucked broken and dying sixteen years before. Queen Odelia had saved his life, and her ladies-in-waiting had nursed him through a series of fevered relapses. But he had survived, and Junith, one of those ladies, had become his wife. He had two sons now, one of whom would be of an age to begin his provenance in another couple of years. He was not unique: almost all the Fimbrians who had survived Armagedir had taken Torunnan wives.

Of the circle of officers and friends which had surrounded the King in those days only he and Aras now remained, and Aras was up in the north holding Gaderion and the Torrin Gap against the Himerians. But there were fresh faces in the army now, a whole host of them. An entirely new generation of officers and soldiers had filled the ranks. They had been youngsters when Aekir had fallen, and the savage struggle to overcome the hosts of Aurungzeb was a childhood story, or something to be read in a book or celebrated in song. In the subsequent years the Merduks had become Torunna's allies. They worshipped the same God, and the same man as his messenger. Ahrimuz or Ramusio, it was all one. There were Merduk bishops now in the Macrobian Church, and Torunnan clerics prayed in the temple of Pir-Sar in Aurungabar, which had once been the cathedral of Carcasson. And in the very bodyguard of King Corfe himself, Merduks served with honour.

But the years of near-peace had bred other legacies. The Torunnan army had been a formidable force back in King Lofantyr's day; now it was widely held to be invincible. Formio was not so sure. A certain amount of complacency had crept through the ranks in recent years. And more importantly, the number of veterans left in those ranks was dwindling fast. He had no doubts about his own countrymen – war ran in their blood. And the tribesmen who made up the bulk of the Cathedrallers viewed war as a normal way of life. But the Torunnans were different. Fully three quarters of those now enrolled in the army had never experienced the reality of combat.

It had been ten years now since the Himerians had sent an army into the Gap. There had been no effort at diplomacy, no warning. It was obvious to the world that the regime headed by one Pontiff could never recognise or treat with the regime which protected another.

The enemy had advanced tentatively, feeling their way eastwards. Corfe had moved with breakneck speed, a forced march out of Torunn that left a tenth of the army by the side of the road, exhausted. He had not paused, but had launched into the enemy with the Cathedrallers and the Orphans alone, and had thrown them back over the Torian Plains with huge losses. Formio remembered the wreckage of the Knights Militant as they counter-charged his lines of pikes with suicidal courage but little tactical insight. The big horses, disembowelled and screaming. Their riders pinned by the weight of their armour, trampled to a bloody mire as the Cathedrallers rode over them to finish the job. The Battle of the Torian Plains seemed to have given the Himerian leadership pause for thought. It was said that the Mage Bardolin had been present in person, though it had never been confirmed.

Not once since then had there been a general engagement. The enemy had built outposts of stone and timber and turf and had advanced them as far into the foothills as he dared, but he had not cared to risk another full-scale battle. The Thurian Line, as this system of fortifications had come to be known, now marked the border between Torunna and the Second Empire.

Ten years, and another turnover of faces. The men of the Torunnan army were as well trained as a professional like King Corfe could make them, but they were essentially unblooded.

This was about to change.

In the Bladehall, the fires had been lit and the map-table was dominated by a representation of Barossa, the land bounded by the Searil and Torrin rivers to east and west, and by the Thurians in the north. Blue and red counters were dotted about the map like gambling tokens. *In some respects*, Formio thought grimly, *that is what they are.*

"How are they shaping up, General?" Corfe asked the Fimbrian. He held an empty brandy-glass in one fist and a crumpled despatch in the other. Surrounding him were a cluster of other officers, several of whom looked as though they had yet to start shaving.

"They're good, but only on a parade-ground. Take them out in the rough and their formations go all to pieces. They need more field-manoeuvres."

Corfe nodded. "They will get them soon enough. Gentlemen, we have despatches just in from Aras in the north. The Sea of Tor is now largely clear of ice, and Himerian transports are as thick upon it as flies on jam. The enemy is massively reinforcing his outposts in the Gap. At least two other armies are marching down from Tarber and Finnmark. They began crossing the Tourbering River on the 15th."

"Any idea about numbers, sir?" a squat, brutal-looking officer asked.

"The Finnmarkan and Tarberan forces total at least forty thousand men. Added to the troops already in position, and I believe we could well be talking in the region of seventy thousand."

There was a murmur of dismay. Aras had less than half that in Gaderion.

"It will take them at least four or five days to cross the river. Aras sent out a flying column last month which burned the bridges, and the Tourbering is in full spate with the meltwater from the mountains."

"But once they're across," the squat officer pointed out, "they'll make good time across the plains south of there. Any word on composition, sir?"

"Very little, Comillan. Local intelligence is poor. We do know that King Skarp-Hedin is present in person, as is Prince Adalbard of Tarber. The northern principalities have historically been weak in cavalry. Their backbone is heavy infantry."

"*Gallowglasses*," someone said, and Corfe nodded.

"Old-fashioned, but still effective, even against horse. And their skirmishers continue to use javelins. Good troops for rough ground, but not of much account in the open. My guess is that the Himerians will send out a screen of the light northern troops before probing with their heavies."

They all stared at the map and its counters. Now the red blocks laid square across the inked line of the Tourbering river had a distinctively menacing air. Similar blocks were set in a line north east of the Sea of Tor. Opposing them all was the single blue square of Aras's command.

"If that's their plan, then it buys us some time," Formio said, breaking the silence. "The northerners will be almost two weeks marching across the Torian Plains."

"Yes," Corfe agreed. "Enough time for us to reinforce Aras.

I plan to transport many our own troops upon the Torrin, which will save time, and wear and tear on the horses."

"This is it then, Corfe?" Formio asked. "The general mobilisation?"

Corfe met his friend's eye. "This is it, Formio. All roads, it seems, lead to the Gap. They may try and sneak a few columns through the southern foothills, but the Cimbriani will help take care of those. And Admiral Berza is liaising with the Nalbeni in the Kardian to protect that southern flank."

"Bad terrain," Comillan said. His black eyes were hooded and he tugged at the ends of his heavy moustache reflectively. "Those foothills up around Gaderion are pretty broken. The cavalry will be next to useless, unless we remount them on goats."

"I know," Corfe told him. They've pushed their outposts right up to the mountains, so we've little room to manoeuvre unless we abandon Gaderion and fall back to the plains below. And that, gentlemen, will not happen."

"So we're on the defensive, then?" a voice asked. The senior officers turned. It was Ensign Baraz. His fellow subalterns stared at him in shock for a second and then stood wooden and insensible. One moved slightly on the balls of his feet as though he would like to be physically dissociated from his colleague's temerity.

"Who in Hell – ?" Comillan began angrily, but Corfe held up a hand.

"Is that your conclusion, Ensign?"

The young man flushed. "Our forces have been brought up thinking of the offensive, sir. It's how they are trained and equipped."

"And yet their greatest victories have been defensive ones."

"The strategic defensive sir, but always the tactical offensive."

Corfe smiled. "Excellent. Gentlemen, our young friend has hit the nail on the head. We are fighting to defend Torunna, as we once fought to defend it from his forefathers – but we did not win that war by sitting tight behind stone walls. We must keep the enemy off-balance at all times, so that he can never muster his strength sufficiently to land a killer blow. To do that, we must attack."

"Where, sir?" Comillan asked. "His outposts are well sited. The Thurian Line could soak up an assault of many thousands."

"His outposts should be assaulted if possible, and in some force. But that is not where I intend the heaviest blow to fall." Corfe bent his head. "Where could we do the most damage, eh? Think."

The assembled officers were silent. Corfe met Formio's eyes. The two of them had already discussed this in private, and had violently disagreed, but the Fimbrian was not going to say a word.

"Charibon," Ensign Baraz said at last. "You're going to make for Charibon."

A collective hiss of indrawn breath. "Don't be absurd, boy," Comillan snapped, his black eyes flashing. "Sir –"

"The boy is right, Comillan."

The commander of the bodyguard was shocked speechless.

"It can't be done," someone said.

"Why not?" Corfe asked softly. "Don't be shy now, gentlemen. List me the reasons."

"First of all," Comillan said, "the Thurian Line is too strong to be quickly overrun. We would take immense casualties in a general assault, and a battering by artillery would give him enough time to bring up masses of reinforcements, or even build a second line behind the first. And the terrain. As was said earlier, our shock troops need mobility to be most effective. You cannot throw cavalry, or even pikemen, at solid walls, or over broken ground."

"Correct. But forget about the Thurian Line for a moment. Let us talk about Charibon itself. What problems does it pose?"

"A large garrison, sir?" one of the ensigns ventured.

"Yes. But don't forget that most of the troops about the monastery city will be drawn eastwards to assault Gaderion. Charibon is largely unwalled. What defences it has were built in the second century, before gunpowder. As fortresses go, it is very weak, and could be taken without a large siege train."

"But to get to it you would have to force the passage of the Thurian Line anyway," Colonel Heyd of the Cuirassiers pointed out. "And to do that, Charibon's field armies would have to be destroyed. We have not the men for it."

"I had not finished, Heyd. Charibon's man-made defences may be weak, but her natural ones are formidable. Look here." Corfe bent over the map on the table. "To the east and north she is shielded by the Sea of Tor. To the south-east, the Cimbrics. Only to the west and north are there easy approaches for an attacking army, and even then the northern approach is crossed by the line of the Saeroth River. Charibon does not need walls. It is guarded by geography. On the other hand, if the city were suddenly attacked, with its forces heavily engaged to the east in the Torrin Gap, then the enemy would have an almost impossible time recalling them to her defence – the problems bedevilling an attacker would suddenly be working against the defender. The only swift way to recall them would be to transport them back across the Sea of Tor in ships. And ships can be burnt."

"All well and good, sire," Comillan said, clearly exasperated, "if our troops could fly. But they can't. There are no passes in the Cimbrics there that I know of. How else do you suggest we transport them?"

"What if there were another way to get to Charibon, bypassing the Thurian Line?"

Dawning wonder on all their faces save Formio's.

"Is there such a way, sir?" Comillan asked harshly.

"There may be. There may be. The point is, gentlemen, that we cannot afford a war of attrition. We are outnumbered and, as Ensign Baraz pointed out, on the defensive. I do not want to go hacking at the tail of the snake – I intend to cut off its head. If we destroy the Himerian Triumvirate, this continent-wide empire of theirs will fall apart."

He straightened up from the map and stared at them all intently.

"I intend to lead an army across the Cimbric mountains, to assault Charibon from the rear."

No-one spoke. Formio stared at the map, at the line of the Cimbrics drawn in heavy black ink. They were among the highest peaks in the world, it was said, and even in spring the snow on them lay yards deep.

"At the same time," Corfe went on calmly, "Aras will

assault the Thurian Line. He will press the assault with enough vigour to persuade the enemy that it is a genuine attempt to break through to the plains beyond, but what he will actually be doing is drawing off troops from the defence of the monastery city. A third operation will be a raid on the docks at the eastern end of the Sea of Tor. The enemy transport fleet must be destroyed. That done, and we have him like a bull straddling a gate."

"But first the Cimbrics must be crossed," Formio said.

"Yes. And of that I shall say no more at present. But make no mistake, gentlemen, we must win this war quickly. The first battles have already begun. I have communications from the west to the effect that the fleet of the Grand Alliance is about to go into action. A Fimbrian embassy has been reported at Charibon. It is likely that Himerian troops have been granted passage through Fimbria to attack Hebrion, and we know that they are massing on the borders of East Astarac. We are not alone in this war, but we are the only kingdom with the necessary forces to win it."

Formio continued to stare at his King and friend. He drew close. "No retreat, Corfe," he said in a pleading murmur. "If you fail in front of Charibon, there is *no retreat*."

"What of the Fimbrians?" Heyd, the square, straight-lipped officer who was commander of the Torunnan Cuirassiers asked.

"They are the great unknown quantity in this equation. Clearly, they favour the Empire for the moment, but only because they consider our armies to be the greater threat. I believe they think they can manage Aruan – think how easy it would be for them to send a great host eastwards to sack Charibon. If we are considering it, you may be sure they have. No, they want the Empire to break us down, along with the other members of the Alliance, and then they will strike, thinking to rebuild their ancient hegemony out of the ruins of a war-torn continent. They are mistaken. Once the true scale of this war becomes apparent, I am hoping they will think again."

"And if they don't?" Formio asked, looking his King in the eye.

"Then we'll have to beat them as well."

SEVEN

THERE WAS A storm, out in the west. For two days now the people of Abrusio had watched it rise up on the horizon until the boiling clouds blotted out fully half the sky. Each evening the sun sank into it like a molten ball of iron sinking into a bed of ash, its descent lit up by the flicker of distant lightning. The clouds seemed unaffected by the west wind that was blowing steadily landwards. They towered like ramparts of tormented stone on the brim of the world, the harbingers of monstrous tidings.

Abrusio was a silent city. For days the wharves had been crowded with people – not dockworkers or mariners or longshoremen, but the common citizenry of the port. They stood in sombre crowds upon the jetties and all along the waterfront, talking in murmurs and staring out past the harbour moles to the troubled horizon beyond. Even at night they remained, lighting fires and standing around them like men hypnotised, watching the sea-lightning. There was little ribaldry or revelry. Wine was passed round and drunk without enjoyment. All eyes were raised again and again to the mole-beacons at the end of the Outer Roads. They would be lit to signal the return of the fleet. To signal victory, perhaps, in a war none of the people standing there truly understood.

They could be seen from the palace balconies, these waterfront fires. It was as though the docks were silently ablaze. Golophin had reckoned there were a hundred thousand people – a quarter of the city's population – standing down there with their eyes fixed on the sea.

Isolla, Queen of Hebrion, stood with the old wizard and looked out at the storm-wracked western ocean from one of those palace balconies. She was a tall, spare woman in her forties with a strong face and freckled skin. Her wonderful red-glinting hair had been scraped back from that face and was covered by a simple lace hood.

"What's happening out there, Golophin? It's been too long."

The wizard set a hand lightly on her shoulder. His glabrous face was dark and set and he opened his mouth to speak, then paused. The hand left her shoulder and bunched into a bony fist. Faint around it grew an angry white glimmer. Then it faded again.

"They're stopping me from going to him, Isolla. It's not Aruan, it's someone or something else. There is a powerful mage out there in that storm, and he has thrown up a barrier that nothing, not ships or wizards or even the elements of the sea and earth itself can penetrate. I have tried, God knows."

"What can cannon and cutlasses do against such magic?"

The wizard's jaw bunched. "I should have been there, it's true. I should have been there."

"Don't torture yourself. We've been over this."

"I – I know. He picked his moment well. Isolla. My only hope is that this mage, whoever he is, will have expended himself maintaining this monstrous weatherworking spell, and so will not be able to aid in any attack on the ships. They will have to be assaulted using more conventional means, and thus, valour, cold steel and gunpowder may yet count for something for those who are trapped out there."

She did not look at him. "And if they do not count for enough? What do we do then?"

"We make ready to repel an invasion."

"An invasion of *what*, Golophin? The country is near panic, not knowing who we war with. The Second Empire, some say. The Fimbrians, say others. In the name of God, what exactly is out there?"

The old wizard did not reply, but traced a glowing shape in the air with one long finger. The shape of a glyph flashed for a second and was gone. Nothing. It was like staring at a stone wall.

"We fight Aruan, and whatever he has brought out of the uttermost west with him. We know not exactly what we fight, Isolla, but we know that it is dedicated to the overthrow of every kingdom in the west. They are out there, in that storm, our enemies, but I cannot tell you what manner of men they are, or if they are men at all. You have heard the stories which have come down through the years, the tales about Hawkwood's voyage. Some are fanciful, some are not. We know there are ships, but we do not know what is in them. There is a power, but we are not sure who wields it. But it is coming. And I fear that our last attempt to rebuff it has failed." His voice was thick with grief and a strangled fury.

"It has failed."

ONE HALF OF the night sky had been obliterated, but the other was ablaze with stars. It was by these that Richard Hawkwood navigated his little craft. He had found a scrap of canvas that afternoon, barely big enough to cover a nobleman's table, and he had rigged up a rude mast and yard from broken ship's timbers. Now the steady west wind was blowing him back towards Hebrion, though the maintop-wreckage that formed his raft was awash in a two-foot swell, and he had to keep one end of the knotted stay that kept his little mast erect bunched round his pus-oozing and skinless fist.

His companion, hooded and anonymous, squatted unconcernedly on the sodden wood as the swell broke over them both and caked them with salt. Hawkwood wedged himself in place, shivering, and regarded the hooded figure with the burning eyes of a fever-victim.

"So you came back. What is it this time, Bardolin? Another warning of imminent catastrophe? I fear you are talking to the wrong man. I am fish-bait now."

"And yet, Richard, you strive to survive at every turn. Your actions contradict the brave despair of your words. I have never seen one so determined to live."

"It is a weakness of mine, I must confess."

The hood shook with what might have been a silent chuckle. "I have news for you. You will survive. This wind will waft you back into the very port you sailed from."

"It's been arranged, then."

"Everything has been arranged, Captain. Nothing is left to chance in this world, not any more."

Hawkwood frowned. Something about the dark figure

seated opposite him made him hesitate. Then he said, "Bardolin?"

The hood was thrown back, to reveal a hawk-nosed, autocratic face and a hairless pate. The eyes were black hollows in the night, like the sockets in a skull.

"Not Bardolin."

"Then who in the hell are you?"

"I have many names, Richard – I may call you Richard? – but in the beginning I was Aruan of Garmidalan." He bowed his head with mocking courtesy.

Hawkwood tried to move, but the murderous lunge he had attempted turned into a feeble lurch. The rope which belayed his little mast had sunk into the burnt flesh of his palm and could not be released. The pain made him retch emptily. Aruan straightened and levered the mast back into place. The canvas flapped, then drew taut again. The two men sat looking at one another as the raft rose and fell on the waves, their crests glittering in the starlight.

"Come to finish the job?" Hawkwood croaked.

"Yes, but not in the way you think. Compose yourself, Captain. If I wished you dead I would not have permitted Bardolin to visit you, and I would not be here now. Look at you – this suffering could have been avoided had you but followed your friend's advice of last night. Your sense of honour is admirable, but misguided."

Hawkwood could not speak. The pain of his salt-soaked burns was a ceaseless shuddering agony, and his tongue rasped like sand against his teeth.

"You are to be my messenger, Richard. You will return to Abrusio and relay my terms."

"Terms?" The word felt like crushed glass in his mouth.

"Hebrion and Astarac are defeated, their Kings dead, their nobility decimated. Their eggs, shall we say, were all in the one basket. Yes, you will tell me that their land armies are intact, but you have seen the forces at my disposal. There is no army in the world which can stand against my children, even if it is commanded by a Mogen, or a Corfe. I was of Astarac myself once upon a time. I have no wish to see these kingdoms laid waste. I am not a barbarian."

"You are a monster."

Aruan laughed softly. "Perhaps, perhaps. But a monster with a conscience. You will survive, as I have always allowed you to survive, and you will go to your friend Golophin. Hebrion and Astarac must surrender to me, unless you wish to see them suffer the same fate as the fleet they sent against me. It may be better this way, now I think of it. You are a very convincing survivor of disaster, Captain, and you are a good witness."

"You go to Hell."

"We are all in Hell already. Imagine my hosts running amok through all the kingdoms of the west. Imagine the blood, the terror, the mountains of corpses. You want that no more than I. And Golophin, especially, will know that I make no idle boasts. I mean what I say. Hebrion and Astarac must surrender to the Second Empire, hand over all that remains of their nobility, and accept my suzerainty. If they do not, I will make of them a desert, and their peoples I will render into carrion."

Aruan's eyes lit up as he spoke with a hungry yellow light that had nothing human about it. His voice thickened and deepened. A powerful animal stink that lingered a moment, and then was swept away by the wind.

Hawkwood stared at the lightning-shot clouds in their wake. His eyes stung and smarted. "What manner of thing are you?"

"The new breed, you might say. The future. For centuries men have been pouring their energies into the fighting of their endless, worthless wars, many started in defence of a God they have never seen. Or else they cudgel their brains to think up more efficient ways of winning them – this they call science, the advance of civilisation. They turn their backs on the powers within them, because these are deemed evil. But what is more evil, the magic that heals a wound or the gunpowder that inflicts it? It is baffling to me, Hawkwood. I do not understand why so many clever men think that I and my kind are such an abomination."

"I never thought so. I've hired weatherworkers before now and been damned glad of them. Torunna's Queen is a witch, it is said, and is respected across the continent. The Mage Golophin has been Abeleyn's right hand for twenty years. And Bardolin –"

"Yes – and Bardolin?"

"He was my friend."

"He is yet."

"I doubt that somehow."

"You see? Suspicion. Fear. These names you drop are isolated instances, the exceptions that prove the rule. Four hundred years ago every Royal court had a mage, every army had a cadre of wizards, and every city a thriving Thaumaturgist's Guild. Hedge-witches and oldwives were a part of ordinary life. That cursed Ramusio changed everything, he and his ravings. This God you people worship has now hounded my people to the brink of extinction. How can you blame us for fighting back?"

"It was your creature, Himerius, who instigated the worst of the purges eighteen years ago now. How was that fighting back?"

Aruan paused. The yellow light flickered again. "That was a means to an end, painful but necessary. I had to separate my folk from yours; make clear to all men the division between the two."

"Otherwise, you might have found wizards ranged against you when you attacked the western kingdoms, fighting for their own kings – your cause would not be so clear-cut. You want power. Don't try to dress it up as a crusade."

Aruan laughed. "You are a perceptive man, Richard. Yes, I want power. Why shouldn't I? But in this world unless you are somebody's son you are nothing. You know that as well as anyone. Why should mankind be ruled by a flock of fools just because they were dropped in a Royal bed? I want power. I have the means to take it. I will take it."

Again, Hawkwood stared past his companion, into the storm-shot western sky where the lightnings shivered and the black clouds blotted out the stars. Those fine ships, those Kings of men and that huge armament with its guns and its banners and its tall beauty.

"All gone. All of them."

"Very nearly all. It is a shock, I know. Men place such confidence in an array of power that it blinds them to its weaknesses. Ships must float, and must have wind to propel them."

"We should have had weather-workers of our own."

"There are none left, not in all the Five Kingdoms. Whatever you say, they are mine now, the Dweomer-folk. They have suffered for centuries under the rule of blind, bigoted fools. No longer. Their hour is come at last. This narrow land, Captain, is about to be fashioned anew."

"Golophin did not turn traitor. Not all the Dweomer-folk think of you as their saviour."

"Ah yes. My friend Golophin. I have not given up on him yet. You and he are very similar – stubborn to the core. Men who cannot be browbeaten or threatened or bought. That is why he is such a prize. I want him to see sense in his own time, and I am willing to wait."

"Corfe of Torunna will never bow the knee to you either."

"No. Another noble and misguided fool. He will be destroyed, along with that much-vaunted army of his. My storm will fell the oaks and leave the willows standing, and this little continent of yours will be a better place for it."

"Save your breath. I caught a glimpse of that better place of yours in the fog. I want no part of it."

"That is a pity, but I am not surprised. These are the labour pangs of the world. There will be pain, and blood, but a new beginning when it is over. The night is darkest just before the dawn."

"Spare me the rhetoric. You sound to me the same as any other grasping noble. You're not making a new world, you're just grabbing at the old and destroying anything that stands in your way. Those who fish the seas or till the land will have a change of masters, but their lives will not change. They'll pay their taxes to a different face, is all."

Aruan bent towards Hawkwood with a smile that was a snarled baring of teeth. "You are wrong there, Captain. You have no idea what I have in store for the world." He stood up, seemingly unaffected by the pitching of the raft. "Take my terms to Golophin. He may take them or leave them; I do not negotiate. This wind will bear you home in another day or two. Stay alive, Hawkwood. Deliver your message, and then find a hole to crawl into somewhere. My forbearance is at an end."

And he was gone. Hawkwood was alone on the raft, the

waves black and cold in the night. His claw-hands were cramped in salt-racked torture and the fever in him beat up a blaze within his blood. He shouted wordless defiance at the empty sea, the blank glitter of the uncaring stars.

DAWN SAW THE Hebros mountains rise blue and tranquil out of the horizon – but they were to the north. Hawkwood was baffled for a few minutes until he realised that some time in the night he must have passed Grios Point. He had travelled some thirty leagues.

The wind had backed several points in the last few hours and was still right aft, but now it was blowing west-south-west. He was being propelled up the Gulf of Hebrion, and the spindrift was flying off the crests of the waves in streamers around him, while the rope that supported his little mast had disappeared into a mound of tight, puffed flesh that had once been his hand.

The sunlight hurt his eyes and he clenched them shut, drifting in and out of delirium. It was the sound of gulls that woke him, a great derisive cloud of them. They were hovering and fighting over a small cluster of herrin-yawls which were hove-to half a league away. The crews were hauling in the catch of the night hand over fist, and even from where he was Hawkwood could see the silver glint of fish-flanks as they squirmed in the bulging nets. He tried to rise, to shout, but his throat had closed and he was too weak to raise so much as an arm. No matter. The breeze was at his back, and sending his unwieldy craft right into their midst. Half a glass maybe, and he would be hauled in along with their glinting catch, bearing his fearsome message for the kingdom. And after that was done, if he still lived, he would follow Aruan's advice, and find a hole to climb into. Or maybe the neck of a bottle.

"WHERE IS HE?" Isolla asked urgently.

"Peace, Isolla. He is being carried here as we speak by a file of marines."

"A file may not be enough. Do you hear the crowds

down there? I have ordered out the garrison. The city is ablaze with torches."

Golophin listened. It was a sound like the surf of a distant, raging sea. Tens of thousands of people in a panicked fever of speculation, clogging the streets, choking the city-gates. A mob maddened by fear of the unknown. All this in the space of a few hours. The yawl which bore the survivor had put in to the Inner Roads late in the afternoon, and the marines sent to fetch him to the palace were moving more slowly than speculation.

"Bad news travels fast. Have you summoned the nobles?"

"What is left of them. They're waiting in the abbey. My God, Golophin, what does it mean?" There were tears in her eyes, the first time he had seen her weep in many years. She truly loved Abeleyn, and now she was jumping to conclusions about his fate like everyone else. Golophin felt a pang of pure despair. He knew in his heart what this castaway they had found would tell him. But he had to hear it aloud, from someone who had been there.

A thump on the door. They had repaired to the Queen's chambers, as all the rest of the palace was in an uproar. Rumour sped faster than a galloping horse, and all over the city men were wailing that the fleet was destroyed, and that they were now about to face an invasion of – what? That was the core of the panic. The ignorance. And all the best officers of the kingdom had been on board those proud ships. All that were left were time-servers and passed-over incompetents. Hebrion had been decapitated.

If the fleet is lost, Golophin reminded himself. The door was thumped again.

"Enter," Isolla called, composing herself. A burly marine with a livid scratch on his face put his head round the door. All the maids had been sent away.

"Your Majesty, we have him here. We brought him on a handcart, but that got snarled up , so we –"

"Bring him in," Golophin snapped.

It was Hawkwood. They had not known that. Isolla's hand went to her mouth as the marines carried him in. They set him on the Queen's own four-poster and then stood like men who have had the wind knocked out of them.

They were all looking at Golophin, then at the wrecked shape on the bed as though waiting for some explanation. In a kindlier voice, Golophin said, "There's wine in the antechamber, sergeant. You and your men help yourselves, and remain there. I shall want to question you later."

The marines saluted and clanked out. As the door banged shut behind them Golophin leaned over the body on the bed. "Richard. Richard, wake up. Isolla, bring over that ewer, and the things on the tray. Water, lots of it. Hunt up one of those bloody maids."

Hawkwood had been terribly injured. Half his beard had been burnt off and his face was a raw, glistening wound which was bubbled with blisters and oozing fluid. His arms and chest had also suffered, and his right fist was a mass of scorched tissue from which a sliced rope's end protruded. He was caked with salt and what looked like old blood.

Golophin trickled water over the split lips and sprinkled drops over the eyelids. "Richard." His fingers wriggled and conjured a tiny white ball of flame in the air. He flicked it as one might bat at an annoying fly, and it smote the unconscious mariner on the forehead, sinking into his flesh in the glimmer of a second.

Isolla returned, a maid behind her bearing all manner of cloths and bottles and a steaming bowl. The maid was wide-eyed as an owl, but fled instantly at one look from her mistress.

Hawkwood opened his eyes. The white of one was flooded scarlet.

"Golophin." A cracked whisper. The wizard trickled more water over his lips and Hawkwood burst into a racking cough.

"Cradle his head, Isolla; raise it up."

The Queen rested the mariner's battered head on her breast, tears sliding silently down her face.

"Richard, can you talk?" Golophin asked gently.

The eyes, one garish red, glared wildly for a second, terror convulsing his body. Then Hawkwood relaxed, like a puppet whose strings have been snipped.

"It's gone. The whole fleet. They destroyed it, Golophin. Every ship."

Isolla shut her eyes.

"Tell me, Captain."

"Weatherworking – a calm and fog. Monsters out of the air, the sea. Thousands. We had no chance."

"They're all –"

"Dead. Drowned. Oh, God." Hawkwood's lips drew back from his black gums and a hoarse cry ripped out of him. "*Pain!* Ah, stop, stop." Then it passed.

"I will heal you," Golophin said. "And then you will sleep for a long time, Richard."

"No! Listen to me!" Hawkwood's eyes blazed with fever and anguish. "I saw him, Golophin. I spoke to him."

"Who?"

"Aruan. He let me go. He sent me back." Hawkwood sobbed dryly.

"*I bear his terms.*"

A hand of pure ice closed about Golophin's heart. "Go on."

"Surrender. Hand over the nobles. Hebrion and Astarac both. Or he'll destroy them. He can do it. He will. They're coming here on the west wind, Golophin, in the storm."

It poured out of him in a stream of tumbled words. The raft. Aruan's appearance. His words – his implacable reasoning. At last Hawkwood's voice sank into a barely audible croak. "I'm sorry. My ship. I should have died."

Isolla caressed his unburnt cheek. "Hush now, Captain. You have done well. You can sleep now." She looked at Golophin and the old wizard nodded, his face grey.

"Sleep now. Rest."

Hawkwood's stared up at her, and the ghost of a smile flitted across his face. "I remember you." Then coughing took him, a fit that made him jump in Isolla's arms. He fought for breath. Then his eyes rolled back, and the air came out of him in a long, tired exhalation. He was still.

"He has suffered too much," Golophin said. "I was impatient. I am a fool."

Isolla bent her head and her shoulders trembled, but she made not a sound.

"He is dead, then," she said at last, calmly.

Golophin set a hand on Hawkwood's chest, and shut his eyes. The mariner's body gave a sudden jolt, and his limbs quivered.

"I will not permit him to," Golophin said fiercely, and as he spoke the Dweomer blazed up in him and spilled out of his eyes, his fingertips. It coiled out of his mouth like a white smoke. "Get away from him, Isolla."

The Queen did as she was told, shielding her eyes against the brilliance of Golophin's light. The wizard had been transformed into a form of pure, pulsing argent. The light waxed until it was unbearable to look at, becoming a shining swirl, a sunburst, and then with a shout it left him, hurled into the inert form on the bed. There was a noiseless concussion that blew out the lamps and sent the bedclothes spiralling into the air even as they crackled and shrivelled away to nothing, and Hawkwood's body thrashed and twitched like the plaything of a mad puppeteer.

The room plunged into darkness save for where Golophin crouched by the bed, breathing hard. The werelight still shone out of his eyes dementedly. Isolla was standing at the far wall as if fixed to it. Something powdery and light was snowing down upon her head, and there was an inexplicable tautness to one side of her face.

"Light a candle," the wizard's voice said. The lambency of his stare faded and the room was pitch-dark. On the bed, something was groaning.

"I – I can't see, Golophin."

"Forgive me." A fluttering wick of werelight appeared near the ceiling. Isolla reached for the tinderbox, and retrieved a candle from the floor. The backs of her hands, her clothing, were covered in a delicate layer of white ash. She struck flint and steel, caught the spark in the ball of tinder, and fed it with the candle-wick. A more human radiance replaced the werelight.

Golophin laboured to his feet, beating the ash from his robes. When he turned to her Isolla caught her breath in shock. "My God, Golophin, your face!"

One side of the old wizard's countenance had been transformed into a tormented mass of scar-tissue, like that of burn long healed. He nodded. "The Dweomer always exacts a payment, especially when one is in a hurry. Ah, child, I am so sorry. You should not have been here for this. I thought that I alone would suffice."

"What do you mean?"

He came forward and stroked her cheek gently, the strange tautness there. "It took you too," he said simply.

She felt her skin. It was ridged and almost numb in a line running from the corner of her eye to her jaw. Something in her stomach pitched headlong, but she spoke without a quaver. "It's no matter. How is he?"

They turned to the bed, holding the candle over the blasted coverlet, the ash-strewn and smoking mattress. Hawkwood's ragged, scorched clothes had disappeared. He lay naked on the bed, breathing deeply. His beard had gone, and the hair on his scalp was no more than a dark stubble, but there was not a mark on his body. Golophin felt his forehead. "He'll sleep for a few hours, and when he wakes, he'll be as hale as ever he was. Hebrion has need of him yet.

"Stay here with him, my dear. I must go and take the temperature of the city – and there are one or two errands to be run also." He looked closely at Isolla, as though deliberating whether to tell her something, then turned away with a passable pretence at briskness. "I may be gone some time. Watch over our patient."

"As I once watched over Abeleyn?" The grief was raw in her voice. She remembered another evening, a different man restored by Golophin's power. But there had been hope back then.

Golophin left without replying.

EIGHT

A PROCESSION OF dreams, all brightly-lit and perfectly coherent, travelled brightly along the trackways of Hawkwood's mind. Like paper lanterns set free to soar, they finally burned themselves up and came drifting sadly back down in ash and smoke.

He saw the old *Osprey* blazing brightly in the night, sails of flame twisting and billowing from her decks. At her rail stood King Abeleyn, and beside him, Murad. Murad was laughing.

He watched as, like a succession of brilliantly wrought jewels, a hundred ports and cities of the world winked past. And with them were faces. Billerand, Julius Albak, Haukal, his long-forgotten wife Estrella. Murad. Bardolin. These last two were linked, somehow, in his mind. There was something they shared which he could not fathom. Murad was dead now – even in the dream Hawkwood knew this, and was glad.

At the last there came a red-haired woman with a scar on her cheek who pillowed him on her breast. He knew her. As he studied her face the dreams faded, and the fear. He felt as though he had made landfall after the longest of voyages, and he smiled.

"You're awake!"

"And alive. How in the world –" and he saw her face clearly now, the line of ridged tissue down one side, like the trail of a sculptor's fingers in damp clay.

Her own fingers flew to it at once, covering it. Then she dropped her hand deliberately, stern as the Queen she was. She had been weeping.

The room was gloomy and cold in the pre-dawn greyness. A fire in the hearth had sunk to smoking embers. How long had he been here? What had been happening? There was no pain, no thirst. His life's slate had been wiped clean.

"Golophin saved you, with the Dweomer. But there was a price. He is far worse than I. It is not important. You are alive. He will be here soon."

Isolla rose from the bedside, his eyes following her every move with a baffled, helpless pain. He ran a hand over his own features and was astounded.

"My beard!"

"It'll grow back. You look younger without it. There are clothes by the side of the bed. They should fit. Come into the antechamber when you are ready. Golophin wants to talk to us." She left, walking stiffly in a simple and unadorned court gown.

Hawkwood threw aside the covers and studied his body. Not a mark. Even his old scars of twenty years had disappeared. He was as hairless as a babe.

Feeling absurdly embarrassed, he pulled on the clothing which had been left out for him. He was parched, and drained at a gulp the silver jug of springwater sitting beside them. He felt as though he must crack every joint in his body to bend it back into shape, and spent minutes stretching and bending, getting the blood flowing again. He was alive. He was whole. It was not a miracle, but it seemed more than miraculous to him. Despite all that he had seen of the workings of magic through the years, certain aspects of it never failed to stun him. It was one thing to call up a storm – it was the kind of thing he expected a wizard to do. But to mould his own flesh like this, to smooth out the burns and heal his cracked, smoke-choked lungs – that was truly awe-inspiring.

What price had been paid for the gift of this life? That lady on the other side of the door. She had paid for his scars with her own. She, Hebrion's Queen.

When he stepped through the doorway his face was sombre as that of a mourner. In his life he had not made a habit of frequenting the bedchambers of royalty and he was at a loss as to whether he should bow, sit down or remain standing. Isolla was watching him, drinking a glass of wine. The antechamber was small, octagonal, but high-ceilinged.

A fire of blue-spitting sea-coal burned in the hearth and there was a pretty tumble of women's things here and there on the chairs, a full decanter on the table, ruby and shining in the firelight, beeswax candles burning in sconces in the walls, their fine scent mingling with Isolla's perfume. Heavy curtains were drawn across the single window, so that it might have been the middle of the night, but Hawkwood's internal clock knew that dawn had come and gone, and the sun was rising up the sky now.

"There is no formality here, Captain. Help yourself to some wine. You look as though you had seen a – a ghost."

He did as he was bidden, unable to relax. He wanted to twitch aside the curtains and peer out to see what was in the morning sky.

"I have met you before, have I not?" she said stiffly.

"I have been at a levee or two over the years, lady. But a long time ago I met you on the Northern Road. Your horse had thrown a shoe."

She coloured. "I remember. I served you wine in Golophin's tower. Forgive me, Captain, my wits are astray."

Hawkwood bowed slightly. There was nothing more to be said.

But Isolla was trying to say something. She stared into he wine and asked at last: "How did he die? The King."

Hawkwood swore silently. What could he possibly tell this woman that would make her sleep any easier at night? That her husband had been ripped apart, drowned? She raised her head and saw what he would not say in his eyes.

"So it was bad, then."

"He died fighting," Hawkwood said heavily. "And truly, lady, it did not last long, for any of them."

"And my brother?"

Of course, she was Mark's sister. This woman was now one of the last survivors of two Royal lines – perhaps the last indeed.

"For him also it was quick," he lied, staring her down, willing her to believe him. "He died scant feet away from Abeleyn, the two on the same quarterdeck." *On my ship*, he thought. *Two Kings and an Admiral died there, but not I.* And the shame seared his soul.

"I'm glad they died together," she said thickly. "They were like brothers in life, save that Mark always hated the sea. How was it that he was not on his own flagship?"

Hawkwood smiled, remembering the green-faced and puking Astaran King being hauled over the side of the *Pontifidad* in a bosun's chair. "He came for a conference and – and kept putting off the return journey."

That made her smile also. The room warmed a little.

A discreet knock at the door, and Golophin came in without further ado. Hawkwood had to collect himself for a moment at the sight of the old man's face. God in heaven, why had they done it?

The wizard was a gaunt mannekin with white parchment skin that rendered his purple and pink scars all the more startling. But he grinned at Hawkwood as the mariner stood with his untasted wine in his fist.

"Good, good. A perfect job. You had us worried there for a while, Captain." Isolla took his heavy outer robe like a girl helping her father, and gave him her own glass. He drained it in one swallow, then stepped across to the window and swept back the curtains.

The window faced west, and looked out into a vast, boiling darkness. Hawkwood joined the wizard to stare out at it. "Blood of God," he murmured.

"Your storm is almost upon us, Captain. It made good time during the night."

The cloud was twisted and stretched into a great bastion of shadow which filled the entire western horizon. It was shot through with the flicker of lightning at its base and writhed in tormented billows with a motion that seemed almost sentient.

"The city has been swarming like a wasp's nest all night, and the sight of that this morning has been enough to tip things over the edge. Already there is a throng of soldiers, sailors and minor nobles in the abbey, all talking without listening. The garrison, such as it is, is out on the streets, but the panic has already begun. They're streaming out of north gate in their thousands, and ships in the harbour have dumped their cargoes and are offering passage out of Hebrion instead, to anyone who has a king's ransom in his purse."

"No-one said a word," Isolla said wonderingly. "One castaway is brought ashore, and the whole country expects the worst. Storm or no storm, have they no faith? It's madness."

"The fishermen found me floating on the broken maintop of a great ship. Some of them recognised me as the captain of the flagship. And I would answer none of their questions," Hawkwood told her gently. "Victory is not so close-mouthed. They know that the fleet has met with some disaster."

"Plus, I believe that a few of the palace maids have been more ingenious in their curiosity than I gave them credit for," Golophin went on. "At any rate, the secret is out. The fleet, and our King, are no more – this much is now common knowledge. Aruan's terms have not yet been bruited abroad, though, which is a blessing. We must have no more maids or valets in this wing of the palace, if it is to stay that way. I have posted sentries further down the passage."

"What do we do now?" Isolla asked slowly, her eyes fixed on the preternatural tempest rolling towards them on the west wind. She was no ingenue, but nothing in her life had prepared her for this sudden, crushing weight of responsibility. She did not even know the name of the officer who now commanded the army.

Golophin looked at Hawkwood, and found that the mariner was watching the Queen with a strange intentness. He nodded to himself. He had been right there, all those years ago, and he was still right. That could be for the good.

He pursed his lips. "Abrusio has a garrison of some six thousand men left to her. The marines went with the fleet, as did all the great ships. All we have left are despatch-runners and a few gunboats. There are small garrisons in Imerdon and up on the border with Fulk, but they are weeks away."

"There are the mole-forts," Isolla said. "In the Civil War they held up Abeleyn's fleet for days."

"These things," Hawkwood said slowly, "can fly."

"What were they, Captain?" Golophin asked. Even at a time like this, he seemed more curious than appalled.

"I saw one once before, in the jungle of the Western Continent. I believe they were men at one time, but they have been warped beyond humanity. They are like great bats with tails, and the talons of a raptor. And they number many thousands. There is a fleet out there also, mostly composed of lesser ships, and on board it are black-armoured warriors with pincers for hands and a carapace like that of a beetle. They swarm like veritable cockroaches in any case. The city cannot stand against that. Her best men died off North Cape and her citizens, from what you tell me, are in no mood to stand and fight."

"Abrusio is doomed, then," Isolla murmured.

Golophin's face was a demonic mask. "I believe so. Hebrion, at least, must accept Aruan's terms, or see bloodshed that will make the Civil War pale into insignificance."

"He wants the nobles handed over too," Hawkwood reminded him. "He intends to extinguish the aristocracy of the whole kingdom."

Both men looked at Isolla. She smiled bitterly. "I care not. My husband and my brother are both dead. I may as well join them."

Golophin took her hand. "My Queen, you have been like a daughter to me, one of the few folk I have trusted in this long, absurd life of mine. This man here is another such, though he has not always known it. Abeleyn your husband was the third, and Bardolin of Carreirida was the fourth. Now only you and Hawkwood remain." As she hung her head he gripped her fingers more tightly. "I speak to you now as a Royal advisor, but also as a friend. You must leave Hebrion. You must take ship with a few of the household whom you in your turn can trust, and sail from these shores. And you must go soon, within the day."

Isolla looked shaken. "Where shall I go?"

It was Hawkwood who answered. "King Corfe still rules in Torunna, and his army is the greatest in the world. You should go to Torunn, lady. You will be safe there."

"No. My place is here."

"Hawkwood is right," Golophin said fiercely. "If Aruan captures you then all hope for the future is lost. The people must have some continuity in the times to come. And you must go by sea; the land route to the east is closed." He raised a hand. "Let us hear no more on this matter. I have already spoken to the Master of Ships down in Admiral's Tower. A state xebec awaits you as we speak. Hawkwood here will captain it. You ought to leave, I am told, with a certain combination of tides, the – the –"

"The ebb tide," Hawkwood told him. "It happens at the sixth hour after noon. The xebec is a good choice. She's lateen-rigged, and with this westerly she'll have a beam wind to work with to get out of the harbour – precious little leeway, mind. But you'll find some other skipper. I'm staying here."

Isolla and Golophin both glared at him.

"I survived my King, my Admiral and my ship – despite being her captain," Hawkwood said simply. "I'm not running away again."

"Bloody fool," Golophin said. "And what service will you render here in Hebrion apart from having that stiff neck of yours chopped through?"

"I might make the same point to you. You're staying, it seems – and for what?"

"I can be in Torunn in the blink of an eye if I so choose."

"You look as though a child could knock you over with a willow-wand."

"He's right, Golophin," Isolla said quickly. "Are your powers in need of recuperation? You do not look well." She appeared momentarily exasperated by her own timidity. Hawkwood saw her jaw harden. But then Golophin, ignoring her, was poking him in the chest with a bony forefinger.

"Aruan told you his forbearance is at an end. Twice now he's let you live, to suit his own ends. He will not do so again. Plus, this ship needs an experienced navigator. You will be travelling the entire length of three seas to reach Torunn.. You are going, Captain. And you, lady – even if I were not your friend I would insist, that as Hebrion's reigning Queen, you must go. And you will, if I have to have you bundled up in a sack. Hawkwood, I charge you with her protection. Now let us hear no more about it. As it happens, I have a reason for staying, and you have given me reason to believe Aruan will not have me slain out of hand.

Nor am I defenceless, so rest your minds from that selfless worry and start preparing for your voyage. There are tunnels under the palace that lead almost to the waterfront; Abeleyn had them dug ten years ago, so you will be able to leave without creating even more of a panic than already exists. Isolla knows where they are. You will leave by them as soon as you possibly can."

"I can't do that – I must speak to the nobility before I go. I can't just sneak away," Isolla protested.

Golophin finally let slip the leash on his temper. "*You can and you will!*" A cold light blazed up in his eyes. They burned like white flames and the fury in them made Isolla retreat a step. "By Ramusio's beard, I thought you had better sense. Do you think you can give a cheery little speech to the nobles and then expect to trip lightly away? This kingdom is about to go enter a dark age that none of us can imagine, and the storm of its wings is almost upon us. I have no more time to sit here and wrangle with stiff-necked fools and silly little girls. *You will both do as I say.*"

The light in his eyes faded. In a more human voice he said, "Hawkwood, a word with you outside."

The mage and the mariner left the shocked Queen behind and stood outside her door. Hawkwood watched Golophin warily, and the old wizard grinned.

"What do you think – did I put the fear of God into her?"

"You old bastard! And into me too."

"Good. The eyes were a nice touch, I think. Listen, Richard, you must get her down to that damned ship by mid-afternoon at the latest. Your vessel is called the *Seahare*, and is berthed in the Royal yards at the very foot of Admiral's Tower. Do not ask how I purloined her; I would blush to tell you. But she is yours, and all the paperwork is..." He grinned again. "Irrelevant. Everything is ready or almost so. They're lading her with extra stores but she's a flyer, not a fighter – so they tell me – and if I start sending marines aboard it'll arouse suspicion. The current captain is on shore leave, no doubt dipping his wick in some bawdy-house. I have spoken to the harbour-master, and you are expected, but your passengers are anonymous nobles, no more."

"Nobles? So who are the others?" Hawkwood asked.

"I'm not yet sure there will be others. That is what I am going to find out now. Just get Isolla down to that ship. And – and look after her, Richard. Quite apart from being Queen, she's a fine woman."

"I know. Listen, Golophin, I haven't thanked you –"

"Don't bother. I need you as much as you needed me. Now I must be gone." Golophin gripped his arm. "I will see you again, Captain, of that you may be sure."

Then he was off, striding down the passageway like a much younger man, albeit one who looked as though he had not eaten in a month.

A FLURRY OF packing – and Hawkwood conscripted into the process by dark little Brienne, Isolla's Astaran maid, who had been with her since childhood. Isolla white-faced and silent, still believing Golophin's rage to be genuine. And then a subterranean journey, the little trio hurrying and stumbling by torchlight, weighed down with bags and even a small trunk. From the palace to Admiral's Tower was the better part of half a league, and the first third of the way was a steep-stepped descent of dripping stone, the Queen leading the way with a guttering torch, Hawkwood and Brienne following, unable to see their own feet for the burdens they carried. Hawkwood stepped once on the wriggling softness of a rat, and stumbled. At once, Isolla's strong hand was at his elbow, helping him to his feet. The Queen's face was invisible under a hooded cloak, but she was as tall as a man, and up to the burden. Hawkwood found himself admiring her quick, sure gait, and the slender fingers that held aloft the torch. Her perfume drifted back to him as they laboured along, an essence of lavender, like the scent of the Hebros foothills in summer.

At last they came to a door, which Isolla unlocked and left open behind them, and stepped out into the lower yards of the Tower. All about them was the tumult of the wharves, the screaming gulls. Sea-scents of rotting fish and tar and wood and salt. A forest of masts rose up into a clear sky before them, and the sunlight was dazzling, blinding after their underground journey. They stood blinking, momentarily bewildered by the spectacle. It was Hawkwood who collected his wits first, and led them to their vessel where it floated at its moorings in the midst of a crowd of others.

THE SEAHARE WAS a lateen-rigged xebec of some three hundred tons, a fast despatch-runner of the Hebrian navy with a crew of sixty. Three-masted, she could run up both lateen and square-rigged yards depending on the wind. She was a sharp-beaked ship with an overhanging counter and a narrow keel, but she was nonetheless wide in the beam to enhance her stability as a sail-platform. Her decks were turtle-built so that any seas which came aboard might run off into the scuppers at once, and above the decks were gratings which ran from the centre-line to the ship's rail so that her crew might work dry-shod whilst the water ran off below them. As Golophin had said, she was built for speed, not warfare, and though she had a pair of twelve-pound bow-chasers her broadside amounted to half a dozen light sakers, more to counter a last-minute boarding than to facilitate any real sea-battle. Hawkwood's arrival was greeted with unfriendly stares, but as soon as the ladies were below he began shouting out a series of orders that showed he knew his business. The first mate, a Merduk named Arhuz, was a small, compact man, dark as a seal. He had sailed with Julius Albak thirty years before, and like all of the other sailors he knew of Richard Hawkwood and his great voyage, as a man remembers the nursery-rhymes learned as a child. Once the knowledge of the new captain's identity had spread about the ship the men set to work with a will. It was not every day they were to be skippered by a legend.

A great deal of stores had still to be taken on board, and the mainhatch was gaping dark and wide as the men hauled on tackles from the yardarms to lower casks and sacks into the hold. Others were trundling more casks from the great storerooms under the Tower, whilst yet more were coiling away spare cables and hauling aboard reluctant goats and cages of chickens. It looked like chaos, but it was a controlled chaos, and Hawkwood was satisfied that they would complete their victualling in time for the evening tide.

The Royal yards had not yet been engulfed by the panicked disorder that was enveloping the rest of the waterfront, but that disorder was audible beyond the massive walls that separated them from the Inner Roads. Fear was rank in the air, and all the while men looked over their shoulder at the approaching storm towering in the west, and swallowing up ever more of the sky as it thundered eastwards. Hawkwood needed no charts in this part of the world; he knew all the coasts around Abrusio as well as the features of his own face, and that face grew grave as he considered what it would be like to beat out of the Inner Roads under a strong westerly. Handy as the xebec might be at dealing with a beam wind, she would have to win some leeway once they made it into the Gulf, or that wind might just push them headlong onto the unforgiving coast of Hebrion. But they would have the ebbing flow of the tide beneath the keel, to draw them out of the bay and into the wider gulf beyond. He hoped that would be enough.

Through the years, Hawkwood had taken ships uncounted out of this port, into the green waters of the Gulf, and then beyond, to Macassar of the Corsairs, to Gabrion which had spawned him and of which he remembered almost nothing now. To the coasts of hot Calmar and the jungles of savage Punt. But all those memories faded into a merry silence beside the one voyage which had made his name. The one that had broken him. No good had come of it that he could see, least of all to himself. But he knew now that it would always be irrevocably linked to him – among mariners at least. He had earned a place in history – more importantly perhaps, he had won a hard-bought right to stand tall in the ranks of the mariners of yore, among the sailors of this present day at least. But he took no pride in it. He knew now that it counted for nothing. Men did things because they had to do them, or because they seemed the only thing to do at the time. And afterwards they were lauded as heroes. It was the way the world worked. He knew that now.

But this woman below, she mattered. She mattered to the world, of course – it was important that she survive – but most of all she now mattered to him. And he dared not delve deeper into that knowledge, for fear his middle-age might come laughing back at him. It was enough that she was here.

For a while Richard Hawkwood, standing on the quarterdeck of another man's ship with doom approaching out of the west, watched the sailors ready his vessel for sea, and knew that she was below, and was inexplicably happy.

A commotion down on the wharves. Two riders had come galloping through the gate and had come to a rearing halt before the xebec, scattering mariners and panicking the gulls. A man and a woman dismounted, tawny with dust, and, without ceremony or introduction, they ran up the gangplank hand in hand, leaving their foam-streaked and blowing mounts standing. Hawkwood, jolted out of his reverie, shouted for the master-at-arms and met them at the rail.

"What the hell is this? This is a King's Ship. You can't –"

The woman threw back her richly embroidered hood and smiled at him. "Hello Richard. It has been a long time."

It was Jemilla.

PART TWO

The SOLDIER KING

But I've said goodbye to Galahad,
And am no more the Knight of dreams and show:
For lust and senseless hatred make me glad,
And my killed friends are with me where I go...

– Siegfried Sassoon

HARDIC SEA
FINNMARK
TAN-THURAN
NORTHERN JAFRAR MOUNTAINS
THURIAN RIVER
ALMARK
TARBER
TOURBERING RIVER
OSTRABAR
OSTIAN RIVER
ORKHAN
THURIAN MOUNTAINS
TORIAN PLAINS
SABROTH RIVER
N
AURUNGABAR
SEARIL RIVER
THURIAN LINE
GADERION
KHEDI ANWAR
BERRONA
TORRIN RIVER
KARDIKIA
BAROSSA
SEA OF TOR
CIMBRIC MOUNTAINS
TORUNNA
CHARIBON
LEAGUES
0
30
ARBORONN
NARIAN HILLS
KARDIAN SEA
TORUNN
NORTH PERIGRAINE
KERDIK

NINE

GADERION HAD BEGUN life as a timber-built blockhouse built on a stream-girt spur of the Thurian mountains. The Fimbrians had stationed troops there to police the passage of the Torrin Gap and levy tolls on the caravans that passed through from west to east, or east to west. When their Empire fell apart the station was abandoned, and the only relic left of their presence was the fine road they had constructed to speed the passage of their armies.

The Torunnans had built a series of staging posts in the Gap, and around these had grown up a straggling network of taverns and livery stables that catered for travellers. But these had withered away over the years, first of all in the retrenchment which had followed the crisis of the Merduk Wars, and then in the years after the Great Schism, when trade between Torunna and Almark had all but died out.

More recently, a Merduk army had begun work on a fortress in the Gap, before suffering defeat in the Battle of Berrona. King Corfe, in the years following Armagedir, had had the entire region surveyed, and at the point where the road was pinched in a narrow valley between the buttresses of the two mountain chains, he had had a hilltop spur levelled, and on its summit had constructed a large fortress-complex which in size at least would come to rival long-lost Ormann Dyke. In the subsequent years the defences had been extended for almost half a league, to command the entire pass, and Gaderion now consisted of three separate fortifications, all connected by massive curtain walls.

To the south-east was the Donjon, on its steep spur of black rock. This was a squat citadel with walls fully fifty feet thick to withstand siege guns. There was a spring within its perimeter, and below it bomb-proofs had been hewn out of the living gutrock to house a fair-sized army, and enough supplies to sustain them for at least a year. Here also were the administrative offices of the garrison, and the living-quarters of the commanding officer. In the midst of these was a taller feature, a blunt spike of rock which in the youth of the world had been a plug of molten lava within the walls of a volcano. The walls had worn away, leaving this ominous fist of basalt standing alone. There had been a pagan altar on its summit when Corfe's engineers had first surveyed it. Now it had been partially hollowed out with immense, costly, dangerous labour, and provided a last-ditch refuge within the Donjon itself, and a lofty look-out giving a bird's-eye view of the entire Torrin river-valley and the mountains on either side. Light guns had been sited in embrasures in its impregnable sides, and they commanded every approach. Men called this ominous-looking tower of stone the Spike.

The Donjon and the Spike loomed over the flat-floored valley, which was perhaps three-quarters of a mile wide. The soil here was fertile and dark, watered by the chill stream which hundreds of miles to the south and east grew into the Torrin River, and the soldiers of the garrison tended plots of land in the shadow of the fortress despite the mountain-swift growing season and the killer frosts of the winter. There were currently twenty-eight thousand men stationed at Gaderion. Many of them had wives who lived nearby, and a scattering of stone and log houses dotted the valley east of the walls. Officially this was frowned upon, but in practice it was discreetly tolerated, else the separation between the men and their families would have been well-nigh unsupportable.

Square in the middle of the valley was a low, circular knoll some fifty feet high, and on this had been built the second of Gaderion's fortresses. The Redoubt was a simple square structure with triangular casemates at each corner to catch any foes who reached the walls in a deadly crossfire. The Northern Road ran through it under the arches of two heavily-defended gates, and before these gates were two redans, each mounting a battery of guns. Within the walls were housed the stables of the Royal couriers who kept Gaderion in touch with the larger world, and it was here also that the main sally force of the fortress was billeted, some eight thousand men, mainly cavalry.

The last of Gaderion's fortresses was the Eyrie. This had been tacked on like a swallow's nest to the steep cliffs of the Candorwir, the mountain whose peak overlooked the valley on its western side. The stone of Candorwir had been hollowed out to accomodate three thousand men and fifty great guns, and the only way they could be reached was by a dizzy single-track mule-path which had been blasted out of the very flank of the mountain. The guns of the Eyrie and the Donjon formed a perfect crossfire that transformed the floor of the Torrin valley into a veritable killing ground in which each feature had been mapped and ranged. The gunners of Gaderion could, if they wished, shoot accurately at these features in the dark, for each gun had a log-board noting the traverse and elevation of specified points on the approach to the walls.

The three fortresses, formidable in themselves, had a weak link common to all. This was the curtain wall. Forty feet high and almost as thick, it ranged in strange tortuous zig-zags across the valley floor, connecting the Donjon to the Redoubt and the Redoubt to the cliffs at the foot of the Eyrie. Sharp-angled bartizans pocked its length every three hundred yards, and four thousand men were stationed along it, but strong though it seemed, it was the weakest element of the defences. Only a few guns were sited in its casemates, as Corfe had long ago decided that it was the artillery of the three fortresses which would protect the wall, not the wall itself. If it were overrun, then those three would still dominate the valley too thoroughly to allow the passage of troops. To force the passage of the Torrin Gap, an attacker would have to take all of them; the Donjon, the Redoubt, and the Eyrie. All told, twelve thousand men manned their defences, which left a field army of sixteen thousand to conduct sorties. Once, this had seemed more than ample, but General Aras, officer commanding Gaderion, was no longer so sure.

SOME SIX LEAGUES to the north and west of Gaderion the narrow, mountain-girt gap opened out into the wider land of the Torian Plains beyond, and in the tumbled foothills which marked the last heights of the mountains, a line of turf and timber structures signalled the beginning of the Thurian Line, the easternmost redoubt of the Second Empire. Here, with the conscripted labour of thousands, the forces of Himerius had reared up a great clay and wood barrier, part defensive wall, part staging-post. It meandered over the grassy hills like a monstrous serpent, bristling with stockades and gabions and revetments. There were few heavy guns stationed along it, but huge numbers of men patrolled its unending length, and to the rear they had constructed sod-walled towns and roads of crushed stone. The smoke of their fires could be seen for miles, an oily smudge on the hem of the sky, and their shanty-towns were surrounded by muddy quaqmires through which columns of troops trudged ceaselessly, and files of cavalry plunged fetlock-deep. Here were garrisoned men of a dozen different countries and kingdoms reaching from Fulk in the far west to Gardiac up in the heights of the Jafrar. Knights of Perigraine, looking like chivalric relics on their magnificently caparisoned chargers. Clanking gallowglasses from Finnmark with their greatswords and broadaxes. Almarkan cuirassiers with pistols strapped to their saddles. Knights Militant, as heavily armoured as the Perigrainians, but infinitely more businesslike. And Inceptines, no longer monks in habits, but now tonsured warriors on destriers wielding maces and clad in black iron. They led ragged columns of men who wore no armour, wielded no weapons, but who were the most feared of all Himerius's soldiers. The Hounds of God. When a troop of these trotted down one of the muddy garrison-streets, everyone, even the hulking gallowglasses, made room for them. The Torunnans had yet to meet these things in battle.

A savage, low-intensity warfare had flickered over this disputed ground between the two defence-lines now for several months. Each side sent out patrols to gather intelligence on the other, and when they met no quarter was asked or given. Scarcely two sennights previously, a Torunnan flying column of a thousand cuirassiers had slipped through the foothills to the north-east of the Thurian Line undetected, and had burned the bridges over the Tourbering River a hundred miles to the north. However, on their way back the Himerians had been ready for them, and barely two hundred of the heavy horsemen had survived to see the walls of Gaderion again.

A SMALL GROUP of lightly armed Torunnan cavalry reined in as evening drew on and prepared to bed down for the night on a low bluff within sight of the endless skein of lights that was the Thurian Line. They had been out of Gaderion three days on a reconnaissance, riding the entire length of the enemy fortifications, and were to return to barracks in the morning. Half their number stood guard while the rest unsaddled, rubbed down and fed their mounts, and unrolled their damp bedrolls. When this had been done, the dismounted troopers remained standing and watchful as their comrades did the same. Five dozen tired, grimy men who wanted nothing more than to get through the night and back to their bunks, a wash, and a hot meal. The Torunnans were forbidden to light fires when between the lines, and thus their camps had been chill and cheerless, their food ration scarcely less so. By the time the horse-lines were pegged out in the wooded ground at the foot of the bluff and the animals hobbled and deep in nose-bags, it had become almost fully dark, the last light edging down behind the jagged sentinel-bulk of Candorwir behind them, and the seven stars of the Scythe bright and stark in a cloudless night sky.

The troopers' young officer, a lanky youth with straw-coloured hair, stood watching the line of lights glittering on the world perhaps ten miles away to the north and west. They arced across the land like a filigree necklace, too delicate to seem threatening. But he had seen them up close, and knew that the Himerians decorated those ramparts with Torunnan heads mounted on cruel spikes. The bodies they left out as carrion within gunshot of the walls.

"All quiet, sir," the troop-sergeant told his officer, a shadow among other, faceless shadows.

"All right, Dieter. Turn yourself in as well. I reckon I'll watch for a while."

But the sergeant did not move. He was staring down at the Thurian Line like his officer. "Funny, behind the walls it's lively as an ant's nest someone has poked with a stick, but there's not hide nor hair of the bastards out here. Not one patrol! I haven't seen the like, and I've been stationed up here these past four years."

"Yes, there's a bad smell in the air all right. Maybe the rumours are true, and it's the start of the war at last."

"Saint's blood, I hope not."

The young ensign turned to his sergeant, his senior by twenty years, and grinned. "What's that? Aren't you keen to have a go at them, Dieter? They've been skulking behind those ramparts for ten years now. It's about time they came out and let us get at them."

Dieter's face was expressionless. "I was at Armagedir, lad, and in the King's Battle before that. I was no older than you are now and thought much the same. All young men's minds work the same way. They want to see war, and when they have seen it, they never want to see it again, providing they live through it."

"No glory, eh?"

"Roche, you've been up here a year now. How much glory have you seen?"

"Ah, but it's just been all this damn skirmishing. I want to see what a real fight is like, where the battle-lines are a mile long and the thunder of it shakes the earth."

"Me, I just want to get back to my bed, and the wife in it."

"What about young Pier? He'll soon be of an age to sit a saddle or shoulder a pike. Is he to follow you into the Tercios?"

"Not if I can help it."

"Ah, Dieter, you're tired is all."

"No, it's not that. It's the waiting, I think. These bastards have been building things up for a decade now, since the Torian Plains Battle. They own everything between the Malvennors and the Cimbrics, right up to the Sultanates in the Jafrar, and still they want more. They won't stop 'til we break 'em. I just want to get on with it, I suppose. Get it over with."

He stopped, listening. In the horse-lines among the trees the animals were restless and quarrelsome, despite being as tired as their riders. They were tugging at the picket-ropes, trying to rear though their forelegs were securely hobbled.

"Something in the wind tonight," the young ensign said lightly, but his face was set and hard.

The night was silent save for the struggling horses. The sentries down at the lines were trying to calm them down, cursing and grabbing at their skewed nosebags.

"Something –" Dieter frowned. "Sir, do you smell that?"

The ensign sniffed the air doubtfully. "There must be an old fox's den nearby. That's what is spooking the horses."

"No, it's different than that. Stronger."

One of the sentries came running up to the two men with his sabre drawn. The metal glinted coldly in the starlight.

"There's something out there in the dark, sir, something moving. It was circling the camp, and then I lost it in that gully down on the left. It's in the trees."

The young officer looked at his sergeant. "Stand-to."

But the nickering of the horses exploded into a chorus of terrified, agonising shrieks that froze them all where they stood. The sentries came running pell-mell from the horse-lines, terrified. "There's something down in there, sergeant!"

"Stand-to!" Dieter yelled at the top of his voice, though all through the bivouac men were already struggling out of their bedrolls and reaching for their weapons.

"What the hell's going on down there?"

"We couldn't see. It came out of the gully, big as a fucking house. Some kind of animal, black as a wolf's throat."

Horses were trying pitifully to drag themselves up the rocky slope to the bivouac where their riders stood, trailing their picket-ropes. But their forelegs were securely hobbled and they reared and screamed and tumbled to their sides and kicked out maniacally to their rear. The men could see the black berry-shine of blood on them now. One had been disembowelled and was slipping in its own entrails.

"Sergeant Dieter," the ensign said in a voice that shook, "take a demi-platoon down to the horselines and see what is happening there."

Dieter looked at him a moment and then nodded. He bawled out at the nearest men and a dozen followed him reluctantly down into the wooded hollow from which the hellish cacophony of dying beasts resounded.

The rest of the men formed up on the bluff and watched them as they struck a path through the melee of terrified and dying beasts that was still struggling out of the trees. Two men were knocked from their feet. Dieter left them there, telling them to unhobble every horse they could. The terror-stricken animals mobbed the men, looking to their riders for protection. Then Dieter's group disappeared into the bottomless shadow of the wood that straggled along the foot of the bluff.

A stream of horses was galloping up the slope now as they were loosed of their restraints. The men tried to catch and soothe them but most went tearing off into the night. The men gathered around the ensign were as much baffled as afraid, and angry at the savagery of the attack on their horses. But it was an animal, or animals, that they faced, not men; many of the mounts that had escaped were marked with slashing claw-marks.

A single shout, cut short, as though the wind had been knocked out of the shouter.

"That was Dieter," one of the men on the bluff said.

There were alder and birch down in the hollow below the bivouac, and now these began thrashing as though men were shaking their branches. Cursing the darkness, those on the hill peered down the slope, past the keening, crippled horses that littered the ground, and saw something huge loom out of the trees like a cliff of black shadow. The smell in the air again, but stronger now – the musk-like stink of a great beast. Something sailed across the night sky and thudded to the ground just short of their feet. They heard a noise that afterwards many would swear had been human laughter, and then one of their number was pointing at the thrown object lying battered and glistening on the earth before them. Their sergeant's head.

The thing in the trees seemed to melt away into the darkness, branches springing back to mark its passing. The men on the hill stood as though turned to stone, and in the sudden quiet even the screaming of the horses died away.

THE LADY MIRREN'S daily rides were a trial to both her assigned bodyguards, and her ladies-in-waiting. Each morning, just after sunrise, she would appear at the Royal stables where Shamarq, the ageing Merduk who was head groom, had her horse Hydrax saddled and waiting for her. With her would be the one among her ladies-in-waiting who had chosen the short straw that morning, and a suitable young officer as escort. This morning it was Ensign Baraz, who had been kicking his heels about the Bladehall for several days until he had caught the eye of General Comillan. He had accepted his new role with as much good grace as he could muster, and now his tall grey stood fretting and prancing beside Hydrax, a pair of pistols and a sabre strapped to its saddle. Gebbia, the lady who was to accompany them, had been assigned a quiet chestnut palfrey which she nonetheless eyed with something approaching despair.

The trio set off out of the north-west postern in the city walls and kicked into a swift canter, Gebbia's palfrey bobbing like a toy in the wake of the two larger horses ahead. Mirren's marmoset clung to her neck and bared its tiny teeth at the fresh wind, trying to lick the air with its tongue. The riders avoided the waggon-clogged Kingsway, and struck off towards the hills to the north of the city. Not until the horses were snorting and blowing in a cloud of their own steam did Mirren rein in. Baraz had kept pace with her but poor Gebbia was half a mile behind, the palfrey still bobbing simple-mindedly along.

"Why a court lady cannot be made to ride a decent horse I do not know," Torunna's Princess complained.

Baraz patted his sweating mount's neck and said nothing. He was regretting the King's momentary interest in him, and was wondering if he would ever be sent to a tercio to do some real soldiering. Mirren turned to regard his closed face.

"You, sir, what's your name?"

"Ensign Baraz, my lady – yes, that Baraz." He was getting tired of the reaction his name produced, too.

"You ride well, but you seem more put out even than Gebbia. Have I offended you?"

"Of course not, lady." And as she continued to stare at him, "It's just that I was hoping for a more – more military assignment. His Majesty has attached me to the High Command as a staff officer –"

"And you wanted to get your hands dirty instead of escorting galloping princesses about the countryside."

Baraz smiled. "Something like that."

"Most of the young bloods are very keen to escort the galloping Princess."

Baraz bowed in the saddle. "I am uncouth. I must apologise, lady. It is, of course, an honour –"

"Oh, stow it, Baraz. It's not as though I blame you. Were I a man, I would feel the same way. Here comes Gebbia. You would think she had just ridden clear across Normannia. Gebbia! Clench your knees together and kick that lazy screw a little harder or you'll lose us altogether."

Gebbia, a pretty dark-haired little thing whose face was flushed with exertion, could only nod wordlessly, and then look appealingly at Baraz.

"We should perhaps walk them a while to let them cool down," he ventured.

"Very well. Walk beside me, Ensign. We shall head up to the hilltop yonder, and then maybe I'll allow you to race me."

The three horses and their riders proceeded more sedately up the long heather and boulder-strewn slope, whilst before them the sun rose up out of a roseate wrack of tumbled cloud on the undulating horizon. A falcon wheeled screaming out of the sun towards Torunn and shrank to a winged speck within seconds, though Mirren followed its course keenly with palm-shaded eyes. The marmoset gibbered happily and she shushed it. "No Mij, it was just a bird is all."

"You understand him?" Baraz asked, curious.

"In a way. He's my familiar," and she laughed as his eyes widened. "Didn't you know that Dweomer runs in the blood of the Fantyrs? The female line at any rate. From my mother I gained witchery and from my father the ability to ride anything on four legs."

"You can cast spells then?"

"Would you like me to try?" She wagged the fingers of one hand at him and he recoiled despite himself. Mirren laughed. "I have little talent, and there is no-one to tutor me save mother. There are no great mages left in Torunna. They have all fled to join Himerius and the Empire, it is said."

"I have never seen magic worked."

Mirren waved an arm, frowning, and Baraz saw a haze of green-blue light follow in its wake, as though trailed by her sleeve. It gathered on her open palm and coalesced into a ball of bright werelight. She sent it circling in a blazing blur round Baraz's astonished face, and then it winked out like a snuffed candle.

"You see? Mountebank tricks, little more." She shrugged with a rare sadness, and he saw at once her father's face in hers. Her eyes were warmer, but the same strength was in the line of the jaw and the long nose. Baraz began to regret his assignment a little less.

Mirren stared at him with the sadness still on her face, then turned to her lady-in-waiting.

"Don't try to keep up with us Gebbia; you'll only fall off." And to Baraz: "Ready for that race?"

Without another word she let out a yell and kicked Hydrax on. The big bay sprang into an instant canter, then quickened into a full-blooded gallop, his black mane flying like a flag. Baraz watched her go, startled, but noting how well she sat, sidesaddle or no, and then dug both heels into his own horse's flanks.

He had thought to go easy on her, and let her stay a little ahead, but he found instead that she was leaving him quickly behind, and had to ride in earnest, his grey dipping and rising under him on the rough ground. Once he had to pull up hard on the reins as the gelding tripped and almost went headlong and it took every ounce of his skill to draw level with her as they reached the broad plateau at the summit of the ridgeline, and she slowed to a canter again, then a trot, and finally a slow walk. Both horses were winded but ready for more and they pranced under their riders like yearlings.

"Not bad," Mirren told him, laughing. The marmoset had wrapped itself around her neck like a scarf and was as bright-eyed as she. "Now, Mij, ease off a little there; you'll have me strangled."

There was a rough upland track here on the ridge, and as they walked their horses along it they could look down on the sprawl of the capital behind them. They were some five or six miles out of the Gates now, and poor Gebbia was a mere dot on the land below, still trotting gamely upwards.

They passed the ruins of a house, or hill croft, its roof beams long since fallen in like charred ribs in the crumbling shadow of its walls.

"My father tells me there were many farms here in the hills outside the city before the war. Then the Merduks came and –" Mirren coloured. "Ensign Baraz, I am so sorry."

Baraz shrugged. "What you say is true, lady. My people raped this part of the world before your father threw them back at Armagedir. It was an ugly time."

"And now the grandson of the great Shahr Baraz of Aekir wears a Torunnan uniform and takes orders from a Torunnan King. Does that not seem odd to you?"

"When the wars ended I was a toddler. I grew up knowing that Ramusio and Ahrimuz were the same man. I have worshipped alongside Ramusians all my life. The older men remember things the way they were, but the younger know only the world the way it is now. And it is better this way."

"I certainly think so."

They smiled at each other in the same moment, and Baraz felt a warmth creep about his heart. But the moment was broken by the urgent squeaks of Mirren's familiar.

"Mij! What in the world is wrong?"

The little animal was clambering distractedly about her shoulders, hissing and crying. She halted her horse to calm it and Baraz took her reins as she bodily seized the tiny creature and stared into its face. It grew quiet, and whimperingly climbed into the hollow of her hood where it lay chittering to itself.

"He's terrified, but all he can show me is the face of a great black wolf." Mirren took back her reins, troubled.

"There's someone on the track ahead of us," Baraz told her. He loosened his sabre in its scabbard. A tall figure was standing some way in the distance, seemingly oblivious of their presence. He was motionless as a piece of statuary, and was staring down at the walls of the capital, mustard-coloured in the morning light, and the blue shine of the estuary beyond where the Torrin widened on its way to the sea.

"He doesn't look dangerous," Mirren said. "Oh, Baraz, stop topping it the bodyguard. It's just a beggar or vagabond. Look – there's another one, sat off to one side. They seem lost, and old, too."

They rode up to the men, who appeared to be absorbed in the contemplation of the city in the distance. One was sat with his back to a stone and a hood which seemed like a monk's cowl pulled over his head. He might have been asleep. The other was dressed in a travel-stained robe, buff-coloured with dust, and a wide-brimmed hat that hid his face in shadow. A bulging haversack hung from one bony shoulder.

"Good morning, fathers," Baraz greeted them as they approached. "Are you heading for the city?"

The man on the ground did not stir, but the other answered. "Yes, that is my goal." His voice was deep as a well.

"You've a fair step to go then."

The man did not reply at once. He seemed weary, if the sag of his shoulders were anything to go by. He looked up at the two riders and for the first time they saw his face and gasped involuntarily.

"Who might you two be then?"

"I am Ensign Baraz of the Torunnan army, and this is –"

"The Princess Mirren, daughter of King Corfe himself. Well, this is a happy chance." The man smiled, and they saw that despite the ruin which constituted one side of his face, his eyes were kindly.

"How do you know who I am?" Mirren demanded.

And now the man sitting on the ground raised his head and spoke for the first time. "Your familiar told us."

Baraz drew his sabre and nudged the grey forward until he was between Mirren and the strange pair. "State your names and your business in Torunna," he rasped, dark eyes flashing.

The man on the ground rose to his feet. He also seemed tired. The two might have been nothing more than a pair of road-weary vagabonds, but for that last statement, and the aura of unquiet power which hung about them.

"They're wizards," Mirren said.

The disfigured older man doffed his wide-brimmed hat. "Indeed we are, my dear. Young man, our business is our own, but as for our names, well I am Golophin of Hebrion, and my companion –"

"Will remain nameless, for now," the other interrupted. Baraz could see a square jaw and broken nose under the cowl, but little else.

"Golophin!" Mirren cried. "My father speaks often of you. The greatest mage in the world, it is said."

Golophin chuckled, replacing his hat. "Perhaps not the greatest. My companion here might bridle at such an assumption."

"What are you doing here in Torunna? I thought you were still in Abrusio."

"I have come to see King Corfe, your father. I have some news for him."

"What of your taciturn comrade?" Baraz asked, pointing at him with his sword.

As he gestured with the blade the weapon seemed to flick out of his grip. It spun coruscating in the air for a second and then flicked away into the heather, stabbing into the ground so that the hilt stood quivering. Baraz shook his hand as though it had been burned, mouth gaping.

"I do not like blades pointed in my face," Golophin's companion said mildly.

"You had best leave us be," Golophin told Baraz. "My friend and I were in the middle of a little altercation when you arrived, hence his testiness."

"Golophin, there is so much I must ask you," Mirren said.

"Indeed? Well, child, you may ask me anything you like, but not right now. I am somewhat preoccupied. It might be best if you said nothing of this meeting. The fewer folk who know I am here the better." Then he looked at his companion, and laughed. The other's mouth crooked under the cowl in answer.

"You may tell your father, though. I will see him tonight, or possibly tomorrow morning."

"What is this news you have come to deliver? I will take it to him."

Golophin's ravaged face hardened into a mask. "No. One so young should not have to bear such tidings." He turned to Baraz. "See the lady safe home, soldier."

Baraz glared at him. "You may be sure I will."

SPRING MIGHT BE in the air, but up here in the hills there was still an algid bite to the air when the wind got up, and as the day drew on Golophin and his companion kindled a fire with a blast of rubescent theurgy and sat on pads of gathered heather warming themselves at the transparent flames. As the afternoon waned and the sun began to slide behind the white peaks of the Cimbrics in the west, Golophin was aware that a third person had joined them, a small, silent figure who sat cross-legged just outside the firelight.

"That is an abomination," the old mage told his companion.

"Perhaps. I am no longer sure I care greatly. One can become accustomed to all sorts of things, Golophin." The speaker had thrown back his cowl at last and now was revealed as a middle-aged man with close-cropped grey hair and a prize-fighter's face. He reached into the breast of his habit and brought forth a steel flask. Unscrewing the top, he took a sip and tossed it across the fire. Golophin caught it deftly and drank in his turn. "Hebrionese akvavit. I applaud your taste, Bard."

"Call it a perk of the job."

"Call it what it is; spoils of war."

"Hebrion was my home also, Golophin."

"I have not forgotten that, you may be sure."

A tension fizzled across the flames between them, and then slackened as Bardolin chuckled. "Why, Golophin, your hauteur is almost impressive."

"I'm working on it."

"It is pleasant, this, sitting here as though the world were not on fire around us, listening to the hunting bats and the sough of the wind in the heather. I like this country. There is an austerity to it. I do not wonder that it breeds such soldiers."

"You met these soldiers in the field I hear, a decade ago now. So are you become a general now?"

Bardolin bowed. "Not much of a one, it must be said. Give me a tercio and I know what to do. Give me an army and I am baffled."

"That doesn't bode well for your master's efforts in this part of the world, Presbyter."

"We have generals, Golophin, ones who may surprise you. And we have numbers. And the Dweomer."

"The Dweomer as a weapon of war. In the days before

the Empire – the First Empire – it is said that certain Kings fielded regiments of mages. But it has never been recorded that they tolerated the presence of shifters in their armies. Not even the ancients were barbarian enough for that."

"You speak whereof you know nothing."

"I know enough. I know that the thing seated across the fire from me is not Bardolin of Carreirida, and the succubus which hides silent in the shadows behind you was not conjured up for his comfort."

"And yet she is a comfort, nonetheless."

"Then why are you here? To sit and wax nostalgic about the old days?"

"Is that so inexplicable, so hard to believe?"

Golophin dropped his eyes. "I don't know. Ten, twelve years ago I thought there was a part of my apprentice which could still be saved. I am no longer so sure. I am consorting with the enemy now."

"It does not have to be that way. I am still the Bardolin you knew. Because of me, Hawkwood is alive."

"That was your master's whim."

"Partly. The survival of the other had nothing to do with me, though, you may be sure."

"What other?"

"The new Lieutenant of Hebrion."

"I don't understand, Bard."

"I can tell you no more. I, also, am consorting with the enemy, do not forget."

The two wizards stared at each other without animosity, only a gentle kind of sadness.

"It is not as though Hebrion has been destroyed, Golophin," Bardolin said gently. "It has merely suffered a change in ownership."

"That sounds like the self-justification of the thief."

"You are so damned wilful – and wilfully blind." Here Bardolin leaned forward so that the firelight carved a crannied mask out of his bluff features.

"The fleet did not make landfall in Hebrion out of a mere whim, Golophin. Your – our – homeland is vital to Aruan's plans. It so happens that Hebrion, and the Hebros Mountains were once part of the Western Continent."

"How can you –"

"Let me finish. At some time in the unimaginable past Normannia and the west were one great landmass, but they split apart aons ago, drifting like great lilypads and letting the ocean flood in between them. Aruan and his chief mages have been conducting research into the matter for many years."

"So?"

"So, there is something, some element or mineral in the very bowels of the Western Continent which is in effect the essence of the energy we know as *magic*. Pure theurgy, running like a vein of precious ore through the very bedrock of the earth. It is that which has made Aruan what he is."

"And you what you have become, I take it."

"This energy runs through the Hebros also, for the Hebros and the mountains of the Western Continent were once part of the same chain. That is why Hebrion has always been home to more of the Dweomer-folk than any other of the Five Kingdoms. That is why Hebrion had to fall. Golophin, you have no conception of the great researches that are underway, in the west, at Charibon, even in Perigraine. Aruan is close to solving an ancient and paramount riddle. What are the Dweomer-folk, and how were they created? Is it in fact possible to imbue an ordinary man with the Dweomer, and make of him a mage?"

Golophin found his bitter reply dying in his mouth. Despite himself, he was fascinated. Bardolin smiled.

"Think of the progress this army of mages can make in the pursuit of pure knowledge, given all the materials they need, allowed to proceed in peace with their studies. Golophin, for the first time in history, the bowels of the library of St. Garaso in Charibon have been opened up and laid bare. There are treatises and grimoires down there that predate the First Empire. They have been sealed away by the Church for centuries, and now they are finally being studied by those who can understand them. I have seen a first edition of *Ardinac's Bestiary* –"

"No! They were all destroyed by Willardius."

Bardolin laughed, and threw his hands up in the air. "I've seen it, I tell you! Golophin, listen to me, think about this. Imagine what a mind like yours, allied to that of Aruan, could mean for the progress of learning, both theurgical and otherwise. An eighth Discipline is only the beginning. This is a precious opportunity, a crux of history right here and now, with the bats squeaking round our ears in the hills north of Torunn. It may be there are things about our regime that you find distasteful – no man is perfect, not even Aruan. But damn it all, our motives are pure enough. To lead mankind down a different path.

"At this time, there is a fork in the road. Man can either follow what he terms as science, and develop ever more efficient means of killing, and build a world where there is no place for the Dweomer, and which will eventually see its death. Or he can embrace his true heritage, and become something entirely different. A society can be created in which theurgy is part of daily commerce, and learning is treasured above the soot-stained tinkering of the artisan. At this point in history, mankind must choose between these two destinies, and that choice will be made in a tide of blood, because that is the way of revolutions. But that, regrettable though it may be, does not make the choice invalid.

"Join us, Golophin, in the name of God. Perhaps we can spare the world some of that bloodletting."

The two men stared intently across the fire at one another. Golophin could not speak. For the first time in his long life he did not know what to say.

"I'm not asking you to decide now. But at least think about it." Bardolin rose. "Aruan has been away from Normannia a long time. It is a foreign country to him. But that is not true for us. Learned though he is, we possess a familiarity with this world of today that he lacks. He respects you, Golophin. And if your conscience still niggles, think on this; I am convinced you would have more influence over his deeds as a counsellor and friend rather than as an antagonist.

"As for me, my friend you have always been, and yet remain – whatever you might choose to believe."

Bardolin rose with the smooth alacrity of a much younger man. "Think about it, Golophin. At least do that. Farewell."

And he was gone, only a slight stirring in the air, a faint whiff of ozone to mark his passing. Golophin did not move, but stared into the firelight like a blind man.

TEN

THE BLADEHALL WAS crowded, bubbling with talk that rose to the tall roof-beams in a babble of surmise. Virtually every senior officer in the country was present, with the exception of Aras of Gaderion, but he had sent a staff officer-cum-courier to represent him and to inform the High Command of recent events at the Gap.

The King entered without ceremony, limping a little as he always did when he was tired. It was common knowledge about the palace that most nights lately he slept in a chair by the Queen's bed. She was very low now, and would not last more than a few more days. Only the day before, a formal embassy had been sent out to Aurungabar on her express orders, and the court was still in a feverish frenzy of speculation as to what it might signify. It was as well to steer clear of the King, though. His temper, never particularly equable, had become truly savage of late.

The Hall hushed as he entered, flanked by General Formio and a tall, horribly scarred old man in travel-stained robes who bore a haversack on one shoulder.. Corfe's personal bodyguard Felorin brought up the rear, watching the stranger's back warily. The little group came to a halt in front of the map-table and Corfe scanned the faces of the assembled officers. They were staring at his aged companion with avid curiosity.

"Gentlemen, I would like to introduce you to the Mage Golophin of Hebrion, one-time chief advisor to King Abeleyn. He is here with tidings from the west which take precedence over all other matters for the moment. Golophin, if you please."

The old wizard thanked Corfe and then stared at the hungry faces that surrounded him much as the King had done. His mellifluous voice was without its customary music as he spoke.

"King Abeleyn of Hebrion is dead, as is King Mark of Astarac, and Duke Frobishir of Gabrion. The great naval armament which they commanded is destroyed. The fleet of the westerners has made landfall in Hebrion, and that kingdom has surrendered to the foe."

A second of stunned silence, and then everyone began talking at once, a tumult of horrified exclamations, questions lost in the clamour. Corfe held up a hand and the noise tailed away. The Torunnan King's face was grey as marble.

"Let him continue."

Golophin, unbidden, had filled a glass from the decanter on the table, and drained it at a draught. He smelled of woodsmoke, sweat, and another evocative stink much like the charged air of a thunderstorm. A vein throbbed like a blue worm in the hollow of one temple.

"Himerian troops are on the march. They are riding out from Fulk, down both sides of the Hebros towards Imerdon and the northern Hebrionese coast. An army has crossed from Candelaria into East Astarac and has defeated the Astarans in the foothills. Garmidalan is about to stand siege, if it is not besieged already. And if my information is correct, another Himerian army is making for the passes of the Malvennors as we speak, to take Cartigella from the rear."

"How do you know all this?" General Comillan asked, his thick moustache bristling like a besom.

"I have a – a reliable source in the Himerian camp."

"Won't they at least put up some resistance?" one Torunnan asked incredulously.

"Not in Hebrion. It has been agreed that there will be no pillage, no sacking of Abrusio, in exchange for a bloodless occupation. In Astarac the military has been caught off-guard, as have we all. They are in full retreat westwards. The garrison of Cartigella is capable enough, though, and will probably stand siege under Cristian, the Crown Prince." Golophin filled his glass again, peered into it as though it were hemlock, and tossed it off.

"But Cartigella's fall is only a matter of time."

"Gentlemen," Corfe said softly, "we are at war. The general mobilisation is under way. I signed the Conscription Decree not half an hour ago. As of now, this kingdom is under martial law, and every able-bodied man in the country is being called to the colours. No exceptions. Comillan, Formio, in the morning you will begin processing the first batch of conscripts. I want them knocked into shape as quick as possible. Comillan, the bodyguard will act as the kernel of the new training cadre –"

"Sir, I protest."

"Your protest is noted. Colonel Heyn, I am drawing up a command for you which you will take north to reinforce Aras within two days. Colonel Melf."

"Sir?"

"You also are to have an independent command. Once the Merduk contingents arrive from Aurungabar you will set off, and take it south, to the port of Rone. Your area of operations will be the southernmost foothills of the Cimbrics, where the mountains come down to the Levangore itself. The enemy may well try to sneak a column round our southern flank that way. You will be liasing with Admiral Berza, of course."

"Sir!" Melf, a tall, lean man who looked like a peasant farmer, beamed.

"What of the main body of the army sir?" Formio asked.

"It will remain here in Torunn for the time being, under my command. That means the Cathedrallers; your Orphans, Formio; and the bodyguard, of course. Ensign Roche, my apologies for keeping you waiting. What news from Aras?"

The young officer seemed to gulp for a second, then jerkily proffered a despatch-case. "Sir –"

"Read it out, if you please. All present needs must hear it."

Ensign Roche flipped off the lid of the leather tube and unrolled the paper within. He cleared his throat. "It is dated six days ago sir.

"*Corfe,*
"*I write in haste and without ceremony. The bearer of this despatch will give you a fuller picture of conditions up here than my penmanship ever can. He has experienced*

them first-hand. But you must know this – we have been swept out of the Plains entirely by a large-scale advance of the enemy. Not one patrol can be sent out without encountering huge numbers of the foe, and in the past week we have lost heavily in men and horses. I have been tempted to essay a large-scale sally, but prefer to wait for your approval before attempting so major an operation. The Finnmarkans and Tarberans are still not yet up, thanks to our bridge-burning, but the Himerians have numbers enough without them, it seems. I would hazard that they have already stripped Charibon of much of its garrison. They mean to take Gaderion, that much is plain.

"There is more. We are encountering something new, something which the bearer will be able to inform you of more fully. These Hounds*, as they are called – they are beasts of some kind, or men that can become beasts at will. The rumours have been flying about the continent for years, as we all know, but I have had patrols, demi-tercios of good men, slaughtered like rabbits by these things, always in the night, half-glimpsed. Our intelligence-gathering is non-existent now. I believe that soon we will be under siege.*

"Man for man, we are better soldiers than the foe, but this new thing we do not know how to fight, and there are no Dweomer-folk about to advise us. I need reinforcements, but also I need a way to fight back. I need to know how to kill these things.

"Officer Commanding Gaderion, Nade Aras."

There was a concussive silence, as though the wind had been taken out of all their mouths. Corfe spoke first. "Ensign Roche, you have encountered these things General Aras speaks of?"

"I have, sir."

Corfe flapped a hand impatiently. "Tell us."

Briefly, tonelessly, Roche recounted the fate which had befallen his patrol two sennights before. The attack of the huge, half-seen beast, the death of his sergeant.

"We found the bodies in the wood after it had gone, sir. They had been torn into pieces, twelve men. We had only heard that one shout. We saddled up what horses remained, doubled up in the saddles, and made our way back into Gaderion that same night."

"You left the bodies unburied?" Comillan snapped.

Roche ducked his head. "I am afraid so, sir. The men were panicked, and I –"

"It's all right, Ensign," Corfe said. He turned to the old mage who stood at his side listening intently. "Golophin, can you enlighten us?"

The wizard sighed heavily and stared into his empty glass. "Aruan and his cohorts have been experimenting for years, perhaps centuries. They have taken normal men and made them into shifters. They have taken shifters and twisted them into new forms. They have bred unnatural beasts for the sole purpose of waging war, and these are now being unleashed upon the world. They destroyed the allied fleet, and now they will take part in the assault upon Torunna."

"I ask you Aras's question; how do we kill these things?"

"It's quite simple. Iron or silver. One nick from a point or a blade made of either and the Dweomer which flows through the veins of these creatures has its current disrupted, and they die instantly."

Corfe seemed slightly incredulous. "That's it?"

"That's it, sire."

"Then they are not so fearsome after all. You hearten me, Golophin."

"The swords and pike-points of the army are made of tempered steel," Formio said wryly. "They will not bite, it seems. Nor will the lead of our bullets." He looked quizzically at the old wizard.

"Correct, General."

"We must get the smithies busy then," Corfe broke in. "Iron blades and pike-points. And I'm thinking maybe some kind of iron barbs which can be fitted onto armour. We'll make of every man a deadly pincushion, so that if these things so much as lay a paw on him, they'll send themselves off to Hell."

The mood in the Bladehall lightened somewhat, and there were even some chuckles. The news from the west was bad, yes, but Hebrion and Astarac were not Torunna, and Abeleyn was no Corfe. The very sea itself might be subjugated to the will of Aruan and his cohorts, but there was no force on earth that would stop the Torunnan army once it had begun to march.

"Gentlemen," Corfe said then, "I believe you all know your duties for now, and Lord knows there's enough to be getting on with. You are dismissed. Ensign Baraz – you will stay behind."

"Corfe," Formio said in a low voice, "have you thought any more on our discussion?"

"I have, Formio," the King replied evenly, "and while you make very valid points, I believe that the possible gains outweigh the risks."

"If you are wrong –"

"There is always that chance." Corfe smiled, and gripped Formio by the shoulder. "We are soldiers, not seers."

"You are a king, not some junior commander who can be spared to hare off on a whim."

"It's no whim, believe me. If it succeeds, it will bring down the Second Empire. That makes the gamble worthwhile."

"Then at least let me come with you."

"No. I need to leave behind someone I trust – someone who could be Regent if the worst occurs."

"A Fimbrian."

"A Fimbrian, who is my closest friend, and most trusted commander. It must be you, Formio."

"The nobility will never wear it."

"The Torunnan nobility is not the fractious beast it once was – I have seen to that. No, you would have the backing of the army, and that is all that matters. Now let us hear no more of this. Continue the preparations, but discreetly."

"Will you let him into our little secret?" Formio asked, nodding at Golophin, who was conversing with Ensign Baraz on the other side of the hall. Nearly all the other officers had left by now and the fire cracked and spat loudly in the sudden quiet. Felorin stood watchful as always in the shadows.

"I believe I will. He may be able to make some suggestion. There is always that bird of his anyway, a hell of a useful thing to have around."

Formio nodded. "There is something, though, Corfe – something about Golophin that does not feel right."

"Explain."

"Nothing, perhaps. It is just that sometimes I feel he should hate more. He has seen his King slain, his country enslaved, and yet I sense no hatred, hardly any anger in him."

"What are you now, some kind of mindreader?" Corfe grinned.

"I find myself not wholly trusting him, is all."

Corfe clapped him on the back. "Formio, you are getting old and cantankerous. I'll see you later down at Menin field. We'll go over those new formations again. But talk to the Quartermaster-General for me. Let's see how much scrap iron we can come up with."

Formio saluted, spun on his heel, and left as crisply as a young officer fresh off the drill square.

"A good man, I think," Golophin said, walking over from the fire. "You are lucky in your friends, sire."

"I have been lucky, yes," Corfe said. Formio's words had unsettled him. He stared at the old wizard closely. "Golophin, you said you had a reliable source in the Himerian camp. Would it be out of place for me to ask who it might be?"

"I would rather that his identity remained secret for now. He is an ambivalent sort, sire, a man unsure as to where his loyalties lie. They are sorry creatures, these fellows who cannot make up their minds what is black and what is white. Do you not think?" The mage's smile was disconcertingly shrewd.

"Indeed." There was a brief moment where their eyes locked, and something akin to a struggle of wills took place. Golophin dropped his gaze first. "Was there anything else, sire?"

"Yes, yes there was. I was wondering if – that is to say –" Now it was Corfe who looked down. Quietly, he said, "I thought you might call in on the Queen. She is very low, and the physicians can do nothing. Old age, they say, but I believe there is more to it than that, something to do with your... realm of expertise."

"I should be glad to, sire." And here the wizard's eyes met Corfe's unflinchingly. "I am flattered that you should trust me in such a grave matter." He bowed deeply. "I shall call on her at once, if that is convenient. Now, if you will excuse me sire, I have things to attend to."

"Your suite is adequate?"

"More than adequate, thank you, sire." The wizard bowed again, and left, his robes whispering about him.

The man had served kings faithfully and unstintingly for longer than Corfe's lifetime. Formio was merely being a cautious Fimbrian, that was all. The King of Torunna rubbed his temples wearily. *God, to get clear of the palace, the city, to get back on a horse and sleep under the stars for a while.* Sometimes he thought that there were so many things contained in his head that one day it would bulge and burst like an overripe melon. And yet when he was in the field it was as though his mind were as clear as the tip of an icicle.

I never should have been King, he thought, as he had thought so often down the years. *But I am here now and there is no other.*

He collected himself, strode across to the fire where Ensign Baraz stood stiff and forgotten.

"You've met the great Golophin, I see. What do you make of him?"

Baraz seemed startled by the question. "He asked me about my grandfather," he blurted out. "But there was not much I could tell him that is not in the history-books. He wrote poetry."

"Golophin?"

"Shahr Ibim Baraz, sire. *The Terrible Old Man* he was called by his men."

"Yes. Sometimes we called him that too, and other things besides," Corfe said wryly. "Whatever happened to him?"

"No-one knows. He left camp and some say he set out for the steppes of his youth, at the very height of his victories."

"As well for Torunna he did. Baraz, Princess Mirren speaks very highly of you. She seems to think that you are a very gallant young officer and has asked that you accompany her on her daily rides from now on. What would you say to such a proposal?"

Baraz's face was a picture of pleasure and chagrin.

"I am honoured by the lady's confidence, sir, and I would esteem it a great privilege to be her morning escort."

"But."

"But I had hoped to be attached to the field army. I have not yet commanded anything more than a ceremonial guard, and I was hoping to be assigned to a tercio."

"You think that your time spent with the general staff is wasted then."

Baraz's dark face flushed darker. "Not at all, sir, but if an officer has never commanded men in the field, what kind of officer is he?"

Corfe nodded approvingly. "Quite right. I'll make a bargain with you, Baraz, one that you had best not give me cause to regret."

"Sir?"

"You will remain the Lady Mirren's escort for the time being, and will remain attached to the staff as interpreter. In fact I will have need of you in that capacity this very evening. But when the time comes I promise that you will have a combat command. Satisfied?"

Baraz smiled uncertainly. "I am at your command, of course, sir – I merely follow orders. But thank you, sir."

"Good. I will wish to see you in the audience wing of the palace at the sixth hour, in your best uniform. Dismissed."

Baraz saluted and left. There was a jauntiness to his stride that made Corfe pause. Before Aekir, there had been something of the young officer's eagerness in himself. That urge to make a name for himself, the desire to do the right thing. But in Aekir his soul had been re-tempered in a white-hot crucible, and had made of him someone else.

THE FACE WAS like that of a bloodless doll, lost in the wasteland of blinding linen that surrounded it. So slight was the wizened form under the coverlet that it might not have been there at all, a mere trick of the lamplight perhaps, a shadow conjured up by the warm flames leaping in the hearth. But then the eyes opened, and life glistened out of them. Bloodshot with pain and exhaustion, they yet retained some of their old fire, and Golophin could well picture the beauty that had once filled the wasted face.

"You are the Hebrian mage, Golophin." The voice was slight but clear.

"Yes, lady."

"Karina, Prio, leave us." This to the two ladies-in-waiting who sat silent as mice in the shadows. They curtseyed, their skirts scraping on the stone floor, and snicked shut the door behind them.

"Come closer, Golophin. I have heard a lot about you."

The wizard approached the bed and, as the firelight fell on his ravaged face, the Queen's eyes widened slightly.

"Hebrion's fall left its mark on you, I see."

"It is a light enough burden, compared to some."

"My husband asked you to come here?"

"Yes, lady."

"That was thoughtful of him, but useless, as we both know. I would have sent for you in any case. There are so few folk of intelligence I can converse with these days. They all troop in here and look dutifully mournful – even Corfe – and I can get little sense out of them. I am near the end and that is that." She hesitated, and said in a more ragged tone, "My familiar is dead. He went before me. I had not imagined there could be such pain, such a loss."

"They are part of us," Golophin agreed, "and with their passing goes something of our own souls."

"You wizards, you can create them, I am told, whereas we Dweomer-poor witches must wait for another to come along. Myself, I shall have no need of another. But I do miss poor Arach." Then she seemed to collect herself. "Where are my manners? You may sit and have some wine, if you do not mind drinking from a glass a queen has used before you. I would call a maid, but then there would be an interminable fuss, and I grow impatient with advancing years."

"As do we all," Golophin smiled, filling the glass. "The old have less time to waste than the young."

She stared at him in silence for a minute and seemed to be testing words in her mouth. Her eyes were bright as fevered jewels.

"What of you now, Master Mage? Where do you call home?"

"I have none, lady. I am a vagabond."

"Will Hebrion see you again?"

"I hope so."

"You would be very welcome here as an advisor at court."

"A Hebrionese wizard? I think you may exaggerate."

"We have all manner of foreigners in Torunna these days. Formio is Fimbrian, Comillan a Felimbric tribesman, Admiral Berza a Gabrionese. Our Pontiff, Albrec, is an Almarkan. The flotsam and jetsam of the world end up in Torunna. You know why?"

"Tell me."

"The King. They are moths to his candle. Even those haughty Fimbrians come trickling over the mountains to join him, year by year. And in his heart he hates it. He would rather be the simple nobody he was before Aekir's fall. I have watched him these seventeen years and seen the joy leech out of him day by day. Only Mirren lifts his heart. Mirren, and the prospect of leading an army into battle."

Golophin stared at Odelia wonderingly. "Lady, your candour is disarming."

"Candour be damned. I will be dead within the week. I want you to do something for me."

"Anything."

"Stay here with him. Help him. When I go there will be only Formio left for him to confide in. You have spent your life in the service of Kings. End it in the service of this one. He is a soldier of genius, Golophin, but he needs someone to guide him through the silken quagmire that is the court. He, also, is less patient than he was, and will brook no opposition to what he sees as right. I would not have such a man end his days a tyrant, hated by all."

"Surely that is not possible."

"There is a black hole in his soul, and once he sets his mind to something he will shift earth and heaven to accomplish it, recking nothing of the consequences. In the years he has been King I have tried to make him see the value of compromise, but it is like trying to reason with a stone. He must have someone of experience in the darker wiles of the world beside him, to help him see that a sword is not the answer to everything."

"You flatter me, lady. But the confidence of a king is not an easily won thing."

"He admires competence and plain speaking. From what I have heard, you possess both. But there is another thing. When I am gone there will not be a single practitioner of the Dweomer at court, save only my daughter. She also needs guidance. There is a wellspring of power in her that quite eclipses anything in my experience. I would not have her explore the Dweomer alone." Odelia looked away. Her withered hands picked restlessly at the heavy weave of the coverlet. "I would she had been born without it. It would make her life easier.

"Your people and mine have chosen a different side in this war, Golophin. The wrong side. They had little choice in the matter, it is true, but they will suffer for it. They may even be destroyed by it."

Something astonishing dawned on Golophin.

"You are against this war."

Odelia managed a tight smile. "Not against it, but I have my doubts about fighting it to the bitter end. The Dweomer runs in my blood as it does in yours, and in my daughter's. I believe this Aruan to be evil, but many of the aims he espouses are not. We will not be fighting Merduks in the time to come, but fellow Ramusians – not that there is much to tell between us all now I suppose. And I do not want a pogrom of the Dweomer-folk to stain Corfe's victory, if he should gain one. There must come an end to this senseless persecution of those who practice magic."

Golophin felt a wave of relief. He was not a traitor, then. His doubts were not his alone. And Bardolin might not be the evil puppet he had feared, but a man trying to do the right thing in difficult circumstances. The thing he had so wanted to be true might well be so.

"Lady," he said, "you have my word that when the time comes I will be by your husband's side. If needs be I will make myself his conscience."

Odelia closed her eyes. "I ask no more. Thank you, Brother Mage. You have eased an old woman's mind."

Golophin bowed, and as he did he found himself thinking that here in Torunna he had found a king and queen who were somehow larger than the monarchs he had known hitherto. Abeleyn, who had become a good ruler before the end, even a great one, seemed now but a boy beside Corfe of Torunna, the Soldier-King. And this frail woman breathing her last before him; she was a worthy consort. There was a greatness here in this country that would remain the stuff of legend, no matter how many centuries passed it by.

He laid a hand on the Queen's forehead and her eyes fluttered open, the lashes feathering against his palm.

"Hush now."

The Dweomer in Odelia had sunk down to a smoking ember. It would never kindle into light again, but it was all that was keeping her alive. That, and this woman's indomitable will. She might have been a mage – the promise was there – but she had never undergone the training necessary to make her powers bloom. Anger stirred in Golophin. How many others, humble and great across this blinkered world, had wasted their gifts similarly? Bardolin was right. The world could have been different, could still be different. There might still be time.

He gave Odelia sleep, a heavy healing sleep, and with his own powers he stoked up that last ember glowing within her, coaxed it into a last flicker of life. Then he sat back, poured himself some more of the fragrant wine, and mused upon the crooked course of this darkening earth.

ELEVEN

AURUNGZEB STIRRED LAZILY with a kiss of silk hissing about his hams. "I like that woman. I have always liked her. As direct as a man, but with as mind as subtle as an assassin's."

He rolled over in the bed and the sturdy hardwood frame creaked under him. The white-limbed girl who shared it with him scurried nimbly out of the way as his vast bulk settled and he sighed comfortably.

Ancient Akran, the Vizier, leant on a staff that had once been ceremonial but now was genuinely necessary. He stood on the other side of a curtain of gauzy silk which hung like fog around the Sultan's monumental four-poster.

"She is... remarkable, my Sultan, it must be said. Making arrangements for her husband's wedding while she, his wife, is yet living. That argues a formidable degree of will."

"He will accept, of course. But I find myself worrying all the same. Perhaps we sent out the embassy too soon. I am not convinced that he will see past the unseemly haste of the thing. Corfe is as cold and murderous as a winter-wolf, but there is a stiff propriety about him. These Ramusians – well, they are not Ramusian any longer I suppose, but our brothers-in-faith after all – they see marriage in a different light to the rest of us. The Prophet, may God be good to him, never said that a man should have one spouse only, and for a monarch, well... How can a man maintain his dignity with just the one wife? How can he be wholly sure of a son to follow him? Torunna's Queen may be a marvellous woman in many respects, but that did not stop her womb from proving as barren as a salted field. Or near as damn it. One child in sixteen years, and a girl at that. And the bearing of it rendered her a virtual invalid by all accounts. If he has any red blood in his veins at all he ought to jump at this chance, Corfe. A beautiful young woman to share his bed and bear him sons? And she *is* beautiful, Akran. As fair as her mother once was.

"No, unseemly haste or not, Torunna's Queen and myself are of the one mind on this matter. And the fruit of this new union will be my grandchild. Think of that, Akran! My grandson on the throne of Torunna!"

Akran bowed, straightening with the aid of his staff and stifling a groan. "And what of this other union, sire? The Prince Nasir is impatient to know more of his intended bride."

Aurungzeb's grin faded into the bristling darkness of his beard. He levered himself into a sitting position, helped by the nude girl beside him, and while she leant against his back to keep him upright, he stroked his bearded chin with one plump, hairy hand, the rings upon it sparkling like a brilliant, tiny constellation.

"Ah, yes. The girl. A good match, a balancing of the scales." He lowered his voice and peered into the grey mist of the surrounding gauze. "They say she is a witch, you know. Like her mother."

"It may be court gossip, sire, no more."

"It matters not; that shall be Nasir's problem, not mine." He boomed with sudden laughter, shaking the slim, straining shoulders of the girl who was supporting him.

"The Prince has expressed a wish to see this girl before he marries her. He is, in fact, relaying through me a request to go to Torunn to meet this Princess Mirren face to face." Akran licked his thin lips nervously.

Aurungzeb frowned. "He will hold his tongue and do as he is told. What does it matter to him how this girl looks? He will plough her furrow and plant in her a son, and then for recreation he shall have a garden of concubines. The young! They hatch such absurd ideas."

"He also would like to visit Torunn in order to –"

"What? Spit it forth."

"He wants to see something of his mother's homeland."

Aurungzeb's eyebrows shot up his face like two caterpillars on strings. "Does something ail the boy?"

Akran coughed delicately. "I believe the Queen has been telling him stories about the history of her people. I beg your pardon, my Sultan. I mean the people she once belonged to."

"I know what you mean," Aurungzeb growled. "And I was aware of it. She has been filling his head with tall tales of John Mogen and Kyle Ormann. She would do better to prate to him of Indun Meruk or Shahr Baraz."

With a titanic heave, the Sultan hauled himself off the bed. He struggled through the flimsy veil that surrounded it, and sashed close his silk dressing-gown. Barefoot, he padded over to a small gilt table that glittered in the light of the overhead lamps. His soles slapped loudly on the marble floor, for he was an immense man with a pendulous paunch. He gently lifted the brindled length of his beard out of the bosom of his robe and poured himself a goblet of sharp-smelling amber liquid from a silver jug.

He sipped at it, his face changing. There was no trace of joviality left in it now. His eyes were black stones.

"What do we know of the current situation at Gaderion?" he snapped.

"There has been fighting in the open country between the two defensive lines, sire, and the Torunnans may have had the worst of it. In any case, our spies tell us that conscription has begun in earnest, and martial law declared."

Aurungzeb grunted. "He will be wanting troops, under the terms of the treaty. I suppose I shall have to give him some. We are allies, after all, and with these marriages..." He broke off, chin sunk in his chest.

"There are times, Akran, when I wonder if it is all but a dream. Everything that has happened since Armagedir. Here are we, two countries whose faith is the same in all but name, who are about to be joined by the closest of dynastic ties – so close that, if they take, then these two Royal lines will become virtually one. And yet twenty years ago we were each striving for the annihilation of the other in the most savage war that history has yet seen. Old habits have not died hard; they have withered away like morning mist as the sun climbs. I try to tell myself that all this is for the best, for all our peoples, but still something within me is astonished by it all, and is still waiting for the war to begin again. And then this Second Empire, arising out of thin air and empty theology to dominate the world –" He shook his head like a baffled old bear. "Strange times indeed."

He mused some more.

"I tell you what, Nasir shall indeed go to Torunn. He shall lead the contingent of reinforcements that the treaty obliges us to render, and he shall see the face of his bride-to-be. But he shall also make a first-hand report on the state of the Torunnan military, and the current situation up at the Gap. His wide-eyed enthusiasm may well get us farther than the shadowed creeping of our spies."

"He is young, sire..."

"Bah, at his age I had already fought in half a dozen battles. The younger generation has no idea –" Aurungzeb halted, interrupted by the boom of the chamber doors as they were rolled back by a pair of bald-pated eunuchs.

Through the ornate doorway strode a tall woman in cobalt blue silk. A veil covered her face but above it grey eyes flashed from under stibium-darkened brows. Her sandal-clad feet clapped on the marble. Behind her a gaggle of veiled women huddled nervously, and dropped to their knees as the Sultan's baleful glare swept over them. In the four-poster, the slim girl pulled the sheets over her head.

"My Queen –" Aurungzeb began with a voice like thunder, but the woman cut him short.

"What is this I hear about a marriage between Aria and the Torunnan King? Is it true?"

The vizier backed away discreetly and signalled for the eunuchs to close the doors again. They did so, the sonorous boom passing unnoticed as Aurungzeb and his Queen stood glaring at one another.

"Your presence in the harem is both awkward and insulting," Aurungzeb bellowed. "A Merduk Queen –"

"*It is true?*"

Something went out of Aurungzeb, some kind of self-righteous outrage. He turned away and studied his forgotten wine-goblet as if reluctant to meet the fire of her eyes. "Yes, it is true. There have been negotiations, and both parties are in favour of the match. I take it you have some objection."

To his surprise she did not speak. He turned back to her enquiringly and found that she was standing rigid as wood, her hands clasped together, and the beautiful eyes alight above the veil with tears that would not fall.

"Ahara?" he asked, startled.

She lowered her head. "Who thought up this match? The man's wife is not yet dead."

"Actually it was she who suggested it, through our regular diplomatic couriers. She is dying, it seems, and wishes her husband's line to be secured. Torunna needs a male heir. And what better way to cement the bond between our two countries? Nasir shall marry Corfe's daughter at the same time. It will be quite touching, I am sure." Here Aurungzeb stopped. "Ahara, what is wrong?"

The tears had slipped down inside he veil. "Please do not do this. Do not make Aria do this thing." Her voice was low and there was a throb in it.

"Why ever not?" Aurungzeb was a picture of exasperation and perplexity.

"She is... she is so young."

Aurungzeb smiled indulgently and took Ahara in his arms. "It is hard for a mother, I know. But these things are necessary in affairs of state. You will become used to the idea in time, as will she. This Corfe is not a bad fellow. A little austere, perhaps, but he will be good to her. He had better be; she is my daughter, after all. With this our two houses will be joined for all time. Our peoples will become even closer." Aurungzeb tried to hug her more tightly. It was like embracing a pillar of stone. Over her shoulder, he nodded meaningfully at Akran. The Vizier rapped on the chamber doors. "The Queen is leaving. Make way."

Aurungzeb released her. He tilted up her chin and kissed her though the veil. Here eyes were empty, expressionless, their tears dried.

"That is more like it. That is the bearing of a Merduk Queen. Now I feel you may need a rest, my sweetness. Akran, see the Queen back to her apartments. And Akran, see that Serrim gives her something to calm her nerves." Another meaningful look.

Ahara, or Heria as she had once been, left without another word. Aurungzeb stood with his hands on his broad hips, frowning. She was Nasir's mother, hence the dam of a future sultan. And he had made her his Queen – almost seventeen years now she had been his wife. But there was some part of her she kept always hidden, even now. Women! So many times more difficult to deal with than men. He thought she confided in old Shahr Baraz, but that was all. And he – you would think he was her father, the way he watched over her.

A purr from the bed. "My Sultan? It grows cold here. I need to be warmed."

He rubbed his chin. Since Nasir was going to get a look at his new wife, why not do Corfe the same courtesy? Yes, Aria would also go, with a suitable chaperone from the harem. Her beauty would melt that stiff-necked propriety of his, and he would see sense. Excellent. Now where might this glorious double-wedding be held? Aurungabar for choice – Pir-Sar would be such a magnificent setting. No, Corfe would insist on it being in Torunn. He was King of Torunna after all. But it must be soon. This war was erupting around their ears, and once it had blossomed into full flower, Corfe would no doubt take the field, perhaps not to return to the capital for months. Yes, let it happen in Torunn, and straight away. In fact, let Aria take the road at once.

Then Aurungzeb remembered that Odelia had not yet breathed her last. He said a quick, furtive prayer of apology to the Prophet for being so presumptuous. He liked and respected Torunna's present Queen; their letter correspondence had been a stimulating challenge. But he needed her dead, soon.

THE QUEEN OF Ostrabar sat in her chambers like a porcelain vase set aside in a velvet-padded box. She sat straight-backed on a divan and stared through the fretwork of an ornately carved shutter at the teeming sprawl of the city below. This place had been her home throughout her life, though in different guises. Once it had been Aekir, and she had been Heria. Now it was Aurungabar, and she was Ahara. She was a queen, and the man who had been her husband was a king. But of different kingdoms.

When she thought about it like that she had to marvel at the joke fate had played upon Corfe and herself. It had been a long time. She was past youth now, sliding into middle age with grown-up children by a man for whom she felt nothing but distaste.

And her daughter was destined, it seemed, to marry the man who had once been her husband.

How could Corfe do this to her, or to himself? Had he changed that much? Perhaps the passing years had healed or hardened him. Perhaps he was entirely a king now, with a politician's pragmatism. A matter of state, was that it?

"You sent for me, mother?" It was Aria by the door, in the Queen's Wing and thus unveiled, a willowy version of herself as a young woman. Perhaps that was it. The resemblance to the ghost of a woman he once had loved.

"Mother?"

"Come sit with me, Aria."

The girl joined her. Heria smoothed back the raven hair from her cheek with a smile. There was a dreamy sense of unreality that fogged her mind, but it was not unpleasant. Serrim, the ageing eunuch, had a small chest full of every potion and herb and drug that the east produced, and he had made her eat a tiny cube of pure *kobhang* an hour before. He and that wizened crow Akran had watched her swallow it down with ill-concealed relief. It was not that they were afraid of her, but they were the butts of Aurungzeb's anger when she committed some transgression, such as walking unaccompanied in the market, or receiving a male visitor without a eunuch present. The rules seemed to have become more stifling over the years, partly because she was the mother of the Sultan's heir, and partly because as a noble matron she was supposed to set an example, to lead a veiled life of discretion and inoffensiveness. She was no longer even allowed to ride a horse, but must be borne in a palanquin like some kind of aged libertine.

"Have you heard the rumours too, Aria?"

"About my wedding? Yes, mother." The girl's eyes fell. "I am to be married to the King of Torunna, and Nasir is to marry his daughter."

"You know, then. I am sorry. You should have heard it from me."

"It's all right. I know what is expected of me. I suppose it will be quite soon now. In the kitchens they are talking about a caravan being prepared for Torunn, and Nasir is to lead an army to help King Corfe. Imagine, mother, Nasir leading an army!" She smiled. She was a quiet, grave girl, but the smile lit up her face.

Heria looked away. "He will be fine, as will you."

"Will you be coming with us?"

The question rocked her. "I – I don't know." A maniac notion filled her head, a vision of herself at her daughter's wedding, flinging herself at the groom, begging him to remember her. She blinked her stinging eyes clear. "Perhaps not."

Aria took her hand. "What is he like, mother? Is he very old?"

She cleared her throat. "Corfe? He is – he is not so old."

"Older than you?"

She gripped her daughter's fingers tightly. "A little older. Some years older."

Aria looked thoughtful. "An old man. They say he is lame, and bad-tempered."

"Who says?"

"Everyone. Mother, my hand –" Heria released it.

"Are you all right, mother?"

"I'm fine my dear. Tired. Ask the maids to bring in a blanket. I believe I may well lie here and doze a while."

Aria did not move. "They've been giving you more of their drugs, haven't they?"

"It calms me, Aria. Don't be worried."

Don't be worried, she thought. *You are to marry a good man. The best of men.* She closed her eyes. Aria eased her back onto the divan and stroked her hair. "It will be all right, mother. You'll see," she whispered, her lovely face grave again.

Heria slept, and from below her closed eyelids the tears trickled down soundlessly.

THERE WAS AN hour before the dawn, in the black throat of the night, when even a city as large as Torunn slept. Corfe's horse picked its way through the streets unhindered and he rode it with the reins loose on its neck as though the tall gelding knew the way better than he. And perhaps it did, for the bay destrier brought Corfe unbidden to the north gate, where he saluted the sleepy gate-guards and they, grumbling and unaware of his identity, opened the tall postern for him to lead his mount through. Once beyond the city walls he let the gelding have its head, and it burst into a fast canter. The moon was riding high and gibbous in a star-brilliant sky, but it was just possible to make out the glimmerings of the dawn speeding its way up over the distant ramparts of the Jafrar in the east. Corfe left the pale ribbon of the Kingsway and headed north, his steed dipping and rising under him with the undulating ground. But he kept his knees clamped to the gelding's sides and a loose bite on the reins, and it almost seemed that he might be afloat in a grey moonlit sea upon some bobbing ship, save for the eager grunts of the horse and the creak of the saddle under him.

He reined in at last, and the steam of his mount's sweat rose around him, clean and acrid at the same time. Dismounting, he hobbled the gelding with the ease of long practice, and after he had slipped off bridle and saddle, he rubbed it down with a wisp of coarse upland grass. The gelding clumped away, happy to nose at the yellow grass and sniff for better fare. And Corfe sat on the swell of the hill, grey in the moonlight, and stared, not east at the gathering dawn, but west to where the Cimbrics loomed up dark and forbidding in the dregs of the night.

Tribesmen's tales told of a hidden pass in those mountain fastnesses, a narrow way where determined men had once forged a passage of the terrible mountains. The journey was semi-legendary – the reputation of the Cimbrics as the harshest peaks in the world had been well-earned – but it had happened. And Corfe had a map of the route.

Almost four centuries before, when the Fimbrians had been lords of the world, they had sent out exploratory expeditions to all corners of the continent. One of those expeditions had had as its mission the discovery of a pass through the Cimbrics. They had succeeded, but the cost had been horrendous. Albrec, High Pontiff of Torunna and all the Macrobian kingdoms, had discovered the text of the expedition's log in the Inceptine archives of Torunn Cathedral. He seemed to consider the discovery of unique and ancient documents to be part of his calling. Or perhaps it was a hobby of his. Corfe smiled at the moonlit night. Even now that Albrec was a middle-aged man at the head of a large and influential organisation, there was something of the enthusiastic boy about him when it came to a dusty manuscript or mouldering grimoire. This ancient record, an untidy bundle of dog-eared and mouldering papers, he had shown to Corfe on a whim, never guessing how important it might prove.

For Corfe intended to use the log to take an army across the Cimbrics and win the war at a stroke.

It was a huge gamble, of course; the log might be a fiction, or at the least hopelessly out of date. But the alternative to such a bold stroke would be either a full frontal assault on the Thurian Line, or a fall back to the purely defensive business of holding Gaderion and hoping for the best. To make a serious assault on the Thurian Line would be foolhardy to the point of lunacy. It was too heavily fortified, and the defenders would outnumber the attackers many times over. As for the magnificent works at Gaderion, formidable though they were, Corfe placed little faith in the merits of a static defence, and had done since Aekir, all those years ago. He had seen supposedly impregnable cities and fortresses fall too often to be sanguine about the chances of containing the Himerians up at the Gap.

There was snow still clinging to the flanks of the Cimbrics, It glowed in the bright moonlight, and the mountains seemed to be disembodied, luminous shapes that hung suspended over the shadowed expanse of the darkened land at their feet. Deep in the midst of the range, the snow remained inviolate all year round, and even among the lesser peaks the drifts would still be deep and cold. Spring took its time in the high places.

The Fimbrian expedition, three hundred strong, had started out in the Year of the Saint 113, with the melting of the first snows, and once they had fought their way into the centre of the range they had travelled along the backs of huge glaciers as though they were a network of roads amid the tall peaks which spawned them. Crevasses and avalanches had killed them by the score, but in the end they had won through thirty leagues of the most forbidding terrain in the world, and had come finally to the shores of the Sea of Tor, and the trading post of Fort Cariabon as it then was. Even with the renowned stamina and endurance of Fimbrians, they had been two weeks on the mountainous section of the journey, and half of them had been left frozen corpses upon the flanks of those mountains.

Corfe had been mulling over the log for months, and had interviewed a succession of Cimbric tribesmen to test its veracity. Nothing they had told him about the region contradicted the account, and he was convinced that the route was still feasible, if difficult. He could see no other way of winning this war.

His horse, bored with the winter-dry grass, nosed his neck and its warm breath blew down his nape. He rubbed the velvet-soft nostrils absently, and turned his head to peer eastwards.

The rising sun had still to clear the Jafrar, but its promise was clear in the lightening sky. A skein of cloud had caught in the summits of the eastern mountains and looked as though it had been set afire from below. Behind it the sky was palest aquamarine, a pink glow riding up it moment by moment.

He turned his gaze north-east to where the Thurians stood, the first flush of the dawn beginning to pale their eastern sides. The world he knew was defined by the brutal majesty of mountains. The Cimbrics, the Thurians, the Jafrar. They gave birth to the rivers which watered the world. The Ostian, the Searil, the Torrin. Somewhere out there in the low country leading down to the Kardian Sea stood Aurungabar, capital of Ostrabar. He had been there as King and had seen the huge labour of rebuilding which the Merduks had undertaken. Myrnius Kuln's vast Square of Victories still remained, opening out from the foot of what had been the cathedral of Carcasson; but was called *Hor-el Kadhar* now, Glory of God. The old Pontifical palace was now the pleasure garden of the Sultan, wherein his harem had been installed. And somewhere among those buildings there slept right at this moment the woman who had been Corfe's wife.

Why he should find himself thinking about her at this moment he did not know, except that it was usually on waking and on going to sleep that he saw her most clearly. Those ill-defined periods of the day between darkness and light. Or perhaps she was lying awake herself in the pre-dawn murk, and thinking of him. The thought made his heart beat faster. But the woman he pictured in his mind was young, not much more than a girl. She would be almost out of her thirties now, a mature woman. And he, he was a greying martinet with a halt leg. They were strangers, complete and utter. And yet the pain remained.

Was she thinking of him at this moment? There was the oddest pain in his breast, a wrench as though something there had suddenly constricted. He pushed the balls of his palms into his eyes until the lights flared, and the pain faded. He was too old to be entertaining such fancies.

He knew he would marry this girl who was his wife's daughter. It was necessary for the good of the kingdom, and he had sacrificed so much to that end that he could not imagine doing otherwise.

But there was a deeper, darker reason for doing so that he would not even contemplate admitting to himself. In marrying Aria, he would possess something of Heria again, and perhaps that would help calm his snarling soul. Perhaps.

TWELVE

In squares and at street-corners the people gathered in subdued crowds, while those who could read relayed the content of the daily bulletins to their fellow citizens.

> *This day were executed Hilario Duke of Imerdon, Lord Queris of Hebriera, and Lady Marian of Fulk, they having been found guilty of conspiring against the Presbyter of Hebrion, Lord Orkh. May Almighty God have mercy on their souls.*
>
> *A reward of five hundred silver crowns is offered for information leading to the arrest and apprehension of the following...*

And here a long list of names followed which those reading the bulletin intoned in stentorian voices, watching always to see if any of the Knights Militant, or worse, an Inceptine were near.

No-one knew how or where the executions took place, and the names of the dead all belonged to the nobility of Hebrion. Thus while the common folk might feel anger, even outrage at this unseen slaughter of their betters, they were largely unaffected by it. And besides, there was a new nobility to get used to.

Thus the life of Abrusio, which had shuddered to a trembling halt for days after the first landings, slowly began to return to something approaching normality. Market-stalls were cautiously opening up again, and taverns began to fill in the evenings as folk became less afraid to walk the streets at night. There was no curfew, no martial law, just the daily bulletins, their wording unchanged but for the names they listed. Even the soldiers of the garrison had been merely told to stack arms and return to barracks. There was talk of a treaty having been signed, a peaceful annexation, and certainly the new rulers of Hebrion were busy men. They had taken up residence not in the palace but in the old Inceptine abbey, as befitted a group of churchmen, and from the abbey the couriers rode in unending streams, while in the harbour every Royal vessel remaining had received a boarding party of Himerians and was frantically readying to put to sea.

It was not so bad, on the whole, and people looked back to the hysteria which had followed the rumours of the fleet's destruction with a kind of abashed wonder. They forget – or chose not to remember – the storm which had smote the city, the thunderheads which had hidden the sun and darkened the face of the waters at noon, and the sea-lightnings which had capered madly, striking people in the streets, setting light to houses. Only the deluge which had followed had stopped the city from burning a second time. The black clouds had burst overhead and people had scurried for cover as the rain came down in rods, flattening the waves which the west wind had reared up, turning the steep streets in the upper city into tawny rivers.

There were those who said that in the heart of the lightnings and the hammering rain the sky had not been empty. Things had been circling below the lowering clouds. Monstrous things which were not birds. But people chose not to dwell on these things now, and those who insisted were ignored and even ridiculed.

As the storm had lifted, and the daylight returned, the horizon had become dark with ships. There were a few fools who wiped the rain out of their eyes and cheered the return of King Abeleyn, but they were soon hushed. Out of the west, the enemy had come to claim his prize.

The soldiers of the garrison, many little more than frightened boys, ran out the great guns of the mole-forts and barricaded the wharves of the waterfront. A few public-spirited citizens helped them, but most locked themselves indoors, as if they could somehow will the invaders away, while many others choked the city gates with waggons and carts and laden mules, and set off for the dubious sanctuary of the Hebros Mountains. Perhaps a hundred thousand of Abrusio's population departed in this manner, churning up the Northern Road in a frenzied exodus. In their midst rode many noblemen with fortunes stuffed into bulging saddlebags, and a canny teamster might line his pockets handsomely if he were willing to sell his waggon to some desperate aristocratic family.

The enemy fleet had backed their topsails within a half league of the moles and there they had ridden out the breeze, which had backed round to south-south-east. Only a few Himerian vessels had put in towards the Inner Roads, flying flags of truce. Archaic, cog-like ships, they had sailed smoothly past the staring gun-crews of the moles and moored at the foot of Admiral's Tower and disgorged not the beasts of nightmare that the populace had feared, but a dignified group of black-clad clerics under a flapping white flag. The gunners of the mole-forts had held their fire in fear as much as anything else, for the fleet which had hove-to beyond Abrusio's massive breakwaters was larger than anything they had ever seen. And what was more, on the decks of those innumerable ships there were massed tens of thousands of armoured figures. They might take a heavy toll of such a host, should the Himerians try to force the passage of the moles, but they would be overwhelmed in the end. Their senior officers, all well-bred second-raters, had fled the city days earlier and so the common soldiery of Abrusio, in the absence of definite orders, waited to see what might happen. They trusted to the white flags of the invaders and the rumours of the mysterious treaty which had been doing the rounds of the city ever since the flight of the Queen.

A few of the more prosperous citizens who possessed some backbone met the Himerian delegation on the waterfront and were told with firm affability that they were now subjects of the Second Empire, members of the Church of Himerius, and as such, guaranteed protection from any form of rapine or pillage. This cheered them considerably, and they went down on their knees to kiss the ring of the dark-skinned leader of the invaders whose eyes were an unsettling shade of amber. He introduced himself as Orkh, now Presbyter of Hebrion, and his accent was strange, with something of the east about it. When he stumbled in his understanding of the Abrusians' babbling a hooded figure at his side clarified their words in a low voice and an accent that was unmistakably Hebrian.

Since then a few more ships had put in, but to the astonishment of the citizenry, the vast Himerian fleet had disappeared. Old sailors mending nets down on the waterfront sniffed the wind, now veering to the west again, and looked at each other, mystified. Square-rigged vessels such as the Himerian cogs ought to have been embayed in the Gulf of Hebrion by such a breeze, or even run aground. But they had sailed away in the space of a night, seemingly against the wind, and against all that was natural to seafaring experience.

Those ships which had put ashore had disembarked perhaps a thousand troops and these were all the occupation force that it would seem the Second Empire deemed necessary to hold Abrusio, though rumours had come in to the city of more armies on the march in the north and the east. There had been a battle on the borders with Fulk, and the Hebrian forces there were in panicked retreat, it was said. Pontifidad, capital of the Duchy of Imerdon, had capitulated to the invaders after defeat in a battle before her very walls. The Duke of Imerdon had fled for his life with Knights Militant in hot pursuit. And there were even hazier rumours, which no one could verify or account for, that the Himerians had landed in Astarac, and were preparing to besiege Cartigella.

The occupiers of Abrusio were a strange and disparate body. Many wore the robes of Inceptines, but over those robes they had donned black half-armour and they went gauntleted and armed with steel maces. They rode shining ebony horses which were tall and gangling as the camels of the east, and gaunt as greyhounds. Very many of these fearsome clerics were black men, who looked as though they might hail from Punt or Ridawan, but they spoke together in a language that even the most well-travelled mariner had never heard before, and many of them rode with an homunculus perched on their shoulders, or flapping about their shaven heads.

There were Knights Militant who rode the same weird breed of horses as their Inceptine Brothers, but who kept their faces hidden, their eyes glinting behind the T-shaped slot in their closed helms. But the most mysterious of the invaders were those whom the foreign clerics referred to simply as the *Hounds*. These were a type of men who went about in straggling troops, always accompanied by a mounted Inceptine, and they looked as though they came from every nation under heaven. They went barefoot, dressed always in rags, and there was something vulpine and horribly eager about their eyes. They spoke seldom, and had little dealings with the populace, the Inceptines leading them like a shepherd his sheep – or an overseer his slaves – but, unarmoured and ill-kempt though they might be, they frightened the folk of Abrusio more than any of the other Himerians.

"THEY HAVE ESCHEWED the coastal route, the shorter voyage, and have struck out for the open sea," lord Orkh, Presbyter of Hebrion, said in his sibilant, heavily accented Normannic.

"And they are already out of the range of our airborne contingents, I take it, or else this conversation would be entirely different."

Orkh licked his lipless mouth. In the darkened room his fulvous eyes glowed with a light of their own and his skin had a reptilian sheen about it.

"Yes, lord. We expected them to make for the Hebrian Gulf, and the direct route to the Astaran coast, but they –"

"They outsmarted you."

"Indeed. This man who captains the *Seahare* is a mariner of some repute, and is known to you, I believe. Richard Hawkwood, a native of Gabrion."

The simulacrum to which Orkh was speaking went silent. It was a shimmering, luminous likeness of Aruan, and now it frowned. Orkh bent his head before its pitiless gaze.

"*Hawkwood.*" Aruan spat the word. Then, abruptly, he laughed. "Fear not, Orkh, I am a victim of my own whim, it would seem. Hawkwood! It would seem that he has more bottom than I gave him credit for." His voice lowered into something resembling the purr of a giant feline. "You have, of course, set in place an alternative plan for the interception of the Hebrian Queen."

"Yes, lord. As we speak, a swift vessel is putting out from the Royal yards."

"Who commands?"

"My lieutenant."

"The renegade? Ah yes, of course. A good choice. His mind is so consumed by irrational hatred that he will fulfil his mission to the letter. How many days' start does Hawkwood have?"

"A week."

"A week! There are weather-workers among the pursuers I take it."

Orkh hesitated a moment and then nodded firmly.

"Good. Then we shall consider that loose end taken care of. What of the Hebrian Treasury?"

Here Orkh relaxed a little. "We captured it almost entirely intact, my lord."

"Excellent. And the nobility?"

"Hilario Duke of Imerdon we executed today. That more or less wipes out the top tier of the aristocracy."

"Aside from your turncoat lieutenant, of course."

"He is entirely ours, my lord, I can vouch for it personally. And his status will be useful once things have settled down somewhat."

"Yes, I suppose it will. He is a tool apt for many uses. I do not regret sparing him as I do Hawkwood. But had I allowed Hawkwood, as well as Abeleyn, to die at that time, I could well have lost Golophin." Aruan's shade settled its chin on its chest pensively. "I would I had more like you, Orkh. Men I can truly trust."

Orkh bowed.

"But Golophin will see sense yet, I guarantee it. Good! Get that money in the pockets of those who will appreciate it. Buy every venal soul you can and handle Hebrion with a velvet glove. It is silver filigree to Torunna's iron. Corfe's kingdom we must crush, but Hebrion, ah, she must be wooed... How soon before we can expect the fleet off Cartigella?"

"My captains tell me that with the aid of their weather-workers they will drop anchor before the city in eight days."

"That will do. I believe that will do. Cartigella will be invested by land and sea, and will be made to see sense as Hebrion has."

"You don't think that the Hebrion Queen is making for her homeland?"

"If she is, the fleet will snap her up, but I doubt it. No, I sense Golophin's hand at work here. He must have healed Hawkwood and spirited the Queen away. He is in Torunn now, and that is where I believe she is going. They are touchingly fond of one another, I am told. All these splendid people we must kill! It is a shame. But then if they were not so worthy, then they would not be worth killing." He smiled, though his face remained without humour.

"Make sure our noble renegade catches this Isolla, Orkh. With her gone, Hebrion will acquiesce to our rule that much more easily. And I will give the kingdom to this man when he kills her. It will doubtless lend even more of an edge to his eagerness when I inform him of his reward. You, I will install in Astarac, for it will prove more troublesome than Hebrion I believe, and you will have to keep an eye on Gabrion. Does that satisfy you?"

For an instant what might have been a thin black tongue flickered between Orkh's lips. "You honour me, lord."

"But now the war in the east gathers pace. The assault on Gaderion will begin soon, and the Perigrainian army is preparing to move on Rone. We will enter Torunna through the back door while knocking at the front. Let their much-vaunted Soldier-King try being in two places at once." Again, the perilous, triumphant smile. The simulacrum began to fade.

"Do not fail me, Orkh," it said casually, and then winked out.

THE *HIBRUSIAN* WAS a sleek barquentine which displaced some six hundred tones and had a crew of fifty. Square-rigged on the foremast, she carried fore-and-aft sails on main and mizzen, and was designed to be handled by a small ship's company. The Hebrian navy had built her to Richard Hawkwood's experimental designs and her keel had been-laid down barely a year before. She had been conceived as a formidable kind of Royal yacht to transport the King and his entourage on state visits abroad, and was luxuriously appointed in every respect. The Himerians had found her laid up in dry dock and had at once launched her down the slipway on Orkh's orders. Renamed the *Revenant* by someone with a black sense of humour, she floated at her moorings now some way from shore in the Outer Roads. Her crew had been trebled by the addition of Himerian troops of all kinds, and she awaited a signal from Admiral's Tower to cast off and go hunting.

The signal came. Three guns fired at short intervals, three bubbles of grey smoke from the battlements preceding the distant boom of their detonation. The *Revenant* slipped her moorings, set jibs and fore-and-aft courses on main and mizzen, and began to carve a bright wake through the choppy sea with the wind square on her starboard beam. On her quarterdeck, the thing which had once been Lord Murad of Galiapeno grinned viciously at the southern horizon, an homunculus perched on its shoulder and chuckling into its ear.

THIRTEEN

"KEEP HER THUS until four bells," Hawkwood told the helmsman. "Then bring her one point to larboard. Arhuz!"

"Skipper?"

"Be prepared to send up the mizzen topsail when we alter course. If the wind backs, call me at once. I am going below."

"Aye, sir," Arhuz answered smartly. He checked the xebec's course on the compass board and then swept the decks with his gaze, noting the angle of the yards, the fill of the sails, the condition of the running rigging. Then he watched the sea and sky, noting the direction of the swell, the position of clouds near and far, all those almost indefinable details which a master-mariner took in and filed away without conscious volition. Hawkwood clapped him on the shoulder, knowing the *Seahare* was in good hands, and went below.

He was exhausted. For days he had been on deck continually, snatching occasional dozes in a sling of canvas spliced to the mizzen-shrouds, and eating upright on the xebec's narrow quarterdeck, with one eye to the wind and another to the sails. He had pushed the crew and the *Seahare* very hard, straining to extract every knot of speed out of the sleek craft and keeping the helmsmen on tenterhooks with minute variations of course to catch errant breezes. The log had been going continually in the forechains and a dozen times a day (and night) the logsman would cast his board into the sea while his mate watched the sands trickling through the thirty-second glass and cry *nip* when the time ran out. And the line would be reeled back in and the knots which had been run out by the ship's passage counted. So far, with a beam wind like this to starboard, the fore-and-aft rig of the xebec was drawing well, and they were averaging seven knots. Seven long sea-miles an hour. In the space of six days, running due south, they had put almost a hundred and ninety leagues between themselves and poor old Abrusio, and by Hawkwood's calculations had long since passed the latitude of northern Gabrion, though that island lay still three hundred miles eastwards. Hawkwood had decided to avoid the narrow waters of the Malacar Straits, and sail instead south of Gabrion itself, entering the Levangore to the west of Azbakir. The Straits were too close to Astarac, and too easily patrolled. But a lot depended on the wind. While veering and backing a point or two in the last few days, it had remained steady and true. Once he changed course for the east, as he would very soon, he would have to think about sending up the square-rigged yards, on the fore and mainmasts at least. Lateen yards were less suited to a stern wind than square-rigged ones. The men would be happier too. The massive lateen yards, which gave the *Seahare* the look of some marvellous butterfly, were heavy to handle and awkward to brace round and reef.

He rubbed his eyes A packet of spray, knocked aboard by the swift passage of the ship's beakhead, drenched the forecastle. The xebec was riding the swell beautifully, shouldering aside the waves with a lovely, graceful motion and almost no roll. Despite this, seasickness had afflicted his supercargo almost from the moment they had left the shelter of Grios Point, and they had remained in their cabins. A fact for which he was inordinately grateful. He had too much to think about to worry about a sparring match between Isolla and Jemilla. And the boy, whose whelp was he? Murad's in the eyes of the world, but Hawkwood had heard court rumours about his parentage. And why else would Golophin have inveigled a passage out of Hebrion for he and his mother if there was not some Royal connection? Here he came now, hauling himself up the companionway and looking as eager as a young hound which has sighted a fox. Alone of the passengers he was unaffected by sea-sickness, and seemed in fact to revel in their swift southward passage, the valiant efforts of the ship. Hawkwood had had several conversations with him on the quarterdeck. He was pompous for one so young, and full of himself of course, but he knew when to keep his mouth shut, which was a blessing.

"Captain! How goes our progress?" Bleyn asked. The other occupants of the quarterdeck frowned and looked away. They had taken to Richard Hawkwood very quickly once he had proved that he was who he had claimed to be, and they thought that this boy did not address him with sufficient respect.

Hawkwood did not answer him for a second, but studied the compass-board, looked at the sails, and seeing one on the edge of shivering barked to the helmsman, "Mind your luff." Then he looked humourlessly at Bleyn. He had been about to go below and snatch some sleep for the first time in days and he was damned if some chattering popinjay was going to rob him of it. But something in Bleyn's eyes, some element of unabashed exuberance, stopped him. "Come below. I'll show you on the chart."

They went back down the companionway and entered Hawkwood's cabin, which by rights should have been the finest on the ship. But Hawkwood had given that one to Isolla, and retained for himself that of the first mate. He had a pair of scuttles for light instead of windows and both he and Bleyn had to stoop as they entered. There was a broad table running athwartships which was fastened to the deck with brass runners, and pinned open upon it a chart of the Western Levangore and the Hebrian Gulf. Hawkwood picked up the dividers and consulted his log, ignoring Bleyn. The boy was staring about himself at the cutlasses on the bulkhead, the battered sea-chest, the cross-staff hung in a corner. At last Hawkwood pricked the bottom left corner of the chart. "There we are, more or less."

Bleyn peered at the chart. "But we are out in the middle of nowhere! And headed south. We'll soon drop off the edge of the map."

Hawkwood smiled and rubbed at the bristles of his returning beard. "If you are being pursued, then nowhere is a good place to be. The open ocean is a grand place to hide."

"But you have to turn eastwards soon, surely."

"We'll change course today or the next, depending on the wind. Thus far it has been steady, but I've never yet known a steady westerly persist this long in the Gulf. In spring the land is warming up and pushing the clouds out to sea. Southerlies are more usual in this part of the world, and heading east we should have a beam wind to work with again. Thus I hesitate to lower the lateen yards."

"They're better when the wind is hitting the ship from the side, are they not?"

"The wind is *on the beam*, master Bleyn. If you're to sound like a sailor you must make an effort to learn our language."

"Larboard is left and starboard is right, are they not?"

"Bravo. We'll have you laying aloft before we're done."

"How long before we reach Torunn?"

Hawkwood shook his head. "This is not a four-horse coach we are in. We do not run to exact timetables, at sea. But if the winds are kind, then I would hazard that we should meet with the mouth of the Torrin Estuary in between three and four weeks."

"A month! The war could be over in that time."

"From what I hear, I doubt it."

There was a muffled thump on the partition to one side, someone moving about. The partitions were thin wood, and Bleyn and Hawkwood looked at one another. It was Jemilla's cabin, though the word *cabin* was a somewhat ambitious term for her kennel-like berth.

"Do you know much about this King Corfe?" Bleyn asked.

"Only what Golophin has told me, and popular rumour. He is a hard man by all accounts, but just, and a consummate general."

"I wonder if he'll let me serve in his army," Bleyn mused.

Hawkwood looked at him sharply but before he could say anything there was a knock at his door. It was opened straight after to reveal Jemilla standing there, wrapped in a shawl. Her hair was in tails around her shoulders and she looked pale and drawn, with bruised rings about her eyes.

"Captain, you have come downstairs at last. I have been meaning to have a word with you for days in private. I could almost believe you have been avoiding me. Bleyn, leave us."

"Mother –"

She stared at him, and he closed his mouth at once and left the cabin without another word. Jemilla shut the door carefully behind him.

"My dear Richard," she said quietly. "It has been a long time since you and I were alone in the same room together."

Hawkwood tossed the dividers on the chart before him with a thump. "He's a good lad, that son of yours. You should stop treating him like a child."

"He needs a father's hand on his shoulder."

"Murad was not the paternal type I take it."

Her smile was not pleasant. "You could say that. I've missed you, Richard."

Hawkwood snorted derisively. "It's been eighteen years, Jemilla, near as damn it. You've done a hell of a job of pretending otherwise." He was surprised by the rancour in his voice. He had thought that Jemilla no longer mattered to him. The fact that both she and Isolla were on board confused him mightily, and though the ship had needed careful handling to enable the fastest possible passage since Abrusio, he had been using that as an excuse to stay up on deck, in his own world as it were, leaving the complications below.

"I'm rather busy, and very tired. If you have anything to discuss it will have to wait."

She moved closer. The shawl slipped to reveal one creamy shoulder. He gazed at her, fascinated despite himself. There was a lush ripeness about Jemilla. She was an exotic fruit on the very cusp of turning rotten, and wantonness in her seemed not a vice but the expression of a normal appetite.

She kissed him lightly on the lips. The shawl slipped further. Below it she wore only a thin shift, and her heavy round breasts swelled through it, the dark stain of the nipples visible beneath the fabric. Hawkwood cupped one breast in his callused palm and she closed her eyes. A smile he had forgotten played across her lips. Half triumph, half hunger. He placed her mouth on hers and she gently closed her teeth on his darting tongue.

A knock on he door. He straightened at once and drew back from Jemilla. She drew her shawl about her again, her eyes not leaving his. "Come in."

It was Isolla. She started upon seeing them standing there together, and something in her face fell. "I will come back at a better time."

Jemilla curtseyed to her gracefully. "Do not depart on my account, your Majesty. I was just leaving." As she passed the Queen in the doorway the shawl unaccountably slipped again. "Later, Richard," she called back over her naked shoulder, and was gone.

Hawkwood felt his face burning and could not meet Isolla's eyes. He scourged himself, not understanding why. "Lady, what can I do for you?"

She seemed more disconcerted than he. "I did not know that the Lady Jemilla and you were... familiar to each other, Captain."

Hawkwood raised his head and met her eyes frankly. "We were lovers many years ago. There is nothing between us now." Even as he said it, he wondered if it were true.

Isolla coloured. "It is not my business."

"Best to have it in the open. We'll be living cheek-by-jowl for the next few weeks. I will not dance minuets around the truth on my own ship." His voice sounded harsher than he had intended. In a softer tone he asked, "You are feeling better?"

"Yes. I – I think perhaps I am gaining my sea-legs."

"Better to go up on deck and get some fresh air. It is fetid down here. Just do not look at the sea moving beyond the rail."

"I will be sure not to."

"What was it you wished to speak of, lady?"

"It was nothing important. Good day, Captain. Thank you for your advice." And she was gone. She banged her knee on the jamb of the door as she left.

Hawkwood sat down before the chart and stared blindly at the parchment, the dull shine of the brass dividers. He knuckled his eyes, his exhaustion returning to make water of his muscles. And then he had to sit back and laugh at he knew not what.

THE SMALL CHANGE of course he had ordered woke him from a sleep as deep and untroubled as any he had had in his life. He climbed out of the swinging cot and pulled on his sodden boots, blinking and yawning. In his dreams he had been terribly thirsty, his tongue swollen in his rasping mouth, and he had been seated before a pitcher of water and one of wine, unable to quench his raging thirst because he could not choose between the two.

He stumped up on deck to find a strained atmosphere and a crowded quarterdeck. Arhuz nodded, checked the compass-board and reported. "Course east-sou'-east, skipper, wind backing to west-sou'-west so we have it on the starboard quarter. Do you want to call all hands?"

Hawkwood studied the trim of the sails. They were still drawing well. "What's our speed?"

"Six knots and one fathom, holding steady."

"Then we'll continue thus until the change of the watch, and then get square yards on fore and main. Rouse out the sailmaker, Arhuz, and get it all set in train. Bosun! Open the main hatch and get tackles to the maintop."

The mariners went about their business with a calm competence that pleased Hawkwood greatly. They were not his *Ospreys*, but they knew their craft, and he had nothing more to tell them. He studied the sky over the taffrail. The west was clouding up once more, banners and rags of cloud gathering on the horizon. To the north the air was as clear as ice, the sea empty of every living thing.

"Lookout!" he called. "What's afoot?" On an afternoon like this, with the spring sun warming the deck and the fresh breeze about them, the lookout would be able to survey an expanse of ocean fifteen leagues wide.

"Not a sail sir. Nor a bird or scrap of weed neither."

"Very good." Then he noticed that both Isolla and Jemilla were on deck. Isolla was standing by the larboard mizzen shrouds wrapped in a fur cloak with skeins of glorious red-gold hair whipping about her face, and Jemilla was to starboard, staring up into the rigging with a look of anxiety. "Captain," she said with no trace of coquetry, "can you not say something to him, issue some order?"

Hawkwood followed her gaze and saw what seemed to be a trio of master's mates high in the foretopmast shrouds.

Frowning, he realised that one of them was Bleyn, and his two companions were beckoning him yet higher.

"Gribbs, Ordio!" he bellowed at once. "On deck, and see master Bleyn down with you!"

The young men halted in their ascent, and then began to retrace their steps with the swiftness of long practice.

"Handsomely, handsomely, there, damn you," and they moderated their pace.

"Thank you, Captain," Jemilla said, honest relief in her face. Then she swallowed and her hand went to her mouth.

"You had best get below, lady." She left the quarterdeck, weaving across the pitching deck as though she were drunk. One of the quartermasters lent her his arm at a nod from Hawkwood and saw her down the companionway. Hawkwood felt a small, unworthy sense of satisfaction as she went. This was his world, where he commanded, and she was not much more than baggage. He had seen her a few times at court in the recent years, a high born aristocrat who deemed it charity when she deigned to notice his existence. The tables had been turned, it seemed. She was a refugee, dependent on him for the safety of her son and herself. There was satisfaction to be had in her current discomfort, and she was not so alluring with that pasty puking look about her.

She will gain no hold on me, Hawkwood promised himself. *Not on this voyage.*

The wind was picking up, and the *Seahare* was pitching before it like an excited horse, great showers of spray breaking over her forecastle and travelling as far aft as the waist. Hawkwood grasped the mizzen backstay and felt the tension in the cable. He would have to shorten sail if this kept up, but for now he wanted to wring every ounce of speed he could out of the blessed wind.

"Arhuz, another man to the wheel, and brail up the mizzen-course."

"Aye, sir. Prepare to shorten sail! You there, Jorth, get on up on that yard and leave the damn landlubber to make his own way. This is not a nursery."

The landlubber in question was Bleyn. He managed a creditable progress up the waist to the quarterdeck until he stood dripping before Hawkwood, his face wind-reddened and beaming.

"Better than a good horse!" he shouted above the wind, and Hawkwood found himself grinning at the boy. He was game, if nothing else.

"Get yourself below, Bleyn, and change your clothes. And look in on your mother. She is taken poorly."

"Aye, sir!" Hawkwood watched him go with an inexplicable ache in his breast.

"He seems a fine young fellow. I wonder he was not presented at court," Isolla said. Hawkwood had momentarily forgotten about her. "You too might be better below, lady. It's apt to become a trifle boisterous on deck."

"I do not mind. I seem to have become accustomed to the movement of the ship at last, and the air is a tonic."

Her eyes sparkled. She was no beauty, but there was a strength, a wholeness about her that informed her features and somehow invited the same openness in return. Only the livid scar down one side of her face jarred. It did not make her ugly in Hawkwood's eyes, but he was reminded of his debt to her every time he saw it.

What am I become, he thought, *some kind of moonstruck youngster?* There was something in him which responded to all three of his passengers in different ways, but he would sooner jump overboard than try to delve further than that. Thank God for the ceaseless business of the ship to keep his thoughts occupied.

He recalled the chart below to his mind as easily as some men might recall a passage from an oft-read book. If he kept to this course he would, in mariner's terms, shave the south-west tip of Gabrion by some ten or fifteen leagues. That was all very well, but if the southerlies started up out of Calmar he would have not much leeway to play with. And then, to play for more sea-room would mean eating up more time. Two days, perhaps.

The figures and angles came together in his head. He felt Isolla watching him curiously, but ignored her. The crew did not approach him. They knew what he was about, and knew he needed peace to resolve it in his mind.

"Hold this course," he said to Arhuz at last. What Bleyn

had said had tipped the scales. They could not be profligate with time. He would have to chance the southerlies and gain leeway by whatever small shifts he could. The decision left his mind clear again, and the tension left the deck. He studied the sail-plan. The lateens on fore and main were drawing well for now. He would let them remain until the wind began to veer, if it did at all. No need to call all hands. The watch below might snore on undisturbed in their hammocks.

"Bosun!" he thundered. "Belay the swaying up of the square yards. We'll stick to the lateens for now. Take down those tackles."

He stood there on the quarterdeck as the crew took to the mizzen shrouds and began to fight for fistful after fistful of the booming mizzen course, tying it up in a loose bunt on the yard. The *Seahare*'s motion grew a little less violent, but as Hawkwood watched the sea and the clouds closely he realised that the weather was about to worsen. A squall was approaching out of the west; he could see the white line of its fury whipping up the already stiffening swell, whilst above the water the cloud bunched and darkened and came on like some purposeful titan, its underside flickering with buried lightning.

He and Arhuz looked at one another. There was something disquieting about the remorseless speed of that line of broken water.

"Where in the world did that come from?" Arhuz asked wonderingly.

"All hands!" Hawkwood bellowed. "All hands on deck! Arhuz, take in fore and main, and make it quick."

The off-duty watch came tumbling up the companionways from below, took one look at the approaching tempest, and began climbing the shrouds, yawning and shaking the sleep out of their heads.

"Is there something the matter, Captain?" Isolla asked.

"Go below, lady." Hawkwood's tone brooked no argument, and she obeyed him without another word.

The mizzen was brailed up and the maincourse was in, but the men were still fighting to tie up the thumping canvas of the forecourse when the squall reached them.

In the space of four minutes it grew dark, a rain-swept, heaving twilight in which the wind howled and the lightnings exploded about their heads. The squall smote the *Seahare* on the starboard quarter and immediately knocked her a point off course. Hawkwood helped the two helmsmen to fight the wicked jerking of the wheel and as the thick, warm rain beat on their right cheeks they watched the compass in the binnacle and by main strength turned one point, then two and then three points until the beakhead pointed east-north-east and the ship was running before the wind.

Only then could Hawkwood lift his gaze. He saw that the forecourse had broken free from the men on the yard and was flying in great, flapping rags, the heavy canvas creating havoc in the forestays, ripping ropes and splintering timber as far forward as the jib-boom. Even as he watched, the sailors managed to cut the head of the sail free of the yard, and it took off like some huge pale bird and vanished into the foaming darkness ahead.

The *Seahare* was shipping green water over her forecastle, and it flooded down the waist as the bow rose, knocking men off their feet and smashing through the companion doorway and thus flooding the cabins aft. Hawkwood found himself staring at slate-grey, angry sky over the bowsprit, and then as the ship's stern rose the waves soared up like dark, foam-tipped phantoms and came choking and crashing over the bow again.

Arhuz was setting up lifelines and double-frapping the boats on the booms. Hawkwood shouted in the ear of the senior helmsman. "Thus, very well thus." The man's reply was lost in the roar of wave and wind, but he was nodding his head. Hawkwood made his way down into the waist as carefully as a man negotiating a cliff-face in a gale. The turtle-deck was shedding the green seas admirably, but they had surmounted the storm-sills of the companionways and he could feel the extra weight of water in the ship, rendering her stiffer and thus more likely to bury her bowsprit. It was a following sea now, and thank God the xebec was not square-sterned like most ships he had sailed and thus the waves which the wind was flinging at them slid under her counter without too much trouble. Hawkwood found himself admiring his sleek vessel, and her winsome eagerness to ride the monstrous swells.

"She swims well!" he shouted in Arhuz's ear. The Merduk grinned, his teeth a white flash in his dark face. "Aye sir, she was always a willing ship."

"We need men on the pumps, though, and those hatchway tarpaulins are working loose. Get Chips on deck to batten them down."

"Aye sir." Arhuz hauled himself aft with the aid of the just-rigged lifelines.

It was the lack of heavy broadside guns that helped, Hawkwood realised. All the weight of a couple of dozen culverins on deck raised the centre of gravity of a ship and made her that much less seaworthy. It was the difference between a man jogging with a pack on his back, and one running unencumbered. The xebec was running before the wind with only a brailed-up mizzen course to propel her, but her speed was remarkable. Perhaps too remarkable. A vision of the chart still pinned to his table belowdecks floated into his mind. They were steering directly for the ironbound western coast of Gabrion now, and there was not a safe landfall to be made there for many leagues in any direction; the promontories of that land loomed out to sea like the unforgiving ravelins of a fortress. They must turn aside if they were not to be flung upon the coast and smashed to matchwood. Hawkwood closed his eyes as the water foamed around his knees. A northerly course was the safer bet. Once they were around that great rocky peninsula known as the Gripe, they would find anchorages aplenty on Gabrion's flatter northern shores. But it would mean giving up on the southern route – they would then be committed to a passage of the Malacar Straits, the one thing he had tried so hard to avoid.

He opened his eyes and stared at the lowering sky again. Sudden squalls such as this were unusual, but by no means unknown in the Hebrian Sea. Mostly they were quick to pass, a brief, chaotic maelstrom most dangerous in the first few minutes. But every horizon was dark now, and the sun had disappeared. This squall would blow for a day or two at least. The southern passage was too risky. He cursed silently. They would have to go north as soon as the ship could bear it.

He blinked rain out of his eyes. For a moment –

And then he was sure. He had seen something up there against the dark racing clouds, a shadow or group of shadows moving with the wind. His blood ran cold. He stood staring with wide eyes, but saw nothing more than the galloping clouds, the flicker of the lightning, and the shifting silver curtain of the rain.

His CABIN WAS swimming in at least a foot of water which sloshed back and forth with the pitch of the ship. A hooded lantern set in gimbals still burned feebly and he opened its slot to give himself more light, then bent over the chart and picked up the dividers. Navigating by dead-reckoning, with a rocky shore to leeward and the ship running full tilt towards it before the wind. A mariner's nightmare. He wiped salt water out of his eyes and forced himself to concentrate, estimating the ship's speed and plotting out her course. The results of his calculations made him whistle soundlessly, and he tossed down the dividers with something like anger. There was nothing natural about this squall, of that he was now sure. It had reared up out of a clear sky at just the right moment, and was meant to wreck them on the rocks of Gabrion. It would blow until its work was done.

"Bastards."

He roused out a bottle of brandy and gulped from the neck, feeling the good spirit kindle his innards, wondering if the xebec could stand a change of course to the north. The wind would be square on the larboard beam then, trying to capsize her. The decision had to be made soon. With every passing minute they were running off their leeway, thundering ever closer to that killer-coast.

A knock on the door of his cabin. It stood open, swinging back and forth with the pressure of the water that sloshed underfoot. He did not turn around, and was unsurprised to hear Isolla's voice, somewhat hoarse.

"Captain, may I speak to you?"

"By all means." He sucked from the neck of the brandy-bottle again as though inspiration might be found therein.

"How long do you suppose this storm will endure? The mariners seem very concerned."

Hawkwood smiled. "I've no doubt they are, lady." The lurch of the ship sent Isolla thumping against the door-jamb. Hawkwood steadied her with one hand. Her cloak was sodden and cold. She was as soaked as he was.

"I believe the Himerians have found us," Hawkwood said at last. "It is they who have conjured up this squall. It's not violent enough to threaten the ship – not yet – but it is making us go where we do not want to go." He gestured to the chart, which was wrinkling with wet. "If I cannot change course very soon we will run full tilt onto the rocks of Gabrion. They timed their weatherworking well."

Isolla looked startled. "How can they cast a spell over so great a distance? Hebrion is hundreds of miles behind us."

"I know. I believe there must be another ship out there, somewhere beyond the walls of this storm. Weatherworkers can only maintain one spell at a time; I believe they have used sorcery to speed their own vessel and draw within range of us, and then have switched their focus and unleashed this storm, which they believe will propel the ship to its doom."

"And will they succeed?"

"Even a preternatural storm can be weathered like any other, given good seamanship and a little luck. We're not beaten yet!" He smiled. Perhaps it was the brandy, or the storm, but he felt a certain sense of license.

"You're wet through. You must try and keep yourself out of the water. Huddle in your cot under a blanket if you have to."

She shrugged, and gave a wry smile. "It's pouring in the door and down from the ceiling. There's not a dry spot in this ship, I believe."

Hawkwood leaned towards her on an impulse and kissed her cold lips.

Isolla jerked back, astonished. Her fingers went to her mouth. "Captain, you forget yourself! Remember who I am."

"I've never forgotten," Hawkwood said recklessly, "not since that day on the road all those years ago when your horse threw a shoe, and you served me wine in Golophin's Tower."

"I am Hebrion's Queen!"

"Hebrion is gone, Isolla, and in a day or two we may all be dead." He reached for her again but she backed away. He cornered her by the door and set his hands on the bulkhead on either side of her, the bottle still clenched in one fist. Around them the ship pitched and heaved and groaned and the water swept cold about their legs and the wind howled up on deck like a live thing, a sentient menace. Hawkwood bent his head and kissed her once more, throwing all sense of caution to the ravening wind. This time she did not draw away, but it was like kissing a marble statue, a tang of salt on stone.

He leant his forehead on her damp shoulder with a groan. "I'm sorry." The moment where all had been possible faded like the mirage it had been, burning away with the brandy fumes in his head.

"Forgive me, lady." He was about to leave her when her hands came up and clasped his face. They stared at one another. Hawkwood could not read her eyes.

"You are forgiven, Captain," she said softly, and then she lowered her face into the hollow of his neck and he felt her tremble. He kissed her wet hair, baffled and exhilarated at the same time. Half a minute she remained clinging to him, then she straightened and, without looking at him or saying another word, she left, splashing up the companionway towards her own cabin. Hawkwood remained frozen, like a man stunned.

WHEN HE FINALLY came back up on deck he felt oddly detached, as though the survival of the ship was no longer important. There were four men on the wheel now, and the remainder of the crew were huddled in the half-deck under the wheel, sheltering from the wind. Hawkwood roused himself and checked their course by the compass-board. They were hurtling east-north-east, and if he was any judge the *Seahare* must be making at least nine knots. Before the squall they had been perhaps fifty leagues to windward of the Gabrionese coast. At their current speed they would run aground in some sixteen hours. There was no time to play with. His mind clear, Hawkwood stood by the wheel, clutched the lifeline, and bellowed at the helmsmen. "Two points to port. I want her brought round to nor'-nor'-east, lads. Arhuz!"

"Aye, sir." The first mate looked as dark and drowned as a seal.

"I want a sea-anchor veered out from the stern on a five-hundred fathom length of one-inch cable. Use one of the topgallant sails. It should cut down on our leeway." Arhuz did not answer, but nodded grimly and left the quarterdeck calling for a working party to follow him below.

The decision was made. They would try and weather the Gripe and strike out for the northern coast. If the southerlies finally kicked in after they had left this squall behind, then they would have the broad reaches of the Hebrian Sea to manoeuvre in instead of fighting for sea-room all along the southern coast of Gabrion. They would have to risk the Straits. It could not be helped.

If we make it that far, Hawkwood thought. He kept thinking of Isolla's arms about him, the salt taste of her lips unmoving under his own. He could not puzzle out what it might mean, and he regretted the brandy she must have tasted on his mouth.

The ship came round, and the blast of the wind shifted from the back of his head to his left ear. The xebec began to roll as well as pitch now, a corkscrew motion that shipped even more water forward, whilst the pressure on the rudder sought to tear the spokes of the ship's wheel from the fists of the helmsmen. They hooked on the relieving tackles to aid them, but Hawkwood could almost feel the ropes slipping on the drum below.

"Steer small!" he shouted to the helmsmen. They had too little sea-room to work with, and her course must be exact.

Bleyn came up on deck wearing an oilskin jacket too large for him. "What can I do?" he shouted shrilly.

"Go below. Help man one of the pumps."

He nodded, grinned like a maniac, and disappeared again. The pumps were sending a fine spout of water out to leeward but the *Seahare* was making more than they could cope with.

As if conjured up by Hawkwood's concern, the ship's carpenter appeared.

"Pieto!" Hawkood greeted him. "How does she swim?"

"We've three feet of water in the well, Captain, and it's gaining on us. She was always a dry ship, but this course is opening her seams. There's oakum floating about all over the hold. Can't we put her back before the wind?"

"Only if you want to break her back on Gabrion. Keep the pumps going, Pieto, and rig hawse-bags forward. We have to ride this one out." The carpenter knuckled his forehead and went below looking discontented and afraid.

Hawkwood found himself loving his valiant ship. The *Seahare* shouldered aside the heavy swells manfully – they were breaking over her port quarter as well now – and kept her sharp beakhead on course despite the wrenchings of her rudder. She seemed as stubbornly indomitable as her captain.

This was being alive, this was tasting life. It was better than anything that could be found at the bottom of a bottle. It was the reason he had been born.

Hawkwood kept his station on the windward side of the quarterdeck and felt the spray sting his face and his good ship leap lithe and alive under his feet, and he laughed aloud at the black clouds, the drenching rain, and the malevolent fury of the storm.

FOURTEEN

CORFE HAD DECREED that the funeral should be as magnificent as that of a king's, and in the event Queen Odelia was laid to rest with a sombre pomp and ceremony that had not been seen in Torunn since the death of King Lofantyr almost seventeen years before. Formio's Orphans lined the streets with their pikes at the vertical, and a troop of five thousand Cathedrallers accompanied the funeral-carriage to the cathedral where Torunna's Queen was to be interred in the great family vault of the Fantyrs. The High Pontiff himself, Albrec, intoned the funeral oration and the great and the good of the kingdom packed the pews and listened in their sober finery. With Odelia went the last link with an older Torunna, a different world. Many in the crowd cast discreet glances at the brindled head of the King, and wondered if the rumours of an imminent Royal wedding were true. It was common knowledge that the Queen had wanted her husband to be re-wedded before even her corpse was cold, but to whom? What manner of woman would be chosen to fill Odelia's throne, now that they were at open war with the might of the Second Empire, and Hebrion had already fallen and Astarac was tottering? The solemnity of those gathered to bid farewell to their Queen was not assumed. They knew that Torunna approached one of the most critical junctures in her history, more dangerous perhaps than even the climax of the Merduk Wars had been. And there were rumours that already Gaderion was beset, General Aras hard-pressed to hold the Torrin Gap. What would Corfe do? For days thousands of conscripts had been mustering in the capital and were now undergoing their provenance. Torunn had become a fortress within which armies mustered. Whither would they go? No-one save the High Command knew, and they were close-lipped as confessors.

When the funeral was over, and Odelia's body had been laid in the Royal crypt, the mourners left the cathedral one by one, and only a lonely pair in the front rank of pews remained. The King – his bodyguard Felorin standing in the shadows – and General Formio. After a brief word Formio departed, laying his hand on the back of the King's neck and giving him a gentle shake. They smiled at each other, and Corfe bent his head again, the circlet that had been Kaile Ormann's glinting on his brow. At last the King rose, Felorin following like a shadow, and knocked on the door of the cathedral sacristy. A hollow voice said "Enter," and Corfe pushed the massive ironbound portal open. The Pontiff Albrec stood within flanked by a pair of Inceptines, who were in the process of disrobing him. His friend Avila, Bishop of Torunn, stood to one side. He bowed as Corfe entered. Behind the clerics gleamed a gallery of chalices and reliquaries and a long rail hung with the rich ceremonial garments a Pontiff must needs don at times like this.

"A noble ceremony," Avila said. "The Queen deserved no less." The years had heightened the aristocratic lines of his face. The ignorant might mistake him for the Pontiff, and not the pigeon-plump, mutilated little man that was Albrec.

"Leave us, Brothers," Albrec said crisply, and the two Inceptines bent low before King and Pontiff, and departed through a small side-door. Avila hesitated a moment, and at a nod from Albrec he bowed once more before the King, and followed them without a word.

"Corfe – will you give me a hand? Albrec asked, tugging at his richly embroidered chasuble.

"Felorin," the King said, "wait outside and see no-one enters."

The tattooed soldier nodded wordlessly and heaved shut the great sacristy door behind him with a dull boom.

Corfe helped Albrec out of his ceremonial apparel and hung it up on the rail behind, whilst the little cleric pulled a plain black Inceptine habit over his head and, puffing slightly, kissed his Saint's symbol and settled it about his neck. The air wheezed in and out of the twin holes where his nose had been.

There was a fire burning in a small stone hearth which had been ingeniously hewn out of a single block of Cimbric basalt. They stood before it, warming their hands like men who have been labouring together out in the cold. It was Albrec who broke the silence.

"Are you still set on this thing?"

"I am. She would have wished it. It was her last wish, in fact. And she was right. The kingdom needs it. The girl is already on the road."

"The kingdom needs it," Albrec repeated. "And what of you, Corfe?"

"What of me? Kings have duties as well as prerogatives. It must be done, and done soon, ere I leave on campaign."

"What of Heria? Is there any word on how she is taking this thing?"

Corfe flinched as though he had been struck. "No word," he said. He stood rubbing one hand over the other before the flames as though he were washing them. "It has been sixteen years since last I saw her face, Albrec. The joy we shared so long ago is like a dream now." Something thickened in Corfe's voice and his face grew hard and set as the basalt of the burning hearth before him. "One cannot live by memory, least of all when one is a king."

"There are other women in the world, other alliances which could be sought out," Albrec said gently.

"No. This is the one the country needs. One day, Albrec, I foresee that Torunna and Ostrabar will be one and the same, a united kingdom wherein the war we fought will be but a memory, and this part of the world will know true peace at last. Anything, any sacrifice, any pain, is worth the chance of that happening."

Albrec bowed his head, his eyes fixed on Corfe's tortured face. *And you, my friend*, he thought, *what of you?*

"Golophin has been transporting messages swiftly as a hawk's flight. Aurungzeb knows of Odelia's death, and we have both agreed on a small, a – a subdued ceremony, as soon as the girl arrives. There will be no public holiday or grand spectacle, not so soon after – after today. The people will be told in time, and I will be able to leave for the war without any more delay. I want you to conduct the ceremony, Albrec." Corfe waved an arm. "In here, away from the gawpers."

"In the sacristy?"

"It's as good a place as any other."

Albrec sighed and rubbed at the stumps where long ago frost had robbed him of his fingers. "Very well. But, Corfe, I say this to you. Stop punishing yourself for what fate has visited upon you. It is not your fault, nor is it anything to feel ashamed over. *What's done is done.*" He reached up and set a hand on Corfe's shoulder. The Torunnan King smiled.

"Yes, of course. You sound like Odelia." A strangled attempt at a laugh. "God's blood, Albrec, but I miss her. She was one of the great friends of my life, along with Andruw, and Formio, and others long dead. She was another right hand. Had she been a man, she would have made a fine king." He pushed the palm of his hand into the hollow of one eye. "Perhaps I should have told her. She might not have been so insistent on this thing."

"Odelia? No, she would still have wanted it, though it would have tortured her much as it is tormenting you. It is as well she never knew who Ostrabar's Queen is."

"Ostrabar's Queen... I wonder sometimes – even now I wonder – about how it was for her, what nightmares she must have suffered as I fled Aekir with my tail between my legs."

"That's enough," Albrec said sternly. "What's done is done. You cannot change the past, you can only hope to make the future a better place."

Corfe looked at the little cleric, and in his bloodshot fire-glazed eyes Albrec saw something that shook him to the core. Then the King smiled again.

"You are right, of course." He tried to make his voice light. "Do you realise that Mirren will have a step-mother younger than she is? They will be friends, I hope." The word *hope* sounded strange coming out of his mouth. He embraced the disfigured little monk as though they were brothers, and then knelt and kissed the Pontifical ring. "I must away, Holiness. A king's time is not his own. Thank you for yours." Then he spun on his heel and thumped the sacristy door. Felorin opened it for him, and they left together, the King and his shadow. Albrec stared unseeing into the depths of the bright fire before him, not hearing his Inceptine helpers re-enter the room and stand reverently behind him. He was still shaken by the light he had seen in Corfe's eye. It was the look of a man who cannot find peace in life, and who means to seek it in death.

IN THE MIDST of the crowded activity that currently thronged Torunn, few remarked upon the entry into the city of a Merduk caravan several days later. It was some thirty waggons strong, and halfway down their column a curtained palanquin bobbed, borne on the shoulders of eight brawny slaves. They had been given an escort of forty Cathedraller cavalry, and entered the city via the north gate, where the guards had been told to expect them. Merduk ambassadors and their entourages were a common sight in Torunn these days, and no-one remarked as the caravan made its stately way to the hill overlooking the Torrin estuary on which loomed the granite splendour of the palace, its windows all draped black in mourning for Torunna's dead Queen.

Ensign Baraz was within the palace courtyard as the heavily-laden covered waggons rattled through the gates, drawn by camels whose heads bobbed with black and white ostrich-feathers. He drew up the ceremonial guard and at his crisp command they flashed out their sabres in salute. The palanquin came to a halt upon the shoulders of the sweating slaves, and a bevy of silk-veiled Merduk maids lifted back the curtains to reveal a barely discernible form within. This shape was helped out with the aid of a trio of footstools and the ministrations of the maids and stood, somewhat uncertain, with the cold spring wind tugging at her veil. Baraz stepped forward and bowed. "Lady," he said in Merduk, "you are very welcome in the city of Torunn and kingdom of Torunna."

He got no farther through the flowery speech of welcome he had devised the night before after the King had peremptorily informed him of his mission. A stout Merduk matron with black eyes flashing above her veil waddled forward and demanded to know who he was and why the King was not here to greet his bride-to-be in person.

"He has been unavoidable detained," Baraz said smoothly. "Preparations for the war –"

"Sibir Baraz! I know you! I served in your father's household ere he was transferred to the palace. My brave boy, how you've grown!" the Merduk matron enfolded Baraz in her huge arms and tugged his head down to rest in her heaving, heavily scented cleavage. "Do you not know Haratta, who wiped your nose when you could barely say your name?"

With difficulty Baraz extricated himself from her soft clutch. Behind him, a fit of coughing had spread throughout the men of the honour-guard and the eyes of the slim girl who had been in the palanquin were dancing.

"Of course I remember you. Now, lady" – this to the girl – "I have been instructed to guide you and your attendants to your quarters in the palace and to make sure that all is as you wish there."

Haratta turned and clapped her hands. In an entirely different tone, a harsh bark, she began to issue orders to the hovering maids, the slaves, the waggoneers. Then she turned back to Baraz, having produced a chaotic turmoil of activity out of what had been stately stillness a moment before, and pinched his burning cheek. "Such a handsome young man, and high in the favour of King Corfe, no doubt. Lead on, Master Baraz! The lady Aria and I would follow you anywhere, I'm sure." She winked with a kind of jovial lechery and, when he hesitated, shooed him on as though he were a chicken clucking in her path.

The procession had something of the circus about it: Baraz leading, with Haratta beside him chattering incessantly, Aria following with her maids about her, and then an incongruous crocodile of burly, sweating men burdened with trunks, cases, rolled carpets, bulging bags and even a flapping nightingale in a cage. But the sombre mourning-hangings which festooned the palace soon put paid to even Haratta's loquaciousness and by the time they reached their destination they were a silent troop, and somewhat subdued.

The palace steward, an old and able quartermaster named Cullan, was waiting for them surrounded by sable-clad courtiers. The Merduk party was installed in a cavernous series of marble-floored rooms which were traditionally reserved for visiting potentates, but which had seen little use since the days of King Minantyr forty years before. Even the braziers which had been lit in every corner seemed to have done little to dispel the neglected chill within. Haratta eyed the suite critically, but was courteous, even restrained, to Cullen and his subordinates. The Merduk slaves deposited a small hillock of luggage in every room, and then were shown away to their own quarters above the kitchens – no doubt warmer and less draughty than the grand desolation their betters occupied.

Baraz turned to go, but Aria laid a hand on his arm. "When will I see the King, Ensign Baraz?"

"I do not know, lady. My orders were to see you comfortably installed here and then to report to him, that was all."

She drew back, nodded. Her eyes were incredibly young and somewhat fearful under the cosmetics painted about them. Baraz smiled at her. "He is a good man," he said kindly, then collected himself and saluted. "A pair of palace maids will be stationed in this wing to see that you have everything you need. Fare well, lady." And he was gone.

Aria's entourage spent the rest of the day converting the cold chambers into something more befitting a Merduk princess, and by the time evening had rolled in – and with it a chill spring rainstorm out of the heights of the Cimbrics – they had transformed the austere suite into an approximation of the luxurious living spaces they were used to. Rich and colourful carpets had been unrolled to cover the bare marble, hangings had been hooked upon the walls, brass and silver lamps had been lit, incense was burning, and the nightingale sang his drab little heart out from the confines of his golden cage.

Aria and Haratta were in the bedchamber unpacking silken dresses and shawls from one of the larger trunks, Haratta enlarging upon the merits and defects of each garment, when one of the doe-eyed maids rustled in and fell to her knees before them.

"Mistress, mistress! The Torunnan King is here."

"What?" Haratta snapped. "Without a word of warning? You are mistaken."

"No! It is he, all alone but for a tattooed soldier who waits down the passage. He wishes to talk with the princess!"

Haratta threw down the costly silk she had been examining. "Barbarians! Send him away! No, no, we cannot do that. My sweet, you must receive him – he is a king, after all, though now I believe those stories about his peasant upbringing. Unheard of – to force himself upon us unheralded, catching us unawares. Veil yourself, girl! I will speak to him and set him to rights." Haratta rose and, twitching her own veil about her pouting mouth, stalked from the chamber in a shimmer of billowing raiment.

In the main antechamber a man of medium height stood warming his hands at the glowing charcoal of a brazier. He was dressed in black and his close-fitting tunic sat on him as trimly as on the body of a youth. But when he turned Haratta saw that his hair was three parts grey and his eyes were sunken, though they gleamed brightly in the lamplight. He wore a simple silver circlet about his temples and no other ornament or decoration of any kind. King or no, Haratta had intended to upbraid him politely but icily for his presumption, but something about his eyes stopped her cold. She curtseyed in the Ramusian way.

"You speak Normannic?" the man asked.

"A small piece, mine lord. Not very goods."

"Haratta your name is, I am told."

"Yes, lord."

"I am Corfe. I am here to see the lady Aria. I apologise for my absence at your arrival, but I was detained by matters of state." He paused, and seeing the look of alarm and incomprehension crossing her face his eyes softened. In Merduk he said:

"I wish only to speak with your mistress for a moment. I will wait, if that is necessary."

Her face cleared. "I will ask her to come at once." There was something in this man's gaze, something which even at first meeting made one eager to obey him.

WHEN ARIA ENTERED the room a few moments later she was swathed in yards of midnight silk, the finest she possessed, and kohl had been applied to her eyelids, the lashes drawn out at the corners of her eyes with black stibium. Haratta followed her and took an unobtrusive seat in a shadowed corner as her mistress walked steadily towards her future husband, a man old enough to be her father.

The Torunnan King bowed deeply and she inclined her head in answer. He did not look as old as she had feared, and had in fact the bearing of a much younger man. He was not ill-looking either, and the first, absurd, girlish fears she had harboured faded. She was not to share a bed with some pot-bellied bald-headed libertine after all.

They exchanged inconsequential courtesies, all the while taking in every detail of the other. His Merduk was adequate, but not fluent, as though it had lately been studied in a hurry. They switched to Normannic at her request, for she was at home in both, thanks to her mother. He had a stern cast to his face, but when she made him smile she saw a much younger man beneath the Royal solemnity, a glimpse of someone else. She found herself liking his gravity, the sudden, unexpected smile which lifted it. His eyes were almost the same shade as her own.

He asked about her mother, turning away to poke at the brazier with a fire-iron as he did so. She was very well, Aria told him lightly. She sent her greetings to her future son-in-law. This last thing she had invented as a empty courtesy, no more, but as she said it the fire-iron went still, and remained poised in the burning red heart of the coals. The King went silent and she wondered what she had said to offend him. At last he turned back to her and she could see sweat glittering on his brow. His eyes seemed to have sunk back into his head and the firelight raised no gleam from them.

"May I see your face?" he asked.

She was taken aback, and had no idea how to deal with such a bold request. She glanced back at Haratta in the shadows and almost called the older woman over, then thought better of it. Why not? He was to marry her, after all. She twitched aside her veil and drew back her silken hood without speaking.

She heard Haratta gasp with outrage behind her, but had eyes only for the King's face. The colour had fled from it. He looked shocked, but mastered himself quickly. His hand came up as if he were about to caress her cheek, then fell away without touching her.

"You are the very image of your mother," he said hoarsely.

"So I have been told, my lord." Their eyes locked and something indefinable went between them. There was a great, empty hunger in him, a grieved yearning which touched her to the quick. She took his hard-planed fingers in her own, and felt him tremble at her touch.

Haratta had reached them. "My lord King, this is no way to be behaving. I am here as chaperone for the princess, and I say that you overstep the mark. Aria, what are you thinking? Cover yourself, girl. A man does not see his bride's face until their wedding night. For shame!"

Corfe's eyes did not leave Aria's for a second. "Things are done differently here in Torunna," he said quietly. "And besides, we are to be married in the morning."

Aria felt her heart flip. "So soon? But I –"

"I have communicated with your father. He has agreed. Your dowry will be sent on with your brother Nasir and the reinforcements he is leading here."

Haratta seemed to choke. She dabbed at her eyes. "Oh my little girl, oh my poor maid. Are you ashamed of her, my lord, that you rush through this thing like – like a thief in the night?"

Corfe's cold stare shut her mouth. "We are at war, woman, and this kingdom buried its Queen this morning. My wife. It is not how any of us would have wished, but circumstance dictates our actions. I must leave for the war myself very soon. Forgive me, Aria. No disrespect is intended – your own father recognises this."

Aria bowed her head. "I understand." She still held his fingers in her own and she felt the pressure as he squeezed them, then released her.

"A covered carriage will be waiting for you in the morning, and will convey you to the cathedral where we are to be married. You may bring Haratta and one other maid, but that is all. Are there any questions?" He seemed to think he was briefing a group of soldiers. His voice had become hard and impersonal; the tone of command. Aria and Haratta shook their heads silently.

"Very good. I will see you in the morning, then." He raised Aria's hand to his lips and kissed her knuckle, a dry feather-touch. "Good night, ladies." Then he turned on his heel and strode away. When the door had closed behind him Aria covered her face with her hands and fought the sudden sobs which threatened to burst free.

THE BELLS WOKE her. There had been a late spring snowfall a few days before, probably the last of the year, and Aurungabar's usual clatter and clamour had been muffled by the white tenderness of the snow. But now all over the city this morning the bells of every surviving Ramusian church were tolling, and chief among them the mournful sonorous pealing of Carcasson's great bronze titans. Heria threw aside the piled coverlets and, shrugging a fur pelisse about her shoulders, darted to the window and tugged aside the ornate shutters.

The cold air made her gasp and the whiteness was blinding after the gloom of the room. The sun was still rising and was nothing more than a saffron burning glimpsed through thick ribands of grey cloud. Some kind of emergency? But the people trudging through the streets seemed unafraid. The wains heading to market in great clouds of oxen-breath trundled obliviously, their drovers yawning muffled figures unpanicked by any news of war or fire or invasion.

A knock on the door, and her maids entered immediately, bearing hot water and towels and her clothes for the day. She closed the shutters without a word and let them undress her; they might have been deaf for all the notice they took of the tolling bells. When she was naked she stepped into the broad, flat-bottomed basin in which the water steamed and they dabbed at her with scented sponges brought up from the jewel-bright depths of the Levangore. They wrapped warm towels about her white limbs and she stepped out of the basin to peruse the garments they had brought for her to choose from.

The Sultan entered the room without fanfare or ceremony, rubbing his ring-bright fingers together. "Ah! I caught you!"

The maids all went to their knees but Heria remained standing. "My lord, I am at my ablutions."

"Ablute away!" Aurungzeb was grinning white out of the huge darkness of his beard. He settled himself on a creaking chair and arranged his robes about his globular paunch. The curved poniard he wore in his sash jutted forth as though it had been planted there. "It is nothing I have not seen before, I am sure. You are still my wife, after all, and a damned fine figure of a woman. Drop those towels, Ahara; even Queens must not stand on their dignity all the time."

She did as she was told and stood like a white, nude statue while the maids cowered at her feet and Aurungzeb eyed her appreciatively, ignoring or unaware of the blazing hatred in her eyes.

"Splendid, still splendid. You hear the bells? Of course you do. I thought I would be the one to tell you. The union I have long sought is concluded. This morning our daughter weds Corfe of Torunna, and our kingdoms are indissolubly linked for posterity. My grandson shall one day rule Torunna. Ha ha!"

Blood coloured her face. "This was not to happen so soon. We were to be at the ceremony. I – I was to give her away. We agreed."

Aurungzeb flapped a hairy-knuckled hand. "It proved impossible, in the event – and what is a little ceremony, after all? They have just buried their Queen. Corfe wanted a quiet wedding, without fanfare. He is leave for the war very soon, and had best try and plant a seed in Aria ere he goes."

Heria stepped dripping from the basin and snatched a dressing-robe from one of the frozen maids, wrapping it about her. Her eyes were blazing but vacant, as if they gazed upon some cruelty only she could see. "I was to be there," she repeated in a murmur. "I was to see them. I was..."

Aurungzeb was becoming irritated. "Yes, yes, we know all that. Matters of state intervened. We cannot have all we wish in this world." He hauled himself out of the chair and padded over to her. "Put it out of your mind. The thing is done." He raised her chin and regarded her face. She stared through him as though he did not exist, and he frowned.

"Queen or no, you are my wife, and you will bend to my will. You think the world will stand still to suit you?" When he released her his fingermarks left red bars on her cheek.

Heria's eyes returned to the room. After a moment, she smiled. "My Sultan, you are in the right of it as always. What do I know of matters of state? I am only a woman." Her hand sought his, raised it, and slipped it inside the loose collar of her robe so that he cupped one of her full breasts. Aurungzeb's face changed.

"Sometimes I must be reminded that I am a woman," Heria said, one eyebrow arching up her forehead. Aurungzeb licked his upper lip, wetting his moustache.

"Leave us," he growled at the maids. "The Queen and I desire a private word together."

The maids rose to their slippered feet and backed out of the room with their heads bowed. When the door had shut behind them Aurungzeb smiled. He reached up and twitched Heria's robe aside. It fell to her waist.

"Ah, still beautiful," he whispered, and grinned. "My sweet, you always knew how –"

Her hand, which had been stroking the sash about his voluminous middle, fastened upon the ivory hilt of the poniard tucked away there. She drew it forth with a flash.

"But you never knew," she said. And she stabbed him deep, deep in the belly, twisting the blade and slicing open the flesh so that his innards bulged out and blood flooded with them. Aurungzeb sank to his knees with an astonished gasp, trying vainly to press his lacerated flesh together.

"*Guards*," but the word came out as little more than a strangled whisper. He fell over on his side in a widening pool of his own blood, his eyes bulging white. His legs twitched and kicked uselessly.

"*Why* –"

His Queen looked down on him contemptuously, the bloody knife still gripped in one small fist. "My name is Heria Car-Gwion of the city of Aekir, and my true husband is, and has always been, Corfe Cear-Inaf, one-time officer in the garrison of Aekir, now King of Torunna." Her eyes bored into Aurungzeb's horrified, dying face.

"*Do you understand?*"

Ostabar's Sultan gurgled. His horror-filled eyes seemed to dawn with some awful knowledge. One hand left his terrible wound and reached for her like a claw. She stepped back, leaving bare footprints in his blood, and watched in silence as his movements grew feebler. He tried again to shout, but blood filled his mouth and came spitting out. She dropped her robe over his contorted face and stood naked, watching him struggle ineffectually under it. At last he was still. Tears streaked her face, but her features were stiff as those of a caryatid.

She blinked, and seemed to become aware of the weapon still clenched in her hand. Her arm was crimson to the elbow. There was a soft, insistent knocking at the door.

She looked around the room through a blaze of tears, and smiled. Then she thrust the keen blade deep into her own breast.

FIFTEEN

THE ROYAL BEDCHAMBER was something of a forbidding
place, the vast four-poster dominating it like a fortress. The
bed seemed to have been sturdily built to accommodate
duties rather than pleasures. Corfe had slept alone in it for
fourteen years.

He stood before a fireplace wide enough to roast a side of
pork, and warmed his hands unnecessarily at the towering
flames. The same room, the same ring on his finger, but
soon a different woman to warm the bed. He reached for
the wineglass that glinted discreetly on the tall mantle, and
drank half its blood-red contents at a gulp. It might have
been water, for all he tasted.

A quiet ceremony indeed. Only Formio, Comillan and
Haratta had been present as witnesses, and Albrec had been
brief and to the point, thank God. Aria had removed her
veil and hood, for she was a Torunnan now, and she had
bowed her head as the Pontiff placed the delicate filigree of
the Queen's crown upon her raven tresses.

Corfe rubbed his chest absently. There had been an ache
there since this morning that he could not account for. It
had begun during the wedding ceremony and was like the
dull throb of a bruise.

"Enter," he said as the door was knocked so softly as to
be barely audible.

A miniature procession entered the room. First came a
pair of Merduk maids bearing lighted candles, then came
Aria, her black hair unbound, a dark cloak about her
shoulders, and finally Haratta bearing another candle.
Corfe watched, bemused, as the three women stood around
Aria as though shielding her. The cloak was dropped by
the bedside, and he caught only a candlelit glimpse of a

white shape flitting under the covers before Haratta and the maids had turned again. The maids left like women in a trance, not flinching as the wax of their candles dripped down the back of their hands, but Haratta paused.

"We have delivered her intact, my lord, and have fulfilled our duty. We wish you joy of her." The look in Haratta's eye wished him anything but. "I shall be outside, if anything is needed."

"You will not," Corfe snapped. "You will return to your quarters at once. Is that clear?" Haratta bowed soundlessly and left the room.

The chamber seemed very dark as the candles were taken away, lit only by the red light of the fire. Corfe threw back the last of his wine. In the huge bed, Aria's face looked like that of a forgotten child's doll. He tugged off his tunic and sat on the side of the bed to haul off his boots, wishing now that he had not had so much wine. Wishing he had drunk more.

The boots were thrown across the room and his breeches followed. Kaile Ormann's circlet was laid with more reverence on the low table by the bed. Corfe rubbed his fingers over his face, wondering at the absurdity of it all, the twists of fate which had brought himself and this girl into the same bed. Better not to dwell on it.

He burrowed under the covers feeling tired and vinous and old. Aria jumped as he brushed against her. She was cold.

"Come here," he said. "You're like a blasted icicle."

He put his arms about her. He was warm from the fire but she was trembling and chilled. She seemed very slim and fragile in his grasp. He nuzzled her hair and the breath caught in his throat. "That scent you're wearing. Where did you get it?"

"It was a parting gift from my mother."

He lay still, and could almost have laughed. He had bought that perfume as a young man for his young wife. The Aekir bazaars sold it yet, it seemed.

He rolled away from the trembling girl in his arms and stared at the flame-light dancing on the tall ceiling.

"My lord, have I offended you?" she asked.

"You're my wife now, Aria. Call me Corfe." He pulled her close. She had warmed now and lay in the crook of his arm with her head resting on his shoulder. When he did not move further she began to trace a ridge of raised flesh on his collar-bone. "What did this?"

"A Merduk tulwar."

"And this?"

"That was... Hell, I don't know."

"You have many scars, Corfe."

"I have been all my life a soldier."

She was silent. Corfe found himself drifting off, his eyes struggling to shut. It was very pleasant lying here like this. He laid a hand on Aria's smooth hip and traced the curve of her thigh. At that, something in him kindled. He rolled easily on top of her, supporting his weight on his elbows, his hands cupping her face. Her mouth was set in an O of surprise.

That face within his hands, the dark hair fanning out from it. It smote him with old memories. He bent his head and kissed her mouth. She responded timidly, but then seemed to catch fire from his own urgency and became eager, or at least, eager to please.

He tried not to hurt her but she uttered a sharp, small cry all the same, and her nails dug into his back. It did not take long. When he was spent he rolled off her and stared at the ceiling once again, thinking *it is done*. His eyes stung and in the dimness he found himself blinking, as though he faced the pitiless glare of the sun.

"Does it always hurt like that?" Aria asked quietly.

"The first time? Yes, no – I suppose so."

"I must bear you a son. My father told me so," she went on. She took his hand under the covers. "It was not so bad as I thought it would be."

"No?" He smiled wryly. He could not look at her, but was grateful for her warmth and the touch of her hand and her low voice. He tugged her into his arms again, and she was still talking when he drifted off into black, blessed sleep.

A HAMMERING ON the door brought him bolt upright in bed, wide-awake in an instant. The fire was a volcanic glow in the hearth. The slats of sky beyond the shutters were black as coal; it was not yet dawn.

"Sire," a voice said beyond the door, "news from Ostrabar. Tidings of the utmost urgency." It was Felorin.

"Very well. I'll be a moment." He pulled on his clothes and boots whilst Aria watched him, wide-eyed, the sheets pulled up to her chin. He hesitated, and then kissed her on the lips. "Go back to sleep. I will return." He smoothed back her hair and found himself smiling at her, then turned away.

The palace was dark yet, with only a few lamps lit in the wall-sconces. Felorin bore a candle-lantern, and as the two men strode along the echoing passageways it threw their shadows into mocking capers along the walls.

"It is Golophin, sir," Felorin told Corfe. "He is in the Bladehall and refuses to speak to anyone save you. Ensign Baraz brought me word of his return. He has been to Aurungabar somehow, by some magic or other, and something has happened there. I took the liberty of rousing out General Formio also, sir,"

"You did well. Lead on."

The Bladehall was a vast cavernous darkness save at one end where a fire had been lit in the massive hearth and a table pulled across, upon which a single lamp burned. Golophin stood with his back to the fire, his face a scarred mask, impossible to read. At the table sat Formio with parchment, quills and ink, and standing in the shadows was Ensign Baraz.

"Golophin!" Corfe barked. Formio stood up at his approach. "What's this news?"

The wizard looked at Baraz and Felorin questioningly.

"It's all right. Go on."

Golophin's face did not change; still that terrible mask empty of expression. "I have been to Aurungabar, never mind how. It would seem that both the Sultan and his Queen were assassinated this morning."

No-one spoke, though even Formio looked stunned. Corfe groped for a chair and sank into it like an old man.

"You're sure?" Baraz blurted.

"Quite sure," the old mage snapped. "The city is in an uproar, panicked crowds milling in the streets. They managed to keep it quiet for a couple of hours, but then someone blabbed and now it is common knowledge." He faltered, and there was something like disgust in his voice as he added, "It is all wearily familiar."

They looked at Corfe, but the King was sitting with his elbows on his knees, his eyes blank and sightless.

"Aruan?" Formio asked at last.

"That would be my guess. He must have wormed an agent into the household."

She was dead. His Heria was dead. Corfe spoke at last. "This morning, you say?"

"Yes sire. Around the third hour before noon."

Corfe rubbed his chest. The ache had gone, but something worse was settling inexorably in its place. He cleared his throat, trying to clear his mind.

"Nasir," he said. "How far along the road is he?"

"My familiar is with him now. He is ten leagues east of Khedi Anwar at the head of fifteen thousand men – the army he was to bring here."

"He knows?

"I told him, sire, yes. He has already broken camp and is marching back the way he came."

"We need those men," Formio said in a low voice.

"Ostrabar needs a sultan," Golophin replied.

"He's a boy, not yet seventeen."

"The army is behind him. And he is Aurungzeb's publicly acknowledged heir. There is no other."

Corfe raised his head. "Golophin is right. Nasir will need those men to restore order in the capital. We must do without them." Heria was dead, truly dead.

He fought the overwhelming wave of hopelessness which was trying to master him.

"Nasir will be five, maybe six days on the road before he re-enters Aurungabar. Golophin, are there any other claimants who could make trouble before he arrives?"

The wizard pondered a moment. "Not that I know of. Aurungzeb has sired other children by concubines, but Nasir is the only son, and he is well-known. I cannot foresee any difficulties with the succession."

"Well and good. Who is in authority in Aurungabar at the moment?"

Golophin nodded at Ensign Baraz, who stood forgotten in the shadows. "That young man's kinsman, Shahr Baraz the Younger. He was a bodyguard of the Queen at one time, and remained a confidant. It was he who took charge when the maids discovered the bodies."

"You have spoken to him?"

"Briefly." Golophin did not relay his own suspicions about Shahr Baraz. The most upright and honourable of men, while he had told the wizard frankly of the assassinations he had nevertheless been holding something back. But, Golophin was convinced, not for his own aggrandisement. Shahr Baraz the Younger was of the old *Hraib*, who held that to tell a lie was to suffer a form of death.

Corfe stood up. "Formio, have fast couriers sent to Aurungabar expressing our support for the new Sultan. Our whole-hearted and, if necessary, material support. Get one of the scribes to couch it in the necessary language, but get three copies of it on the road by dawn." Formio nodded, and made a note on his parchment. The scrape of his quill and the crack and spit of the logs in the hearth were the only sound in the looming emptiness of the Bladehall.

"We will be short of troops now," Corfe continued steadily. "I will have to weaken Melf's southern expedition in order to make up the numbers for the main operations here." He strode to the fire and, leaning his fists on the stone mantle, stared at the burning logs below.

"The enemy will move now, while our ally is temporarily incapacitated. Formio, another despatch to Aras at Gaderion. He should expect a major assault very soon. And get the courier to repeat the message to Heyn on the road north. Henceforth he will move by forced marches.

"As for Torunn itself, I want the field army here put on notice to move at once. We have wasted enough time. I will lead them out within the week."

Formio's scratching quill went silent at that. "The snows are still lying deep in the foothills," he said.

"It can't be helped. In my absence you will remain here, as Regent."

"Corfe, I –"

"You will obey orders." The King turned from the fire

and smiled at Formio to soften his words. "You are the only person I would trust with it."

The Fimbrian subsided. From the tip of his quill the ink dripped to blot a black circle on the pale parchment. Corfe turned to Golophin.

"It would ease my mind were you to remain here with him."

"I cannot do that, sire."

Corfe frowned, then turned away. "I understand. It is not your responsibility."

"You misunderstand me, sire. I am going with you."

"What? Why in the world –"

"I promised a dying woman, my lord, that I would remain by your side in this coming trial." Golophin smiled. "Perhaps I have just gotten into the habit of serving Kings. In any case, I go with you on campaign – if you'll have me."

Corfe bowed, and some life came back into his eyes. "I would be honoured, Master Mage." As he straightened he turned to Ensign Baraz, who had not moved.

"I would very much like to have you accompany me also, Ensign."

The young man stepped forward, then came stiffly to attention once again. "Yes, sir." His eyes shone.

"There is one more thing." Corfe paused, and as they watched him they saw something flicker in his eyes, some instantly hidden agony.

"Mirren must go to Aurungabar at once, to be married."

Formio nodded but Baraz looked utterly wretched. It was Golophin who spoke up. "Could that not wait a while?" he asked gently. "I have barely begun her tuition."

"No. Were we to delay, it would be seen as uncertainty about Nasir. No. They sent us Aria, we must send them Mirren. When she marries Nasir the whole world will see that the alliance is as strong as ever, despite the death of Aurungzeb, the turning back of the Merduk reinforcements."

"It is the clearest signal we can send," Formio agreed.

And it is only right, Corfe thought, *for me to suffer something of what Heria suffered*. There was an ironic symmetry about it all, as though this were all laid on for the amusement of some scheming god. So be it. He would shoulder this grief along with the others.

"Ensign Baraz," he said, "fetch me the palace steward, if you please. Formio, get those notes off to the scribes and then rouse out the senior staff. We will all meet here in one hour. Felorin, secure the door."

When only he and Golophin remained in the hall's vast emptiness, Corfe leant his forehead against the hot stone of the mantle.

"Golophin, how did she die?"

The old mage was taken aback. He seemed to take a moment to comprehend the question. "The Merduk Queen? A knife, Shahr Baraz told me. There were maids close-by but they heard nothing. So he says."

Corfe's tears fell invisibly into the flames below, to vanish with not so much as a hiss to note their passing.

"Sire – Corfe – is there something else the matter?"

"This is my wedding night," the King said mechanically. "I have a new wife waiting for me."

Golophin set a hand on his arm. "Perhaps you should go back to her for a little while, before she hears the news from someone else."

Dear God, he had almost forgotten. He raised his head with a kind of dulled wonder. "You are right. She should hear it from me. But I must talk to Cullen first."

"Herc, then. Have a swallow of this." The wizard was offering him a small steel flask. He took it automatically and tipped it to his mouth. Fimbrian brandy. His eyes smarted and ran as he filled his mouth with it and swallowed it down.

"I always keep a mote of something warming about me," Golophin said, drinking in his turn. "Nothing else seems to keep out the cold these days."

Corfe looked at him. The mage was regarding him with a kindly surmise, as though inviting him to speak. For a moment it was all there, crowding on his tongue, and it would have been a blessed relief to let it all gush forth, to lean on this old man as other Kings had before him. But he bit back the words and swallowed them. It was enough that

Albrec alone knew. He could take no sympathy tonight. It would break him. And others would need sympathy ere the night was done.

Footsteps the length of the hall, and Baraz was returning with the grizzled old palace steward. Corfe drew himself up.

"Cullen, you must have the Princess Mirren woken at once. She is to pack for a long journey. Have the stables harness up a dozen light waggons, enough for a suitable entourage. Ensign Baraz, you will, with my authority, pick out a tercio of cuirassiers as escort."

"Where shall I tell the princess she is going, sire?" Cullen asked, somewhat bewildered.

"She is going to Aurungabar to be married. I will see her before she goes, but she must be ready to leave by daybreak. That is all."

The steward stood irresolute for a second, his mouth opening and closing. Then he bowed and left hurriedly, drawing his night-robes closer about him as if the King exuded some baleful chill. Baraz followed him unhappily.

A blessed quiet for a few minutes. Corfe felt an overwhelming urge to go down to the stables, saddle up a horse, and take off alone for the mountains. To run away from this world and its decisions, its complications, its pain. He sighed and drew himself up. His bad leg was aching.

"You had best stay here," he said to Golophin. "I will be back soon." Then he set off to tell his new wife that she was an orphan.

THE TROOP-TRANSPORTS TOOK up four miles of river-frontage. There were over a hundred of the wide-beamed, shallow-draught vessels, each capable of carrying five tercios within its cavernous hold. They had been taking on their cargoes for two days now, and still the wharves of Torunn's waterfront were thronged with men and horses and mules and mountains of provisions and equipment. A dozen horses had been lost, and several tons of supplies, but the worst of the embarkation was over now and the transports would unmoor with the ebb of the evening tide in the estuary, and would begin their slow but sure battle upstream against the current of the Torrin River.

"The day has come at last," Formio said with forced lightness.

"Yes. At one time I thought it never would." Corfe tugged at the hem of his armoured gauntlets. "I'm leaving you three thousand of the regulars," he told Formio. "Along with the conscripts, that will give you a sizeable garrison. With Aras and Heyd at Gaderion, and Melf and Berza in the south, they should not even have to see battle."

"We will miss those Merduk reinforcements ere we're done," Formio said gravely.

"Yes. They would have eased my mind too. But there's no use crying after them now. Formio, I have been over all the paperwork with Albrec. As soon as I step aboard the transports you become Regent, and will remain so until I return. I've detached a few hundred of your Orphans to take over the training from the bodyguard. The rest are already boarded."

"You're taking the cream of the army," Formio said.

"I know. They have a hard road ahead of them, and there's no place for conscripts upon it."

"And the wizard goes too."

Corfe smiled. "He may be useful. And I feel he is a good man."

"I do not trust him, Corfe. He is too close to the enemy. He knows too much about them, and that knowledge he has never explained."

"It's his business to know such things, Formio. I for one shall be glad of his counsel. And besides, we shall face wizardry in battle before we're done. It's as well to be able to reply in kind."

"I would I were going with you," Formio said in a low voice.

"So would I, my friend. It has seemed to me that the more rank one acquires in this world, the less one is able to do as one prefers."

Formio gripped Corfe by the arm. "Do not go." His normally closed face was bright with urgency. "Let me take them out, Corfe. Stay you here."

"I cannot do that. It's not in me to do that, Formio. You know that."

"Then be careful, my friend. You and I have seen many battlefields, but something in my heart tells me that this one you are setting out for shall be the worst."

"What are you now, a seer?"

Formio smiled now, though there was little humour in his face. "Perhaps."

"Look for us in the early summer. If all goes well we shall march back by way of the Torrin Gap."

The two men stood looking at one another for a long moment. They had no need to say more. Finally they embraced like brothers. Formio moved back then and bowed deep.

"Farewell, my King. May God watch over you."

HALF THE CITY came down to the waterfront to see them off, waving and cheering as ship after ship of the transport fleet pulled away from the wharves and nosed out into the middle of the estuary. The fat bellied vessels set their courses to catch the south-east wind that was blowing in off the Kardian and in line astern they began the long journey upriver.

Torunna's sole princess had already left for Aurungabar and her wedding, but the kingdom's new Queen was there in the midst of a cloud of ladies-in-waiting, courtiers and bodyguards. She raised a hand to Corfe, her face white and unsmiling, the eyes red-rimmed within it. He saluted in return, then turned his gaze from the cheering clouds and stared westwards to where the Cimbric Mountains loomed bright in the sunlight, their flanks still deep in snow, clouds streaming from their summits. Somewhere up in those terrible heights the secret pass existed which led all the way down to the Sea of Tor, and that was the path this great army he commanded must take to victory. He felt no trepidation, no apprehension at the thought of that mountain-passage or the battles that would follow. His mind was clear at last.

PART THREE

NIGHTFALL

Men worshipped the dragon, for he had given his authority to the beast, and they worshipped the beast, saying, "Who is like the beast, and who can find against it?"

– Revelation ch. 13 v. 4

SIXTEEN

THE SUN WAS a long time clearing the Thurian Mountains in the mornings, and down in the Torrin Gap it remained drear and chill long after the surrounding peaks were bright and glowing with the dawn. The sentries paced the walls of Gaderion and cursed and blew into their hands, whilst before them the narrow valley between the mountains opened out grey and shadowed, livid with frost, and out in the gloom the campfires of the enemy gleamed in their tens of thousands.

General Aras walked the circuit of the walls with a cluster of aides and couriers, greeting the sentries in a low voice, halting every now and then to look out at the flickering constellations burning below. This he did every morning, and every morning the same view met his eyes, as it had for eleven days now.

The defenders of Ormann Dyke must have experienced something like this, back in the old days. The knowledge that there was nothing more to do than to wait for the enemy to move. The nerve-taut tension of that wait. The Himerian general, whoever he was, knew how to bide his time.

Finally the sun reared its head up over the white-frozen Thurians, and a blaze of red-yellow light swept down the flanks of Candorwir in the western arm of the valley. It lit up the blank, pocked cliff-face that was the Eyrie, travelled along the length of the curtain wall and kindled the stone of the Redoubt, the sharp angles of the fortifications thrown into perfect, vivid relief, and finally it halted at the foot of the Donjon walls, leaving that fortress in shadow. Only the tall head of the Spike was lofty enough to catch the sun as it streamed over the white peaks behind it. In the Donjon itself Aras heard the iron triangles of the watch clanging, summoning the night watch to breakfast, and sending the day watch out to their posts. Another day had begun at Gaderion.

Aras turned away. His own breakfast would be waiting for him in the Donjon. Salt pork and army bread and perhaps an apple, washed down with small beer – the same meal his men ate. Corfe had taught him that, long ago. He might eat it off a silver plate, but that was the only indulgence Gaderion's commanding officer would allow himself.

"The last of the wains go south this morning, do they not?" he asked.

His quartermaster, Rusilan of Gebrar, nodded. "Those are the last. When they have gone, it will be nothing but the garrison left, and several thousand fewer mouths to feed, though it's hard on the family men."

"It'll be easier on their minds to know their wives and children are safe in the south, once the real fighting starts," Aras retorted.

"The real fighting," another of the group mused, a square-faced man who wore an old Fimbrian tunic under his half-armour. "We've lost over a thousand men in the last fortnight, and are now penned in here like an old boar in the brush, awaiting the spears of the hunters. Real fighting."

"A cornered boar is a dangerous thing, Colonel Sarius. Let him move within range of our guns and he will find that out."

"Of course, sir. I only wonder why he hesitates. Intelligence suggests that the Finnmarkans and Tarberans are all up now. He has his entire army arrayed and ready, and has had them so for at least four days. His supply-lines must be a Quartermaster's nightmare."

"They're convoying thousands of tons of rations across the Sea of Tor in fishing boats," Rusilan said. "At Fonterios they have constructed a fair-sized port to accommodate them all, now that the ice is almost gone. They can afford to wait for the summer if they choose; the Himerians can call on the tribute of a dozen different countries."

The report of an artillery piece silenced Rusilan, and the group of officers went stock-still. High up on the side of the Spike, the smoke of the gun was hanging heavy as wool in the air, and before it had drifted a yard from the muzzle of the culverin that had belched it, the alarm-triangles were ringing.

Aras and his party ran along the curtain wall to the Donjon proper, against a tide of soldiers coming the other way. When they had passed through the small postern that linked the wall with the eastern fortifications, they climbed up to the catwalks there and peered out of an embrasure whilst all around them the gun-crews were swarming about their weapons.

"Our adversary is on the move, it seems," Colonel Sarius, the keen-eyed Fimbrian, remarked. "I see infantry formations, but nothing else as yet."

"What strength?" Aras asked him.

"Hard to gauge; there are still hordes of them forming up in front of their camps. Two or three grand tercios at the least. A mile of frontage – but that's only the front ranks. I do believe it's a general assault." The Fimbrian's hard eyes sparkled as though some great treat were in store for him.

"Horse-teams coming up from the rear – yes, he's bringing forward his guns. That's what it is. He's decided to begin siting his batteries. And in broad daylight! What can he be thinking?"

"Ensign Duwar," Aras barked. "Run up to the signallers. Have them hoist *General Engagement, Fire at Will*."

"Aye sir!" The young officer took off at a sprint for the signal-station on top of the Spike.

"Gentlemen," Aras said to the more senior officers remaining, "to your posts. You all know what to do. Rusilan and Sarius, remain with me. We shall repair to the upper battlements I think, and get ourselves a better view. It's apt to grow somewhat busy down here once the action starts."

There was a strange gaiety in the air, Aras realised. Even the common soldiers of the gun-crews were grinning and chattering as they loaded their pieces, and their officers seemed afire with anticipation. For days, weeks even, they had been harried and beaten back by the enemy until they had no option but to retreat behind the stout walls of Gaderion. Now that those walls were about to be assaulted, they knew they would be able to wreak a bloody revenge.

On the topmost battlement of the Donjon, with the blank stone of the Spike's towering menace at their back, Aras and his remaining colleagues halted, breathless from having run up several flights of stairs. They could see the entire valley spread out below them: the sharp-angled shape of the Redoubt, the snaking curtain wall, the sun glinting on the iron barrels of the Eyrie's guns as they were run out of the rock of the very mountain opposite. And all along that intricate and formidable series of defences, thousands of men dressed in Torunnan sable were labouring in the casemates or loading their arquebuses or running here and there in long lines bearing powder and shot and wads for the batteries.

"Here they come," Sarius said dryly.

"I wish I had your eyes, Colonel," Aras told him. "What are they?"

"Rabble from Almark. He won't waste good troops in the first wave. He's got to know we have that entire valley ranged. "Look at their dressing! They've never so much as smelled a drill-square, this lot."

A mile and a half away, Aras could now see that the dark crowd of men darkening the face of the land was moving in a broad line. Behind that line there came another, this one more ordered. And behind that, the beetling mass of scores of horse-teams hauling guns and limbers and caissons.

The first wave came on very swiftly, keeping no formation beyond that of a broad, ragged line. They were clad in Almarkan blue, some carrying pikes and swords, others jogging along with arquebuses resting on their shoulders. On the valley floor before them, a scattered line of thin saplings had been planted years before with a half-furlong between each tree. This marked the extreme range of the Torunnan guns. Aras held his breath as the host approached them. His men had been trained to hold their fire until the enemy was well beyond the treeline.

All along the walls of Gaderion's fortresses the crowded activity gave way to an intent stillness. The smell of slow-match drifted about the valley. *The Perfume of War,* old soldiers called it.

A puff of smoke from one of the Redoubt casemates, followed a second later by the dull boom of the explosion. Right in the middle of the enemy formation a narrow geyser of earth went up, flinging aside the ragged remains of men, tearing a momentary hole in the carpet of tiny figures.

A second later every gun in the entire valley opened up. The air shook, and Aras felt the massive stone of the battlements trembling under the soles of his boots. The noise of that opening salvo was experienced by the entire body rather than just heard by the ears. Waves of hot air and smoke came billowing up from the embrasures like a wind passing the gates of Hell.

And Hell came to earth instants later for the men of the Himerian vanguard. The valley floor seemed to erupt in bursting fountains of stone and dirt. It reminded Aras of the effect a heavy rainstorm has on bare soil. The lead enemy formations simply disappeared in that tempest of explosions. The Torunnan gunners were using hollow shells packed with powder for the most part. When these detonated they sent wicked showers of red-hot metal spraying in a deadly hail, tearing men apart, maiming them, tossing them through the air. In the lower embrasures, however, the batteries were loaded with solid shot, and these skimmed along at breast height, cutting great swathes of bloody slaughter through the close-packed enemy, each shot felling a dozen or a score of men and sending their sundered fragments flying among their fellows. Aras found he was beating his fist on the stone of the merlon as he watched, and his face had frozen open in a savage grinning rictus. There were perhaps fifteen thousand men in that first wave, and they were being torn to pieces while still a mile from Gaderion's mighty walls. From those walls he could hear a hoarse roaring noise. The gunners were cheering, or baying rather, even as they reloaded and ran out the culverins again. A continuous bellowing thunder rang out, magnified and echoed by the encircling mountains until it was almost unbearable and could hardly be deciphered from the hammering beat of the blood in Aras's own heart. The smoke of the bombardment reared up to blot out the morning sunlight and cast a shadow on the heights of the Cimbrics in the west. It seemed impossible that such a noise and such a shadow could be made by the agency of men.

"They're coming on," Colonel Sarius shouted in disbelief.

Out of the broken, smoking ground, the enemy were struggling onwards, leaving behind them the shattered corpses of hundreds of their comrades; and now the massed roar of their voices could be heard amid the thunder of the guns.

"They're going to make it to the walls," Aras said, incredulous. What could make men move forward under that murderous fire?

The entire valley floor seemed covered with the figures of running men, and among them the shells rained down unceasingly. It could be seen now that many of them carried spades and baulks of wood and others had the wicker cages of empty gabions strapped to their backs. In their midst, armoured Inceptines urged them on from the backs of tall horses, waving their maces and shouting furiously.

Back up the valley, a second assault wave started out. This one was heavily armoured and disciplined, and moved with forbidding alacrity. Tall men in long mail coats with steel cuirasses. They bore two-handed swords or battleaxes, and all had matchlock holsters slung at their backs. gallowglasses of Finnmark, the shock infantry of the Second Empire.

The men of the first wave had now halted well short of arquebus range, and there went to ground as if by prior order. The Almarkan soldiers began digging frantically amid the shellbursts, throwing the frozen soil up over their shoulders and shoring up the sides of their hasty scrapes with slats of wood and hastily filled gabions. Hundreds more died, but the shells that killed them broke up the ground and aided them in their digging. As the holes grew deeper, the Torunnan artillery had less effect. The culverins of Gaderion fired on a flat trajectory, so once the enemy was below ground level it was almost impossible to depress the guns low enough to bear.

Aras fumbled in his pouch for pencil and parchment. Leaning on the merlon he hastily scratched out and signed a note, then turned to one of the couriers who stood waiting as they had stood throughout the assault. "Take this along the walls and show it to all the battery commanders. They are to switch fire – do you understand me? They are to switch fire to the second wave. Go quickly."

The young man sped off with the note in one fist and his sword-scabbard held high in the other.

"I see it now," Sarius was saying. "The enemy is cleverer than we thought. He's sacrificing the first wave to gain a secure foothold for the second. But it still won't do him any good – they'll just sit there and get plastered by our guns."

"Perhaps not," Aras said. "Look up the valley, beyond the gallowglasses."

Sarius whistled soundlessly. "Horse artillery, going full tilt. He can't mean to bring them all the way up to the front! It's madness."

"I believe he does. Whoever the enemy general is, he is an original thinker. And a gambler too."

As the courier's message went along the walls, the guns of Gaderion shifted their aim, and began to seek out the second enemy wave, which was making steady and relatively unhindered progress up the valley. As soon as the first shells began to land in the midst of the gallowglasses their orderly formation scrambled and began to open out. They increased speed from a slow jog to an out-and-out sprint. Aras could see many of them falling, tripped by the broken ground and the weight of their armour. There were perhaps eight thousand of them, and they had half a mile to run before they gained the shelter of the trenches their Almarkan comrades were so frantically digging.

"Sarius," Aras said, "go down to the Redoubt. We will attempt a sortie. Take half the heavy cavalry, no more, and hit the Finnmarkans. They'll be winded by the time they reach you."

"Sir!" Sarius took off, running like a boy.

Aras turned to another of his young aides. "Run along the walls. All battery-commanders. We are about to make a sortie. Be prepared to hold fire as soon as our cavalry leaves the gates."

Minutes passed, while Aras stood chafing and the gallowglasses struggled closer to the line of crude trenches. They were taking casualties, but not so many as the first wave had, a tribute to their superior armour and more open ranks. The roar of the battle was a dull thumping in the ear now, every man in the valley partially deafened.

The great gates of the Redoubt swung open and files of Torunnan cavalry began to ride out and form up beyond the covering redan. The Himerian troops in the southern half of the valley seemed to pause, and then redouble their efforts, though Aras saw many throw aside their spades to pick up arquebuses.

Sarius formed up his men on sloping ground before the redoubt. Four lines of horsemen some half a mile long. As soon as they were in position, Aras saw Sarius himself, together with a trio of aides and a banner-bearer, place themselves square in the front rank. Then there was the flash of a sword blade, the bright gleam of a bugle-call in the smoke-ridden murk, and the first line of four hundred horsemen began to move. When it had gone a few horse-lengths the second started out, and then the third, and the fourth. Sixteen hundred heavy cavalry in sable armour with matchlock pistols held cocked and ready at their shoulders.

In the makeshift trenches three furlongs to their front the Almarkans dropped their spades and reached for weapons instead. The guns of the Redoubt and the curtain wall had ceased fire, masked by the cavalry, but those up in the Eyrie and the Donjon were still pouring a storm of shot and shell into the ranks of the gallowglass infantry who were now almost at their goal. Fully five hundred of them had fallen, but the remainder knew their only hope of survival was to gain the shelter of the line of trenches. If they had to retreat back the way they had come they would be destroyed.

Aras watched the Torunnan cavalry charge forward. The instant before impact there was a sudden eruption of smoke all along their line as they fired their matchlocks at point-blank range. They were answered by the arquebuses of the Almarkans, and horses began to stumble, and fall, men toppling from their saddles.

Into the trenches. Some riders leapt their steeds across the line of earthworks, some halted at the lip, and not a few tumbled cartwheeling into them. The second line reined in and fired their matchlocks where they could. Sarius's banner was waving but Aras could not make him out in that terrible maelstrom of men and horses and jetting smoke. He had been busy, though: the third and fourth ranks of cavalry broke off and wheeled to the flanks before charging home in their turn.

All across the floor of the valley the fighting was savage and hand-to-hand. The Almarkans were no match for the peerless heavy cavalry of Torunna, but what they lacked in training and morale they made up for in numbers. Sarius was outmatched nine to one, and the gallowglasses were forging along that last quarter-mile relentlessly. Once they joined battle, the cavalry would be swamped.

Men in blue livery running in one and twos, then by squads and companies out of the killing-floor of the trenches. The Almarkans were beginning to break. Too late.

The gallowglasses joined the line, swinging their great swords or two-handed axes. Aras saw a destrier's head cut clean from its neck by a swing from one of the huge blades. Sarius's banner was still waving, pulling out of the scrum. Riderless horses were screaming and galloping everywhere. Faint and far-off in the huge tumult of battle there sounded the silver notes of a bugle. Sarius was sounding the *Retreat*.

The cavalry broke off, firing their second matchlocks over the rumps of their steeds as they went. There was little attempt to dress the ranks; the gallowglasses pressed them too closely for that. A formless mob of mounted men streamed away from the mounded dead of the earthworks and began a retreat up the slope to the redan, where two hundred arquebusiers of the garrison were waiting to cover their return. Sarius's banner, scarlet and gold, was nowhere to be seen.

The cavalry thundered up the incline, many two to a horse. Other unhorsed troopers hung on to tails or stirrups and were dragged along. The great guns of Gaderion began to thunder out again, the gunners maddened by the slaughter of their comrades in the cavalry. The Himerian earthworks became a shot-torn hell of flying earth and bodies. The gallowglasses and Almarkans broke off the pursuit and cowered in their trenches as the sky turned black above them and the very earth screamed below their feet. But the rage of the Torunnans was impotent. The Almarkans had held on just long enough for the trenches to be reinforced in strength, and the enemy would now be impossible to dislodge. Perhaps fifteen thousand men were now dug-in within a half-mile of Gaderion's walls.

Aras ran down the great stairs to the curtain wall, and became enmeshed in the fog of battle-smoke. Grimy, soot-stained men were still working the guns maniacally, and the air in the casemates seemed to scorch his lungs. Finally he made it out to the courtyard in the centre of the Redoubt, where the cavalry were still streaming in through the tall double-gates.

"Where is Sarius?" he demanded of a bloody-browed officer, only to be met with a mad vacancy. The man's mind was still fighting out in the trenches.

"Where is Sarius?" he asked another, but was met with blankness again. At last he caught sight of Sarius's banner-bearer being carried away and halted the litter-bearers.

"Where is your Colonel?"

The man opened his eyes. He had lost his arm at the elbow and the stump spat and dribbled blood like a tap.

"Dead on the field," he croaked.

Aras let the litter-bearers carry him away. The courtyard was a milling crowd of bloody men and lacerated horses. Beyond them, he heard even over the roar of the artillery the great gates of Gaderion boom shut as the last of the rearguard came in. He wiped his face, and began to make his way back up to the fuming storm of the battlements.

CARTIGELLA, LIKE MANY of the Ramusian capitals, had started life as a port. The chief city of the tribal King Astar, it had fallen to the newly-combined Fimbrian tribes over eight hundred years before, and Astarac, as the region about it became known, had become the first conquest of what would one day be the Fimbrian Empire. The city rebelled against its northern conquerors within a hundred and fifty years of its fall, but was besieged and crushed by the great Elector Cariabus Narb, who had also founded Charibon. Those rebels who survived the sack scattered southwards for the most part, into the jungles of Macassar, and their descendants became the corsairs. Some, however, kept together and under a great sea-captain named Gabor they sailed through the Malacar Islands, seeking some place they might live in peace, untroubled by fear of Fimbrian reprisals. They settled a large island to the south-west of Macassar, and that place became Gabrion.

It would be almost four hundred years before Astarac finally threw off the decaying Fimbrian yoke, and in those centuries the Fimbrians made of ruined Cartigella a great city. But they deliberately refused to fortify it, remembering the agonies of the year-long siege it had taken to reduce the place. So Cartigella's walls were later constructs of the Astaran monarchy – for Astar's bloodline had somehow survived the long years of vassalage – and they were perhaps not so high or formidable as they might have been, had they been constructed by Imperial engineers.

And now Cartigella was besieged again.

The Himerian army had started out from Vol Ephrir at midwinter, and by the time the first meltwaters were beginning to swell the rivers tumbling out of the Malvennors, they were on the borders of East Astarac, the hotly contested duchy which King Forno had wrested from the Perigrainians scarcely sixty years before. So well had they hidden their movements with Dweomer-kindled snowstorms, and so unexpected was this midwinter march, that King Mark had left with the fleet for his rendezvous with the rest of the allied navy off Abrusio unaware that his kingdom was about to be invaded.

The Astaran army, left under the command of Mark's son Cristian, was caught completely by surprise. The Himerians advanced deep into East Astarac before they were challenged, and in a confused battle which took place in a blizzard in the Malvennor foothills the Astarans were worsted, and thrown into retreat. Their retreat became a rout as they were harried night and day by Perigrainian cavalry and packs of huge wolves. Most fell back in disorder upon the city of Garmidalan, and there prepared to fight to the last. But the Himerians merely surrounded the city and began to casually starve it into submission.

The main body of the Empire's forces had not joined in the pursuit. Instead, they struck off westwards for the Malvennor passes, which were lightly guarded by an Astaran rearguard. They marched down from the heights largely unmolested, and carved a bloody swathe across King Mark's kingdom, driving the Astaran troops and their inexperienced Crown Prince before them, until finally they came to a halt before the walls of Cartigella, the capital.

Outnumbered many times over by an army that employed weatherworking and legions of beasts, Prince Cristian nonetheless held out some hope. The sea-lanes had not yet been closed, and thus Cartigella might yet be saved by reinforcements from her ancient ally Gabrion, or perhaps even the Sea-Merduks. He sent out swift despatch-runners to every free kingdom of the west, and strengthened his walls, and waited, whilst the Himerians brought up siege artillery and began to bombard the city from the surrounding hills.

On the day of Sultan Aurungzeb's death, the first breach was made in Cartigella's defences, and fighting began to rage in the wall-districts of the city. The Astarans, soldiers and civilians alike, fought with savage heroism, but were pushed back from the outer fortifications by Inceptine warrior-monks leading companies of werewolves. Thousands died, and Cristian withdrew to the Citadel of Cartigella itself. There the Himerian advance was halted, foiled by the impregnable fortress on its high crag which dominated the lower city. From there the Astaran gunners poured a torrent of artillery fire into the ranks of the Himerian beasts that even werewolves could not withstand. The Himerians drew back, and the garrison of the citadel under their young prince dared to believe that they might hold out.

But the next morning a vast fleet appeared in the bay below, and from the holds of its vessels issued a foul swarm of flying creatures. These descended upon the citadel like a cloud of locusts, and overwhelmed the defenders. Cristian was slain and his bodyguard died in ranks around him. Cartigella was sacked with a brutality which surpassed even the legendary excesses of the Fimbrians, and the smoke of its burning climbed up in a black pillar which could be seen for many miles in the clear spring air.

Within three days, Astarac had capitulated, and was incorporated into the Second Empire.

SEVENTEEN

"AND NOW IS Hell come to earth,
And in the ashes of its burning will totter
All the schemes of greedy men.
The Beast, in coming, will
Tread the cinders of their dreams.

"Thus spake Honorius the Mad, four and a half centuries ago, and he was never wrong in his predictions – though he was cursed in that they were fated to be dismissed in his lifetime as the ravings of an insane anchorite. My friends, we are tools of history, instruments in the Hands of God. What we have done, and what we will do in the time to come, is but a fulfilment of His vision for the good of the world. So set your minds at rest. Out of blood and fire and smoke shall dawn a new sunrise, and a second beginning for the scattered peoples of the earth."

Aruan did not seem to raise his voice, but every man in the vast host heard his words, and as they did, something about their hearts kindled and uplifted them, and each one straightened his shoulders as if the Vicar-General were speaking to him alone.

On the waterfronts they listened, and in the rigging of the ships, and all through the streets of ancient Kemminovol, capital of Candelaria. As he spoke, the night drew back from the margins of the horizon and the sun sprang up above the grey silhouette of the great promontory to the east, touching the mastheads of the tallest ships with gold.

"So go now about your work, and know that it is the work of God you do. His blessing is upon you this day."

Aruan raised a hand in benediction, and the listening crowds bent their heads as one. Then he left the rough dais which had been cobbled together out of old fish-boxes, and the men who had been listening sprang into a swarm of activity, and the ships moored there were thick with their sweating and hauling companies.

Bardolin supported the Archmage as he climbed down from his wooden podium. Aruan was white-faced and perspiring. "I'll not do that again for a while. I believe I misjudged the effort required. What a task it is, to lift men's hearts!"

"There were many thousands listening to you – you are not telling me you touched every one," Bardolin said gruffly.

"Oh yes. I can bend the will of armies, but it takes an effort. I must sit down, Bardolin. See me to the carriage will you?"

They climbed inside the closed box of the four-wheeler and in its padded leather confines Aruan threw his head back and closed his eyes. "Better, much better.

"With Almarkans and Perigrainians it is easier; they have traditional antagonisms with Astarans and Torunnans – a matter of history, you understand. But the Candelarians have been a nation of merchants for centuries, opening their doors to whatever conqueror comes along and then going on with business as usual. I had to fire them up a little, you might say."

"They will be the first wave then?"

"Yes. The main host of the Perigrainians will follow up the seaborne assault with an advance on Rone, crossing the Candelan River up in the southern foothills. Southern Torunna is lightly defended; it will fall quickly. Our intelligence reports that the Torunnan King is finally on the move with his main army. He is going north by ship, to the Gap. All that is left in the capital are a scattering of regulars and a mob of conscripts. By the time the great Corfe realises what we're at, we'll be sitting in Torunn and he will be caught between two fires."

"And Gaderion? How hard do you want the Torunnans pressed there?"

"Very hard, Bardolin. Corfe must be persuaded that his presence at the Gap is essential to prevent its fall, so the assault must be pressed home with the utmost ferocity. If it falls, so much the better. But it does not have to fall; its role is to suck in the main Torunnan armies and keep them occupied."

Bardolin nodded grimly. "It shall be so."

"What of Golophin? Have you had any more words with him?"

"He has disappeared. He has cloaked his mind and cut himself off. He may not even be in Torunna any longer."

"Our friend Golophin is running out of time," Aruan said tartly, mopping his bald pate. "Track him down, Bardolin."

"I will. You may count on it."

"Good. I must rest now. I will need all my strength in the days to come. Four of the Five Kingdoms are ours now, Bardolin, but the fifth, that will prove the hardest. When it falls we will be close to matching the Fimbrian Empire of old."

"And the Fimbrians, what of them?" Bardolin asked. "We've heard no word since their embassy left Charibon, weeks ago now."

"They're waiting to see how Torunna fares. Oh, I have plans for Fimbria also, make no mistake. The Electors have stood aloof too long; they think their homeland is inviolable. I may have to prove them wrong." Aruan smiled, his eyes gazing upon a vision of a single authority that spanned the continent. Firm yet benign, harsh at times, but always fair.

"You shall be Presbyter of Torunna, once it falls," he told Bardolin, smiling. Then his eyes narrowed. He pursed his full lips. "As for master Golophin, I shall give him one last chance. Find him, speak with him. Tell him that if he comes over to us with a full heart and a clear conscience, he shall have Hebrion to govern in my name. I cannot say fairer than that."

Bardolin's eyes shone. "That will do it; I'm sure of it. It will be enough to tip the scales in our favour."

"Yes. We will have to disappoint Murad, of course, but I am sure we will find something else for him to do, once he has slain the Hebrian Queen and her mariner. Good! Things are progressing, my friend. Orkh is already installing himself in Astarac and our armies are poised for the final campaign. I believe I will sleep for a while before returning to Charibon. You must go back to Gaderion and begin hammering on those walls again." He smiled tiredly, and gripped Bardolin by the hand. "My mage-general. Get me Golophin's loyalty, and the three of us will together set this unhappy world to rights."

THE VAST, FOAM-FLECKED and moonlit expanse of the Levangore, stirred into a stiff swell by an inconstant wind blustering out of the south-south-east. Above it a sky empty of cloud, the stars brilliant pin-points in that black vault, the moon as bright as a silver lantern.

Richard Hawkwood fixed his eye on the North Star and stared through the two tiny sights on his quadrant. The plumb-line of the instrument hung free and he swayed easily with the ship, compensating without conscious effort for the pitch and roll. When he was satisfied he caught the plumb line and read off the numbers on the scale. The ship was six degrees south of Abrusio's latitude. Those six degrees of latitude corresponded to over a hundred leagues. By his dead-reckoning, they had made some two hundred leagues of easting in the past eleven days. They were south of Candelaria, not far off the latitude of Garmidalan, and two thirds of their journey was behind them.

Hawkwood checked the pegs of the traverse board. They were headed north-north-east, and the wind was on the starboard quarter. He had sent up the square yards on fore and main at last, retaining the lateen only on the mizzen, and the *Seahare* rode the swells easily under courses and topsails, making perhaps five knots. Sprightly though her progress might be, an experienced observer would note that much of the rigging had been knotted and spliced several times over, and her foremast had been fished with beams of oak and line after line of woolding to hold together the crack which ran through it from top to bottom.

They had outpaced the storm, and had run through the Malacar Straits at a fearsome clip, Hawkwood on deck day and night, the leadsman in the forechains continually calling out the depth. The wind had backed round after that, and had slowly become a natural thing once more, the seasonal airs of the Hebrian Sea replacing the Dweomer-birthed gale. But that had not ended the hard labour on board. The *Seahare* had taken a severe battering in her race with the squall and while she could neither pause in her voyage nor put in to shore, her crew were able to start the work of restoring her to full seaworthiness.

The repairs had taken the better part of a week, and even now the ship was making more water than Hawkwood liked, and the pumps had to be manned for half a glass in every watch. But they were still afloat, and they seemed to have outrun their pursuers with a mixture of luck, good seamanship, and the valour of a swift-sailing ship. The ship's company were a crowd of whey-faced ghosts who dropped off to sleep as soon as they were off their feet, but they were alive. The worst was over.

Hawkwood put the traverse board away in the binnacle-housing, noted the ship's position in the crowded chart that was his mind, and yawned mightily. His belt hung slack about his waist; he must make another hole in it soon. But at least he had hair on his head once more, a salt-and-pepper crop which stood up like the bristles of a brush on his scalp.

Ordio, one of the more capable master's mates, had the watch. He was scrutinising the brilliant night sky with studied nonchalance, standing by the larboard rail. They were two glasses into the morning watch, and it would be dawn in another hour. When they had finally made landfall, Hawkwood promised himself, he would sleep the clock around. He had not had more than an hour or two's uninterrupted rest in weeks.

"Call me if the wind changes," he told Ordio automatically, and went below, staggering a little with his ever-present tiredness. The blankets in his swinging cot were damp and smelled of mould, but he could not have cared less. He drew off his sodden clothes and crawled under them gratefully, and was asleep in moments.

He woke some time later, instantly alert. The sun had come up by now despite the darkness in the cabin, and the *Seahare* was still on her course, though by the tone of the water running past the hull she had picked up a knot or so. But it was not that which had woken him. There was someone else in the cabin.

He sat up, throwing the blankets aside in the closed darkness, but two hands on his shoulders stopped him from getting to his feet. He flinched as a pair of cold lips were placed on his own, and then the warm tongue came questing over his teeth. His hands came up to cup the face of the one who kissed him, and he felt under his fingers the ridged scar-tissue on the otherwise smooth cheek.

"Isolla."

But she said no word, only pushed him back down into the cot. There were rustlings and the click of buttons, and she climbed in beside him, shivering at the touch of the fetid blankets on her skin. Her hair was down and covered both their faces with its feather-touch as they sought each other in the darkness. The cot swung and the ropes supporting it creaked and groaned in time with their own smothered sounds. When they were done her skin was hot and moist under his hands and their bodies were glued together by sweat. He started to speak, but her hand covered his mouth and she kissed him into silence. She climbed off the cot and he heard her bare feet padding on the wood of the deck as she dressed. He raised himself up on one elbow and saw her slim silhouette in the cracks of light which slipped under the cabin-door.

"Why?" he asked.

She was tying up her hair, and paused, letting it tumble once more about her shoulders. "Even queens need a little comfort now and again."

"Would you still need it, if you were not a queen of a lost kingdom?"

"If I were not a queen, Captain, I would not be here – nor you either."

"If you were not a queen I would marry you, and you would be happy."

She hesitated, and then said quietly "I know." Then she gathered her things and slipped out the door as silently as she must have arrived.

Two more days passed in the bright spring blue of the sea, and the routine of the ship became a way of life for all of them, ruled by bells, punctuated by unremarkable meals. As the *Seahare* sailed steadily onwards it became their entire world, self-contained and ordered. They had a fair wind, a sky uncluttered save by a little high cloud, and no sight of any other ship, though the lookouts were kept at the masthead day and night. It seemed strange to Hawkwood. The Levangore, especially the Western Levangore, was crossed by the busiest sea-lanes in the world, and yet in all their passage of it thus far they had sighted not a single sail.

The wind kept backing round until it was east-south-east, and in order to preserve some of their speed, Hawkwood altered course to north-north-east so it was on the beam. To larboard they could see now the blue shapes of the Malvennor mountains that formed the backbone of Astarac, Isolla's birthplace. She spent hours standing at the leeward rail, watching the land of her childhood drift past. The lookouts kept their gaze fixed on the open sea, and thus it was she who came to Hawkwood in the afternoon watch, and pointed at the south-western horizon.

"What do you make of that, Captain?"

Hawkwood stared, and saw dark against the blue shadows of the mountains a sombre stain on the air, a high column rising blackly against the sky.

"Smoke," he said. "It's some great, far-off fire."

"It is Garmidalan," Isolla whispered, "I know it. They are burning the city."

All day she remained on deck staring over the larboard quarter at the distant smoke, and as the daylight faded it was possible for all to see the red glow on the western horizon which had nothing to do with sunset.

Bleyn appeared on deck at dusk, having stayed dutifully by his sick mother all day, and joined Isolla at the rail. An unlikely friendship had grown up between the two, and when Hawkwood saw the both of them standing together at his ship's side with the swell of the sea rising and falling behind him he felt an almost physical ache in his heart, and knew not why.

"Sail ho!" the lookout called down from the masthead.

"Where away?"

"Fine off the port quarter, skipper. She's hull down and with not too much canvas abroad, but I do believe she's ship-rigged."

Hawkwood dashed up the starboard shrouds, then the futtock-shrouds into the maintop. The lookout was on the crossyards above him. He peered back along their wake, slightly phosphorescent in the gathering starlight, and caught the nick on the red and yellow glimmer of the horizon. He wiped his watering eyes but could make out nothing more. The strange ship, if ship it were, was on almost the same course as they, but it must have no more than reefed courses up or he'd have seen them pale against the sky. Not in a hurry then.

He did not like it all the same, and began bellowing orders from the maintop.

"All hands! All hands to make sail! Arhuz, send up topgallants and main and mizzen staysails."

"Aye sir. Rouse out, rouse out, you sluggards! Get up that rigging before I knot me a rope's end."

In minutes the rigging was full of men, and a crowd of them climbed past Hawkwood on the way to loose the topgallantsail. As the extra canvas was sheeted home and the yards braced round he felt the ship give a quiver, and the dip of her bow became more pronounced. Her wake grew even brighter with turbulence and he could feel the masts creaking and straining. The *Seahare* picked up speed like a spurred thoroughbred. Hawkwood stared aft again.

There – the pale shapes of sails being unfurled. Despite their extra speed, the stranger was hull-up now. She must be a swift sailer indeed, and have a large crew to cram on so much extra sail in so little time. Fore and aft sails on main and mizzen – so she was a barquentine then. God almighty, she was fast. Hawkwood felt a momentary chill settle in his stomach.

He looked down at the deck below. They were lighting the stern-lanterns at the taffrail.

"Belay, there! Douse those lights!"

The mood on board changed instantly. He saw pale faces looking up into the rigging at him, and then over the stern to where the strange ship was visible even from the quarterdeck, she was coming up so fast.

Hawkwood swallowed, cursing the sudden dryness in his mouth. A row of lights appeared along the barquentine's sides. She was opening her gun-ports. He hung his head a moment and then called out hoarsely:

"Master-at-arms, beat to quarters. Prepare for battle."

He climbed slowly down from the maintop whilst the deck exploded into a crowded, frantic activity below him. The enemy had caught up with them once more.

EIGHTEEN

THE LAST OF the waggons had been abandoned and now the men of the army were bent under the weight of their packs, while at the rear of their immense column a clanking, braying cavalcade of heavily-burdened mules were cursed forward by their drovers. They had left behind the last paved road and were now forging upwards along a single stony mountain track. Above them, the Cimbrics reared up in peak on peak, and the snow blew in streaming banners from their summits.

They were ten days out of Torunn, and the first, easy stage of their journey was behind them. They had been three days on the river, and after the interminable disembarkation had been five days more marching across the quiet farmland of northern Torunna, cheered to the echo at every village and town and freely given all the food supplies they needed. A thousand mules and seven thousand horses had cropped the new spring grass of every pasture in their path down to the roots, and the Torunnan King had every evening summoned the local landowners about him and had compensated them in gold coin from his own hand.

But the kindly plains were behind them now, and so were the lower foothills. They were on the knees of the Cimbric mountains, highest in the western world, and their sweating faces were set towards the snows and glaciers of the high places. And the battle which would be fought on their other side.

CORFE SAT HIS horse on the brow of a tall, crag-faced hillock, and watched as his army streamed past. Beside him were Felorin, General Comillan of the bodyguard, Ensign Baraz, and a sable-clad man on foot, Marshal Kyne, commander of the Orphans now that Formio was left behind in the capital.

The Cathedrallers were in the van, five thousand of them leading their warhorses by the bridle, most of them natives of these very hills. Next came ten thousand picked Torunnans armed with arquebuses and sabres, then the Orphans, ten thousand Fimbrian exiles with their pikes balanced on their shoulders, and then the straggling length of the mule train. Bringing up the rear would be the five hundred heavy cavalry of Corfe's bodyguard in their black *Ferinai* armour.

In the midst of both the Torunnan infantry and the Orphans, light guns were being manhandled along, sometimes lifted bodily over deep-running streams and broken boulders that had tumbled from the heights above. They were six-pounder horse-artillery, three batteries' worth in total. All that Corfe dared try and take across the mountains.

All told, more than twenty-six thousand men were trekking westwards into the fastnesses of the Cimbrics this bright spring morning, and their column stretched along an inadequate track which bore them for almost four miles. It was not the largest army Torunna had ever sent forth to war, but Corfe felt that it must surely be one of the most formidable. The best fighting men of four disparate peoples were represented in that long column; Torunnans, Fimbrians, Cimbric tribesmen, and Merduks. If they succeeded in making their way through the mountains, they would find themselves alone and unsupported on the far side, and arrayed against them would be armies from all over the remainder of the world. They would have to take Charibon then, or they would be destroyed, and with them the last, best hope of this earth.

The end was very close now – the climax of the last and greatest war that men would fight in this age of the world. Hebrion was gone, as was Astarac, and Almark and Perigraine were subjugated. Of all the Monarchies of God, Torunna alone now stood free.

I will raze Charibon to the ground, Corfe thought as he sat his horse and watched his army march past. *I will slaughter every wizard and shape-shifter and witch I find. I will make of Aruan's fall a terrible lesson for all the future generations of the world. And his Inceptine Order I shall wipe from the face of the earth.*

A gyrfalcon wheeled in a wide circle about his head, as though looking for him. Finally it came to earth as swiftly as though it were stooping on prey, and perched on the withered branch of a rowan tree to one side. Corfe rode away from his officers so that he might speak without being overheard.

"Well, Golophin?"

"Your path exists, Corfe, though perhaps *path* is an optimistic word. The sky is clear halfway through the Cimbrics, but on their western flanks a last spring blizzard rages, and the snow there is deepening fast."

Corfe nodded. "I expected no less. We have it from the Felimbri that winter lies longest on the western side of the divide; but the going is easier there all the same." He gestured to where the army marched before him, like a barbed serpent intent on worming its way into the heart of the mountains. "Once we leave the foothills behind us and get above the snowline, we will meet with the tail of the great glacier that the tribes name Gelkarac, the *Cold-Killer*. It will be our road through the peaks."

"It is a dangerous road. I have seen this glacier. It is pitted and creviced like a pumice-stone, and avalanches roar down on it from the mountains about."

"If wishes were horses, beggars would ride," Corfe said with a wry smile. "I would we all might sprout wings and fly across the mountains, but since we cannot, we must take whichever way we can." He paused, and then asked, "How go things where – where you are now, Golophin?"

"Aurungabar has been cowed by the return of Nasir with his host, and he has been recognised by all as the Sultan of Ostrabar. He will combine his coronation and his wedding in one ceremony, as soon as Mirren enters the city."

Corfe's breath clicked in his throat. "And how far has she to go?"

"Another five days will see her within the gates. She has left the waggons behind and has been making her way very swiftly with a small entourage on horseback."

Corfe smiled at that. "Of course she has. And you, Golophin – when do you return to the army?"

"Tonight, I hope, when you camp. I meet this evening with Shahr Baraz the Younger. He has something on his mind, it seems. After that, I will remain with the army until the end. It seems to me you will need my help ere you are done with the Cimbric Mountains, sire. Fare well."

And with that the gyrfalcon took off from its perch, leaving the wizened rowan shaking behind it, and disappeared into the low cloud that hung over the peaks of the nearest mountains. Corfe nudged his mount back to where his officers stood patiently.

"Tomorrow, gentlemen," he said, his eyes following the bird's flight, "we will enter the snows."

BUT THE SNOWS came to them first. As they were pitching camp that evening a chill gale of wind came roaring down from the heights, and in its train whirled a swift, blinding blizzard of hard snow, dry as sand and almost as fine. Many men were caught unawares, and saw their leather tents ripped out of their hands to billow high in the air and vanish. Cloaks were plucked out of packs and sent flying, and the campfires were flattened and quenched. The mules kicked and panicked and some broke free from their drovers and galloped back down the way they had come, while a few, crazed by the impact of a flapping tent which had come tumbling out of the snow at them like a fiend, jumped over a low cliff and landed in broken agony on the rocks below, their packs smashing open and spraying black gunpowder upon the snow.

The blizzard created a wall about the huddled thousands who darkened the face of the hills, and it was several hours before some kind of order was restored, tents made fast to crags and weighted down with stones, mules hobbled and picketed into immobility, and the troops wolfing down cold rations about the smoking embers of their campfires.

The wind eased off with the rising of the moon, and Corfe, standing outside his skewed tent, looked up to see that the sky was clearing, and the stars were out in their millions, flickering with far-off flames of red and blue and casting faint shadows on the drifts of deep, fine snow that now crunched underfoot. They had been somehow transported to a different world, it seemed; one of blank, twinkling greyness lit up by the moon so that the drifts seemed strewn with tiny diamonds, and men were black silhouettes in the moonlight whose breath steamed and clouded about them.

In the morning, the troops were up well before the dawn, and the tent-sheets were stiff as boards under their numb fingers. The water in their canteens had thickened to a slush that made the teeth ache, and if bare metal touched naked skin it clutched it in a frozen grip painful to break free of.

Comillan trudged through the snow to the King's tent. Corfe was blowing on his gauntleted hands and looking up at the way ahead through the narrow passes whilst behind him the dawn was a pale blueness in the sky, and the stars still twinkled coldly above.

"Eleven mules lost, and one hapless lad who went out for a piss in the night and was found this morning. Aside from that, we seem to be in one piece." When the King did not respond, Comillan ventured, "It will be heavy going today I'm thinking."

"Aye, it will," Corfe said at last. "Comillan, I want you to pick thirty good men and send them forward on foot – they can leave their armour behind. We need a trail blazed for the main body. Tribesmen like yourself, for preference."

"Yes, sir."

"Are these sudden blizzards usual this late in the foothills?"

"In spring? No. But they are not unknown. Last night was just a taster. But it sharpened up the men at least. The winter-gear is being dug out of packs, and they're gathering wood while they can. I'll load as much as I can on the mules. We'll need it in the high passes."

"Very good."

"I take it the wizard did not return, sire?"

"No, he did not. Perhaps mages are as blinded by blizzards as the rest of us."

An hour later the sun was over the horizon and rising fast, into an unclouded blue sky which seemed as brittle and transparent as glass. The world was a white, glaring brightness and the soldiers smudged the hollows of their eyes with mud or soot to reduce the glare while some held leaves between their teeth to prevent the blistering of their lower lips. Comillan's trailblazers forged ahead with the easy pace of men who are in familiar country, while behind them the great column grew strung-out and disjointed as the rest of the army trudged wearily upwards, even the cavalry afoot and leading their snorting mounts by the bridle. Entire tercios were assigned to each of the artillery pieces, and dragged them up the steep, snowbound track by main force.

When Corfe paused, gasping, to look back, he could see the green land of Torunna blooming out below him like some kindlier world forgotten by winter, and sunlight shining off the Kardian Sea in a half-guessed glitter on the edge of the horizon. The Torrin river snaked and meandered across his kingdom, bright as a sword-blade, and here and there were the dun stains of towns leaking plumes of smoke to bar the cerulean vault overhanging them.

The sky held clear for two more days, and while no more snow fell, and the wind remained light and fitful from the south-east, the temperature plummeted so that men walked with their cloaks frosted white by frozen breath, and icicles hung from the bits of the horses. The snow became hard as rock underfoot, which made for better going, but on the steeper stretches men had to go ahead of the main column and hack rude stairs out of the ice with mattocks, or else there would have been no purchase for the thousands of booted and hoofed feet following.

They were high up in the mountains now, and far enough within their winding flanks that the view of the land below was cut off, and they were surrounded on all sides by spires of frozen rock, blinding snowfields, and hoar-white slopes of scree and boulder. In the dark freezing nights Corfe halved the length of sentry-duty, for an hour at a time was as much as the men could bear out of their blankets, and few fires were lit, for they were trying to conserve their meagre store of wood for some future emergency.

So, they came to the end of all man-made tracks, and found themselves at the foot of the Gelkarak glacier, and stared in wonder at what seemed to be a broken and tumbled cliff of pale grey translucent rock. Except that it was not stone, but ancient ice which had come oozing down from the mountainsides in millennia of winters to form a vast, solid river fully half a mile wide, and many fathoms deep.

"We'll have to rig up ropes and pulleys at the top to haul up the animals and the guns," Corfe said to Comillan and Kyne, who stood swathed in furs beside him. "We'll work through the night; there's no time to play with. Comillan, you handle the horses. Kyne, give Colonel Rilke a hand with his guns." The King stared at a sky, which was still largely clear, but ahead of them sullen clouds gathered on the peaks, heavy with snow.

They were two days and a night hauling up the horses and mules and artillery pieces one by one to the top of the glacier. There was little engineering skill about it. The commanders had teams of up to three hundred men hauling on a cat's cradle of ropes at the lip of the glacier, and even the most recalcitrant mule could not argue with that amount of brute force.

On the second day of this rough portage the clouds arrived above them and snow started in again. Not the wicked blizzard of before, but a heavy silence of fat white flakes which accumulated with amazing speed, until the teams at the top of the glacier were labouring thigh-deep, and the ropes were buried. Yet more men were put to clearing the snow from the bivouacs, and half a dozen fell into hidden crevasses and were lost. A company of Felimbric tribesmen from the Cathedrallers then explored up the glacier for several miles, roped together and feeling their way step by step. They marked each crevasse with an upright pike thrust into the snow, a dark rag flying from the tip, and thus blazed a safe road for the army to follow. And still it grew colder, and the men's lungs began to labour in the thinning air.

They lost a field piece and six mules as a whole series of rime-stiff ropes snapped in the same instant and they tumbled down the cliff of the glacier's end, but at the end of their fifth day in the mountains proper, the army was united on the back of Gelkarak itself, and the advance went on.

The glacier wound like a vast, flat-backed snake through the heights of the surrounding mountains. A wide, safe highway, it seemed, with its concealing blanket of snow, but below that snow it was pitted and fissured and cracked, and in the dark, windless nights they could hear it groaning and creaking under their feet, so that it seemed they were crawling like ants stop the spine of some enormous, unquiet beast. Its course ran roughly westwards, and every now and then a lesser ice-tributary would snake down from the high surrounding valleys to join it. In three more days of travel Corfe lost fifteen men staking out the trail for the main body. Even the tribes had never come this deep into the Cimbrics.

Golophin returned at last, appearing at the door of the King's tent late one icy night and entering with a nod to Felorin, who stood stamping his feet nearby. The wizard's gyrfalcon was perched like a grey frosted sculpture on his forearm, and his face was livid with tiredness.

Corfe was alone, poring by candlelight over the ancient, inadequate text which Albrec had discovered in Torunn. A small charcoal brazier burned in a corner of the tent, but it did little to heat the frigid air within. He looked up as Golophin entered, and frowned. "You're late," he said shortly.

The wizard sat down on a camp stool and let his familiar hop to the foot of Corfe's cot. He took off his wide-brimmed hat, letting fall a glittering shower of unmelted snow. "My apologies."

Corfe handed him a leather bottle and he gulped from the neck before wiping his mouth and replacing the cork. "Ah, better. Thank you, sire. Yes, I am late. I have travelled far since last you saw me, farther than I had intended. The Eighth Discipline is a great gift, but it sometimes tempts one to overdo things, such is the thirst for news in men."

"What news?"

"Your daughter reached Aurungabar today, and is to be married in the morning. The new Sultan of Ostrabar will be crowned and wed in the same ceremony. After it is done, Nasir will ride forth with the men promised you by his father. Fifteen thousand, mostly heavy cavalry."

"Good," Corfe said, though he looked anything but relieved.

"Colonel Heyd has reached Gaderion, and the Himerians there are gearing up for a second assault. I bring General Aras's compliments. He will hold as long as he can, but his losses are high, while the Himerians seem to multiply daily. They have breached the curtain wall in three places but have not yet established a foothold beyond it. Communications with the south are still open. For the moment."

Corfe nodded silently. His face was gaunt and grey with cold. "Is that all?"

"No. I save the most startling news for last. In Aurungabar I talked again to Shahr Baraz the Younger. The Sultan and his consort are in their tomb and Ostrabar's succession is now established, but still he is a haunted man."

Corfe stared at the old wizard but said nothing. His eyes glittered redly in the light of the brazier.

"He is convinced – and much persuading it took for him to admit it – that Aurungzeb died not at the hand of an assassin," Golophin hesitated, "but at the hand of his own Queen."

Corfe went very still.

"Not only that, but he then believes she turned the knife on herself. This Ramusian lady, the mother of his children, his wife of seventeen years. She must have harboured an enduring hatred in secret all that time. What finally made her act on it, no man can say. Shahr Baraz loved her like a daughter. It is he who put about the story of foreign assassins in the pay of Himerius, and the court and harem believed him. Why should they not? Not even Nasir suspects the truth, and it is perhaps best left that way. But I thought you would like to know."

The King had turned his face and it was in shadow. Golophin watched him closely, wondering.

"Sire, I cannot help thinking there was something between you and the Merduk Queen. Something..." Golophin tailed off.

The King did not move or speak, and the old mage rubbed his chin. "Forgive me, Corfe. I am like a woman fishing for gossip. It's a besetting fault of old age that when you start a hare you feel you must run it to ground. My mind has become over-subtle with the passing years. I see connections and conspiracies where there are none."

"She was my wife," Corfe said quietly.

"*What?*"

The King was staring into the red gledes at the heart of the brazier, unblinking. "Her name was Heria Car-Gwion, a silk-merchant's daughter of Aekir. And she was my wife. I thought her dead in the fall of the city. But she lived. She lived, Golophin, and was taken by Ostrabar's Sultan and made his Queen. Her own daughter I took to wife. Because it was the right thing to do for the kingdom. And now you tell me that when she died it was by her own hand. On the day I wed the girl who should by rights have been my own daughter. My child.

"She was my *wife*."

Golophin rose to his feet hurriedly, knocking over the camp stool. Corfe had turned to stare at him through bright, fire-filled eyes, and in that moment the wizard was mortally afraid. He had never seen such torment, such naked violence in another man's face.

Corfe laughed. "She is at peace now, dead at last. I wished her dead over the years, because I could not forget. I wished myself dead also. I might rest, I think, if I were laid in the tomb beside her. But even in death we will never be together again. Once I would have torn every Merduk city in the world brick from brick to get her back. But I am a king now, and must not think only of myself."

His smile was terrible, and in that moment he radiated more menace than any great mage or shifter that Golophin had ever known. The air seemed to crackle about him.

Corfe rose, and Golophin backed away. His familiar flew to his shoulder with a harsh, terrified screech. The King smiled again, but there was some humanity in his face now, and the terrible light had left his eyes.

"It's all right. I am not a madman or a monster. Sit down, Golophin. You look as though you had seen a ghost."

Golophin did as he was bidden, soothing his frightened familiar with automatic caresses. He could not get past the stunning realisation which was flooding his mind.

There was Dweomer in this man.

No, that was not correct. It was something else. An adamantine strength greater than the craft of mages, an *anti*-Dweomer perhaps. He could not fully explain it, even to himself, but he realised that here was a man whose will would never be tamed, whom no spell would ever subdue. And this also; Odelia's dying instincts had been correct. In victory, this man might well revel in an enormous bloodletting. His wife's fate had kindled an unassuageable pain in him which sought outlet in violence. And Golophin, in ignorance, had just stoked the fires of his torment higher.

THREE MORE DAYS the army laboured painfully and slowly up the Gelkarak glacier. They were struck by a series of brief, vicious snowstorms which cost them dearly in horses and mules, and they lost another artillery piece to a crevasse, as well as the two dozen men who were roped up to it. There was a crack like a gunshot, and it sank through the crust of snow and ice and dragged them screaming to their deaths like a series of fish snared on a many-hooked line. The troops were warier after that, and their speed decreased as they realised that it was to some extent a matter of luck whether a man put his foot in the wrong place or not. Pack-mules were unladen and harnessed up to the guns in the place of men, but this meant that the army marched more heavily burdened than ever. They were making at best two and a half leagues a day, and often much less, and Corfe estimated that no more than half their journey was behind them.

The air grew thin and piercing, and even the fittest of them gasped for breath as he marched. Mercifully, though, the weather cleared again, and though the intense cold was a torture in the star-bright nights, the days remained fine and sunlit. Many of the animals became lame as the surface crust of the snow gashed their legs, and the cavalry quickly learned to bind wrappings about the hocks of their mounts. But the cold was wearing down both animals and men. Soon there were many cases of frostbite and snow-blindness, mostly among the Torunnans, and after a meeting of the senior officers it was decided that those so afflicted would be left behind with a small guard to make their way back eastwards as soon as they were able. With them stayed scores of worn-out animals that might yet bear the weight of men, and a good store of rations.

But they were over the highest point of their passage now, and had left the great glacier-road behind. There was a narrow pass leading off to the west-south-west and this they took, following the ancient trail described in Corfe's text. It was a harder road than the glacier, being much littered and broken with boulders and shattered stones, but it was less treacherous, and the men's spirits rose.

And at last there came the evening, twenty-four days out of Torunn, when the army paused on the opening of a great glen between two buttresses of rock, and looked down to see the vast expanse of the Torian Plains darkling below under the sunset, and closer by, almost at their feet it seemed, there glittered red as blood the Sea of Tor.

The army was fewer by over a thousand men and several hundred mules and horses, but it had accomplished the crossing of the Cimbrics and there were now only thirty leagues of easy marching between it and Charibon.

NINETEEN

AURUNGABAR HAD SEEN a sultan and his queen buried, and a new sultan and his queen wed and crowned, all in the same month. The city was still unsettled and volatile, but the presence within its walls of a great host of soldiery entirely loyal to Sultan Nasir had a great soothing effect. The harem had been purged of all those who had fomented intrigue in the brief interregnum and Ostrabar's absolute ruler had proved his mettle, acting swiftly and without mercy. A youth he might be, but he had an able vizier now in the shape of Shahr Baraz the Younger, and it was rumoured that his new Ramusian wife was a great aid to him in the consolidation of his position. A sorceress of great power she was reputed to be, even mightier than her witch of a mother. Unruly Aurungabar had been swiftly cowed, therefore, and it was rumoured throughout the city that the Sultan already felt sure enough of his position to wish to set out immediately for the wars of the west.

He was closeted now with his new vizier in one of the smaller suites off the Royal bedchamber. He sat at a desk, leafing through a pile of papers, whilst Shahr Baraz stood, looking over his shoulder, pointing something out now and again, and the spring rain lashed at the windows and the firelight sprang up yellow in the hearth to one side. A set of Merduk half-armour stood on a wooden stand by the door, and a scabbarded tulwar had been set on the mantelpiece.

At last Nasir rubbed his eyes and straightened back from the desk with a mighty yawn. He was slim and dark, with olive skin and grey eyes, and he was dressed in a robe of black silk which shimmered in the firelight.

"All this can wait, Baraz. It's frivolous stuff, this granting of offices and remission of taxes."

"It is not, Nasir," the older man said forcefully. "Through such little boons you buy men's loyalty."

"If it must be bought it is not worth having."

Shahr Baraz gave a twisted smile. "That sounds like your mother speaking."

Nasir bowed his head, and his clear eyes darkened. "Yes. I never thought I would get it this way, Baraz. Not this way."

The vizier laid a hand on his shoulder. "I know, my Sultan. But it rests on your shoulders now. You will grow into it in time. And you have made a fair beginning."

Nasir's face lit up again, and he turned round. "Only fair?" They both laughed.

The door was knocked, and without further ceremony the Queen entered, also clad in midnight silk. Her golden hair was down and her marmoset clung to her shoulder chittering gently, its eyes bright as jewels.

"Nasir, are you ever coming to bed? It's hours past the middle of the –" She saw Shahr Baraz and folded her arms.

Nasir rose and went to her. The vizier watched them as they looked upon each other, half shy still, but an eagerness in their eyes. That, at least, had turned out well, he thought. One must be thankful for small mercies. And those not so small.

"I'm being drowned in dusty details," Nasir told his wife, "when all I want is to get on the road with the army."

"Are you sure that is all you want, my lord?" They grinned at one another like mischievous children, and indeed they were neither of them yet eighteen years of age.

"The army marches in the morning, my Queen," Shahr Baraz said, his deep old voice bringing them up short.

"I knew that," Mirren said with the laughter gone from her face. "Golophin spoke to me. He has been in and out of here for days. "If Nasir is to be up before the dawn he must have some rest at least."

"I quite agree," Shahr Baraz said. "Now the Sultan and I have some last business to attend to, lady, and the night is passing."

Mirren's eyes narrowed, and the marmoset hissed at Shahr Baraz. The rebellion in her face faded, however, seeing the vizier's implacable eyes. She kissed Nasir on the mouth and left. When the Sultan turned around with a sigh he found the old man shaking his head and smiling.

"You make a handsome pair, the dark and the gold. Your children will be fair indeed, Nasir. You have found yourself a fine queen, but she is as strong-willed and stubborn as an army mule." When Nasir's mouth opened in outrage Shahr Baraz laughed, and bowed. "So says Golophin. For he has spoken to me also, the old meddler. She is her father's daughter in more ways than one. And in truth she reminds me somewhat of –" and then he stopped, though they both knew what he had been about to say.

THE MERDUK ARMY marched out before sunrise, when the streets were as quiet as they ever became in the capital. They formed up in *Hor-el Kadhar* where once the statue of Myrnius Kuln had frowned, and then led off in long files by prearranged streets to the west gate. It was a cold, clear night with the sun not yet begun to glimmer over the Jafrar in the east, and King Corfe of Torunna, who had once fled through this very gate as Aekir burned about him, was not yet in the high foothills of the Cimbrics. Nasir was leading fifteen thousand heavily armoured cavalry westwards to the aid of the kingdom which had once been his people's bitterest foe. But he was young, and dwelt seldom on such ironies. Besides, half of his own blood belonged to that people. As did his new wife, whom he already knew he loved.

THAT SAME DAWN found two ships coursing swift as cantering horses across the eastern Levangore. Their masts were rigid with almost every sail they possessed and their decks were black with men. All through the previous evening and the night they had been hurtling north-north-east with the freshening wind on their larboard quarters, and now to port loomed the purple shapes of the southern Cimbric Mountains as they marched down to the sea east of the Candelan River. Torunna, last free kingdom of the west, rising up in the dawn light, with the snow on the summits of the mountains catching the sun first, so that they tinted scarlet and pink and seemed to be disembodied shapes floating over the darker hills below.

Murad stared at that sunrise briefly and then focused once more on the ship ahead. The xebec had tried to lose them in the night, but the moonlight had been too bright and the eyes of the pursuers too keen. She was little more than four cables ahead now, almost within gunshot, and the *Revenant* was closing the gap.

The thing which had once been the Lord of Galiapeno glanced aft to see a man in the black of an Inceptine habit standing before the mainmast, solid and unyielding as a stone gargoyle despite the pitch and roll of the barquentine. From him there seemed to hum a silent vibration which could be felt underfoot in the wood of the decks. A soundless thrumming which, Murad knew, was responsible for the present speed, or part of it.

For Richard Hawkwood was too canny a sailor to be caught by conventional seamanship. He had survived the storm sent to sink him and they had almost lost him in the great sea-wastes of the Levangore, until one of Murad's homonculi had glimpsed him by chance as it flew high and far beyond its master in search of news. There would be no second storm – such tactics were obviously inadequate. No, to Murad's great joy Aruan had given him leave to capture the *Seahare* intact if he chose, and dispose of her crew in any way he wished – provided Hebrion's queen met her end in the process. What a pleasure it would be to meet up with his old shipmate and comrade again, and to preside over his unhurried death.

Murad knew much of death. On the night of the fleet's destruction he had become lost in the fog on his way back from the flagship, and thus had watched from his longboat as that great armada was reduced to matchwood all about him. He remembered prising the fingers of desperate drowning survivors from the gunwales of his little craft less they swamp it in their panic. He had bade his men row them out, far out into the fog, and there they had leant on their oars and watched the ships burning through the mist, listening to the screams. They had escaped that great slaughter, or so he had thought.

Then the mage had come in a furious storm of black

flame which incinerated Murad's companions in a flashing second and seemed like to do the same to himself. But a curious thing had happened.

I know you, a voice had said. Murad had lain in the smoking bottom of the longboat with the swells washing around his charred body and the thing had hovered over him like a great bat. He felt he were being turned this way and that for inspection, though he had not been touched.

Kill him, another voice said, a familiar voice. But the first laughed.

I think not. He may well prove useful.

Kill him!

No. Put aside your past hates and prejudices. You and he are more similar than you think. He is mine.

And thus had Murad of Galiapeno been taken into the service of the Second Empire.

And he had been willing to serve. All his life he had hated mages and witches and the workings of the Dweomer, but more than that, Murad had chafed at his subordination to men he deemed less able than himself, even Hebrion's last King. Now he took orders from one he acknowledged to be his superior, and there was a strange comfort in it. He was at last glad to merely do as he was told, and if the orders he received chimed with his own inclinations, so much the better. As for the Dweomer, well, he had become reconciled to it, for was it not now a part of him?

And what was more, he would be ruler of Hebrion once this woman he pursued was dead. It had been promised, and Aruan always kept his promises.

"RUN OUT THE bow-chasers," he said, and his crew jumped to do his bidding. A few of them were ordinary mercenaries, sailors of many navies, but most were tall, gleaming black men of the Zantu. They had cast aside their horn carapaces and now teams of them hauled, sweating, on the cables which trundled out the forward-aimed guns of the ship until they came to bear on the stern of their prey.

"Usunei!"

"Yes, lord."

"Let us see if we cannot scratch his paintwork. Fire when ready."

The grunting gun-crews levered the two culverins round with handspikes while the gun-captains sighted along the bronze barrels with smoking slow-match grasped in their fists. At last they were content and held up their free hands. As the bow of the ship rose, they whipped the match across the touch-holes, springing aside with the grace of panthers as the culverins went off as one and leapt inboard, squealing on their trucks. A cloud of smoke went up and was quickly winnowed into nothing by the wind and the speed of the ship's passage. Watching intently, Murad saw two splashes just short of the *Seahare's* stern.

"Good practice! More elevation there, and we shall have her."

The next shots could be followed by those with quick eyes; two dark blurs which punched holes in the chase's mizzen-course and sent splinters flying from something in her waist. Murad laughed and clapped his hands, and the guncrew's faces split in wide, fanged grins.

A minute later the chase's wounded mizzen-course split from top to bottom and flapped madly from the yard. Spray struck Murad in the mouth and he licked the salt-tang of it away, his eyes shining. The *Seahare* lost speed. The next pair of shots went home in the mizzen-rigging and he saw a small, wriggling figure blown off the yard and flung into the sea.

"More speed!" Murad screamed. "You there, give us another two knots and we'll have them before breakfast!"

The hooded Inceptine to whom he spoke did not answer, but he seemed to hunch over within his robe, and the tone of the vibration filling the ship rose by an octave. The *Revenant* dipped deeply and water came flooding in the chaser gunports, green and cold. The masts creaked and complained and the backstays were wringing taut, but nothing gave away. The weather-worker was not moving the ship, but the water within which it travelled, and spreading out all around the ship's hull was a violent turbulence of broken, foaming spray at odds with the natural swell of the sea about them. The ship trembled and shook as though it were being rattled in the grip of some undersea giant, and several of the crew were knocked off their feet, but Murad stood on the wave-swept forecastle gripping one of the foremast shrouds, and the light in his eyes grew to a yellow fire. They drew nearer to their prey. Now only a cable and a half – three hundred yards – separated the tip of the barquentine's bowsprit and the *Seahare*'s taffrail.. In half a glass they would be abreast. Murad raised his voice. "All hands, prepare for boarding!" and a homonculus wheeled out of the rigging and settled on his shoulder. About him on the forecastle clustered a great mob of the Zantu, now clad again in their black horn armour and clicking their pincers impatiently. The armour began as a natural construct of horn and leather, but when a man donned it, he became somehow part of it, and it augmented his strength as well as protecting his flesh. The Zantu were fearsome warriors in their own right, but when wearing their black harness they were well-nigh invincible.

"Remember!" Murad yelled, "the captain is to be taken alive, and the woman's body I must see with my own eyes. The rest are yours."

The Zantu had fasted for days in anticipation of this hour, and from the depths of their shining masks their eyes glittered with hunger and anticipation.

Murad could actually recognise Hawkwood now. He stood at the stern of his ship with an oddly familiar dark-haired boy beside him, and shouted orders that were lost in the wind and the foaming tumult of the waves. The *Seahare* suddenly yawed hard a-port so that she revealed her full broadside, such as it was. Six gun-ports gaping, and then the side of the ship disappeared in a bank of smoke, and a heartbeat later came the roar of the reports. Murad felt the wind of one shot pass his head, and it staggered him. The rest smashed down the full length of the *Revenant*, leaving chaos in their wake. Blocks and fragments of rigging were hurled through the air and the close-packed boarding party was blasted to pieces, so that the scuppers ran with blood and fragments of men were blown as far aft as the quarterdeck.

The humming tremble of the ship's hull ceased, and looking aft Murad saw that one cannonball had cut his weatherworking Inceptine in two. The *Revenant* lost speed and the foaming water about her began to settle into a more rational wake.

"Get me back my speed!" he shrieked at the ship's master, a renegade Gabrionese who stood white-faced by the wheel. "Shoot them! Catch them. Sink them, for the love of God!"

The master put the wheel about and the barquentine yawed in her turn, exposing her much heavier metal. "Fire!" he shouted, and the gun-crews collected their wits and sent off a ragged broadside.

But the Zantu were not the well-trained sailors of Hawkwood's crew. Murad saw three of the balls strike home amidships, and a hail of wood splinters went flying as the *Seahare's* larboard rail was demolished, but most went high, slicing cables in the rigging but doing little serious damage.

Both ships had lost speed now, and both were turning back to starboard, into the wind. An arquebus ball zipped past Murad's ear and he ducked instinctively. Hawkwood had several sailors with small-arms firing from his stern. There were a series of splashes in the xebec's wake; they were throwing their dead overboard. Murad beat his fist on the forecastle rail in his frustration and his homunculus jumped up and down on his shoulder, screeching.

"More sail!" he shouted to the master. "If they escape then your life is forfeit, Master Mariner."

The crew raced up the shrouds and began piling on every scrap of canvas the barquentine possessed. Staysails and jibs were flashed out and the *Revenant* began to accelerate through the water at something approaching her previous rate. The xebec still had not sent up a new mizzen-course, and they were gaining again. Murad ignored the arquebus balls that whined and snicked about him, and helped the depleted chaser-crews run out their guns once more. They fired on the rise and this time the shots smashed square into the *Seahare's* stern, sending timbers flying through the air and tossing one of the arquebusiers into the sea. Murad laughed again, and called for more men to come forward.

Another party of Zantu joined him by the chasers. Aboard the *Seahare* a party of men were busy on the quarterdeck and the odd ball came hissing overhead from their arquebusiers.

Barely fifty yards separated the two ships now. Murad could see Hawkwood clearly; he was manning the ship's wheel himself, watching the barquentine as it came up hand over fist. That dark boy was helping him, and to one side of them was Isolla herself. She was aiming an arquebus. Murad, startled, saw the smoke spurt from its muzzle, and something thumped the side of his head. He went down and the homunculus squawked harshly. Labouring back to his feet he realised he was deaf on one side, and when he put up a hand it came away wet. Isolla had shot off half his ear.

Furious, he opened his mouth, but at that moment the *Seahare* made a sharp turn to port, going directly before the wind. As she turned her guns went off in measured sequence, and the *Revenant* was raked again, the cannonballs passing the full length of the ship.

Her sails shivered, then banged taut, and she fell away before the wind. Looking aft, Murad saw that the ship's wheel had been splintered into pieces and the master lay dead beside it along with the helmsman. The decks were slimy and slick with blood and everywhere fragments of jagged wood and scraps of flesh lay piled amid sliced cables and shattered blocks. Murad dashed aft to the companionway and shouted at the Zantu who staggered there, dazed and bewildered. "Get below to the tiller and steer her from there! You others, get back to your guns and commence firing!"

He climbed to the quarterdeck, slipping in blood and cursing, his hand held to the ragged meat where his ear had been. The two vessels were sailing directly before the wind now, on parallel courses less than a cable's length apart. They were pointed at the long inlet which housed the Torunnan port of Rone; Hawkwood was making a run for shore.

Both ships began firing again, broadside to broadside now. The *Revenant* had heavier guns and more of them, but the *Seahare's* were better served, and more accurate. She was slower in the water now, though, and her pumps were sending thick jets of water out to port – Murad must have holed her below the waterline.

The lean nobleman's spirits rose. His crew had taken severe casualties, but there were still enough of them to board the enemy. He shouted down the hatch to the tiller-deck below. "Hard a-starboard!"

The *Revenant* made the turn sluggishly, but managed two points into the wind until her beakhead pointed square at the xebec's larboard forechains. The gap closed frighteningly quickly, and before Murad could even shout a warning the ships had collided with a massive jolt that knocked everyone aboard them both from their feet. The *Revenant's* bowsprit splintered with a sickening crash and tore loose to rake down the xebec's side, only to be halted again by the mainchains. There it stuck in a fearsome snarl of broken wood and cordage and iron frapping, and the two ships continued before the wind hopelessly entangled, both out of command.

Murad recovered his wits and his feet quickly, and drew his rapier. "Boarders away!" he shrieked, and ran down the length of his ship to where the wreckage of the bow joined her to the enemy xebec. Two dozen unarmoured Zantu gunners followed him clutching boarding-axes and cutlasses and roaring like beasts. They crossed the perilous bridge of wrecked spars with the sea foaming below them and charged down onto the waist of the xebec. The *Seahare* was low in the water now; they had indeed breached her hull with their gunfire, and she was sinking under them.

Three or four gunshots met the invaders, and one of Murad's followers was blown off the side to plunge into the sea. Then Hawkwood was there – *Hawkwood, at last* – with a cutlass in one hand and a pistol in the other, and the two were glaring naked hate at one another while all about them their ship's companies engaged in a savage hand-to-hand fight in the waist and along the gangways of the *Seahare*.

Hawkwood's pistol misfired, a flash in the pan and no more. Murad laughed and closed with him, darting in the flicker of the rapier whilst his homunculus went for the mariner's eyes.

The pair were in the midst of a murderous mob of fighting men, but they might have been alone in the world for all the notice they took. Hawkwood drew his dirk and stabbed at the flapping homunculus even while clashing Murad's blade aside. The little creature screamed and fastened itself on the back of his neck, biting, reaching round for his eyes with its needle-claws, flapping its wings. Murad lunged forward, still laughing, and the tip of the rapier pierced the mariner's thigh a full three inches. He twisted the blade as he withdrew and Hawkwood fell to one knee. The homunculus had clawed out one of his eyes but he dropped the dirk and seized the little beast in his fist. He clenched his fingers about it and popped its tiny ribs, then threw it, dying, at Murad.

Murad batted it aside. It was not a familiar, merely a messenger, and thus no loss to him. He sprang forward again, a great joy rising in him, and drew back his sword for the kill.

But he was buffeted by the melee which raged about them, and thrown off-balance. Cursing now, he reached forward again but something struck him in the side, a blunt blow that knocked the breath out of him. He hissed in pain. A woman stood over Hawkwood – *it was Isolla*. Her face was scarred by fire but he knew her at once, though she wore a seaman's jacket over her skirts. Her face was white and resolute, fearless. She fired the arquebus at point-blank range.

And missed. In the push and shove of the scrum the barrel was knocked aside. The muzzle-blast scorched Murad's hair and half-blinded him. He grabbed the barrel with his free hand and stabbed at her with his rapier. His blade caught her below the collar-bone and sank deep, deep through her heart. She crumpled and slid off the bloody steel to lie on top of Hawkwood. Murad grinned and raised the rapier to finish the job.

But there was a sudden, savage blow to the side of his neck. It numbed his left arm and made him stumble in astonishment and pain. His lemon-yellow eyes flickered as the Dweomer which bound his burned limbs together faltered. He turned, and the rapier slipped from his nerveless fingers.

Bleyn stood there, his own stepson. And in his hand Hawkwood's dirk, bloody to the hilt. The boy's face was livid and glaring, though his cheeks were running with tears. Murad reached out his good hand towards him, utterly baffled. "*What*?" he began.

But Bleyn darted forward and punched the dirk into his chest. It stuck there, grating through his breastbone, and Murad sank to his knees.

"How?"

Hawkwood was staring at him, his remaining eye glittering, Isolla's body cradled in his arms. The inhuman light in Murad's own eyes winked out, and for a few seconds his old dark gaze met Hawkwood's maimed stare in startled disbelief. "I didn't know –"

Hawkwood simply gazed on him, without hatred or anger, and watched the life flit from Murad's face. The nobleman's chin sank on his breast and he toppled over onto the bloody deck, mere burnt carrion. Around him his followers saw their leader's death and faltered, and were beaten back into the sea.

THEY ABANDONED THE *Seahare* and tossed flaming torches up onto the decks of the *Revenant* as they took to the boats. In the gathering dusk the waves were full of dark faces and others were diving off the sides of the barquentine and swimming out to them. They shot them in the water or hacked their hands from the sides of the boats as they tried to climb on board. Finally they drew clear, their wake lit by the blazing ship behind them, and landed the ship's boats on the shelving shore east of Rone, and stood a while with the surf beating about their knees and watched the *Revenant* burning against the evening sky. At last the fire reached the powder-room, and the barquentine vanished in a bright explosion that echoed and re-echoed in a sharp, brief thunder about the hills of the inlet. For a long while afterwards the wreckage tumbled and splashed down in the quiet waters of the bay, and the evening darkened into night upon the waters.

RICHARD HAWKWOOD HAD fulfilled his mission, and had brought Hebrion's Queen to Torunna; and they buried her on a hilltop overlooking the sea and set a cairn of stones upon her grave.

TWENTY

THE COURIERS ARRIVED in Torunn in the red light of dawn, their mounts near foundering, streaked with foam and slathered with mud. The men slid from their saddles in the courtyard of the palace and then half-staggered, half ran to the great doors. The gate-guards there took their despatches and, after a quick, urgent word, ran pelting to the Bladehall.

Formio, Regent of Torunna, stood before the blazing hearth therein and behind him on the massive mantle there was a lighter space where once the Answerer had hung. But it was gone to war in the hands of the king, and who knew if it would ever hang there again? The Fimbrian was rubbing his hands together absently at the fire and when the guards burst in with the despatch cases he did not seem much surprised. He looked at the seals, nodded grimly, and spoke to the panting soldiers who had brought them.

"Rouse out his Majesty the Sultan and bid him come here – humbly, mind. And then relay to Colonel Gribben my compliments, and he is to stand-to the entire garrison at once, and then join me here also."

As the men left him alone again, Formio snapped open the despatch-cases and read their uncurled contents, frowning.

Rone, 20th Forialon
The Himerians have struck here in the south. We knew they might, but they have arrived in much greater strength than we had expected and have incorporated the host of Candelan into their ranks. My command was worsted in a battle five miles east of the Candelan River and we have fallen back on Rone, where Admiral Berza's ships are based. Most of his vessels are in dock, being refitted, and he has agreed to turn over his marines to my command. I

shall hold as long as I can, but I need reinforcements. The Perigrainians alone muster some twenty-five thousands. The enemy are infantry in the main, but they have also some of these accursed Hounds in their ranks, and the fear of them is out of all proportion to their numbers.

I believe that this is no mere raid, but a full-scale invasion. The enemy intends to overrun the entire kingdom from the south while our forces are engaged far to the north. I need men, quickly.

Yours in haste,
Steynar Melf,
Officer Commanding, Army South

Formio's lips moved in silent oaths as he read the despatch. There came attached a muster and casualty list and a rough map of operations. Melf was a professional if nothing else, but he was no military phoenix. And even with Berza's marines he had less than five thousand men left to withstand this great Himerian army.

Formio looked as the Merduk Sultan strode down the hall, flanked by two bodyguards. With him came Colonel Gribben, second in command of the garrison of Torunn, and a pair of aides. All of them had that bleared, dull look of men who have been roused out of sleep.

"My lord Regent," Nasir said, "I hope that this is –"

"How soon can you put your men back on the road, Sultan?" Formio asked harshly.

Nasir's mouth snapped shut. His eyes opened wide. "What has happened?"

"How soon?"

The young man blinked. "Not today. We have just made a long march. The horses need more rest. Tomorrow morning, I suppose." Nasir rubbed his unlined forehead, his eyes darting to left and right under his hand.

"Good. Gribben, I want you to pick out ten thousand of the best men of the garrison. They must be fit also, capable of a long forced-march."

"Sir!" Gribben saluted, though his face was a picture of alarm and perplexity.

"The combined force will move out at dawn tomorrow,

and it will travel light. No mules or waggons. The men will carry their rations on their backs. No artillery, either."

"Where are we going?" the Sultan asked, sounding for a moment very like the boy he had so lately been.

"South. The Himerians have invaded there and defeated our forces. They have stolen a march on us, it seems."

"Who will command, sir?" Gribben asked.

Formio hesitated. He looked at Nasir and gauged his words carefully.

"Majesty, you have not yet commanded an army in war, and this is not the time to learn. I – I beg you to let a more experienced man lead the combined army." And here Formio nodded at Gribben, who had fought in all the Torunnan army's battles since Berrona, seventeen years before, and had been lately promoted by Corfe himself.

Nasir flushed. "That is out of the question. I cannot turn over the cream of Ostrabar's armies for you to do with as you will, not while I am here with them. I shall command them, no other."

Formio watched the young man steadily. "Sultan, this is not a game, or a manoeuvre on the practice fields. The army that goes south cannot afford to lose. I do not doubt your valour –"

"I will not stand aside for a mere colonel. I could not do so, and still look my men in the face. But do not mistake me my lord Regent. I am not some foolish boy dreaming of glory. If anyone takes overall command, it must be you, the Regent of Torunna, the great Formio himself. You, they will obey." Nasir smiled. "As will I, Sultan or no."

Formio was taken aback, but made his decision at once. "Very well, I shall command. Gribben, you will remain here in the capital. Majesty, I salute your forbearance. We have much to do, gentlemen, and only one day to do it in. By this time tomorrow we must be on the road south."

IN THE NIGHT, the wind dropped and the sky was entirely free of cloud. The little group of castaways huddled around their campfire in a dark, silent ring, but one of them, a broad-shouldered young man with sea-grey eyes, stood apart on a small rise some distance away and peered towards the horizon with the waning moon carving shadows out of his face.

"Another city burns," Bleyn said wearily. "Which one might that be?"

Hawkwood stared south and west with his good eye, shivering. "That would be Rone, the southernmost city of Torunna. As well we never reached it."

"The world is gone mad," Jemilla said. "All the old seers were right. We are at the end of days."

Hawkwood cocked his head towards her. Bleyn's mother was sat upon a folded blanket, hugging her knees to her breasts, and her hair hung about her face in a rat-tailed hood. She had lost weight during the voyage, for seasickness had prostrated her the greater part of it, and there were lines running from the corners of her mouth and nose that had not been so noticeable before. Age had claimed Jemilla at last, and she no longer held any allure for Richard Hawkwood.

She seemed to know this, and was almost diffident in his company. She had gathered wildflowers to set atop Isolla's cairn, something the old Jemilla would have scorned, and when she spoke her voice held none its old ringing bite. But Hawkwood sensed something about her, some secret knowledge which was gnawing at her soul. When he had been supported by Bleyn in their limping stumble inland he had found her watching the pair of them with an odd expression on her face. It held almost a note of regret.

He dropped his head again and continued to work on the rude crutch he was fashioning from a broken oar, then paused. His dirk still had some of Murad's blood on it. He wiped the cold-running perspiration from his face.

Jemilla was right perhaps. The world had indeed run mad, or else those unseen powers which fashioned its courses were possessed of a bitter humour. Well, this particular race was almost run.

For a moment the light of the fire was a broken dazzle in Hawkwood's remaining eye. He had been loved by a queen, only to lose her almost as soon as he found her. And Murad was dead at last. Oddly, he could take no joy in the nobleman's end. There had been something in his dying eyes which inspired not triumph, but pity. A baffled surprise perhaps. Hawkwood had seen that look in the faces of many dying men. No doubt he would one day wear it himself.

"I know nothing of this part of the world," Bleyn said. Whither shall we go now?"

"North," Hawkwood told him, fighting himself upright and trying out the crutch for size. His breath came in raw, ragged gasps. "We are in the country of friends; for now, at any rate. We must stay ahead of the Himerians and get to Torunn."

"And what then?"

Hawkwood hobbled unsteadily over to him. "Then it'll be time to get drunk." He clapped the boy on the shoulder, unbalancing himself, and Bleyn helped him keep his feet.

"We'll need horses and a cart, then. You won't get far on that."

Jemilla watched them as they stood together beyond the firelight, so alike, and yet so different. Father and son. She wiped her eyes angrily, covertly. That knowledge would remain sealed in her heart until the day she died.

"Bleyn is now the rightful king of Hebrion," she said aloud, and the sailors about the fire looked at her. "He is the last of the Hibrusid Royal house, whether born on the wrong side of the blanket or no. You all now owe him your allegiance, and must aid him in any way you can."

"Mother –" Bleyn began.

"Do not forget that, any of you. When we get to Torunn his heritage will be made public. The wizard Golophin already knows of it. That is why we were told to take ship with you."

"So the rumours were true," Arhuz said. "He is Abeleyn's son."

"The rumours were true. He is all that is left of the Hebrian nobility."

Hawkwood nudged Bleyn, who stood wordless and uncertain. "I beg leave for leaning on the Royal shoulder, Majesty. Do you think you could stir the Royal legs and go hunt us up some more firewood?" And both Bleyn and the mariners about the fire laughed, though Jemilla's thin face darkened. The boy left Hawkwood and went out into the moonlit darkness on his errand, while the mariner stumped back to the fire.

"Jemilla," he said sharply, and she glared at him, ready for argument. But Hawkwood only smiled gently at her, his eyes fever-bright.

"He'll make a good king."

THE NEXT MORNING the early sunlight rose over the world to reveal bars of smoke rising up from the south-western horizon. The nearest was scarcely ten miles away. The castaways climbed out of their blankets, shivering, and stamped their feet, staring at the besmirched sky. There was little talk, and less to eat, and so they started off at once, hoping to come across some friendly village or farm that would speed them in their journey.

Villages and farms they found in plenty, but they were all deserted. The inhabitants of the surrounding countryside had seen the smoke on the air also, and had decided not to await its coming. Bleyn and Arhuz ranged far ahead of the rest of them and procured food in plenty, and extra blankets for the chill nights, but all manner of steed and vehicle had left with their fleeing owners, and so they must needs limp along on foot, their faces always set towards the north, and Hawkwood the slowest of them all, the dressing on his eye weeping a thin continual stream of yellow fluid.

Four days they proceeded in this manner, sleeping in empty farmhouses at night and starting their daily marches before dawn. On the fifth day, however, they finally caught up with the streams of other refugees heading north and joined a straggling column of the dispossessed that choked the road for as far as the eye could see. The crutch-wielding Hawkwood was found space on the back of a laden waggon, and Jemilla joined him, for the mariner's fever had risen inexorably over the past few days, and she kept him well wrapped and wiped the sweat and the pus from his burning face.

The days were becoming warmer as late spring edged into an early summer, and the crowds of people that choked the roads sent up a lofty cloud of dust that hung in the air to match the palls of smoke behind them. Talking to the fleeing Torunnans, Bleyn learned that Rone had fallen after a bitter assault, and its defenders had been massacred to a man. The ships docked in the harbour had been burned and the land about laid waste. The Torunnan commander, Melf, and Admiral Berza of the fleet were both dead, but their stand had bought time for the general population to get away from the jubilant Perigrainians and Candelarians persuing them. But ordered companies of disciplined men will always make better time than mobs of panicked civilians, and the enemy were gaining. What would happen when the Himerian forces caught up with the refugees no one would speculate upon, though many of them had lived through the Merduk wars and had seen it all before. *Where is the King?* they asked. *Where is the army? Can they all be up in Gaderion or have they given any thought to the south at all?* And they trudged along the dusty roads in their tens of thousands, holding their children in their arms, and hauling hand-carts piled high with their possessions, or urging along slow-moving ox-waggons with a frantic cracking of whips.

"HELP ME GET him off the waggon," Jemilla told her son, and together the two of them lifted the delirious Hawkwood from the bed of the overburdened vehicle as it trundled forward relentlessly in the heat and the dust. The mariner jerked and kicked in their arms and mumbled incoherently. The heat of his body could be felt even through the sodden blanket in which he was wrapped.

The other sailors had long deserted them, even Arhuz, becoming lost in the trudging crowds and teeming roadsides. So it was with some difficulty that Jemilla and Bleyn carried their mumbling burden off the road and through the ranks of refugees, until they were clear of the exodus and could lay the mariner down on a grassy bank not far from the eaves of a green-tipped beech wood. Jemilla laid her palm on his hot brow and thought she could almost feel the poison boiling within his skull.

"His wound has gone bad," she said. "I don't know what we can do." She took the mariner's hand and his brown fingers clenched about her slender pale ones, crushing the blood out of them. But she said no word.

Bleyn knuckled his eyes, looking very young and lost. "Will he die, mother?"

"Yes. Yes, he will. We will stay with him." And then Jemilla shocked her son by bowing her head and weeping silently, the tears coursing down her pale, proud face. He had never in his short life seen his mother cry. And she clung to this man as though he were dear to her, although during the voyage she had treated him haughtily, as a noblewoman would any commoner.

"Who was he?" Bleyn asked her, amazed.

She dried her eyes quickly. "He was the greatest mariner of the age. He made a voyage which has passed already into legend, though small reward he received for it, for he was of low blood. He was a good man, and I – I loved him once. I think perhaps he loved me, back in the years when the world was a sane place." The tears came again, though her face remained unchanged. More than anything she wanted to tell Bleyn who this man really was, but she could not. He must never know, not if he were to make his claim to Hebrion with any conviction.

Even to herself, Jemilla's reasoning seemed hollow. The Five Kingdoms were gone, their last hope, Torunna, falling to pieces in front of her eyes. There would soon be no room in the world for herself and her son and the old order of things. But she had come too far to relinquish hope now. She remained silent.

The day passed around them unnoticed as they sat on the grass, a trio of lost people to one side of a great concourse of the lost and the fearful and the fleeing.

HE REMEMBERED THE *light of the sun on the warm waters of the Levangore, the green light through the waves, the white beaches of the Malacars. He saw again the empty horizon of the west, and out of it the violent emerald jewel of the Western Continent arising, a whole new world. He smelled salt, and felt the deck tilt under his feet, and smiled because he was where he should be; on his ship, with a fair wind on the quarter and the whole wide world awaiting him.*

Hawkwood's eye opened, and he gripped Jemilla's hand until the bones creaked under his strong fingers.

"Clew up, clew up, there," he whispered in a cracked, dry voice. "Billerand, set courses and topsails. Steer due west with the wind on the quarter."

Then he sighed, and the pressure of his fingers relaxed. The light faded from his eye.

Richard Hawkwood's long voyaging was over.

TWENTY-ONE

ARUAN WOKE OUT of sleep with the knowledge that something had changed in the black hours of the night, some balance had shifted. He was a master of Soothsaying, as he was of every other Discipline, but this feeling had nothing to do with the Dweomer. It was more akin to an old man's aches before a storm.

He rose and called for his valet and was quickly washed and robed in the austere splendour of the Pontifical apartments, for he resided there now, though Himerius and not he was Pontiff in the eyes of the world. He looked out of the high window upon the cloisters of Charibon below and saw that the dawn had not yet come and the last hours of the night still hung heavy above the horns of the cathedral and the library of St. Garaso.

He clenched and unclenched one blue-veined fist and stared at it darkly. He had over-tired himself in his travels, bending the wills and raising the hearts of men up and down the length of the continent. But now Rone had fallen and Southern Torunna was being invaded with little resistance, while at Gaderion, Bardolin had laid the curtain wall in ruins and the Torunnans there were besieged within their three great fortresses, relief column and all. Hebrion and Astarac and Almark and Perigraine were conquered, their peoples his to command, their nobility extinguished. Only Fimbria now stood alone and aloof from the convulsions of the world, for the Electorates had sent no word since the departure of their embassy months before. Well, they would be dealt with in time.

But still he was afflicted by a restless uneasiness. He felt that he had overlooked some piece of his opponent's upon the gaming board of war, and it troubled him.

As DAWN FINALLY broke open the sky in bands of scarlet behind the white peaks of the Cimbrics, King Corfe Cear-Inaf brought his army down from the foothills to the shores of the Sea of Tor, and where the land levelled out into the first wolds of the Torian Plains, he set his men into line of battle, a scant four miles from the outskirts of Charibon itself. It was the eleventh day of Enderialon in the Year of the Saint 567, and it was thirty-one days since he had set out from Torunn.

The army he led was a good deal smaller than that which had taken ship on the Torrin River those weeks before. Many had died in the unforgiving mountains, and over two thousand men, Fimbrians and Torunnans and tribesmen, had been detached while still high up in the foothills, their mission to destroy the Himerian transports docked at the eastern shore of the Sea of Tor, and thus cut the supply-lines of the army which was entrenched in the Thurian Line and before Gaderion.

So it was with less than twenty-two thousand troops that Corfe descended from the high places to give battle to the forces of the Second Empire before the very gates of their capital. It was still dark as he set his men into line, and despite their depleted numbers their ranks stretched for over two and a half miles.

He rested his right flank on the shore of the Sea itself, and there three thousand Torunnan arquebusiers were placed in four ranks, each half a mile long. To their left was the main body of the Orphans, eight thousand Fimbrian pikemen under Marshal Kyne, with a thousand more arquebusiers mingled in their files. The pike phalanx bristled nine ranks deep and had a frontage of a thousand yards. Next to them stood another three thousand arquebusiers, and out on the far left was the main body of the Cathedraller cavalry, four thousand heavy horsemen in four ranks, armed with lance and sabre and matchlock pistols, their lacquered armour gleaming red as blood in the morning light. Comillan had been newly made their commander, their previous leader having died in the snows. Hidden in their midst were three batteries of horse-artillery and their teams, awaiting the signal to unlimber and begin firing.

Behind this first wave, and closer to the left of the line than its centre, rode the Torunnan King himself at the head of his five-hundred strong bodyguard. He kept back with him a mixed formation of some two thousand Fimbrians and Torunnans to act as a general reserve, and also to bolster the open flank. For off on that flank, on the higher ground leading down to Charibon, the Citadel of the Knights squatted, a grey low-built fortress around which were the tents and baggage of a small army. As the Torunnans advanced towards Charibon proper, they would have this fortress and encampment in their left rear. Not only that, but the fast-riding Cathedraller scouts who had been scouring the land about the army for days had only yesterday reported seeing a large body of infantry bivouacked some fifteen miles to the west of Charibon, square upon the Narian Road. They had not drawn close enough to the force to ascertain its nationality, but there was little doubt that it consisted of more levies on their way to swell the ranks of the Empire. And so Corfe had hurried his men through the night, to attack Charibon before this fresh army came up.

He had no illusions about the slimness of the thread from which his men's survival hung, and he knew that even if they were victorious before the monastery-city, there was little hope of their ever returning to Torunna. But this was the head of the snake here before him, and if it were destroyed, the west might yet rise again and throw off the yoke. That chance was worth the sacrifice of this army. And as for his own life, he knew that it had been twisted beyond hope of happiness, and he would be content to lay it down here.

Ahead of the Torunnans and Fimbrians as they formed up on the plain, more tent encampments sprawled amid a web of gravel roads, and beyond them the tricorne tower of the cathedral of the Saint loomed tall and stark, matched in height by the library of Saint Garaso and the Pontiff's palace close by, all connected by the long cloisters. That was the heart of Charibon, and of the Second Empire itself. Those buildings must all be laid in ruin and their inhabitants destroyed if the head of this snake were to be cut off.

Albrec had passionately disagreed when Corfe had told him of his intentions back in Torunn, but Albrec was not a soldier, and he was not here, staring at the vast factory of war that Charibon had become. Corfe would rather a thousand books burn than he needlessly lose a single one of his men, and he would see the history of ages go up in smoke rather than let one scion of Aruan's evil brood escape. This he had impressed upon his officers and his men in a council of war held up in the hills, although Golophin, who had attended, had said nothing.

"They have no pickets out," Ensign – Haptman rather – Baraz said, incredulously. "Sir, I believe they're all asleep."

"Let us hope so, Haptman." Corfe looked up and down at the line which stretched out of sight in the raw dawn light. Then he breathed in deep. "Alarin, signal the *Advance*."

Corfe's colour-bearer was a Cimbric tribesman, a close kinsman of Felorin's. He now stood up in his stirrups and waved the sable and scarlet banner of Torunna forward and back, for no bugle-calls were to be used until the army had joined battle. The signal was taken up all down the line, and slowly and in silence the huge ordered crowd of men began to move, and became a muffled creeping darkness which edged closer to the tents of the enemy, bristling with barbed menace. Anyone looking closely at the war-harness of the army's soldiers would have rubbed their eyes and stared, for every man had welded short iron nails to his armour, and even the horses' chamfrons and breastplates were similarly adorned, whilst the spear-points of the Fimbrians and lanceheads of the Cathedrallers were not bright winking steel, but black iron also. Save for the scarlet of the Cathedrallers, the appearance of the army was sombre as a shadow, with hardly a gleam of bright metal to be seen.

When they had advanced two miles Corfe ordered the reserve to edge farther out on the left, for they were passing the camps of the Knights Militant about their Citadel. There was activity there now where there had been none before, and he could see squadrons of cavalry mounting their horses. And then a bright series of horn-calls split the morning and from the summit of the citadel's tower a grey smoke went up.

"It would seem the enemy has clambered out of bed at last," he said mildly. "Baraz, ride to Colonel Olba with the reserve and tell him to drop back further and cover our left rear. He is to go into square, if necessary, but he is to be prepared to ward off the Knights Militant from the main body."

"Sir!" Baraz galloped off.

"Ensign Roche."

"Yes, sir." The young officer's horse was dancing under him and his eyes were bright as glass. He was about to see a real battle at last.

"Go to Marshal Kyne in the middle of the phalanx, and tell him that he is to keep advancing for Charibon itself, even if he loses contact with the arquebusiers on his left. He has my leave to detach a flank guard if he sees fit, but he must keep moving regardless. Clear?"

"Yes, sir!" Clods of turf flew through the air like birds as Roche wheeled his horse away in turn.

Yes, the enemy were awake all right. A mile in front of the army, men were tumbling out of their tents and forming up with confused haste. They were in Almarkan blue, arquebusiers and sword-and-buckler men. Many thousands of them were now preparing to bar the way into Charibon. As they milled about, the bells of the cathedral of the Saint, and those of every other church in the monastery city, began to peal the alarm, and Corfe could see that the streets of Charibon were clogging with troops rushing south and east to meet him. Out to the west of the city he could see other formations moving on the plain: Finnmarkan gallowglasses, according to the word of his scouts. They had vast camps out there, but had two miles to march before they would be on his flank. Corfe drew the Answerer, and the ancient pattern-welded iron of John Mogen's sword glittered darkly as it left the scabbard. He raised it in the air and led the bodyguard out to the left rear of the Cathedrallers. The Torunnan army was eating up the yards to Charibon at a great pace, and was now deployed in a great L-shape with the base of the L facing west. Not a single battlecry or shout came from the ranks; the only sound was the dull thunder of all those thousands of hooves and feet.

"Ensign Brascian," said Corfe to another of his young staff who clustered about him. "Go to Colonel Rilke of the artillery. You will find him with the Cathedrallers. Tell him to deploy his guns to the west at once and commence to engage the Knights Militant. Then find Comillan and say he is to charge the Knights at his own discretion, but he is not to pursue. He is not to pursue, is that clear?"

"Very clear, sir."

"He is to pull back as soon as the enemy is halted and in disorder, and the guns will cover his withdrawal. Then he is to hold himself in readiness for further orders."

Seven or eight thousand of the Knights Militant had now formed up in a long line facing east, in front of their citadel and the tents pitched at its foot. They would advance very soon, and must be neutralised. Corfe watched Brascian pelt off, slapping his horse's rump with the flat of his sabre. He disappeared into the sea of red-armoured horsemen that was the Cathedrallers, and scant minutes later the ranks of the cavalry parted and the gun-teams began to emerge and set up before them. The Cathedrallers halted behind the line of six-pounders and dressed their ranks. For all that they were composed mainly of the Cimbric tribes, they were as well disciplined as Torunnan regulars now, and Corfe's heart swelled at the sight of them. What had once been a motley band of ill-armed galley slaves had over the years become the most feared body of cavalry in the world.

The Knights Militant began to advance, a tonsured Presbyter out to their front and waving them on with his mace. They too were heavily armoured, with the Saint's Symbol picked out in white upon their breastplates, and their faces were hidden behind their closed helms. Their horses were of the fine, long limbed strain which had been bred as hunters and palfreys on the Torian Plains for centuries by the aristocracy of Almark, but they were smaller in stature than the massive destriers of the Cathedrallers. The horses of Corfe's mounted arm were descended from those brought east by the Fimbrians, back in the ancient days when some of their troops still went mounted, and the best of these had been stolen and raided by the tribesmen of the Cimbrics over the years and for centuries after had been selected and bred purely for size, and courage. For war.

The startling boom of a gun as the first six-pounder went off, followed by a close-spaced salvo from all three batteries. Rilke had trained his gun-teams well. Hardly had the cannon jumped back on their carriages than his men were levering them forward again, worming and sponging them out, and reloading. They were using canister, hollow metal shells filled with scores of arquebus-balls, and as the smoke cleared the carnage they produced was awesome to see. All along the front of the Knights' line horses were tumbling screaming to their sides, crushing their riders, or rearing up with their bowels exposed or backing frantically away from the deadly hail to crash into their fellows behind them. The Knights' advance stalled in bloody confusion. The horse of their Presbyter was galloping riderless about the field with gore streaming from its holed neck and flanks, and its owner lay motionless in the grass behind it, his tonsure pale as a porcelain bowl on the trampled turf.

"*Now*," Corfe whispered, banging his gauntleted hand on his knee. "*Go now.*"

Comillan seemed to have read his thought, for as soon as the artillery had fired their second salvo he spurred out to the front of his men with his colour-bearer in tow, and with a wordless cry ordered them forward. The hunting-horns of the Cimbrics sounded full and clear over the screams of maimed horses and men, and the huge line of armoured cavalry began to move, like some monstrous titan whose leash had been slipped. Corfe's heart went with them as they quickened into a trot, and then a canter, and the lances came down in a full-blooded charge to contact. The earth trembled under them and the tribesmen now began to sing the terrible battle-paean of their native hills, and still singing they ploughed into the enemy formations like the blade of a hot knife sinking into butter. The first and second lines of Cathedrallers made a deep scarlet wedge in the ranks of the Knights Militant, and the smaller horses of the Himerians were knocked off their feet by the impact of the charge. The Cathedrallers discarded their broken and bloody lances and fired a volley of matchlock pistols at point-blank range, adding to the carnage and the panic. Then the silver horn-calls signalled the *Withdrawal*, and the first two lines turned about and fell back, covered by the advance of the third and fourth ranks, who rode through their files, formed up neatly and fired a rolling pistol-volley in their turn. Comillan's command trotted back across the field unmolested and seemingly unscathed, though Corfe could see the scarlet bodies which littered the plain they left behind them. But these were as nothing compared to the great wreckage of carcasses and steel-clad carrion which had once been the proud ranks of the Knights Militant.

The survivors of the charge, many now on foot, streamed back across the plain through the trampled debris of their tented camp, and sought sanctuary about the walls of their citadel. The Torunnan advance continued.

ARUAN, AGHAST, WATCHED the ruin of his Knights from the high tower of the Pontifical palace. Inceptine clerks and errand-runners clustered about him like black flies settling on a wound, but none dared meet their master's blazing eyes. As his gaze went hither and thither across the wide battlefield, he saw the Almarkan troops south of Charibon stand to fire a volley of ragged arquebus fire. The oncoming Torunnans were not even checked, but closed up their ranks and marched over the bodies of their dead. Even as he watched, the pikes of the Orphans came down from the vertical and became a bristling fence of bitter points which reflected no light. The Almarkans could not withstand that fearsome sight, and began to fall back to the dubious shelter of their encampment, pausing to fire as they went. The Torunnan phalanx paused, and the thousand arquebusiers within its ranks fired in their turn. Then out of the smoke the Orphans marched on once more. They did not seem to be men, but rather minute cogs in some great, terrible engine of war, as unstoppable as a force of nature.

Aruan's eyes rolled back in his head and a great snarling came from his throat. His aides backed away but he was utterly indifferent to them. He gathered his strength and launched a bolt of pure, focused power into the east, like a puissant broadhead propelled by a bow of immense force. This lightning-swift Dweomer-scrap carried the message of his mind's demand.

Bardolin, to me.

He came back to himself and snapped at his aides without looking at them, his eyes still fixed on the vast panorama of the smoking battlefield below.

"Loose the Hounds," he said.

THE TORUNNAN LINE opened out. As the main body of the infantry advanced, the Cathedrallers turned north and covered their open flank, and with them came Rilke's guns. But in the gap left by the departure of the red horsemen, Colonel Olba's reserve formation shook out from column into line of battle, and faced west to guard against any fresh attack by the remnants of the Knights. Near the apex of these two lines the Torunnan King, his standard rippling sable and scarlet above him, took up position surrounded by his bodyguard.

From the north-west the long columns of glittering mail-clad gallowglasses, the stormtroopers of the Second Empire, approached, while from their camps along the shores of the Torian Sea trotted fresh contingents of Almarkans and Perigrainians and Finnmarkans. The blue sky was dotted with the tiny flapping shapes of homonculi running their masters' errands. Aruan was recalling every tercio that remained between the Cimbrics and the Narian Hills to the defence of Charibon. And still the bells tolled madly in the churches, and the Torunnans came on like a wave of black iron.

It was Golophin who sensed their coming first. He stiffened in the saddle of the army mule which was his preferred mount and seemed almost to sniff the air.

"Corfe," he cried. "The Hounds."

The King looked at him, and nodded. He turned to Astan his bugler. "Sound me the *Halt*."

Clear and cold over the tumult of the battle the horn-call rang out. As soon as the notes had died the buglers of other companies and formations took it up, and in seconds the entire battle-line had stopped moving, and the Orphans grounded their pikes. Those two miles and more of armed men and stamping horses paused as though waiting, and the field became almost quiet except for stray spatters of gunshots here and there and the neighing of impatient destriers. To the north the bells of Charibon had fallen silent.

Golophin seemed to be listening. He stood up, tense and stiff, in his stirrups, while his mule shifted uneasily under him. Soon all the men of the army could hear it. The mad, cacophonous chorus of a wolf-pack in full cry, but magnified so that it rose up over the trampled and bloodstained and scorched grass of the battlefield and seemed to issue from the very air about their heads. The Torunnans shifted in their files, men looking sidelong at one another, licking their lips. The fear could almost be smelled rising from their ranks.

"Arquebusiers stand by!" Corfe shouted, raising the Answerer, and down through the army the order was repeated, while the Cathedrallers clicked open their saddle-holsters and reached for their matchlocks.

"Hold fast! Stand your ground and let them come to us!"

And come they did. They ran in a huge pack, hundreds, thousands of them. From the centre of Charibon they poured along the streets in a fanged, hairy torrent, their eyes glaring madly and their claws clicking and sliding on the cobbles. The human troops of Aruan made way for them in terror, shrinking against walls and ducking into doorways. But the Hounds ignored them. Running now on four legs, now on two, they burst out of the narrow streets and formed up vast as a cloud on the plain before Charibon, marshalled by mail-clad Inceptines. Lycanthropes of every shape and variety imaginable milled there, yapping and snarling and hissing their hatred at the silent ranks of the Torunnans, a tableau from some primeval nightmare.

"Holy God," Corfe said, appalled despite himself. The ranks of the Torunnan army seemed to twitch, to shudder like the hide of a horse twitching off a fly; then they were stock-still again.

The Almarkans who were caught between the two lines streamed west in utter panic, collapsing the last of their tents behind them, some dropping their weapons as they ran. They were not professionals but shepherds of the Narian Hills, fishermen from the shores of the Hardic Sea, and they wanted no part of the slaughter to come.

Corfe stared narrowly at the mobs of shifters who snapped and spat by the thousand before his men, but yet obeyed the commands of their Inceptine leaders and remained in place.

He shaded his eyes and looked up at the high buildings of Charibon itself, less than a mile away now, and wondered if perhaps one of the figures he saw standing there was the architect of these monstrosities. A small group of men watching from the tower next to the cathedral – one of them must be Aruan, surely. And even as he watched the air seemed to shimmer about them, and ere he looked away, rubbing his watering eyes, he was sure their number had increased by one.

Even in that moment, the Hounds of God sprang forward. They loped through the ruined camp of the Almarkans, looking from afar like a tide of rats, and the roaring, howling and snarling they made as they came on made the horses rear up and fight their bridles in fear. Corfe gave no order, for his men knew what to do. The Hounds ran straight up to his line in a boiling mass, and with them came an overpowering, awful stink, heavy as smoke.

With forty yards to go the Orphans levelled their pikes once more, and every firearm in the entire army was discharged in one long, stertorous volley that seemed to go on for ever. The front of the army was hidden in a solid wall of smoke and a moment later hundreds and hundreds of werewolves and shifters of all shapes and misshapes came hurtling out of it and threw themselves upon the Torunnan front rank.

The army seemed to shudder at the impact, and was at once engaged in hand to hand combat all along its length, and Corfe could see soldiers being flung through the air and smashed and clawed off their feet. The formations of Torunnans and Orphans and tribesmen were smashed in on themselves, ranks intermingling, order breaking down under that preternatural assault.

Beside Corfe, Ensign Roche had returned from his errand and was praying loudly, repetitively, wholly unconscious of it, his wide eyes staring at the horrors before him.

Hard to see what was going on at the front line. The arquebuses had fallen silent; there was no time or space to reload them in that murderous mob. The smoke of that single volley was hanging thick and low to the ground, and in and out of it men battled shapes out of nightmare.

But the army's position was not so parlous as it seemed. Every time a shifter struck one of Corfe's men, it set its flesh against the barbed metal which armoured them. Soon, at the feet of the Orphans and the Torunnans of the front line, a horrible tide-mark built up, a barricade of nude bodies. For when the shifters were so much as grazed by the spiked iron of Torunnan armour, the Dweomer left them, and their beast-bodies melted away.

As the smoke of the initial volley cleared and drifted in rent patches out to sea, it was possible to perceive the carnage that the arquebusiers had wrought. Thousands of naked corpses littered the plain, in places lying piled in mounds three and four deep. The grass was dark and slimy with their blood. And the Torunnan formations were recovering. They pushed forward as they regained their courage, reforming their ranks and hacking madly at the lycanthropes who were battling in their midst. They were beasts to be slaughtered, animals with a fatal flaw.

The attack of the Hounds faltered. Even through the blood-rage that impelled them they finally realised their mistake, and began to pull back from that deadly line of iron-clad men. They streamed away in their hundreds, trampling their Inceptine officers or snarling and beating them aside.

But there was to be no chance even in retreat. As soon as they broke off the army's arquebuses were levelled again, and Corfe heard the voices of his officers bellowing out. Another volley, and another. Every round his men fired was made not of lead, but of pure iron, and the bullets snicked and whined and scythed across the battlefield so that the surviving Hounds were cut down in swathes as they withdrew. When the smoke finally cleared again, the plain was empty of life, and the corpses of Aruan's most feared troops littered it like a ghastly windfall. They had been utterly destroyed. An eerie silence fell over the field, as though all men were astounded by the sight.

Corfe turned to Astan his bugler and simply nodded. The tribesman put his horn to his lips and blew. The Torunnan advance began again.

"Golophin has betrayed us, lord," Himerius said, his voice quavering with anger and the rattle of an old man's phlegm.

"He has told the Torunnans how to kill us."

Bardolin stood with the last shifting threads of the Dweomer dwindling about him. His clothes smelled slightly scorched and his face was wan with fatigue. "Any hedge-witch could have told them the same."

"There are none left in Torunna now, Bardolin." Aruan stood between them, his hawk-nosed face pensive, eyes glowering.

"No, it was your friend Golophin. He has chosen his side at last. A pity. I thought he would see sense in the end." Aruan's eyes seemed slightly out of focus, as if they could not quite take in the enormity of the spectacle before them.

"Their infantry are entering the city," Himerius cried. "Bardolin, in God's name, what kind of men are these? Does nothing daunt them?" The wattles beneath his chin shook, and he bunched up one liver-spotted fist and raised it impotently.

The Hebrian mage did not answer his question. "The Hounds have failed us, for the moment. There are others we can call on when the time is right. But for now we must fight the enemy sword to sword. Reinforcements are on their way from the north, and the south. Corfe has made a brave fight of it, but he cannot win, not against the numbers we will bring to bear on him."

Aruan clapped him on the shoulder. "That is what I like to hear. I am glad you came, Bardolin. I have need of your good sense. A man must be a stone not to lose a little of his equilibrium at a time like this."

"Then I had best give you my news before you lose any more. Yesterday an army of Torunnans and Merduks under Formio defeated our forces in a battle near the town of Staed in southern Torunna. The invasion has failed."

"Failed," Himerius repeated. He looked withered by the news.

Aruan did not move or speak, but a muscle clenched and unclenched like a restless worm under the skin of his jaw. "Is that all?"

"No. Our spies tell me that, after the battle, Formio received a young man at his headquarters who claims to be heir to the throne of Hebrion, Abeleyn's illegitimate son by his one-time mistress. He told the Fimbrian Regent that Queen Isolla is dead. Murad killed her in the Levangore before being slain himself."

"Jemilla," Himerius snarled. "Still ambitious, after all this time. I knew of her years ago, when I was prelate in Abrusio. She was indeed the King's mistress. So the line of the Hibrusids survives after all."

Bardolin looked down, and his voice changed. "Richard Hawkwood is dead also."

Aruan nodded. "Well, we must be thankful for what we are given, I suppose. Our plans have gone awry, my friends, but the set-back is temporary. We have fresh forces on the way which will weigh heavy in the scales, as you say." He smiled, and the perilous lupine-light burned in his eyes, gloating now with secret knowledge.

An Inceptine who was leaning over the tower parapet with his fellows threw back his hood and pointed south. His voice quavered. "Lord, the Torunnans are advancing up the very streets. They are approaching the cathedral!"

"Let them," Aruan said. He rested his hands on the shoulders of Himerius and Bardolin, and squeezed their flesh.

"Let the doomed have their hour of glory."

THE BATTLEFIELD HAD grown, so that now the monastery-city itself had been swallowed by it. Corfe had wheeled the Orphans westwards once more so that their right flank was resting on the complex of timber buildings that constituted the southern suburb of Charibon. Those arquebusiers who had been positioned on the shore of the Sea of Tor now advanced northwards and began pushing towards the great square at the heart of the city while the Cathedrallers formed up south of the Orphans to protect their open flank, and Olba's reserve began moving at the double northward to join in the taking of the city. Buildings were burning here and there already and the Himerian troops trying to hold back the Torunnan advance were confused and leaderless. The hard-bitten Torunnan professionals herded them like sheep, advancing tercio by tercio so that the once tranquil cloisters of Charibon rang with the thunderous din of volley-fire and the screams of desperate men. No quarter was given by the iron-clad invaders, and they cut down every man, woman and black-garbed cleric in their path until the gutters ran with blood.

But the Second Empire had not yet committed all its strength. From the west the glittering ranks of mail-clad gallowglasses advanced in unbroken lines with their two-handed swords resting on their shoulders and their faces hidden behind tall, masked helms. And beyond them, more regiments of Almarkans and Perigrainians were forming up on the plain, preparing to push the Torunnans into the sea.

A wind off the Torian carried the smoke and stink of the battle inland and the sun came lancing in great banner-bright beams though the curling battle-reek, making of the armed formations brindled silhouettes. For three square miles south of Charibon the wreck and smirch of war covered the earth, as though the battle were some dark flaming brush-fire that left blackened carrion in its wake. And it was not yet mid-morning.

Rilke's artillery began to bark out once again and create flowers of red ruin among the ranks of the advancing gallowglasses. However, these Finnmarkans were not the frightened boys that the Almarkan conscripts had been, but the household warriors of King Skarp-Hethin himself. They continued advancing, closing their gaps as they came, so that Corfe could not help but admire them.

He studied the battlefield as though it were some puzzle to which he must find the answer. Huge masses of men had almost completed dressing their lines behind the gallowglasses; the foremost had already begun to advance in their wake. He was outnumbered several times over, and it would not be long before someone in the enemy high command had the wit to move around his left and outflank him. He could either pull his men back now and await the enemy onslaught, or he could throw caution aside.

He looked north. The outskirts of Charibon were on fire and his men were fighting their way street by bloody street into the heart of the city. That was where the battle would be decided; in the very midst of the hallowed cloisters and churches of the Inceptines. He must make a deliberate choice. Battlefield victory was now impossible; he knew that. Now he must either fight this battle conventionally, harbouring his men's lives and hoping that they could stage a fighting withdrawal through the hordes pitted against them. Or deliberately send the thing he loved to its destruction, throw away the tactics manual and chance everything on one throw of the dice. All to accomplish the death of a single man.

If he failed here – if Aruan and his cohorts survived this day – then the west would become a continent of slaves and the magicians and their beasts would rule it for untold years to come.

Corfe looked at Golophin, and the old wizard met his eyes squarely. He knew.

Corfe turned to Ensign Roche, who was wide-eyed and sweating beside him.

"Go to Comillan. He is to charge the gallowglasses, and follow up until they break. Then go to Kyne. The Orphans must advance. They will keep advancing as long as they are able."

The young officer took off with a hurried salute.

And as easily as that, it was done, and the fate of the world thrown into the balance. Corfe felt as though a great weight had been raised off his shoulders. He spoke to Haptman Baraz.

"I am taking the bodyguard into the city. Tell Olba to follow up with his command." And when the young officer had gone, he turned to Golophin again.

"Will you be there with me at the death?" he asked lightly.

The old wizard bowed in the saddle, his scarred face as grim as that of a cathedral gargoyle. "I will be with you, Corfe. Until the end."

TWENTY-TWO

BARDOLIN WATCHED THE charge of the Cathedrallers from the roof of a building off the great square. In all the houses around he had gathered together what he could of the retreating Almarkans and had stationed them at windows and on balconies, ready to fire down on the Torunnan invaders as they came. More reinforcements were still flooding through the city from the north, and while the Torunnans were burning and killing their way forward, he and Aruan had set in place many thousands of fresh troops to bar their way, rearing up barricades across every street and positioning arquebusiers at every corner.

But out on the plains beyond the city the red horsemen of Torunna were advancing side by side with a Fimbrian pike phalanx, eight or nine thousand strong, to meet the gallowglasses of Finnmark. Something in Bardolin stirred at the sight, some strange grief. He watched as the Cathedrallers charged forward, a scarlet wave, and the terrible pikes of the Orphans were lowered as they followed up. Scarlet and black upon the field, the colours of Torunna. He heard faintly over the roar of the battle the battle-paean of the Cimbric tribes come drifting back to the city, fearsome and beautiful as a summer storm. And he watched as the gallowglasses were shunted backwards and the lines intermingled silver and red as the Cathedraller's legendary charge struck home. The Finnmarkans fought stubbornly, but they were no match for the army that Corfe Cear-Inaf had created, and eventually their line broke, and splintered, and fell apart. And the Orphans came up to finish the bloody work, their pikes as perfect as though they were being wielded in a parade-ground review.

A nudge, a subtle spike in his brain.

Now, do it now.

Bardolin rose with tears in his eyes. He raised hands to heaven and called out in Old Normannic. Words of summoning and power which shook to its foundations the building whereon he stood. And he was answered. For out of the south came a dark cloud that sullied the spring sky. It drew closer while the battle below it opened out heedlessly below and the smoke of Charibon's burning rose to meet it. At last other men saw the looming darkness, and cried out around him in fear. In a vast flock of many thousands, the Flyers of Aruan came shrieking down out of the sun and swarmed upon the advancing armies of Torunna like a cloud of locusts. Even the destriers of the Cathedrallers could not withstand the sudden terror of that attack from above, and they reared and threw their riders and screamed and milled in confusion. The scarlet armour of the tribesmen was hidden as by a black thunderhead and in the midst of it, dismounted, buffeted by their panicked steeds, they began a savage fight for survival. The remnants of the gallowglasses, and the great regiments of Himerians behind them, took heart, and began to advance. The Orphans moved to meet them, and Corfe's Fimbrians fell under the cloud also, and all that part of the battlefield became a whirlwind of shadow and darkness within which a holocaust of slaughter was kindled.

THE SUNLIGHT HAD gone, and a premature twilight had fallen upon the world. Great tumbling clouds had come galloping up from the south, propelled by smatterings of lightning, and a chill had entered the air. It began to rain, and with the rain fell long slivers of ice which scored men's flesh and rattled like knives off their armour. The battle-plain began to soften, and the churned footfalls of soldiers and horses sank into mud below them so that a vast quagmire was created, and within it heavily burdened men swung their weapons at each other and battled with the unthinking ferocity of animals.

Such was the press and congestion in the streets of the city that Corfe and his bodyguard had to dismount and leave their horses behind. Armed with sabres and pistols, the five hundred men in raven-black *Ferinai* armour picked their way forward on foot, the rain dripping from their fearsome helms. They were tribesman and Torunnan, Fimbrian and Merduk; the cream of the army. As the regular Torunnans fighting there in the shadow of the burning houses saw them they set up a great shout. "The King is come!"

The bodyguard walked on until they came to the first of the street barriers behind which Almarkan arquebusiers were firing and reloading frantically. There came a sound like heavy hail rattling off a tin roof, and several of the bodyguard staggered as arquebus bullets slammed into them. But their armour was proof against such missiles. They walked on, shielding the match in their pistols from the rain, and delivered a volley at point-blank range. Then they discarded their firearms and drew their sabres and began climbing over the barricades. The Almarkans ran.

The Torunnans marched on. Men were still firing at them here and there from upper windows, but for the most part the Himerians had fallen back to the great square before the cathedral and the library of St. Garaso. They gathered there and were placed in order by Bardolin and Aruan and Himerius and dozens of Inceptines. A few surviving Hounds squatted snarling on the cobbles and homonculi wheeled overhead like vultures.

Corfe and his men burst out of the streets and into the square itself. The rain had quenched every scrap of slow-match between both armies and now the arquebusiers had thrown aside their useless firearms and drawn their swords. The tall helms of the bodyguard as they formed up in the square made them seem like black towers alongside their more lightly armoured comrades, and behind them in the streets Olba's reserve, a thousand of whom were Orphans, were coming up at the double, their pikes resting on their shoulders, the sharpshooters felling them by the dozen as they advanced.

Charibon's great square was almost half a mile to a side. At its north end stood the library of St. Garaso, greatest in the world since the sack of Aekir. To the west loomed the towers of the Pontifical palace, a newer construction much expanded in the last decade. And to the east was the triple-horned cathedral of the Saint. The square, for all its size, was hemmed in by tall buildings on all sides and resembled nothing so much as a huge amphitheatre. Across it Corfe could now see two glittering figures who must be Aruan and Bardolin. They wore antique half-armour worked with gold, and it flashed and gleamed in the rain. The stooped cleric in the black habit beside them – that must be Himerius. Even as Corfe watched, he saw one of the armoured figures straighten before his troops, heedless of the invaders, and lift his arms to the lowering sky and the ice-mingled rain. He was saying something in a strangely beguiling chant, and as he did his troops straightened, lifted their heads, looked at the fearsome Torunnans across the short distance of the square, and were no longer afraid. They began to cheer and howl and beat sword-blade against breastplate; a deafening din of clattering metal rose up under the rain.

Corfe's Torunnans had dressed their lines, and now stood motionless and silent. The bodyguard formed the front rank, with a thicker knot of them about the King. Behind them came a thousand Orphans, their pikes projecting over their shoulders, and behind them two thousand more Torunnan arquebusiers, fighting now with sabres alone.

Golophin stood beside the King, the only man in all that densely packed line who wore no harness and carried no weapon. Corfe looked at him. "Which one is which?"

"Aruan is the bald one with the hawk nose. Bardolin's nose is broken and he looks like a soldier. That is him on the right."

"And Himerius, he's the third, the monk?"

"Himerius is near eighty now. He'll not be wearing armour. Yes, it is him."

Golophin was not far off that age himself, Corfe realised. He set a gauntleted hand on the wizard's shoulder. "Maybe you'd best go to the rear, Golophin."

The wizard shook his head, and his smile was not altogether pleasant. "No weapon will bite me today, sire. And I am not without weapons of my own."

Corfe raised his voice to be heard over the clamour of the Himerians and the hissing rain.

"Then help me kill him."

Golophin nodded, but said no word. He turned so that his wide-brimmed hat hid his eyes.

At that moment the Himerian troops in the square charged, screaming like fiends. They came on in a frenzied rush and, crashing into the tall armoured line of the bodyguard, began to hammer upon the Torunnans like men possessed.

Corfe's line bent but did not break. The Orphans of the reserve came forward and leant their weight to the melee, some stabbing blind with their pikes, others drawing their short, broad-bladed swords and pitching in where a falling bodyguard left a gap.

The discipline of the Torunnans mastered even the Himerians' Dweomer-fed rage, and indeed that rage caused many of the enemy to leave themselves open as they neglected to defend themselves in their haste to kill. They pulled down many of the tall Torunnans, three and four of them attacking a single soldier at a time, but Olba's Fimbrians strode forward to fill the gaps and the line remained unbroken.

Corfe felt the moment when all was poised, and the initiative began its slip away from the enemy, like the moment when a wave crests the beach and must begin to ebb.

"Sound the *Advance*!" he shouted at Astan, and the horn-call blew loud and clear over the tumult of battle. A hoarse animal roar came from the throats of the Torunnans, and they surged forward. The spell broke under the strain, and the Himerians began to fall back like men in a daze.

"Come with me," Corfe said to those around him, and a group of men clustered under his banner and began cutting a path through the retreating enemy to where Aruan and Bardolin and Himerius stood on the steps of the library of St. Garaso with a great crowd of soldiery about them. Baraz was with the King, and Felorin, and Roche, and Golophin, and Astan and Alarin and two dozen more. They held together with the compact might of a mailed fist and when their foes saw the light in Corfe's eye they blenched and fell back.

The Torunnans poured across the square in the wake of their King. Before them the enemy retreat degenerated into a rout. The Himerians had fought Hebrians and Astarans; they had cowed the petty kingdoms and principalities of the north and they had set their stamp across two thirds of the known world. But faced by the elite of Torunna's warriors and their Soldier-King, they were hopelessly outmatched, and not even the wizardry of Aruan could make them stand fast.

Corfe and his followers strode across the corpse-choked square until they were scant yards from the triumvirs of the Second Empire and their last bodyguards crowded on the library steps. Aruan looked like a man exhausted, but there was a deadly light in his eyes and he stood straight and arrogant. At his shoulder Bardolin stood, his armour covered in other men's gore, a short-bladed broadsword in his fist. Himerius was a shrunken figure in black who was being supported by an armoured monk.

The darkness of the day was deepening, for Charibon was on fire all about them now, and shrouds of smoke hid the sky. The rain poured down in shining rods and leapt up bloody from the cobbles. Across the square a quiet fell, though all around them in the distance they could hear the great battle raging on beyond, as though Charibon were groaning in its death-throes.

Corfe pointed at Aruan with the tip of the Answerer's blade. "It ends here."

Astonishingly, the Archmage laughed. "Does it, indeed? Thank you for the warning, but I fear, little king, that you are misinformed. Golophin, be a good fellow and tell him. You know the truth of it. You have seen it with your Farsight."

Golophin frowned, and Corfe spun on him. "What does he mean?"

"Sire, the Cathedrallers and the Orphans are defeated and surrounded upon the field. They are gathering for a last stand. This thing's flying legions have broken their lines, and more troops are on their way from the west, a great army tens of thousands strong. The battle is lost."

Corfe turned to Aruan again and, to the astonishment of all, smiled. "So be it. They have done their job, and now I must do mine." He raised the Answerer and kissed the dark blade, then began to march forward.

His men came with him, and the tribesmen among them began singing. Not a battle-paean this time, but the mournful song raised by hunters at the place of the kill.

Aruan's mouth opened and closed. Then he shut his eyes and his body shimmered and seemed to grow transparent. Just when it seemed he would disappear entirely, a bolt of blue light came lancing across the heads of his men and smote him to the ground. He grew solid again in the blink of an eye and fell to his hands and knees gasping.

Golophin lowered his still-smoking fist. "No-one runs away," he said. "Not today."

A last, bitter fight took place on the steps of Charibon's ancient library, wherein, long before, Albrec had discovered the document which united the great religions of the world. The Himerians fought with a savagery hitherto unseen, the Torunnans like dreadful machines of slaughter. The bodies tumbled down the steps and built up at their foot, but all the while Corfe cut his way ever closer to Aruan and Bardolin and Himerius. As the last of their defenders fell, the great doors of the library opened behind them, and a fresh wave of their troops poured out, yelling madly. But they could not drown out the sombre death-hymn of the tribes, and these too were pushed back by a black hedge of flailing iron blades, until the melee had moved and retreated into the tall dimness of the library itself. There it opened out, and by lamplight and torchlight amid the tall shelves and stacks of books and the ash-grey pillars of the building the fighting went on, and men scattered trying to flee or trying to kill. But Corfe and those about them held together and followed the gleam of Aruan's bright armour, and pursued him back through the shadows of the library. There, the elderly Himerius tripped and fell and lay weeping until Felorin bent and cut his throat. The tribesman straightened, eyes ashine with the battle-rage of his people.

"Now there is only one Pontiff again."

They forged on through the shelf-stacks, the learning of the ages knocked down and trampled underfoot, precious manuscripts falling through the air like flapping birds, bookcases toppled like trees, the tall stone of the library echoing with the crash of them, the clash of metal, the screams of desperate men. The Himerians were cut down without mercy, whether they fought to the last, or dropped their swords and begged for their lives. There was to be no quarter given or taken this day. This was the end of a world.

The Torunnans spread out in the shadowed vastness of the library, scattering for the hunt. Knots of them cut their way through and through the ranks of the enemy until the building was full of disparate mobs of struggling men, and all order was lost, and each combat a fight of individuals.

They harried Aruan until at last he stood at bay with few about him, cornered in a dark wing of the ancient building deep in shadows, his eyes glaring hatred and a kind of madness, and the stench of the beast rising about him. Corfe stood before him, on his face the calm smile of a man who has almost finished his day's work.

Bardolin strode forward then and clashed swords with Corfe himself, but the Torunnan King seemed to have grown in the shadows of the ancient building until he loomed like some giant warrior out of legend. He knocked Bardolin aside with one mailed fist, and kept going with his eyes fixed on Aruan.

The beast erupted out of the Archmage, uncontrollable and baying. The armour it wore burst its straps and fell from its body and it became a huge monolithic darkness within which yellow eyes gleamed and long fangs clashed in its slavering muzzle. It lunged forward and, careering into a tall shelf full of books, sent it tumbling over. The heavy wood caught Corfe on his left side and knocked him off his feet. The Answerer skittered across the stone floor. The wolf-Aruan towered over him, and then bent to bite out his throat.

But two more shapes sprang forwards, their swords stabbing out above their prone King. Felorin and Baraz, charging like champions at the huge shifter, yelling defiance. The wolf leaped back with preternatural speed and ripped free a heavy shelf from the wall. This it swung in a great arc that caught Baraz across the side of the head and broke his neck. It raised the heavy wood again, but Felorin ducked under the swing and stabbed upwards. He missed, but the wolf fell back swiftly, holding the shelf before it like a shield.

Then Felorin's mouth opened and he dropped his sword to the floor with a clatter. He half-turned, but something smote him deep once again, and he sank to his knees.

Bardolin pulled his sword free and stepped back as Felorin collapsed face-up on the floor. There was a haziness to his outline, as if he possessed more than one shadow, and indeed as he turned back to the King it could be seen that a second shadow detached itself from him and left to be lost in the gloom of the library. He strode forward, and behind him the great wolf followed.

Corfe's left arm was broken, and the ribs on that side had been cracked and displaced. He tasted blood in his mouth and a harsh gasp of pain left his lips as he struggled to his feet, then bent to retrieve his sword. His bugler and colour-bearer were dead behind him, at whose hand he knew not, and though fighting could be heard all through the library, here at this end he stood alone.

He bowed his head a moment, looking first at Felorin's dead, surprised face, and then at young Baraz, whose grandfather had once taken Aekir. A single tear glittered under his eye, but his face was as set and stern as that of an ancient warrior on his sarcophagus. The kill-song of the tribes seemed to resonate in his mind, louder even than the sounds of fighting still echoing through the library. A fine, dark song to end with.

He would not call for help, not today.

Bardolin faced him while the wolf padded off to one side, circling. Corfe stood swaying and the Answerer seemed impossibly heavy in his good fist. He pointed the sword into the floor like a staff to steady himself and stared at the man who had been Golophin's protégé, his apprentice, his friend. He had, as the wizard had said, a soldier's face, and Corfe knew, looking at him, that at another time or in another world they would have been friends. He smiled. That other world awaited him now, and was not so far away.

Bardolin nodded as if he had spoken his thought aloud, but there was something else in his eye. It looked beyond Corfe, behind him –

The wolf attacked. Corfe, warned by the movement of Bardolin's eye, wheeled round, forgetting his pain. The

Answerer jumped up, light as a bird again in his hand, and as the great beast's paws came raking down he stabbed inwards, felt the point break flesh and sink half a handspan, no more. The claws raked the flesh from his face and fell away. There was a shrieking bellow, like the sound of an animal caught in a trap, and the wolf tumbled to the ground stiffly as a felled tree. Before it hit the flags of the floor it was no longer an animal, but a naked man in old age. And Aruan lay there with blood trickling from a wound over his heart, and he lifted up his head, hatred burning out of his eyes. He aged as Corfe stood there, his face becoming lined and withered, his muscles melting away, his skin darkening like old leather. He dwindled to bare, sinew-frapped bone and his stare was lost in the twin orbits of an empty skull.

Corfe staggered. His flesh hung in rags below his eyes and the blood was pouring in a black stream down his breastplate. Now Bardolin strode forward, and his broadsword came up. His expression had not changed, and his face wore still a mask of gentle grief.

Corfe managed to beat aside his first lunge. The second smote his breastplate and knocked him backwards. He came up against a scribe's angled desk and knocked away a third.

"No!"

There was a sudden blazing radiance, and Golophin stepped between them with the werelight spilling out of his eyes and burning around his fists. He was breathing heavily, and even his breath seemed luminous. Bardolin retreated before him, though there was no fear in his eyes. "Get back, Golophin," he said calmly.

"We did not agree to this!"

"No matter. It is necessary. He must die, or else it has all been for nothing."

"I will not let you do this, Bardolin."

"Do not try to stop me. Not now, when we are so close. Aruan is gone – that was the bargain. But he must go too."

"No," Golophin said steadily, and the light in him increased.

Bardolin's cheeks were wet with tears. "So be it, master." He dropped his sword and out of him a light flooded to match Golophin's.

Corfe shielded his eyes. It seemed to him that there was stroke and counter-stroke in the midst of a storm of whirling and leaping brilliances. Books caught fire and blazed to ashes, the stone floor was blackened, but he felt no heat. The ground under him trembled and shook.

The light winked out, and when Corfe had blinked away the searing after-images he saw that Golophin was standing over a prostrate but conscious Bardolin, his chest moving in great heaves.

"I'm sorry, Bard," he said, and cocked one fist, upon which a globe of blue werelight shimmered like a broadhead trembling at full draw.

But then a shadow flew out of the gloom of the wrecked library, and as it approached it took on shape and definition until it seemed to Corfe to be a young girl with a head of heavy bronze-coloured hair. He shouted at Golophin but his voice was no more than a harsh croak in his throat. The girl-shadow sprang upon the old wizard's back and his head came back and he screamed shrilly. She seemed to melt into his body, and his werelight was sucked into a growing darkness near his heart. For a moment he metamorphosed into a writhing, grotesque pillar of wildly gyrating limbs and faces, and there was a last, blinding flash of light, and the pillar crumpled to the floor like a bundle of tortured rags.

THE ONLY SOUND was the cutting rasp of Corfe's breathing. The air was heavy with the stink of the wolf, and another reek, like old burning. Corfe grasped his sword and crawled one-handed over to Golophin's body, but there was nothing there except a shredded robe. The fighting in the library seemed to have ended, and though men's voices could be heard far down the aisle of book-stacks none but the dead seemed to remain around him.

He crawled on, until he came across Bardolin's body in the gloom, and there he halted, utterly spent. It was done. It was over.

But Bardolin stirred beside him. He raised his head and Corfe saw his eyes glitter in the darkness, though no other part of him moved.

"Golophin?"

"He is dead."

Bardolin's head fell back and Corfe heard him weeping. Moved by some feeling he could not explain, he released his grip on the Answerer and took the wizard's hand.

"He could not do it, in the end," Bardolin whispered. "He could not betray you." Corfe said nothing, and Bardolin's fingers tightened about his own.

"There should have been a better way." He said in the same, wracked whisper. His eyes met Corfe's again. "There must be a better way. It cannot always be like this."

He looked away, and Corfe thought he could almost feel the life slipping out of him. It was growing lighter. The darkness outside the tall windows of the library was clearing. Lifting his eyes, Corfe saw a shard of blue sky breaking through the clouds far above. From farther down the library came the sound of men approaching, Torunnans by their speech.

"It will be different now," he told Bardolin. But the wizard was already dead.

OUT ON THE fuming expanse of the battlefield, the remnants of the Torunnan army had come together in a great circle, and were beleaguered there by a sea of foes while behind them Charibon burned unchecked, its smoke hiding the light of the sun. Around them were piled a monstrous mound of corpses, and the teeming regiments of the Himerians attacked with merciless persistence, men clambering over the bodies of the dead to come at each other. The Torunnan circle shrank inexorably as thousands upon thousands more of the enemy came up on all sides and the flyers beat black in the air above their heads, and within the dwindling circle men cast away hope, and resolved to sell their lives dearly, and their discipline held firm despite their shrinking numbers. They would make an end worth a song, if nothing else.

Another army came marching over the horizon out of the west, and the Torunnans watched its advance with black despair while the Himerians were inspired to fresh heights of violence. But the keen-eyed on the battlefield paused as they watched it, and suddenly a rumour and a strange hope swept the struggling tercios and regiments that battled there.

The approaching army opened out and shook into battle-line with the smooth efficiency of a machine. And now all on the western edge of the field could see that it was clad in black, and its soldiers carried pikes on their shoulders. As they drew near, the Himerian attack faltered, and the rumours grew until they were being shouted from man to man, and the Torunnans lifted their heads in wonder.

Thus the Fimbrian army, fifty thousand strong, came marching to the aid of their old foes the Torunnans, and the forces of the Second Empire took one look at that sable juggernaut, and began to flee.

TWENTY-THREE

THE SKY WAS striped with the smoke of the burning.
Charibon was aflame, and from the blazing wreck of its
streets the clerics of the monastery city were streaming in
black crowds, like nothing so much as rats fleeing their
nest. The armies had encamped about the Citadel of the
Knights to the south-west, and thousands of Torunnans
and Fimbrians were lining the hills, watching as the capital
of the Second Empire consumed itself.

On the battlements of the citadel, Comillan of the
Cathedrallers, Marshal Kyne of the Orphans, and a pair
of Fimbrian officers stood and watched. Couriers came
and went, presenting despatch-scrolls to the silver-haired
Fimbrian who wore a circlet on his head.

"And so it ends," he said with satisfaction. "A close-run
thing, at the end. We were not sure if we would make it
on time."

Comillan and Kyne said nothing. They were blackened
and bloodied, painted dark with the residue of carnage. In
their eyes were the memories of what they had seen and
endured. They seemed to be staring at something far away.
The silver-haired Fimbrian looked them up and down
with his head tilted slightly to one side, a professional
appraisal.

"He did well, gentlemen. He did what he came to do. He
saved the west."

"No other could have done it," Comillan rasped, black
eyes flashing.

"Had you been half a day quicker, he'd be standing here
now, and half our army with him," Kyne said quietly.

"We did our best," the Fimbrian said with a shrug. "It
was a hard march."

Comillan and Kyne looked at one another. There was something beaten in their eyes.

"If you'll excuse us, gentlemen, we must go. I have tercios mopping up in the south. We'll dine later." The silver-haired Fimrian bowed slightly and withdrew. His comrade leaned on the stone of the battlement after he had gone, and spat over the edge.

"Who is he?" Comillan asked the man.

"Him? Name's Briannon. He was Elector of Neyr once."

"What is he now?" Kyne asked.

"Well, as of a few weeks ago, he's been voted Emperor of Fimbria."

"Emperor?" Comillan cried.

"That's what they call him. This here army is going to finish the job you Torunnans started. We're going to beat out whatever sparks are still alight of this Second Empire, hunt out every shifter and witch and wizard that's still on its feet in this part of the world, and torch them, every one. So I hear say, anyway."

The Fimbrian paused. "You fought this one well, as well as men can fight. I'm sorry about your King. He was a soldier." The Fimbrian turned and left them, following in the wake of his Emperor.

When he had gone, Comillan leaned his elbows on the battlement and hid his face in his hands.

THE SCROLL QUIVERED in Mirren's grasp, trembling with the beat of her heart. She looked out the window, and stared across the teeming streets of Aurungabar to the horned Temple of Pir-Sar, which had once been the cathedral of Carcasson. It was full summer now, and the air above the city shimmered with heat, as though shuddered into ripples by the busy clamour of the streets below.

In her hands, the scroll crackled as her fingers closed upon it, clenching white. Her eyes filled with tears.

The chamber door was opened, and in breezed her husband, dark, smiling Nasir. She looked at him, and smiled back, even as his face fell.

"News from the west," she said. The scroll fell from

her hands. Her marmoset squeaked and leapt up to her shoulder, ringing her neck with its tail. She soothed it, burying her face in the soft fur.

Nasir knelt before her. "I couldn't find you," he said. "I looked everywhere."

"I wanted a view of the Temple. I wanted quiet."

"I have heard rumours, but this is the first despatch."

"Yes. They brought it to me. I am Torunna's Queen now." She paused. "I knew what was in it. I knew by his face. The man who brought it looked as though it was his own father who had died. He wept as he gave it to me. Torunna is in mourning already."

Nasir groaned. He grasped her hand and kissed it. "I am so sorry, Mirren."

"Now we are both orphans," she said. She smiled, and stroked his face. "I must not weep for him. He succeeded. He saved us all." More briskly she said, "Now up, Nasir, off the floor. Sit beside me. We have much to discuss."

Side by side they looked out at the hot brightness of the day beyond, and smelled the breeze of summer which played about the city. A king and a queen, who loved one another, and were not much more than children. They spoke quietly together of the future, of the fate of two peoples, and the ways in which these would one day be brought together.

EPILOGUE

THE DREAMING HEIGHTS of the Jafrar Mountains were
wrapped in everlasting snow, but down on their knees a
summer evening was blue with the approaching dusk, and
the first stars had begun to burn bright and clear in an
empty sky.

About the campfire two old men sat warming their hands
while behind them their mounts nosed at the fresh grass:
one a common mule, the other a fine-limbed grey gelding
such as the Merduks had bred upon the eastern steppes for
generations. The two men said nothing, but watched the
approach of a third rider as he made his way up into the
empty hills towards them. He was clad in a black cloak, and
a circlet of silver was set on his head. He carried a sword
of great lineage, and yet his face was ridged and scarred as
by the claws of some beast. He halted at the limit of the
firelight and dismounted, and as he walked towards them
they saw that he was lame in one leg.

"I saw your fire, and thought I might join you," he said,
and, wrapping his cloak about himself, he sat close to the
embers of the wind-flapping flames.

"You are weary," one of the two others told him, a kind-
eyed man with a monk's tonsure and a grey beard.

"I have come a long way."

"Then you shall stay with us and have peace," the third
said, and he was a white-haired old man with the face of
a Merduk.

"I would like that."

The three sat companionably enough about the fire as the
night swooped in around them and the mountains became
vast black shadows against the stars. Finally the scarred
man stirred, rubbing his leg.

"I almost lost my way, back down there. I almost took the wrong path."

"But you did not," the tonsured one said, smiling, and there was a great compassion in his eyes. "And now, perhaps, all will be well at last. And you may rest."

The other sighed and nodded.

"I never thought I would have to travel so far. But there are others now to take my place, and their world is better than the one in which I lived. I am no longer needed."

"But you will not be forgotten."

It seemed that some last thing troubled the scarred man.

"Who are you, lord?" he asked in a low voice.

"Men called me Ramusio, when I dwelled among them. And my friend here was named Shahr Baraz. If you wish, you shall stay with us."

"I would like that," the man said, and he seemed to slump, as though a last burden had been taken from him.

"And what may we call you?" Shahr Baraz asked gently.

The man raised his head, and it seemed a much younger face now looked out at them, and the scars thereon had disappeared.

"My name is Corfe," he said. "I was once a king."

His two companions nodded as though it were something they already knew, and then the trio sat quiet in the night staring into the firelight whilst above them the great vault of the night sky glittered and under their feet the dark heart of the earth turned on in its endless gyre amid the stars.

Acknowledgements:

John McLaughlin and Jo Fletcher,
for their enormous patience.

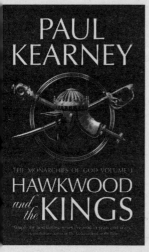

PAUL KEARNEY'S THE MACHT

THE TEN THOUSAND

UK: ISBN: 978 1 844166 47 3 • £7.99
US: ISBN: 978 1 844165 73 5 • $7.99

On the world of Kuf, the ferocity and discipline of the seldom-seen Macht are the
stuff of legend. For centuries they have
remained within the remote fastnesses of
the Harukush Mountains, while in the world
beyond, the teeming races of the Kufr have
been united within the bounds of the vast
and invincible Asurian Empire.

But now the Asurian Great King's brother
means to take the throne by force, and has
sought out the legend to do so. He has hired
ten thousand mercenary warriors of the
Macht, to lead into the heart of the Empire.

CORVUS

UK: ISBN: 978 1 906735 76 0 • £7.99
US: ISBN: 978 1 906735 77 7 • $7.99

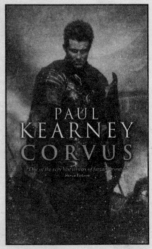

It is twenty-three years since a Macht army
fought its way home from the heart of the
Asurian Empire. Rictus is now a hard-bitten
mercenary captain, middle-aged and tired,
and wants nothing more than to become the
farmer that his father was. But fate has different ideas. A young warleader has risen in
the very heartlands of the Macht, taking city
after city, and reigning over them as king.

His name is Corvus, and the rumours say
that he is not even fully human. He means to
make himself absolute ruler of all the Macht.
And he wants Rictus to help him.

  WWW.SOLARISBOOKS.COM

Follow us on Twitter! www.twitter.com/solarisbooks